# THE SCHUBERT SONG COMPANION

After a career as a schoolmaster, and as a BBC producer and administrator, John Reed retired to a busy life as a writer. His first book, *Schubert: The Final Years* was published by Faber and Faber in 1972. As well as many other books and articles, he is also author of a full-length critical biography of the composer published in the Dent 'Master Musicians' series. In 1986 the *Schubert Song Companion* was awarded the Vincent Duckles Prize by the Music Library Association of America. John Reed became an honorary member of the *Internationales Franz Schubert Institut* of Vienna in 1989, and is Chairman of the recently formed Schubert Institute.

*To Roger Fiske, friend and mentor*

# The Schubert Song Companion

JOHN REED

*With prose translations by*
NORMA DEANE
CELIA LARNER

*and a Foreword by*
DAME JANET BAKER

*faber and faber*
LONDON BOSTON

First published in 1985
by Manchester University Press,
Oxford Road, Manchester M13 9PL

This paperback edition published in 1993
by Faber and Faber Limited
3 Queen Square London WC1N 3AU

Printed by Clays Ltd, St Ives Plc

A CIP record for this book is available
from the British Library

ISBN 0 571 166652

10 9 8 7 6 5 4 3 2 1

# Contents

# Foreword

Here at last is a reference book for which all students of Schubert have been waiting. It will be of enormous value to the scholar, the serious performer and the serious listener alike.

If the *Companion* is used as it should be we may look forward to a generation of recital audiences arriving at a concert hall properly prepared with so good a knowledge of the text, translation and background of each song that communication between artist and audience in non-German-speaking countries will reach new levels. I can think of no contribution more valuable to the understanding of the Schubert Lied nor adequate words of gratitude to John Reed for undertaking a labour of such magnitude.

JANET BAKER

# Preface

One book, it seems to me, has been conspicuously missing from the shelves of the singer and song lover, a comprehensive guide to Schubert's songs. More than 150 years have elapsed since the composer's death, and his vast legacy of song has been gradually explored and revealed. Its astonishing variety and universality are no longer in question; Schubert is to modern song what Shakespeare is to the drama, a nonpareil, the only begetter and exemplar. Yet there is no book to which the scholar or music-lover can turn in the certain expectation of finding information, not to mention illumination, about any one particular song. Faced with the news that the promising young baritone Herr Schönstimme proposes to begin his recital with a Schubert group consisting of *Klage*, *Sehnsucht*, *An den Mond* and *Am Flusse*, even the most conscientious critic is likely to find himself at a loss. True, if Deutsch numbers are available (nowadays they usually are), and if he is lucky enough to have access to the excellent new German edition of the Deutsch Thematic Catalogue, he will at least be able to discover which of the twenty or so songs covered by these titles the artist really intends to sing. If he is so persistent, however, as to want to know what the songs are about, and something of their literary and musical background, he will have to do the best he can with Richard Capell's brilliant and perceptive study of the songs, now nearly sixty years old; or with Dietrich Fischer-Dieskau's more recent book, both of which deal with most of the songs (but by no means all of them) in their own discursive and selective way. And if, like most of us, his German is inadequate, and he needs the help of a straightforward prose translation of the text, he may have to wait until the programme becomes available, and even then he will sometimes wait in vain.

If I were asked, therefore, why this book was written, I should be obliged to turn Leigh Mallory's famous remark about Everest on its head, and say: 'because it wasn't there'. Several years have passed since the project was set in train, years in which the completion of the task has sometimes seemed as remote and inaccessible as Everest itself. But I have never doubted that the songs themselves justify all the time and effort involved. Not only do they provide unique insights into the development of Schubert's mind and art; they leave the student with the impression of a lyrical genius which was truly Shakespearean in its bulk and humanity, and in the phenomenal assurance with which it advanced from tentative beginnings to great masterpieces. Schubert not only discovered a new world, the world of the Romantic *Lied*; he mapped out the territory, opened up the routes which later adventurers were to follow, and himself left the best descriptions of the terrain.

A word about the entries in Part I of the book, which are arranged so as to lead from factual information to more subjective matters like critical comment and interpretation. Modern research into paper types and script characteristics has helped to solve many of the chronological problems associated with the songs. In general I have relied for guidance on the new German edition of the Thematic Catalogue, and on the pioneer work of Ernst

Hilmar and Robert Winter. But many dates remain uncertain. I have tried to present the arguments fairly in disputed cases, but have not been afraid to express a personal view. Different settings of the same text are distinguished by arabic numbers; settings of different poems by the same author with identical titles are distinguished by roman numbers.

The key quoted is normally that of the original autograph, where it still exists, or of the first edition, where it does not. However, this rule of thumb gives way to a host of special cases. Schubert sometimes changed his own mind about keys, as he did about *Frühlingsglaube*, for instance, and about four of the *Winterreise* songs. Moreover, he often left variant autographs of a song in different keys, so that it is not always easy to decide which is the original key. Where the first edition appeared in the composer's own lifetime, and differs from the autograph, I have usually assumed that the change of key carried his approval, or at any rate his assent.

The translations are intended to give the sense of Schubert's text, taking account of his own changes, omissions and repetitions; and as far as possible to give an indication of the poetic tone of the original. The paragraphing follows the stanza form; but where a musical structure is superimposed on the verse form this is usually noted in the commentary. A few long narrative poems of no special artistic merit are presented in summary translation.

A book of this size and scope can hardly be produced single-handed. I am indebted to a team of skilled collaborators; in particular to Norma Deane and Celia Larner, who shared the formidable task of translating all Schubert's song texts from the original German into English; and to Sheila Ralphs, who gave similar assistance with the Italian songs. Paulène Fallows edited the typescript with an expert eye for clarity, accuracy and consistency of detail, and Malcolm Bothwell designed and drew the music examples. Mrs Alice Wragg, to whose friendly and conscientious co-operation I owe much over the years, typed the fair copy for the main parts of the book, though she did not live to complete the task. John Banks, of Manchester University Press, has given patient and sympathetic support in spite of inevitable difficulties and delays.

A special bond seems to unite lovers of Schubert's music, and there are some to whom I owe a more personal debt of gratitude. Father Reinhard van Hoorickx OFM not only put his unrivalled knowledge of the song fragments and sketches at my disposal; he read through the whole of Part I in draft, made many helpful comments and suggestions, and saved me from many errors and mis-judgments. Professor W. E. Yates of the University of Exeter gave invaluable help with the Grillparzer/Schubert relationship and the cultural life of Vienna in the 1820s. Ward Gardner and Michael Waugh commented usefully on the problem of Schubert's illness. I have also learnt much on particular songs from the writings and conversation of my friends, including Roger Fiske, Eric Sams and Susan Youens. To all these, and to Dame Janet Baker, who generously agreed to write a foreword for this book, I offer my warm thanks.

Didsbury                                                                    John Reed
July 1984

# Abbreviations

## I SOURCE MATERIALS

App.—Appendix

D—O.E. Deutsch, *Schubert: Thematic Catalogue of all his Works*, London, 1951

D2—W. Dürr, A. Feil, C. Landon and others, *Franz Schubert: thematisches Verzeichnis seiner Werke in chronologischer Folge von Otto Erich Deutsch*, NSA VII vol.4 Kassel, 1978 [rev. and enlarged trans. of D]

*Docs.*—O.E. Deutsch, ed., *Schubert: a Documentary Biography*, London, 1946/R1977 [trans. from Ger. original, Munich, 1914]

GA—E. Mandyczewski, J. Brahms and others, eds., *Franz Schuberts Werke: kritisch durchgesehene Gesamtausgabe*, Leipzig, 1884–97/R1964–9 [ser., no.]

Kreissle—H. Kreissle von Hellborn, *Franz Schubert*, Vienna, 1865 [Eng. trans., 1869]

*Memoirs*—O.E. Deutsch, *Schubert: Memoirs by his Friends*, London, 1958 [trans. from Ger. original, Leipzig, 1957]

*Nachlass*—*Franz Schuberts Nachgelassene musikalische Dichtungen für Gesang und Pianoforte*, 50 vols., Vienna, 1830–50 [published by A. Diabelli]

NSA—W. Dürr, A. Feil, C. Landon and others., eds., *Franz Schubert: Neue Ausgabe sämtlicher Werke*, Kassel, 1964– [ser., vol., p.]

Peters—M. Friedländer, ed., *Franz Schubert: Gesänge für eine Singstimme mit Klavierbegleitung*, 7 vols., Leipzig, 1885–7 [published by Peters]

*Rev. Ber.*—E. Mandyczewski; ed., *Revisionsbericht*, GA, Leipzig, 1897/R1969

ser.—series

suppl.—supplement

trans.—translated by, translation

## II LOCATION OF AUTOGRAPHS

BL—British Library, London

DS—Deutsche Staatsbibliothek, East Berlin

GdM—Gesellschaft der Musikfreunde, Vienna

HNL—Hungarian National Library, Budapest

LC—Library of Congress, Washington, DC, USA

MGV—Männergesang-Vereïn, Vienna

ÖNB—Österreichische Nationalbibliothek, Vienna

PML—Pierpont Morgan Library, New York

SB—Stadt– und Landesbibliothek, Vienna

SLB—Sächsische Landesbibliothek, Dresden

SMf—Stiftelsen Musikkulturens främjande, Stockholm

SPK—Staatsbibliothek Preussischer Kulturbesitz, West Berlin

UB—Universitätsbibliothek, Lund, Sweden

## III BIBLIOGRAPHY

*AMZ—Allgemeine musikalische Zeitung*
*M and L—Music and Letters*
*MMR—The Monthly Musical Record*
*MQ—The Musical Quarterly*
*MR—The Music Review*
*MT—The Musical Times*

*ÖMZ—Österreichische Musikzeitschrift*
*RMA—Proceedings of the Royal
    Musical Association*
*SKW—O. Brusatti, ed., Schubert-
    Kongress Wien 1978, Graz, 1979*
*ZfK—Weiner Zeitschrift für Kunst,
    Literatur, Theater und Mode*

## IV REFERENCES

M. J. E. Brown, *Schubert: a Critical
Biography*, London, 1958/R1977 [*CB*],
—, *Essays on Schubert*, London, 1966
[*Essays*]
R. Capell, *Schubert's Songs*, London,
1928/R1967, rev. 3/1973 by Martin
Cooper
A. Craig Bell, *The Songs of Schubert*,
London, 1964
A. Einstein, *Schubert: a Musical Portrait*,
New York and London, 1951
A. Feil, *Franz Schubert: Die schöne
Müllerin, Winterreise*, Stuttgart, 1975
D. Fischer-Dieskau, *Schubert: a Bio-
graphical Study of his Songs*, London,
1976 [trans. of Ger. original]
M. Friedländer, *Das deutsche Lied im 18.
Jahrhundert*, Stuttgart and Berlin, 1902/
R1970
T. Georgiades, *Schubert: Musik und Lyrik*,
Göttingen, 1967

G. Moore, *The Schubert Song Cycles*,
London, 1975
E. G. Porter, *Schubert's Song-technique*,
London, 1961
E. B. Schnapper, *Die Gesänge des jungen
Schubert*, Berne and Leipzig, 1937
M. and L. Schochow, eds., *Franz Schubert:
die Texte seiner einstimmig kompo-
nierten Lieder und ihre Dichter*,
Hildesheim and New York, 1974
J. M. Stein, *Poem and Music in the
German Lied*, Cambridge, Mass., 1971
F. W. Sternfeld, *Goethe and Music*, New
York, 1979
*Studies*: E. Badura-Skoda and P.
Branscombe, eds., *Schubert Studies:
Problems of Style and Chronology*,
Cambridge, 1982
*Symposium*: G. Abraham, ed., *Schubert: a
Symposium*, London, 1947/R1969

# I The Songs

**ABEND** Evening
**Ludwig Tieck**

January 1819
G minor D645  Not in Peters  Not in GA

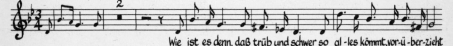

Wie ist es denn, daß trüb und schwer so al-les kömmt, vor-ü-ber-zieht

Why is it that everything is so heavy and dull, as it comes and goes, and this poor heart, inconstant, tormented, always empty, grows faint?

Scarce have I come than I must go; scarce kindled into life, all joys must fade, and the dark cloud of misery descends.

From the light of those eyes that make my heart rejoice I am cast back into darkness, into barren, tormented life. How fleeting is my joy! Parting's heavy sorrow lasts a long and weary space! How can I turn back, and live without you.

Before I had ever seen you, then I could live with longing. The wind of hope fanned my desires, the future looked bright. Now I can only remember what I scarcely perceived before it was dispelled.

Again I must wander, grieving, among the vulgar crowd through an unknown land, the golden thread of happiness lost to me. I feel your touch still, your kisses as in a dream; still your loving glances follow me, and the feeling that I am bereft remains behind with me.

O Hope, O Longing, Pangs of Love, how I thirst for the sweetness of tears. O comfort me, vain fancy, empty and dead and worthless as you are. Must you abandon me so fleetingly?

The verses belong to a sequence of four poems called *Der Besuch* ('The Visit'), published in Tieck and A. W. Schlegel's *Musenalmanach* for the year 1802. The autograph, in private possession in the USA, is dated January 1819. The voice line is written out for 119 bars, breaking off at line 38 of the poem; there are a few sketchy indications for the accompaniment. The sketch was made when Schubert's involvement with the Romantic poets was at its height. It seems strange, therefore, that it was not completed, and that this is the only attempt he made to set a poem of Tieck's. For an authoritative discussion of Schubert's relationship with the Schlegel circle, and of the background to the song, see Berke. A completion of the song has been made by Reinhard van Hoorickx.

D. Berke, 'Schuberts Liedentwurf "Abend" und dessen textliche Voraussetzungen', *SKW* pp. 305–20

## ABENDBILDER Evening Scene

**Johann Petrus Silbert**                                                    February 1819

A minor  D650  Peters III p.134  GA XX no.352

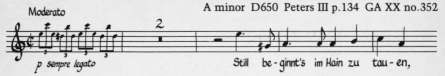

In the grove, quietly the dew begins to fall. Gently the sinister twilight weaves through the light of day, distorting the green bushes in the fields.

The nightly ravens swoop on distant oaks; the breeze smells sweet. Echo tenderly recalls Philomel's magic songs.

Hark how the angelus tells the sons of men to turn their hearts from earthly joys to heaven.

The skies, barred with cloud, sparkle with a thousand shining stars. The moon, mirrored in clear waters, scatters its gold afar on field and hill.

In its full light, the mossy church roof gleams, while all around cold stones stand guard above the sleepers' limbs.

Rest, beloved, from all travail, until at the resurrection God shall call us upward to eternal bliss.

Silbert's poems had been published early in 1819. He was a follower of the Redemptorist priest Clemens Hofbauer, and his nocturne makes the conventional gesture towards the 'long last sleep' at the end. The autograph (Yale University) is dated February 1819. There is a copy in the Spaun–Cornaro collection, in private possession in Vienna. The song was first published in book 9 of the *Nachlass* in 1831.

The new pianistic freedom and independence that are characteristic of the songs of 1818 and 1819 give *Abendbilder* much of the quality of a sonata movement. The tolling-bell effects in the third verse and elsewhere are neatly combined with the triplet figure which persists throughout the song, at some risk to the listener's close attention. Schubert was to put the figure to much more expressive use later in *Der Lindenbaum*. In form and style *Abendbilder* points the way to, for instance, the Seidl songs; but, impressive as it is, it does not touch the heights.

Capell, 158–9; Einstein, 189; Fischer-Dieskau, 119

## ABENDLIED Evening Song

**Author unknown**                                                    24 February 1816

F major  D382  Not in Peters  GA XX no.190

The evening sun shines gently on these quiet fields, laving every creature in peace and joy. It paints the flower-strewn grass with light and shade, and the green meadows glitter with crystal dew.

As breezes play and birds sing, rapture fills my breast. Every breath fills me with sweet delights. Sorrow and pain flee in the gentle evening light.

To you, who spread the twilight glow over the heavens, and filled the country-side with the sweet sounds of night, I consecrate this heart suffused with pure gratitude; may it still beat with joy when life ends.

The autograph, a first draft dated 24 February 1816, is now in the PM Library New York. The song first appeared in the *Gesamtausgabe* in 1895. This strophic setting is an 'evening hymn' of unpretentious charm, without any of the atmospheric quality of Schubert's mature nocturnes, and is entirely classical in form and idiom.

## ABENDLIED Evening Song

**Matthias Claudius**                                        November 1816

Ruhig                         B flat major  D499  Peters VII p.30  GA XX no.278

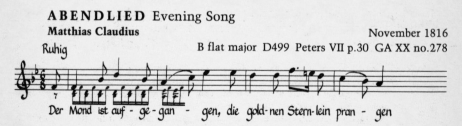

Der Mond ist auf - ge - gan - gen, die gold-nen Stern-lein pran - gen

The moon is risen, the golden stars shine clear. Dark and silent are the woods, and white above the meadows hangs the enchanted mist.

How still the world, how intimate and close in twilight's folds. Like a quiet room, where the tumult of the day should sleep forgotten.

Do you see the moon standing up there? It is half-hidden now, though round and fair. So it is with many other things, which we deride because we do not see them.

We proud sons of men are poor ignorant sinners. We weave our fantasies and seek out skills, yet wander further from our goal.

God, show us your grace, that we may shun all transitory things, spurn all that is vain. Grant us simplicity, that we may live on earth like children, innocent and glad.

The poem has two more verses, in the same pious vein as the fifth, which Schubert did not use. The autograph is lost, but the catalogue of the Witteczek–Spaun collection (Vienna, GdM) dates the song November 1816, and the first edition has December 1816. The song first appeared in 1885 in vol.VII of the Peters collected edition, which used as its source a copy in the Witteczek–Spaun collection.

Much more Romantic in feeling than the previous song, this delightful strophic setting, with its perfectly shaped tune and gently moving accompaniment, catches the mood of quiet meditation perfectly. Significantly, the pianist has the best of it in the four-bar postlude. The hidden counter-theme in the right hand is pure Schubert.

## ABENDLIED Evening Song

**Friedrich Leopold, Graf zu Stolberg-Stolberg**              28 August 1815

Ruhig, mäßig                              A major  D276  Not in Peters  GA XX no.133

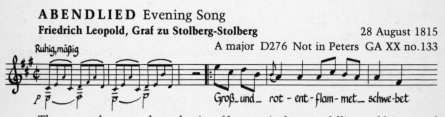

Groß und rot - ent - flam-met schwe-bet

The great red sun stands on the rim of heaven, its last rays falling on blue sea and shore. The moon, rising from the beechwood, presages peace to her sister earth.

The red glow darkens on the swollen clouds, and softer colours play upon the rocks. Quails call amid the corn, and the shepherd makes answer with his pipe.

Sweet-scented are the meadows, and the dew falls from the shrubs to where warm-lipped flowers sip, and the grasses, drooping with liquid pearls, drink deep.

The ring-doves and the drowsy pigeons coo; and the bats beat their wings to the glassy mere. The roving beetles swarm, and the sentinel owl hoots as he mounts his watch.

Our songbirds slumber now, heads tucked under wing. Their songs are silent.

Even the raucous starlings rest in the swaying reeds. Only the nightingale exults in the moonlight.

As night falls, busy mothers make sure that their little ones lie down to sleep, rewarding each goodnight with a soft kiss.

Thus when day's toils are done eternal love looks down through the starry heavens. It hears the first stirrings of the awakening earth, and the late prayer of him who prays alone.

Lift up your spirit, my soul, when nightingales pipe up. Hearken to me, O Father, in the first flush of day. Spirit, transcend this earth and all its woes. As the meadows fill the air with their sweet scents, let your dew, Father, descend upon us!

The poem was written in 1793. The autograph (London, BL) is dated 28 August 1815. Only the first verse is written out, but the music has repeat marks at the end. There is a dated copy in the Witteczek–Spaun collection (Vienna, GdM). *Abendlied* was first published in 1895, in the *Gesamtausgabe*. It is an unremarkable song, with (for Schubert) a rather weak postlude.

## ABENDLIED DER FÜRSTIN The Princess's Evening Song

**Johann Mayrhofer**                                      (?) November 1816

F major D495 Not in Peters GA XX no.271

The vale is red with evening light; Hesperus softly glows. The beechwood is silent, and quieter the sound of the river.

Gold-rimmed clouds sail by the clear sky. The heart exults, the heart dreams, free from the cares of the world.

The huntsman stretched out on the green hillside falls fast asleep, then rouses to sudden thunder, and the lightning's hiss.

Where are you, blessed evening glow? And you, mild Hesperus? So every pleasure turns to grief and pain.

The autograph (DS) has neither date nor tempo indication. The Witteczek–Spaun catalogue (Vienna, GdM), however, gives 1816 and Kreissle's list November 1816. The song was first published in 1868, by Wilhelm Müller of Berlin.

The unexpected thunderstorm is central to the poem, since it enables Mayrhofer to point his pessimistic moral. The pastoral outer sections in 6/8 rhythm, with their unexpected swing away into E flat major, are delightful. But the principle of faithfulness to the text seems to be at war with the principle of unity of mood in the song, so that the very realistic thunderstorm in the middle section makes its effect at the cost of destroying the unity of the song.

R. Winter, 'Schubert's undated works: a new chronology', *MT*, CXIX, 1978, p.500.

# ABENDLIED FÜR DIE ENTFERNTE Evening Song:
## For the Distant Beloved
**August Wilhelm von Schlegel**                    September 1825

F major D856 Peters III p.52 GA XX no.482

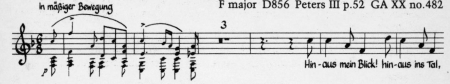

Eyes, look out towards the valley, where life in its richness abides; and refresh yourself with blessed moonlit peace. Hearken, heart, to gentle sounds which press in upon you from far away, for joy or sorrow.

They crowd in so wondrously they rouse all my longing. Are these feelings real, or mere illusion? Will my eyes one day smile in unalloyed pleasure, as they do now in tears? Will my heart, often uplifted, one day find blessed peace?

When hope and memory unite before our eyes, then at dusk the shadows on the soul grow softer. O, were reality not laced with dreams, how colourless and dull human life would be!

The heart hopes on faithfully to the grave; investing the moment with love, it counts itself rich in possessions, those which it creates itself, and which fate cannot plunder. It lives and works in warmth and strength, in faith and trust.

Though all around lie dead in misty darkness, the heart has long since forged itself a shield. In troubled times it plays its part with proud defiance. And so I sleep, and wake again; if not in joy, then in peace.

The poem was written in 1807. Schubert omitted the third verse, which speaks more directly of the conflict of reason and hope in human affairs. The autograph is lost. The Witteczek–Spaun catalogue (Vienna, GdM) dates the song September 1825. It was published by Thaddäus Weigl in December 1827 as op.88 no.1.

Here the pastoral song, in its traditional 6/8 F major dress, comes to full maturity. The strophic form is subtly adapted to the words; a mood of thoughtful melancholy suffuses the whole song, varied and enlivened by Schubert's command of modulation and by the echo phrases in the accompaniment; and the shift into the minor for the third verse gives a suggestion of tripartite form to the song. There is a close affinity with the Andante of the A minor Sonata of 1823 (D784).

Capell, 218

# ABENDRÖTE Sunset Glow
**Friedrich von Schlegel**                    (?) 1820–March 1823

A major D690 Peters V p.7 GA XX no.376

The sun sinks lower, all the world breathes peace. Day's work is done, the children laugh and play.

The green earth glows more greenly in the sun's last rays; the flowers waft sweet scents that charm the soul and steal the senses.

The small birds, distant figures, soaring peaks, and the great silver stream that winds its sinuous way along the valley – the poet knows their meaning. They speak to him and become a unified choir, one voice with many songs.

The poem forms the introduction to part I of the sequence called *Abendröte*, written in 1800–1 and later published in the Tieck–Schlegel *Musenalmanach*. But Schubert's source was probably the collected edition of Schlegel's poems published 1822–5. Schubert's autograph (Stockholm, SMf) is a fair copy, headed 'Abendröte: Erster Teil', which suggests that he intended to set all the poems in the cycle and was preparing a fair copy of the whole work. In fact he set only eleven of the twenty poems in the cycle.

The autograph is dated March 1823, though Deutsch read the date as March 1820. But the other texts from the cycle belong to the years 1819 and 1820, either certainly or probably. Even if the fair copy of this one was made in March 1823, therefore, it is still possible that the song was written some years earlier. *Abendröte* was first published in October 1831 in book 7 of the *Nachlass*.

The piano part is an elaborate nocturne, a theme with variations, full of decorative trills and arpeggio figures – not very different from the sort of nocturne John Field was then writing. The singer's discrete phrases are counterpointed, often in contrary motion, in the piano part. The dynamic level hardly rises above *p*. The whole song is suffused with serenity and stillness: 'one voice with many songs'. Unlike *Im Abendrot* and *Nacht und Träume*, remarkable for the weight of subjective emotion they carry, *Abendröte* is pictorial, Romantic in feeling and conception, but outward-looking. It is one of the most remarkable examples of the song style of Schubert's middle years, uniquely successful in conveying the sense of the unity of man and nature which inspires the poem.

Capell, 165–6; Fischer-Dieskau, 124; D. Berke, 'Schuberts Liedentwurf ''Abend'' und dessen textliche Voraussetzungen', *SKW* pp.305–15

## ABENDS UNTER DER LINDE Evening under the Linden Tree (1)

**Ludwig Kosegarten**

24 July 1815

F major D235 Not in Peters GA XX no.100

Whence comes this nameless longing in my breast? Whence these bittersweet tears that cloud my eyes? O evening glow, O moonlight, shine paler beneath the linden tree.

There is a rustling in the leaves of the linden and acacia trees. The evening breeze caresses, sweet and soft, filled with spirit voices, light as an angel's kiss.

The dark fields glow, the grey boughs of the linden tree quiver. Is it you, transfigured heavenly forms, that hover round me? I feel the touch of your kiss, O Julie, O Emilius!

Stay, fortunate ones, in your Eden! The breath of life blows hot and heavy here, through silent grievous wastes. But where you are peace reigns, and the coolness of dawn. So fare you well! Forever fare you well!

The autograph is a first draft, dated 24 July 1815, with *Huldigung* D240 on the other side (Berlin, DS). This first version has been published only in the *Gesamtausgabe* (1894). See the following entry.

## ABENDS UNTER DER LINDE (2)
**Ludwig Kosegarten**                                                      25 July 1815
F major D237 Not in Peters GA XX no.101

For translation, see the preceding entry. The autograph, in private possession, is dated
25 July 1815. A fair copy, auctioned in 1958, has since disappeared. There is a dated copy
in the Witteczek–Spaun collection (Vienna, GdM), which differs in some details from
the autograph. The song was published by J. P. Gotthard in 1872 as no.10 of 'Forty Songs'.

The two settings of this song, written on successive days, seem to have evolved from
the same germ-cell, as a glance at the melodic contour of the opening bars will show. But
the second has a much more developed personality, with a clearer harmonic structure
and a firmer rhythm. It is rare indeed for Schubert to revise so radically the musical
elements of a piece, as though searching (in the Beethoven manner) for the right expression
of a preconceived idea. Significantly perhaps, neither version makes a really successful
song. The second is better but seems unable to carry the weight of emotion suggested
by the text and by the direction *Langsam*.

## ABENDSTÄNDCHEN: AN LINA Evening Serenade: To Lina
**Gabriele von Baumberg**                                               23 August 1815
B flat major D265 Not in Peters GA XX no.125

Evening, be soft as her soul, merry as her glance, and let my faithfulness bring me joy!
    When the world sleeps, and the lamplight glows dim, only unrequited love
weeps its bright tears.
    If I could sing a love song beneath her window, perchance my languishing looks
and plaintive strumming might move her more, inclining her cold heart to love.
    Aroused from slumber by my songs, hearing my anguish half in dreams, then
she may fearfully arise, aware at last of the sufferings of her minstrel.
    Beloved moon, shine down from on high, that I may see her tears reward my
pain.

According to Deutsch the poem was written 'after an unidentified French poem', but if
so it remains unidentified. Schubert's autograph (Washington, LC) is a first draft dated
23 August 1815. There is a dated copy also in the Witteczek–Spaun collection (Vienna,
GdM). The song was first published in the *Gesamtausgabe* in 1895.

All Schubert's settings of Gabriele von Baumberg's poems except one very early one
belong to August 1815, a month when he was much taken up with Goethe and Schiller. All
of them are strophic, and all have a somewhat archaic eighteenth-century charm, which
seems strange when one considers that the vein of passionate feeling is close to the surface
in the poems. This one is as shapely and pleasing as a Haydn canzonetta, with a well-
moulded climax. The singer's B flat on the first beat of bar 12 in the *Gesamtausgabe* is
a misprint for C.

## ABENDSTERN Evening Star

**Johann Mayrhofer**

March 1824

A minor D806 Peters V p.133 GA XX no.459

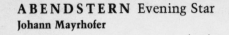

Why do you linger lonely in the sky, fair gentle star? Why do your bright companions flee your face? 'I am the faithful star of love, and love they shun.'

If you are love, then go at once to them, for who can resist you? O sweet and wayward light! 'I sow no seed, I see no fruit, and bear my grief alone.'

The poem was included in the first volume of Mayrhofer's verse, published early in 1824. Schubert's name, oddly enough, does not appear on the list of subscribers, but it may have been the appearance of this collection that turned his attention again to Mayrhofer's work after a gap of some three years. The autograph, dated March 1824, is in Vienna (GdM). It seems to have been part of a larger sheaf of manuscripts, for the draft of *Abendstern* follows the last eleven bars of *Der Sieg* D805, the beginning of which has been lost. There is a copy, also dated March 1824, in the Witteczek–Spaun collection (GdM). The song was first published in 1833 in book 22 of the *Nachlass*.

Mayrhofer sees in the evening star the symbol of his own loneliness. Schubert turns a familiar rhythm (dotted crotchet followed by three quavers), that of *Suleika I* and *Du liebst mich nicht*, to the same purpose, slowing it down and keeping the modulations well within range of the tonic A minor. The mood of resigned sadness and isolation is akin to that of *Der Leiermann*. The epigrammatic sharpness of *Abendstern* sets it apart from all the other Mayrhofer songs. At bar 19 the tempo indication should probably be *Etwas schneller* (as in the *Gesamtausgabe*). There should be no sudden change of pace.

Capell, 205; Fischer-Dieskau, 193–4; Porter, 67

**ABSCHIED** see RELLSTAB SONGS no.7

## ABSCHIED. NACH EINER WALLFAHRTSARIE

Farewell. Based on a Pilgrims' Song

**Johann Mayrhofer**

September 1816

G major D475 Peters VII p.18 GA XX no.251

Over the hills you go, where the green places are. I must return alone. Farewell, so be it.

Parting, leaving those we love, saddens the heart. The woods and hills, the smooth lakes all fade, the echo of your voices dies away.

Parting, leaving those we love, saddens the heart.

In September 1816 Mayrhofer went on a walking tour in Lower Austria with the son of Professor Watteroth, in whose honour Schubert wrote the cantata *Prometheus*. The poem, entitled simply *Lunz* (a village in Lower Austria), may have been written on that excursion. Schubert's autograph has been lost, but two contemporary copies in the Witteczek–Spaun collection (Vienna, GdM) are dated September 1816. One is headed as above, the other 'Lunz, oder Abschied'.

The tune on which the song is supposedly based has never been identified. It seems not to have been noticed that the opening bars of the melody are identical with the passage from the lost *Prometheus* cantata which Leopold Sonnleithner many years later wrote down from memory (*Memoirs* p.444). The cantata had been written in June 1816, only three months earlier, and would surely still be very much in the composer's mind.

A version of the song for piano solo by J. P. Gotthard was published by Kratochwill of Vienna in 1876. The first appearance of the authentic version was in 1885, in the Peters edition. In that edition the song is confusingly set out with repeat signs. The performers are intended to play through to the *Da capo* sign at bar 51 and then go back to the double barline. At the end of the third verse (misleadingly marked 'Fine') it is necessary to turn to the postlude (ten bars) at the end. The layout is much clearer in the *Gesamtausgabe*.

This haunting and unusual song might suggest that Schubert had somewhere heard the sound of the alpenhorn echoing round the valleys. Yet so far as we know he had not in 1816 ever been far from Vienna. The curiously wistful prelude music, with its slow dropping thirds and sixths, which serves also as postlude and interlude, seems to provide an emotional rather than a pictorial setting for the foursquare pilgrims' chant.

Fischer-Dieskau, 76–7

## ABSCHIED VON DER ERDE Farewell to the World
**Adolf von Pratobevera**                                                            February 1826

F major D829 Peters VII p.109 GA XX no.603

Fare you well, fair earth! Only now, as joy and sorrow pass away. do I understand you. Fare you well, Sir Care, I go with tearful thanks. Joy I take with me, you I leave behind.

Teach men with gentleness, that they may turn to God. Lighten the darkest night with streaks of dawn.

Make men aware of love, and soon or late they will give thanks. Life will be sweet, and grief will wear a smile. Joy will dwell in the pure tranquil heart.

The poem forms the envoi to Pratobevera's one-act verse play *Der Falke* ('The Falcon'), written in 1825. It was privately performed at Pratobevera's house on 17 February 1826, to mark the birthday of his father Karl (*Docs.* p.509), and Schubert's music was presumably written for this occasion. It is the only example of melodrama – spoken verse with musical accompaniment – among the songs. The autograph (Vienna, GdM) has no title or date; the assumption that the piece was written for the performance in February 1826 is however confirmed by a comparison of the music paper used with other 1826 manuscripts (see Winter). There is an undated copy in the Witteczek–Spaun collection (GdM), headed 'Abschied. Melodramatisch'. The work was first published as the appendix to August Reissmann's biography, *Franz Schubert: sein Leben und seine Werke* (Berlin, 1873).

*Abschied von der Erde* remains almost unknown and unperformed. Yet it is quintessential Schubert, the great Schubert moreover of the final phase. The tone of inner stillness and reconciliation, the steady pulse and slow harmonic pace, the emotionally charged modulations, all call to mind the slow movements of the String Quintet and the last piano sonata. There seems even to be a thematic link with the opening movement of the latter work in the cadence (twice repeated) of bar 9. In bar 27 the penultimate quaver chord in the pianist's left hand should be D, F and C, not E, G and C as in the Peters edition.

> P. Branscombe, 'Schubert and the melodrama', *Studies*, pp.139–40; Fischer-Dieskau, 110–11; R. Winter, 'Schubert's undated works: a new chronology', *MT*, CXIX, 1978, p.498

## ABSCHIED VON DER HARFE  Farewell to the Harp
**Johann Gaudenz von Salis-Seewis**                                     March 1816

Etwas langsam                          E minor  D406  Peters VII p.83  GA XX no.208

Harp, sound once more; you sing only what we feel. Tenderly, your voice softly fading, sing that swan song which reconciles us to the misery along life's way.

In the morning of our days you sounded clear and bright. Who can preserve that sound? In our search for experience the pure source of your song fades and dies.

In our late youth we hear its voice, loving and anxious now, like the sound of frightened birds. In our adolescent pain the heart and the harpstrings quiver with love and song.

Then in the summertime of life the strings fall mute. They still call to us, like the nightingale, touching us, though more rarely now, singing of melancholy.

O play in the darkening heart of life's sad eventide, when fate enfolds our dreary lives. Play then, and awake our longing for immortality.

A first draft, dated March 1816 and marked 'Etwas geschwind', is in the Curtis Institute Library, Philadelphia. The fair copy (Vienna, SB) is dated April 1816 and marked 'Etwas langsam'. A copy in the Witteczek–Spaun collection (Vienna, GdM) marked 'Etwas bewegt' seems to have provided the source for the published versions. According to Deutsch the song was published by C. A. Spina in 1860, but no copy has come to light. It was included in vol.VII of the Peters edition in 1887. A rather conventional song, which is better at the brisk pace suggested by Schubert's later marking.

## ABSCHIED VON EINEM FREUNDE  Farewell to a Friend
**Franz Schubert**                                                    24 August 1817

B minor  D578  Peters V p.169  GA XX no.586

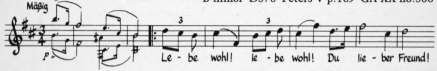

Farewell, dear friend, you go to a far place. Take this ring of friendship and wear it faithfully upon your hand.

Farewell, dear friend. Hear in this sad song the voice of my inmost heart, heavy and afraid.

Farewell, dear friend, parting is a bitter word, that calls you hence to the place where you must go.

> Farewell, dear friend, should this song touch your heart, then shall my friendly spirit hover near, playing upon the strings of my soul.

The 'dear friend' was Franz von Schober, who had to leave Vienna to look after his brother Axel, an officer in the Austrian army who was ill in France. Schubert had been living as a guest in the Schober household and he wrote the song out in Schober's album (Dresden, SLB), doubtless as a gesture of gratitude and affection. The autograph, in the Paris Conservatoire, is signed and dated 24 August 1817. There is a dated copy also in the Witteczek–Spaun collection (Vienna, GdM). The song was published in book 29 of the *Nachlass* (1838). The Peters edition includes only three of the four verses.

This lovely little song is one of the earliest examples of Schubert's ability to invest the key of B minor with a special poignancy. In particular the modulation from B minor to its relative major here takes on a special Schubertian tone, which he was to exploit in many later songs (cf. for instance the beginning of *Vor meiner Wiege*). The song has a touching directness and sincerity.

## ADELAIDE
**Friedrich von Matthisson** 1814

A flat major  D95  Peters VI p.35  GA XX no.25  NSA IV vol.7 p.3

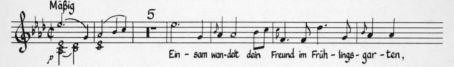

Lonely your lover wanders in the garden of spring, lapped in the mild enchantment of its light, that shimmers through the swaying blossom-boughs. Adelaide!
In the water's mirror, in the alpine snow, in the golden clouds of the departing day, in heaven's star-strewn meadow, there shines your image, Adelaide!
Evening breezes whisper in the tender leaves; May's murmuring grass is full of silver bells; waves softly break, the nightingale trills forth: Adelaide!
One day, O miracle! A flower will blossom on my grave, engendered in the ashes of my heart; and on each crimson petal will shine clear: Adelaide!

Matthisson's poem was written in 1788; the musical properties of the name Adelaide, however, had been exploited in verse before that. Some commentators have suggested that the poem was based on an earlier French model.

Schubert's autograph is lost, but there are several contemporary copies. The two in the Witteczek–Spaun collection are dated 1815, but another, for the song album of Albert Stadler (Lund, UB), was made, it is stated, in 1814. The earlier date is almost certainly correct; the song belongs, in all probability, to the autumn of that year. Schubert may well have made a fair copy of the song at a later date. All these copies are in the key of A flat and marked 'Mässig'. When the song came to be published in 1848, in book 42 of the *Nachlass*, it appeared in the key of G major, and with the tempo indication *Sehr mässig*. These changes were doubtless made by Diabelli in an attempt to mitigate the difficulties imposed by the song's high tessitura.

Schubert's setting has been overshadowed by the popularity of Beethoven's great song, and its usual fate is to be damned with faint praise. Schubert himself is reported to have told Josef Hüttenbrenner that he was reluctant to compose it, 'because he would have to write it exactly as Beethoven did' (*Memoirs* p.77). In fact there are many felicitous and characteristic touches in the song. The motto phrase, and the whispering triplets in verse 3, are pure Schubert, and if the song fails to match the vigour of Beethoven's setting, it has a lyrical tenderness of its own.

Capell, 32, 83; Einstein, 69–70; Fischer-Dieskau, 29, 30

## ADELWOLD UND EMMA  Adelwold and Emma

**Friedrich Anton Bertrand**                                                   June 1815

F major  D211  Not in Peters  GA XX no.79

Hoch, und e - hern schier von Dau-er,   ragt ein Rit - ter-schloß em-por.

[*Synopsis*] Adelwold, a penniless landless orphan, raised by a knightly foster father among his own children, loves and is loved by Emma, the old knight's daughter. To flee the father's curse, and to avoid betraying the knight's trust, Adelwold goes on pilgrimage to the Holy Land. The knight, old and lonely, bereft of his wife and all his sons, who have fallen in battle, realises at last that Emma is all he has left, and prays that some noble bridegroom may help her to restore his proud name. But Emma, fallen into a decline since Adelwold's departure, wastes away to the point of death. The distraught father pledges his all in return for Emma's life. Adelwold, drawn back by some nameless dread, arrives in time to bring her back to life. The old knight, touched by the sincerity of their love and by Adelwold's purity of heart, lifts the curse and gives their marriage his blessing.

The ballad consists of forty eight-line verses, and Schubert's alterations are numerous. Nothing seems to be known of the author; the poem appeared in a collection published in 1813. The autograph (Vienna, SB) is dated 5 June 1815 at the beginning and 14 June 1815 at the end. There is a copy in the Witteczek–Spaun collection (Vienna, GdM). The song first appeared in the *Gesamtausgabe* in 1894.

At 628 bars, *Adelwold und Emma* has the dubious distinction of being Schubert's longest song. A certain stamina is required to play it through, and performances are unlikely, to say the least. The naivety of the pictorialism – at the episode of the ghost in the night, for instance, and the burning of the town – fatally suggests to modern ears the early days of the silent cinema. But the arioso sections, as one might expect, are pleasantly singable. One can only regard the piece as a sort of do-it-yourself opera for voice and piano, complete with dramatic effects. Yet it remains something of a mystery that the naivety of the concept could co-exist in Schubert's mind with the Third Symphony and the Goethe settings of 1815.

## ADIEU

D2 Anhang I 31  Peters VI p.130

This song is not by Schubert, but by August Heinrich von Weyrauch. It was first published in 1824, to a text by Karl Friedrich Gottlob Wetzel. Schubert's name was first attached to the song in 1843, when it was published by Schlesinger in Berlin with words translated from the French. The author of the French text to which the song is now sung ('Voici l'instant suprême ...') is thought to have been Edouard Bélanger. The song has been adopted into the Schubert family and appears in many collections of Schubert songs.

# ALINDE
**Johann Friedrich Rochlitz**

January 1827

A major  D904  Peters II p.154  GA XX no.287

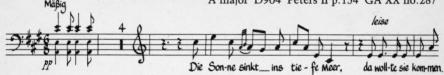

The sun sinks in the depths of the ocean. She said she would come. Quietly the reaper goes by. My heart aches. 'Have you not seen my love, reaper? Alinde!' 'I must go home to wife and children, no eyes have I for other maids. They are waiting for me under the lime tree.'

Moonrise, and still she does not come. The fisherman puts his boat to sea. My heart aches. 'Fisherman, have you not seen my love? Alinde!' 'I must see to my oyster creels. No time have I for girls. See what a catch I've made!'

The stars come out, and still she comes not. The huntsman hurries by at a brisk pace. My heart aches. 'Huntsman, have you not seen my love? Alinde!' 'I must chase the red deer. I don't enjoy looking for girls. There he goes in the evening breeze.'

Here stands the grove, in darkest night, and still she does not come. Lonely and alone I wander, anxious and afraid. To you, Echo, I confess my grief. Alinde! 'Alinde', echoed softly back. And then I saw her by my side. 'So faithfully you sought me. And now you have found me!'

Rochlitz, founder and editor of the Leipzig *AMZ*, had met Schubert in Vienna in 1822 and was an admirer of his work. *Alinde*, written in 1804, had been published in 1822. The autograph (Vienna, SB) is dated January 1827 and has the censor's stamp on it. The song was published by Haslinger with two other Rochlitz settings as op.81 in May 1827. This unusual haste suggests that Haslinger was anxious to get the publication out, in view of Rochliz's considerable reputation as a critic and literary figure. The opus was dedicated to the author.

The song owes its popularity to the infectious lilt of the barcarolle rhythm. Schubert's dependence on a tonal image to set his imagination at work is nicely illustrated, for the 6/8 lilt is also the rhythm of the serenade, and the speaker is of course serenading his lover. The piece thus has something of the immediacy of a dramatic scene, and the modified strophic setting is skilfully adapted to the words.

Capell, 128; Fischer-Dieskau, 247

# ALLES UM LIEBE All for Love
**Ludwig Kosegarten**

27 July 1815

E major  D241  Not in Peters  GA XX no.104

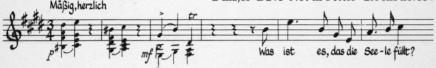

What fills the soul? Love. Not gold, nor its worth, nor worldly desires, but love.

What stills our longings? Love. Not titles, power, rank, nor sounding fame, but only love.

What is the heart's desire? Love. It does not seek dalliance, nor lust's delight, but love.

Gladly I'd give my all for love: the frothy glamour of riches, the round of pleasure, dreams of fame; without love, what are they?

Sweeter far, in poverty, to lie upon the loved one's breast, than to while away one's days or to sleep lapped in lust, unloved and loveless.

My love loves me through good and ill. Let fate take all I have. Take peace, renown, fame and fortune, my love is all I need.

Nor should I languish, far away, did I but know you loved me, dear. Who then could pity me?

Were I a slave in desolate lands, yet knew you to be true, then slavery would be sweet, and the wilderness paradise.

And if, my love, the darkness of death dimmed your light, or if I died, mourned only by you, why then death would be bliss.

Better by far to die in love's embrace, young, strong and bold, than to grow old and waste away, sated with tasteless, empty joys.

The autograph (Berlin, DS) is written on the last side of a manuscript originally used for the first version of Schiller's *Des Mädchens Klage* D6. It is dated 27 July 1815. There are also two fair copies, one of them now in ÖNB. A dated copy is in the Witteczek–Spaun collection (Vienna, GdM). The song was not published until 1894, in the *Gesamtausgabe*. The tuneful sweetness of the setting matches the poem; there is no need to insist on all the verses.

## ALS ICH SIE ERRÖTEN SAH  When I saw her blush
**Bernhard Ambros Ehrlich**                                          10 February 1815
G major  D153  Peters VI p.18  GA XX no.41  NSA IV vol.7 p.135

All my doing, all my being is for you, my love. My senses weave a picture of you, enchantress. You set my heart aflame and inspire my song. More than the muses, you excite and bewitch me.

The tranquil gaze of your blue eyes shines through the tempests of the soul, and the sweetness of your smile paints the future with a rosy glow. Though the crimson flush of the sun adorns the fringes of the sky, a lovelier light is in your face when my intoxicated glances, my delighted eyes, behold the scarlet beauty of your blush.

The incomplete autograph, dated 10 February 1815 is in private possession. There are two copies in the Witteczek–Spaun collection (Vienna, GdM), one of them with a different title (*Die entfernte Geliebte*), a short prelude and variant readings. The song was published in book 39 of the *Nachlass* (1845).

Schubert's prodigious output of songs in 1815 is a mixture of the conventional and the predictive. This song is one of the important few that seem to hold within themselves the seed of future greatness. The fluent on-running melody is subject to a process of continuous adaptation; the pianist's semiquaver figure might belong to a *Schöne Müllerin* song, *Wohin!* perhaps. And the song has a wonderful spontaneity and plasticity, to such an extent do the phrases seem to grow out of each other. If it were not for the dated autograph we might be tempted to place it much later.

Capell, 89; Einstein, 108; Fischer-Dieskau, 54

## ALTE LIEBE ROSTET NIE Old love never tarnishes

**Johann Mayrhofer**

September 1816

B major D477 Not in Peters GA XX no.253

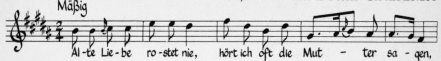

Old love never tarnishes, I often heard my mother say. Old love never tarnishes: now, alas, I know it's true.

She surrounds me, like the air, she whom I once called mine, and truly loved, who sent me out into the world.

Since I lost her I have travelled far and wide, but I remained unmoved by the fairest flower of womankind.

For in my mind her image rose chiding, as though opposing them, and such is her magic power, there was only one end to that contest.

There is the garden, there the house, where so often we caressed. What do I see? She is there! Will old love never tarnish?

Mayrhofer's title was *Alte Liebe* and his first line 'Alte Liebe rostet nicht'. Schubert put 'nie' for 'nicht' and used the first line as his title. He also made changes in the sense of verse 4. The autograph, in private possession, is a first draft, dated September 1816. There are dated copies also in the Witteczek–Spaun collection (Vienna, GdM). The song did not appear until 1895, in the *Gesamtausgabe*.

A simple setting in Schubert's folksong manner, with an attractive postlude. The tempo indication *Mässig* seems to mean *andantino* rather than *allegretto*, in view of the nostalgic mood of the song.

## AM BACH IM FRÜHLING By the Brook in Springtime

**Franz von Schober**

(?) 1816

D flat major D361 Peters IV p.120 GA XX no.272

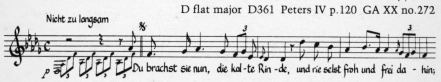

Now you have broken through your icy crust, and ripple free and merrily along. The winds blow soft again, and mossy grass grows fresh and green.

Alone and heavy-hearted I walk by the waterside as of old. The flowering of all the earth brings no joy to my heart.

For me the winds blow ever chill, my spirits do not lift with hope, save that I find a flower here – blue, as the flowers of yesteryear

[*The first two verses are repeated at the end of the song.*]

The autograph is in private possession; the usually accepted date rests only on the catalogue of the Witteczek–Spaun collection (Vienna, GdM). It is the only Schober setting of 1816. The song was published by Diabelli in 1829 as op. 109 no. 1.

The conventional theme – the contrast between vibrant nature and blighted youth – here strikes a responsive chord in Schubert. The lovely D flat melody turns sadly to the minor in the second verse and then, enharmonically, to E major and C sharp minor. The personal affirmation of verse 3 demands different treatment. Schubert sets it in an accompanied recitative which is integrated with great subtlety into the main fabric and then repeats the opening section to give the song a satisfying ternary form. If the song is indeed of 1816, it carries an unusual weight of feeling for that date. The low tessitura suggests that it was written for bass voice.

Capell, 126

**AM ERLAFSEE** see ERLAFSEE

## AM ERSTEN MAIMORGEN On the First May Morning
**Matthias Claudius**                                                      (?) 1816
G major  D344  Not in Peters  Not in GA

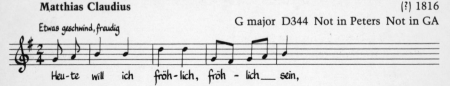

Today I shall be merry, hear no wise word or moral text. I shall rush out and shout for joy. The king himself shall not stop me.

Schubert set only the first verse of Claudius's three-verse poem. The autograph is included in the songbook which Schubert assembled for his sweetheart Therese Grob (see GROB), probably in November 1816. *Am ersten Maimorgen* is the last song in the album, now in private possession in Switzerland. It is an unpretentious little song in Schubert's folksong manner. It has been edited and privately published by Reinhard van Hoorickx.

**AM FEIERABEND** see DIE SCHÖNE MÜLLERIN no.5

## AM FENSTER At my Window
**Johann Gabriel Seidl**                                                March 1826
F major  D878  Peters III p.77  GA XX no.492

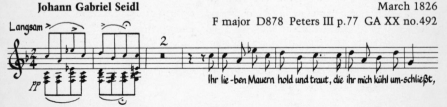

Dear friendly walls that keep me cool and safe, towering silver in the light of the full moon! Once you looked down so sadly as I sat, head sunk in weary hands, my thoughts turned in upon myself, whom none could understand.

But then another light dawned, and sadness fled. Now many keep me company along life's blessed way. Fortune can never rob me of them. They are ever there in my heart, my inmost soul, where fate can never reach.

Do you imagine that I am troubled, as once I was? Quiet joy is mine. When now I see you shine in the moonlight, my heart leaps up. I seem to see at every window-pane a friendly face looking toward heaven, and thinking of me too.

Seidl's poems were published early in 1826 in two volumes, and these were presumably Schubert's source. The autograph manuscript, dated March 1826, originally contained four songs (D878–81), but it has been divided into two, and the autograph of this song, together with that of *Sehnsucht* D879, is now in Washington (LC). *Am Fenster* was published by Czerny of Vienna as op.105 no.3 in November 1828.

The song splendidly illustrates the metaphorical nature of Schubert's musical language in his maturity. The short, hesitant motif from which the song grows, with its flattened seventh, unemphatic accents and short phrases, exactly defines the mood of low-key contemplative content. The music seems to turn back on itself introspectively after a brief glimpse of the dominant in bar 9, while the unexpected pauses heighten the effect of happy solitude. The middle section, in D flat major, leads back to the tonic not directly but by way of a characteristically eloquent excursion into A major/minor. *Am Fenster* is not heard as often as the other Seidl songs; because of its air of understatement, it is not easy to bring off in performance. But it is hauntingly beautiful.

Capell, 223 Fischer-Dieskau, 237–8

## AM FLUSSE By the Stream (1)
**Johann Wolfgang von Goethe**                27 February 1815

D minor  D160  Not in Peters  GA XX no.47

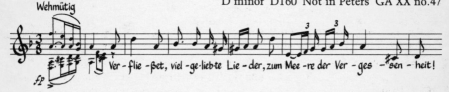

Flow far away, songs I once loved so well, into the ocean of oblivion. No enraptured youth will ever sing you now, or maiden in the springtime of her life.

You were the songs that told my tale of love, but now they hold my faithfulness to scorn. Since you were written on the water, flow far away, even as the waters flow.

The poem was written in 1768–9, and published in Schiller's *Musenalmanach* for 1799. The autograph (Berlin, SPK) is a first draft dated 27 February 1815. There are two copies in the Witteczek–Spaun collection (Vienna, GdM), one of them in C minor. The song was first published in the *Gesamtausgabe* in 1894.

Goethe's poem expresses all the heartache of youthful passion. Schubert catches the mood of vain regret perfectly. The song is deeply felt, wonderfully inflected as only Schubert knew how (the E flat in bar 6 for instance), and within the limits of its classical language it manages to reflect all the changing emotions of the poem. The song is a perfect miniature. How it managed to escape publication for so long is a mystery.

Capell, 100; Fischer-Dieskau, 53

## AM FLUSSE (2)
**Johann Wolfgang von Goethe**                December 1822

D major  D766  Not in Peters  GA XX no.418

For translation, see the preceding entry. The autograph manuscript (Berlin, SPK), dated December 1822, contains four Goethe songs, of which this is the third. There are two dated copies in the Witteczek–Spaun collection (Vienna, GdM). The song was published as no.3 of 'Forty Songs' by J. P. Gotthard in 1872.

In this second setting the attention is focussed not on the emotion but on the image of the stream, for Schubert had, in the intervening seven years, become a master of *Bewegung*. The gently flowing quavers carry the poetic associations along with them on the smooth surface of the stream; but it has to be admitted that the song looks only at the surface of the poem, not into the poetic depths. This is one of the few occasions when it may seem reasonable to prefer Schubert's first setting to his second. The simplicity, not to say facility, of this one is captivating, and it calls to mind a much greater song, *Fischerweise*. But it does not seem right for the young Goethe. (See Brown for a contrary view.)

Brown, *CB*, 203; Capell, 54, 181; Fischer-Dieskau, 167–8

## AM GRABE ANSELMOS By Anselm's Grave
**Matthias Claudius** 4 November 1816
E flat minor D504 Peters II p.14 GA XX no.275 NSA IV vol.1 pp.56, 216

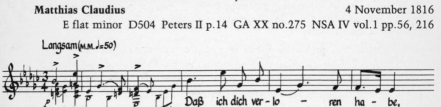

That I have lost you, that you are no more, that my Anselm lies here, in this grave – oh, that is my grief.
  See, we two loved one another, and so long as life shall last joy will never return to my heart.

The poem was written in 1792 or 1793, under the title *Bei dem Grabe Anselmos*. This title also appears on Schubert's autograph first draft, which is dated 4 November 1816 and bears the marking *Langsam*. A fair copy, however, written in the album of Therese Grob (see GROB) probably also in November 1816, is headed 'Am Grabe Anselmos' and marked 'Sehr langsam'. There are other minor differences between the two versions, which are both printed in the *Neue Ausgabe*. The earlier editions all follow the first draft. There are copies in the Stadler album (Lund, UB) and the Spaun–Cornaro collection (Vienna, privately owned). The song was first published in August 1821 as op.6 no.3 by Cappi and Diabelli on commission and dedicated to J.M. Vogl.

The Claudius songs of November 1816 have great expressive power and subjective feeling, but these are achieved by a refinement of the classical language, and not by the use of new Romantic motifs. Schubert's 'graveside songs' illustrate the point perfectly. His imagination responds in the same way to the same emotional stimulus, so that this song and the companion piece *Bei dem Grabe meines Vaters*, and the much later, and greater, song *Ihr Grab*, are all in E flat major, all have a vocal line based on the contour of the tonic arpeggio, and all explore the tonal relations of E flat on the flat side. Two of them, it may be added, have an off-key introduction, a symbol perhaps of emotional disturbance. The effect is quite different from 'Romantic' songs like *Grablied für die Mutter* and *Vor meiner Wiege*. The tone of *Am Grabe Anselmos* is one of mingled sorrow and consolation, a dignified sorrow before the inevitable face of death. The vocal line is adapted to the text with meticulous care.

Capell, 120; Fischer-Dieskau, 86

**AM MEER** see HEINE SONGS no.5

## AM SEE By the Lake
**Franz von Bruchmann**

(?) 1817/1822

E flat major D746 Peters V p.29 GA XX no.422

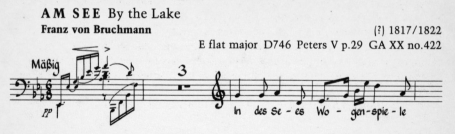

Into the rippling waters of the lake, down through the sunshine, stars come falling
– oh, so many! – flashing, gleaming down. If man too becomes like the lake, into
the rippling waters of his soul the stars come falling, down from the very gates of
heaven: oh, so many!

The autograph, now in Vienna ÖNB, is a single leaf, undated, headed 'Am See, by
Bruchmann'. The song cannot be precisely dated. In the list of works appended to
Kreissle's biography it is dated March 1817, but no supporting evidence has come to light.
The only two Bruchmann songs which can be firmly dated belong to the winter of
1822–3, and in the absence of any clear evidence this one is usually assigned to the same
period, when the relations between Schubert and the Bruchmann circle were closest. On
purely stylistic grounds the earlier date seems more likely than the later. The song was
published, together with *Abendbilder* and *Der zürnende Barde*, in book 9 of the *Nachlass*
in April 1831.

As so often, what turns the ignition switch of Schubert's creative imagination is
a sensuous image, exactly transmuted into a musical figure, a precise *Bewegung*.
Everything is contained in the smoothly rocking figure which runs through every bar of
this barcarolle. For the long flowing melody itself seems to be carried along on that figure,
like a boat rocking lazily on the waves. And the lingering appoggiaturas of the singer's
final bars mirror the eternity of a summer day.

Capell, 47, 176; Fischer-Dieskau, 159

## AM SEE By the Lake
**Johann Mayrhofer**

7 December 1814

G minor D124 Peters VII p.42 (corrupt version) GA XX no.36 NSA IV vol.7 pp.65, 194

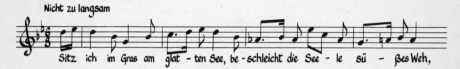

I sit on the grass by the glassy lake, sweet anguish stealing through my soul. Then
comes a witching nameless sound, as of Aeolian harps.

The sighing rushes bend, the flowers from the bank greet me, the birds cry
and the breezes blow. Would I might die of grief!

How strong the surge of life within me, now darkly seething, now clear as
a mirror.

The consciousness of my own inner strength floods me with joy. Into that
flood I cast myself, to struggle for the highest good.

O life, how beautiful you are, both in your heights and in your depths! Should I ignore your friendly light, and tread the gloomy path to Hades?

Yet you are not the highest goal to me; I sacrifice you gladly to duty. A radiant image draws me on, and for it I would risk my life.

Tears often stain this bright image, as it burns in my breast. Then I dash those tears from my cheeks, and die a thousand deaths.

Great Leopold, you were so manly, pure, and good, humanity so wrung your heart, it brought you the sacrificial crown. Thus crowned, you sprang down into your watery grave for mankind. Thermopylae and Marathon pale before your deed, O noble Prince! The sighing rushes bend, the flowers greet me from the bank, the birds cry and the breezes blow. Would I might die of grief!

The poem commemorates Duke Leopold of Brunswick, a nephew of Frederick the Great, who was drowned in April 1785 in an attempt to save his threatened subjects from a flood. The event made a big impression, and was celebrated in verse by Herder and Goethe, among others. Schubert had the poem in manuscript from the poet, via his friend Josef von Spaun. The autograph sketch of the first 57 bars is in Vienna (SB). The source for the full version published in the *Gesamtausgabe* was the copy in the Witteczek–Spaun collection (Vienna, GdM), marked 'Nicht zu langsam', and dated 7 December 1814.

The first Mayrhofer song gives no indication of the riches to follow. The complete song is bitty, a cantata-like setting in which the climaxes seem forced. The best part is the opening section, to an attractive 6/8 pensive G minor tune, which Friedländer published in the Peters edition as a complete song! To this strophic tune he set the first two verses of Mayrhofer's poem, suitably edited, and added two more specially written by Max Kalbeck. One may sympathise with Friedländer's critical judgment, if not with his editorial practice.

## AM STROME By the Stream

**Johann Mayrhofer** March 1817

B major D539 Peters II p.25 GA XX no.306 NSA IV vol.1 p.82

Ist mir's doch, als sei mein Le - ben

My life, it seems, is linked to the lovely stream; for have I not known both joy and sorrow on its banks?

Yes, you are like my soul, sometimes green and tranquil, and sometimes, when the winds blow, foaming, restless, furrowed.

Onward flow to the distant sea: not for you to settle here at home. I too long for kinder shores. I find no joy here on earth.

The only surviving autograph (Vienna, SB) is a fragment consisting of the last twenty-two bars, undated and without any tempo indication. This manuscript also contains the autograph of *Philoktet* D540, which is dated March 1817. The first edition was presumably based on a lost fair copy. The song was published as op.8 no.4 by Cappi and Diabelli in May 1822, and dedicated by Schubert to Johann Karl, Count Esterházy.

Like *Auf der Donau*, *Am Strome* uses the 'river of life' image to convey the poet's own longing for a better world. But here Schubert's mood is more complaisant, and the music more sweetly lyrical. There are, indeed, interesting pre-echoes of *Die schöne Müllerin*, not only in the main tune, but also in the way the middle verse resorts to a

form of declamation, switching the focus from the external scene to the narrator himself. But it is the placid flow of the outer verses that has given the song its deserved
popularity.

Capell, 138

## AM TAGE ALLER SEELEN see LITANEI

## AMALIA
**Friedrich von Schiller**                                    19 May 1815

A major D195 Peters VI p.106 GA XX no.71

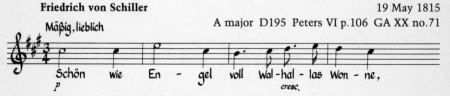

Fair as angels full of Valhalla's bliss, he was the fairest of all the youths; his glances
heavenly kind, like the May sun reflected in the blue mirror of the sea.

His kisses brought a touch of paradise; as two flames intertwine, as the
strains of the harp mingle in heavenly harmony, so our two spirits met, flew, fused
together.

Lips and cheeks burned and trembled, soul melted into soul; earth and heaven
swam, as though dissolved, about the lovers!

He is gone: in vain, in vain I sigh. He is gone: and all life's joy flows from me
in one forlorn lament.

The poem comes from Schiller's play *Die Räuber* ('The Robbers'), Act III Scene 1. Amalia,
sitting in her garden, is thinking of her banished lover, Karl. Schubert used the slightly
shorter version published in the collected edition of 1810. The autograph has been missing
since October 1869. There are, however, several contemporary copies, including one in
the Witteczek–Spaun collection (Vienna, GdM) dated 19 May 1815, and another, similarly
dated, in the album of Anton Schindler (Lund, UB). The song was published by C. A. Spina
in 1867 as op.173 no.1.

The dramatic situation here resembles that of Gretchen at her spinning-wheel;
Amalia's soliloquy moves, like Gretchen's, from composure and recollection through
passionate imaginings to a recognition of her own loneliness and despair. But there the
resemblance ends. In *Gretchen* the musical motif that defines and unifies the song is the
one that represents the spinning-wheel. Here Schubert's model is the operatic aria of several
cumulative sections, each with its own pace and movement. The form is seen at its best
in later songs like *Ganymed*. *Amalia* is a splendid song for a dramatic soprano, with an
orchestrally written recitative leading to a fine climax.

In his diary (*Docs.* p.60) Schubert records that he performed *Amalia* at a musical
party in June 1816, and remarks that it was not so well received as Goethe's *Rastlose Liebe*.
This he attributes to Goethe's genius as 'a musical poet'; and certainly many of the Schiller
songs seem to lack the emotional commitment which is so marked a feature of the Goethe
settings.

## AMMENLIED The Nurse's Song

**Michael Lubi**                                                December 1814

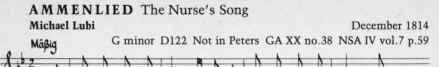

G minor D122 Not in Peters GA XX no.38 NSA IV vol.7 p.59

Am ho-hen, ho-hen Turm___, da weht ein kal-ter Sturm___ :

High about the tower a chill wind blows. Patience! The bells chime, the sun gleams from afar.

Deep in the valley a waterfall rushes. Patience! A little further on runs a merry streamlet.

Bare are the branches around the sheltering dove. Patience! Soon the meadows will be green, and it will build its nest.

You are frozen, little daughter mine, no friend bids you come in. But when the time comes angels will welcome you, and God keeps the best little room in his house for those he loves.

Little is known about Michael Lubi except his dates (1757–1808) and the fact that his poems were published in Graz in 1804. The autograph is missing, but a copy in the Witteczek–Spaun collection (Vienna, GdM) is dated December 1814. According to a manuscript catalogue of Schubert's songs made by Diabelli the song belongs to the beginning of that month. The first publication was in 1872, as no.12 of 'Forty Songs', by J. P. Gotthard; only the first verse of the poem was printed. The others were added in the *Gesamtausgabe* from the collected edition of the poems. But since the copy in the Witteczek–Spain collection also has only one verse, it is quite possible that Schubert intended only one verse to be sung. An attractive strophic song in Schubert's folksong manner, full of playful tenderness.

## AMPHIARAOS

**Theodor Körner**                                                1 March 1815

G minor D166 Not in Peters GA XX no.52

Etwas langsam, mit Kraft          Recit.

Vor Thebens siebenfach gähnenden To-ren

[*Summary translation*] The princes' army lay before the seven yawning gates of Thebes, ready for battle, sworn to kill, girt in their shining armour, dreaming triumphantly of victory: all except noble Amphiaraos, Apollo's mighty son.

In the stars' eternal course he read what threatened, saw the dice fall, saw fate lie waiting with its bloody claws. But the heroes mocked his heaven-sent words.

He knew what the fates held in store and went to battle, doomed, shamelessly betrayed by his own wife, yet conscious of the divine flame within him. For a god's heart beat within his breast.

'Am I, who have spoken with the gods, to die in ignoble strife, slain by Periklymenos? Rather would I die by my own strength, that the bards might tell how boldly I went down to endless night.'

So when the bloody fight began, amid the tumult on the plain he cried despairingly: 'My fate draws nigh. But I have divinity in my blood, and must die a worthy death.'

He turned his horses, raced his chariot beside the swift river. The stallions snorted, their hooves pounding the track; the clattering chariot flew like a whirlwind, ever faster.

The watery gods, appalled, raised their reed-crowned heads from the flood. Then suddenly a thunderbolt rent the clear air, cleaving the earth. Exultantly the son of Apollo cried out: 'My thanks, mighty one; my covenant is kept. Your thunder is my seal of immortality. I follow you, Zeus!'

Then, gathering up the reins, he drove the horses down into the abyss.

The autograph (Vienna, SB) is a first draft, dated at both the beginning and the end 1 March 1815. At the end Schubert has added 'In 5 hours'. A copy in the Witteczek–Spaun collection (Vienna, GdM) is similarly dated. The song was first published in the *Gesamtausgabe* in 1894.

Amphiaraos, son of Apollo, was persuaded by his wife Eriphyle to take part in the expedition of the seven against Thebes. Foreseeing his own fate, he charged his children to avenge his death by killing their mother. As he fled from the beleaguered city Zeus dispatched a thunderbolt and the ground opened to swallow him up. Schubert's setting is almost unknown, yet it is a brilliant and dramatic piece, and a splendid vehicle for a powerful and flexible voice. The fluency and vividness of the piano writing, and its superficiality, suggest early film music. There is no undercurrent of subjective emotion, except perhaps in verse 4 ('Am I, who have spoken with the gods, to die in ignoble strife?'), where the strong *sf* bass octaves descend chromatically from C to F below the stave, reminding us of a favourite Schubertian image of death. *Amphiaraos*, in short, has the dramatic vividness of a Loewe ballad.

Capell, 91

## AN CHLOEN To Chloe

**Johann Georg Jacobi**                                    August 1816

Etwas geschwind                     A flat major D462 Not in Peters GA XX no.244

Bei__ der Lie - be rein - sten Flam-men glänzt das ar - me Hüt -ten - dach:__

The humble rooftop gleams with love's purest flames. Forever we are together, my darling, dreaming or awake.

Sweet tender embrace when dawn dispels the dark; secret longing stirs when the dews of evening fall.

Bliss is there on every hilltop, bliss in the valley and joy is here! We are free to bar the door of our little hut.

A song of praise in the darkness, where none lurks nearby to envy us; where we no longer need to fear the lightest breeze when we kiss!

And we share all our joys, sun and moon and starlight, every blessing, every pain, work, and prayer, and dancing.

So the sweet contest ends in the pure flames of love; at peace we drift together, my darling, towards heaven.

The autograph is lost, but there is a copy in the Witteczek–Spaun collection (Vienna, GdM) dated August 1816, which provided the source for the *Gesamtausgabe* when the song was first published in 1895. An unremarkable strophic setting.

## AN CHLOEN To Chloe
**Johann Peter Uz**

1816 (?June)
G major D363 Not in Peters Not in GA

[Bars 1-5 incomplete]     [ent-]-gan-gen; der Mund will kaum ein Lä-cheln wa-gen;

My cheeks are wan, my eyes have lost their sparkle, my mouth scarce dares to smile.
Like flowers at noon, when Flora languishes and Zephyr dies, my feeble frame can
scarce hold up.

And yet I notice that when Chloe comes my eager gaze is eloquent, my lips
come alive, a rosy glow is in my face, and I am all young again, like flowers bathed
in dew.

I gaze on her with anxious longing; I cannot turn away. The grace that wakes
in her eyes and laughs in her young cheeks coaxes me to look again, drawing me
back with fetters of gold.

My blood flows fast, I burn, I tremble with desire to kiss her. I seek her out
with frantic looks, stifled with impatience, for in my longing I can see her but not
fold her in my arms.

This strophic song was complete when Schubert wrote it, but the autograph (Lund, UB)
was mutilated by a later owner. Bars 7–23 survive, but the first six bars have only the
bass line of the accompaniment. The manuscript also contains another Uz setting, *Die
Nacht* D358. The only authority for the date of composition is the catalogue of the
Witteczek–Spaun collection (Vienna, GdM) but all the surviving dated autographs of Uz
songs belong to June 1816. The song has been completed and privately printed by Reinhard
van Hoorickx, and this performing version has been recorded (DG 1981007). It is a song
of grave and contemplative beauty, and undoubtedly one of the best of the Uz settings.

**AN CIDLI** see FURCHT DER GELIEBTEN

**AN DEM JUNGEN MORGENHIMMEL** see DON GAYSEROS no.3

## AN DEN FRÜHLING To Spring (1)
**Friedrich von Schiller**

6 September 1815
F major D283 Peters VI p.103 GA XX no.136

Mäßig, heiter

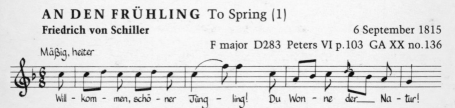

Will-kom-men, schö-ner Jüng-ling! Du Won-ne der— Na-tur!

Welcome fair youth, nature's delight. Welcome to these meadows with your basket
of flowers.

Ah, you are come again, so dear and beautiful; our hearts are joyful as we haste
to greet you.

Do you still think of my sweetheart? Ah, do think of her, my friend. For there
my girl loved me, and she loves me still!

I asked for a host of flowers for her. Now I come and ask again, and you –
you give it me.

Schiller's poem was written in 1782. Schubert set it three times, twice for solo voice and
once (D338) for male-voice quartet. The autograph of this first version, a first draft dated

6 September 1815, is in the Taussig collection (Lund, UB). There are two dated copies in the Witteczek–Spaun collection (Vienna, GdM). The song was published as op.172 no.5 in 1865 by C.A. Spina.

Schiller repeats the first verse at the end, making five verses in all. Schubert here uses only the first four verses, linking two verses together in his strophe. Because of the confusion over the date of the other solo setting (see the following entry), this song was long regarded as Schubert's final version, and as such was highly praised, as it deserves to be, for its purity of style and perfection of form.

## AN DEN FRÜHLING (2)
**Friedrich von Schiller**

October 1817

A major D587 Peters VII p.34 GA XX no.107(b)

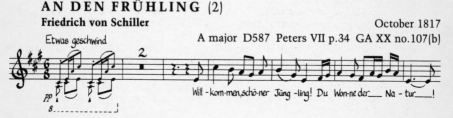

For translation, see the preceding entry. There are two variants entered separately as D587 and D245 in the thematic catalogue (but see D2 under 587). The first draft (New York, privately owned) is in A major and dated October 1817. The fair copy of this A major version belonged to a sheaf of songs which was auctioned in Vienna 1906 and is now in WSLB, Vienna. There are two copies in the Witteczek–Spaun collection (Vienna, GdM). A later fair copy, in B flat major, has written on it in an unknown hand the date August 1815. This seems to be the result of a double mistake. It misled Deutsch into believing that the B flat version must be the earlier, though the calligraphic evidence points to its being later. Both autographs are in private hands. Both versions are printed in the *Gesamtausgabe*. The song, in the A major version, first appeared in vol. VII of the Peters edition (1885). The prelude is a Ländler closely resembling, say, op.9 no.17 or no.19, and its infectious gaiety sets the tone for this delightful song.

## AN DEN MOND To the Moon
Fragment without text

1815

A major D311 Not in Peters Not in GA

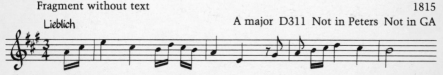

The fragment, consisting of twelve bars of the melody line, without text or accompaniment, was written on the last page of a manuscript which includes two songs (D318–19) dated 19 October 1815. The page is headed 'An den Mond'. This autograph is in Vienna (SB). The tune has been edited and printed by Reinhard van Hoorickx, with a text borrowed from a folksong.

## AN DEN MOND To the Moon (1)

**Johann Wolfgang von Goethe**                    19 August 1815

E flat major  D259  Peters VI p.57  GA XX no.116

Once more you fill the woods and valleys silently with your misty light, and at last my soul is quite set free.

Your healing gaze is spread over my fields, watching over my fate with a friendly eye.

My heart feels every echo of happy times and sad; joy and sorrow mingle in my loneliness.

Flow on, sweet river. I shall never be happy. For so too love and laughter have drifted away, and faithfulness.

A precious thing I once possessed, which, though it tortures me, I cannot forget.

Murmur on through the valley, ever onward without cease, whispering your tunes to my song;

as when in winter nights your raging waters overflow, or when you drench the young buds in springtime glory.

Happy is he who, feeling no hatred, shuts himself off from the world, clasps one friend to his heart, and with him enjoys those things which, unknown or unconsidered by men, wander through the labyrinth of the heart in the night hours.

Goethe's famous poem was written in the winter of 1777–8, as a 'parody' of a poem by Heinrich Wagner which had been set to music by Goethe's friend Philip Kayser. The inverted commas are necessary to make it clear that the intention was not in any sense satirical, but prompted by the appeal of the verse rhythm as realised in Kayser's setting, in a spirit of admiration and creative emulation. *An den Mond* is a love poem; when it was finished Goethe sent it, with Kayser's music, to Charlotte von Stein. When in 1786 Goethe deserted Weimar and Charlotte and fled to Italy, Charlotte made her own version of the poem to express her grief, and some of her emendations were embodied in the final version of the text which Goethe made on his return.

The interdependence of verse and music in the pre-Romantic period carried with it certain obligations for the composer, who was expected to provide a strophic setting matching the prevailing tone of the poem, and its metre, but leaving the expressive details to the skill of the singer. His job was to 'set' the poem, not to provide a musical composition in its own right which distorts the text for its own purposes. This modest role is accepted in this first version, but Schubert is not so successful as Zelter was with his strophic setting in catching the reflective spirit of the poem; the tone is too jaunty. Nor can the strophic form reflect the progression of thought or Goethe's complex pattern of ideas and emotions, or his ability to comprehend past, present and future in the poetic moment. Indeed, since Schubert's stanza covers two verses of the poem, not all the nine verses can be sung.

Schubert's two versions thus fall on opposite sides of the great divide between pre-Romantic and Romantic song. The first was written, along with four other Goethe songs, on 19 August 1815. There is a dated autograph, with *Bundeslied* on the reverse side, but it disappeared in the 1950s. A fair copy was made for Goethe, probably in the autumn of 1816; it is now in the Paris Conservatoire. There are also two copies in the Witteczek–Spaun collection (Vienna, GdM). The song was published in 1850 in book 47 of the *Nachlass*. The four-bar prelude included in the Peters edition appears to be spurious.

# AN DEN MOND (2)

**Johann Wolfgang von Goethe**

(?) 1819

A flat major D296 Peters VII p.50 GA XX no.176

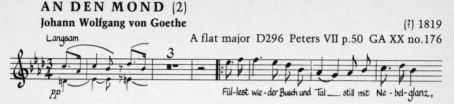

For translation, see the preceding entry. The date of this second version is uncertain. The autograph (Berlin, SPK) is undated, and there is no other firm evidence. Deutsch suggested autumn 1815, but this is unlikely in view of the enormous advance which it shows on the setting of August 1815. Recent work on the autograph, however, has established that the paper used is of the same type as that of *Adrast* and other dramatic works on which Schubert was occupied in 1819–20. It is a reasonable guess, therefore, that this mature version belongs, with *Prometheus* and *Die Liebende schreibt*, to October 1819. There are copies, undated, in the Witteczek–Spaun collection (Vienna, GdM). The song was published in 1868, as no.3 of 'Six Previously Unpublished Songs', by Wilhelm Müller of Berlin.

The form chosen is again basically strophic, but this time the music pierces to the heart. The singer's first notes, the lift of the voice which gives to the 'seventh on the seventh' a magical new expressive force, seems to contain within itself the essence of the song. Schubert again combines two verses in one strophe, but so modifies the structure as to give it the depth and subtlety of the poem and a basically tripartite form. The first five verses are set to the same music in the tonic A flat. Verses 6 and 7 undergo extensive modulation to G flat and C flat and are given a melodic treatment of their own; the last two verses return to the opening music and the tonic.

It can be said – and it has been – that the song does not truly mirror the development of the poet's thought. The music for the placid opening and the existential questioning of the last verses is the same. The link between verses 4 and 5, which are both concerned with the sense of lost innocence, is destroyed; and the musical climax, in verses 6 and 7, comes in a sense in the wrong place, since the poem is not about the river but about one man's complex state of mind as he stands watching it in the moonlight. All this is true, and it can be added that the verbal emphasis is by no means impeccable; but it is unimportant. What matters is that Schubert has matched the *Innigkeit* of the poem with music of a comparable grandeur and depth; this inwardness, this sense of the voice as a kind of vehicle for the soul, makes *An den Mond* an important landmark in the history of the Romantic lied.

> Capell, 102–3; Einstein, 108; Fischer-Dieskau, 52–3; Stein, 17–27; Sternfeld, 103; R. Winter, 'Schubert's undated works: a new chronology', *MT*, CXIX, (1978), p.500

# AN DEN MOND To the Moon I (Geuss, lieber Mond)

**Ludwig Hölty**

17 May 1815

F minor D193 Peters II p.116 GA XX no.69

Pour your silver light, beloved moon, through the beech trees' green, where fancies and dream figures flee before me.

Shine forth, that I may find the place where oft my sweetheart sat, forgetful of the gilded town among the waving beech and linden boughs.

Shine forth, that I may see the leafy sprays that whispered to her in the breeze, and strew a wreath on every meadow where she once listened to the brook.

Then, dear moon, veil your face once more, and mourn your friend. Weep down through the cloudy ranges of the sky, as I, forsaken, weep.

The first draft of the song, dated 17 May 1815, but without the piano prelude, is in Vienna (SB). The copies made by Albert Stadler and Johann Leopold Ebner (Lund, UB) have no prelude either, so it is reasonable to assume that Schubert added it when the song was published as op.57 no.3 in April 1826 by Thaddäus Weigl. This setting was the only one of the Hölty songs to be published in the composer's lifetime.

Doubtless the resemblance to Beethoven's 'Moonlight' Sonata in the accompaniment has contributed to the song's popularity, though there is no need to assume any conscious borrowing. Schubert had used these flowing triplets before in an earlier nocturne (*Geisternähe*) and he probably knew Mozart's *Abendempfindung*. The pastoral melancholy of the 12/8 tune which frames the song is evocative, but the middle section does not quite sustain the same poetic level.

Capell, 92; Fischer-Dieskau, 58–9

## AN DEN MOND II (Was schauest du so hell und klar)
**Ludwig Hölty**
7 August 1816

A major D468 Not in Peters GA XX no.243

Why do you look down, so bright and clear, through the apple trees, where once your friend was happy, dreaming sweet dreams? Veil your silver light, and glimmer as when you dimly light the funeral wreath of the young bride.

In vain you look down upon these boughs, so bright and clear; nevermore will you find the happy pair beneath their shade. Dark, cruel fate has robbed me of my love; no sighs, no tears of longing, can weave a spell to bring her back.

If she should one day come back to where I rest, then let your melancholy light make my grave-flowers bright. She will sit weeping on my grave, where the roses droop, and pluck a flower, and press it to her cheek.

The autograph (Vienna, SB) is dated 7 August 1816. The song first appeared in the *Gesamtausgabe* in 1895. In contrast to the Romantic tone of *Geuss, lieber Mond* of the previous year (see the preceding entry), Schubert here reverts to the more formal and classical manner which characterises so much of his work in 1816. But the song is not lacking in feeling, and indeed it could be argued that its Mozartian simplicity and major–minor pathos is more in keeping with Hölty's period style than the earlier song.

Capell, 117

## AN DEN MOND IN EINER HERBSTNACHT To the
Moon on an Autumn Night

**Alois Schreiber**                                           April 1818

A major D614 Peters V p.88 GA XX no.337

Your face is kind, son of heaven; softly you pace across the vastness of the sky, fair companion of the night.

Your gentle glimmer comforts like a friendly word, when fear preys on the soul. You see so many tears, so many smiles; you hear the lovers' whispered secrets, as you light them on their quiet way. Hope streams down from you upon the silent sufferer, as he travels his thorny path in loneliness.

You gaze upon my friends too, scattered in distant lands. You shed your beams upon the happy hills, where I often played as a boy, a strange longing clutching at my young heart as you smiled down upon me.

You shine also upon the place where my loved ones sleep, where the dew falls upon their graves, and the grass above them waves in the evening breeze.

Yet your light does not penetrate into the dark chamber where they rest from their toil, and where I too shall soon rest. You will go, and return again; you will see many more smiles still; but then I shall no longer smile, or weep, and none will call me to mind on this fair earth.

This is the first of four Schreiber songs, all composed in 1818. An edition of the poems was published in 1817 at Tübingen and another in Vienna. The autograph, dated April 1818, is now in LC Washington DC. There is a copy in the Witteczek–Spaun collection (Vienna, GdM). The song was first published in 1832 (*Nachlass* book 18).

The Schreiber songs, noteworthy for their pure lyrical style and for the freedom of their accompaniments, occupy an important place in the development of Schubert's art, pointing forward to the masterpieces of his middle years. The new tone is set in the opening bars of the song, which sound like the beginning of a slow movement from a Schubert sonata, and have the slow contemplative gait which is so characteristic of the composer. The postlude ends, too, with a phrase which anticipates the theme of the Andante of the A minor Sonata (D784); but since this is an echo of the singer's final cadence, it seems to be a coincidental likeness.

*An den Mond in einer Herbstnacht* is predictive in a much more significant way. As the poem turns to thoughts of the grave, to the dark chamber where the light of the moon cannot penetrate, the movement changes to that of measured speech, and then, as we hear the descending chromatic line of a characteristic death motif, to recitative. But at the end, the declamatory tone returns, in a sort of quasi-recitative. This ability to change the focus of the song at will is one of the glories of the great song cycles, here clearly adumbrated. Indeed, bars 78–88 ('Du blickst auch auf die Stätte') are a striking pre-echo of one of the great moments in *Winterreise* (*Frühlingstraum*, bar 27).

Capell, 144; Einstein, 165–6; Fischer-Dieskau, 112–13

## AN DEN SCHLAF To Sleep
**Author unknown**                                              June 1816

A major  D447  Not in Peters  GA XX no.232

Komm und sen-ke die um-flor-ten Schwingen, sü - ßer Schlummer, auf den mü-den Blick!

Come and rest your weary wings, sweet slumber, on my tired eyes. Blessed friend,
comfort and balm come quickly in your arms, when happiness has fled.

The autograph is lost. A copy in the Witteczek–Spaun collection (Vienna, GdM) names
Johann Peter Uz as the author, but the poem is not to be found among his published works.
The same copy is the only authority for the date of the song. The first publication was
in 1895, in the *Gesamtausgabe*. The repeat marks at the end, and the three-bar postlude,
suggest that the lines may have formed only the first verse of a longer poem. The song
has the poise and formal clarity of the classical canzonet.

## AN DEN TOD To Death
**Christian Friedrich Schubart**                                      1817

B major  D518  Peters V p.84  GA XX no.326

Tod,          du Schre-cken der Na - tur!        im - mer rie -selt dei - ne Uhr

*Verses 1, 2:* Death, thou scourge of nature, thine hour-glass runs unceasing. The
swinging scythe flashes, and grass, stem and flower, falls. Do not cut down in-
discriminately this little flower just open, this rose half-blown. Be merciful, O death!

*Verses 14, 16:* (When will you come, death, my desire, to draw the dagger from my
breast, to strike the fetters from my wrists and cover me with sand?
    So if it please thee, Death, release the prisoners from the world. Come, end
their misery; be merciful, friend Death.)

The poem has sixteen verses. Schubert set the first two, as a continuous composition.
He wrote out two more – verses 14 and 16 – supposedly to be used as a kind of optional
repeat. The Peters edition refuses to regard this as a strophic song, and prints only the
first two verses.

    The autograph is lost, and there is no firm evidence as to the date of composition.
There is a copy in the third volume of Albert Stadler's song album (Lund, UB), which
was compiled in 1817. The song was published by the Lithographic Institute of Vienna
in 1824. It appeared first as a supplement to the Vienna *AMZ* on 26 June 1824, and later
that same year as a separate publication. Diabelli included it in book 17 of the *Nachlass*,
published in 1832. Friedländer was surely right to print only the first two verses. It is quite
clear that Schubert did not intend all the verses to be sung, and that being so, there is
little point, either musically or poetically, in the repeat performance.

    *An den Tod* is a puzzle. It cannot be dated later than 1817, if the implications of
Stadler's copy are accepted, yet it seems to belong rather to the world of *Nacht und Träume*,
with which it has tonal affinities. It lacks any obvious thematic links with roughly contemporary songs like *Der Jüngling und der Tod* and *Auf der Donau*, and seems to have
more in common with songs on classical themes like *Fahrt zum Hades*; for the tone
is awesome and mysterious rather than apprehensive and personal. The adventurous

modulations (B major – C major – B flat major – B major) are surely meant to suggest mystery rather than 'passionate protest' (Capell). The marking 'Mit Pedal' (see the *Gesamtausgabe*) must mean with sustaining pedal through to the end of the phrase.

Brown, *CB*, 45; Capell, 135; Fischer-Dieskau, 107 – 8; Porter, 110 – 11

## AN DIE APFELBÄUME WO ICH JULIEN ERBLICKTE
To the Apple Trees where I Espied Julia
**Ludwig Hölty** 22 May 1815
A major D197 Peters VI p.76 GA XX no.73

Langsam, feierlich

*pp*

Ein hei - lig Säu-seln und ein Ge - san - ges - ton

Let a solemn murmur, and the sound of song, stir the tree-tops above your shadowy paths, where the ecstasy of love first disturbed my heart.

The evening sunlight quivered like bright gold through purple blossoms, quivered like bright gold about the silver veil of her breast. I melted in a shudder of delight.

Let a faithful youth, after long separation, greet his beloved wife with an angel's kiss, and in this blossomy darkness plight his undying troth to his chosen bride.

When we are dead, may a flower blossom on this grass, where her footsteps trod, and may it bear on every one of its leaves the name of my glorified love.

The autograph, a first draft dated 22 May 1815, has been split up, and the first fifteen bars, written on the back of *An die Nachtigall* (D196), have disappeared. The remaining thirteen bars (with *Seufzer* D198) are in the Paris Conservatoire. There is a dated copy in the Witteczek – Spaun collection (Vienna, GdM). The song was first published in 1850, as no.1 of book 50 of the *Nachlass*.

*An die Apfelbäume* has been undeservedly neglected by both singers and critics. It breaks away from the strophic mould of most of the Hölty songs and presents us with a long flowing melody in a 12/8 movement. The lilt is interrupted for verse 3, where the young man's expression of love is set to a free recitative in the minor. Like the earlier (February 1815) song, *Als ich sie erröten sah*, this one looks forward to the free flowing style of *Wohin?*

Craig Bell, 25

## AN DIE DIOSKUREN see LIED EINES SCHIFFERS AN DIE DIOSKUREN

## AN DIE ENTFERNTE To the Distant Lover
**Johann Wolfgang von Goethe** December 1822
G major D765 Peters VII p.54 GA XX no.417

Langsam

So hab ich wirk - lich dich ver - lo - ren?

> <=*f* >*p*

Have I really lost you? Have you forsaken me, beloved? Every word, every inflection still lingers in the familiar way in my ear.

As the traveller's gaze searches the morning sky in vain, when the hidden lark sings high aloft in the blue dome, so do my anxious eyes range back and forth, on field, and grove, and woodland.

All my songs call to you: 'Come back to me, beloved; beloved, oh, come back!'

The poem was written after Goethe's return from Italy in 1788; it was occasioned by the breach with Charlotte von Stein. Schubert's setting is one of a group of four Goethe songs written in December 1822 (D764–7). The autograph (Berlin, SPK) contains all four, and is dated December 1822. There is a dated copy also in the Witteczek–Spaun collection (Vienna, GdM). The song was first published in 1868 by Wilhelm Müller of Berlin.

The song's belated publication, and its comparative neglect, are difficult to explain. The unity of words and music is so close that it achieves the effect of soliloquy, each phrase finding its true and individual expression within the pervasive mood of tenderness and remorse. Yet it also preserves the spontaneity and immediacy of the poem, as though spoken without artifice and without premeditation.

Capell, 181; Einstein, 254; Fischer-Dieskau, 161–2

## AN DIE FREUDE Ode to Joy
**Friedrich von Schiller**                                                        1815

E major  D189  Peters IV p.126  GA XX no.66

Joy, fair spark divine, daughter of Elysium, we approach your sanctuary, heavenly one, drunk with ardour. Your magic reunites what harsh custom separates; all men become brothers where your gentle wing hovers. Take this embrace, ye millions! This kiss is for all the world! Brothers, a loving father must dwell above the starry vault of heaven.

He who has been fortunate, enjoyed true friendship, won a dear wife, let him mingle his joy with ours. Yes – even he who has but one soul on earth to call his own. And whoever has not achieved this, let him steal away weeping from this brotherhood! Whoever dwells on this great globe, let him pay homage to sympathy, for it leads to the stars, where the Unknown is enthroned.

All earth's creatures drink joy from Nature's breasts; good men and bad follow her rosy path. She gave us kisses, and wine, gave us a friend well tried in death; the worm was endowed with lust, and the cherub stands before God. Ye millions, do you fall down and worship? World, do you sense the Creator? Seek him beyond the firmament, for he must dwell beyond the stars.
[*The poem has five more verses.*]

The poem, written in the summer of 1785 (and so some years before the outbreak of the French Revolution), embodies the political ideals of the Enlightenment. It is not to be wondered at therefore that in the revolutionary era it became a kind of battle hymn for liberals, an ode to freedom as well as to joy. Beethoven contemplated a setting of it at various times from 1793 onwards, and finally used it in the Finale of his Ninth Symphony. The autograph of Schubert's setting is lost. In the list of works appended to Kreissle's biography the song is attributed to 1815; there appears to be no authority for a more precise date. It was published early in 1829 by Josef Czerny as no.1 of op.111.

Schubert's strophic setting with unison chorus may well have been written for some special – possibly scholastic – occasion. The *Gesamtausgabe* prints all eight verses, but in the absence of the autograph it is not clear how many Schubert intended should be sung. The song catches the exalted mood of the poem in all its strength and simplicity; it is a pity that the right occasion for a complete performance rarely offers itself. The superficial resemblance between Schubert's tune and Beethoven's is not surprising; there are other examples in 1815. It is certain also that Schubert knew Beethoven's Fantasy for Piano, Chorus and Orchestra op.80, and to judge from Schwind's later painting (called *The Symphony*) he took part in performances of it. He may have caught the tone of his song from the finale of that work.

> Fischer-Dieskau, 194–5

## AN DIE FREUNDE To his Friends

**Johann Mayrhofer**

March 1819

A minor  D654  Peters VI p.28  GA XX no.356

Bury me in the forest, in silence, with no cross or stone. For whatever you heap upon my grave will be covered over with winter's snow and ice.

And when the earth is young again and brings her flowers out upon my grave, then rejoice, good friends, rejoice. All this means nothing to the dead.

And yet – and yet your love spreads its branches into the spirit world, and as it leads you to my grave, so it draws me ever more strongly down.

In 1819 Schubert was living in Mayrhofer's rooms in the inner city. He must have received the poem in manuscript from his friend. The autograph (Vienna, GdM) is a first draft dated March 1819. It is in A minor, and bears no tempo indication. A copy in the Witteczek–Spaun collection (GdM) is marked 'Langsam' and transposed to F minor. It is annotated 'To Kenner from Mayrhofer'. When the song came to be published in book 40 of the *Nachlass* (c. 1842) the text was mistakenly attributed to Josef Kenner. Diabelli printed the F minor version, which differs from the autograph in some significant details, and added the marking *Mässig*. The *Gesamtausgabe*, following the autograph, prints the A minor version without tempo indication. It omits the octaves in the pianist's prelude, and writes out the singer's appoggiatura on the first beat of bar 59, where the F minor version has a minim A.

The poem calls to mind the ironic cry in *Trockne Blumen*: 'Then all you flowers, come out, come out! Spring has come, and winter is done!' But Schubert's staccato quavers are an image of the funeral procession, and put him in the position of an observer. In the second half the detached quavers become legato crotchets, but the solemn gait is unchanged. Only once in the song is it broken, at the phrase 'All this means nothing to the dead'; and here a personal sense of loss shows itself, with the neapolitan shift up from F major to G flat major, and the downward-plunging voice line. When the steady gait is resumed, it is with a certain sense of anticlimax. It is difficult to avoid the feeling that Schubert's imagination was not fully engaged. The slow four-in-a-bar pacing movement is one of the commonest Schubert rhythmic fingerprints.

> Capell, 160; Einstein, 189; Porter, 82–3

## AN DIE GELIEBTE To the Beloved

**Josef Ludwig Stoll**

15 October 1815

G major D303 Peters VII p.108 GA XX no.151

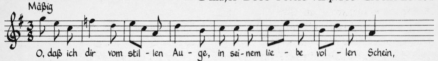

O, daß ich dir vom stil-len Au-ge, in sei-nem lie-be vol-len Schein,

Oh, let me drink the tears from your quiet shining eyes and from your cheek, before they sink into the earth.

    They linger hesitantly upon your cheek, a witness to your constancy. Now, when I capture them with a kiss, your grief too is mine.

The autograph, now in ÖNB, is a first draft, dated 15 October 1815. There is a dated copy in the Witteczek–Spaun collection (Vienna, GdM). The song was first published by Peters of Leipzig in 1887.

    The song was written, along with seven others, on the name day of Schubert's first love Therese Grob, so there is little doubt about the identity of 'die Geliebte'. The curious thing is that a year later, in November 1816, he used the same musical idea as the basis for a much greater song, his setting of the Claudius poem *An die Nachtigall* (D497). This too is a love song, and more personal in tone than *An die Geliebte*. A comparison of the two songs tells us more about the development of Schubert's genius between October 1815 and November 1816 than about his love-life. For whereas *An die Geliebte* is very singable, the Claudius song is a masterpiece, which uses the off-key opening to much better purpose.

## AN DIE HARMONIE To Harmony

**Johann Gaudenz von Salis-Seewis**

March 1816

A major D394 Not in Peters GA XX no.199

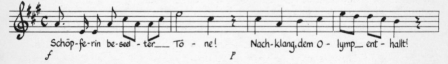

Schöp-fe-rin be-seel-ter__ Tö-ne! Nach-klang, dem O-lymp__ ent-hallt!

Goddess mother of heavenly music, from the echoing heights of Olympus you send to us on earth such music as uplifts, emboldens, comforts; you daughter of heaven, sweet Harmony.

    Our sighs, our tears, vanish in your healing stream, and tender feelings bloom again in our breasts.

    You are our lost dreams, you are love's imaginings which lie like shadowy moonlight round about us. In life's autumnal fields violets flower anew.

    Your sweet voice regenerates the wasteland of our spirits.

    Better than words is your melodious chant, bringing consolation to the distracted mind.

    Lead us back from the path of sorrow to the land of peace. Our lives need music and song to keep hope alive in the soul.

    When the future looms dark, sing your soft lullabies to the prisoners in life's dungeon, bringing them golden dreams of a better life.

    Teach man to weep, to love, and in him life will be renewed.

    Music has powers to unite men's souls, for all our deepest feelings are expressed in music not words.

    Yours is the voice of heaven that must lead us, like the swan's song, through the dark vale of death, gently unravelling the bonds of life, upward to the fields of bliss, sweet Harmony!

Salis-Seewis entitled the poem *Gesang an die Harmonie*. Schubert's autograph is lost, but a copy in the Witteczek–Spaun collection (Vienna, GdM) is dated March 1816. To judge by this copy, Schubert's title was *An die Harmonie*. The song was first published in the *Gesamtausgabe*, in 1895.

Schubert's setting is not a march, but a hymn. If the marking *Mässig* is observed, and the piece sung with enough rubato to give sense and feeling to the words, this makes a very attractive song. The only reservation is that ten verses are too many. Schubert probably intended only two to be sung. Although it was published as a solo song, the piece has the tone and attack of a male-voice chorus, and may have been intended as such.

## AN DIE LAUTE To the Lute
**Johann Friedrich Rochlitz**

January 1827

D major D905 Peters IV p.62 GA XX no.288

Whisper more softly, little lute, whisper my secret to that window there. Send your message to my mistress like a ripple of soft airs, like moonlight, and the scent of flowers.

The neighbours' sons are envious, and a solitary light still gleams in my beauty's window. So play yet more softly, little lute, so that my love may hear you but not – ah, not – the neighbours!

Rochlitz was the editor of the Leipzig *AMZ* and an influential figure in the musical world. He first met Schubert in 1822, during a visit to Vienna, and became an admirer of his work. *An die Laute* is one of three Rochlitz songs written in January 1827 and published in the following May by Tobias Haslinger as op.81. The work was dedicated to Rochlitz by the publisher 'in friendly esteem'. Rochlitz was sufficiently well known to be good for sales, and the circumstances in which the songs were written and quickly published suggest that Haslinger encouraged – perhaps even proposed – the project. The autograph, containing both op.81 songs, is in Vienna (SB). It is dated at the beginning January 1827 and was stamped by the censor on February 26.

This 'bewitching little serenade', as Capell justly calls it, speaks for itself. It needs a light touch, a light heart, and a confidential manner; then it is irresistible.

Capell, 128; Fischer-Dieskau, 247

## AN DIE LEYER To the Lyre
**Franz von Bruchmann**

(?) Winter 1822–3

E flat D737 Peters II p.110 GA XX no.414

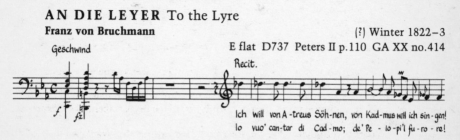

Fain would I sing of Atreus's sons, and Cadmus too, but the sound from my strings tells of nought but love! I changed the strings, would I could change the lyre. Then might the victorious march of Alcides thunder from its mighty heart. But these strings too will sing of nought but love. Farewell, then, heroes; for my strings, though they might ring with fierce heroic songs, will sing of nought but love.

The autograph is missing, and there is no clear evidence as to the date of the song. However, relations between Schubert and Bruchmann were really close only in 1822, and the only Bruchmann songs that can be firmly dated belong to November 1822 and February 1823, so it is probable that this one belongs to the same winter. *An die Leyer* (together with *Willkommen und Abschied* and *Im Haine*) was published in July 1826 as op.56 by A. W. Pennauer.

The poem is a free translation of verses by Anacreon (6th century BC), playfully ironic and erotic in tone. Schubert takes it at its face value, dramatising the poet's conflicting moods, turning the epic sentiments into impassioned recitative and the amatory ones into a long flowing *nobilmente* line, and then juxtaposing them rather than linking them so as to give the maximum musical effect to the contrast. The effect is to turn the song into a paean of praise for heavenly rather than earthly love, agape perhaps rather than eros. This would have won the approval of the high-minded Bruchmann, if not of Anacreon. *An die Leyer* is splendidly effective in performance, especially in the hands of a strong dramatic baritone. In the combination of vigorous recitative and a strong melodic line it calls to mind the setting of Klopstock's *Dem Unendlichen* D291.

Capell, 175; Einstein, 254; Fischer-Dieskau, 186–7

## AN DIE MUSIK To Music
**Franz von Schober** March 1817

D major D547 Peters I p.236 GA XX no.314 (a) and (b)

Thou lovely art, how often in dark hours, when life's wild tumult wraps me round, have you kindled my heart to loving warmth, and transported me to a better world.
Often a sigh, escaping from your harp, a touch of heavenly sweet harmony, has opened up a paradise for me.
Thou lovely art, I thank thee for this gift.

The text does not appear in the collected edition of Schober's poems, but there is a handwritten copy in Vienna (SB). Deutsch has pointed out (*Docs.* p.348) that it closely resembles a passage in the second canto of Ernst Schulze's epic poem *Die bezauberte Rose* ('The Enchanted Rose'). Schubert knew this work well, and planned to use it as the basis of an opera; moreover, the Schulze passage begins in much the same way ('Du holde Kunst melodisch süsser Klagen' – 'Thou lovely tuneful art of sweet complaints'); however, *Die bezauberte Rose* was not published until 1818, so conscious imitation appears to be ruled out.

There are two versions of the song, with minor but significant differences. The first goes back to the original autograph, which is dated March 1817 and marked 'Etwas bewegt'. Its present whereabouts are not known. Two fair copies of this first version are known to exist: one, undated, in the Paris Conservatoire and another, dated 24 April 1827, which Schubert copied out in the album of the piano virtuoso Albert Sowiński and signed 'in friendly remembrance'. This is the version published in the *Gesamtausgabe* as no.314(a). The more familiar version goes back to 1827, when the song was published as op.88 no.4 by

Thaddäus Weigl. The tempo indication here is *Mässig*, the expression marks are more detailed, and the small note B is added in bar 5. More significant still, the bass line in bars 4 and 13 is altered (and improved), suggesting that Schubert revised the song for publication. An autograph copy of this version is preserved now in BL London.

By any reckoning, *An die Musik* must be among the best-known and best-loved songs in the world. Its greatness is inseparable from its simplicity. The broad sweep of the melody grows inevitably out of the opening phrase, and leads inevitably to the echo phrase at the end. It hardly diverges from the tonic. The pianist's gesture towards the dominant in bar 10 serves only bring us back firmly to the tonic, while the move to the subdominant in bars 14–17 is a preparation for the concluding cadence. The tone of devotion is underlined by the steady pulse of the repeated triadic chords. But perhaps the secret of the song's greatness is the strength of the bass line which underpins the voice line; a dialogue between voice and piano which is in itself an image of that 'touch of heavenly harmony' of which the poem speaks. And if there is also about the song a touch of *Gemütlichkeit*, that too is thoroughly Schubertian.

Capell, 141–2; Craig Bell, 46–7; Einstein, 143; Fischer-Dieskau, 83–4

## AN DIE NACHTIGALL To the Nightingale

**Matthias Claudius**                                                  November 1816

G major  D497  Peters I p.252 and IV p.96  GA XX no.276

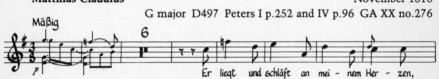

He lies and sleeps against my heart; my guardian angel sang him lullabies; and I can be merry and make sport, enjoy every flower and leaf.
O nightingale, do not wake my love with your song!

The poem appeared in 1771. The autograph is missing, and the only external evidence for the date is an entry in the catalogue of the Witteczek–Spaun collection (Vienna, GdM). The song was published in July 1829 as op.98 no.1 by Diabelli. The opus number may have been assigned by Schubert himself.

The greatest songs of Schubert's early maturity – and this is one of them – combine in a uniquely characteristic way purity of style and intensity of feeling. Here there is nothing strikingly novel or 'Romantic' about the musical language. The texture is clear and sparse and the harmonic sequences familiar. The most original feature of the song, the off-key opening, is taken over from another song, *An die Geliebte*, written a year earlier. Yet the simple succession of tonics and dominants, and the sudden switch to the minor at 'Nachtigall, ah!', pierces to the heart: a wonderful example of Schubert's ability to give to the classical language an altogether new emotional force. In its *Innigkeit* the song foreshadows the emotional world of Romantic song.

Einstein, 161

## AN DIE NACHTIGALL To the Nightingale

**Ludwig Hölty**                                                                22 May 1815

F sharp minor  D196  Peters VI p.100  GA XX no.72

Unruhig, klagend. Im Zeitmaße wachsend bis zur Haltung

Geuß nicht so laut der lieb - ent-flamm-ten Lie - der ton-rei-chen Schall

*p*        *cresc.*                                                    *f*

Pour not so loudly the melodious strain of your impassioned songs down from the bough of apple-blossom, O nightingale!

The music of your sweet throat awakens love in me; already my inmost soul trembles at your melting cry.

Then sleep once more forsakes this couch, and I gaze, pale and drawn, towards heaven with moist eyes. Fly, nightingale, to the green darkness of the woodland thicket, and there in your nest lavish your kisses on your faithful partner. Fly away, away!

The poem was written in 1772, but Schubert used the complete edition of 1804, in which the poem is shortened and substantially 'improved' by the editor, Johann Voss. The autograph has been missing since 1872. There is a copy in the Witteczek–Spaun collection (Vienna, GdM) dated 22 May 1815, and another in the Stadler collection (Lund, UB). The first publication was in 1865 by C.A. Spina, as no.3 of op.172: 'Eight Songs by Franz Schubert'. There are minor differences in the expression marks and in the melody between the Peters edition and the *Gesamtausgabe*.

Einstein calls this one of the simplest and loveliest of Schubert's songs, and sees it as 'a confession of love for the inevitability of death and farewell'. Certainly it is full of Romantic longing, which in Schubert is never far removed from the thought of mortality. But in 1815 he was in love with poetry rather than with death. There is nothing in the slightest degree morbid about this rapturous song; it re-creates the 'moment one and infinite' with rare passion and immediacy, but it has been overshadowed by Brahms's splendid setting.

Einstein, 360

## AN DIE NATUR To Nature

**Friedrich Leopold, Graf zu Stolberg-Stolberg**                    (?) 15 January 1816

F major  D372  Not in Peters  GA XX no.183

Mäßig

Sü - ße, hei - li - ge Na-tur, laß mich gehn auf dei - ner Spur,

Sweet, blessed nature, let me walk in your ways; lead me by the hand, like a stumbling child.

Then when I am tired I shall sink down upon your breast, and breathe heavenly joy at your motherly bosom.

Ah, what bliss it is to be with you! I shall love you for ever.

Let me walk in your ways, sweet blessed nature.

The poem was written in 1775. The date of composition is uncertain. Schubert seems to have discovered Stolberg's poems in August 1815, and the first draft, in F major, with only the first verse beneath the stave, could have been written then. The autograph

(Vienna, SB) has subsequently been amended and the second and third verses added. It is dated 15 January 1816, but whether this date refers to the original composition or the subsequent revision is an open question. A copy of the song in the Witteczek–Spaun collection (Vienna, GdM) is dated 15 February 1816.

Therese Grob, Schubert's first love, told Kreissle that this was the first song of Schubert's she ever saw. Since his relations with the Grob family were close at any rate from October 1814 onwards, this might suggest the earlier date as more probable. The fair copy of the song included in the Therese Grob album (see GROB) is transposed to A major, to suit Therese's high soprano voice. The top of the sheet has been cut away, possibly because it contained some personal message. Schubert's strophic folksong-like setting matches the simple piety of the verses.

Kreissle, I, 35

## AN DIE SONNE To the Sun

**Gabriele von Baumberg** (?) August 1815

Sehr langsam E flat major D270 Peters IV p.150 GA XX no.127

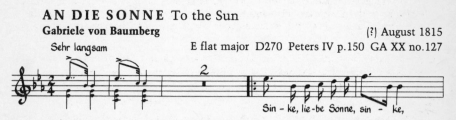

Sin - ke, lie - be Sonne, sin - ke,

Sink, friend sun, sink! Finish your cloudy course, and quickly summon the moon to take your place.

But rise again tomorrow, more splendid and more beautiful, and bring my love with you, friend sun.

The title of the poem in the Vienna edition (1800) of the poet's works is *Als ich einen Freund des nächsten Morgens auf dem Lande zum Besuche erwartete* ('As I waited in the country for the visit of a friend on the following morning'). Schubert's title is as above. The autograph is lost, and the evidence for the date is not quite conclusive. In favour of it is the fact that the surviving manuscripts of Baumberg songs (D263–5), are all dated August 1815. Moreover, in the catalogue of the Witteczek–Spaun collection (Vienna, GdM) *An die Sonne* is dated 25 August 1815. However, this precision is somewhat suspect, for there is another Schubert song with the same title (see next entry) which is quite certainly dated 25 August 1815, and the entry for this one may be due to confusion between the two. The song was published in June 1829 by Josef Czerny as op.118 no.5, but the opus number was not of course authorised by Schubert.

*An die Sonne* is an eloquent miniature, in Schubert's key of peace and reconciliation. The key, the mood, and some of the cadences anticipate a later song to the setting sun, Kosegarten's *An die untergehende Sonne*. But unlike that later song, *An die Sonne* retains its classical poise and restraint throughout.

## AN DIE SONNE To the Sun

**Christoph August Tiedge** 25 August 1815

Mit Majestät E flat major D272 Not in Peters GA XX no.129

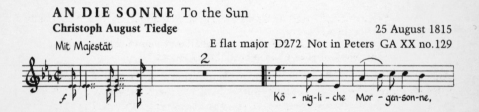

Kö - nig - li - che Mor - gen-son-ne,

Majestic morning sun, I greet you in your joy and splendour. Already the hills are mantled with your golden light, and in every wood the birds begin to wake. [*The poem has four more verses.*]

Schubert set only the first verse but put repeat marks at the end. The author was identified only in recent years by the Norwegian scholar Odd Udbye. The poem appeared in W. G. Becker's 'Pocket-book and Almanach of Sociable Pleasures' for 1795, published in Leipzig. The autograph, a first draft dated 25 August 1815, is in private possession. A note on it (not in Schubert's hand) names the author as Gabriele von Baumberg, but this must be due to confusion between this song and the previous one. There is a dated copy in the Witteczek–Spaun collection (Vienna, GdM). The song was first published by J. P. Gotthard in 1872, as no.9 of 'Forty Songs'.

A solemn invocation to the rising sun which fully justifies the instruction 'With majesty'. The most striking feature is the contrast between the simple diatonic harmonies of the opening bars and the postlude on the one hand, and on the other the long chromatic climb up to the top E flat in bars 12–15. This culminates in the tonally ambiguous seventh chord on C flat, marked 'piano', Schubert's equivalent of a hush inspired by awe.

## AN DIE TÜREN WILL ICH SCHLEICHEN I shall
### steal along from door to door
**Johann Wolfgang von Goethe** September 1816

A minor D479 (D2 478 no.3) Peters II p.33 GA XX no.255(a) and (b)

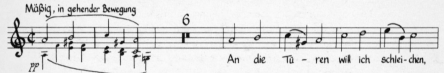

I shall steal along from door to door, and stand there silent and humble. A kindly hand will offer food, and I shall go on my way. Men will think themselves happy when they picture me before them; they will shed a tear, and I shall not know why they weep.

See HARFENSPIELER. The song comes from book 5 of *Wilhelm Meister*. Schubert's autograph, now split up, is headed 'Aus Wilhelm Meister. Harfenspieler. Göthe' and dated September 1816. In this manuscript *An die Türen* appears as the second of the three songs, but when the songs came to be published the order of nos. 2 and 3 was reversed. The fair copy made for the printer in 1822 is missing, but there is a copy in the Witteczek–Spaun collection (Vienna, GdM). When he revised the songs for publication Schubert left this one substantially unchanged, contenting himself with a new tempo indication (see below), and a shortened postlude. Both versions of the song are published in the *Gesamtausgabe*. The song was published (on commission) by Cappi and Diabelli in December 1822, as op.12 no.3, and dedicated to Johann Nepomuk von Dankesreither, Bishop of St Pölten, 'with profound respect'.

*An die Türen* is the creative germ from which *Winterreise* was to grow. The blind Harper is the forerunner of the Wanderer, and the even-paced crotchets to which he sings have the same pace and movement as *Gute Nacht*. Schubert himself seems to confirm this associative link, for the tempo indication on the final version of *An die Türen* is *Mässig, in gehender Bewegung* (the earlier version was simply *Mässig*); and this same untranslatable phrase appears on his autograph of *Gute Nacht*, which sets the pace and the tone for the cycle. The image of the dispossessed, the alienated man, which was to haunt

Schubert's imagination all his life, finds its first clear realisation in the Harper's songs, and particularly in this one.

Capell, 122; Einstein, 141

## AN DIE UNTERGEHENDE SONNE To the Setting Sun

**Ludwig Kosegarten**                                                July 1816–May 1817

E flat major  D457  Peters IV p.45  GA XX no.237

Son-ne, du sinkst_, Son-ne_,du_ sinkst_,

Sun, you are setting. Sink down in peace, O sun!
    Calm and tranquil is your going, touching and solemn is your silent farewell. Your kindly eye smiles sadly, tears fall from your golden lashes; blessings rain down on the fragrant earth. Ever deeper, ever fainter, ever more serious and solemn you sink down in the heavens. Sun, you are setting. Sink down in peace, O sun!
    Earth's peoples bless you. Breezes murmur, meadows are wreathed in mist as you pass by; the winds ripple through your curly hair, the waves cool your burning cheeks; your watery bed spreads far and wide. Rest in peace, sleep in peace! The nightingale is fluting lullabies. Sun, you are setting. Sink down in peace, O sun!

The poem was written in 1787. The original title was *An die scheidende Sonne* ('To the Departing Sun'). There are four long stanzas, of which Schubert used only the first two, and each is framed within the three-line 'refrain' 'Sonne, du sinkst'. There is a sketch of the first 21 bars, breaking off at the beginning of the first stanza, which Schubert seems to have set aside, perhaps uncertain what form the song should take. This is dated July 1816. Ten months later he wrote out a complete version of the song. The autograph, dated May 1817, is in private possession. The first publication was in January 1827 as op.44, by Diabelli.

    The song provides a fascinating glimpse into the development of Schubert's genius, for the hymnlike setting of the refrain is pre-Romantic Schubert, and the fact that he abandoned the first attempt to set the poem is evidence that he was already, in July 1816, reaching out towards a more personal form of expression. The final version, a year later, certainly does that. At the end of the second A flat major episode the music moves into B major enharmonically and suddenly the nightingale is fluting with a lyrical intensity which anticipates *Suleika I*. The song is thus something of a hybrid, but a most interesting and impressive one.

Capell, 117

## AN EINE QUELLE To a Spring

**Matthias Claudius**                                                    February 1817

A major  D530  Peters IV p.124  GA XX no.273

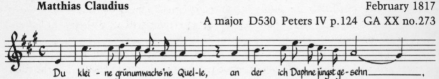

Du  klei - ne grünumwachs'ne Quel-le,    an  der  ich Daphne jüngst ge-sehn_____,

Bowered in green you lie, little spring, where lately I espied Daphne. Your water was so still, so clear, and Daphne's mirrored face so fair.
    O, should she appear again by your side, hold her lovely image fast. Then will I stealthily approach with tear-filled eyes and tell her picture all my plight; for when we two are face to face, o then I am struck dumb.

The poem was written in 1760. The autograph is a fair copy, dated February 1817, now in the Bodmer Library, Geneva. It was evidently used for the later publication, for it carries the censor's stamp, dated 8 July 1829, and a French translation of the text, which may have been made for the Paris edition of 1838. The four-bar prelude is editorial, though it is based on Schubert's postlude. The song was first published by Diabelli as no.3 of op. 109 in July 1829.

There is more than a touch of convention about Claudius's lovesick youth, yet the sentiment is natural and sincere. It matches the clarity and freshness of Schubert's musical idiom in his first-stage maturity perfectly; the unity of tone and text, the sharpness and pliancy of the musical invention within its Mozartian constraints, give to the song a serene perfection. How exactly and inevitably does the melodic line point up the words at 'so schön', and at 'meine Not zu klagen'. The song is a minor masterpiece.

Fischer-Dieskau, 87

## AN ELISA see TROST, AN ELISA

## AN EMMA To Emma
**Friedrich von Schiller**                                    17 September 1814

F major  D113  Peters II p.118  GA XX no.26(a), (b) and (c)

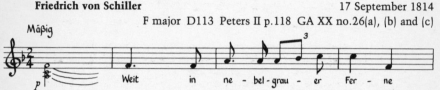

Far in the grey misty distance lies my past happiness. My gaze still lingers fondly on one lovely star alone; but like the splendour of the star, it is only an illusion of the night.

If the long sleep of night had closed your eyes my grief might still possess you; you would live on in my heart. But oh, you live in the light, but you do not live for my love.

Emma, can love's sweet longing fade and die? That which is past and gone, Emma – can that be love? Can the heavenly glow of its ardour die, like some earthly possession?

The poem was written in 1797. There are three versions; the last is the one usually heard, and the one included in the Peters edition. The *Gesamtausgabe* prints all three. The original autograph has disappeared, and only a cancelled draft of the first nine bars survives (Vienna, SB). This is in 2/4 time, marked 'Andante' and dated 17 September 1814. On 30 June 1821 a version in 6/8 time marked 'Etwas langsam' was published as a supplement to the *ZfK* under the title *An Emma*. Finally, in April 1826 the song was published by Thaddäus Weigl as op.56 (later op.58) no.2 with the title *Emma* and the tempo indication *Mässig*. This version, published in the composer's lifetime, was presumably prepared or authorised by Schubert himself. It reverts to 2/4 time, and two extra bars are inserted to give expressive emphasis to the words 'Aber ach, du liebst in Licht'.

It is usual to assert that Schiller's intellectuality and Schubert's lyrical genius were out of harmony. But until Goethe comes on the scene with *Gretchen am Spinnrade*, the best Schubert sings are the Schiller settings *Der Jüngling am Bache* and *An Emma*, and both show a remarkable freedom of form and rhythm. In *Emma* the phrase lengths are continually varied, so that the music seems to cling to the words without losing their lyrical impetus, pausing only to point up the bitterness of 'Aber ach, du liebst in Licht' and the sadness of 'Emma, kann's vergänglich sein?' And although no two phrases are melodically exactly alike, each one flows naturally from its predecessor. Its early publication suggests that it was among the first Schiller settings to win popularity.

Einstein, 70

## AN GOTT  To God
**C. C. Hohlfeld**

D863

The poem was published in 'Songs for the Blind and by the Blind' in 1827 with a note 'Music by Franz Schubert'. But the song has never been discovered. The first line is: 'Kein Auge hat Dein Angesicht geschaut' – 'No eye has e'er beheld thy face'.

## AN LAURA  To Laura
**Friedrich von Matthisson**                        2–7 October 1814

E major  D115  Peters V p.173  GA XX no.28  NSA IV vol.7 p.48

Hearts that upward turn towards heaven, tears that tremble from quiet eyes, sighs that softly issue from the lips, cheeks aglow with devotion, fond glances, radiant with delight – all give you thanks, harbinger of grace!

Laura, listening to these strains the souls of angels must grow in beauty, saints see heaven open before them, heartsick doubters still their complaints, callous sinners beat their breasts and pray like the angel Abbadona!

With the strains of the victorious song came the foretaste of my passing, from the darkness of the tomb to the glow of transfiguration! As though I heard angels singing, I imagined, earth, that I had left you behind and saw the stars dance beneath me.

The gentle breath of heaven surrounded me. Joyful I beheld the Elysian fields, where the river of life flows on amid the palms. Glowing from the brilliance of God's presence, my trembling spirit wandered through the vales of Paradise.

The full title is *An Laura, als sie Klopstocks Auferstehungslied sang* ('To Laura, when she was singing Klopstock's Resurrection song'). The poem dates from 1783, and refers to Carl Heinrich Graun's famous setting of Klopstock's poem *Die Auferstehung* ('The Resurrection'). The autograph (Vienna, SB) is dated 2 October 1814 at the beginning and 7 October 1814 at the end. There are dated copies in the Witteczek–Spaun collection (Vienna, GdM) and another in Stadler's album (Lund, UB). The song first appeared in book 31 of the *Nachlass* in 1840, together with two other Matthisson songs.

This song, and the contemporary *Die Betende*, introduce us to what might be called Schubert's devotional hymn style. He was to use it to the end of his life, in songs like *Der Kreuzzug* (1827) and *Der Pilgrim* (1823), and adapt it to more secular emotions in the *Wanderers Nachtlied*, *Der Tod und das Mädchen* and other songs. *An Laura* does not have quite the intensity of feeling and economy of form of the strophic *Die Betende*. It is through-composed, and the block harmonies are not so compelling. Even Schubert's favourite modulation to the flattened sixth at the end of the first verse sounds here a little self-indulgent.

Capell, 83; Fischer-Dieskau, 30

## AN MEIN HERZ To my Heart
**Ernst Schulze**                                                         December 1825

A minor D860 Peters V p.73 GA XX no.485

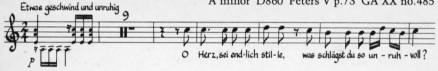

Be still, my heart: why do you beat so wildly? It is heaven's will that I should leave her.

And if your young life was nought but delusion and pain, why, if it made her happy, then it was well spent.

And though she never understood either your love or your grief, you kept faith, and God was your witness.

While our tears can still flow, let us endure it bravely, and dream of happier days, long since gone.

And if you see the flowers bloom, and hear the birds sing, you may well shed a secret tear, but must no more complain.

For there above us the eternal stars move on in golden light, smiling down from afar in friendly fashion, though they have no thought for us.

In the *Poetisches Tagebuch* ('Verse Journal') the poem is entitled simply *Am 23sten Januar 1816. An mein Herz* is Schubert's title. The autograph, in private possession, is a first draft, undated. On the same manuscript is the end of another Schulze song, *Um Mitternacht*, which certainly belongs to December 1825. This agrees also with the date given in the catalogue of the Witteczek–Spaun collection (Vienna, GdM). The song was published in 1832, in book 13 of the *Nachlass*.

The obsessive crotchet–quaver–quaver rhythm runs like a heartbeat through the 119 bars of the song, quickened to the brisk pace (*Etwas geschwind und unruhig*) of a man fleeing from his own loneliness. Moreover, the repeated return to A major at the end of the sentence – all but one of the verses end thus – gives to the song a tone almost of desperation, of inescapable doom. In this it has something in common with *Der Zwerg*. There are no marked changes of pace, so that the performers have to do their best, by an occasional subtle rubato, to prevent the listener from tiring. Both the style and the sentiment foreshadow *Winterreise*.

Capell, 216; Fischer-Dieskau, 223

## AN MEIN KLAVIER To my Piano
**Christian Friedrich Schubart**                                              c. 1816

A major D342 Peters VII p.23 GA XX no.238

Soft-toned piano, what delights you bring me, while the spoilt beauties flirt, I pledge my love to you, beloved piano.

I whisper my inmost thoughts to you, pure as heaven, innocently playing. Virtuous thoughts speak from you, beloved instrument.

And if I sing with you, golden-voiced piano, what heavenly peace you whisper to me. The strings catch the tears of joy, silvery sound carries the song along.

Soft-toned piano, what delights you bring me. When cares surround me, sing to me, faithful piano!

Schubart died in 1791, so the instrument he was talking about was probably a fortepiano, though it could have been any keyboard instrument. The poem is entitled *Serafina an ihr Klavier* ('Serafina to her Piano') and has six verses, of which Schubert omitted the third and fifth. The spurious title 'Schubert an sein Klavier' was invented by Fox-Strangways in his English version of the songs (London, 1928).

The autograph is lost, and there is no clear evidence as to the date of composition; the Schubart settings belong to the 1816–17 period. There is an undated copy of the song in Stadler's song album (Lund, UB). A corrupt version, with accompaniment for piano duet, was published in 1876 by V. Kratochwill of Vienna. The authentic version first appeared in 1885 in vol.VII of the Peters edition.

The simplicity of the song matches the poem, which is about a young girl at her practice, and not a personal confession of faith, like *An die Musik*. It hardly needs the sentimental associations that have attached themselves to it, for in its own way it is direct and moving.

Capell, 118–19; Fischer-Dieskau, 108

## AN MIGNON  To Mignon

**Johann Wolfgang von Goethe**                                     27 February 1815
*Etwas geschwind*                       G minor  D161  Peters II p.49  GA XX no.48(a) and (b)

Over the valley and stream the sun's chariot passes on its untroubled way. Ah, in its course it stirs my grief and yours, deep in our hearts, new again each morning.

Nor can the night any longer comfort me, for now even dreams come in mournful guise, and I feel the secretly growing power of this anguish silent in my heart.

For many a fair year I have watched the ships below, sailing each to its appointed place. But oh, the waters do not bear away the abiding pain that lodges in my heart.

I must come in fine clothes, they are taken from the closet; for today is a holiday. None suspects that in my inmost heart I am cruelly riven with pain.

In secret must I ever weep, and yet outwardly I can seem so cheerful, and even ruddy with the glow of health. But had these pains the power to kill my heart, then were I long since dead.

The poem was written in 1796 and published in the following year in Schiller's *Musenalmanach* in Zelter's setting. Mignon is Goethe's nearest approach to true tragedy. The unhappy waif, with her inheritance of sin and sorrow, seems to have a religious significance for him, as a symbol of the problem of evil. Hence the title – 'To Mignon' – and the penitential tone of the poem. There are two versions, both printed in the *Gesamtausgabe*. The first is in G sharp minor, marked 'Klagend mässig', the second in G minor, marked 'Etwas geschwind'. The original autograph (Berlin, SPK) is in G sharp minor, dated 27 February 1815. The fair copy made for Goethe (Berlin, DS) now lacks the last four bars. A fair copy of the second version is in the Fitzwilliam Museum, Cambridge. The song was published in the G minor version in 1825 as op.19 no.2 by Diabelli. Schubert dedicated the opus to Goethe (without permission) and sent two copies to the great man with a fulsome covering letter, but he received no reply.

Schubert's plaintive G minor setting makes an interesting comparison with Zelter's

F major one. Zelter is good, but Schubert is better; as one might expect, Schubert brings to the song a sense of concealed grief, of emotional disturbance, which is absent from the earlier setting. The difference may be pointed by reference to the words 'Tief im Herzen', which Schubert intensifies by a wrenching lift from the implied G minor to the 'neapolitan' key of A flat.

Capell, 100

## AN ROSA To Rosa I

**Ludwig Kosegarten**                                                                 19 October 1815

A flat major D315 Not in Peters GA XX no.162

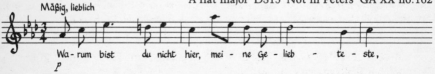

Why are you not here, beloved, your arm about me, your comforting hand in mine, pressing me to your beating heart?

Rosa, do you love me? Rosa, none ever loved you more than I, nor shall again; none of the sons of earth or heaven.

My fond heart could not beat for you more warmly, more tenderly, if we had been born of one womb, suckled at one breast.

The spring refreshes the thirsty, the evening star the weary. The moon comforts the lost traveller, the flush of dawn the sick. But for me, beloved, your embrace is the best balm of all.

Why are you not here, my dearest one, that my arm might enfold you, that I might whisper a sweet greeting, and press you ardently to my beating heart?

The poem dates from 1787. Kosegarten wrote four poems 'to Rosa'. Schubert set the second and third. The autograph, headed 'An Rosa I' and dated 19 October 1815, is now in LC, Washington DC. A fair copy containing both the *An Rosa* songs is in the library of the Northwestern University, Evanston, Illinois. There is a dated copy in the Witteczek–Spaun collection (Vienna, GdM). The first publication was in the *Gesamtausgabe* in 1895.

Schubert wrote seven songs to Kosegarten texts on 19 October 1815. The problem with these songs, however, is not one of quantity versus quality, for Schubert was quite capable of writing a masterpiece in the course of such a busy day's work: it is a question of scale; however enjoyable in its unpretentious way, the song is too slight for public performance.

## AN ROSA To Rosa II

**Ludwig Kosegarten**                                                                 19 October 1815

A flat major D316 Not in Peters GA XX no.163(a) and (b)

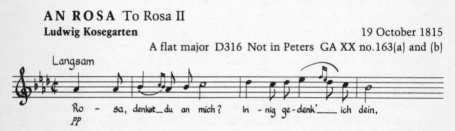

Rosa, do you think of me? I think of you tenderly. The sunset glow glimmers through the green forest, and the whisper of eternity rustles through the fir-tops.

If you were here, Rosa, I should watch the evening light glow in your cheeks, the evening breeze ruffle your hair. Dear soul, bliss would be mine.
[*The poem has four more verses.*]

This is the third of Kosegarten's 'An Rosa' poems. Schubert's title is *An Rosa II*. There are two versions, both printed in the *Gesamtausgabe*. The autograph of the first is dated 19 October 1815. The second is written on the back of *An Rosa I*. Both manuscripts (originally part of a set of Kosegarten songs) are now in LC, Washington DC. There is a copy in the Witteczek–Spaun collection (Vienna, GdM) and another in that of Johann Leopold Ebner (Lund, UB). First publication was in the *Gesamtausgabe* in 1895.

The second version has a much stronger climax in the subdominant D flat before the cadence. Both this and the previous song are in A flat major, Schubert's key of devotion, but the mood of sweetness and tenderness is more impressive in this one.

## AN SCHWAGER KRONOS To Brother Time the Coachman
**Johann Wolfgang von Goethe** (?) 1816

D minor D369 Peters II p.44 GA XX no.263

Hurry on, Time, on at a rattling trot! The road runs downhill, your dawdling makes things swim before my eyes. On at a brisk pace, over stick and stone, stumbling headlong into life!

Now once more toiling uphill, out of breath – up then, no slacking, upward striving and hoping.

High, wide, and glorious the prospect of life rings us round. The eternal spirit soars from peak to peak, full of intimations of eternal life.

A shadowy doorway beckons you aside across the threshold of the girl's house, and her eyes promise refreshment. Take comfort! For me too, lass, that sparkling draught, that fresh and healthy look.

Down then, faster down! See, the sun sinks. Before it sets, before the marsh-mist envelops me in my old age, with toothless gnashing jaws and tottering limbs; snatch me, drunk with the sun's last ray, a sea of fire boiling up before my eyes, blind and reeling through the dark gate of hell.

Blow your horn, brother, clatter on at a noisy trot. Let Orcus know we are coming, so that mine host will be there at the door to welcome us.

The poem is subtitled: 'In the postchaise, 10 October 1774'; Goethe was twenty-five when it was written. *Schwager* is literally 'brother-in-law', a colloquial term for a postilion. The autograph is lost, and the date of composition cannot be determined precisely. The index of the Witteczek–Spaun collection (Vienna, GdM) attributes it to 1816, but there are no contemporary copies. Deutsch, without adducing any evidence, says 'Beginning of 1816', in the belief perhaps that it was written to send to Goethe in that year. But it does not seem to have been included in either of the songbooks prepared for Goethe in 1816, and it was not published until the summer of 1825, when it appeared from Diabelli as op.19 no.1.

Goethe's defiant assertion of the pride and invulnerability of youth is a text made for Schubert's hand, not simply because like was speaking to like (for Schubert himself in his twentieth year was, as he himself was soon to put it, 'composing like a god'), but because the sense of movement, the gait, always the key which unlocked Schubert's imagination, is here the very essence of the poem. There is only one tempo indication

(*Nicht zu schnell*) and the galloping quavers never falter; yet Schubert finds the precise musical equivalent for the change of tone at every turn in the journey; the climb up the hill (from D minor to E flat major), the wide and glorious prospect of life from the commanding heights of youth, the easing of tension (but not of pace) as the girl's smiles beckon from the doorway, the plunge down into the chromatic depths of hell, and the cheerful horncalls (switch to D major) that welcome the travellers at the end of the day. And all this is achieved with an inevitability and a power of visual evocation which make this one of the greatest of the Goethe songs. Its impetuous sweep, and its mastery, call *Erlkönig* to mind. And like that song, it offers a challenge to the pianist, who should note that the instruction 'staccato' in bar 2 applies throughout.

> Capell, 123–5; Craig Bell, 34–7; Einstein, 142; Fischer-Dieskau, 63–4; Stein, 70–71

## AN SIE To Her
**Friedrich Gottlieb Klopstock**                    14 September 1815

A flat major D288 Not in Peters GA XX no.142

Time, harbinger of the greatest joys, close happy Time, I have wept too many sad tears in search of you in faraway lands.
> And yet you come. Yes, angels send you to me, angels who were once human, and loved like me, and now love as immortals do.
> You come down from heaven with the eternal spring, on the wings of peace in the morning breezes, bright with the dew of the smiling day.
> For the soul is fulfilled and the heart enraptured when, in the ecstasy of love, it knows it is beloved.

The poem dates from 1752. The autograph is a first draft, with several Klopstock settings, dated 14 September 1815 (Berlin, DS). There is a dated copy in the Witteczek–Spaun collection (Vienna, GdM). The first publication was in the *Gesamtausgabe* in 1895.

The text is one of three Klopstock songs which the poet addressed to his first wife, Meta ('Cidli'), who died four years after their marriage. Schubert's strophic settings catch the devotional tone of the poems beautifully, with words and music evenly matched. Though not so well known as *Das Rosenband*, *An Sie* is a lovely song.

> Fischer-Dieskau, 46

## AN SYLVIA To Sylvia
**William Shakespeare**                              July 1826

A major D891 Peters II p.202 GA XX no.505

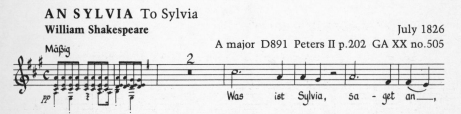

The song comes from *The Two Gentlemen of Verona*, Act IV Scene 2, and in the original runs:

Who is Sylvia? what is she,
That all our swains commend her?
Holy, fair, and wise is she;
The heavens such grace did lend her,
That she might admired be.

Is she kind as she is fair?
For beauty lives with kindness.
Love doth to her eyes repair,
To help him of his blindness,
And being helped, inhabits there.

Then to Silvia let us sing,
That Silvia is excelling:
She excels each mortal thing
Upon the dull earth dwelling:
To her let us garlands bring.

Schubert took the German text from the Vienna *Shakespeare-Ausgabe* of 1825. The translation is by his friend Eduard von Bauernfeld. The word-setting is not particularly happy
even in German, and the song fits the English words well enough, with a slight adjust-
ment in verse 2 at bar 22. The autograph is contained in a small pocket-book, the staves
ruled out by Schubert himself. The booklet is dated on the front page 'Währing, July 1826'
Währing was then a small village just outside the city, where Schubert was spending a
holiday with his friend Franz von Schober. This first draft (Vienna, SB) is headed simply
'Gesang' and has no tempo marking. A fair copy, marked 'Mässig', was made for the first
edition. The title (*Gesang*) has been crossed out and *An Sylvia* put in its place in some
other hand. This manuscript formerly belonged to Schober; it was discovered in Budapest
(HNL) only in 1969. *An Sylvia* was published early in 1828 by the Lithographic Institute
of Vienna, then under Schober's management. The edition was dedicated to Marie Pachler,
Schubert's hostess and patroness at Graz, and *An Sylvia* was substituted for *Edward* as
one of the four songs included. In 1829 Diabelli republished the volume as op.106.

The mythical anecdotal accretions about the composition of the Shakespeare songs
– autographs written on the backs of menu cards and the like – are understandable even
if unfounded. The autograph is both a first draft and a finished composition. The echo
phrases were an afterthought, squeezed in above the stave, but otherwise the masterpiece
seems to have been written down as it came into the composer's head. As with *An die
Musik*, the magic lies at least partly in the perfect balance of piano and voice: the forward
movement, firm but unhurried, the flowing melody never straying far from the tonic and
underpinned by the marching bass line, the dotted fourth beat of which gives a steely
strength to the mood of devotion. There are many more profound songs, and more elaborate
ones, but none greater than this one. Its perfection of form and expression is absolute.

Capell, 225; Fischer-Dieskau, 233

## ANDENKEN Remembrance

**Friedrich von Matthisson**                                      April 1814

Etwas geschwind        F major D99 Not in Peters GA XX no.16 NSA IV vol.7 p.11

Ich  den - ke  dein__,wenn durch__ den__  Hain__

I think of you, when the grove resounds with the sweet song of the nightingale. When do you think of me?

I think of you at twilight, as the shadows fall. Where do you think of me?

I think of you with sweet anguish, with anxious longings and hot tears. How do you think of me?

Oh, think of me until we meet in a better world. In that far distance, I shall think of none but you!

The poem, written in 1792–3, set a fashion, and a whole series of similar verses beginning 'Ich denke dein' followed, including Goethe's famous *Nähe des Geliebten*, which Schubert was also to set. There are two versions of the song with slight variations. The original autograph is lost, but there are two copies in the Witteczek–Spaun collection (Vienna, GdM), both dated April 1814. On this first version the tempo indication is *Allegretto*. This was the only known source when the song was first printed, in the *Gesamtausgabe* in 1894. A fair copy of the song was made for the Therese Grob song album in 1816 (see GROB). This is marked 'Etwas geschwind', and shows minor differences. Both versions are included in the *Neue Ausgabe*.

The unusual stanza form, with its questioning last line, presents a problem which Schubert solves as successfully as Beethoven does in his quite different setting. By leaving the sense and the harmony suspended on a dominant seventh Schubert makes a dramatic point and links the verses together neatly. The song has however been superseded by the setting of Goethe's poem on the same theme, *Nähe des Geliebten*, a greater song altogether.

Capell, 83

## ANTIGONE UND OEDIP  Antigone and Oedipus

**Johann Mayrhofer**                                        March 1817

Langsam (M.M. ♩=54)   C major  D542  Peters IV p.3  GA XX no.309  NSA IV vol.1 p.50

*Antigone:* Ye high and heavenly powers, hear a daughter's heartfelt plea. Let the cool breath of comfort waft into my father's great soul. Take this young life to assuage your wrath; let your avenging stroke destroy this deeply grieving sufferer. Humbly I clasp my hands. The sky is calm and clear; only mild breezes rustle through the ancient grove. Pale-faced, my father sighs and moans. I sense that some dreadful vision disturbs his light sleep. He starts up and speaks.

*Oedipus:* I dream a grievous dream. Did not this right hand wield the sceptre? But mighty forces brought your majesty to dust, old man! In happier times I drank your golden light, O Helios, in my ancestral halls, amid the songs of heroes and the blare of trumpets; that I can never see again. From every side I hear destruction call: 'Prepare yourself for death, your earthly task is done.'

While the blind Oedipus sleeps, faithful Antigone begs the gods to vent their wrath upon her instead of her father. But Oedipus, waking, foresees his death at Colonos. The text was given to the composer in manuscript, and it was set as a duet with Oedipus's melody written in the bass clef, presumably with J.M. Vogl in mind. The first draft (Paris Conservatoire) is dated March 1817, but the fair copy has disappeared. The copy in the Witteczek–Spaun collection (Vienna, GdM) is annotated 'Altered by J. M. Vogl' and gives a fascinating insight into Vogl's habit of 'interpreting' the melody of the songs he sang and adding his own embellishments. (See the discussion, and examples, in the introduction to NSA IV vol.7, p.xii.) The song was published by Cappi and Diabelli in August 1821 as op.6 no.2 and dedicated to Michael Vogl 'with high regard'. The vocal line is written in the treble clef throughout. The Peters edition follows this first version, but the *Gesamtausgabe* restores the original.

For this dramatic scena Schubert turns to the epic style he had adopted for *Hermann und Thusnelda* and was to develop in the Walter Scott songs, with its horn calls and other arpeggio-based figures and long-breathed melodic phrases. The nervous motif marked 'Etwas geschwinder' admirably suggests Antigone's agitation, and the song's climax has a certain operatic grandeur and nobility, characterised by the neapolitan lift from G to A flat, the wide leaps in the voice line, and the dramatic crescendos in the accompaniment.

Capell, 136–7; Fischer-Dieskau, 96

**ARIA DELL'ANGELO** see QUELL'INNOCENTE FIGLIO

**ARIA DI ABRAMO** see ENTRA L'UOMO ALLOR CHE NASCE

**ARIETTE DER CLAUDINE** see LIEBE SCHWÄRMT AUF ALLEN WEGEN

**ARIETTE DER LUCINDE** see HIN UND WIEDER FLIEGEN PFEILE

## ATYS
**Johann Mayrhofer**                                    September 1817

Etwas geschwind                    A minor  D585  Peters V p.124  GA XX no.330

Der Kna-be seufzt ü-bers grü-ne Meer,

Sighing, the youth looks down over the green sea. He came from a far shore, and had he strong wings to fly he would return, for he is sick with longing.

'O longing for home, unfathomable pain that tortures the young heart – can love not suppress you? I love, I rage. I saw her ride the wind, her chariot drawn by lions. Take me with you, I begged. My life is dull and desolate. Will you deny my plea?

Smiling she looked on me. The lions bore us away to Thrace, where I serve as her acolyte.

A blissful happiness possesses the madman, but when he wakes he shudders with horror, and no god is near to lend him aid. Beyond the mountain, in the sunset glow, my native valley slumbers. Oh, that I might cross the seas.'

Thus sighs the youth. But the clash of cymbals heralds the goddess, and down he plunges into the woody depths.

The poem is based on the legend recounted by Catullus, of the Phrygian shepherd boy who was abducted by the goddess Cybele. The autograph is a first draft dated September 1817 (Vienna, SB). There is also an incomplete fair copy which includes only the last thirty-four bars, originally part of a sheaf of papers containing several Mayrhofer and Schiller songs. The missing bars are however to be found in another copy recently discovered in Vienna (MGV). The song was published in book 22 of the *Nachlass*, together with three other Mayrhofer songs (D805, 806, 669), in 1833.

Atys, like Mayrhofer himself, longs for a homeland beyond his reach. But Schubert ignores the symbolic meaning of the poem, giving to the song the narrative smoothness of a ballad. The plaintive 6/8 minor key melody which characterises the outer sections might form the basis of a good sonata movement (indeed, there is a suggestion of the first movement of the 'Arpeggione' Sonata of 1824 about it). The eleven-bar postlude (Schubert's longest?) is almost a miniature movement in itself. Maybe the song reflects the composer's absorption in the piano sonata during the summer months of 1817. Whatever the reason, there is little attempt at dramatic immediacy, and the song fails to make a very deep impression, in spite of its pleasing melodiousness.

Capell, 137; Porter, 128

**AUF DEM FLUSSE** see WINTERREISE no.7

## AUF DEM SEE On the Lake

**Johann Wolfgang von Goethe**                                              (?) March 1817

Mäßig                    E flat major D543 Peters II p.172 GA XX no.310(a) and (b)

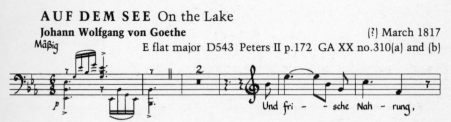

I draw fresh nourishment, new blood from this wide world. How gracious and good is Nature, who holds me to her breast. Our boat is cradled on the waves, and the cloud-capped mountains come to meet us as we move to the rhythm of the oars.
    Why should my eyes be cast down? Golden dreams, will you ever return? Dreams, begone, golden as you are; here too is love, and life.
    A thousand swaying stars twinkle in the waves; faint mists engulf the looming distances; the morning breeze takes wing across the shadowed bay, and the ripening fruit is mirrored in the surface of the lake.

The verses were written in the summer of 1775, during a holiday in Switzerland which the young Goethe spent with his friends the Stolbergs. The lake is Lake Zurich, and the 'golden dreams' of the second stanza are said to refer to his relations with Lili Schönemann. There are two versions of the song, the first in E major, marked 'Mässig, ruhig', and the second, the published version, in E flat, marked 'Mässig'. The second version is also twelve bars longer, with an extended prelude and postlude, and the vocal line is substantially altered and improved, doubtless by Schubert himself. Both versions are printed in the *Gesamtausgabe*. No autograph survives, so the date of composition is not altogether certain, but a copy of the original version made for Josef Hüttenbrenner is dated March 1817, and we know that Schubert was occupied with Goethe songs during that month. *Auf dem See* appeared with two other Goethe songs as op.92 no.2 in July 1828. Originally the opus was numbered 87, but that number had already been used for an earlier group of songs and the publisher Leidesdorf corrected the mistake in later issues. The publication was dedicated by Schubert to Frau Josefine von Franck, the widow of a well-known patron of the arts in Vienna.

    The key, and the rhythmic figure in the accompaniment, call to mind the Bruchmann song *Am See*. But a close comparison of the two songs shows with what subtlety Schubert can define a particular *Bewegung* from the infinite variety offered by the 6/8 rhythm. In *Am See* the single strong beat comes in the middle of the bar, so that each bar seems to advance and recede, like a wave. In *Auf dem See* there are two strong beats to the bar, as though to suggest the rhythmic pull of the oars, while the semiquaver figures in the pianist's right hand image the lapping of the waves. Moreover, the basic movement is cleverly modified to match the changing moods of the poem. At bar 19 the boat emerges from the shelter of the shore into the choppy waters of the lake, and at bar 50 the movement changes to a brisk 2/4, so that the boat seems now to be dancing over the waves in the morning sunlight. Most remarkable of all, when in the second verse the poet's thoughts turn inward to his own uncertainties, Schubert manages to suggest this change of mood without damage to the basic rhythmic pattern. *Auf dem See* is thus a more complex song to suit a more complex text. The extension of the last verse – 'A thousand stars twinkle in the waves' – beautifully catches the poet's absorption in the moment.

Capell, 132; Fischer-Dieskau, 89

## AUF DEM STROM On the River
**Ludwig Rellstab**

March 1828

E major  D943  Peters III p.100  GA XX no.568

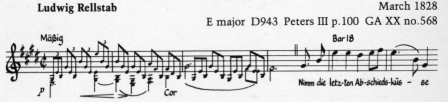

Take the last kisses of farewell, the last greetings I wave ashore, before you turn away. Already the stream is tugging at the boat; but my tear-dimmed gaze is constantly drawn back.

And so the waves bear me swiftly hence. Already the meadows where happily I found her have disappeared. Blissful days, you are gone for ever! Hopelessly my complaint echoes round the fair homeland where I found her love.

See, how the shore rushes past. And how it draws me over, with invisible bands, to land by the little house, to tarry beneath the trees. But the river flows on ceaselessly, bearing me on to the sea.

Oh, how I shudder with horror before that dark wilderness, far from every friendly shore, where no island is to be seen! No song can reach me from the shore, to bring sad tears. Only the storm blows cold across the grey and angry sea.

If the sweep of my longing eyes can no longer make out the shore I shall look upward to the stars there in the hallowed distance. By their soft light I first called her mine. There perhaps, O happy fate, there I shall meet her glance again.

Rellstab's poem is about separation and reunion, about a passage from light to dark, from day to night, a metaphorical passage from life to death. It would therefore recommend itself to Schubert in its own right, quite apart from the fact that it may have come to him from Beethoven's *Nachlass*. On the chronology, see RELLSTAB SONGS.

The autograph, in the Houghton Library, Harvard University, is dated March 1828. The song was performed at Schubert's public concert on 26 March, and the arrangement with horn obbligato must have been made with that public occasion in mind. A copy in Berlin (DS) has the obbligato part written for cello. It is said to have belonged to Anna Milder, for whom Schubert wrote his only other comparable 'public' song, *Der Hirt auf dem Felsen*, later in the year. This version was performed by Anna Fröhlich and the cellist Josef Linke at the memorial concert of 30 January 1829. The published version (op.119, Leidesdorf, October 1829) includes both cello and horn parts as alternatives. In the following year Diabelli published an arrangement for piano and solo voice, transposed to C major; it is this version which is included in the Peters edition.

There are signs in *Auf dem Strom* of an anxiety not to expect too much of public taste, not unreasonable perhaps in view of the failure of Schubert's Fantasia for violin and piano at Slavik's concert of January 20. Its homophonic style, strong melodic lines and familiar harmonic sequences seem deliberately to exclude the virtuosic brilliance of the Fantasia. But Hallmark has shown that the structure is carefully designed to match the changing sentiment of the poem, and that it is conceived as a tribute to Beethoven, in admiration of *Die ferne Geliebte*. In particular, the minor tune to which the second verse is set derives from the Funeral March in the second movement of the 'Eroica' Symphony. This enables us to see the work in a quite new light, as an attempt to combine a popular idiom with philosophical depth, to pay a tribute to a departed hero – Beethoven himself – and to acknowledge at the same time the presence of the shadow of death in Schubert's own life.

Capell, 247; Einstein, 346–7; Fischer-Dieskau, 274; R. Hallmark, 'Schubert's *Auf dem Strom*', *Studies*, pp.25–46

## AUF DEM WASSER ZU SINGEN To be Sung on the Water
**Friedrich Leopold Graf zu Stolberg-Stolberg**                                    1823

Mäßig geschwind                        A flat minor D774 Peters I p.216 GA XX no.428

Mit - ten im Schimmer der spie - geln - den Wel - len

'Mid the glimmer of sparkling waves the swaying boat glides like a swan; ah, the soul glides onward like the boat, on gently gleaming waves of joy. For the sunset glow, shining down from heaven upon the waves, dances round the boat.

The rosy light beckons us above the treetops of the western wood; beneath the branches of the eastern wood the reeds whisper in the rosy light; in the reddening glow the soul breathes the joy of heaven, the peace of the grove.

For me, alas, time itself vanishes on dewy wings in the cradle of the waves. Tomorrow time will fly onward on glistening wings, as it did yesterday and today, until I myself escape from time's inconstancy on loftier, more glorious wing.

The poem, written in 1782, is headed 'Lied auf dem Wasser zu singen. Für meine Agnes'. Schubert's title is as above. The autograph is lost, and no precise date of composition can be given. The song is dated 1823 in the catalogue of the Witteczek–Spaun collection (Vienna, GdM), and this fits in well enough with its appearance as a supplement to the *ZfK* on 30 December 1823. There is a copy in the Witteczek–Spaun collection (in A minor) and another in the Spaun–Cornaro collection (Vienna, privately owned). In March 1827 the song was published by Diabelli as op.72.

There is no more perfect strophic song in all Schubert than this one. The repeated last line, with its heart-easing shift to the major, brings a sensuous shock of delight, so that each verse increases our pleasure and sense of anticipation. Yet it is essential neither to the verbal nor to the musical sense. Another composer might have been content to end at bar 25, basing the whole song on the attractive alternation between minor key and relative major. It is that characteristically Schubertian tailpiece that turns a fine song into an incomparable one.

The poem may not be great literature, but it gives Schubert all he needs: a strong dactylic rhythm, and a simple stanza form which falls easily into a symmetrical four-bar structure; above all, a unifying tone of creative idleness, and an image of the waves lapping gently against the boat, which Schubert is able to transmute into rippling semiquavers. As always, it is a sensuous image which fires Schubert's imagination, and gives him the rhythmical figure he needs as the starting-point for a song.

Capell, 73; Fischer-Dieskau, 188–9

## AUF DEN SIEG DER DEUTSCHEN On the Victory of the German Armies

**Author unknown**                                                    Autumn 1813

Andante                                    F major  D81  Not in Peters  GA XX no.583

Ver - schwunden sind die Schmer - zen,

The suffering is over, for sighs are not heard from full hearts. So rejoice, Germans, for the accursed whip has cracked its last.

The creatures of France turned German fields into bloody altars. For more than twenty years the greedy hyenas devoured our noble sons.

The struggle is now decided. Soon peace will come in blessed form. Rejoice then, Germans, for the hated whip has cracked its last.
[*The poem has five more verses.*]

This juvenile piece was written for solo voice, two violins, and cello. Almost certainly it was intended for the family performers, a youthful *jeu d'esprit* meant perhaps for some family occasion, in which case the very easy cello part and rather more difficult first violin part were tailored to match the capabilities of Schubert's father (cello) and brother Ferdinand (violin). At the end of each verse the music turns into a little dance of jubilation. The battle celebrated in these unsophisticated verses – which may be by Schubert himself – is that fought at Leipzig on 16–19 October 1813. Here Napoleon was totally defeated by the Austrian and Prussian forces ranged against him, and the battle marked the end of his European empire. It raised patriotic feeling in the German lands to an unprecedented height.

The autograph parts (undated) are in the Taussig collection (Lund, UB). There is a copy of the score in the Witteczek–Spaun collection (Vienna, GdM) with all eight verses written out below. The first publication was in the *Gesamtausgabe* in 1895.

## AUF DEN TOD EINER NACHTIGALL On the Death of a Nightingale (1)

**Ludwig Hölty**                                                      25 May 1815

Langsam                               F sharp minor  D201  Not in Peters  Not in GA

Sie   ist     da - hin_____, die  Mai - en - lie - der  tön - te,

She is gone, the sweet singer of May songs, who filled the whole grove with beauty. She is gone! She whose song echoed in my heart, as I lay among the flowers by the brook which babbles through the undergrowth at evening.

From deep in her full throat came the silvery notes, and echo softly answered from the mountain clefts. The rustic melody and the trumpet call were in her song. Maidens would dance to it in the evening light.

Lying on a mossy bed a youth listened enraptured to that sweet sound, and the young bride hung languishing upon her lover's glances; and hands would touch at each repeated phrase. They heard nothing of other songsters. O nightingale!

They listened until the angelus tolled in the village and the evening star drew out from behind the clouds like a golden snowflake. Then they went to their cottage in the cool of the May evening, their hearts full of tenderness and sweet peace.

The poem, written in 1771, was originally entitled *Elegie auf eine Nachtigall*. Schubert used the version published in the 1804 posthumous edition of the poems, in which there are many editorial 'improvements'. This first attempt at a setting was left unfinished, though the melody lacked only the last three notes, and enough survives to show how the accompaniment would have continued. The autograph is lost, but a copy made by Ferdinand Schubert survived and is now in Vienna (GdM). It is dated 25 May 1815. The song has been completed and privately published by Reinhard van Hoorickx. His completion was also published, together with a facsimile of Ferdinand's transcription, in the *Revue belge de musicologie*, XXIV, 1970, pp.92–3.

Why Schubert left this attractive song incomplete is not clear. It is in the same key, and has something of the same poetic mood, as the Hölty song *An die Nachtigall*, written only three days before; perhaps he felt too near to that song to find the right form for this one.

## AUF DEN TOD EINER NACHTIGALL (2)

**Ludwig Hölty**                                    13 May 1816

A minor  D399  Not in Peters  GA XX no.218

For translation, see the preceding entry. The autograph of this second version is in Washington (LC). It is a first draft, dated 13 May 1816. It first appeared in the *Gesamtausgabe* in 1895. The plaintive 6/8 type of melody which Schubert had exploited in *Ins stille Land* and other songs of 1816 is here used to express the elegiac tone of the verses. The effect is more formal, almost conventional. Schubert's first thoughts a year earlier seem to be better than his second.

Einstein, 135; Fischer-Dieskau, 59

## AUF DER BRÜCKE On the Bridge

**Ernst Schulze**                                    (?) March 1825

A flat major  D853  Peters II p.176  GA XX no.477

Trot briskly on, good horse, through the dark and the rain, without stopping or staying. Why do you shy at the bushes and boughs, why stumble on the rough paths? However dark and thick the woods, they must give way at last, and a friendly light will greet us from the valley.

On your slender back I could happily ride far away over mountain and plain, enjoying all the gay pleasures and the charming sights of the world. Many a laughing eye meets mine, promising peace and love and joy, and yet I hurry on, back to my waiting sorrow.

For three days now I have been far from her, to whom I am for ever bound. For three days the sun and stars, heaven and earth have vanished from my sight. Of the joy and sorrow in my heart, soon wounded, soon made whole, in her presence, I have known for three days only the pain. Ah, what joy I had to miss!

Across land and water we see the birds fly far away to warmer pastures. How then should love deceive itself and lose its way? So trot bravely on through the night! Though the track disappear into the dark the bright eye of longing keeps watch, and sweet forebodings guide me safely on my way.

The poem comes from Schulze's *Poetisches Tagebuch* ('Verse Journal'), where it is entitled *Auf der Bruck, den 25sten Julius 1815*. Bruck is the name of a look-out point on a hill near Göttingen, but the confusion between the place name and 'die Brücke' (bridge) has led to endless uncertainty about the proper title. What Schubert's title was we do not know, because the autograph is missing. Deutsch claimed that the mistake was the publisher's, and certainly the first edition gave the title as *Auf der Brücke*. This could however have been taken from Schubert's fair copy, and since the copy in the Witteczek–Spaun collection (Vienna, GdM) is also headed 'Auf der Brücke' it seems quite possible that the original misunderstanding was Schubert's. He gave his own title to all the extracts from the *Poetisches Tagebuch* which he set, so it is reasonable to assume that he also did so here. In any case it is much too late to change the title of this well-known song.

*Auf der Brücke* was published with its companion piece *Im Walde* as op.90 – later changed to op.93 – in May 1828. The edition was engraved and published in Graz, and the publisher, J. A. Kienreich, claimed that the songs had been written during Schubert's stay in Graz in the previous September. In fact they were more than two years old when Schubert negotiated the deal during his visit in September 1827. The catalogue of the Witteczek–Spaun collection dates them both March 1825, and though another entry puts the date of *Auf der Brücke* as August 1825, the earlier date seems much more likely, both because the two poems are close together in the original text and Schubert's attention was probably attracted to both at the same time, and because in August 1825 he was on holiday at Gastein and much occupied with other matters. In 1835 Diabelli, who had acted as Kienreich's agent for the 1828 edition, republished the two songs as op.93. *Auf der Brücke* appeared (under that title) in the key of G major. As the Witteczek–Spaun copy is also in G major it seems likely that this was the original key, and that Schubert himself transposed the song to A flat when he wrote out his fair copy for Kienreich in 1827. It is, however, the A flat version which has become familiar through the Peters edition and the *Gesamtausgabe*, neither of which prints the G major version.

It has often been pointed out that the passion and pathos of the Schulze songs foreshadow *Winterreise*. If *Im Walde* can be regarded as a kind of preparation for *Erstarrung*, *Auf der Brücke*, with its blend of courage, hope, and misgiving, might be compared to *Muth*. The relentless quavers drive on for nearly 150 bars, an image both of the rhythm of the trotting horse and of the rider driven on by his passion and self-doubt. In this strophic setting the risk of monotony is avoided by the subtle changes in the voice line, and by the richness of the tonal palette by means of which Schubert adapts the music to the sense.

Capell, 215–16; Einstein, 304

## AUF DER DONAU On the Danube

**Johann Mayrhofer**                                                    April 1817

E flat major/F sharp minor D553 Peters IV p.14 GA XX no.317 NSA IV vol.1 p.148

The boat swims on the mirror of the waves; ancient castles soar heavenwards. There is a ghostly stirring in the pinewoods and our hearts grow faint.

For all men's creations pass away. Where are the towers, the gates, the ramparts? Where are the strong men themselves, who sheathed in armour stormed out to war or to hunt? Where?

Sadly the briars grow rank, while the power of the pious myth fades. And we grow fearful in our little boat, for the waves, like time itself, threaten destruction.

The only evidence as to the date of the song comes from the catalogue of the Witteczek–Spaun collection (Vienna, GdM), where it is annotated 'April 1817'. The autograph is lost, and there are no contemporary copies. *Auf der Donau* was published in June 1823 by Sauer and Leidesdorf as op.21 no.1. The opus, consisting of three Mayrhofer songs all for bass voice, was dedicated by Schubert to the poet.

This fine song is one of the most original and disturbing of all the Mayrhofer settings, and it points forward to the mood of Schubert's final years. As so often with Mayrhofer, the natural peace and beauty of the scene are turned to his own pessimistic purposes. What surprises us is Schubert's wholehearted acceptance of the theme. The song begins with a musical image of the rocking boat which is so precise and captivating that we confidently assume that it will dominate the song, as Schubert's watery motifs usually do. But soon a 'ghostly stirring' is heard in the accompaniment, and we find ourselves unexpectedly in the remote key of C flat. In the second verse the movement becomes choppy, and a series of ominous trills sound in the bass, the precursors surely of the trills which echo equally menacingly through the first movement of the B flat Piano Sonata D960. Moreover Schubert here denies us the consolation of a ternary structure. Although the last verse returns to the opening piano figure, it returns in the key of F sharp minor, and the last twelve bars resound to the one word 'Untergang' ('destruction'), as we hear once again the long slow descent of the bass line to F sharp, one of the most remarkable instances of Schubert's familiar death motif. So a song which begins like a placid barcarolle ends in total desolation.

In view of its unconventional structure and sombre tone, not to mention the challenge it poses to the voice, it is not surprising that *Auf der Donau* is rarely heard. Yet it is a wonderful song, in which text and music, voice and accompaniment, are blended in a tonal texture that is rich and seamless.

Capell, 60, 138–9; Fischer-Dieskau, 97; Porter, 129–30

## AUF DER RIESENKOPPE On the Giant Peak

**Theodor Körner**                                               March 1818

D minor/D major/B flat  D611  Peters VI p.68  GA XX no.336

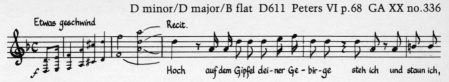

High on the peak of the mountains, holy heaven-storming summit, I stand amazed, and glowing with rapture.

My ravished gaze ranges far into the distance; everywhere is life, luxuriant growth, everywhere sunshine.

There are flowering meadows, shining towns; I see the happy kingdoms of three kings, am carried away by heartfelt delight.

I see the frontiers of my native land too, where life began happily for me, and love's sacred longing first possessed me.

Dear homeland, accept my blessing from afar. Blest be the land of my dreams, home of my loved ones.

The poem is entitled *Sonnenaufgang auf der Riesenkoppe* ('Sunrise on the Giant Peak'). The mountain chain called the Riesengebirge is not far from Körner's native Dresden. The autograph (Stockholm, SMf) is dated March 1818. There is a dated copy in the Witteczek–Spaun collection (Vienna, GdM). *Auf der Riesenkoppe* was published in book 49 of the *Nachlass* (c. 1850).

The song is comparatively little known, but it is remarkable for the freedom and originality of its tonal structure. A bold recitative in D minor leads to a bland melody in D major which takes an unexpected route through F major, G major and C major before finally coming to rest in A major. The final section is in B flat major, and makes effective use of the flattened sixth G flat. In spite of the episodic structure, the song preserves a unity of tone and feeling. There is a close relationship between the D major and the B flat major sections, expressed not only by the key but also by the melodic shape and rhythm. The recitatives are skilfully linked with the rest of the song; Schubert seems to be feeling his way towards the looser structure of the *Müllerlieder*. Indeed, the closing sequences of the song plainly look forward to *Pause*.

Fischer-Dieskau, 26

## AUF EINEN KIRCHHOF On a Churchyard

**Franz Xaver von Schlechta**                                 2 February 1815

A major  D151  Peters VI p.69  GA XX no.39  NSA IV vol.7 p.119

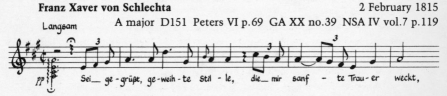

I salute you, holy stillness, which fills me with gentle melancholy; where kindly nature spreads her bright mantle over your graves.

Lightly borne on the clouds, the sun dips in her course; above the darkened earth the red glow flames aloft.

Ah, you too, my dead brethren, have run your course. Was your descent into the dread darkness of the grave so splendid?

Sleep softly, you cold hearts, in your long dark rest. The gentle earth covers your wounds and your pain.

The wheel of time drives on, destroying and creating anew; the force hidden in the earth blossoms afresh in the meadow.

And you too, mortal frame, will one day sink down trembling, and will blossom anew in splendour, like a flower on the grave.

You will flicker like a flame through the tombs, a wandering light over the fens, a shaft soaring up into the heavens, a sweet sound echoing aloft.

But you, the spirit that dwells in me, will you also become a prey to worms? Whatever uplifts and delights me, are you too but vain dust?

No, what I feel within me, that which uplifts and delights me, is the pure spirit of the Godhead, the breath that lives in me.

Schubert must have had the poem in manuscript from Schlechta, who was one of his earliest friends and admirers. It was entitled *Im Kirchhofe* ('In the Churchyard'), but Schubert's autograph (Vienna, SB) is headed as above and dated 2 February 1815. Schlechta made substantial alterations to the poem before it was published. There is a copy of the song in the Witteczek–Spaun collection (Vienna, GdM). It was published about 1850 in book 49 of the *Nachlass*. ·

Schubert's setting is through-composed, and relies on recitative to serve as a link between the changes of mood. The song begins well, but as a whole it lacks unity and cumulative effect. The brisk, lighthearted tone of the final section seems also out of sympathy with the contemplative poem.

Capell, 89; Fischer-Dieskau, 74

**AUFENTHALT** see RELLSTAB SONGS no.5

## AUFLÖSUNG Dissolution

**Johann Mayrhofer**                                                  March 1824

Nicht zu geschwind                    G major  D807  Peters V p.196  GA XX no.460

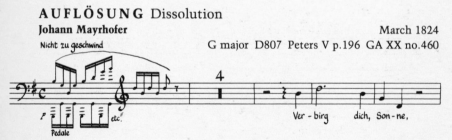

Hide yourself, sun, for I burn with rapture. Be silent, sounds; spring beauty, flee away, and leave me to myself.

From every corner of my soul sweet powers well up and encompass me with heavenly singing. Dissolve, world, and never more disturb the sweet ethereal choirs.

The autograph, dated March 1824, is in the archive of the Deutsches Sängerbund, Cologne. There is also a dated copy in the Witteczek–Spaun collection (Vienna, GdM). The song was published in 1842 in book 34 of the *Nachlass*.

There is no other song like *Auflösung* in Schubert, nor, one is tempted to say, elsewhere. The poem is a kind of secular version of Pope's poem which Schubert set in *Verklärung*: 'The world recedes, it disappears/ Heaven opens on my eyes, my ears/ With sounds seraphic ring.' But what worlds away from the conventional piety of that earlier (1813) song is the rhapsodic afflatus of this one. The concept is Wagnerian. The first verse consists essentially of the continuous sounding of the chord of G major for nineteen bars (*pp*), reinforced by a vocal line confined almost entirely to the tonic arpeggio and by an accompaniment which gives an orchestral dimension to the same tonal structure. At bar 11 there is a two-bar feint towards B minor, which serves only to emphasise the pull of

G major as a kind of symbol of eternity itself. The next verse is in the neapolitan key of A flat major (*ff*). This moves enharmonically towards a climax in B major. But again Schubert brings us back to G major, with insistent *sforzando* chords, and to the poet's arrogant assertion of his own immortality: 'Dissolve, world, and never more disturb the sweet ethereal choirs.'

This extraordinary song is contemporary with the 'Death and the Maiden' quartet, and with *Der Sieg*, another Mayrhofer song with which it makes a contrasted companion piece. Both songs are about death, one in proud resignation, the other in a kind of poetic rhapsody. It is a strange and moving song to emerge from the imagination of the normally phlegmatic Schubert, the tonal equivalent perhaps of the 'holy fire' of Novalis which he failed to match in the Novalis settings themselves.

Capell, 204–5; Einstein, 303; Fischer-Dieskau, 192

## AUGENBLICKE IM ELYSIUM Moments in Elysium
**Franz von Schober**                                                      D582 (D2 990B)

In the second edition of Schober's poems this one is annotated 'with music by Schubert'. But no such song has yet been found. The poem begins: Vor der in Ehrfurcht all mein Wesen kniet,/Jetzt scheb' hernieder, Urbild ew'ger Schöne! (Come down now, image of eternal Beauty, Before whom my whole being kneels in reverence).

## AUGENLIED To her Eyes
**Johann Mayrhofer**                                                        (?) Early 1817
F major  D297  Peters VI p.80  GA XX no.171

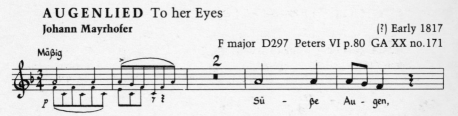

Sweet eyes, clear fountains, my torment and my bliss truly all come from you. My songs I dedicate to you. Where I linger, when I hasten, lovingly you shine on me, lighting my path, bedewing it with tears.

Never fade, faithful stars, lead me on to Acheron, and with your last gleam let my life too ebb away.

The autograph is lost, and no precise date can be given for the song. The only solid evidence comes from Spaun's memoir of the composer, in which he says that at Schubert's first meeting with the singer Michael Vogl he played over this song, 'which he had just composed' (*Memoirs* p.22). This meeting took place in the spring of 1817. There are various contemporary copies, in which the song appears in two versions. The one in the Witteczek–Spaun collection (Vienna, GdM), with no piano prelude and marked 'Etwas geschwind', may have been based on Schubert's original autograph. A second version, with a four-bar piano prelude and marked 'Mässig', exists in several copies, and one of these, belonging to the monastery at Kremsmünster in Upper Austria, is signed by Schubert, so that this version also may claim to be authentic. It is reproduced in the Peters edition. The *Gesamtausgabe* follows the earlier version without prelude. *Augenlied* was published in 1850, in book 50 of the *Nachlass*.

In his account of the first meeting between Schubert and Vogl, Spaun describes how the singer 'took up the nearest sheet of music, containing Mayrhofer's poem *Augenlied*, a pretty, tuneful, but not very significant song. Vogl hummed rather than sang, and then said coldly "Not bad!"' (*Memoirs* p.132). The account carries conviction, not least in its estimate of the song.

## AUS 'DIEGO MANAZARES': ILMERINE From *Diego Manazares*

**Franz Xaver von Schlechta**                                                   30 July 1816

*Etwas bewegt*                                       F minor D458 Not in Peters GA XX no.242

Where are you wandering through the lonely caverns of the night? My life, my happiness, where are you?
Already the night stars have risen from their dewy darkness, but ah, my beloved has not yet returned.

*Diego Manazares* is the title of a play, and Ilmerine is the heroine. Schubert must have had the text in manuscript from Schlechta. The autograph, headed as above, is dated 30 July 1816 (Paris Conservatoire). There are dated copies also in the Witteczek–Spaun collection (Vienna, GdM). The song was published by J. P. Gotthard in 1872 as no.25 of 'Forty Songs'. In this first edition the title appears erroneously as *Diego Manzanares*.

The universal indifference to this attractive song is difficult to understand. Schubert has written an effective operatic aria on a small scale which beautifully conveys the restless anxiety of the lover. There is an operatic quality about the piano writing too. How well that opening figure would sound with plucked strings and woodwind! Yet the song does not appear in the Peters volumes, and the commentators ignore it.

## AUS 'HELIOPOLIS' From *Heliopolis* I (Im kalten, rauhen Norden)

**Johann Mayrhofer**                                                             April 1822

*Mäßig*                                       E minor D753 Peters III p.33 GA XX no.404

In the cold, raw north I heard tell of a city, the city of the sun. Where rides the ship, where does the road beckon, which will take me to its courts? Men could not tell me, for they were crazed with strife. I turned to the flower beloved of Helios, which ever looks towards him – and was enraptured: 'Like me, turn your face to the sun! There is bliss, there is life. Be constant, like a faithful pilgrim, and doubt not. In the light you will find peace. Light kindles ardour, sows the seeds of hope, engenders noble deeds!'

The poem is the fifth in the sequence entitled *Heliopolis*, which Mayrhofer wrote in the autumn of 1821. The beginning of Schubert's autograph (Oslo, UB) has not survived, but the copy in the Witteczek–Spaun collection (Vienna, GdM) is headed 'Heliopolis no.5', and the companion piece from the same sequence is called 'Heliopolis no.12'. The two *Heliopolis* songs were published separately. *Im kalten, rauhen Norden* appeared in November 1826 as op.65 no.3 (Cappi and Czerny). Schubert worked from Mayrhofer's manuscript, now in Vienna (SB): The sequence is prefaced by a verse motto which reads: 'We mean to ring the changes on an old theme, recited in olden times. Though we stumble and lose our way we may still dare to look towards the sun.' In the collected edition of Mayrhofer's poems the sequence is dedicated 'To Franz Schober'. The autograph has been split up, and only the last nineteen bars survive in the Udbye collection at Oslo. The catalogue of the Witteczek–Spaun collection dates the song April 1822.

The steady four crotchets to the bar, and the bare unisons, foreshadow the first movement of the A minor Piano Sonata of 1825 D845. This is the 'cold, raw north'. Schubert's minor–major symbolism here works beautifully, however; the music warms to the thought of Mayrhofer's mythical 'city of the sun', and the texture thickens, so that the closing bars seem to glow with hope and confidence. There is little doubt that the *Heliopolis* cycle was written for Schubert, and that the intention was that it should become a song cycle. Why the plan fell through we do not know; maybe the sequence lacked the narrative interest Schubert was looking for. Maybe the estrangement between poet and composer intervened. Whatever the reason, it is a pity that this fine song is not heard more often.

Capell, 177; Fischer-Dieskau, 120

## AUS 'HELIOPOLIS' From *Heliopolis* II (Fels auf Felsen hingewältzet)

**Johann Mayrhofer**                                                    April 1822

Geschwind und kräftig                C minor D754 Peters III p.204 GA XX no.405

Fels auf Fel – sen hin – ge-wäl – zet,

Rock piled upon rock, solid ground and firm foothold, waterfalls, gusts of wind, power beyond comprehension. On the lonely mountain peak stands a monastery or castle ruin: engrave them on the memory, for the poet lives by experience. Breathe the hallowed air, let your arms embrace the world. Dare to remain devoted only to the great and the worthy. Let the passions swell in brassy harmony; when the fierce storms rage you will find the right word.

The poem is no.12 in the *Heliopolis* sequence, and in both the autographs the heading is *Heliopolis 12*. In the collected edition of the poems (1824) this one is entitled *Im Hochgebirge* ('On the Mountain Tops') and printed separately. The first draft is in Vienna (ÖNB) and the fair copy in Berlin (SPK). Neither is dated; the catalogue of the Witteczek–Spaun collection (Vienna, GdM) gives April 1822, and one of the two copies is similarly dated. The fair copy is written for bass voice. The song was published in book 37 of the *Nachlass* (1842).

The leaping unison theme which dominates the song wonderfully captures the 'quick, powerful, energetic strokes' of the climber, and his exhilarating energy. There is a tremendous dynamic energy in the piece, as though the power of nature itself had been inspiring the climber. Indeed, in the powerful C major peroration the chromatically rising top line set against the vocal line calls to mind the climax of the 'Great' C major Symphony.

Capell, 177; Einstein, 253; Fischer-Dieskau, 120

**AVE MARIA** see ELLENS GESANG III

## BALLADE
**Josef Kenner**                                                      (?) Early 1815

G minor D134 Peters IV p.152 GA XX no.99 NSA IV vol.7 p.77

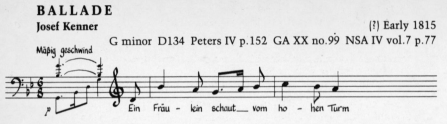

[*Synopsis*] A maiden looks down from the tower across the wide sea. Sadly she sings to the mournful notes of the zither. 'This castle holds me prisoner here; my rescuer tarries long.'

'Take comfort, noble maid. See, behind the white cliffs a warship sails into the darkness of the bay. Your rescuer comes, with the eagle's plume and roses upon his shield.' Already the hero's horn sounds to battle.

'Welcome, fair youth. Soon I shall hack the gold flowers from your sable shield. Your royal bride will find the eighteen flowers by the water's edge stained with your blood. Come, draw your sword.'

Hearing the noise of battle die away at last, the waiting bride hastens to the shore where her oppressor lies slain. But alas, the blood-bespattered body of the hero lies pallid in death.

She strews the body of her lover with roses. As the tears fall on his wounds she says: "Tis I have done the deed.'

A henchman of the robber band, in vengeance and lust for blood, despatches an arrow through her chaste breast.

They lowered her body into her bridal chamber, still and small, to join her lover on the pebbled shore. They lie there under a stone which still stands, overgrown with thistles by the ruined water.

The poem was written in June 1814, and may well have been given to Schubert in manuscript, since Kenner was one of his earliest associates. It seems to have been modelled on Matthisson's *Das Fräulein im Thurme* (see *Romanze*) which Schubert set in September 1814. The autograph is missing and there are no copies, so the date of the song is uncertain; but it probably belongs, like the other Kenner songs, to the early months of 1815. It was published as op.126 in January 1830 by Josef Czerny.

The song is one more proof of the fascination this sub-Ossianic balladry held for Schubert and his friends. The trumpet calls and march rhythms are scene-painting of a conventional kind, but the gently undulating thirds and sixths in the final section are more interesting . Schubert often uses this figure to suggest grief and loneliness, and it became quite a feature of his Ossian style.

**BEI ANSELMOS GRABE** see AM GRABE ANSELMOS

## BEI DEM GRABE MEINES VATERS  At my Father's Grave
**Matthias Claudius**                                               November 1816

E flat major D496 Peters VII p.28 GA XX no.274

Peace be to this stone, the gentle peace of God. Ah, they have laid a good man to rest; to me he was far more. He showered blessings on me, like a star from a better world; and I can never repay what he gave me.

He slept, and they laid him here. May the dear·consolation of God, and the promise of eternal life, keep his bones sweet, until Jesus Christ, in his glory and greatness, gently wakens him again.

Oh, they have laid a good man to rest, and to me he was far more.

The poem appeared in 1773. The autograph is lost, but there is a copy in the Witteczek–Spaun collection (Vienna, GdM) and the date given in the catalogue is November 1816. The first publication was in 1885, in vol. VII of the Peters collected edition.

There is a striking contrast between the tone of the Claudius songs of bereavement of November 1816 and the more personal and Schubertian tone of the death songs written a few months later in the spring of 1817. It is not simply that the latter are more deeply felt, for this song and its companion piece *Am Grabe Anselmos* are moving in their sincerity and compassion. But the feeling is contained within the restraints of a classical structure. The tonal scheme is confined to the primary relations of E flat major, and there is something Beethovenish about the expressive dialogue between the pianist's right hand and the voice at the words, 'I can never repay him what he gave me.' The subdominant feeling which makes itself felt at the very beginning is characteristic too of a later song in the same vein, *Ihr Grab*. The stress distribution is by no means perfect, but this fine song is grateful to the voice. It seems to be more popular with singers than with the commentators.

## BEI DIR ALLEIN With you alone
**Johann Gabriel Seidl**                                   (?) Summer 1828
A flat major D866 no.2  Peters III p.66  GA XX no.509

With you alone I feel I am alive. I am filled with the spirit of youth, a carefree world of love invests me. I rejoice in my being with you alone!

With you alone is the breeze so refreshing, the meadows so green, the flowering spring so gentle, the evening so fragrant, the grove so cool!

With you alone pain's bitterness is lost and every joy enhanced! In you is my heart's natural heritage fulfilled. I feel I am myself, with you alone!

The second of 'Four Refrain Songs', published by Thaddäus Weigl in August 1828 as op.95. The date of these songs is uncertain. Seidl's poems were published in two volumes in 1826 and may have come into Schubert's hands then. However, a sketch for the first of the four songs appears on the second sheet of a manuscript which also contains a sketch for the fourth movement of the C minor Piano Sonata D958, finished in September 1828. This suggests that Schubert may have worked on the songs, as well as on the last piano sonatas, during the summer of 1828. No autograph of *Bei dir allein* has survived. The four songs were published as op.95 and dedicated to the author.

A refrain song is one in which all the verses end with the same line, used however in a changed context and sometimes in a different sense, as in the Ballade. The publisher's blurb claimed the four songs were 'of a merry comic nature'; the publication was clearly an attempt to come to terms with prevailing taste. All four are lighthearted in tone, but *Bei dir allein* is a straightforward love song. The impetuous triplet figure runs right through the song to its final flourish in the last bars, symbolising the young lover's irrepressible ardour. The tonal structure reflects Schubert's favourite key relationship: outer verses in A flat, middle verse in E major, enharmonically the flattened sixth. The song calls for a strong tenor voice able to cope with the wide range (middle C to top A flat); in a good performance it is irresistible.

> Capell, 223–4

## BEIM WINDE Windy Weather
**Johann Mayrhofer**                                                                                October 1819

G minor D669  Peters V p.129  GA XX no.365

Dreaming, the clouds, stars, moon, trees, birds, flowers and stream lull themselves to sleep and nestle down in still places, dewy beds, and private bliss. But the rustle of leaves and the rippling of the waves herald an awakening; the gusty winds moan, restless and hurrying, first a gentle stirring, then a wild commotion; dreams are swallowed up in the opening spaces.

Keep your dear ones close to your heart, unsullied; the blood pulses, so that you may protect the sacred flame from raging storms.

The autograph (Berlin, SPK) is dated October 1819. There is a copy in the Witteczek–Spaun collection (Vienna, GdM). The song first appeared as a supplement to the *ZfK* in June 1829 and was subsequently published in book 22 of the *Nachlass* (1833).

Schubert repeats the first ten lines (as far as 'private bliss') at the end of the song. The outer sections are delightful in the manner of the *Schöne Müllerin* songs. Indeed, *Beim Winde* might almost be a sketch for *Der Müller und der Bach*, which it closely resembles not only in the major–minor alternations but even in some harmonic sequences (see, for instance, bars 13–18). In the middle sections Schubert follows the sense closely, at some risk to the lyrical thread. The pause and double bar in the middle of the third verse seems to contravene the sense, moreover. None the less, *Beim Winde* is pure Schubert–Mayrhofer and should be much better known than it is.

> Capell, 161

## BERTAS LIED IN DER NACHT Bertha's Lullaby
**Franz Grillparzer**                                                                                February 1819

E flat minor D653  Peters VI p.26  GA XX no.355

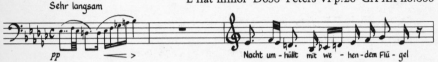

Night on hovering wing envelops valley and hill, summoning to rest. Softly she whispers to Sleep, the sweet child: If you know of a troubled, wakeful eye, sweet Sleep, close it for me. Do you feel him approaching? Have you a sense of peace? All things are restored in sleep. Do you sleep also.

The poem is linked, not altogether clearly, with the first production of Grillparzer's play *Die Ahnfrau* ('The Ancestress'), which took place in January 1817. During the ensuing weeks Grillparzer revised the text for publication, and it was at this stage that he wrote

*Bertas Lied in der Nacht*, presumably to be sung in the first act. But it was never incorporated in the text, and it survives as a separate poem. The autograph (Vienna, GdM) is a first draft dated February 1819. It is in E flat minor, but when the song was published about 1842 (*Nachlass* book 40 no.2) it was transposed to D minor. The original key, which suits the song better, is used in the *Gesamtausgabe*.

This is Schubert's only setting of words by Grillparzer, but it is a very fine one, and one of the most atmospheric of his night pieces. The unison passages in the opening bars seem to invest the song with the mystery of night. The syncopated quaver C's have a hypnotic effect. The dynamic level changes only from *pp* to *ppp* at the end, when the song seems to resolve into the clarity of sleep. The rhythmic freedom and originality of the song contrast strikingly with the conventional build of a song like *Nachtgesang* (Kosegarten), written in October 1815.

Capell, 167–8; Einstein, 189; Fischer-Dieskau, 117–8

## BLANKA
**Friedrich von Schlegel**                                        December 1818

A minor D631 Peters VII p.44 GA XX no.348

Wenn mich ein - sam    Lüf - te fä - cheln,      muss___ ich lä - cheln,

When in my loneliness soft breezes fan me, then must I smile, as when I dally childlike with the rose. Were it not for these new pangs, then would I jest. If I could say what I feel, I should complain and ask, anxiously hoping, what fate holds in store for me. If I jest and flirt with roses, still I have to temper my complaints with smiles.

The poem, entitled *Blanka*, was written about 1800 and appeared in Schlegel's 'Poetic Pocket-book' for 1806. Later, under the title *Das Mädchen*, it was incorporated in the cycle *Stimmen der Liebe* ('Voices of Love'). Schubert's autograph is a pencil sketch inked over, headed 'Blanka. Schlegel' and dated December 1818, in private possession. The song was published in 1885 in the Peters edition. The direction *Mässig* is editorial. An arrangement for piano solo by J.P. Gotthard had appeared in 1876.

The varied phrase-length, the major–minor shifts and the gently wayward movement all contibute to the mock-serious mood. The song is sometimes called *Das Mädchen*, but it is better to reserve this title for the better-known setting, of February 1819, of the rather similar Schlegel poem.

Capell, 145; Einstein, 186; Fischer-Dieskau, 124

## BLONDEL ZU MARIEN  Blondel to Mary
**Author unknown**                                        September 1818

Sehr langsam

E flat minor D626 Peters V p.200 GA XX no.343

*p*

In   düst - rer Nacht  wenn Gram mein füh-lend Herz um-zie - het,

In the dark night, when sadness invests my loving heart, and the sun of good fortune escapes me, a friendly star shines in the far distance, like a bright jewel in the crown of love.

And amid joys and sorrows its reflection stays pure for ever in my faithful loving heart. So your sweet and gentle image will keep watch over me, as by magic, though I be far away.

The autograph, written in E flat minor and dated 1818, belonged for many years to the Esterházy family, which suggests that the song was written during Schubert's residence in Zseliz. It was auctioned at Sotheby's in April 1935; its present whereabouts are unknown. There is a copy in the Witteczek–Spaun collection (Vienna, GdM) in C minor, but a note states that the original is in E flat minor; the catalogue gives the date of the song as September 1818. The copy gives the name of the author as Grillparzer, but the song does not appear in any authoritative edition of his works. Einstein suggests that the author was Alois Schreiber, who wrote three other poems set by Schubert at Zseliz in 1818, but he adduces no real evidence. The song was first published, in C minor, early in 1842 as no.2 of book 34 of the *Nachlass*.

Blondel de Nesle was the troubadour friend of Richard the Lionheart. According to legend he discovered the imprisoned king's whereabouts by singing a song under his window and pausing so that the king could complete it. An essay in the melismatic style, the song needs a light tenor voice to do it justice. Not all the vocal embellishments, however, sound authentic; some may well derive from J.M. Vogl.

Capell, 146–7; Einstein, 184

**BLUMENBALLADE** see VERGISSMEINNICHT and VIOLA

## BLUMENLIED Flower Song
**Ludwig Hölty**
May 1816
E major D431 Peters VII p.100 GA XX no.223

It is halfway to heaven to see the flowers spring up from the clover like the flowers of paradise, and to hear the birds sing from blossom-laden branches, now in the garden, now by the stream.

But the sweetest flower of all is a fine woman, a good soul and comely, in the flush of youth. We leave the flowers alone to gaze at that young woman, and delight in her goodness.

The poem, based on one of Walter von der Vogelweide's love songs, was written in January 1773. It is worthy of note that the ten Hölty songs of May 1816 strike a quite different note from those written a year earlier. It is a note of unaffected joy, free of the wistful melancholy so characteristic of earlier songs like *An den Mond* and *An die Nachtigall*. Significantly, five of the May 1816 songs are in E major, a key of innocence and rejoicing. *Blumenlied* is a good example; it has much the same infectious gaiety as *Seligkeit*, though not such a good tune.

**BRÜDER, SCHRECKLICH BRENNT DIE TRÄNE** see LIED

## BUNDESLIED Comrades' Song

**Johann Wolfgang von Goethe**                                    August 1815

Mäßig                        B flat major D258 Not in Peters GA XX no.115

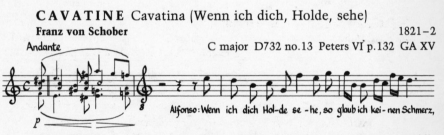

In al - len— gu - ten Stun - den, er - höht von Lieb— und— Wein,

Whenever, inspired by love and wine, we celebrate the good times, united we shall sing this song; and God, who brought us hither, will revive the flames he once kindled.

So, with warm hearts and in unity drink this glass of purest wine to renewed joy; clink glasses and kiss, making the old bonds between us new again.

As we pass swiftly along life's way we look toward heaven, with gaze ever serene; though all things rise and fall we shall never fear; and may we long remain so, united for ever.

The poem was written in September 1775. Schubert probably used the 1806 collected edition. There are five verses, of which the third and fourth are sometimes omitted in performance. The autograph, in private possession, is dated 19 August 1815. There is also (in Vienna, SB) a fair copy made for Goethe in 1816. The song was published in 1887 by Weinberger and Hofbauer of Vienna. This hearty drinking-song originally ended with an emphatic tum-ti-tum, but when he copied out the song for Goethe Schubert replaced it with a single *sforzando* chord.

## CAVATINE Cavatina (Wenn ich dich, Holde, sehe)

**Franz von Schober**                                              1821–2

Andante                    C major D732 no.13 Peters VI p.132 GA XV

Alfonso: Wenn ich dich Hol-de se - he, so glaub ich kei-nen Schmerz,

When I behold you, fair one, then pain no longer exists, for your mere presence fills my heart with bliss. Sorrows flee, that once racked my breast. A thousand suns light up this world aflame with pleasure, and new powers invade my giddy heart. Yes, I will protect you, I will be your servant.

This tenor aria comes from Schubert's grand opera *Alfonso und Estrella*, and the only reason for including it here is that it appears in vol. VI of the Peters edition of the songs, where it is given the spurious title 'Cavatina' and transposed into B flat major. At the beginning of Act II Alfonso, son of the deposed King Troila, comes upon Estrella, the daughter of the usurper, lost in a wood. In a succession of tender arias and recitatives they fall in love. The opera was written between 20 September 1821 and 27 February 1822. The autograph is in Vienna (GdM).

**CLÄRCHENS LIED** see DIE LIEBE (Goethe)

**COLMAS KLAGE** see KOLMAS KLAGE

# CORA AN DIE SONNE Cora to the Sun

**Gabriele von Baumberg**                                   22 August 1815

Langsam, mit Ausdruck                    E flat major  D263  Peters VI p.33  GA XX no.123

Nach so vie-len trü-ben Ta-gen send uns wie-de-rum ein-mal,

After so many dismal days have pity on us, dear sun; send us once more your soft and gentle beams.

Dear sun, drink up the rain that threatens to fall, your rays are a blessing to us, your glances bliss.

Shine, dear sun, ah shine! Every joy I owe to you; all spiritual joy and heart's delight, light and warmth all come from you.

The autograph, together with another Baumberg song, *Abendständchen*, is in Washington (LC). It is a first draft, dated 22 August 1815. There is a dated copy in the Witteczek–Spaun collection (Vienna, GdM). The song was published in book 42 of the *Nachlass* (1848) with a spurious two-bar prelude presumably by Diabelli. This appears also in the Peters edition. The tune makes a single span of twelve bars without leaving the home key. Schubert's melodic gift in these early songs shows a classical sense of line and form, though the song has not quite the charm of its companion piece *Abendständchen*.

# CRONNAN

**James Macpherson (Ossian)**                              5 September 1815

Langsam                         C minor  D282  Peters IV p.174  GA XX no.188

Ich sitz bei der moo-sig-ten Quel-le,

Macpherson's text reads:

I sit by the mossy fountain, on the top of the hill of the winds. One tree is rustling above me. Dark waves roll over the heath. The lake is troubled below. The deer descend from the hill. No hunter at a distance is seen. It is midday, but all is silent. Sad are my thoughts alone. Didst thou but appear, O my love, a wanderer on the heath! Thy hair floating on the wind behind thee; thy bosom heaving on the sight; thine eyes full of tears for thy friends, whom the mist of the hill had concealed. Thee I would comfort, my love, and bring thee to my father's house!

But is it she that there appears, like a beam of light on the heath? Bright as the moon in autumn, as the sun in a summer storm, comest thou, O maid, over rocks, over mountains to me. She speaks: but how weak her voice, like the breeze in the reeds of the lake!

'Returnest thou safe from the war? Where are thy friends, my love? I heard of thy death on the hill; I heard and mourned thee, Shilric.'

Yes, my fair, I return; but I alone of my race. Thou shalt see them no more; their graves I raised on the plain. But why art thou on the desert hill? Why on the heath alone?

'Alone I am, O Shilric, alone in the winter-house. With grief for thee I fell, Shilric; I am pale in the tomb.'

She fleets, she sails away, as mist before the wind! And wilt thou not stay, Vinvela? Stay and behold my tears! Fair thou appearest, Vinvela, fair thou wast, when alive!

By the mossy fountain I will sit, on the top of the hill of winds. When midday is silent around, O talk with me Vinvela! Come on the light-winged gale, on the breeze of the desert, come! Let me hear thy voice, as thou passest, when midday is silent around.

See OSSIAN SONGS. The text comes from the prose poem *Carric-Thura*. The story tells how Fingal came to the rescue of Cathulla, King of Inistore, who was besieged in his palace of Carric-Thura by Frothal, King of Sora. But this is only the framework within which the bardic episodes can be fitted: 'Cronnan, said Ullin of other times, raise the song of Shilric; when he returned to his hills, and Vinvela was no more. He leaned on her grey mossy stone; he thought Vinvela lived. He saw her fair-moving on the plain, but the bright form lasted not: the sunbeam fled from the field, and she was seen no more. Hear the song of Shilric, it is soft but sad ...' Schubert used the translation by Edmund von Harold.

The autograph, dated 5 September 1815, has been divided, and the first part, containing the first 113 bars, is now in private possession in Vienna. The last 17 bars appear with a sketch for the finale of the 'Tragic' Symphony (no.4 in C minor) and the Claudius song *Zufriedenheit* (Vienna, SB). The song was published in July 1830, as no.1 in book 2 of the *Nachlass*. Diabelli made many changes in the text, which are followed in the Peters edition. The source for the version published in the *Gesamtausgabe* was the autograph, which itself differs in detail from the Harold translation. There is nothing to suggest that Schubert intended the piece to be performed as a duet. It is a dramatic scena for solo voice and piano.

*Cronnan* is one of the best of the Ossian songs, and of special interest because of its use of repeated motifs in a quasi-Wagnerian fashion. The undulating thirds and sixths seem to be Schubert's portrayal of the mist and the moor, while the upward-curving semi-quavers, usually in thirds, stand for Vinvela's loyalty and beauty. The depth and economy of expression suggest once again that the idea of a large-scale Wagnerian drama haunted Schubert's imagination. These marks of what might be called Schubert's 'Ossian style' are to be found again in *Die Nacht*.

Capell, 94

**DA QUEL SEMBIANTE APPRESI** see VIER CANZONEN no.3

**DANKSAGUNG AN DEN BACH** see DIE SCHÖNE MÜLLERIN no.4

## DAPHNE AM BACH Daphne by the Brook
**Friedrich Leopold, Graf zu Stolberg-Stolberg**                    April 1816
D major D411  Peters VII p.87  GA XX no.209

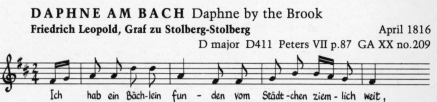

Ich  hab ein Bäch-lein fun - den vom Städt-chen ziem-lich weit,

Far from the town I have found a brook, and I linger quietly there alone for hours. I choose a spot on the cool moss; there I sit, and let the tears rain down in my lap.

My young blood throbs for you, and I whisper your name to the stream. Fearful that some deceiver from the town may overhear, even the rustling of the leaves in the poplar trees alarms me.

I long for the most fleeting pleasure again; every moment I feel your parting kiss; happy, yet sad in your embrace, as your tears fell on my cheeks.

Long I watched you go from the hillock, and I longed to have wings, like the dove. Now every moment I feel close to death. If you wish to see your love again, then come back soon!

The poem was written in 1775. Schubert's autograph, a first draft dated April 1816, is in the Spaun–Cornaro collection, in private possession in Vienna. The song was first published in 1887, in vol. VII of the Peters edition. The attractive strophic setting is nothing special in itself, but it points to greater things (*Wohin!*, for instance) with its running semiquavers and clinching final phrase.

## DAS ABENDROT The Sunset Glow

**Alois Schreiber**                                                   November 1818

E major  D627  Peters VI p.123  GA XX no.344

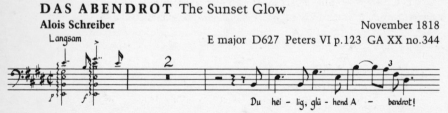

Blessed glow of evening! The sky melts into splendour. So martyrs take their leave, smiling as they die for love. The mountains still and grey in the dawn; the bright fires of the day's dying; the swan on the crimson waters, and every blade shining in silver dew!

O Sun, light of God, you are never more glorious than in your going. Gladly would you draw us after you to the source of your splendour.

The autograph (Washington, LC) is dated 'November 1818, Zseliz'. The song is for bass voice, and was evidently written for Johann Karl, Count Esterházy, in whose household Schubert served as tutor. A copy formerly in the possession of Karoline, Countess Esterházy, has been lost. *Das Abendrot* was published in 1867, as op.173 no.6, by C. A. Spina. The voice part, though written in the treble clef, is marked 'Bass'.

This splendid bass song is a fine example of the lyrical extension and pianistic freedom typical of the Schreiber songs. It is something of a showpiece, indeed, calling for a voice of considerable power and flexibility with a good E below the stave. It is written with great assurance and attention to the words (note the discreet scene-painting in the second verse, and the familiar *Wanderer* sequence at bars 25–8, where the poem speaks of the day's dying). The song lacks any great depth of subjective feeling, it is true, but it is an impressive achievement for all that.

Capell, 145; Einstein, 184–5; Fischer-Dieskau, 112

## DAS BILD The Vision

**Author unknown**                                               11 February 1815

F major  D155  Peters VI p.90  GA XX no.42  NSA IV vol.7 p.140

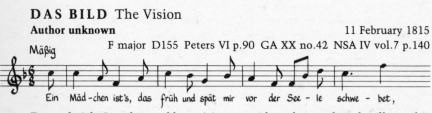

Day and night I am haunted by a vision, a maiden who stands and walks, and is woven of all heaven's charms.

I see her when the dawn's soft light shines through my window, and when the gentle evening star beckons.

The image follows me most faithfully, in calm or strife, deep in the earth and even in the sky.

It haunts me in the fields and woods, it glimmers above the flower-beds. It shines forth from the angel's face at the altar where I pray.

But is this image that haunts me day and night only fantasy – the stuff of air and dreams? Oh no, this angel vision that my love paints for me is but a shadow of the loveliness that gilds the maiden herself.

The autograph is missing, but a copy in the Witteczek–Spaun collection (Vienna, GdM) is dated 11 February 1815. When the song was published in 1862 by C. A. Spina as op.165 no.3, it was transposed down to E flat major and an introductory bar was added. This version is followed in the Peters edition. The most attractive feature of this innocent little song is the way the tune pauses for breath just before the end of the strophe, while the accompaniment heads away in the direction of the subdominant and then thinks better of it.

## DAS ECHO The Echo

**Ignaz Franz Castelli** (?) 1826–8

B flat major D868 (D2 990C) Peters II p.204 GA XX no.513

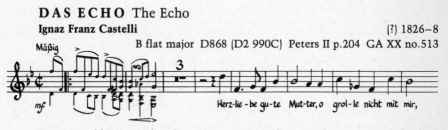

Herz-lie-be gu-te Mut-ter, o grol-le nicht mit mir,

Do not scold me, mother dear. You saw Hans kiss me, but I cannot help that. Patience! For I will tell you everything. The hillside echo is to blame.

He spied me sitting in the meadow but kept his distance, saying: 'Gladly I'd come nearer, if you would not take it amiss. Say, shall I come?' 'Come!' rang out the echo.

So he came and sat beside me, called me his lovely Liese, put his arm around me, asked if I would be kind, for he would accept that gladly. 'Gladly!' rang out the echo then.

At this he drew near, thinking these were *my* words. Tenderly he said: 'Will you be my bride, and let me give you loving kisses?' 'Kisses', shouted back the echo.

So you see how it happened that Hans was kissing me. That wicked, wicked echo has caused me so much trouble. When he comes you will see him, and he will respectfully ask you if I may be his bride.

If you think, dear mother, that Hans is not the man for me, then tell him that it was the echo played this trick on him. But if you think that we would make a good wedding pair then you must not hurt him. You may pretend that *I* was the echo.

The autograph is lost, there are no contemporary copies, and the date of the song is an open question. However, the poem's arch manner is strongly reminiscent of the Seidl *Refrain Lieder*, which Schubert set in 1828. In the last years of his life Schubert was urged by his publishers to make more concessions to public taste and to write more songs of 'a merry, comic nature', as one reviewer put it. Significantly, when *Das Echo* was published by Thaddäus Weigl as op.130 in July 1830, it was advertised as the first of a group of six 'humorous songs'. So *Das Echo* may well have been written some time in the last three years of the composer's life.

The poem has seven verses, and it is impossible to say how many Schubert intended to be sung. The first edition prints them all, but when the song was reissued by Diabelli in 1832 verse 7 was omitted, thus depriving the poem of much of its point. The Peters edition, on the other hand, omits verse 4, as above. Echo effects are a Schubert fingerprint, and this attractive strophic setting makes the most of them. The playful manner is strongly suggestive of the drawing-room ballad; it looks as though the whole project for a group of 'humorous songs' was inspired by Weigl, whose dealings with Schubert began in 1826.

## DAS FINDEN The Find
**Ludwig Kosegarten**                                                   25 June 1815

Etwas langsam, unschuldig                    B flat major D219 Peters VI p.32 GA XX no.85

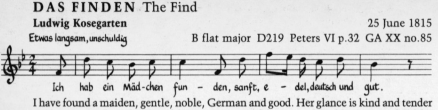

Ich hab ein Mäd-chen fun - den, sanft, e - del, deutsch und gut.

I have found a maiden, gentle, noble, German and good. Her glance is kind and tender
as the sunset glow; her hair like gossamer, and her eyes deep blue. Songs fall like
dew from the rosy chalice of her lips.

I found her wandering, chastely clad, the breezes playing in her rippling hair,
singing her sweet songs amid the trees.

In the clover by the brook I lay, then started up and watched her. Stay, fair
one; I too am German, noble, true and good.

She turned and hesitated, then beckoned me. I flew delighted to her side. She
stood before me, pure and fair.

I took the fair maiden by the hand and strolled with her along the banks of
the stream. I won her love. I know she is fond of me. So let my song be her own,
her very own.

The poem has seven verses, some of them shortened in the translation above. The Peters
edition prints only the first and the last. Schubert's autograph, now in ÖNB, Vienna, has
the first verse only written out between the staves and a note saying 'six more verses'.
It is dated 25 June 1815. The two-bar prelude in the Peters edition is editorial. A fair copy
earlier with Karl and Faber of Munich seems to have disappeared. There is a dated copy
in the Witteczek–Spaun collection (Vienna, GdM). The song was published in book 42
of the *Nachlass* in 1848.

*Das Finden* is one of the best of the Kosegarten songs, and it matches the innocence
of the verses admirably. Only domestic performers, however, will feel inclined to sing
all the verses.

## DAS FISCHERMÄDCHEN see HEINE SONGS no.3

## DAS FRÄULEIN IM THURME see ROMANZE

## DAS GEHEIMNIS The Secret (1)
**Friedrich von Schiller**                                               7 August 1815

A flat major D250 Not in Peters GA XX no.105

Sehr langsam

Sie konn - te mir kein Wört - chen sa - gen, zu vie - le Lauscher wa - ren wach;

Not a word could she say to me; too many listening ears were there. I could only
shyly read the look she gave me, and I understood what she meant. Softly I come
to the stillness of the leafy beech-grove. Oh, may the lovers be hidden under your
green canopy from the eye of the world!

From afar comes the confused murmur of the busy day, and through the hum
of voices I recognise the beat of the heavy hammers. So man wrests his scant reward
from a cruel heaven; yet happiness falls unearned from the lap of the gods.

May no-one ever discover how happy our love makes us! For those who have
never known joy can only spoil our own. The world looks askance at happiness;

it is a prize to be snatched. You must steal it before envy takes you by surprise.
It comes on tiptoe, loves stillness and the night; and, fleet of foot, it vanishes
when the betrayer's eye is near. O gentle fount of love, enfold us like a mighty stream,
and defend this sanctuary with your angry waves!

The poem, written in 1797, was a tribute to Schiller's betrothed, Charlotte von Langefeld.
The autograph, in private possession, is dated 7 August 1815. There is a dated copy also
in the Witteczek–Spaun collection (Vienna, GdM). The song was published in 1872 by
J. P. Gotthard as no.28 of 'Forty Songs'.

Schubert's tonal analogue for the idea of complicity is the musical equivalent of
walking on tiptoe, the staccato quavers (ppp) marching along steadily against the legato
line of the voice. And it is a remarkable proof of the persistence of these musical images
in Schubert's mind that when he returned to the poem eight years later he produced not
an entirely new setting but something more like an elaborate version of this one. A glance
at the opening bars of the later version will show that, so far as the *Bewegung* and the
melody are concerned, the two versions grow from the same cell; though whether this
is a case of unconscious memory, of independent reinvention or of straight revision it
is impossible to say. This first version expresses very successfully the innocence, the new-
discovered joy, of the lovers' secret. It may be said that the simple strophic setting does
not adequately convey the depth and subtlety of Schiller's famous poem. It seems a pity,
none the less, that this one remains almost completely unknown.

## DAS GEHEIMNIS (2)

**Friedrich von Schiller**                                                    May 1823

Langsam                              G major  D793  Peters VI p.109  GA XX no.431

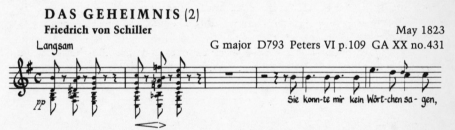

For translation, see the preceding entry. The autograph (Berlin, DS) is a first draft, in G
major, and dated May 1823. A fair copy in the key of F major, formerly in the possession
of Karoline, Countess Esterházy, has disappeared. It was probably made during Schubert's
residence in Zseliz in 1824. Two copies in the Witteczek–Spaun collection (Vienna, GdM)
are wrongly dated March 1823 (probably a misreading), but the catalogue of the collection
gives the correct date. The Esterházy manuscript seems to have been the source for the
first edition in 1867. The song was published in F, as op.173 no.2, by C. A. Spina, and
the Peters edition followed suit. The *Gesamtausgabe* on the other hand, follows the first
draft.

The basic strophe which underlies the song's subtle changes of mood and movement shares the melodic shape and the 'tiptoeing' accompaniment of the earlier setting,
but it is adapted to match the words with such melodic bravura and richness of invention
that the first setting is quite eclipsed. For the second half of the stanza Schubert summons
up a rocking motif with a triplet rhythm (the dotted quavers in the accompaniment are
clearly broken triplets) which has a Viennese lilt about it. The sober realities of the
workaday world are deftly portrayed in verse 2, but the mood of bubbling happiness cannot
be suppressed; at the end the dancing triplets convey a mood of subdued ecstasy.

Schubert approached the organic unity of the song from two different directions;
one way – the modified strophic way – preserves the strophic form at least in outline,

and relies on changes in the accompaniment to match the words; the other – the through-composed way – starts with a pianistic figure which unifies the song, and relies on tonal manipulation to reflect the changes of mood. It is noteworthy that Schubert seems never to have adopted the latter method with Schiller. *Das Geheimnis* is among the greatest of the Schiller songs, and deserves to be better known. Accompanists using the Peters edition should note that there is a misprint in the left hand on the second beat of the penultimate bar (C–A should read C–B flat).

Einstein, 255

## DAS GESTÖRTE GLÜCK Frustrated Bliss

**Theodor Körner**                                                    15 October 1815

F major  D309  Not in Peters  GA XX no.157

Ich hab ein hei - ßes jun - ges Blut, wie ihr wohl al - le wißt,

I am young and hot-blooded, as you well know, yet never have I kissed. For though I love my maiden fair, it seems as though it will never happen. In spite of all I do, I've never kissed her yet.

The neighbour's daughter is fond of me. I followed her, early one morning, into the meadow, and put my arm about her. But then I pricked my hand on a pin in her bodice; it bled, and I ran home. No kiss for me that day.

Then, walking idly by the stream, I met her, slid my arm round her waist, begging for a kiss. She pursed her pretty mouth, but along came her old watchdog, and bit me on the leg, so the kiss had to wait.

Next time, I sat expectant by her door, and when she gave me her dear little hand, I drew her to my breast. Then out jumped her father, who had been listening all along behind the door, and as you might expect, that put paid to my third kiss.

Only yesterday I met her, and she called me softly in. 'I'll expect you tonight – my window overlooks the courtyard.' But when I came, aflame with love, and put my ladder it broke in two beneath me, and that was the end of kissing.

That's how things are every time for me; it's really hard to endure. If I don't get a kiss soon, I'll never be happy. I don't know what a poor wretch like me has done to deserve such a cruel fate. So who will take pity on me, and be kind and kiss me?

The autograph, in private possession, is dated 15 October 1815. A fair copy, known to exist in 1865, has since disappeared. There is a dated copy in the Witteczek–Spaun collection (Vienna, GdM). Schubert's lively 6/8 tune neatly underlines the payoff at the end of each strophe. The direction, *Lustig*, says all that is needed.

## DAS GRAB The Grave
**Johann Gaudenz von Salis-Seewis**

Between December 1815 and 1819 Schubert made or attempted five different choral settings of this poem, which was written in 1783. Strictly speaking none of them has any place in a book on the solo songs, but for no apparent reason Mandyczewski included three of them in series XX of the *Gesamtausgabe* and omitted them from series XVI and XVII, where they properly belong. One of them (D569) has even found a place in the Deutsche Grammophon collected recording of the solo songs. To avoid further confusion the details relating to the individual settings are given below, together with a translation of the poem:

Beyond its awful brink, the grave is deep and silent; its black shroud covers an uncharted land. No nightingales sing in its depths; only the roses of friendship fall on the mossy grave.

Forsaken brides wring their hands in vain, nor does the orphan's weeping penetrate its depths.

Yet nowhere else is longed-for peace to be found; only through the dark portals of death do men go home.

Poor, mortal, storm-tossed hearts never find their true peace until they cease to beat.

(1) D2 329A (Not in D) Not in Peters Unpublished December 1815 C minor. A fragmentary sketch of a setting for unaccompanied mixed chorus in canon. The sketch breaks off after twelve bars. On the other side of the manuscript (Lund, UB) is

(2) D330 Not in Peters GA XX no.182 28 December 1815 G minor. A setting in block harmony for male voices.

(3) D377 Not in Peters GA XX no.186 11 February 1816 C minor. For male voices, similar in style and mood to (2). The song was published in 1872 by J. P. Gotthard as no.5 of 'Nine Partsongs'.

(4) D569 Not in Peters GA XX no.323 June 1817 C sharp minor/major. For unison male-voice choir. The most effective setting.

A. Weinmann: 'Zwei neue Schubert-Funde', ÖMZ, XXVII, 1972, p.75.

(5) D2 643A (Not in D) Not in Peters Not in GA 1819 E flat major (SATB). A setting for mixed voices, a copy of which was recently discovered in the monastery of Seitenstetten in Lower Austria.

## DAS GROSSE HALLELUJA The Great Hallelujah
**Friedrich Gottlieb Klopstock**                                           June 1816
E major D442 Not in Peters GA XX no.227

Glory be to the Most High, the First, the Father of Creation! To whom we sing with faltering tongue, although the Wonderful One is inexpressible and incomprehensible.

A flame from the altar at his throne is kindled in our souls. The joy of heaven is ours, that we exist and can stand in awe of him.

From us, at the graveside, be glory also to him, even though the archangel has laid his crown at the foot of his throne, and sings his rapturous praise.

Glory, and thanks, and praise be to the Most High, the First, who is without beginning and without end, who gave immortality even to creatures of dust.

Glory be to thee, Most High, Father of Creation! The Ineffable! The Inconceivable One!

The poem was written in 1766. Of the six verses, Schubert omitted the fifth. The autograph is a first draft, together with *Julius an Theone* (D419) which is dated 30 April 1816. The song is written out on two staves only, and marked simply 'Song and Pianoforte'. The present whereabouts of this manuscript are unknown. There is a copy in the Witteczek–Spaun collection (Vienna, GdM), dated June 1816. Diabelli published the piece in 1848 as a trio for female voices (*Nachlass* book 41 no.2). The *Gesamtausgabe*, however, includes it among the solo songs in series XX.

*Das grosse Halleluja* is a sacred song rather than a lied, and the layout of the composition, with its 'walking bass' and three-part writing on the upper stave, strongly suggests that it was intended as a vocal trio. It may, indeed, have been written for performance in church, which would help to explain the archaic liturgical style.

### DAS HEIMWEH Longing for Home
**Theodor Hell**                                                      July 1816

F major D 456 Peters VII p.64 GA XX no.241

Often in quiet lonely hours I have felt a yearning, strange and wondrous, like a quiet intimation of a far-off better world up above among the stars.

The old trees bow their heads above the house there on the edge of the forest. Quiet! Let me listen. From afar I hear the soft murmur: come back home!

Who will repay my love? No longer shall I come and go in the land of strangers. Yonder in the starry vaults under the golden boughs of heaven my homeland awaits me.

Theodor Hell was the pseudonym of Karl Gottfried Winkler, the librettist of Weber's *Die drei Pintos* and translator of the text of *Oberon*. The poem has six verses. Schubert wrote out the first under the stave and omitted the others but put repeat marks at the end of the song. When the song was published in the Peters edition in 1887, Max Friedländer commissioned Max Kalbeck to write a second and third verse and produced a hybrid text which is translated above. The full original text is given in the *Gesamtausgabe* and in Schochow p.704. The autograph (Paris Conservatoire) is dated July 1816. There is a copy, similarly dated, in the Witteczek–Spaun collection (Vienna, GdM).

*Das Heimweh* is a minor masterpiece, with the perfection and economy of form combined with a gravity and weight of feeling which characterise the best songs of 1816. Elisabeth Schumann, in a fine recording, rescued it from oblivion in 1938, but it is still not well known.

### DAS HEIMWEH Homesickness
**Johann Ladislaus Pyrker**                                         August 1825

G minor D851 Peters II p.142 GA XX no.478(a) and (b)

A son of the mountains is attached to his homeland with a childlike love. As the alpine flower withers when torn away from the mountain, so he withers when severed from his native soil.

Always he pictures the cosy cottage where he was born, among fragrant green meadows, sees the dark pinewoods, the towering cliff above him, peak upon peak looming up fearfully, and rosy in the glow of evening.

Always the image hovers before his eyes, obscuring everything else around him.

He listens anxiously, expecting to hear the cattle lowing in the woods, or the tinkling bells from the alps, the shepherd's call, the voice of the dairymaid as it echoes joyfully in yodelling song.

It rings in his ears all the time. The smiling charm of the plains cannot hold him back; he flees alone from the constricting walls of the town, and with moist eyes looks up from the foothills towards his native peaks.

Ah, they draw him back with irresistible longing!

Schubert's meeting with Archbishop Pyrker, epic poet and Patriarch of Venice, at Gastein in August 1825, was one of his most treasured memories, and both songs to Pyrker texts were written during that month. However, *Das Heimweh* was not written, as Deutsch suggested, specially for Schubert; it had been published years earlier.

The autograph (Berlin, DS) is dated Gastein, August 1825. It shows that Schubert wrote the song in A minor, and then radically revised it. The first version runs to 250 bars, and carries the scherzo-like major section (3/4 *Geschwind*) through to the end of the song with much repetitive emphasis on the last two lines of the poem. Schubert must have realised on reflection that this emphasises the homesick traveller's impetuous return rather than his longing for home. The second and shorter version, after an abrupt pause, returns to the mood and key of the opening theme for the final pages. But the curiously *sehnsuchtsvoll* sequence in bars 171–4 is taken over from the first version and cleverly incorporated in the new ending.

Both Pyrker songs were published by Haslinger as op.79 in May 1827 and dedicated to the poet by Schubert 'with profound respect'. Both were transposed, if not on Schubert's authority, then at least with his acquiescence. *Das Heimweh* appeared in G minor. The *Gesamtausgabe* prints both the original (A minor) versions.

*Das Heimweh* has been overshadowed by the popularity of the companion piece, *Die Allmacht*, yet it is equally impressive in its structurally more complex and evocative way. It is a locus classicus for Schubertian images of *Sehnsucht*: the bare octaves, the dotted rhythms, the tonic–German sixth–tonic sequences which so abound, the successive descending phrase (*pp*) that precede the section marked 'Geschwind' (3/4), and above all the curious feint towards G flat major at the words 'Irresistible longing', as though striving to escape the tonality of G minor, but failing. Despite the sectional form, the unity of mood is preserved.

Capell, 212–13; Fischer-Dieskau, 215–16

## DAS LIED IM GRÜNEN The Song of the Greenwood
**Friedrich Reil**                                                                     June 1827

Mäßig                              A major D917 Peters IV p.132 GA XX no.543

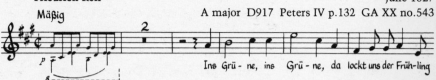

To the greenwood! That darling youth Spring invites us, leading us on with his flower-decked staff to where the larks and thrushes sing – to the woods, the fields, the hills, the brook – to the greenwood!

In the greenwood life is bliss, and we love to roam; even from a distance our eyes are riveted upon it. As we wander there with merry hearts, a childlike pleasure laps us round, in the greenwood!

In the greenwood, where our rest is so sweet, and our feelings so fine; where we gently muse on this and that; our cares are charmed away, and the heart rejoices, in the greenwood!

In the greenwood how bright shine the stars, those guiding lights of the wise men of old; the little clouds drift gently by, our hearts are light, and our senses clear, in the greenwood!

In the greenwood our little schemes take wing, and the future looks bright. Our eyes are refreshed and our gaze is serene; we dally with our fancies, in the greenwood!

In the greenwood, in the intimate stillness of morning and evening, how many songs and poems of fun and of longing have been written; for light is the spirit, and open the heart, in the greenwood!

Let us joyfully follow that friendly youth to the greenwood! And if one day life no longer smiles on us we shall not have missed the green springtime; we shall at least while it lasted have enjoyed our dreams, in the greenwood!

Schubert may have met Reil, actor, journalist and occasional poet, at Dornbach, a village outside Vienna where he stayed intermittently during May and June 1827. There is no doubt, at any rate, that he set the poem from Reil's manuscript. It first appeared on 13 October 1827 in the Vienna *Allgemeine Theaterzeitung*, with an explanatory note from the author: 'Was often sung in the meadows hereabouts during the summer by a merry· company to a lively and agreeable tune by Schubert.'

The autograph (Stanford University, California) is a carefully written first draft dated· June 1827. An insertion above the stave in bar 9 shows that the echo phrase in the accompaniment was an afterthought. Schubert set seven verses, and only seven were published in October 1827. However, when the song came to be published in June 1829 repeat signs were added to bars 105–20, and an extra verse beginning 'O gerne im Grünen bin ich schon als Knabe' was inserted before the last verse. But whether this was part of the original draft or was added by the poet after Schubert's death is not clear. All the printed versions of the song include it, though it is not in the autograph. *Das Lied im Grünen* was published by M. J. Leidesdorf as op.115 no.1 in June 1829 and reprinted by Diabelli in 1830. Underneath the song three more verses, specially written by Reil in memory of the composer, were appended with a dedication by the author. The verses are reprinted in Schochow p.466. There is a copy of the song in G major in Schindler's collection (Lund, UB), which also contains the memorial verses.

This is Schubert's loveliest spring song, and a perfect example of his skill in adapting the strophic song to the expressive demands of a longish poem. The running quavers in the pianist's right hand murmur on unceasingly for 158 bars. The steady, unhurried movement gives an effect of timelessness that matches the mood of the song. The song is built up on two related but complementary tunes: the first stays securely within the tonality of A major, and the second (verses 3 and 4) is based on the subdominant D major, but wanders further afield into B flat. Verses 6 and 7 return to the main tune, but wonderfully inflected both tonally and melodically to match the sense, so that at one point the quavers become the running feet of the boys at play, and at another the sudden switch to D minor reminds us of death, the last enemy. But the key, like the thought, is shrugged off, and the last haunting cadence – 'in the greenwood!' – brings this magical song to a close.

Capell, 244; Fischer-Dieskau, 246–7

# DAS LIED VOM REIFEN Song for a Frosty Morning
**Matthias Claudius**                                   February 1817

A flat major D532 Not in Peters GA XX no.303

Seht mei - ne lie - ben Bäu - me an, wie sie so herr - lich stehn____,

See how my beloved trees stand so splendid, each branch clad in frosty beauty.
From foot to crown each twig is hung with white, crisp, fine and delicate;
nothing could be more fair.
And far and wide the trees around stand bedecked in like dignity and splendour.

The poem, written in December 1780, is entitled *Ein Lied vom Reiffen*. There are fifteen
verses, but it is clear from Schubert's autograph that he meant only three to be sung. The
autograph has been cut into two pieces and badly mutilated. The larger section (Lund,
UB) consists of the first ten bars, dated February 1817. It has another Claudius song (*Täglich
zu singen*) on the reverse. A second sheet, which originally contained the remaining five
bars, and the text of the second and third verses followed by the attribution to Claudius,
has been mutilated in the interests of *Der Tod und das Mädchen*, the first twelve bars
of which appear on the reverse (Vienna, GdM). None the less, when the song was first
published in the *Gesamtausgabe* (1895) it could be reconstructed complete except for the
final bar.

In the postlude the running semiquavers make their own contribution – a kind
of contredanse – to this innocently tuneful song. But it seems that Schubert's intention
in the postlude has been confused by the mutilation of the manuscript. The likely solution
is that bars 11 and 12 are first-time bars, and bars 13 and 14 last-time bars only. Bar 14
does not appear in the *Gesamtausgabe*; it is to be found on a copy in Vienna (GdM). The
song is thus no longer, strictly speaking, a 'fragment'.

**DAS MÄDCHEN** I (Wenn mich einsam Lüfte fächeln) see **BLANKA**

**DAS MÄDCHEN** The Maid II (Wie so innig, möcht ich sagen)
**Friedrich von Schlegel**                                      February 1819
Langsam, zart                          A major D652 Peters III p.211 GA XX no.354

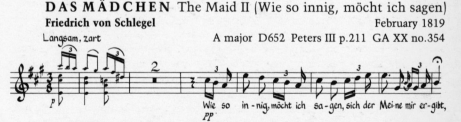

Wie so in-nig, möcht ich sa-gen, sich der Mei-ne mir er-gibt,

I would like to say that my lover is so passionate with me only to still my complaints
that he does not really love me. But when I try to put it into words, they fly away.
If I had music in me I would pour out my love in harmony, for that is what it is.
Only the nightingale can say how passionate he is with me, to still my
complaints that he does not really love me.

The poem is from the cycle called *Abendröte*, written 1800–1. The autograph (Vienna,
GdM) is dated February 1819 and has no tempo indication. A dated copy in the Witteczek–
Spaun collection (GdM) is marked 'Langsam, zart', and another copy in the Spaun–
Cornaro collection (Vienna, privately owned) is headed 'Aria' and marked 'Mit Innigkeit'.
These manuscripts are in A major. When the song was published about 1842 (*Nachlass*
book 40 no.1) it was transposed to G major. This version, possibly based on a lost manu-
script, is followed in the Peters edition, but the *Gesamtausgabe* follows the autograph.

The major–minor alternations, the pauses and the reflective movement perfectly
hit off the uncertainty, the mingled joy and anguish, of first love. The tone and style of
this delightful song recall that of *An die Nachtigall* of 1816. The pianist's dotted quavers
conform to the singer's triplets.
Capell, 164

## DAS MÄDCHEN AUS DER FREMDE The Strange Maid (1)

**Friedrich von Schiller** 16 October 1814

A major D117 Not in Peters GA XX no.30

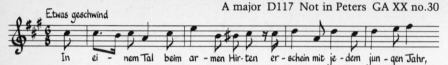

Each year in spring, when the first larks were on the wing, a strange and lovely maid appeared to some poor shepherds in a valley.

She was not born there; none knew whence she came. And when she left, scant trace she left behind.

Her presence was bliss; every heart was open to her; and yet a certain majesty, some nobility, set her apart.

Flowers she brought, and fruits ripened elsewhere, under a different sun, where nature was more kind.

She shared these gifts, gave this one fruits and that one flowers; each youth, each old man leaning on his staff, went home enriched.

All guests were welcome; but if perchance two lovers came, to them she gave the choicest gifts, the loveliest flowers of all.

This vaguely allegorical poem was written in the summer of 1796. It reflects perhaps the then current intellectual fashion for extolling peasant virtues. The autograph, in private possession, is dated 16 October 1814 both at the beginning and at the end. There is a dated copy in Ferdinand Schubert's hand in the Witteczek–Spaun collection (Vienna, GdM). This first version is available only in the *Gesamtausgabe*.

See the following entry.

## DAS MÄDCHEN AUS DER FREMDE (2)

**Friedrich von Schiller** 12 August 1815

F major D252 Peters VII p.92 GA XX no.108

For translation, see the preceding entry. The autograph is in private possession. The source for the published version is a copy in the Witteczek–Spaun collection (Vienna, GdM) made by Ferdinand Schubert and dated 12 August 1815. The first publication was in vol.VII of the Peters edition (1887).

Both settings are strophic and unpretentious, the first in the pastoral manner (A major, 6/8) with the verses grouped in pairs, and the second (F major 2/4) in Schubert's vernacular style. The later setting is the more memorable, and it has a Haydnesque sweetness about it, though it would be difficult to sustain the interest over six verses.

## DAS MÄDCHEN VON INISTORE The Maid of Inistore

**James Macpherson (Ossian)** September 1815

C minor D281 Peters IV p.202 GA XX no.148

The original text reads:

> Weep on the rocks of roaring winds, O maid of Inistore! Bend thy fair head over the waves, thou lovelier than the ghost of the hills, when it moves in a sunbeam, at noon, over the silence of Morven. He is fallen! thy youth is low, pale beneath the sword of Cuthullin! No more shall valour raise thy love to match the blood of kings. Trenar, graceful Trenar, died, O maid of Inistore! His grey dogs are howling at home; they see his passing ghost. His bow is in the hall unstrung. No sound is in the hills of his hinds.

See OSSIAN SONGS. Inistore is the Celtic name for Orkney. The autograph is incomplete, lacking the last five bars. Its present whereabouts are unknown. The song is dated September 1815 in the catalogue of the Witteczek–Spaun collection (Vienna, GdM). There are copies in the Stadler and Ebner collections (Lund, UB). *Das Mädchen von Inistore* was first published with the other Ossian songs in 1830 (*Nachlass* book 4).

Why Schubert should have chosen this short passage from the long prose poem *Fingal* is something of a puzzle, although the maiden lamenting over the fallen hero was, so to speak, a stock Romantic situation. Here he seems concerned to secure the maximum effect of pathos by means of dynamic contrasts. At the words 'He is fallen', for instance, we go from *ppp*, after a long pause, to *ffz*, and in the concluding bars ('No sound is in the hills of his hinds') the music dies away to a whisper. Unlike the other Ossian songs, there is little attempt at the *tonmalerisch*. The melancholy C minor tune is almost operatic.

## DAS MARIENBILD  The Madonna

**Alois Schreiber**                                                                    August 1818

Mit heiliger Rührung                    C major D623 Peters V p.38 GA XX no.341

Sei ge-grüßt, du Frau der Huld   und der rei - nen, schö-nen Min- ne,

Hail, Lady, full of grace, of pure fair love, spotless and guiltless, humble of mind. Here in this oak-tree bole a simple chapel is raised to you in pious innocence. No pillars here, no entrance.

Birds on every bough sing lullabies to your child, and the shining angels move up and down among the branches. Here each sorrowing heart grows light, the pilgrim draws comfort from the fount of grace.

Would I might build a cabin here in this quiet wood, so that this star of the sea might illumine every hour. So in this small space I should feel near to heaven, and no evil disquieting dream disturb my last sleep.

The autograph is lost, but a copy in Schindler's collection (Lund, UB) is annotated 'composed August 1818'. The song was published in 1831 in book 10 of the *Nachlass* (*Geistliche Lieder* no.3). *Das Marienbild*, presumably written at Zseliz during Schubert's residence there as tutor, is the least attractive of the four Schreiber settings, though there is a certain rather sanctimonious charm about the chromatic inflections and suspensions. One suspects that it may have been composed 'by request', for Schubert was not at this time in sympathy with orthodox piety.

Capell, 145

## DAS ROSENBAND The Rose Garland

**Friedrich Gottlieb Klopstock**     September 1815

A flat major  D280  Peters V p.160  GA XX no.139

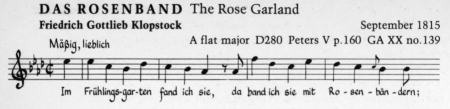

Im Frühlings-gar-ten fand ich sie, da band ich sie mit Ro - sen - bän -dern;

I found her lying in the spring sun, and bound her fast with a rose garland; all unaware she slumbered on. I gazed on her, our lives were bound one to the other. I sensed it, yet I knew it not.

I murmured wordlessly to her, and made the garland of roses rustle. She woke from sleep; she looked at me; with that look our lives were bound together, and all around was paradise.

The poem was written in 1753 for Klopstock's wife, 'Cidli'. The autograph disappeared in the nineteenth century, and the only surviving source is a copy in the Witteczek–Spaun collection (Vienna, GdM). This has no prelude. The catalogue of the collection dates the song September 1815. The song was published in 1837 in book 28 of the *Nachlass*. The four-bar prelude, which also appears in the Peters edition, is probably editorial.

The three 'Cidli' songs – this one, *Furcht der Geliebten* and *An Sie* – are all in A flat, and are set in a spirit of hymnlike devotion. *Das Rosenband* is the best of them. Schubert's setting covers both verses, and the long-breathed phrases lead perfectly to the final cadence. Though the language is purely classical, the song invests that language with *Innigkeit*.

Capell, 95; Einstein, 111; Fischer-Dieskau, 48

## DAS SEHNEN Longing

**Ludwig Kosegarten**     8 July 1815

A minor  D231  Peters VI p.101  GA XX no.94

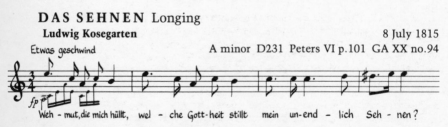

Weh - mut,die mich hüllt, wel - che Gott-heit stillt mein un-end - lich Seh - nen?

Melancholy wraps me round. What god can calm my ceaseless longing? It moistens my eyes with nameless grief. Flow, tears, flow!

Tell me what ails me, moon that shines kindly, lovingly, in through my window. Stars that glimmer above with a warm friendly greeting, tell me what plagues me.

Light shivers flutter about me, the sweet supplication of love hovers in the dusk. The scent of rose and violet perfumes the enchanted air. Gentle voices whisper.

My being, uplifted, reaches out into the distance as though on hovering wings. Strange impulse, secret power, nameless passion, oh, make me whole again!

Melancholy oppresses me in my fear, stifling breath and speech. We languish in solitary pain and grief, alone in the wilderness of life.

Is there then no arm to hold me tenderly, in joy and sorrow? Is there no loving heart, to which I may pour out my own heart, in pleasure and pain?

You who, alone and unbefriended, pour out your troubles at daybreak, or when night falls – ah, you scorn good fortune, you languish and pine away.

Kosegarten's title is *Sehnsucht*; Schubert's is as above. The autograph, in private possession, is dated 8 July 1815. There is also an autograph fair copy (Vienna, SB) and a dated copy in the Witteczek–Spaun collection (Vienna, GdM). The song was published in 1866 by C. A. Spina as op.172 no.4. The attractive tune flows briskly forward to an accompaniment of broken chords in the pianist's right hand. The style suggests the canzonet, but the mood is closer to impatient protest than to Kosegarten's 'nameless grief'.

## DAS TOTENHEMDCHEN The Shroud
**Eduard von Bauernfeld**                                           D864

The verses appeared in the 'Album of Austrian Poets' (Vienna, 1850) and in the collected editions of Bauernfeld's verse, with a note 'Music by Franz Schubert', but the song has never been discovered.

> The child died. Ah! by day the mother sat and wept; she sat and wept by night.
> The little child came back, so pale in its little shroud, and said to the mother: 'Lie down. Look, my little shroud is grown so wet with your fond tears, and I cannot sleep, mother!'
> The child vanished again, and the mother wept no more.

## DAS WANDERN see DIE SCHÖNE MÜLLERIN no.1

## DAS WAR ICH That was I (1)
**Theodor Körner**                                           26 March 1815

G major  D174  Peters VI p.22  GA XX no.56

Lately, in a dream, I spied a maiden walking on the sunlit hills bathed in the morning light; so pure, so sweet, that she was just like you. A young man knelt before her, seemed to draw her to his breast; and that was I.

Soon the scene changed, and now the lovely maid was struggling in the flood, her frail strength gone. A youth rushed to her aid, plunged in, and dragged her from the waves; and that was I.

It was a happy dream, for everywhere I looked love was triumphant; and you were at the centre of it all, walking in perfect freedom there, and silently following after you came the faithful youth; and that was I.

When I awoke at last, the new day brought new longing. Your sweet beloved face was all around me still. I saw you responding to the warmth of his kisses, saw your happiness in the young man's embrace; and that was I.

The poem was published posthumously in 1815. It has six verses, all printed in the *Gesamtausgabe*. The Peters edition prints only the first four, which seem in fact to provide a better end to the song. The autograph (New York, PML) is dated 26 March 1815. It contains also the incomplete first version of another Körner setting, *Liebesrausch*. The song was published in book 39 of the *Nachlass* (1845).

*Das war ich* is an early and striking example (the setting of Matthisson's *Andenken*, written a year earlier, was perhaps the first) of Schubert's ability to give psychological depth to a song by bringing the key phrase sharply into focus and changing the singer's role from that of narrator to that of actor. Everything in the song, from the off-beat entry of the voice in the first bar (marked 'Erzählend', 'as though telling a story') and the beautifully detailed accompaniment to the final crescendo leading to the *sf* chord of C major, is designed to highlight the singer's final declaration – 'and that was I'. This delightful song is one of the best of Schubert's early strophic settings.

## DAS WAR ICH (2)
**Theodor Körner**

(?) June 1816

D major D174 Not in Peters Not in GA

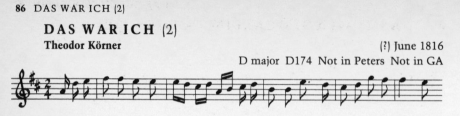

For translation, see the preceding entry. This fragment consists of six bars of the voice line, without accompaniment or text, written on the back of the *Fragment aus dem Aeschylus* D450. It is headed 'Das war ich. Körner', and is assumed to be the start of a second setting of the poem. D450 dates from June 1816. The fragment was published in the *Revisionsbericht* to the *Gesamtausgabe*. It has been completed and privately printed by Reinhard van Hoorickx.

## DAS WEINEN Weeping
**Karl Gottfried von Leitner**

Autumn 1827

Ziemlich langsam

D major D926 Peters II p.199 GA XX no.546

Gar tröst-lich kommt ge - ron - nen der Thränen heil' - ge Quell,

The blessed fount of tears brings comfort as it flows like a healing spring, so bitter, hot and clear. Therefore, you wounded heart, so full of grief and quiet pain, if you would soon be whole, bathe in that spring.

Its waters have a secret, magic power, a healing ointment for your wounds; its power increases as your torments grow. From your heart it lifts the stone of evil that would crush you, rolling it away.

This have I felt in my own vale of tears as, swathed in crepe, I stood by the graves of loved ones. In mad frenzy I railed against my God, but my tears kept the frail ship of hope afloat.

And so, when you too are held fast in the darkest night of sorrow, take refuge in the wondrous strength of tears. Soon, when your eyes are red with weeping, a new day will be born, for already the morning shows bright.

The poem was written in 1821. The autograph (Budapest, HNL) is a fair copy made for the printer, and undated. But according to Leitner (*Memoirs*, p.197) Schubert was introduced to the collected edition of the poems by Marie Pachler during his stay at Graz in September 1827. The collection of songs that Schubert dedicated to her included two Leitner settings, though it seems clear from Jenger's letter to her of 26 April 1828 (*Docs.* no.1088) that this one was not actually written at Graz, but soon after. The song was published by the Lithographic Institute of Vienna, then under Schober's management, in the spring of 1828 as no.2 of 'Four Songs', and dedicated to Marie Pachler. The collection was reissued by Diabelli in February 1829 as op.106.

There is something devout, penitential even, about this simple hymnlike setting with its characteristic descending four-note motif at the beginning of each phrase. Fischer-Dieskau suggests that it may reflect Schubert's own feelings of anguish and remorse at a recurrence of his own illness in the autumn of 1827.

Fischer-Dieskau, 252–3

**DAS WIRTSHAUS** see WINTERREISE no.21

## DAS ZÜGENGLÖCKLEIN The Passing Bell

**Johann Gabriel Seidl**                                                   (?) March 1826

A flat major D871 Peters III p.36 GA XX no.507

Kling die Nacht durch, klin - ge, sü - ßen Frie - den brin - ge

Ring, ring the night through, bring sweet peace to him you ring for. Ring out afar, for so you reconcile the pilgrim to the world. But who would journey after the dear loved ones who have gone before? For though he may gladly ring the bell, he trembles on the threshold when a voice bids 'Enter'.

Does it ring for the erring son, who curses the sound for its sacredness? No, it tolls more loudly, for a godfearing man whose race is run.

But if it is some weary one bereft of kin, in whom only some loyal beast has kept his faith alive, call him, O God, to thee.

If it rings for one of fortune's blest, who shares in the joy of pure love and friendship, allow him still the bliss of life beneath the sun, while he gladly tarries here.

Seidl's collected poems were published early in 1826. This one belongs to a sequence called *Lieder der Nacht* ('Poems of the Night'). The autograph (Berlin, DS) is undated and has no tempo indication. The manuscript contains also the first draft of *Der Wanderer an den Mond*. A fair copy made for the printer is now in the Kolbenheyer Gesellschaft, Nürnberg. Three Seidl songs – this one *Der Wanderer and den Mond* and *Im Freien* were published as Op.80 by Haslinger in May 1827. For this published version the tempo indication *Langsam* was added for *Das Zügenglöcklein*. The Seidl songs which can be firmly dated all belong to March 1826, and it reasonable to suppose that *Das Zügenglöcklein* does too. The song is dated 1826 in the catalogue of the Witteczek–Spaun collection (Vienna, GdM).

'Das Zügenglöcklein' is a small tolling bell (*zügen*, 'to pull') rung in Austrian churches, when a parishioner is dying, as a call to prayer. A contemporary notice of the song (*Docs*. no.1014) says that it 'touches the keys and the heart profoundly' and praises the way Schubert keeps the bell tolling in the pianist's right hand throughout the song, while the 'melody and very choice harmony move on quite free and unconstrained'. It is as good an example as any of the way Schubert gratefully seizes on any tonal image offered by a poem, and turns it to his own purposes. Within this unifying figure the melodic and harmonic variations reach out beyond the pious sentiments of the poem to a deeper humanity and compassion.

Capell, 222

## DASS SIE HIER GEWESEN She has been here!

**Friedrich Rückert**                                                          (?) 1822

C major D775 Peters III p.30 GA XX no.453

Daß der Ost - wind Düf - te hau - chet in die Lüf - te,

The east wind blows gently, scenting the air; and so it tells me that you have been here.

Because the tears fall here you will know, even if you were not told, that I have been here.

Beauty or love – can either remain concealed? The scented breezes, and the tears, reveal that she has been here.

The poem was written in 1819 or 1820. Like the other Rückert texts set by Schubert, it comes from the collection called *Östliche Rosen* ('Oriental Roses') published in 1822 or perhaps late 1821. It was not given a separate title. *Dass sie hier gewesen* was probably Schubert's own working title, but we cannot be sure, because the autograph has disappeared. None of the Rückert songs can be precisely dated, but it is reasonably certain that they belong to the second half of 1822 and the first half of 1823. This one was published with two other Rückert songs, one of which (*Du bist die Ruh*) is dated 1823 in the catalogue of the Witteczek–Spaun collection (Vienna, GdM). The song was published as op.59 no.2 in September 1826 by Sauer and Leidesdorf of Vienna (*Vier Gedichte von Rückert und Graf Platen*). When the opus was reissued by Diabelli in 1830 the title *Dass sie hier gewesen!* was added.

It is Schubert's unique sense of tonal ambiguity, his instinctive feeling for the centrality and security of the home key and for the disruptive tendencies inherent in chromatic harmonies, that characterises the best work of his middle years; and it is this perhaps above all which gives the Rückert songs their special originality and expressiveness. The essence of *Dass sie hier gewesen* is the contrast between the sighing, constantly shifting German sixths which conjure up an unstable world of disoriented feeling and sensation – a sort of tonal no-man's land – and the solid emotional home-ground of C major ('Dass sie hier gewesen') which makes the point of the poem. Schubert was to explore this same conflict in some of his greatest work (the 'Unfinished' Symphony, for instance, also written during this eventful winter of 1822–3, and the G major string quartet). What is most remarkable about this song is the economy and refinement with which it is made to serve the words. Not until bar 13 is the tonic revealed. It is reserved for the assurance of the motto phrase and of one other line – 'Beauty or love – can either remain concealed?' The song is a favourite with Schubert lovers, though it still makes only an occasional appearance in recitals.

Capell, 200–1; Fischer-Dieskau, 196

## DELPHINE
**Christian Wilhelm von Schütz**                                         September 1825

Mäßige Bewegung            A major D2 857 no.1 Peters III p.126 GA XX no.484

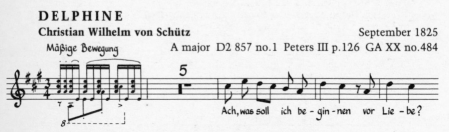

Ach, was soll ich be - gin - nen vor Lie - be?

Ah, how shall I begin, for love? It fills my inmost being.

Young man, the smallest part of me, from top to toe, is yours alone.

Flowers, you may fade; once the soul has known love, you are no use.

I would do nothing, know nothing, have nothing, but think only of love, which holds me in its power.

I keep wondering what else love might inspire me to do, but it holds me so fast, there is nothing else.

Now that I am in love, I want to live first and then die. Now I am in love, I want to burn brightly and then wither.

What's the use of planting out flowers and watering them? Their leaves fall.

As he perceives, love saps my strength. As the rose fades, so will my cheeks. Its glory is ruined, as clothes grow shabby.

Young man, how is it that love is mixed with pain for me, when it is your love that brings me joy?

The text comes from Act IV of Schütz's play *Lacrimas*, which was edited by A.W. von Schlegel and published in Berlin in 1803. The author was not named, and when the song was published in 1829 the text was wrongly attributed to Schlegel. The autograph has not survived, and the date is not altogether certain. In the Witteczek–Spaun catalogue (Vienna, GdM) it is dated September 1825. The song was published together with the companion piece *Florio* in October 1829 as op.124 by A.W. Pennauer.

The Witteczek–Spaun date is plausible, for the unbroken rhythmic flow over six pages of music, the complete domination of a single pianistic idea, and the technical difficulty of the piece for both singer and accompanist, have much in common with other works of the summer of 1825, including the 'Great' C major Symphony. The music seems to be absorbed in itself, much as Delphine is absorbed in her love. Yet the basic idea seems to be symphonic rather than purely lyrical; the vocal line has a certain lack of independent interest, and it is difficult to avoid a sense of monotony. In the hands of a dramatic soprano the song sounds impressive, but it is not another *Suleika I*.

Capell, 219; Fischer-Dieskau, 220–1

## DEM UNENDLICHEN To the Infinite One
**Friedrich Gottlieb Klopstock**                                    15 September 1815

Sehr langsam          G major D291 Peters V p.31 GA XX no.145(a), (b) and (c)

Wie er-hebt sich das Herz, wenn es dich, Un-end-li-cher, denkt!

How the heart leaps, Infinite One, when it thinks of you! How it sinks when it turns its gaze on itself, wretched and lamenting, and upon night and death.

You alone summon me from the night of misery and death. Then I remember that you, Mighty One, created me. Lord God, no grateful hymn of praise, from the grave or by thy throne, can match thy glory.

Bow down, tree of life, to the sound of the harp! Crystal stream, murmur to the harps' sound! You whisper and rustle, and the harps play, but never wholly satisfy, for 'tis God whom you praise!

Thunder forth, you worlds, in solemn measure, to the chorus of trumpets! Make a loud noise, all you suns along the shining way, to the chorus of trumpets!

Thunder, you worlds, and trumpet choirs, ring out. But you never praise him fully, never fully; for it is God whom you praise!

The poem was written in 1764. There are three variant autographs: (1) A first draft, dated 15 September 1815, is in Vienna (GdM). This has the preludial recitative in F major, marked 'Sehr langsam'. The main section, in E flat major, is marked 'Langsam mit aller Kraft'.

(2) A fair copy (New York, PML) differs only in detail, mainly of dynamics and expression marks. It appears with the closing bars of D290 and D322, suggesting a date in September or October 1815.

(3) A later fair copy, together with Goethe's *Hoffnung* and *An den Mond* (2) and Mayrhofer's *Abendlied der Fürstin*. This manuscript (Berlin, SPK) is signed and entitled by Schubert 'Four German songs for solo voice with pianoforte accompaniment'. It was evidently intended for a projected publication which failed to materialise, and must therefore be regarded as the definitive version. It has the opening recitative in G major and the main section (*Langsam mit Kraft*) in E flat major as before. There are consequential changes in bars 16–18, and the postlude has an extra bar. There are good reasons for believing that this manuscript is much later than the others (see Winter).

All three versions are printed in the *Gesamtausgabe*; only the second (F major) version elsewhere. There are copies of (2) in the Stadler and Ebner collections (Lund, UB), that in the former made in 1816. The song was published in 1831 in book 10 of the *Nachlass* (*Geistliche Lieder* no.1). The source was (2) above. There are good musical as well as textual reasons for preferring the G major version, which exploits Schubert's favourite tonal relationship, that between the tonic and the flattened sixth. Unfortunately this is at present available only in the *Gesamtausgabe*.

Schubert's Klopstock style seems to be derived from Gluck. It is represented at its best by the contemplative 'Cidli' songs and, in a more operatic style, by the strength and sublimity of *Dem Unendlichen*. Here, in this splendidly fashioned recitative and aria, are the foundations of Schubert's epic style, later to flower in the Pyrker and Scott songs.

Capell, 95; Einstein, 111; Fischer-Dieskau, 46; R. Winter, 'Schubert's undated works: a new chronology', *MT*, CXIX, 1978, p.500.

## DER ABEND Evening
**Ludwig Kosegarten**                                    15 July 1815

B major D221 Peters IV p.146 GA XX no.95

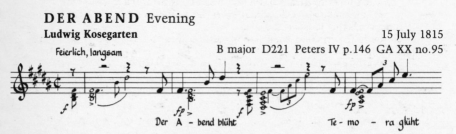

The evening is glorious. Temora glows in the sun's last light. Sinking, it kisses the sea, which trembles in awe and bliss.

A greyness fills the air, wreathes Daura's golden fields; round about murmurs the darkening sea, and ominous dusk rules over all.

Dear land, blessed strand! Peerless meadows, whence sprung the flower which shamed all other flowers. As the snow is like the lily, so is this fair flower like the blush of roses.

The meadow, garlanded with scent and light, awards it the prize, for it is matchless.

Far and near its fragrance scents the air, and if this song lives on then one day its fame will reach to the stars.

Dear land, noble strand, be proud of your fairest flower. The sacred sea, and the ring of islands pay homage to its glory.

Night covers the shore; Temora has faded; the last light has burnt itself out. The ocean roars, and the full moon, glowing red, rolls over behind the murky waves.

Temora was the name of the royal castle belonging to the legendary kings of Ireland in Ossian's *The Death of Cuthullin*. But Schubert seems here to be indulging his own enthusiasm for Ossian; in the original the name is Arkona, in the island of Rügen, where Kosegarten lived for several years. The autograph, now in ÖNB, Vienna, is not dated, but the catalogue of the Witteczek–Spaun collection (Vienna, GdM) gives the date as 15 July 1815. The song was published as op.118 no.2 by Josef Czerny of Vienna in June 1829.

In Schubert's tonality B major usually has associations with rhapsody or devotion, whether the context be religious (*Die Betende*), erotic (*Suleika I*), or romantically transcendental (*Nacht und Träume*). *Der Abend* is an early example of the key's transcendental associations, and though this strophic setting is content to stay within an eighteenth-century mould, the mood of exaltation, and the weight of emotion carried even by the tonic–dominant alternation of the beginning, foreshadow greater things. (There is a similar reliance upon the emotive power of tonic and dominant in the short B major section towards the end of *An die untergehende Sonne* of 1817). The song is well worth a hearing, though it would be unwise to insist on all seven verses.

## DER ABEND Evening

**Friedrich von Matthisson**                                           July 1814

Andante con moto     D minor  D108  Not in Peters  GA XX no.22  NSA IV vol.7 p.31

The fir-clad hills are touched with purple after the sun's farewell.
The flickering gleam of lovely Hesperus is mirrored in the brook.
In the poplar grove dusk falls with the chill of death, and all the birds go to sleep among the whispering leaves.
Only the cricket's evening song rises from the dewy grass, a sad melody in the enchanted dusk.
Will it sound one day on the evening breeze over my early grave?
Will you sing your lament from the rosy wreaths laid there by my friends?
My spirit will listen for you always as I listen now, while you murmur like this breath of summer over the flowery hill.

The poem was written in 1780, originally with a different fourth verse. Schubert's autograph is missing, but a copy in the Witteczek–Spaun collection (Vienna, GdM) is dated July 1814. The song was first published in the *Gesamtausgabe* in 1894. It is a good example of the early Matthisson songs, entirely conservative in idiom yet conveying a sense of personal conviction, heightened by the intervention of recitative for the sixth verse. This brings an added immediacy, a touch of 'direct speech', to the song, as well as providing a ternary form.

## DER ALPENJÄGER The Huntsman on the Mountain

**Johann Mayrhofer**                                                 January 1817

F major  D524  Peters II p.35  GA XX no.295(a) and (b)  NSA IV vol.1 p.104

Frisch, doch nicht zu schnell

Up on the mountain ridge where everything is green and fresh it is the huntsman's delight to look down through the drifting mists upon the land below.
As the paths wind their way up more steeply and dangerously his beating heart exults. He thinks more tenderly of his distant beloved still at home.
And when his goal is reached a sweet image crowds the stillness. The golden sunbeams weave a picture of his chosen one down in the valley.

There are three versions: (1) In E major, marked 'Froh und frei'. There are no introductory chords. The autograph of this first draft is lost, but there are copies in the Stadler and the Ebner collections (Lund, UB), that in the former made in 1817. There is a roughly contemporary copy also in the library of the monastery at Seitenstetten, Lower Austria.

(2) In D major, marked 'Lebhaft', the voice line written in the bass clef. This copy

was made for Count Esterhazy in 1818, during Schubert's residence at Zseliz. It remained with the Esterházy family for many years, but seems to have been lost during World War II. There is a photocopy in Berlin (SPK).

(3) In F major, marked 'Frisch doch nicht zu schnell'. This fair copy, now lost, was made for the first edition in 1822. No dated autograph survives, but the catalogue of the Witteczek–Spaun collection (Vienna, GdM) gives the date as January 1817, and this is consistent with the dated copy made for Stadler.

The song was published as op.13 no.3 by Cappi and Diabelli in December 1822, and dedicated by Schubert to his friend Josef von Spaun. The *Gesamtausgabe* prints both the original (E major) version and that in F. The D major version appears only in the *Neue Ausgabe*.

The sentiments are conventional, but not necessarily bogus. They belong within the pastoral tradition, but the zest and spontaneity of the song are sufficient proof that that tradition was still very much alive. Schubert's key, rhythm and horn calls in the accompaniment reinforce the pastoral tone of the song, and the ternary form reflects the changing moods of the poem. The song is more than a period piece, *pace* Capell. It belongs with *Erlafsee* and *Schlaflied*, among the most popular of the Mayrhofer settings.

Capell, 139

## DER ALPENJÄGER The Huntsman on the Mountain

**Friedrich von Schiller**                                   October 1817

Mäßig                                   C major  D588  Peters IV p.28  GA XX no.332

Willst du__ nicht das Lämm-lein hü-ten? Lämm-lein ist so fromm und sanft

Will you not tend the lamb, so meek and mild? It feeds on the flowers of the field, and plays beside the brook. 'Mother, let me go hunting in the high hills.'

Will you not entice the flock with the horn's merry note? Sweetly the bells ring out in the woodland's glad song. 'Mother, let me go roving over the wild peaks.'

Will you not cherish the friendly flowers in their beds? No garden will welcome you out there on the bare mountain tops. 'Let me go, mother; leave the flowers to bloom by themselves.'

And the youth went hunting, driving on further and further without rest or heed, to the remote parts of the mountain. The trembling gazelle flees like the wind before him.

He pursues it with his deadly bow as it climbs lightly up the bare crags, crossing the chasms with daring leaps.

Now it clings to the jagged ridge above the gorge, where the path ends and the cliffs drop sheer below, while behind the enemy draws near.

With mute distress it pleads with the cruel huntsman, but in vain, for already his bow is drawn ready to shoot. Suddenly from a rocky cleft the spirit of the mountain steps forth.

And with his godlike hands he protects the tormented beast, and cries: 'Must you bring death and misery even here to me? The earth has room for all. Why do you persecute my flock?'

The poem was not finished until 1804, but it may have been begun much earlier. There are two versions of the song: (1) The first draft, in the Fitzwilliam Museum, Cambridge, is in E flat major, and has a single introductory chord. It is now incomplete, though it is believed that originally it contained the missing final section. As it now stands it includes only the strophic sections of the song, the 2/4 and 6/8 sections to which the first six verses are set, a total of 34 bars. This first version is printed in the *Revisionsbericht* to the *Gesamtausgabe*. This autograph is dated October 1817.

(2) A fair copy in C major. This is lost, but an incomplete copy in the Witteczek–Spaun collection (Vienna, GdM) shows that the concluding section began in D major and ended in E major. There is also a copy in the Spaun–Cornaro collection (Vienna, privately owned); it has no introduction.

The song was published in February 1825 by Cappi as op.37 no.2 and dedicated to Schubert's friend Schnorr von Carolsfeld. For this publication Schubert must have made another fair copy, altering the concluding section and adding the four-bar prelude.

The poem is a broken-backed affair, and it is not surprising that Schubert was defeated by the melodramatic appearance of the schoolmasterly *deus ex machina* at the end. The original tonal sequence for the concluding section seems to have been F–G major. In the transposed version this became D–E major, but changes in the middle section led Schubert to the final G–A major. The song begins well, if a little blandly, and if it had not been for the problem inherent in the conclusion it might have made an attractive duet, rather in the manner of Schubert's early operas. But in its surviving form it is too episodic to make an effective song.

**DER ATLAS**  see HEINE SONGS no.1

## DER BLINDE KNABE  The Blind Boy
**Colley Cibber trans. Jacob Nicolaus Craigher**          February or April 1825
B flat major  D833  Peters II p.196  GA XX no.468(a) and (b)

The original English text runs:

>O say! what is that thing called Light,
>Which I must ne'er enjoy;
>What are the blessings of the sight,
>O tell your poor blind boy!

>You talk of wondrous things you see,
>You say the sun shines bright;
>I feel him warm, but how can he
>Or make it day or night?

>My day or night myself I make
>When'er I sleep or play;
>And could I ever keep awake
>With me 'twere always day.

>With heavy sighs I often hear
>You mourn my hapless woe;
>But sure with patience I can bear
>A loss I ne'er can know.

>Then let not what I cannot have
>My cheer of mind destroy:
>Whilst thus I sing, I am a king,
>Although a poor blind boy.

The poem, published in 1734, seems to have been well known in the Schubert circle. According to Deutsch (*Docs.* p.471) it had already been set to music by Franz Lachner and Simon Sechter in a translation by Count Majláth. Craigher was an amateur poet on the fringe of the circle, and a follower of Friedrich von Schlegel. He describes in his diary (*Docs.* p.470) how he agreed to provide Schubert with translations 'in the metres of the originals, which he will then set to music and have published with the original text'. *Der blinde Knabe* seems to have been a first experiment with this procedure, and it can in fact, at the risk of a few dubious stresses, be sung to the original words.

Craigher's meeting with Schubert took place in October 1825, but *Der blinde Knabe* is certainly earlier. Of the two surviving autographs, one (Vienna, SB) is associated with another Craigher setting which can be dated April 1825. The other (New York, PML) is associated with a fair copy of *Im Abendrot* which is dated February 1825. The song first appeared as a supplement to the *ZfK* on 25 September 1827. The poem was attributed to Craigher both there and on Schubert's autographs. Later the song was published as no.2 of 'Four Songs' (H.A. Probst, Leipzig, December 1828) under the opus number 101.

The pianist's gently swaying semiquavers suggest the deliberately cautious movement of the blind, a kind of graceful uncertainty, while the staccato repeated quavers in the left hand are surely a perfectly precise image of the tapping stick. This through-composed song is organised in three paired verses, the last being repeated; the constant variation of the melodic line is balanced by the simple tonal scheme with a middle section in the dominant, and by the unifying accompaniment figure. Schubert at least ignores the note of complacency and sentimentality in the poem. For the mood of the song, as a whole, is one of sweetness, even serenity.

Capell, 207; Fischer-Dieskau, 244

## DER BLUMEN SCHMERZ The Flowers' Anguish

**Johann, Count Majláth**                                   September 1821

Mäßig, zart                          E minor  D731  Peters VI p.116  GA XX no.399

How I shudder at the sound of the first breath of spring. How sad I am when the flowers are reborn.

They lay quietly in their mother's arms, and now, poor things, they must struggle up into the busy world.

The tender children shyly raise their heads: 'Who summons us to life from the stillness of the night?'

Spring, breathing sweet desire, entices them with magic words through the dark portals, away from their mother's breast.

Like brides, festive and bright, the flowers come in splendour; but already the groom has gone, and the strong sun glows fiercely.

Now their fragrance tells of their great longing; the scent that lies upon the balmy air is born of pain.

The flowers droop, turning their gaze to the earth: 'O Mother, receive us again, for life is but pain.'

The withered leaves drop, and the snow gently covers them. 'O God, so is it for us all. Only in the grave do we find rest.'

Majláth, Hungarian by birth, went to Vienna for medical treatment and maintained himself there as a freelance journalist and poet. He was a member of the Schubert circle in the

1820s. Schubert presumably set these cosily gloomy verses from his manuscript. There are two versions. That in the *Gesamtausgabe* is based on the only surviving complete autograph, contained in an album which belonged to Alois Fuchs and is now in private possession. It is dated September 1821, and there are copies in the Witteczek–Spaun collection (Vienna, GdM) and in Schindler's album (Lund, UB). In the Peters edition, however, Friedländer prints a quite different version, which omits the last verse, concludes with a somewhat different postlude, and has a variety of embellishments in the vocal line. This may date back to a 'performing version' made by Vogl or by another member of the circle; the source does not seem to have been identified. The song was performed by Karl Gross at an 'evening entertainment' of the Philharmonic Society on 3 February 1825. *Der Blumen Schmerz* was published as a supplement to the *ZfK* on 8 December 1821. It did not appear again until 1868, when C. A. Spina published it as op.173 no.4.

If the fashionable pessimism, and smooth flow of the verses, remind the reader of Müller, this fine song foreshadows in a remarkable way the Schubert of the song cycles. In its sweet disenchantment, in the minor–major play of light and shade, in the layout of the melodic line and the accompaniment, it reminds us constantly of *Trockne Blumen*, *Der Wegweiser*, and *Der Müller und der Bach*. But it is a lovely song in its own right and deserves to be as well known as they are.

Capell, 170; Einstein, 252

## DER BLUMENBRIEF Message of Flowers

**Alois Schreiber**                                                                                          August 1818

Mit Empfindung                         D major  D622  Peters II p.225  GA XX no.340

Euch Blüm-lein will ich sen-den zur schö-nen Jung - frau dort,

I will send you, little flowers, to that fair maiden. Entreat her to end my suffering with one kind word.

You, rose, can tell her how I burn with love, how I pine for her, weeping night and day.

You, myrtle, whisper my hopes to her. Say to her: 'You are the only star that shines for him on life's way.'

You, marigold, explain to her the pain of despair. Tell her: 'Without you, his heart becomes a prey to death.'

The poem appeared in a collected edition of Schreiber's poems published at Tübingen in 1817. Schubert seems to have come across the volume in April of that year, and to have taken it to Zseliz with him in July. *Der Blumenbrief* was written in August, while he was in residence there. The autograph (Vienna, SB) is in D major, marked 'Mit Empfindung' and dated August 1818. When Diabelli published the song in 1833 (book 21 of the *Nachlass*) he transposed it to B flat and added the tempo indication *Mässig*. The copy in the Witteczek–Spaun collection (Vienna, GdM) is also in B flat, so that both it and the first edition may have been based on another autograph, since lost.

*Der Blumenbrief* stands out from the few other songs of 1818 because of its perfection of form, lyrical sweetness and sincerity. The equality of interest between voice and piano is complete, so that the pianist's four-bar link between the two halves of the stophe seems like a continuation of the melody. The second half of the tune clings hopefully to the dominant, then dies with a sigh.

Capell, 145

**DER DOPPELGÄNGER** see HEINE SONGS no.6

**DER 13. [DREIZEHNTE] PSALM** see entry following DER PILGRIM

## DER EINSAME The Recluse

**Karl Lappe**                                                     (?) January 1825

Mäßig, ruhig                           G major  D800  Peters II p.92  GA XX no.465(a) and (b)

Wann mei-ne Grillen schwirren, bei Nacht, am spät er-wärmten Herd,

When crickets chirrup in the night, by the late warmth of my hearth, I sit cosily by the fire and gaze contentedly into the flames, at ease, and light of heart.

For one sweet peaceful hour it is good to linger by the fire, stirring the embers when the blaze dies down, musing, and thinking: Another day is done.

Once more we run over in our minds the joy or sorrow it has brought us. Only the bad is cast aside, lest it should disturb the night.

Gently we prepare ourselves for pleasant dreams, and when a lovely image comes unsought and fills our soul with tender joy, we yield to rest.

O how I love this tranquil country life. The restless heart, held captive in the world's mad tumult, can never find content.

Chirp away, friendly cricket, in my narrow little cell. I will happily put up with you, for you don't disturb me at all. When your song breaks the silence, I am no longer quite alone.

Lappe's poems appeared in collected form in 1836. Schubert may have found the poem in a periodical or in an earlier (1801) volume. The autograph has not survived, and there is some uncertainty about the date. However, the song was sung by Vogl at Sophie Müller's on 7 March 1825 (*Docs.* no.537) and published as a supplement to the *ZfK* on 12 March 1825. Sophie Müller regarded it as a 'new song', and the catalogue of the Witteczek–Spaun collection (Vienna, GdM) also attributes it to 1825. A strong tradition existed in Kreissle's day that the song was composed during one of Schubert's spells in hospital. If this is so, it points to a date in January 1825, since Schubert's movements in February are accounted for in some detail. The singer's high G's in the concluding bars were added when the song was republished by Diabelli as op.41 in January 1827. The *Gesamtausgabe* includes both this and the earlier version. On 23 November 1826 the tenor Ludwig Tietze sang *Der Einsame* at one of the evening entertainments of the Gesellschaft der Musikfreunde.

The song is a splendid example of Schubert's ability to conjure up not merely a visual picture, but a particular state of mind also, in a single rhythmical figure. There is something complacent, or at any rate *gemütlich* about the staccato quavers that run like the notes of a solo bassoon through the song's seventy-nine bars. The little semiquaver figure like a turn that occurs intermittently through the song is the friendly chirp of the cricket, sounding now low down, and at the end higher and more distant. Within this basic pattern Schubert manages to fit a wealth of expressive detail: the breaking-up of the voice line in verse 2 as the speaker ruminatively pokes at the dying embers; the gentle sinking down to F major for 'Another day is done', and to E major when he speaks of yielding to sleep. Schubert's mastery of the modified strophic form is complete; nothing disturbs the mood of cheerful introspection, yet the song reflects the course of the poem with infinite resource.

Capell, 206; Fischer-Dieskau, 236

## DER ENTFERNTEN To the Distant Beloved
**Johann Gaudenz von Salis-Seewis**                              (?) Spring 1816

E flat major  D350  Peters VII p.40  GA XX no.203

Wohl denk__ ich al - lent - hal - ben, o   du   Ent - fern - te,   dein,

Wherever I am I think of you, my beloved, far away! At early morning when the
clouds grow pale, and late by the light of the stars; against the golden ground of the
dawning, and in the red glow of evening, your sweet beloved vision hovers round me.

Where noisier, darker, the rushing river cleaves the mountains, its sound
carries over to me, and my soul recognises it. When I scale the peak no man has
yet reached, I listen for that voice. But no sound echoes from the abyss.

Where in the twilight the gleam of the pines wavers through the night, I see
your beloved form fleeing through the air like a hesitant ghost. But when my longing
arms reach out to touch you, the image has vanished, swept away like morning mist.

The poem was written in 1789, an early example of the 'Ich denke dein' theme, which
predates Matthisson's *Andenken*. Schubert used three of the five verses, omitting verses
2 and 3. The autograph (Stockholm, SMf) is undated. But all the securely dated settings
of Salis poems belong to the spring of 1816, and this one probably does too. An arrangement for piano solo by J. P. Gotthard was published in 1876. The authentic version appeared
only in vol.VII of the Peters edition in 1885. This slight but attractive setting has a
spontaneity and a rhythmic flexibility which are very Schubertian.

## DER ENTSÜHNTE OREST Orestes Purified
**Johann Mayrhofer**                              (?) March 1817

Sehr langsam, mit Kraft                     C major  D699  Peters V p.42  GA XX no.383

*mf*                                    Zu  mei - - - nen  Fü - ßen  brichst du dich,

O sea of my homeland, whose waves break at my feet and softly murmur 'Triumph!
Triumph!' I wield my sword and spear.

Mycene honours me as king, gives me freedom to act, and above my head
rustles the golden tree of life.

Spring decks my path with early roses, and my little boat glides onward on
the waves of love.

Diana approaches; priestess-deliverer, hear my prayer! Grant me my heart's
desire, to return to my fathers.

Schubert set the poem from Mayrhofer's manuscript. The published version includes some
later revisions. The autograph is lost, and the song's date is uncertain. In general the
classical songs to Mayrhofer's words belong to 1817, and most of them to March 1817.
Certainly the companion piece, *Orest auf Tauris*, does, on the evidence of a dated
autograph. The catalogue of the Witteczek–Spaun collection (Vienna, GdM) ascribes *Der
entsühnte Orest* to September 1820, but it seems unwise to rely on this, particularly
because the same authority erroneously attributes *Orest auf Tauris* also to September 1820.
There seems no reason to reject the obvious conclusion that both songs belong to the main
phase of Schubert's neo-classical enthusiasm. The song was published with three other
Mayrhofer songs in April 1831 as book 11 of the *Nachlass*.

As a punishment for the murder of Aegisthus and Clytaemnestra Orestes was sent into exile for a year. During this period he was pursued by the Furies and driven to madness, but after undergoing rites of purification in the rivers of Argolis he returned to Athens and put himself under the protection of Athene. It is difficult to think of another song with the nobility of utterance of this one, unless it be *Antigone und Oedip*. The opening arioso, with its wide leaps in the voice and sustained arpeggios, is Wagnerian, and the impression is oddly confirmed at bar 8, with its Wotan-like reference to 'sword and spear'. The strength and simplicity of the tonal structure – middle section characteristically in A flat and outer sections in C major – also contribute to the effect. The pictorialism of the lapping waves in the first section and the rocking boat in the second is pure Schubert.

Capell, 162–3; Fischer-Dieskau, 199

## DER FISCHER The Fisherman
**Johann Wolfgang von Goethe**                                             5 July 1815

B flat major  D225  Peters II p.9  GA XX no.88  NSA IV vol.1 pp.42, 243

Maßig (M.M. ♩ = 60)

Das  Was - ser rauscht', das  Was - ser schwoll, ein  Fi - scher saß dar - an,

The water swirled and murmured; a fisherman sat tranquilly watching his rod, cool to his very heart. And as he sits and listens the waters part, and from their troubled depths a water-nixie rose.

She sang to him, she talked to him: 'Why do you lure my brood with human guile and human wiles up to the deadly light? If you only knew how happy these little fish are down below you would climb down, just as you are, and at last be made whole. Do not the sun and the moon themselves bathe in the sea? Are they not twice as beautiful reflected in the waves? Does not the heavenly depth tempt you with its watery blue? Does not your own face draw you down here into the dewy depth of eternity?'

The water swirled and murmured, moistened his naked foot. His heart was full of longing, as though his beloved called. She spoke to him, she sang to him, then it was all up with him. Half dragged, half willing, down he sank, and nevermore was seen.

Goethe's famous ballad appeared in 1779 in Seckendorff's *Volks und andere Lieder*, and later in the same year Herder put it at the beginning of his *Stimmen der Völker*, holding it up as a model to be followed by other poets. It was probably written in the preceding year. The autograph (London, BL) is dated 5 July 1815; on that day Schubert wrote three Goethe songs, all masterpieces. The printed versions, which include the mordents in bars 5 and 9, are based on the copy made for Goethe early in 1816 (Berlin, DS). Both versions are given in the *Neue Ausgabe*. *Der Fischer* was published as op.5 no.3 with four other Goethe settings in July 1821 and dedicated by Schubert to Anton Salieri.

The universal appeal of the poem rests on its concreteness, its simplicity, and the sense it conveys of the unfathomable mystery of nature. It draws its strength from the superstitious dread of the primitive forces inherent in nature, while retaining the rational tone of ironic detachment. Schubert's achievement is to have found a setting which at least accommodates the poem's subtlety. The tone is light without being trivial; the music combines the simplicity of the folksong with the sophistication of the lied.

Capell, 104–5; Fischer-Dieskau, 43

# DER FLÜCHTLING The Fugitive

**Friedrich von Schiller**                                18 March 1816

Ziemlich langsam, feierlich                B flat major  D402  Not in Peters  GA XX no.192

*Frisch at - met des Mor-gens le - ben-di-ger Hauch;*

The lively morning breeze is fresh; the early light gleams red through the dark pine trees, and sparkles from the bushes. The cloud-capped peaks blaze into flame. The awakening larks carol their joyful song to greet the laughing sun, which glows with youthful bliss in dawn's embrace.

Blessings upon you, light; your beams flow down to warm the fields and meadows; from the silvery pastures a thousand suns shimmer in the dew.

In the cool whispering dawn young nature begins to frolic. The breezes caress the roses and sweet fragrance pervades the smiling plain.

The clouds of smoke rise high above the city; horses and bullocks neigh and snort, while creaking wagons lumber along the valley. The woods are alive; eagles, falcons, and hawks hover in the dazzling light.

Whither shall I turn my steps to find peace? This smiling world decked out in youthful gear is but a grave for me!

Rise up, glow of morning, and kindle every grove and field with your kiss. Whispering sunset, softly sing the dead world to sleep. Morning, you light up a landscape of death. Evening glow, you do but murmur around my long sleep.

The poem is roughly contemporaneous with *Die Räuber* (The Robbers; 1780), and reflects the sympathy with the outcast fashionable in the *Sturm und Drang* period. There is a fragmentary autograph (Vienna, SB), consisting of the first twenty-two bars only, dated 18 March 1816. A fair copy of the complete song, earlier in private possession in Vienna, has disappeared. There is a copy (complete) in the Witteczek–Spaun collection (Vienna, GdM), which served as the source for the *Gesamtausgabe* when the song was first published in 1895.

The sentiment in verse 5 seems muted and conventional. As Capell nicely observes, 'it seems to be only by force of romantic obligation that the poet, after many agreeable reflections, lapses into misery'. At all events, Schubert was unmoved; the setting of the later verses is perfunctory, and in the end the sectional form outstays its welcome.

Capell, 114

# DER FLUG DER ZEIT The Flight of Time

**Ludwig von Széchényi**                                    (?) 1821

A major  D515  Peters IV p.10  GA XX no.301  NSA IV vol.1 p.63

Etwas geschwind (M.M. ♩ =112)

*Es floh die Zeit im Wir - bel - flu - ge*

Time flew by like a whirlwind, carrying away with it the plan for life. It was rough going on the journey, often difficult and unpleasant.

It went on from age to age, through childhood years, and the happiness of youth; through valleys where joy dwells, remembered in thought with longing.

Until time, with gentler flight, reached the sunny uplands of friendship, and folded its swift wings at last in sweet repose.

Count Széchényi was an influential member of the Philharmonic Society, and an amateur poet and musician. No autograph of the song has survived. It is usually ascribed to 1817, but a later date is much more likely. See the discussion of this point under the companion piece *Die abgeblühte Linde*. The song was published in November 1821 as op.7 no.2 and dedicated to the author.

*Der Flug der Zeit* is a slight and superficial treatment of the theme of the 'river of life', which coming from more prestigious poets inspired some of Schubert's most ambitious efforts. Here it suggests the rhythm of the barcarolle, enlivened by several enharmonic modulations into the flattened sixth. The result is less impressive than the companion piece.

> Capell, 143

## DER FLUSS The River
**Friedrich von Schlegel**

March 1820

B major D693 Not in Peters GA XX no.375

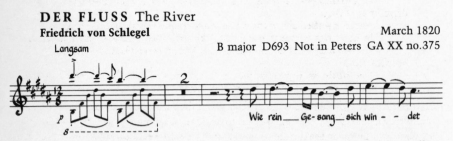

Wie rein__ Ge-sang__ sich win - - det

Like pure song which threads its way through the wondrous harmony of the swelling strings, and finds itself renewed, however much the tunes deceive; so that the listeners are constantly filled with new delight;
>So the pure silver stream flows on, winding snake-like through the waving bushes, held spellbound to see themselves freshly mirrored in its surface;
>Where the hills and bright clouds like to show their gently trembling likeness; when the pale stars climb out of the deep blue distance and the sun's bleary eyes sink down.
>So for the childlike mind the face of Being shines, the mind which, singled out for beauty by the high favour of the gods, preserves the fleeting blossom in the crystal stream.

The poem comes from part I of the *Abendröte* sequence, written in 1800–1. On the autograph (SB) the first twelve bars are missing. It is undated, but there are two complete copies in the Witteczek–Spaun collection (Vienna, GdM) dated March 1820. The song was published in 1872 as no.27 of 'Forty Songs', by J.P. Gotthard.

The Schlegel songs mark a new stage in the evolution of Schubert's art, and nowhere is this more obvious than in *Der Fluss*. The long-breathing 'Italian' melodic line, the rhapsodic key, the unexpected emotional weight which the simple harmonic structure is made to carry, the pianistic figures which fall so readily under the accompanist's hand, all these contribute to the realisation of a single moment, and a single mood, in song. Such are the concentration and the fluency that Schubert seems suddenly to have brought Romantic song within measuring distance of Richard Strauss. The way in which voice and piano move in contrary motion towards the climax of the song is particularly striking. Whether the song matches the complexity of the poem is another matter. Schubert is content to take his cue, as so often, from a single image, that of 'pure song' which constantly renews itself – a metaphor which perfectly describes his own compositional method. The song is not often heard, mainly because it does not appear in the Peters edition.

> Capell, 165; Fischer-Dieskau, 199–200

**DER FRÜHLING** see AM ERSTEN MAIMORGEN

## DER GEISTERTANZ The Ghost Dance (1)

**Friedrich von Matthisson** c. 1812

C minor D15 Not in Peters GA XX no.590 NSA IV vol.7 p.188

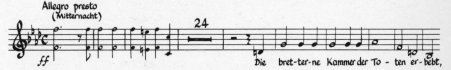

Die bret - ter-ne Kam-mer der To - ten er-bebt,

The boarded chamber of the dead trembles as midnight's hammer strikes twelve.
Round the graves and mouldering limbs we spirits lead the dance.
Why do the dogs whine as their masters sleep? They scent from afar the ghosts
dancing in a ring.
From the ruined abbey the ravens flutter, and fly off past the graveyard gates.
Up and down we tumble and jest, like will-o'-the-wisps over the dank moor.
O heart, whose magic was our martyrdom, now you lie at rest, frozen in silent
stupefaction.
Deep in the gloomy chamber of the grave you have hidden our suffering.
Happy are we, as we whisper you a glad farewell!

Matthisson's attempt to make the flesh creep in the fashionable 'Monk' Lewis manner
was written in 1797. The poem seems to have made a big impression on the young
Schubert, for he made two attempts to set it while still a schoolboy, and then returned
to it two years later. He also set it as a quintet for male voices in November 1816 (D494).
The autograph, in private possession, also contains the second version. It is undated.

This first version, like the 1811 songs, follows the Zumsteg model, and attempts
a sectional treatment of the poem. The seven introductory bars are one more version of
Schubert's earliest horror motif. The setting breaks off after fifty-one bars. The fragment
has been completed by Reinhard van Hoorickx.

## DER GEISTERTANZ (2)

**Friedrich von Matthisson** c.1812

F minor D15 (D2 15A) Not in Peters GA XX no.590 NSA IV vol.7 p.190

Allegro presto
(Mitternacht)

Die bret-ter-ne Kammer der To - ten er-bebt,

For translation, see the preceding entry. This further attempt seems to have been conceived
on a more ambitious scale than the first. It has descriptive subtitles – 'The howling wind',
'Solemn stillness', and so on, and much use is made of German sixths and diminished
sevenths. It breaks off after the third verse. There is an interesting anticipation of the
minim–crotchet–crotchet rhythm, as in *Der Tod und das Mädchen*, at bar 29, to
accompany the first line of the poem.

## DER GEISTERTANZ (3)
**Friedrich von Matthisson**                                     14 October 1814

Mässig langsam    C minor  D116  Peters II p.237  GA XX no.29  NSA IV vol.7 p.52

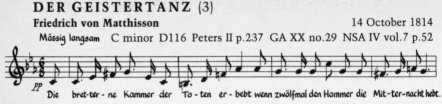

Die  bret-ter-ne  Kammer der  To-ten  er-bebt wenn zwölfmal den Hammer die  Mit-ter-nacht hebt.

For translation, see *Der Geistertanz* (1). The autograph is an incomplete fair copy dated 14 October 1814, containing the first thirty bars. There is a dated copy in the Witteczek–Spaun collection (Vienna, GdM). The first publication was in book 31 of the *Nachlass* (1840).

Here, two years or more after the first attempt, the principle of formal unity asserts itself, and a minor masterpiece results. Elements of the earlier version are still present – the unison themes and the 6/8 macabre dance, for instance – but movement has become form; the 6/8 dance has become the song, and the short recitatives are skilfully integrated into that pervasive gait. In its way the song asserts the independence of the lied as a musical form in its own right as notably as *Gretchen am Spinnrade*, written three days later.

> Einstein, 69; Fischer-Dieskau, 30–1; Schnapper, 81

## DER GOLDSCHMIEDSGESELL The Goldsmith's Apprentice
**Johann Wolfgang von Goethe**                                     May 1817

F major  D560  Peters VI p.66  GA XX no.122

Es  ist  doch  mei-ne  Nach-ba-rin  ein  al-ler-lieb-stes  Mäd-chen!

I have a pretty neighbour, a darling girl: and in the morning, at my bench, I gaze up at her window.

I file away, and sometimes I file clean through the thin gold links. My master grumbles, hardhearted man! He knows the window was to blame.

And when the daily tasks are done she reaches for her spinning wheel. Well I know what she means to spin; the darling girl has expectations.

The little foot goes treadling on. My thoughts are of the leg above, and of her pretty garter. I gave it to the darling girl!

My sweetheart lifts the fine thread to her lips. Oh if only I could take its place. How I should kiss her!

The poem was written in 1808. There are seven verses, of which Schubert omitted the second and third. The autograph (Paris Conservatoire) is a rough draft, undated. But the same manuscript contains two other songs (D558 and 559), dated May 1817. The song was published in 1850 in book 48 of the *Nachlass*. In the process of publication the two leaves of the autograph were separated and were not reunited until 1897, when they were both acquired by Charles Malherbe. *Der Goldschmiedgesell* is a cheerful strophic setting, somewhat overshadowed by the wit and sparkle of its companion piece *Liebhaber in allen Gestalten*.

## DER GONDELFAHRER see GONDELFAHRER

# DER GOTT UND DIE BAJADERE The God and the Dancing-girl

**Johann Wolfgang von Goethe**                    18 August 1815

Mäßig                    E flat major  D254  Peters VII p.106  GA XX no.111

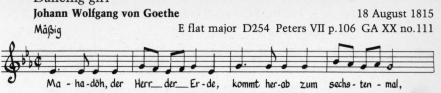

Ma - ha - döh, der Herr___ der___ Er - de, kommt her-ab zum sechs- ten - mal,

[*Synopsis*] Mahadeva, Lord of the Earth, comes down to earth to live among men, for if he is to judge them he must first know them. In human form he roams about the town, watching and observing.

And when at nightfall he goes on his way he encounters, on the outskirts of the place, a lovely maiden, exotic and forlorn. She tells him she is a temple dancer, and begins a sinuous dance for him, enticing him into her 'house of love'.

To test her, he bids her perform ever more degrading tasks, but in the end her cheerful acquiescence makes him rejoice to find a human heart amid so much corruption.

He kisses her, and she weeps in the anguish of love. Waking in the morning after a night of love she finds her lover dead at her side. When he is laid on the funeral pyre the priests drive her away, for only a wife may join her husband in death.

But with outstretched arms she leaps into the flames. Then the divine youth rose from the pyre, and carried her aloft in his arms.

The poem, subtitled *Indische Legende* ('Indian Legend'), was written in 1797. The first draft of the song, known to be in private possession in 1953, has since disappeared. But a fair copy made for Goethe in 1816, and dated August 1815, is in the Paris Conservatoire, and there are copies in the Witteczek–Spaun collection (Vienna, GdM) dated 18 August 1815. The song was published in 1887 by Weinberger and Hofbauer of Vienna in a collection of previously unpublished songs. In the same year it appeared in vol. VII of the Peters edition.

Schubert's passion for a text to set seldom led him completely astray, but it seems to have done so here. What can have persuaded him that this solemn symmetrical chant would make a suitable vehicle for Goethe's vivid and disturbing parable? Was he concerned only to find some technical solution to the metrical problem posed by the unconventional stanza form, with its double quatrain in trochaic rhythm followed by a three-line envoi of tripping dactyls? If so, his success is achieved at the expense of the poem, for the subtle suggestion that there is here a meeting of two worlds is lost.

Perhaps the eighteen-year-old composer was simply content to adopt Goethe's own strongly held view that the composer's function is to find a musical strophe that matches the prevailing tone of the poem, leaving the singer to express the poetic nuances by subtle modifications of tempo and dynamics. Some such view seems to be implied by Schubert's own note on the autograph: 'Bei diesen Strophen sowohl als bei den übrigen muss der Inhalt derselben das Piano und Forte bestimmen' ('In these verses as well as in the others the content must determine the dynamics'). But it does not seem to have occurred to him that the poem is too long, too metrically complex, and too full of descriptive detail, for such strophic treatment. For a different view, however, see Capell. There are nine verses, and the *Gesamtausgabe* prints them all. The Peters edition omits verses 4, 5 and 7.

Capell, 105; Fischer-Dieskau, 45

## DER GRAF VON HABSBURG The Earl of Habsburg

**Friedrich von Schiller**
(?) 1818

G major D990 Not in Peters Not in GA

Zu Aa-chen in sei - ner— Kai-ser-pracht, im al - ter-tüm-li-chen Saa - le,

At Aachen, in the imperial splendour of his ancient hall, Kind Rudolph in his anointed majesty sat at his coronation feast.

The Count Palatine bore in the food, while the Lord of Bohemia poured the sparkling wine. And all the seven electors, ranged like a choir of stars round the sun, stood ready to serve the lord of the world, proud of their high office.

[*The poem has eleven more verses.*]

The poem was written in 1803. The autograph (Vienna, SB) is a sketch on two staves. Only the first verse of the total of twelve is written out, but there are repeat marks at the end.

In 1853 Schubert's brother Ferdinand, then the director of a training college for teachers, published *Der kleine Sänger* ('The Young Singer'), a collection of vocal duets for schools. This included, among other compositions, several arrangements of songs by Franz Schubert, including *Der Graf von Habsburg*, arranged by Ferdinand for two voices and bass accompaniment. In 1816 Ferdinand had been appointed to a post at the Imperial Orphanage in Vienna, and over the next two years he performed several works by Franz there, some specially written for him. While the date of *Der Graf von Habsburg* is an open question, it seems likely that it belongs to this period. According to Ernst Hilmar the script and the paper of the autograph point to late 1818.

> E. Hilmar, *Verzeichnis der Schubert-Handschriften in der Musiksammlung der Wiener Stadt- und Landesbibliothek*, Kassel and Basel, 1978, p.81; R. van Hoorickx, 'About some early Schubert manuscripts', *MR*, XXX, 1969, p.118, and 'Schubert songs and song fragments not included in the collected edition', *MR*, XXXVIII, 1977, pp.273−4.

## DER GREISE KOPF see WINTERREISE no.14

## DER GUTE HIRT The Good Shepherd

**Johann Peter Uz**
June 1816

Vertrauensvoll
E major D449 Not in Peters GA XX no.234

Was sor - gest du? Sei stil - le,mei-ne See - le!

Why so beset with care? Be still, my soul, for God is a faithful shepherd; and even if I am not tormented, he will let me lack for nothing.

He feeds me in flowery meadows, and leads me to fresh streams; and brings me, in the cool dewfall, to tranquil evening peace.

Nor does his loving kindness cease to shield me, and shade me from the heat of the day. In his bosom he shelters me from storms, and the raging of dark evil.

And when through dark valleys he leads me, or through the wilderness, I shall fear nothing; for by my side the faithful shepherd walks.

I will praise him and thank him, I put my trust in my Shepherd; and my faith shall be unswerving, when all else fails.

The poet's metrical paraphrase has seven verses, of which Schubert omitted the fifth and sixth. The autograph (Vienna, SB) is a first draft, lacking the prelude and postlude, and dated June 1816. There is a dated copy, complete, in the Witteczek–Spaun collection (Vienna, GdM), which may have been made from a later autograph. The song was published by J. P. Gotthard in 1872, as no.7 of 'Forty Songs'.

We should hear this attractive song more often, no doubt, if it had not been eclipsed by the much more famous four-part setting of the psalm written in December 1820. It is the resemblances between the two, however, which strike the listener. The identity of mood and of movement, the gently moving broken chords in the right hand, the fact that they move at the same harmonic pace – all this is a clear proof that (whether consciously or unconsciously) the idea of a song communicates itself with Schubert first and foremost in the form of a particular *Bewegung*.

## DER HERBSTABEND Autumn Evening

**Johann Gaudenz von Salis-Seewis**  March 1816

Langsam  F minor  D405  Not in Peters  GA XX no.202

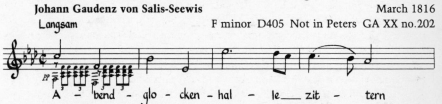

The evening bells send forth their trembling sound, muted by the marshland breeze. Behind the churchyard railings the scarlet blush of twilight pales.

Dead leaves swish down from the storm-tossed linden boughs, and on her grave wan grasses bend their heads.

Dear friend, soon the grass will tremble in the evening wind over my grave; the leaves will swirl about the linden tree restlessly in the humid air.

When only your withered wreath remains on the greensward above me, and my misty image disappears upon Lethe's gentle stream,

Listen then! In the shower of falling flowers a message will be borne: beyond the grave all grief shall fade, and faithful love be born again.

The poem, published in 1808, was subtitled *An Sie*. Schubert's first draft (Berlin, SPK) is an incomplete sketch, lacking the final bar. On the reverse is *Ins stille Land* (D403), which is dated 27 March 1816. A fair copy (Vienna, SB) is dated April 1816. There are several contemporary copies of this original version. Later in the year Schubert made another copy for inclusion in Therese Grob's song album (see GROB), and for this he added a two-bar prelude. This version has been privately printed by Reinhard van Hoorickx. The song had to wait until 1895 before it was published, in the *Gesamtausgabe*. *Der Herbstabend* is one of the best of the Salis songs; the mood of tender melancholy is finely enhanced by the rhythmic independence of the voice line.

## DER HIRT The Shepherd

**Johann Mayrhofer**  8 October 1816

Mäßig  D minor  D490  Not in Peters  GA XX no.267

Clocktower, your soaring height deepens my pain, a constant, cruel reminder of what I lost.

She loves another, and lives in the hamlet there. My poor heart bleeds, pierced by the sharpest dart.

There was no hint of faithlessness in her fair eyes; they spoke only of love and sweet grace.

Now wherever I turn my steps, the clocktower follows me. It marks the hours – would that instead it told her what it is that destroys me.

The autograph (Vienna, GdM) is a first draft, dated October 1816. A copy in the Witteczek–Spaun collection (GdM) is dated 8 October 1816. The song was first published in the *Gesamtausgabe* in 1895. The shepherd with time on his hands to grieve over his lost love is a conventional poetic conceit, and Schubert's plaintive tune, attractive though it is, carries no great weight of feeling.

## DER HIRT AUF DEM FELSEN The Shepherd on the Rock
**Wilhelm Müller, Helmina von Chézy**                    October 1828

B flat major  D965  Peters VI p.134  GA XX no.569

When on the highest rock I stand, and gaze down into the depths of the valley, and sing, the echo from the ravines floats up from far away out of the deep dark valley. The further my voice reaches, the clearer comes back the answer from below. My darling dwells so far from me, and so I long so fervently for her over there.

Deep grief consumes me, my joy is gone. Now earthly hope has forsaken me; I am so lonely here.

So the song rang out ardently through the wood, so ardently it echoed through the night, drawing hearts heavenward with wondrous power.

The spring will come, the spring, my joy; now I shall make ready to go a-wandering.

The song was written for the soprano Anna Milder-Hauptmann and scored for voice and piano with clarinet obbligato. Schubert made up a composite text in order to meet Madame Milder's request for an extended piece with contrasted sections. The first four verses come from the beginning of Wilhelm Müller's poem *Der Berghirt* ('The Alpine Shepherd'), and the last verse from the same poet's *Liebesgedanken* ('Thoughts of Love'). The authorship of the middle section ('In tiefem Gram …') is not certain, but it is usually attributed to Helmina von Chézy on the authority of Friedländer (see *Rev. Ber.* p.358).

The autograph score (Vienna, GdM) is written on four staves for voice, piano and clarinet, and dated October 1828. There are two annotations in Ferdinand Schubert's hand. The first, dated 2 September 1829, indicates that he has sent a copy of the score to Anna Milder in Berlin through the agency of J. M. Vogl. The second, dated 24 September 1829, states that he has sold the copyright of the song to Haslinger. Haslinger published the song in June 1830 as op.129, advertising the obbligato as for clarinet 'or violoncello', though there is no warrant for this in the autograph. The Peters edition omits the obbligato altogether.

Anna Milder was a pupil of Salieri and of J. M. Vogl, and prima donna at the Kärntnertor Theatre in Vienna from 1808 to 1816, when she moved to Berlin. Schubert had been enthusiastic about her talents ever since he heard her sing opposite Vogl in Gluck's *Iphigenie auf Tauris* in 1813. Later she became equally enthusiastic about Schubert's songs but seems to have regarded them as beyond the appreciation of the public at large, which, according to her, was interested only in 'treats for the ear' (*Docs.* no.538). In 1825 in a letter to Schubert she suggested that he write an extended piece for her with contrasting sections and a brilliant conclusion. At that time Schubert did not take up the suggestion, but now three years later he appears to have followed her brief carefully.

It is clear from the scale and sectional structure, as well as the brilliant style, of *Der Hirt auf dem Felsen* that it is designed for public performance. Like the Fantasie in C major for piano and violin, it was written as a medium for the talents of a virtuoso performer. In the hands of gifted artists it is irresistible. The sheer bravura of the piece, and the purity of the melodic writing, are pure Schubert. And yet the supportive role of the piano, and the uniformly eurhythmic nature of the work, seem strangely anachronistic in the month before Schubert's death, as though he had set out to provide merely a banquet for the ear, in the hope of popular success. What other composer could have written so serene and luminous a work as a successor to the String Quintet and the last piano sonatas?

Capell, 247; Einstein, 347; Fischer-Dieskau, 283, 299–300

**DER JÄGER** see DIE SCHÖNE MÜLLERIN no.14

**DER JÜNGLING AM BACHE** The Youth by the Brook (1)
**Friedrich von Schiller** 24 September 1812
Allegretto F major D30 Not in Peters GA XX no.5

An der Quel - le saß der Kna - be, Blu - men__ wand er sich__ zum__ Kranz,

By the spring there sat a youth, twining flowers to make a wreath, and saw them snatched from him to drift away on the dancing waves.

'So too my days fly away, like the streamlet, without stay. So too my youth fades, and quickly withers, like the wreath.

Ask not why I mourn in the blossom time of life. All things rejoice and hope, when spring returns. But the thousand voices of awakening nature kindle in the depths of my heart only heavy grief.

What shall the joy of the fair spring avail me? There is but one I seek, who is near, and ever far. I open my yearning arms to grasp her dear shadowy form, but ah, I cannot reach it, and my heart is troubled still.

Come down, fair sweet maid, from your proud castle. Flowers born of the spring will I scatter in your lap. Hark! the grove resounds with song, and the rippling stream flows clear. The smallest hut has room enough, for a happy loving pair!'

The poem dates from 1803. The autograph (Vienna, SB) is dated 24 September 1812. The song was first published in the *Gesamtausgabe*.

*Der Jüngling am Bache* is the first setting of a true lyric by Schubert which can be precisely dated. Up to this point he had been concerned almost exclusively with dramatic narratives of an epic and horrific kind; this is probably his first excursion into the field of pure song. Anton Salieri, who had been Schubert's tutor since the early summer of 1812, may claim some of the credit for it. One of the exercises that Schubert wrote out for Salieri (D17 no.1), an aria for soprano solo to a text by Metastasio, bears an obvious resemblance to this song. There is no doubt that Salieri set out, among other things, to stimulate and refine the young composer's melodic gifts. It is not only that there is something Italian here about the shape of the melody; the dramatic and declamatory elements which are seized upon so skilfully in the second verse and the last give the song a quasi-operatic tone. *Der Jüngling am Bache* has a good claim therefore to be the first true Schubert lied. Thanks to its freshness and spontaneity it is the earliest song to have kept its place in the repertory. The later (1819) version maintains the elegiac tone throughout, and so misses the youthful assurance which is so effective in the climax of this one.

Capell, 79–80; Einstein, 45, 48; Fischer-Dieskau, 22

## DER JÜNGLING AM BACHE (2)

**Friedrich von Schiller**                                          15 May 1815

Mäßig, erzählend, trauernd            F minor D192 Peters VII p.90 GA XX no.68

For translation, see the preceding entry. The autograph (Vienna, SB) is a first draft, dated 15 May 1815. There are copies in the Witteczek–Spaun collection (Vienna, GdM). The song was first published in vol. VII of the Peters edition in 1887. This second version recasts the tune in the minor mode and eliminates the operatic elements which enliven the first. But the changes are not obvious improvements, and something of the spontaneity of the first version is lost.

## DER JÜNGLING AM BACHE (3)

**Friedrich von Schiller**                                              April 1819

Mäßig                     C minor D638 Peters II p.158 GA XX no.359(a) and (b)

For translation, see *Der Jüngling am Bache* (1). There are two versions. The first draft is in D minor and the autograph (Vienna, SB) is dated April 1819. When the song was published by A. W. Pennauer in August 1827 it appeared in C minor. There are also changes in the vocal line (designed to make it easier) and in the accompaniment. The song was published erroneously as op.84 no.3, later changed to op.87 no.3. A fair copy, formerly in private possession in Vienna but now lost, may be the C minor version made for the printer. The *Gesamtausgabe* prints both versions.

Schubert's final version is much the best known. Again, it is strophic and cast in the minor mode. Einstein professes to find each version an improvement on the last and judges this one 'insusceptible of any further alteration'. Capell justly calls it 'a sweetly melodious and plaintive piece', but reveals his true feelings by saying the fourth repetition of the music seems one too many. The piece is the smoothest, perhaps the most accomplished, of the four settings, but it still lacks the spontaneity of the first, not to mention the horn calls which lift the heart in the final stanza of that version.

Capell, 158; Einstein, 48

# DER JÜNGLING AN DER QUELLE The Youth by the Spring
**Johann Gaudenz von Salis-Seewis** (?) 1821

Etwas langsam A major D300 Peters VI p.3 GA XX no.398

Lei - se, rie -selnder Quell, ihr wal - lenden, flis-pernden Pap-peln

Softly purling brook! You waving and whispering poplars, your sleepy murmurs, waken in me only feelings of love. I came to you for solace, to forget her, who is so cold. But ah, the leaves and the brook all sigh for you, Louise!

In the original, the last line of the poem reads: 'Ach! und Blätter und Bach seufzen: Elisa! mir zu.' Schubert altered the last three words to 'Louise, dir nach!' Mandyczewski in the *Gesamtausgabe* restored the words 'mir zu'. Schubert must have used the Vienna edition of the poems published in 1815, for the poem does not appear elsewhere.

No autograph has survived, and the date of the song is open to question. On the one hand, all the securely dated Salis settings belong to 1815 or 1816, and it is reasonable to suppose that this one does too. On the other hand, one of the two copies in the Witteczek–Spaun collection (Vienna, GdM) is clearly dated 1821. August Reissmann (*Franz Schubert: sein Leben und seine Werke*, Berlin, 1873) gives 12 October 1815 as the date of the song, but that appears to be due to a misunderstanding of an entry in the list of songs appended to Kreissle's biography. The author is not identified in the early editions of the song; it is likely therefore that Schubert's autograph did not identify him either, which weakens the main argument for the earlier date. As for the stylistic evidence, it is true that the song could have been composed either in 1816 or 1821. But its mastery sorts better with the more assured lyricism of 1821. It was published in 1842 in book 36 of the *Nachlass*.

*Der Jüngling an der Quelle* would be unlikely even now to appear on most lists of the twenty best-known Schubert songs. Yet it seems to encapsulate, as hardly any other song does, his genius as a song-writer. Nowhere is the contrast between the simplicity of the ingredients and the rounded perfection of the whole more striking. The voice line is content for the most part to traverse the notes of the common chord; the middle line moves similarly but in contrary motion; except for one bar at the song's climax the bass consists of only two notes, A and E; and the semiquaver figure in the pianist's right hand ripples gently and unceasingly from beginning to end. The words themselves are a fairly conventional example of the Romantic fallacy. Yet out of such simple materials Schubert fashions a song of such subtlety and grace that it defies analysis. The alteration of the text to suit the musical expression at the end is a masterstroke.

Capell, 170; Einstein, 220; Fischer-Dieskau, 152

# DER JÜNGLING AUF DEM HÜGEL The Youth on the Hill
**Heinrich Hüttenbrenner** November 1820

E minor D702 Peters II p.16 GA XX no.385 NSA IV vol.1 p.68

Nicht zu langsam

Ein Jüngling auf dem Hü - gel mit sei-nem Kummer saß____,

A youth sat on the hillside, his heart heavy; his eyes grew dim and moist with tears.

He watched the lambs gambolling on the green slope, and the brook ripple happily through the bright valley.

Butterflies sipped at the red mouth of the flowers; the clouds circled overhead like morning dreams.

All the world was gay, everything swam in happiness; only the rays of joy did not reach into his heart.

Ah, now the muffled funeral bell tolled in the village, and in the distance a mournful dirge was heard.

Now the lights appeared, and the black cortège. He began to weep bitterly, for they bore away his Rosie.

Now they lowered the coffin; the gravedigger came to return to the earth what God had once made from it.

Then the youth ceased lamenting and looked upward in prayer, foreseeing happier days when they would meet again in bliss.

And as the stars came out and the moon sailed up the heavens, he read in those stars a message of hope.

The poet, the younger brother of Anselm and Josef Hüttenbrenner, both closely associated with Schubert, was a law student in Vienna when he wrote the poem. The autograph (Vienna, GdM) is a first draft dated November 1820 and entitled *Auf dem Hügel*. The full title was restored by Josef Hüttenbrenner, who acted as a kind of honorary business manager for the composer in his middle years. The song was published as op.8 no.1 by Cappi and Diabelli in May 1822.

Hüttenbrenner's conventional gloss on the well-worn theme of youth, love and death inspire for the most part conventional responses from Schubert. The verses are set individually, the gambolling lambs rather lamely. The funeral bell music, and the brief quote of the 'death rhythm' as the cortège bears the young lady to the grave, is more impressive, but the shift to the major (6/8) for the final pious gesture is sentimental.

Capell, 168

# DER JÜNGLING UND DER TOD The Youth and Death

**Josef von Spaun**                                                   March 1817

Sehr langsam          C sharp minor D545 Peters VII p.56 GA XX no.312(a) and (b)

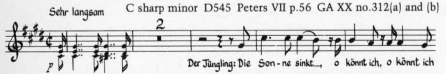

*The Youth:* The sun is sinking: O that I too might take my leave, and depart with its dying rays; escape these nameless torments, and move on to fairer worlds!

O come, death, and loose these bonds. I smile on you, spectre of death; lead me gently away to the land of dreams. O come, and let me feel your touch!

*Death:* You will rest cool and gentle in my arms. You call – I will have compassion on you in your agony.

The text, clearly inspired by the success of *Der Tod und das Mädchen* in the previous month, was never published separately. It is the only poem by his close friend and patron Josef von Spaun that Schubert set. There are two versions, with different endings. Schubert first wrote the music for Death's answer to the youth in G minor, but he seems to have realised immediately that this makes a very awkward tessitura for one voice. So he rewrote the last ten bars on a separate sheet, transposing the voice part to D minor, and introducing the 'death rhythm' (so familiar from the earlier song) in the postlude and in the introductory bars. The autograph is dated March 1817, but it has been split up, and the main part is now missing. The separate sheet with the new ending is now in private possession in New York. The song was published in 1872 by J. P. Gotthard as no.18 of 'Forty Songs'. Both versions are printed in the *Gesamtausgabe*.

It is the *Weltschmerz* of youth that dominates this song, rather than the merciful hand of death. Schubert's music draws on all the familiar themes; the opening bars with their chromatic descending bass line, the sighing appoggiaturas, the falling melodic line at the words 'O come, and let me feel your touch', and the sinister tread of the 'death rhythm' – all this makes the song a kind of compendium of 'doom and death' themes. Yet it is deeply moving, such is Schubert's power to convey the acceptance of the fact of death without sentimentality and without resentment. The introduction is a restatement of the *Wanderer* theme, in a form which points forward to the Piano Fantasia op.15. At the entry of the voice, bars 6–9, with their contrary motion between the inner and outer parts, foreshadow *Freiwilliges Versinken*, an interesting example of verbal association with the sunset.

Einstein, 161; Porter, 108–9, 114

# DER KAMPF The Struggle
**Friedrich von Schiller**

November 1817
D minor D594 Peters Vi p.164 GA XX no.333

No – I will fight this fight no longer, this titanic struggle of duty. If you cannot cool the burning ardour of my heart, then, Virtue, do not demand this sacrifice.

For I have sworn, yes, I have sworn to master myself. Here is your crown, may it be lost to me for ever. Take it back, and leave me to sin.

Let us tear up the treaty we have made. She loves me – may your crown be forfeit. Happy is he who, sunk in intemperate bliss, makes light of his headlong fall as I do.

She sees the worm gnawing at the flower of my youth, the spring of life fly away; calmly she marvels at my heroic self-denial, and generously decides to reward me.

Beware, fair soul, of this angelic kindness! Your pity arms me for a traitor's role. Is there, in the whole vast realm of life, another, fairer prize then you?

Or than the crime I meant to shun for ever? O, despotic fate! The one reward, that was to crown my virtue, is virtue's end.

The poem, published in 1786, originally had twenty-two verses. Schubert used the later shortened version, consisting of verses 1, 2, and 6–9. The subtitle is 'Freigeisterei der Leidenschaft. Als Laura vermählt war im Jahre 1782' ('Passion of the Freethinker. When Laura was married in 1782'). The autograph, earlier in the possession of Josef Hüttenbrenner, is lost. There is a copy in the Spaun–Cornaro collection, in private possession in Vienna. In the catalogue of the Witteczek–Spaun collection (Vienna, GdM) the date of the song is given as November 1817. *Der Kampf* was published as op.110 by Josef Czerny in January 1829.

The conflict between love and duty is one of the oldest themes in the operatic business, and Schubert's dramatic scena is conventionally operatic, with its arpeggio-based unison sequences, wide vocal leaps, agitated rhythm and *con fuoco* manner. *Der Kampf* is reported to have been Vogl's favourite Schubert song, and there is little doubt that it was written as a display piece for him. The ingredients belong to what might be called the mental conflict aria, and anyone who wants to see what Schubert could make of it needs only to look at Simon's F minor *molto allegro* aria in the second act of *Lazarus*. As might be expected, *Der Kampf* wins applause as a show of rhetoric, but it has something of the feeling of an exercise about it. Schubert the consummate musician is much in evidence, but not Schubert the poet.

Capell, 130–31; Fischer-Dieskau, 98–9

## DER KNABE The Boy

**Friedrich von Schlegel**                                                          March 1820

A major  D692  Not in Peters  GA XX no.374

If I were only a bird, ah, how merrily would I fly, and vanquish all the other birds far and wide.

If I am such a bird, then I may catch anything I like, and nibble at the topmost cherries. Then off I fly to mother. If she is cross, then I can fondly snuggle up to her, and very soon dispel her serious mood.

I could flutter bright feathers and light wings in the sun, so that the air vibrated with sound. I would know naught of curb or bridle. If I were once beyond those hills, ah then merrily would I fly, and vanquish all the other birds far and wide.

The poem comes from part I of the *Abendröte* cycle. There is a fragmentary first draft, consisting of the first fifty-one bars only, and without any tempo indication (Berlin, SPK). A complete copy in the Witteczek–Spaun collection (Vienna, GdM) is dated March 1820 and marked 'Heiter'. The song was published in 1872 by J.P. Gotthard as no.22 of 'Forty Songs'.

This delightful essay in the vernacular manner has been sadly underestimated. It does not appear in the Peters edition, and reputable critics have been known to dismiss it as trivial. The innocent high spirits of the piece are largely compounded of tonics and dominants but are none the worse for that. In the hands of a light and flexible soprano, the song is irresistible.

Capell, 165; Einstein, 188

## DER KNABE IN DER WIEGE The Baby in the Cradle

**Anton Ottenwalt**                                                          September 1817

Etwas lebhaft                                           C major  D579  Not in Peters  GA XX no.335

He sleeps so sweetly; his mother's gaze hangs on her darling's lightest breath; so long and anxiously she carried him with quiet longing under her heart. With joy she sees his round cheeks glow, half hidden in his golden curls, and gently covers up the little arm flung outward in his sleep.

Ever more gently she rocks the cradle, softly singing the tiny baby to sleep; a smile plays round his sweet features, but his eyes stay peacefully closed. When you awake, little one, ah, smile once more, and look up into your mother's face:

so you will see pure love look down on you, though as yet you don't know what love is.

But soon you will learn about it from her eyes, and from her heart, when it beats against your tiny heart, in a rapture of motherly delight. And you will learn to speak at the prompting of the heart, stammering at first the sounds your mother makes, and soon many another sweet word of love, and so gain confidence in your own words.

Also you will learn to know the loving Father, hastening toward him from your mother's breast; learn to distinguish things and to name them, feel the un-accustomed delight of thought. And from your mother's mouth you will learn to pray, following the simple pious ways of her heart. In the quiet evening hours, the Father will show you the way to the stars.

Where dwells the Father of mankind, who loves you and all his children, who rewards all goodness like a father and bestows the gift of joy upon all. So you will make your way on earth untainted and in good spirits, your heart faithful, tender and good. Stay thus, my sweet, if you would be happy, for of such is the kingdom of heaven.

Ottenwalt was a prominent member of the artistic circle in Linz and a close friend of Josef von Spaun, whose sister he married in 1819. It was doubtless Spaun who provided Schubert with a manuscript copy of the poem. A letter from Ottenwalt to Spaun dated 7 October 1817 (*Docs.* no.109) expresses pleasure that Schubert should have composed the song, and suggests that it was already written.

The autograph of Schubert's first draft, in C major, is missing. There is however a copy, headed as above, in the Witteczek–Spaun collection (Vienna, GdM), marked 'Etwas lebhaft'. Another copy of this version, formerly in the possession of the publisher Diabelli, was the source for the first edition. There is a fragmentary fair copy (Paris, Conservatoire) in A flat major. It is dated November 1817 and marked 'Etwas bewegt', and it breaks off after thirty-eight bars. This version is given in the *Revisionsbericht* to the *Gesamtausgabe*. The song was published by J.P. Gotthard in 1872, as no.16 of 'Forty Songs'.

*Der Knabe in der Wiege* is a charming lullaby, which rocks gently between tonic and dominant with almost hypnotic effect. The extended strophe, which has a second half beginning in the subdominant, covers two verses, though its changes of tonality give it a generally ternary form. In spite of the repeat marks at the end, it seems doubtful whether Schubert really intended all the verses to be sung.

## DER KÖNIG IN THULE The King of Thule

**Johann Wolfgang von Goethe**                                        Early 1816

D minor  D367  Peters II p.12  GA XX no.261  NSA IV vol.1 p.45

Etwas langsam (M.M. ♩=66)

Es war ein Kö-nig in Thu - le,    gar__ treu bis an____ das Grab,

There was a king in Thule, faithful even to the grave, to whom his dying mistress a golden goblet gave. Above all else he loved it, drained it at every feast, and every time he drank his eyes would brim with tears.

And when he came to die he counted all the towns in his kingdom, and gave all he had to his heirs, except only the goblet. He sat at the royal banquet, surrounded by his knights, there in his father's lofty hall in the castle by the sea.

There stood the old tippler, and drank to life's last glow, then cast the sacred goblet down to the waves below. He watched it fall and fill, and sink deep into the sea; then his eyelids drooped, and nevermore drank he.

The ballad comes from *Faust*, part I scene 8. Gretchen sings the song quietly to herself as she muses upon her first encounter with Faust. The song was written for inclusion in the first collection of Goethe songs, which was sent to Weimar in April 1816. The catalogue of the Witteczek–Spaun collection (Vienna, GdM) dates it 1816, and it probably belongs to the first months of that year, though it could be earlier. There are copies in the Stadler and the Ebner collections (Lund, UB), both marked 'Etwas langsam, romanzen-artig'. It was published with four other Goethe songs in July 1821 as op.5 no.5 by Cappi and Diabelli on commission, and was dedicated by Schubert to Anton Salieri.

Schubert's setting has much in common with Zelter's, which was widely known. The square triadic harmonies and absence of sevenths are clearly designed to suggest the antique balladry of the verses. Schubert does not here match the rhythmic and melodic simplicity of Zelter, though his setting is better suited to the soprano voice. The six verses of the poem are grouped in pairs.

Capell, 122–3; Fischer-Dieskau, 79–80

## DER KREUZZUG The Crusade

**Karl Gottfried von Leitner**                                                November 1827

Ruhig und fromm                          D major D932 Peters II p.232 GA XX no.549

A monk stands by the grey window-bars of his cell: a knightly host comes riding through the meadow in shining armour.

They sing devout songs in solemn chorus; the crusaders' flag, of silken soft-ness, flies aloft in their midst.

They embark on the tall ship at the water's edge. Soon it sails away on its green way like a swan.

The monk still stands at the window and gazes out after them. 'Though I stay here at home, I am a pilgrim like you.

Life's journey, over the raging billows and across hot desert sands, is also a pilgrimage towards the promised land.'

According to the author (*Memoirs* p.197), it was during Schubert's stay in Graz in September 1827 that his attention was drawn to Leitner's poems. The autograph (Vienna, SB) contains this song and two other Leitner settings. The first page is dated November 1827. The copy in the Witteczek–Spaun collection (Vienna, GdM) is similarly dated. *Der Kreuzzug* was written in the key of D major. Publication of the Leitner songs was promised by Tobias Haslinger early in 1829, but the songs failed to appear. *Der Kreuzzug* was first published in January 1832 as a supplement to the Vienna *Allgemeiner musikalischer Anzeiger*. Subsequently Diabelli published the three songs together as book 27 of the *Nachlass* (October 1835). *Der Kreuzzug* was transposed to E major, and the Peters edition follows the printed version.

The key, the square harmonies, and the steady four-in-a-bar link the song with early ones like *Die Betende* and *An Laura* and with contemporary ones like *Das Weinen*, all religious or at any rate devotional in tone. This 'evensong manner', as Capell calls it, is suspect to modern taste, but here it is redeemed by skilful melodic and harmonic variation, and especially by the treatment of the final verses, in which the solo voice takes over the harmonic bass, leaving the pianist to play the tune. It is worth noting also that the plodding four-in-a-bar was much in Schubert's mind at this time. It runs through *Winterreise* (see in particular *Der Wegweiser*) and reappears in the first of the four Impromptus op.90. Michael Vogl sang *Der Kreuzzug* at Schubert's public concert on 26 March 1828.

Capell, 245

**DER LANDENDE OREST**  see OREST AUF TAURIS

## DER LEIDENDE  The Sufferer

**Author unknown**                                                                    May 1816

B minor  D432  Peters VI p.79  GA XX no.224(a) and (b)

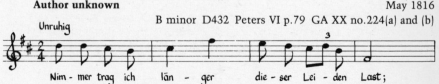

No longer will I bear this burden of suffering; take the weary pilgrim soon to yourself. My heart grows ever more oppressed, the light of my eyes more dim. No longer will I bear this burden of suffering!

Open your heaven to me, kind and gracious God, let me sink with my sorrows in the grave. Too many torments plague my soul. All hope is fled, fled is the warmth of my heart. Open your heaven to me, kind and gracious God!

The text was formerly attributed to Hölty, but it is not to be found in his published works. There are two versions of the song, both written on the same sheet of a longer manuscript which is dated May 1816. The alterations in the second version are in red pencil superimposed on the original. This autograph is in private possession. Both versions are printed in the *Gesamtausgabe*. There is a fair copy of the original version in the Therese Grob songbook, which was compiled about November 1816 (see GROB). It is there entitled *Klage* ('Complaint'). There are also several contemporary copies of the first version, including two in the Witteczek–Spaun collection (Vienna, GdM). The song was published in the original version in 1850, as no.2 of book 50 of the *Nachlass*.

For another setting of the same words, probably not by Schubert, see also under KLAGE.

The words are a cry from the depths; yet the song moves with a delicate plaintiveness. Perhaps its chief claim to fame is that it was a source for one of Schubert's best-known orchestral pieces, the second episode (Minore II) in the B flat major Entre-Act in the incidental music for *Rosamunde*, written in November 1823. In that year Schubert himself had been so desperately ill that at one time he seems to have despaired of his life. Was it perhaps the memory of this cry for mercy that led him to resurrect the tune?

Capell, 116

**DER LEIERMANN**  see WINTERREISE no.24

## DER LIEBENDE  The Lover

**Ludwig Hölty**                                                                    29 May 1815

B flat major  D207  Not in Peters  GA XX no.76

Happy, happy he who looks on you, and drinks the heaven of your sight; who reads in your face, full of angelic light, the greeting of peace.

A tender glance, a sign, a nod shines upon me like the spring sun. I think of it the livelong day, and swim in heavenly bliss.

Your dear image leads me gently along as by a chain of flowers. It wakes within my warm embrace, and follows me to bed.

Happy, happy he who looks on you, and drinks the heaven of your sight; who is summoned to sweet kisses by a tender glance, a sign, a nod.

The autograph (Vienna, GdM) is dated as above, and there is a dated copy also in the Witteczek–Spaun collection (GdM). The song was first published in the *Gesamtausgabe* in 1894. *Der Liebende* is an unknown gem, too slight perhaps for the concert hall, but a gem nevertheless. The music fits the words like a glove, gasping with impatience, sighing with happiness, and singing for sheer joy. These varied moods are all contained within the Haydnesque fabric of Schubert's early style.

## DER LIEBLICHE STERN The Lovely Star

**Ernst Schulze**                                                       December 1825

Etwas langsam                        G major  D861  Peters III p.140  GA XX no.486

When I see you shining down so amiably, little stars, silent in the firmament, playing on the surface of the sea , then for weal or woe my heart grows grave and sad.

Over the watery green surface the sky trembles in the spring gusts. I saw many a tiny star blossom and die. Yet never can I find the loveliest star, which used to shine on my love.

Nor can I climb up the sky to seek that friendly star. The clouds hide it from me forever. Down below, there I may succeed in reaching the haven of peace; down below, there would I love to find rest.

Winds, why do you cradle the rocking boat in your gentle play? Drive it forward on a rougher passage, down into the whirlpool! Deep down in the raging cool waters let me draw near to that lovely star!

The poem comes from Schulze's *Poetisches Tagebuch* ('Verse Journal'), where it is headed simply 'Am 28sten April 1814'. The manuscript containing the autograph of this song, together with the first draft of *Über Wildemann*, was split up shortly after publication in 1832 into two parts. The first, entitled as above but undated, contained bars 1–34. The second section was further divided sometime in the 1950s, but the present whereabouts of all three sections are unknown. *Der liebliche Stern* was published in January 1832 in book 13 of the *Nachlass*.

As with all the Schulze songs, *Der liebliche Stern* grows from a single cell; the semi-quaver figure in the pianist's right hand seems to conjure up the freshness of the spring evening, with the stars dancing high above. And though there is much play with minor and major, for the friendly star which guides lovers to happiness is forever beyond our reach, Schubert ignores the tragic hints in the last two verses of the poem. Poised between heaven and the blue depths, like a symbol of the Romantic imagination itself, the song is content to celebrate our love and our longing.

Capell, 216

## DER LIEDLER The Minstrel

**Josef Kenner**

(?) January 1815

Mäßig geschwind

A minor D209 Peters IV p.33 GA XX no.98

Gib, Schwe-ster, mir die Harf her-ab,

[*Synopsis*] The minstrel loves the noble daughter of the count but, poor and lowly-born, he must see her betrothed to another. Brokenhearted he wanders o'er many lands, singing only of his love; finally he takes up arms to seek repose in death, but death escapes him. Unable to resist the call of his homeland, he finds his native mountains in the grip of winter. When he reaches the castle, he encounters the lovely Milla, leaving by torchlight with her bridegroom to ride across the mountains. Suddenly a werewolf attacks, the horses bolt, and Milla falls senseless to the ground. The minstrel leaps at the monster, who savages his arm; but with one look at his love the minstrel gathers his strength and kills the wolf with his harp. Hurling the beast over the precipice, he perishes with it in the depths below. All pilgrims find rest in the grave!

Kenner was a fellow student of Schubert's at the Imperial College, and his naive exercise in the chevaleresque tale was written in 1813. This sort of thing had been fashionable particularly since Friedrich and Dorothea Schlegel popularised it in their Paris years. The main story-line has a good deal in common with early Romantic operas like *Euryanthe* and *Rosamunde*. *Der Liedler* itself must have had something of a vogue, at least in the Schubert circle, for Schwind planned a series of sepia illustrations to it which are reprinted in O.E. Deutsch's *Franz Schubert: sein Leben in Bildern*, pp.195–201.

The autograph, in private possession, is a fair copy with inscribed title pages, including a dedication to the author. It is dated 12 December 1815, but a pencilled note on the title page gives the date of composition as January 1815. The catalogue of the Witteczek–Spaun collection (Vienna, GdM) dates the song July 1815, but the earlier date seems more likely. The song was published by Cappi as op.38 in May 1825 in a revised version which presumably stems from Schubert himself. The differences between the autograph and the first edition are set out in the *Revisionsbericht*.

Basically the song is a reversion to the form and style of the early cantatas modelled on Zumsteeg. As a kind of do-it-yourself opera it has much to recommend it, some good tunes, some astonishingly bold Schubertian modulations, and a good deal of ingenuity in the use of familiar chromatic death motifs. The battle with the werewolf and the plunge into the abyss are handled with picturesque realism. But the form is, to modern ears, intolerable; the piece outstays its welcome long before the end.

## DER LINDENBAUM see WINTERREISE no.5

## DER MONDABEND Moonlit Evening

**Johann Gottfried Kumpf**

1815

Lieblich, etwas geschwind

A major D141 Peters IV p.158 GA XX no.43

Rein und freund - lich lacht der Him-mel nie-der auf die dunk-le Er - de,

The heavens look laughing, innocent and kindly, upon the earth below. A thousand golden eyes twinkle lovingly in men's hearts, and the moon's pale disc sails serenely through the blue.

The silver drops of sweet melancholy tremble on the golden beams and gently with light breath touch the loving heart, moistening my eyes with the tender dew of longing.

The evening star sparkles in the light-strewn vault and plays through the web of light with diamond flashes. Many a cherub strews lilies round the stars.

Majestic and lovely are the heavens in the wondrous evening light. But the stars of my life inhabit the smallest circle; they have all been charmed away into my Silli's glance.

Kumpf's verses appeared in various periodicals under the pseudonym Ermin. The original publication of this one has not been traced. The autograph is missing, but there is a copy in the Stadler collection (Lund, UB) dated 1815. The song first appeared in a collection published in November 1830 by Josef Czerny, which also included *Trinklied* (D148) and *Klaglied* (D23). In later offprints it was given the opus number 131. *Der Mondabend* is a pleasant surprise. Largely unknown, it ripples along happily, matching the words in their innocent assurance.

## DER MORGENKUSS The Morning Kiss
**Gabriele von Baumberg** 22 August 1815

E flat major D264 Peters VI p.45 GA XX no.124

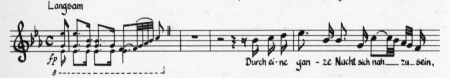

To be near one another all night long, to linger hand in hand, and arm in arm, to feel so much that cannot be imparted – that is delicious torment!

Ever to gaze soul upon soul, seeing into the heart's most secret desire; to say so little, and yet to understand each other – that is the sublime joy of martyrdom!

And then at daybreak, as reward for time perforce wasted, to press mouth to mouth and heart to heart warmly, with rapture – oh, that is the ecstasy that angels feel!

In the collected edition of von Baumberg's poems (Vienna, 1800) the title is *Der Morgenkuss nach einem Ball* ('Morning Kiss after a Ball'), but Schubert's title is as above. There are two versions. The first draft, dated 22 August 1815, is in E flat major. The manuscript, auctioned in 1920 in Berlin, is now missing. But there is a similarly dated copy in the Witteczek–Spaun collection (Vienna, GdM), which provided the source for the *Gesamtausgabe*. When the song was published in 1850 (book 45 of the *Nachlass*), it appeared in a spurious version transposed to C major, with a shortened prelude and the note values doubled. This version is printed in the Peters edition.

What is remarkable, in view of the scarcely concealed eroticism of the poem, is the classical poise of Schubert's setting. This quality, however, is lost in Diabelli's 'improved' version, which sentimentalises the piece.

Einstein, 107

## DER MORGENSTERN The Morning Star

**Theodor Körner**                                                     12 March 1815

Lieblich                                   G flat major D172 Not in Peters Not in GA

Star of love, image of splendour, glowing like the bride of heaven, you wander through the field of light to announce that morning dawns.

Kindly you come, kindly you hover in the sky, twinkling through the airy billows, lighting men's hearts with beams of hope.

As the purple grape swells bravely in the foaming goblets, so your rays illuminate the awakened spring.

As the glorious gold is locked in the noble rocks, so do you shine, star of love, as you tranquilly greet the dawn.

And you continue to shine brightly in the dark after the other stars have fled. Could I but once go with you, over the mountains, far away.

Take me, take me, blessed rays, fling your golden arms around me, that I may flee from this earthly torment into a happy land!

But I cannot lay hold upon you, cannot reach you – you stand so far. Can I ever be free of longing? Blessed star of heaven, is that permitted?

A fragment consisting of the first five bars of a song on a manuscript dated 12 March 1815 which also contains other Körner settings (Houghton Library, Harvard University). The song has been completed and privately printed by Reinhard van Hoorickx. On 26 May 1815 Schubert set these verses as a duet for voices or horns (D203).

## DER MÜLLER UND DER BACH see DIE SCHÖNE MÜLLERIN no.19

## DER MUSENSOHN The Son of the Muses

**Johann Wolfgang von Goethe**                                   December 1822

Ziemlich lebhaft                    G major D764 Peters I p.253 GA XX no.416(a) and (b)

Roving through field and forest, piping my song; thus I go from place to place, and the world keeps time to my beat, and moves in rhythm with me.

Scarce can I wait for the first garden flower, or the first blossom on the tree. My songs welcome them, and when winter comes again, I still dream of them in my song.

I sing of them far and wide, up and down the icy world, when winter blooms in beauty. But this flowering too passes, and new joy is discovered there on the upland farms.

For when by the lime tree I chance upon young folk I rouse them at once. The country yokel puffs out his chest, and the prim maiden dances to my tune.

You lend wings to my feet, and drive your darling over hill and dale far from home. Dear kindly Muses, when at last shall I find rest on the bosom of my love?

The date of the poem is uncertain, but it is usually attributed to the 1770s. The surviving autograph (Berlin, SPK) is part of a manuscript which contains four Goethe songs (D764–7)

and is dated December 1822; a reference in a letter from Schubert to Spaun of 7 December 1822 (*Docs*. no.328) makes it clear that the four songs were finished early in the month. In this original version the song is in A flat major. The song was published in July 1828 as op.92 no.1, by M.J. Leidesdorf of Vienna. The opus, originally given the number 87 by mistake, was dedicated to Josef von Franck. In this first edition the song is transposed to G major; whether this was done with Schubert's approval or acquiescence is not clear. Both versions are given in the *Gesamtausgabe*.

The popularity of this splendid song bears witness to the truth of the saying that a song is more than a setting. It can truthfully be objected that Schubert misses an essential element in the poem, the Ariel-like longing for release which finds expression in the last verse, and which serves perhaps as a symbol of the artist's voluntary self-dedication to his task. There are no such ironic shadows in the song, which dances along in its own irresistible way. But there is no justification for making it gallop rather than dance. The direction is *Ziemlich lebhaft* – 'Quite lively'. The song's magic lies in the complementary nature of the alternating strophes, the tunes so closely matched and the tonalities (a third apart) so interdependent that each verse seems like a new beginning. In this way Schubert gives to the strophic song the scale and continuity of the through-composed song; folksong, as Fischer-Dieskau puts it, has become art song, without losing the its strophic feel and its vernacular style.

Capell, 180–1; Craig Bell, 55–6; Einstein, 254–5; Fischer-Dieskau, 161; Stein, 71

**DER NEUGIERIGE** see DIE SCHÖNE MÜLLERIN no.6

**DER PILGRIM** The Pilgrim
**Friedrich von Schiller**                                                                     May 1823
Mäßig                                   D major D794 Peters IV p.24 GA XX no.432

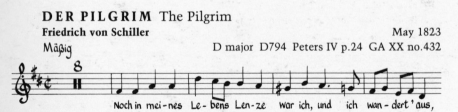

I was still in the springtime of my life when I wandered forth, leaving the merry dance of youth in my father's house.

All my inheritance, all my possessions I cast aside, happy in my faith, and innocent in thought I took my leave with my pilgrim's staff.

For a great hope spurred me on, and a dark word of faith. 'Go,' was the cry, 'the way is open, ever toward the east.

Until you reach a golden gate; then enter in, for there earthly things become immortal.'

Evening came, and morning, never did I stop, but what I seek, what I desire, stays ever hidden.

Mountains barred my way, rivers stayed my feet, I spanned the abyss and bridged the raging torrent.

I came to the bank of a river which flowed east, and I cast myself upon its bosom, happily trusting to follow its course.

Its swirling waves bore me to a great ocean, which lies before me in its vast emptiness. I am no nearer to my goal.

Ah, no bridge will take me there. Ah, the sky above will never touch the earth, and There is never Here!

The poem was written in May 1803. The surviving autograph is an unfinished first draft in E major, consisting of the first eighty-five bars (Berlin, SPK). It is dated May 1823. A complete copy of this E major version made by Ferdinand Schubert, and also dated May 1823, is in private possession. The song was published in February 1825 by Cappi as op.37 no.1, and dedicated by Schubert to his friend Ferdinand Schnorr von Carolsfeld. This published version is in D major, and shows a number of improvements and refinements, which must stem from the composer himself. Peters follows this first edition, but the *Gesamtausgabe*, somewhat illogically, incorporates the changes while retaining the original key.

If evidence were needed for the oft-repeated assertion that Schubert's genius failed to respond to Schiller's intellectualism, *Der Pilgrim* would provide it. The 'message' of the poem – life seen as a pilgrimage towards the unattainable – and the allegorical form, are of a kind to appeal to Schubert, and it is not difficult to think of songs on similar themes which are notably successful. But here he sets all but the last verse to a solemn processional hymn whose square four-bar phrases outstay their welcome. The chromatic harmonies which accompany the description of the raging torrent and the abyss enliven the piece, but in the next verse it returns to the tune it first thought of, with only broken octaves in the accompaniment to improve matters. It is true that Schubert could work wonders with a steady four-in-a-bar beat – witness *Winterreise* and the first of the four Impromptus op.90 – but here the magic fails to work. Only in the last verse, with a change of tonality to B minor and a change of pace, does the song spring suddenly into dramatic life, and there indeed one can hear pre-echoes of *Winterreise*.

Capell, 186–7; Einstein, 255; Fischer-Dieskau, 189

## DER 13. PSALM
**Bible trans. Moses Mendelssohn**                                          June 1819

B flat minor D663 Not in Peters Not in GA

Ach Herr, wie lan-ge willst du mein so ganz ver-ges-sen?

In the Authorised Version the psalm reads:

How long wilt thou forget met, O Lord? For ever? How long wilt thou hide thy face from me?

How long shall I take counsel in my soul, having sorrow in my heart daily? How long shall mine enemy be exalted over me?

Consider and hear me, O Lord my God: lighten mine eyes, lest I sleep the sleep of death;

Lest mine enemy say, I have prevailed against him; and those that trouble me rejoice when I am moved.

But I have trusted in thy mercy; my heart shall rejoice in thy salvation.

I will sing unto the Lord, because he hath dealt bountifully with me.

Schubert set a German translation by Moses Mendelssohn, the grandfather of the composer. The autograph, now missing but formerly with the Schubert family, is an incomplete fragment, lacking the concluding bars only. It is dated June 1819 and headed 'XII. Psalm'. This may simply be a mistake, or possibly Schubert relied on the old (Vulgate) numbering, in which the psalm is no.12. Since the surviving fragment fills both sides of a sheet, and includes all the words, it is almost certain that the final sheet has been lost.

Attempts to complete the song have been made by Mandyczewski, Hans Gál, Peter Gradenwitz, and Reinhard van Hoorickx, whose version, with a translation by Maurice Brown, is reproduced in *MR*, XXVIII, 1977, p.280. Schubert set the psalm in three sections, with a short recitative ('Lest mine enemy … I am moved') leading to the third. The right-hand triplets in the accompaniment are a familiar feature of his psalm settings. This fine song, with its concluding section in the tonic major, moves like the psalm from a mood of dark penitence to one of warm assurance.

## DER RATTENFÄNGER The Rat-catcher

**Johann Wolfgang von Goethe**                                        19 August 1815

Etwas geschwind                         G major  D255  Peters VI p.54  GA XX no.112

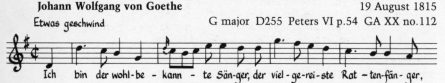

Ich  bin der wohl-be - kann - te Sän-ger, der viel-ge-rei-ste Rat - ten-fän- ger,

I am the celebrated singer, the much travelled rat-catcher, of whom this famous old city assuredly has need. And however many rats there may be, and even if the weasels join in too, I'll rid the place of every one: they must go, one and all.

Then this good-natured singer is also occasionally a child-catcher, who can tame even the naughtiest with his golden tales. However sulky the boys may be, and however suspicious the girls, when I pluck at the strings they all have to follow on behind.

And then this versatile musician is sometimes a catcher of girls. He never enters a town without charming many a one. However shy the girls may be, and however prudish the wives, they all become lovesick at the sound of his magic lute and his song.

The autograph is a first draft, in G major, dated 19 August 1815. The manuscript, which contains two other Goethe settings written on the same day (D256 and 257) is in the Taussig collection (Lund, UB). A fair copy made for Goethe in 1816, also in G major, is in the Paris Conservatoire. There is a dated copy in the Witteczek–Spaun collection (Vienna, GdM). Diabelli published the song early in 1850 in book 47 of the *Nachlass*, transposing it to F major and adding a spurious four-bar prelude. This published version is followed in the Peters edition. The *Gesamtausgabe* adheres to the autograph.

For Schubert, Goethe's 'pied piper' is a cheerful tuneful fellow with no sinister over-tones. Inevitably, the song has suffered by comparison with Wolf's more subtle setting; as might be expected, however, Schubert is much nearer to the folksong origins of the verses than is Wolf.

## DER SÄNGER The Singer

**Johann Wolfgang von Goethe**                                        February 1815

D major  D149  Peters III p.94  GA XX no.45(a) and (b)  NSA IV vol.7 pp.90, 97

Mäßig, heiter                    Recit.

Was hör ich  draußen vor dem Tor,  was auf der Brü - cke schallen?

What do I hear outside the gate? What echoes from the bridge? Let the song resound through the hall in our ears. So spake the king. The page came running. The king cried: 'Bring the old man in.'

'Greetings to you, noble lords; greetings, ladies fair! What a fine constellation, star upon star! Who can know your names? Here in this many-splendoured hall stay closed, my eyes. This is no time to feast and wonder.'

The minstrel closed his eyes, and sang out roundly. Gallantly the knights looked on, and the ladies lowered their gaze. The king, well pleased, sent for a golden chain to honour him for his song.

'Give the golden chain not to me, but to your knights, before whose bold countenance the hostile lances shatter. Give it to your chancellor, and let him carry the golden weight of it with his other burdens.

I sing as the birds sing who live in the trees. The song that issues from my throat is rich reward enough. But if I may beg one boon, let it be this. Bring me a measure of your best wine in a cup of purest gold.'

He put it to his lips and drank – 'O draught of sweetest balm! O blessed be the house, where such a gift seems trifling. If you prosper, then think of me, and thank God as warmly, as I thank you for this drink.'

The ballad was written about 1783. It was incorporated in book 2 of *Wilhelm Meister* when the *Lehrjahren* ('Years of Apprenticeship') were published in 1796. On his first unexpected appearance the Harper sings it to the assembled guests at the inn.

There are two versions of the song, and it is not altogether certain which is the earlier. The surviving autograph (Paris Conservatoire) is a fair copy made for Goethe early in 1816. It is marked 'Mässig, heiter', and dated February 1815. The song was published as op.117 in June 1829 by Josef Czerny in a version which is longer by twenty-two bars, with more recitative. The marking is *Heiter, mässig geschwind*. It is sometimes assumed that this version is based on Schubert's first draft, but it seems more likely that it represents his final revision for publication. Both versions are published in the *Gesamtausgabe* and in the *Neue Ausgabe*..

Capell sums up the song as 'a ballad of idealized mediaevalism', and it has a pleasantly archaic ring. The 'court music' at the beginning is attractive, and the subsequent sections revolved neatly round the 'circle of thirds, D major, B flat major, and F major. But the centre point of the story – the minstrel's song – is missing, and without it it is difficult to sustain the tension of the opening. The archaic style extends to the notation, which is strictly eighteenth century.

Capell, 98; Fischer-Dieskau, 42

## DER SÄNGER AM FELSEN The Singer on the Rock

**Karoline Pichler** September 1816

Unruhig, klagend E minor D482 Not in Peters GA XX no.264

Mourn, my flute, mourn for the vanished, lovely days, and the spring's swift flight here in the sere landscape, where my spirit searches in vain for the traces of sweet accustomed joy.

Mourn, my flute! Your lonely voice cries out to the day which wakes too late, to pain. My lonely songs ring out; only the echo sends them back through the shades of the still night.

Mourn, my flute, mourn for the lovely days long fled, when a heart that beat for me alone hearkened to your gentle songs, resentful of the rustling breeze, and of the slightest sound.

Mourn, my flute! Never will those days return. The anxious longing in my songs leaves Delia unmoved; she whom I often saw lost in rapture at your sound.

Mourn, my flute! Soon the harsh fates will cut short the thread of my life. Mourn then by the banks of Lethe to any kindly shade, mourn for my love and for my torment!

Schubert used the first thirty lines of a much longer poem called *Idylle*, first published in 1803. The autograph, in private possession, is a first draft dated September 1816. There are several contemporary copies, including one in the Witteczek–Spaun collection (GdM), also dated September 1816. The first publication was in 1895, in the *Gesamtausgabe*.

On the autograph Schubert wrote 'Flöte' at the beginning over the treble stave, as though to indicate that the song might be performed as a duet between voice and flute. In any case the six-bar prelude is to be repeated at the end of the song, and possibly also between verses. The song catches the elegiac mood of the poem perfectly and is much too attractive to be left in oblivion.

## DER SCHÄFER UND DER REITER The Shepherd and the Cavalier

**Friedrich de la Motte Fouqué**                                        April 1817

Mäßig, heiter          E major  D517  Peters III p.7  GA XX no.293  NSA IV vol.1 p.95

A shepherd sat amid the green, with his sweetheart in his fond embrace. Through the beech tree tops the sun shone warmly down.

Merry and blithe they talked sweet nothings. Then a cavalier came riding by past the happy pair.

'Dismount, and find some shade!' the shepherd cried to him: 'Soon the oppressive midday heat will bid you quietly rest.

Here the shrubs and flowers laugh in the pride of the morning, and my sweetheart plucks the fresh flowers to make you a garland.'

Then the stern cavalier said, 'Woods and meadows never delayed me. Fate drives me on, and ah, my solemn vow!

I sold my young life away for wretched money. Happiness I can never aspire to, at best only fame, and gold.

So trot on briskly, my good steed, past where the flowers bloom. Some day perhaps a peaceful grave will reward the toil and strife.'

The poem, entitled *Schäfer und Reiter*, was published in 1816, in a volume entitled *Gedichte aus dem Jünglingsalter* ('Poems of Youth'). The autograph is missing. The date derives from an entry in the catalogue of the Witteczek–Spaun collection (Vienna, GdM).

There are two versions. The first survives only in a copy made by Ferdinand Schubert in March 1829, and in an incomplete copy probably made by Johanna Lutz, still in the possession of her descendants. The published version is a few bars longer. It appeared as op. 13 no. 1 in December 1822. Since these early publications were published on commission by Cappi and Diabelli it seems certain that the revision was made by Schubert himself. The opus was dedicated by Schubert to Josef von Spaun.

The poem is a charming parable about the incompatibility of two attitudes to life, as a quest for happiness or a search for power. Schubert is content to treat it as an invitation for scene-painting. The galloping 6/8 theme for the cavalier is sharply contrasted with the shepherd's music, a playful little motif which sways gently between tonic and dominant, a kind of tonal analogue for the Latin tag 'Dulce est desipere in loco'. This turns the piece into a captivating duet, at the cost of some damage to its essential unity.

## DER SCHATZGRÄBER  The Treasure-seeker

**Johann Wolfgang von Goethe**                                           19 August 1815

Mäßig                              D minor/major  D256  Peters VII p.102  GA XX no.113

Poor in purse, sick at heart, I dragged myself through the long days. Poverty is the greatest scourge, riches the greatest boon! And to put an end to my anguish, I went out to dig for treasure. You shall have my soul! I signed it away with my own blood.

I drew circles within circles, set wondrous flames around, and herbs and bones. The spell was wrought. Then in the appointed place and in the prescribed way, I dug for the old treasure. The night was black and stormy.

And then I saw a distant light approaching like a star from the furthest distance, just as it struck twelve. And with no warning suddenly it grew brighter from the light of the brimming cup borne by a fair youth.

I saw his friendly eyes gleam under the garland of flowers. He stepped into the circle in the heavenly glow from the libation, and kindly he bade me drink. And I thought: this youth, with his lovely, shining gift, can truly not be the Devil!

'Take courage to live the pure life. Then you will understand my message, and never return, with fearful incantation, to this place. Dig no more in vain here. For the future, let your magic formula be hard work for the day, good company in the evening, laborious workdays and happy holidays.'

The poem, written in 1797, was inspired by an illustration in a German edition of Petrarch. It was published in the *Musenalmanach* in 1798. The autograph (Lund, UB), is a first draft dated 19 August 1815. There is a dated copy in the Witteczek–Spaun collection (Vienna, GdM). The song appeared in the final volume of the Peters edition in 1887.

Goethe's enigmatic poem ends with what seems like a quotation from the 'Gods of the Copybook Headings'. Schubert's modified strophic setting does not make much of it; the last three verses are set in the major, but the whole thing seems undercharacterised. Carl Loewe's witty and lively setting makes far more of the poem's changes of mood. The song was not included in the songbook sent to Goethe in 1816.

Capell, 105

## DER SCHIFFER  The Boatman

**Johann Mayrhofer**                                                          (?) 1817

E flat major  D536  Peters II p.52  GA XX no.318  NSA IV vol.1 pp.152, 263

I travel the river in wind and storm, my garments soaked by the pouring rain. I lash the waves with powerful strokes, filled with hopes of a bright day.

The waves chase the creaking boat, ahead looms the whirlpool, and the reef; rocks tumble down from the cliff top, and fir trees sigh like moaning ghosts.

So must it be; I have willed it so. I hate a life that goes on and on comfortably. And even if the waves were to engulf the creaking boat, I should still cherish the way I chose.

So let the waters roar in impotent rage; there wells from my heart a fount of bliss, renewing my courage – O heavenly joy, to brave the storm like a man!

The poem was published in 1818 in the second volume of *Beiträge zur Bildung für Jünglinge* ('Contributions towards the Education of Young Men'), a periodical started by Schubert's friends as a vehicle for mildly liberal and cultural ideas, and edited by Mayrhofer.

There are two versions of the song. The autograph in Vienna (MGV), marked 'Feurig', has the voice part in the treble clef. There is also an incomplete manuscript, partly in the hand of Leopold von Sonnleithner, containing the voice part and the words, in Berlin (SPK). The published version is two bars longer, marked 'Geschwind und feurig', and is written for bass voice. It appeared in June 1823 as op.21 no.2 with two other Mayrhofer settings (D553, 525), all arranged for bass voice. The opus was dedicated to the poet 'by his friend Franz Schubert'. Both versions are published in the *Neue Ausgabe*. None of the three songs that make up op.21 can be dated with certainty, and there is no firm evidence as to the date of *Der Schiffer*. On the assumption that the poem was written shortly before it appeared in the *Beiträge*, one might make a plausible guess at autumn 1817 as the date of the song.

Many of the best Mayrhofer songs move progressively forward towards a climax, reflecting the changing moods or conceptual ideas of the poem. But *Der Schiffer*, as Einstein puts it, is 'composed in one *single* passionate stroke'. A single musical idea encompasses the whole; yet the strophic form is so cunningly varied in the alternate verses that the song moves irresistibly forward from beginning to end. The forward drive itself, unusually, seems to have as much a psychological as a pictorial significance. True, there is the violence of the storm in it, but also, as the last verse makes clear, a kind of intoxication: 'O heavenly joy, to brave the storm like a man!'

Capell, 139–40; Einstein, 164; Fischer-Dieskau, 98

## DER SCHIFFER The Boatman

Friedrich von Schlegel                                    March 1820

Ziemlich langsam                    D major D694 Peters V p.190 GA XX no.377

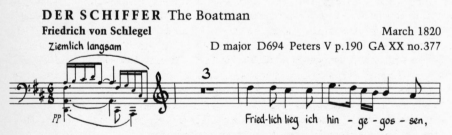

Fried-lich lieg ich hin - ge - gos - sen,

Peacefully I lie stretched out here, turning the oar this way and that, breathing the cool moonlit air, dreaming in a mood of sweet tranquillity. And I let the boat drift, look down into the shining waters where the bright stars glimmer, and again I move the oar.

If only that fair-haired girl sat opposite me, resting on the thwart and softly singing tender songs, I should feel I were in heaven. I should let the child tease me, and flirt with the good-hearted creature again.

Peacefully I lie stretched out here, dreaming in a mood of sweet tranquillity, breathing the cool moonlit air, moving the oar back and forth.

The poem was written in 1800–1 and published in *Erste Frühlingsdedichte* ('First Poems of Spring'). The autograph, in private possession, is a fair copy dated March 1820. A copy made by Ferdinand Schubert in 1840 is in the Witteczek–Spaun collection (Vienna, GdM). *Der Schiffer* was published in 1842 in book 33 of the *Nachlass*.

Schubert's genius for the tonal analogue is beautifully illustrated here. The opening figure rocks gently between tonic and dominant, as though symbolising a state of creative idleness, a trancelike immobility. The notes glide along under the pianist's hand like the drifting boat itself. The whole song is sung in a subdued *mezza voce*, which never rises above *piano*. The second verse moves to the relative minor with a slightly more choppy motion but returns in a manner that matches the poem, to the opening music. The last bar in each verse is usually intoned wordlessly. It may be, however, that Schubert intended the words of the previous bar to be repeated. The song is a striking example of the new sensuousness and fluency that come into Schubert's songs in the years 1820 and 1821.

Capell, 166; Fischer-Dieskau, 123

## DER SCHMETTERLING The Butterfly

**Friedrich von Schlegel**                                          (?) March 1820

Etwas geschwind                        F major D633 Peters IV p.49 GA XX no.179

Wie soll—ich nicht tan-zen,es macht kei-ne Mü-he,

Why should I not dance? It's no trouble, and enchanting colours shimmer here on the greensward. My gaily coloured wings gleam ever more brightly, and the scent of the blossoms is sweeter and sweeter. I feast on the flowers, you cannot protect them.

What a joy it is, late or early, to flit wantonly over hill and dale. When the evening murmurs you see the clouds aglow. When the light is golden the meadows shine with a deeper green. I feast on the flowers, you cannot protect them.

The *Abendröte* cycle was published in two parts, each containing ten poems. *Der Schmetterling* is no.7 of part I. The poems all date from 1800–1. The autograph, a first draft containing two of the settings from the cycle, is now lost, and the date of the song is uncertain. Various other poems from part I of the cycle are attributed in the Witteczek–Spaun catalogue (Vienna, GdM) to March 1820, and this one probably belongs to the same period. The song was published in April 1826 as op.57 no.1 by Thaddäus Weigl.

The poem is sometimes printed as a continuous whole, but the structure, with its refrain couplet, shows that it is really in two verses. Schubert's strophic setting matches that structure perfectly. And his genius for the invention of the precise tonal image, so marked a feature of the Schlegel songs, is again evident here. The brief introduction catches the butterfly's fluttering, inconstant movement perfectly.

## DER SIEG The Victory

**Johann Mayrhofer**                                          Early March 1824

Mäßig langsam                        F major D805 Peters V p.122 GA XX no.458

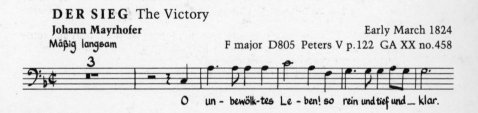

O un - bewölk-tes Le - ben! so rein und tief und— klar.

O unclouded Life, so pure and deep and clear! Age-old dreams hover wondrously over the flowers.

The spirit broke through the bonds of the body's leaden weight; it ranges large and free. The imagination is renewed by the fruits of Paradise. The ancient curse is lifted.

Whatever I may have suffered, the victor's palm is won, my longing appeased.

The Muses themselves sang the serpent to his death-sleep. My own hand struck the blow.

O unclouded Life, so pure and deep and clear! Age-old dreams hover wondrously over the flowers.

The poem appeared in the collected edition of Mayrhofer's poems at the beginning of 1824. The autograph (Vienna, GdM) was originally part of a longer manuscript containing several songs. This has been split up and most of *Der Sieg* is lost, only the last eleven bars surviving in association with another Mayrhofer setting of the same month, *Abendstern*, which is dated March 1824. Schwind refers to these songs in a letter to Schober of 6 March 1824 (*Docs*. no.441). The song was written for bass voice, and the original marking was *Mässig langsam*, which appears also on the copy in the Witteczek–Spaun collection (GdM). In June 1833 the song was published in book 22 of the *Nachlass*. The voice part was written in the treble clef, and the marking changed to *Langsam*.

*Der Sieg* is a little-known song and yet one of the most moving, so eloquently, and with such calm assurance, does it express that longing for the world beyond, the pure intellectual pessimism of the Schubertians. No other poem, moreover, embodies so clearly the complementary claim that it is the artist who holds the key to this victory over death and dissolution; 'the Muses themselves sang the serpent to his death. My own hand struck the blow'. It is a kind of apologia for Mayrhofer's long-contemplated, inevitable suicide.

Schubert's solemn hymn of praise matches the mood of serenity and catharsis in the opening lines. But the tragic implications do not escape him, so that the lines quoted above become the unforgettable emotional climax of the song, the chromatically descending bass line leaving us in no doubt about their meaning. The four sustained chords which follow take us from G flat back to the serenity of F major, a piece of Schubertian harmonic magic. Inexplicably, Mayrhofer's 'Schlange' (serpent) is changed in the *Gesamtausgabe* to 'Sphinx', making nonsense of his allusions to 'the ancient curse'. *Der Sieg* is a companion piece to the contemporary *Auflösung*. Both songs salute the prospect of eternity, *Der Sieg* with solemn awe, *Auflösung* with rapture.

Capell, 204; Fischer-Dieskau, 193

## DER STROM The River

**Author unknown**                                    (?) Autumn 1817

Schnell                    D minor D565 Peters VII p.65 GA XX no.324

Mein Le - ben wälzt___ sich mur-rend fort,

My life rolls grumbling on, rising and falling in curling billows; here it rears up, there plunges down, leaping wildly, curving high.

It hurries through the still valley, the green fields, gently rippling, longing for peace, and delighting in the tranquil life.

> Yet never finding what it seeks, and, ever longing, rages on; it rolls onward in endless flight, unsatisfied, never glad, never serene.

The autograph (Vienna, SB) is a first draft written on two sheets of old music paper. Under the title there is an inscription: 'Zum Andenken für Herrn Stadler' ('In remembrance, for Herr Stadler'). On the same manuscript is the autograph of the fourth version of *Das Grab* (D569), which is dated June 1817. Schubert's old schoolfriend Albert Stadler left Vienna in 1817 to take up an official position in his native city of Steyr, and the song clearly has some connection with this departure. It may have been written to mark the occasion, or (more likely, in view of the inscription) afterwards. It may be significant that on 17 October 1817 another of Schubert's schoolfellows, Anton Holzapfel, wrote to Stadler (*Docs.* no.110) apologising for Schubert's silence and promising that 'he will improve, and really let you hear something from him'. The authorship of the text is a mystery. Stadler himself has been suggested, also Anton Ottenwalt, with whose poems Schubert became acquainted about this time. While there is no certainty about it, these circumstances, and the internal evidence, all point to a date in the second half of 1817. Brahms owned a copy of the song, and it was at his suggestion that it was first published in the autumn of 1876. In 1887 it was included in vol.VII of the Peters edition.

In its Romantic feeling and powerful forward drive, *Der Strom* foreshadows the Schulze songs written ten years later. It is a splendidly dramatic vehicle for a strong baritone voice. Yet the text is an unremarkable treatment of a conventional theme. One might have expected a strophic setting, with some Schubertian scene-painting to match the sense. Instead, Schubert takes his cue from a single phrase in the last verse – 'never finding what it seeks' – and writes a song dominated by a mood of restless striving, and by a single pianistic figure. The descending line of the accompaniment is complemented by the singer's wide leaps, and note the separation of the vocal phrases at the words 'never finding what it seeks'; the integration of voice and piano is so complete that each would be meaningless without the other.

> Capell, 143–4

## DER STÜRMISCHE MORGEN see WINTERREISE no.18

## DER TAUCHER The Diver
**Friedrich von Schiller**                          September 1813 – end of 1814
D minor D77  Peters V p.49  GA XX no.12(a) and (b)  NSA IV vol.6 pp.78, 114

[*Synopsis*] 'Who dares to plunge into the whirlpool? Will no knight or squire fetch me the golden goblet that I now cast into the black mouth of hell? He who does may keep it.' At the king's words all are silent. Again he asks, and again. At last a noble youth, casting off belt and cloak, looks down into the raging waters and plunges into the roaring flood. 'Farewell, brave youth' – the words catch in every throat. If the king were to cast his crown into those seething depths, no one would risk his life for it in that graveyard of proud ships and gallant men. But see, a white arm appears, brandishing the golden cup. Amid cries of joy the youth breathed long and deep, greeted the light of heaven, and cried 'God save the King!'

Then he described the horrors of that underworld hell; how he found the cup dangling from a coral branch above a yawning abyss inhabited by fearsome monsters of the deep.

The king was mightily astonished, and said: 'The cup is yours, and so is this ring, adorned by the most precious stone, if you will brave the deep once more and bring news of what you see on the lowest bed of the sea.'

His daughter pleaded: 'Give up that cruel sport, father. He has done what no one else can do. If you cannot subdue your heart's desire, let the knights put the youth to shame.'

At this the king grasped the cup again and cast it into the deep. 'If you bring it back again, you shall be my noblest knight, and she who now pleads for you shall be your bride.'

Then, seized with heavenly power, the brave youth dived once more into the depths – never to return.

Schiller's splendid poem was finished in June 1797. Presumably the source was some Germanic version of the Beowulf saga, for the story has obvious links with Beowulf's fight with the monster in the undersea cavern. There are twenty-seven verses. Schubert made many alterations in the text.

The first version is dated 13 September at the beginning of the autograph and 5 April 1814 at the end. The second version, finished in August 1814, is a radical revision, which makes a much sharper distinction between the arioso and the recitative sections. Both versions have the voice part in the bass clef. At the end of 1814, Schubert revised the work once again, adding a long piano interlude before the last verse and redrafting the King's last speech. For this version only sketches and a fair copy made for Johann Leopold Ebner with the voice part in the treble clef survive. The song was first published as book 12 of the *Nachlass* (1831).

*Der Taucher* is the most ambitious and in many ways the most impressive realisation of Schubert's obstinate belief in the song as a miniature music drama, a reduction of grand opera to the scale of the drawing room. The early epic/horror motifs are very much in evidence; the opening bars give us an arresting version of the familiar theme with which *Hagars Klage* begins. The running semiquavers, the isolated demisemiquaver groups, and the descending scale passages are all familiar; the piano interlude is an astonishing tour de force which links the ominous repeated quavers with a rising chromatic line, irresistibly suggesting a later masterpiece, *Gruppe aus dem Tartarus*. Archaic as the form now seems, this music still has power to move.

App. IV; Capell, 81; Introduction to NSA IV vol.6; Schnapper, 60–2

## DER TOD OSCARS The Death of Oscar

**James Macpherson (Ossian)** February 1816

Mäßig, in schmerzlicher Erinnerung  C minor D375 Peters IV p.204 GA XX no.187

The text is a translation by Edmund von Harold of a prose poem by Macpherson, here reproduced in a shortened version:

My eyes are blind with tears, but memory beams on my heart. Oscar, my son, shall I see thee no more! He fell as the moon in a storm, as the sun from the midst of his course. Chief of the warriors, Oscar my son, shall I see thee no more!

Dermid and Oscar were one: they reaped the battle together. Their friendship was strong as their steel, and death walked between them to the field.

They killed mighty Dargo in the field, Dargo who never fled in war. His daughter was fair as the morn, mild as the beam of night. The warriors saw her and loved; their souls were fixed on the maid. Each must possess her or die. But her soul was fixed on Oscar. She forgot the blood of her father, and loved the hand that slew him. They fought by the brook of the mountain, by the streams of Branno. Blood tinged the running water, and curled round the mossy stones. The stately Dermid fell, and smiled in death.

And fallest thou, son of Diaran! Dermid who never yielded in war, do I thus see thee fall! – He went, and returned to the maid of his love; but she perceived his grief.

What shades thy mighty soul?

Though once renowned for the bow, O maid, I have lost my fame. Fixed on the tree by the brook is the shield of the valient Gormur, whom I slew in battle. I have wasted the day in vain, nor could my arrow pierce it.

Let me try, son of Caruth, the skill of Dargo's daughter. My hands were taught the bow: my father delighted in my skill.

He stood behind the shield. Her arrow flew, and pierced his breast. Blessed be that hand of snow, and that bow of yew! Who but the daughter of Dargo was worthy to slay the son of Caruth? Lay me in the earth, my fair one, by the side of Dermid.

Oscar, the maid replied, I have the soul of the mighty Dargo. My sorrow I can end. She pierced her white bosom with the steel. She fell, she trembled, and died.

By the brook of the hill their graves are laid; a birch's unequal shade covers their tomb.

The text was not attributed directly by Macpherson to 'Ossian' but was included in the notes to *Temora* in the edition of 1762. Harold's translation was published in 1782. See OSSIAN SONGS. The autograph is lost. The song is dated February 1816 in the catalogue of the Witteczek–Spaun collection (Vienna, GdM). It was published in July 1830 as book 5 of the *Nachlass*. Macpherson's prose poem, with its three deaths and a battle, is not the most cheerful of his works, and Schubert's episodic setting, consisting of recitative and short arioso passages, does little to reconcile us to it. The vigour and verve that inform Schubert's earliest solo cantatas seem to be missing in this last of the Ossian songs.

## DER TOD UND DAS MÄDCHEN Death and the Maiden
**Matthias Claudius**

February 1817

D minor D531 Peters I p.221 GA XX no.302

*The Maiden:* Pass me by, ah, pass me by, fearsome spectre. I am still young. Go away, loved one, and touch me not.

*Death:* Give me your hand, you fair and tender creature. I am your friend, and do not come to chastise. Be of good cheer. I am not to be feared. You will sleep softly in my arms.

The poem was published in the Göttingen *Almanach*, 1775. The original autograph belonged to Ferdinand Schubert and came into the possession of the composer's half-brother Andreas in 1860. Andreas divided it up into eight pieces which he used as prizes to distribute among his favourite pupils. Six of the pieces, including one which bears the date February 1817, are now in Vienna (GdM). A seventh is in private possession, and the eighth is missing. The song is written for solo voice, not as a vocal duet. It was published on commission by Cappi and Diabelli as op.7 no.3 in November 1821 and dedicated by Schubert to Ludwig, Count Széchényi. The metronome marking in brackets appears on the copies made for Albert Stadler and J. L. Ebner (Lund, UB) and stems presumably from Schubert himself. The copy made for the printer has not survived.

The song is a splendid illustration of Schubert's ability to give to old and familiar harmonic sequences new emotional force. But its fame is largely due to extraneous circumstances: first, to the poem itself, an eloquent statement of the more merciful view of Death which supplanted the grotesque horrors of the medieval view for Schubert's generation. In 1824, influenced no doubt by the popularity of the song, he adapted the piano prelude and part of the accompaniment to the second half for use as the theme of the variation movement in his D minor String Quartet ('Death and the Maiden'), thus underwriting the song's claim to immortality. Nowadays it is the quartet theme rather than the song which sounds inevitable in its progression.

Spaun's verses, *Der Jüngling und der Tod*, were clearly written as a kind of tribute to the success of *Der Tod und das Mädchen*, and were set by Schubert in March 1817.

Capell, 134–5; Fischer-Dieskau, 85–6

## DER TRAUM The Dream
**Ludwig Hölty**                                                                                    17 June 1815

A major  D213  Peters VI p.96  GA XX no.80

I dreamt I was a little bird, and flew into her lap. To pass the time, I pulled undone the bows upon her breast, and then flew skittishly onto her white hand, then back to her bodice, pecking at its red ribbon.

Then I fluttered onto her fair hair, and twittered with pleasure, and, when I tired, came to rest on her snowy breast. No bed of violets in paradise surpasses this couch. How sweetly, sweetly, could one sleep, there on her filmy breast.

As I sank deeper, her fingers caressed me gently, which thrilled me body and soul, rousing me from happy slumber. So wondrous kind she looked at me, and offered me her mouth, so that I cannot describe how glad I was.

Then I hopped on one leg, and playfully fanned her red cheeks cool with my little wing. But ah! no earthly joy endures, whether by day or night. My sweet dream quickly vanished, and I awoke.

The poem, originally entitled *Ballade*, was written in 1775. The autograph is lost, but there is a copy in the Witteczek–Spaun collection (Vienna, GdM) dated 17 June 1815 and another in the Stadler collection (Lund, UB). The song was published in 1865 by C. A. Spina as op.172 no.1 (*Sechs Lieder ... von Franz Schubert*). Holty's embarrassingly twee poem is set to a 6/8 strophe marked 'Tändelnd. Sehr leise' ('Flirting. Very light'). The effect is tuneful, but slight.

# DER UNGLÜCKLICHE The Forlorn One

**Karoline Pichler**

January 1821

B minor D713 Peters IV p.70 GA XX no.390(a) and (b)

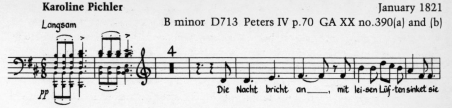

Die Nacht bricht an____, mit lei-sen Lüf-ten sinket sie

Night falls, sinks down with light airs upon tired mortals; soft sleep, death's brother, beckons them, and lays them kindly to their daily rest.

Now only cunning and pain perchance keep watch over the earth, bereft of light. Now let your wounds bleed, poor heart, since nothing can disturb me.

Sink into the depths of your misery; and if half-forgotten sorrows have slept in the tormented breast, then rouse them with bitter-sweet delight.

Reckon up lost happiness, count all the flowers in paradise, from which the harsh hand of fate banished you in the golden days of youth.

You have loved, you have found happiness, before which all earthly pleasure fades; you have found a heart to understand you, and your keenest hopes have been fulfilled.

Then the cruel voice of authority cast you down out of heaven and destroyed your peace of mind. Your vision, all too beautiful, returned to the better world from whence it came.

Now all the bonds of sympathy are rent asunder: no heart beats now for me in all the world.

The poem comes from the novel *Olivier*. Its last six lines are omitted by Schubert. There are two versions: the first, in 12/8 time, exists in an incomplete sketch on two staves of the first seventy-one bars and in a complete fair copy dated January 1821. Both manuscripts are in Vienna (SB). The published version, however, is in 6/8 time, with other minor variations. The fair copy made for the printer is lost. The song was published in August 1827 as op.84 (later changed to op.87) no.1 by A.W. Pennauer. Both versions are published in the *Gesamtausgabe*.

According to Vogl's wife Kunigunde (*Memoirs* p.217) it was this song that featured in a famous story, often called in evidence to prove the unconscious workings of Schubert's imagination. Shown a manuscript of a song which Vogl had performed some weeks earlier, Schubert is supposed to have said: 'That's not bad! Who's it by?' *Der Unglückliche*, however, hardly suggests genius working with somnambulistic unselfconsciousness: on the contrary, there seems to be something contrived about it, something which led Capell to dismiss the song as 'more a parade of emotion than emotion itself'.

In January 1821 Schubert was much concerned with the production of concert pieces (it is the month of Schiller's *Sehnsucht*, of A.W. von Schlegel's *Die gefangenen Sänger*, and possibly of Széchényi's *Die abgeblühte Linde*). Whatever lay behind Schubert's possibly ironical remark, it is likely that *Der Unglückliche* was intended as a concert aria for Vogl to sing at one of Karoline Pichler's prestigious receptions. There is an element of pastiche about it, suggested by the thematic echoes – the Andante of the A major Sonata (D664) in the opening section, *Marie* at the close, and in the B minor passages eloquent pre-echoes of the 'Unfinished' Symphony. Yet at the same time it is a splendid dramatic scena, faithful to the text and, in the hands of a powerful and sympathetic artist, brilliantly effective.

App. IV; Capell, 169–70; Einstein, 179; Fischer-Dieskau, 140

## DER VATER MIT DEM KIND The Father with his Child

**Eduard von Bauernfeld** January 1827

Langsam D major D906 Peters III p.172 GA XX no.514

Dem Va - ter liegt das Kind im Arm, es ruht so wohl, es ruht so warm,

The child lies in his father's arms, resting so safe and so warm; smiles sweetly: 'Dear father mine' – and with the smile he falls asleep.

The father stoops, scarce breathing, and listens to the dreaming child; thinking of times gone by with melancholy tenderness.

And a tear from the depths of his heart falls on the child's mouth; quickly he kisses the tear away, and rocks him gently to and fro.

He would not give up his darling child to gain a whole world. Happy the man in this world, who can cradle his happiness in his arms.

This is the only surviving setting of words by Schubert's friend Bauernfeld; it must have been set from the author's manuscript. The autograph, a first draft dated January 1827 (Vienna, GdM), shows that Schubert first sketched the song in 6/8 time. A copy in the Witteczek–Spaun collection (GdM) is similarly dated. The published version, in 2/2 time, is presumably based on Schubert's fair copy. But it did not appear until May 1832, when it was included in book 17 of the *Nachlass*.

Schubert's uncertainty about the basic rhythm seems symptomatic of a lack of conviction in the song, not surprising perhaps in view of the sentimental text. In *alla breve* time it is difficult to avoid making the song sound halting and monotonous; in the year of *Winterreise* it can only rank as a near miss.

## DER VATERMÖRDER The Parricide

**Gottlieb Conrad Pfeffel** 26 December 1811

Allegro con moto C minor D10 Not in Peters GA XX no.4 NSA IV vol.6 p.46

Ein Va - ter starb von des Soh - nes Hand.

A father died by his son's hand. No wolf, no tiger, but man, the prince of beasts, invented parricide.

The evildoer fled to the forest, to escape the law's revenge, but he could not escape the inner judge.

There the sheriff came across him, wasted and haggard, mute and pale, his clothes in tatters, like a demon of despair.

The savage man, incensed, destroyed a nest with a stone and murdered all the fledglings.

'Stop!' cried the sheriff, 'What right have you, accursed evildoer, to plague the innocent little creatures so?'

'Innocent?' said he, stammering with fury. 'I did it because the hellish brood called me a parricide.'

The man looked at him; his mad expression betrayed his deed. He seized the murderer, who was punished for his knavery on the wheel.

Blessed conscience, you are the last friend of virtue. The thunder of your voice is a fearful song of triumph to your enemy.

Pfeffel's 'Poetic Essays' were published in Vienna in 1802. But the author is not named on the autograph, and Schubert may not even have known who he was. He was identified by a Dr Engelmann of Vienna after the song had been published in the *Gesamtausgabe* in 1894. The autograph (Vienna, SB) is a first draft dated 26 December 1811. On the reverse is a cancelled sketch for Schubert's first opera, *Der Spiegelritter*.

This last of the four dramatic ballads written by the schoolboy composer in 1811 is perhaps the least interesting. Like the others, it is inspired by the example of Zumsteeg, and the idiom has much in common with *Hagars Klage* and *Leichenfantasie*, but its originality is less striking than in those earlier songs. Schubert's stock of compositional motifs is still comparatively limited, and their significance is not precisely differentiated. So the 'flight motif' which emerges here at bar 26 is clearly related to the 'boiling water' motif which plays an important part in *Der Taucher* and elsewhere.

Fischer-Dieskau, 27–8; Schnapper, 98–9

## DER WACHTELSCHLAG The Quail's Cry

**Samuel Friedrich Sauter**
(?) 1822

Etwas lebhaft
A major D742 Peters II p.134 GA XX no.401

Ach! mir schallts dorten so lieb-lich her-vor: Fürchte Gott! fürchte Gott!

Ah, how sweet that sound from yonder comes: 'Fear the Lord! Fear the Lord!' The quail's cry rings in my ears. As he sits concealed among the stalks in the cornfield he warns the listener: 'Love the Lord! Love the Lord!' He is so good and kind.

Again comes that leaping call, saying: 'Praise the Lord! Praise the Lord!' who can commend you. Consider the wonderful fruits of the field, and ponder them in your hearts, you dwellers upon earth. 'Thank the Lord! Thank the Lord!' For he feeds and sustains you.

And if the Lord of Nature affrights you in the storm, 'Pray to God! Pray to God!' He spares the good earth when it calls upon his aid. When you fear for the dangers of warriors in battle, 'Trust in God! Trust in God!' See, he will not tarry long.

The poem, written in June 1796, was published at Heilbronn in 1798 in Carl Lang's 'Almanach of Domestic and Sociable Pleasures'. It was earlier believed to have been a translation from Metastasio. But Friedländer has shown that it is a reworking of a folksong widely known in the eighteenth century. In German folklore the quail, whose dactylic call forms the basis of Schubert's (and Beethoven's) setting, is noted for its piety.

The autograph is lost. The only hard evidence as to the date of the song is the fact that it first appeared on 30 July 1822 as a supplement to the *ZfK*. In May 1827 it was republished by Diabelli as op. 68 in a slightly revised version, doubtless authorised by the composer. The first line, which originally ran, 'Ach! mir schallt's dorten so lieblich hervor', now became 'Horch, wie schallt's dorten ...'. This was followed by Friedländer in the Peters edition. The 1827 edition also carried a translation of the text into Italian, probably by Jacob Nicolaus Craigher.

Schubert's modified strophic version, with its minor inflection in the third verse, is much nearer to the folksong tradition than Beethoven's more elaborate setting. Like many other songs of 1822 (e.g. the Bruchmann songs *Im Haine* and *Am See*) it seems to show a renewed concern for the strength and simplicity of the vocal line. Critical opinion has been rather reserved – 'not outstanding' is Friedländer's judgment – but it deserves to rank as the definitive setting of the verses.

Capell, 173; Friedländer, 450

## DER WALLENSTEINER LANZKNECHT BEIM TRUNK
### Wallenstein's Lancer in his Cups
**Karl Gottfried von Leitner**                      November 1827

G minor D931 Peters III p.198 GA XX no.548

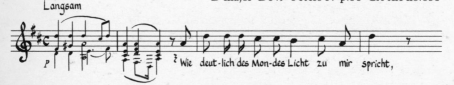

Mäßig

*Hel schen-ket mir im Hel - me ein! der ist—des Knap-pen Be - cher,*

Ho! Pour it into my helmet, which is the soldier's cup. It is not shallow or small, and that suits the hearty drinker.

It has shielded me a thousand times from club, and sword and spear, and how it serves me as a tankard, and as my pillow at night.

Just lately at Lützen it was struck by a spear – I was almost felled to the ground. Yes, had it gone through, I would never have drunk another drop.

But it didn't happen so, thanks to you, my trusty helmet! The Swede soon paid for it, and bit the dust.

Well, God comfort him. Fill her up! Fill her up! My tankard has deep wounds. But it can still hold good German wine, and I shall oft enjoy it.

The poem, written in 1819, had been published in 1825. The autograph (Vienna, SB) and a copy in the Witteczek–Spaun collection (Vienna, GdM) are dated November 1827. Haslinger, who owned the manuscript, advertised his intention to publish the song early in 1829. However, it appeared first as the supplement to an almanac published by Anton Strauss in 1830, and was republished in 1836 as book 27 of the *Nachlass*. Leitner's poem may owe something to Schiller's treatment of the subject in part I of *Wallenstein*. Schubert's setting is a rollicking drinking song, with something appropriately raw and archaic about the modulations.

## DER WANDERER The Wanderer
**Friedrich von Schlegel**                          (?) February 1819

D major D649 Peters IV p.58 GA XX no.351

Langsam

*Wie deut-lich des Mon-des Licht zu mir spricht,*

How plainly the moonlight speaks to me, to cheer me on my way: 'Follow faithfully the old way, choose no country for your home, lest harder times bring endless trouble. You must move on to other lands, lightly casting away every care.'

Thus in the darkness I take my way, sunk in thought: gentle ebb and high flood tide. Climbing boldly, singing cheerfully, the world seems good to me. Smoothly reflected everything seems clear; nothing is distorted, or withered in the heat of the day. Happy in my surroundings, though alone, I go.

The poem comes from part II of the cycle *Abendröte*. The autograph (SB) is undated, but two other songs from part II of the cycle (D642, 656) can be firmly dated January–February 1819, and the catalogue of the Witteczek–Spaun collection (Vienna, GdM) gives February 1819 also for this one. A copy in the Spaun–Cornaro collection (Vienna, privately owned) has the tempo indication 'Mässig'. The song was published by Cappi and Czerny in November 1826 as op.65 no.2. The author is wrongly given as A. W. von Schlegel.

The subtlety of the word-setting in this haunting but little-known song is remarkable. The poem divides into four irregular verses rhyming AABBA. Schubert organises them into two strophes, but treats the voice line and the accompaniment with such finesse that the piece has something of the quality of a through-composed song. The Romantic irony of the verses is matched by a harmonic structure which contrasts diatonic stability in the first half of the strophe with a kind of groping chromaticism in the second, so that the serenity of D major, like that of the moon, seems ever present yet elusive; the flattened sixth at the end (bars 13 and 25) somehow sums up the sadness of human striving after perfection. With what subtlety also does Schubert inflect the harmony at bars 9 and 22 to reinforce the text. Masterly in its suggestion of loneliness (note the unison octaves between voice and piano) and a kind of troubled serenity, *Der Wanderer* shows how Schubert in his middle years reached out towards what might be called the Wolfian ideal of the lied.

Capell, 164–5; Einstein, 187–8; Fischer-Dieskau, 121–2

## DER WANDERER The Wanderer

**Georg Philipp Schmidt von Lübeck**                              October 1816

C sharp minor  D489, 493  Peters I p.184  GA XX no.266(a) and (b)  NSA IV
vol.1 pp.26, 200, 204

Down from the mountains have I come. The valley steams, the ocean roars. I wander on silent and unhappy, and, sighing, ask myself constantly: Where?
  The sun seems too cold to me here, the flower is faded, and life is old; and what men say has an empty ring, I am a stranger everywhere.
  Where you are, my beloved land, sought after, dreamed of, yet never known. The land, the land, so green with promise, the land where all my roses bloom.
  Where all my friends together roam, and where my dead friends rise again; the land which speaks in my own tongue, O land, where are you?
  I wander on silent and unhappy, and, sighing, ask myself constantly: Where? In a ghostly whisper comes the answer: 'There, where you are not, there is happiness!'

Schmidt of Lübeck, an otherwise obscure doctor and public administrator, achieved a limited fame through this one poem, which succeeds at least in encapsulating neatly and memorably the essence of Romantic yearning for that which lies out of reach. It was first published in Leipzig in 1808, under the title *Des Fremdlings Abendlied* ('The Stranger's Evening Song'), in Becker's 'Pocket-book of Sociable Pleasures'. An extended version appeared in 1811. But Schubert's source was an anthology published in Vienna in 1815 by Deinhardstein entitled *Dichtungen für Kunstredner* ('Poems for Recitation'). In this the poem's title is *Der Unglückliche* ('The Unhappy One'), and the author is named as Werner (presumably Zacharias Werner, whose poems were known to Schubert). *Der Wanderer* was Schubert's own title. This version reverts to five verses. In these transformations the famous last line underwent some changes. Originally it ran: 'Da, wo du nicht bist, blüht das Glück!' In the 1815 version this becomes: 'Dort, wo du nicht bist, ist das Glück!' which Schubert himself changed to 'Dort, wo du nicht bist, dort ist das Glück!'

There are three versions of the song: (1) The original autograph (Vienna, GdM), dated

October 1816, in C sharp minor. (2) A fair copy transposed to B minor, and written out for bass voice, for many years in the possession of the Esterházy family. There is a photocopy in Berlin (SPK). (3) The published version in C sharp minor, marked Sehr langsam'. This appeared in May 1821 as op.4 no.1 (Cappi and Diabelli on commission), dedicated to Johann Ladislaus Pyrker.

*Der Wanderer* and *Erlkönig* contributed most to Schubert's fame as a songwriter during his lifetime. The former hit off unerringly both the mood and the taste of the time; not surprisingly bars 23–30 provide us with the most familiar version of Schubert's most significant harmonic sequence, the 'Sehnsucht' motif, which he himself used as the theme of the 'Wanderer' Fantasy six years later. Schmidt's mediocre poem provided Schubert with the prototype of the alienated man, the refugee from life and fate, who is the central figure of the song cycles and of so many of the songs of the last years. But the song itself no longer moves us in quite the same way, though its remains a splendidly dramatic essay in the ballad form.

Capell, 114–15; Fischer-Dieskau, 80–2

## DER WANDERER AN DEN MOND The Wanderer Addresses the Moon

**Johann Gabriel Seidl** (?) March 1826

Etwas bewegt    G minor D870 Peters IV p.59 GA XX no.506

Ich auf der Erd, am Himmel du, wir wandern bei-de rü-stig zu:-

I on earth, you in heaven, both of us moving sturdily on; I sad and cheerless, you so gentle and clear, what can the difference really be?

I go as a stranger from one region to another, so homeless and unknown; uphill, downhill, in and out of the forests, but ah, nowhere do I make my home.

But you traverse up and down, from your cradle in the west to your grave in the east, sail in and out of every land, and yet you are at home wherever you are.

The heavens, endlessly outstretched, are your beloved native land. Happy is he, who wherever he goes, stands ever on his native soil.

The autograph (Berlin, SPK) is a first draft on the same manuscript as *Das Zügenglöcklein*. The catalogue of the Witteczek–Spaun collection (Vienna, GdM) dates both songs 1826. They were published with another Seidl song, *Im Freien*, which can be confidently dated March 1826, by Tobias Haslinger as op.80 in May 1827. This opus was dedicated by Schubert to Joseph Witteczek. *Der Wanderer an den Mond* was originally included in the programme for Schubert's public concert on 26 March 1828, but in the event it was replaced by *Fischerweise*. The autograph made for the first edition is now in the Kolbenheyer Gesellschaft, Vienna.

*Der Wanderer an den Mond* foreshadows *Gute Nacht*. We hear in it the lilt, the *gehende Bewegung*, of the beginning of *Winterreise*, heightened in this song by the strumming of the wanderer's guitar in the prelude. It anticipates also another salient feature of *Gute Nacht*, in the use of the minor–major change as a structural element in the song. For the change is more of a metamorphosis than a modulation, symbolising as it does the gulf between our shadowy human existence and the clarity and perfection of the heavens. The song might carry as its motto the words from *Gute Nacht* 'Es zieht ein Mondenschatten als mein Gefähre mit' ('A shadow cast by the moon is my companion'). Not surprisingly, it has proved the most popular of the Seidl settings, and perhaps the best known of Schubert's 'moon songs'.

Fischer-Dieskau, 197–8

**DER WEGWEISER** see DIE SCHÖNE MÜLLERIN no.20

## DER WEIBERFREUND The Philanderer

**Abraham Cowley trans. J. F. von Ratschky**                    25 August 1815

Scherzhaft                          A major  D271  Not in Peters  GA XX no.128

Noch fand von E-vens Töch-ter-scha-ren ich kei - ne, die mir nicht ge-fiel.

The text was identified by Odd Udbye of Oslo. The ultimate source is a poem by Abraham Cowley (1609–72) called *The Inconstant*. The first two of its seven verses run:

> I never yet could see that face
> Which had no dart for me;
> From fifteen years, to fifties space,
> They all victorious be.
> Love thou'rt a Devil; if I may call thee One,
> For sure in Me thy name is Legion.
>
> Colour, or Shape, good Limbs, or Face,
> Goodness or Wit in all I find.
> In Motion or in Speech a grace,
> If all fail, yet 'tis Woman-kind;
> And I'm so weak, the Pistol need not be
> Double, or treble charg'd to murder Me.

A free translation of this by Josef Franz von Ratschky appeared in Becker's 'Pocket-book of Sociable Pleasures', published in Leipzig in 1795, where, presumably, Schubert found his text. The autograph (Vienna, SB) is a first draft dated 25 August 1815. There is a dated copy in the Witteczek–Spaun collection (Vienna, GdM). The song has repeat marks at the end, but it is not clear how many verses Schubert intended to be sung. The song was first published in the *Gesamtausgabe* in 1895. Schubert's marking, *Scherzhaft*, suggests that this is no more than a pretty trifle; but it is a well-crafted one, with something of the canzonet about it.

## DER WINTERABEND The Winter Evening

**Karl Gottfried von Leitner**                           January 1828

Nicht zu langsam                    B flat major  D938  Peters V p.148  GA XX no.551

Es ist so still, so heim - lich um mich,

It is so still and secret all about me. The sun has set, the day has gone; how quickly now the evening grows grey. I like it so; the day is too loud for me.

But now all is peaceful: no hammering from the blacksmith or the plumber, people have gone away, tired. And the snow has spread her blanket over the streets, so that the carts do not rumble on their way.

How good it is to have this blessed peace. There in the dark I sit, quite withdrawn, quite self-concerned: only the moonlight enters softly here in my room ...

It knows me and leaves me to my silence, and just gets to work, taking up spindle and gold thread, and spins and weaves smiling sweetly, and drapes the furniture and the walls all round with its shimmering veil. It is indeed a quiet, well-loved visitation, which does not disturb the house in the least. If it wants to stay, there is plenty of room, and if it finds no joy here, then off it goes.

I like to sit silent at the window then, and look up at the clouds and the stars, thinking back to the lovely vanished days of long, ah very long, ago. I think of her, and of love's happiness, and quietly I sigh, and think, and think.

The poem had already appeared in the *ZfK* in 1825, but it did not attract Schubert's attention until after his visit to Graz in September 1827. The autograph (New York, PML) and a copy in the Witteczek–Spaun collection (Vienna, GdM) are dated January 1828. Leitner's title was *Winterabend*. Schubert omitted three lines from the middle of the poem. Shortly after Schubert's death Tobias Haslinger announced his intention to publish the song, but it had to wait until October 1835, when Diabelli published it as book 26 of the *Nachlass*.

A mood of stillness and serenity can be established either by music that scarcely moves at all (e.g. *Meeres Stille, Nacht und Träume*) or by music that is constantly in motion, like a dance. In this song, and in the companion piece written in the same month (*Die Sterne*), Schubert uses the second method. In *Der Winterabend* the sense of security, of inner calm, is established not only by the repetitive semiquavers in the pianist's right hand; the effect is reinforced by one of the happiest of Schubert's melodic fingerprints, the little group of four semiquavers which circle the tonic as the singer returns to it at the end of each sentence. The effect is enchanting, though the length of the song (ninety-six bars) and the discursive nature of the verses impose a certain strain on the formula. Capell complains that the mood needs to be more fully defined, but the trouble seems rather to be that it is difficult to sustain. However, there are no obstacles to the success of the song that cannot be overcome with the help of a little discreet rubato.

Capell, 246; Fischer-Dieskau, 270

## DER ZUFRIEDENE The Contented Man

**Christian Ludwig Reissig**                                        23 October 1815

A major  D320  Not in Peters  GA XX no.167

Mäßig

Zwar schuf das Glück hie - nie - den mich we - der reich noch groß,

Though fortune has made me neither rich nor great here on earth, yet I am as happy as if the fairest lot were mine. A friend was vouchsafed to me quite after my own heart. For he too is in his element kissing, drinking and jesting.

In merry mood and wise many a bottle have we drained together; for wine is the best steed on the journey of life.

If perchance a worse fate should befall me, then I reflect: there is no rose without thorns in this world.

The autograph, which is in private possession, is dated 23 October 1815, and so also is the entry in the catalogue of the Witteczek–Spaun collection (Vienna, GdM). The song was first published in the *Gesamtausgabe* in 1895. It seems to be more than coincidence that both the songs Schubert wrote on 23 October 1815 had previously been set by Beethoven, in the same key and manner. In *Der Zufriedene* the resemblance extends to the triplet figures in the accompaniment.

# DER ZÜRNENDE BARDE The Angry Bard

**Franz von Bruchmann**                                    February 1823

Geschwind, kraftvoll                        G minor D785 Peters V p.26 GA XX no.421

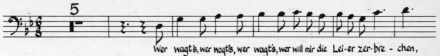

Wer wagt's, wer wagt's, wer wagt's, wer will mir die Lei-er zer-bre - chen,

Who dares, who dares, who seeks to destroy my lyre? It is still day, still day; still burns my strength, to avenge myself.

> Come then, all of you, whoever will make so bold. My lyre grew green out of the rocky cliffs.

> I split the wood from the giant oak beneath which our forefathers danced at Odin's feet.

> For the strings I stole the sun's bright crimson beams, as it sank once in bliss into the flowery vale.

> My lyre will never forsake the ancestral oaks, and the red gold of evening, so long as the gods smile on me.

Bruchmann's poems were never published. Schubert must have set the text from the manuscript. The autograph, in private possession, is dated February 1823, and has the voice part in the bass clef. It appears to have been used as the source for the first edition, for a note at the beginning (not in Schubert's hand) reads: 'NB To be set in the treble clef'. There is a copy in the Witteczek–Spaun collection (Vienna, GdM). Diabelli published the song in April 1831, in book 9 of the *Nachlass*.

As Capell hints, the song has little regard for the intellectual aspect of the poem, which is surely intended as a passionate protest against the stifling of the artist in Metternich's illiberal and materialist Vienna. But it is a splendidly powerful song none the less, and in the hands of a baritone with an edge to the voice and a strong sense of rhythm it is irresistible. The printed versions (except the *Gesamtausgabe*, which follows the autograph) have the voice line in the treble clef.

> Capell, 176; Fischer-Dieskau, 158

# DER ZÜRNENDEN DIANA To the Angry Diana

**Johann Mayrhofer**                                    December 1820

Risoluto                        A flat major D707 Peters II p.75 GA XX no.387(a) and (b)

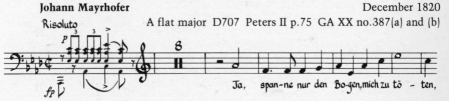

Ja,    span-ne nur den Bo-gen,mich zu tö - ten,

Yes, draw your bow to slay me, goddess; flushed with anger you are even more lovely. Never shall I regret

> That I espied you on the leafy bank, surpassing all the nymphs as they bathed; spreading beauty through the wilderness like rays of light.

> Your image will gladden me in death. He to whom you have revealed your glory unveiled will breathe more cleanly, more freely.

> Your arrow struck home – yet gently flow the warm waves from the wound. My dull senses still tremble at the vision of this last sweet hour.

There are two versions. The first draft (Vienna, GdM), dated December 1820, is in A major and marked 'Entschlossen' ('resolute'). It is entitled *Die zürnende Diana*, but this has been corrected by another hand. There are pencilled corrections on the draft, many of which are embodied in the revised version. The fair copy (Vienna, SB), also dated December 1820, is in A flat and marked 'Feurig'. The main changes are in the middle section, which is slightly longer. This autograph has the same title as the first draft. This second version was published by Cappi and Co. in February 1825 as op.36 no.1 and dedicated by Schubert to Frau Katharina von Lácsny. Both versions are published in the *Gesamtausgabe*. The song was performed by Johann Hoffmann at a Philharmonic Society 'Evening Entertainment' on 24 February 1825.

On the thirteen lines of Mayrhofer's poem Schubert builds an extended aria of 170 bars. Both the voice line and the accompaniment are operatic in scale and style; the unrepentant Endymion finally expires in an ecstasy of sighing phrases over two and a half pages of music. The song is a splendid vehicle for a *Heldentenor*, and an impressive achievement, but like many of the numbers in Schubert's mature operas, it is open to the criticism that it 'protests too much' – that the lyrical extension exceeds the permissive limits of the drama. To compare the impassioned flow of *Der zürnenden Diana* with the classical poise of *Iphigenia* (1817) is to realise that the influence of the theatre on Schubert's style in the intervening years had not been entirely beneficial.

Capell, 161–2; Einstein, 192; Fischer-Dieskau, 204

## DER ZWERG The Dwarf
**Matthäus von Collin** (?) November 1822

A minor D771 Peters II p.55 GA XX no.425 NSA IV vol.1 p.160

In the grey light the mountains already fade away; the ship drifts on the sea's smooth swell. On board, the queen sails with her dwarf.

She gazes up at the high curving vault, at the far blue distance, woven with strands of light, crossed by the pale band of the milky way.

She cries out: 'Never yet have you lied to me, stars. Soon I shall depart. You tell me so. In truth, I'll gladly die.'

The dwarf steps towards the queen, to tie the red silk cord about her neck; and weeps, as though he meant to blind himself with grief.

He speaks: 'You yourself are to blame for this wrong, because you have forsaken me for the king. Now only your death can kindle joy in me. I grant that I shall hate myself for ever, because I have brought about your death with this my own hand; still must you pale before your early grave.'

She lays her hand on her young heart, and the heavy tears run down from her eyes, which she would raise to heaven in prayer.

'May you reap no anguish from my death,' she says. Then the dwarf kisses her pale cheeks, and forthwith her senses fail.

Bemused by death the dwarf gazes upon the lady, and with his own hands commits her to the deep. His heart burns with longing for her. He will never more set foot on any shore.

The poem was published in 1813 in *Selam*, an annual miscellany which appeared in Vienna. The original title was *Treubruch* ('Perfidy'), and a contemporary copy of Schubert's setting made for Karl Haugwitz and now in the Moravské Museum in Brno has the same title, so presumably Schubert used it. However, the autograph is lost, so the assumption cannot be verified.

*Der Zwerg* was published as op.22 no.1 by Sauer and Leidesdorf in May 1823 under its familiar title and was dedicated by Schubert to the author. The date of composition is not certain. According to a report by the painter Franz Stohl (*Memoirs* p.374), it was sung at a reception given by Karl Pinterics towards the end of 1822, and certainly Vogl sang it at St Florian in the spring of 1823 (*Docs.* no.364). It was among the first Schubert songs published by Sauer and Leidesdorf, and according to a story attributed to Randhartinger, Schubert came under some pressure from the publishers to finish it. '*Der Zwerg* is allowed', he writes, 'to be a masterpiece, which the composer dashed off, when pressed by his publisher to write a song off-hand, without any preparation, keeping up a conversation all the while with a friend who had come to take him out for a walk' (Kreissle, I, 317). Like most of Randhartinger's stories, this should be treated with reserve; but in autumn 1822 Schubert decided to break with Diabelli and made a new agreement with Leidesdorf, which lends some support to the view that the song was written before the end of 1822. The internal evidence (see below) suggests November 1822.

Collin's poem is a true ballad, which sustains an atmosphere of mystery and terror with disturbing undertones of sexual domination. What the literary antecedents of the story are is not known. Collin's dwarf is doubtless some kind of cousin many times removed of Quasimodo, since they are both expressions of the Romantic cult of the grotesque and the daemonic; but Hugo's *Han d'Islande* did not appear until 1823, by which time the poem was at least ten years old.

Schubert's through-composed setting entirely supersedes the sectional form of earlier ballad masterpieces like *Erlkönig* or *Der Wanderer*. Its 150 bars all stem from a single rhythmic–harmonic cell given out in the opening bars. Critics have called in evidence the 'fate motif' of Beethoven's C minor Symphony, and even the Wagnerian leitmotif. But the source of this thematic cell lies much nearer home, in the first movement of the 'Unfinished' Symphony, and in *Suleika I* and *Du liebst mich nicht*. Only Einstein seems to have noticed this thematic link between the song and the 'Unfinished' Symphony; it adds powerful support to the notion that the dot–dot–dot–dash rhythm common to all these works held strong erotic associations for Schubert at that time. The opening bars of *Der Zwerg* are little more than a transposition of the 'Unfinished' theme into another key. There are also strong emotional and thematic links with another, later, tragic masterpiece, the setting of Heine's *Der Atlas*. There too we find the tremolando right-hand chords in the accompaniment, and the powerful bass line, with its characteristic drop of a diminished fourth, which is anticipated at bars 116–25 of *Der Zwerg*. It may be noticed finally that the obsessive pulse is precisely that – a rhythmical symbol of the erotic obsession which is the subject of the ballad.

Capell, 183–4; Einstein, 256; Fischer-Dieskau, 169–71

**DES BACHES WIEGENLIED** see DIE SCHÖNE MÜLLERIN no.20

## DES FISCHERS LIEBESGLÜCK The Fisherman's Bliss
**Karl Gottfried von Leitner**                                      November 1827
Ziemlich langsam                    A minor D933 Peters II p.234 GA XX no.550

Dort blin-ket durch Wei-den und win-ket ein Schimmer

A faint light twinkles there through the meadows, a glimmer from my darling's bedroom shines out for me.

It flickers like a will–o'–the–wisp, and the reflection sways softly in the circle of the rippling lake.

I gaze longingly into the blue waves, welcoming the reflected gleam,

And spring to the oar, and turn the boat, away on its smooth glassy course.

Fondly my sweetheart steals down from her room and joyfully hastens to me in the boat.

Then the breezes gently waft us away from the elder tree on the shore out into the lake again.

Veiled in the pale evening mists our silent innocent play is concealed from prying eyes.

And as we kiss the waves lap round us, rising and falling, so no one can hear.

Only the distant stars overhear, as they swim deep down below the path of the drifting boat.

So happily we drift in the darkness, high above the twinkling stars.

We weep, and we smile, and think ourselves free of the earth, and already up there in heaven.

The poem dates from 1821. Schubert's autograph, on a manuscript dated November 1827 (Vienna, SB) has been broken up, and only the first four bars survive; but there is a complete copy, similarly dated, in the Witteczek–Spaun collection (Vienna, GdM). Publication of this and two other Leitner songs was projected by Haslinger in 1829, but all three subsequently appeared as book 27 of the *Nachlass* in October 1835.

This enchanting barcarolle is a splendid example of Schubert's mature mastery of the strophic song. Leitner's eleven short-lined stanzas are grouped together (with a repeat in verse ten) to fit into a long-breathed strophe which moves with sensuous relaxation from minor to major. In earlier years Schubert might have been tempted to set the verses progressively, moving from brisk anticipation to fulfilment. Instead, he takes his cue from the end of the poem and gives us a simple evocative tune that matches the bliss of the lovers in their private heaven.

Capell, 245; Fischer-Dieskau, 255–6


**DES LEBENS TAG IST SCHWER** see DIE MUTTER ERDE


## DES MÄDCHENS KLAGE The Maiden's Lament (1)

**Friedrich von Schiller** (?) 1811

Allegro agitato D minor D6 Not in Peters GA XX no.2

Der Eich - wald brau-set,    der Eich - wald brau - set,

The oak trees roar, the clouds race by, the maiden sits by the grassy shore. The breakers roll with all their might, and she sighs to the darkness of the night, her eyes dimmed with weeping.

'My heart is dead, the world is empty, gives back no echo of my desire. Holy one, call back your child. I have enjoyed earthly happiness. I have lived, and loved!'

Her tears run their vain course; no lament can awaken the dead. But say, what can comfort and heal the heart, when the joy of sweet love is gone? I, daughter of heaven, will not fail in it.

'Let the tears run their vain course; your lamenting will not wake the dead. For the heart in mourning the sweetest happiness, when the joy of fairest love is gone, is the pain and the plaint of love.'

In Act III of *The Piccolomini* (the second part of Schiller's dramatic trilogy on the life of Wallenstein, published in 1799) Thekla is left alone after being parted from her lover Max Piccolomini. She picks up the guitar that is lying on the table and, 'after playing a melancholy prelude, begins to sing'. Schubert probably found the text in the 1804 edition of the poems, which prints all four verses, whereas only the first two appear in the play. The autograph (Berlin, DS) belongs almost certainly to 1811, though one side of the manuscript has been used for the later *Alles um Liebe* (D241), of July 1815. The song first appeared in the *Gesamtausgabe* in 1894.

In this first setting of the ballad Schubert seems unaware of – or deliberately ignores – the fact that it was written as a short lyrical interlude in the drama, and turns it into an extended episodic composition like *Hagars Klage*. Nothing in it, however, quite matches the expressive power of the best parts of that earlier song, still less of *Leichenfantasie*, with which it is probably roughly contemporary. The roaring wind and the rolling breakers of the first verse are vividly portrayed, and the first half of verse 2 builds up to a strong passage underpinned by Schubert's familiar descending chromatic bass. But the more lyrical setting of the rest of the verse ('I have enjoyed ...') seems by comparison bland and unremarkable. Perhaps the most significant part of the song is the beginning: the impetuous running semiquavers and repeated quavers are the prototype of many similar themes expressive of emotional disturbance and fear of the unknown.

Einstein, 44

## DES MÄDCHENS KLAGE (2)

**Friedrich von Schiller**                                    15 May 1815

C minor  D191  Peters I p.210  GA XX no.67(a) and (b)

For translation, see the preceding entry. This is the familiar strophic version. There are two variants. Schubert's first draft (Vienna, SB) is dated 15 May 1815 and marked 'Langsam'. It has no prelude and a short postlude. The published version has a four-bar prelude and postlude and is marked 'Sehr langsam'. The voice line, however, is shorter, because the two concluding lines of the stanza are not repeated. This revised version was published by Thaddäus Weigl in April 1826, but Schubert's fair copy has not survived. The opus number, originally given as 56, was later changed to 58. Both versions are included in the *Gesamtausgabe*.

The plaintive tune is beautifully shaped to suit the five-line stanza, and the sighing appoggiaturas catch the mood of dignified grief exactly. The song's unity of mood and economy of means of contrast with the version written four years earlier.

Fischer-Dieskau, 41; Porter, 110

## DES MÄDCHENS KLAGE (3)

**Friedrich von Schiller**                                    March 1816
Langsam

C minor  D389  Not in Peters  GA XX no.194

For translation, see *Des Mädchens Klage* (1). The autograph is lost. Schubert wrote out the title on a manuscript containing two other Schiller songs and dated March 1816, but got no further. There is a dated copy also in the Witteczek–Spaun collection (Vienna, GdM). This third attempt to set Schiller's lyric first appeared in August Reissmann's *Franz Schubert: sein Leben und seine Werke* (Berlin, 1873).

The song resembles the second setting in key and in tone, and in its melodic and harmonic shape; but the broken chords in the pianist's right hand simulate more effectively the guitar accompaniment. The voice line is adjusted to accommodate more easily all four verses of the poem, and it can be argued that the song in this version builds up to a more effective climax, but its absence from the Peters edition means that this final version is hardly ever heard.

Porter, 110

**DES MÜLLERS BLUMEN** see DIE SCHÖNE MÜLLERIN no.9

## DES SÄNGERS HABE The Minstrel's Treasure
**Franz Xaver von Schlechta**                                   February 1825
*Etwas geschwind*                    B flat major  D832  Peters V p.2  GA XX no.466

Schlagt mein ganzes Glück in Splitter, nehmt mir al-le Ha-be gleich

Shatter all my happiness, take all I have; only leave me my zither, and I shall still be glad, and rich.
When the clouds of sorrow gather it breathes comfort into my heart; and from its golden strains spring all the flowers of my delight.
If love does not answer, and friendship fails in its duty, I can proudly do without them both, but not without my zither.
When the sinews of my life are rent asunder it will serve me as a pillow, and its sweet notes will lull me to my last sleep.
Then within the grove of fir-trees, lay me softly down in earth, and instead of a tombstone, place the zither upon my grave.
So that when at midnight the spirits rise from death's dark realm to dance their silent round, I may touch its strings.

Schubert in effect rewrote his friend's poem, reducing it from seven verses to six and making substantial alterations. Most significant of all, he changed the pronouns in the last two verses from the third person to the first, as though to emphasise its application to himself. The obvious inference is that he saw the poem as an allegory of his own situation after the onset of his tragic illness, when his creative gift was his only solace in adversity. The autograph (Paris Conservatoire) is a first draft dated February 1825. The song was published at the end of 1830 in book 7 of the *Nachlass*.

This strangely moving and revealing song is Schubert's tribute to the saving grace of his creative gift. The gods shattered the lyre of Orpheus, the symbol of his art; I can bear any other loss, says the song, so long as my zither, the symbol of my genius, remains untouched. *Des Sängers Habe* is a strange mixture of moods – exhilaration, defiance, despair and reconciliation – and of styles. It is full of echoes and pre-echoes. The pre-echo of the first movement of the B flat Piano Trio in the triplet theme at the beginning of the song is plain, a symbol perhaps of the composer's joy in creation. The dotted theme at bars 23–5 recalls the resolute theme in *Todesmusik* (bars 24–31). The last two verses are dominated by thoughts of death, symbolised by the familiar descending bass line in octaves in the key of G flat. The unexpected shift from G flat to B flat major at bar 56 reminds us of the similar cadence in *Pause*, perhaps indicating a verbal association of lute and zither. There is something suggestive of the mood of the B flat Piano Sonata D960 in the mixture of dancing rhythms and solemn undertones. In the light of Schubert's deliberate alteration of the text, and these illuminating thematic links, it is impossible to doubt the autobiographical element in the song.

Capell, 214; Einstein, 317

## DIDONE ABBANDONATA Dido Abandoned
**Pietro Metastasio**                                                December 1816

E flat major D510  Not in Peters  GA XX no.573

See how much I love you still, ungrateful one. With a single glance you disarm me. Have you the heart to betray me, to leave me?

  Ah, do not leave me, my beautiful idol. If you deceive me, whom shall I trust? In bidding you farewell my life would fail me, for I could not live in such torment.

The text comes from Act II Scene 4 of Metastasio's first full-length opera libretto, *Didone abbandonata*, first produced in 1724. Schubert's autograph (Vienna, SB) contains three incomplete sketches and a fair copy headed 'Aria' and dated December 1816. This final version appears to have been scrutinised and amended by Salieri. The second sketch, which is for the most part limited to the melody and the bass line, is shorter and easier than the first, and it has been edited in a performing version by Reinhard van Hoorickx. The song was first published in the *Gesamtausgabe* in 1895. *Didone abbandonata* is an operatic scena for dramatic soprano in the grand manner and in the classical style, which even in 1816 must have seemed a little outmoded. Yet there is something unmistakably Schubertian about its assured musicianship and sense of style. Why, one wonders, should Schubert have taken so much trouble over the piece? Was he even then angling for an appointment at the opera house, when he asked Salieri to vet the work before sending it on elsewhere? Whatever the circumstances, it is a remarkable song and a wonderful vehicle for a powerful soprano with a confident top C for the final peroration.

Capell, 127

## DIE ABGEBLÜHTE LINDE The Faded Lime Tree
**Ludwig von Széchényi**                                                (?) 1821

C major D514  Peters IV p.7  GA XX no.300

Will you keep the vow you made, when time has turned my hair grey? Since you went away beyond the mountains reunions do not come easily.

Change is the child of time, which threatens us at parting; and what the future holds in store, is a paler glow of life.

See, the lime tree is still in flower, as you take your leave today; you will find it here when you return, though evening will rob it of its blossoms.

Then it will stand alone, people will pass by unmoved, hardly noticing it. Only the gardener will remain faithful, for he loves the tree itself.

The Hungarian-born Count Széchényi was high steward to the Archduchess Sophie, a member of the Philharmonic Society and a prominent dilettante. Schubert set two of his poems (D514 and 515), presumably from the manuscript since they were not then published. The songs, however, were published on commission by Cappi and Diabelli in November 1821 as op.7 nos.1 and 2 and dedicated by Schubert to the author 'with high regard'. The autographs have not survived, and the date of the two Széchényi songs is uncertain. For no better reason than that they appeared with *Der Tod und das Mädchen* they are sometimes ascribed to 1817. But this seems improbable, if only because Schubert can hardly have been in touch with the author before about 1820. The more likely hypothesis is that the songs were written in 1821 with the publication (and the dedication) in mind.

For what it is worth, the stylistic evidence also points to a later date than the one usually given. The song has the sectional build and the cumulative effect of a concert piece. In that, and in its lack of subjective emotion, it resembles the setting of Schiller's *Sehnsucht* made at the end of 1820 or in January 1821. In its slightly operatic way *Die abgeblühte Linde* is a fine song which deserves to be better known.

Porter, 25

## DIE ALLMACHT Omnipotence
**Johann Ladislaus Pyrker**                                         August 1825

Langsam, feierlich                      C major  D852  Peters II p.150  GA XX no.479

Great is Jehovah, the Lord, for heaven and earth proclaim his might. It is heard in the roar of the storm, in the loud uplifted cry of the forest stream, in the murmur of the greenwood. It is seen in the waving fields of gold, in the radiant glow of the lovely flowers, in the splendour of the star-strewn sky.

It sounds awesomely in the thunder's roll, and flares in the lightning's quivering flight. But if you look up in prayer, hoping for grace and mercy, then your beating heart will make known even more sensibly the power of Jehovah, the eternal God.

The lines come from *Perlen der heiligen Vorzeit* ('Pearls from Holy Antiquity'), a poem in hexameters on biblical themes published in 1821. Schubert met Pyrker during his stay at Bad Gastein 14 August – 4 September 1825) and treasured the memory of the encounter as one of the happiest moments of his life. Both the Pyrker settings were written at Bad Gastein. The autograph of this one, in private possession as late as 1887, has disappeared, but there is a copy, in the key of A major, in the Witteczek–Spaun collection (Vienna, GdM), marked 'Langsam'. The printed versions, however, are in C major and are marked 'Langsam, feierlich'. The two Pyrker songs were published together as op.79 in May 1827 by Tobias Haslinger and dedicated by Schubert to the poet. The high tessitura of the C major version makes it suitable only for a powerful high tenor or soprano; and since the song was presumably intended originally for Vogl the probability is that it was written in A major and transposed for publication (cf. *Das Heimweh*). In January 1826 Schubert sketched another setting of the poem for SATB (D2 875A). The incomplete autograph was discovered only in 1958 at Bratislava.

Schubert was a true Romantic in his devotion to the idea of God apprehended in nature, and in August 1825, exhilarated by the majesty of the Gastein scenery, he found the evidence of the truth of his religion everywhere about him. So much is clear from his letters, and from the compositions which flowed from his pen during those climactic weeks. His feelings found their most eloquent and concentrated expression in this song. Pyrker's hexameters served his purpose well, for they imposed no rhythmic pattern, but left him free to compose a free-ranging tone poem. The close affinity of mood between *Die Allmacht* and the 'Great' C major Symphony, on which Schubert worked also at Gastein, is evident in the vocal line and in the wide-ranging tonal sequences. The repetition of the first line at the end, with its tremendous reach from C major to G flat major and back, is a master stroke. Unlike some of Schubert's climaxes, this one is both cumulative and concentrated, and it brings the most sublime of all his songs to an unforgettable conclusion.

Capell, 213–14; Fischer-Dieskau, 216–18

**DIE ART, EIN WEIB ZU NEHMEN** see IL MODO DI PRENDER MOGLIE

**DIE BEFREIER EUROPAS IN PARIS** The Liberators of Europe in Paris
**Johann Christian Mikan**                                     16 May 1814
G major D104  Not in Peters  GA XX no.584. NSA IV vol.7 pp.180, 182, 24

They are in Paris, the heroes, the liberators of Europe! The father of Austria, the ruler of the Russians, and he who reawakened the valiant Prussians! The happiness of their people was precious to them. They are in Paris! Now we are certain of peace.

The verses celebrate the entry of Franz I into Paris on 15 April 1814. They were published in a Vienna periodical called *Der Sammler*. There are eight verses in all, but Schubert wrote out only the first verse under the stave and put 'da capo' at the end. The autograph (Vienna, SB) is a double page, dated at the end 16 May 1814. There are two heavily corrected and cancelled sketches for the song on the inner pages, and a final version on the outside pages. All three versions are given in the *Neue Ausgabe*. The final version was printed for the first time in the *Gesamtausgabe* in 1895.

This youthful *jeu d'esprit* witnesses, if nothing else, to the fact that the young Schubert shared in the general wave of patriotic feeling in 1814. The most interesting thing about the naive piece is perhaps the eight-bar postlude, which enacts a kind of dance of joy over Napoleon's downfall.

## DIE BERGE The Mountains

**Friedrich von Schlegel**                                    (?) March 1820

Lebhaft                               G major  D634  Peters IV p.51  GA XX no.180

*Sieht uns der Blick ge-ho — ben, so glaubt das Herz die Schwere zu be-sie - gen,*

When we see with eyes uplifted, we believe in our hearts that we can vanquish gravity; we will press onward and fly to the gods above. Man, once soaring aloft, believes himself already beyond the clouds.

Soon he perceives in astonishment that we are for ever grounded in our own nature. Then all his efforts are concentrated upon enduring tasks; he strives never to lose his hold on that foundation, and builds a rocklike edifice of thought.

And then, with new delight, he sees the bold cliffs hang mockingly. Forgetting all his suffering, he feels only the longing to jest in the face of the abyss, for high courage swells in his noble breast.

The poem is the first in the sequence called *Abendröte*, written 1800–1. The autograph has been missing since about 1850, and the date of the song is not certain. However, three other songs from part I of *Abendröte* belong to March 1820, according to Witteczek's copies (Vienna, GdM). It seems possible that at that time Schubert contemplated setting the whole cycle, and if so, he would probably start at the beginning. So it is reasonable to assume that *Die Berge* also belongs to March 1820. The song was published in April 1826 as op.57 no.2 by Thaddäus Weigl.

Man, forever poised uneasily between heaven and earth, is the subject of Schlegel's very characteristic poem, but Schubert is content to look at the external imagery rather than the contemplative centre. The outer sections rely on familiar motifs like the upward-striding arpeggios and horn calls in the accompaniment, while the middle section moves to the flattened sixth and bare unisons in the minor key to suggest man's inescapable limitations. The commentators are silent about *Die Berge*, and indeed it is a strangely unconvincing song.

## DIE BETENDE Laura at Prayer

**Friedrich von Matthisson**                                    Autumn 1814

Adagio         B major  D102  Peters V p.171  GA XX no.20  NSA IV vol.7 p.21

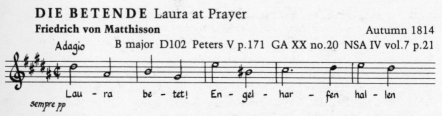

*Lau - ra be - tet! En - gel - har - fen hal - len*
sempre pp

Laura is praying. The sound of angelic harps brings the peace of God to her afflicted heart, and her sighs are wafted heavenward like the scent of Abel's sacrifice.

As she kneels, lost in her devotions, she is as beautiful as innocence painted by Raphael, already transfigured by the glory that surrounds those who dwell in heaven.

Ah, she feels the presence of the All-highest in the soft and gentle air; already she sees in her mind the palm-clad heights where the crown of light awaits.

So to observe this saintly maid in prayer, her angel-pure bosom filled with devotion and with trust in God, is to glimpse that world beyond.

The poem was written in 1778. There is a fragmentary sketch of the voice-part on a manuscript (Vienna, SB) which contains two other songs of autumn 1814, one of them (*An Emma*) dated 17 September 1814. The complete autograph has been missing since

1895. There are several contemporary copies, including one in the Stadler collection (Lund, UB) made in 1814. A copy in the Witteczek–Spaun collection (Vienna, GdM) is marked 'Langsam, feierlich'. The song was published in book 31 of the *Nachlass* in June 1840. There, and in Stadler's copy, the marking is *Adagio*. Although September 1814 seems the most likely date, it is by no means impossible that it dates (as Deutsch thought) from the spring of that year. Schubert used the opening bars of the song in his sketch for no.20(c) of his opera *Der Grav von Gleichen*, a curious example of the composer's habit of reworking earlier ideas in the last years of his life.

*Die Betende* is Schubert's first venture into the transcendental key of B major (the key of *Am Strome* and *Nacht und Träume*). It is also the first of Schubert's secular hymns, adapting the manner and movement of the eighteenth-century hymn to what is in effect a love song. The key of B major seems to have had an association for Schubert with the purity of erotic feelings, so that Laura in this song is the forerunner of Suleika (cf. the closing pages of *Suleika I*) and Mignon (*So lasst mich scheinen*).

### DIE BLUMENSPRACHE The Language of Flowers
**(?) Anton Platner**                                    (?) October 1817
B flat major  D519  Peters VI p.120  GA XX no.299

Flowers show what the heart is feeling, they speak many a secret word. They droop intimately on their swaying stems as though impelled by love. They hide bashfully in the concealing foliage, as though desire had betrayed them to the ravisher.

They embody, in a soft bewitching image, the natural disposition of women and maidens. They stand for beauty, grace and gentleness, they stand for the rewards of life. Like the bud, hidden away so secretly, youth finds in them the pearl of hope.

Their fragrant dress is colourfully interwoven with thoughts of longing and of grief. The hateful barriers of separation do not matter, for flowers proclaim our sorrow. What we may not say aloud, with our guarded speech, kindness may dare to lament, with flowers.

The poem appeared in W. G. Becker's 'Pocket-book of Sociable Pleasures' for 1805 over the signature 'Pl.'. This is taken to refer to Anton (or Edouard) Platner (1787–1855) but the ascription is doubtful. The author's name does not appear on Schubert's autograph. There are four verses, of which Schubert omitted the last. The most likely date for the song is October 1817. An incomplete sketch of the voice line, untitled and without text or acompaniment, appears on a manuscript (New York, privately owned) containing *An den Frühling*, dated October 1817. There is an autograph fair copy in the Sibley Music Library, University of Rochester, NY, and another fair copy, probably written for Johann Karl, Count Esterházy, was for many years in the possession of the Esterházy family but is now missing. The song was published by C. A. Spina in October 1868 as op.173 no.5.

*Die Blumensprache* is a wonderful song, very little known, and deserves to be at least as popular as *Frühlingssehnsucht*, which it closely resembles. Disregarding the sentimental anthropomorphism of the verses, Schubert chooses to set them as a passionate song in praise of spring. The impetuous triplets hurry along (but not too fast!) with a tonal freedom and lyrical impetus that seem somewhat anachronistic for the date; indeed, the form and the style suggest rather the Schulze or Rellstab songs.

Capell, 143

## DIE BÖSE FARBE  see DIE SCHÖNE MÜLLERIN no.17

## DIE BÜRGSCHAFT  The Hostage
**Friedrich von Schiller**                                      August 1815

D246 Peters V p.11 GA XX no.109

Zu Di - o - nys, dem Ty - ran - nen, schlich Möros, den Dolch im Ge - wande;

[*Synopsis*] Möros, attempting to slay the tyrant king of Syracuse, is apprehended in the act. When the king orders his execution he declares himself willing to die, but begs three days' grace so that he may give his sister in marriage. His best friend will act as hostage. 'Kill him, if I fail you, in my place.' The king agrees, the loyal friend embraces Möros and delivers himself up to the king.

On the third morning Möros, having fulfilled his family duties, sets out on his return home. But the heavens open, and when he reaches the river he finds the bridge swept away by the floods. When his pleas to Zeus fail to abate the storm, he plunges into the flood and reaches the other side. As he makes his way through the forest he is waylaid by bandits. 'All I have is my life,' he cries, 'and that is the king's.' But he defends himself so skilfully that three of the robbers are killed and the others flee.

At the point of exhaustion, Möros comes upon a crystal stream in which he refreshes his burning limbs and slakes his thirst. He overtakes two travellers, who tell him that his friend is already prepared for execution. As evening draws on he meets his old steward Philostratus, who urges him to save himself, since it is too late to save his friend. But Möros replies, 'If he dies then I die too. The tyrant shall not think I have broken my word.' As the sun sets he reaches the place of execution. 'Hang me in his place,' he cries, 'for it is I for whom he stands hostage.' The two friends fall weeping into each other's arms.

Even the tyrant is moved to relent. 'Loyalty is no vain delusion,' he says. 'Accept me as the third in your fellowship.'

The ballad was finished in August 1798. In May 1816 Schubert began an opera on the same subject, to a libretto by an unidentified author, but left it unfinished. Schubert's autograph is missing, but there is a copy dated August 1815 in Vienna (ÖNB). The song was published in October 1830 as book 8 of the *Nachlass*.

Schubert set Schiller's poem in the 'loose' form he had inherited from Zumsteeg, as an assemblage of recitative and arioso sections, with the piano doing the linking and the scene-painting. The declamatory passages are written with strength and conviction, and if the lyrical interludes (especially the tyrant's final conversion) seem a little bland for their context, there are many touches of authentic Schubert in them. As a whole, though, the song cannot be said to transcend the limitations of its form, which now seems to us inescapably pre-*Erlkönig*. The piano writing, however, in its freedom and pictorialism, is still remarkable for its time. What a film composer Schubert would have made, with his instant realisation of the drenching rain and the fight with the robbers, his sudden pauses and his touches of sentiment. And there is one moment, at the climax of the story, which reveals a dramatic imagination of quasi-Wagnerian proportions. At the final entry of the tyrant Schubert sums up the solemnity and the drama with a simple succession of *fortissimo* chords punctuated by pauses: D flat, A and finally B major. It is a motif as effective in its way as Scarpia's famous three chords, and very similar in conception.

## DIE DREI SÄNGER The Three Minstrels

**Friedrich Bobrik**

23 December 1815

D329 Not in Peters GA XX no.591

The king sat at his festive board among his knights and ladies. The goblets were passed round, and many a glass was drained.

Then came the sound of golden strings, sweeter than golden wine, and lo! – three strange minstrels stepped forward into the hall and bowed.

'Greetings, sons of song,' began the king jovially, 'in whose hearts dwell the love of music and the secret of song. If it is your will to compete in noble contest that would please us mightily, and the victor shall be the ornament of our court.'

The first minstrel touched the strings, and sang of days gone by. He made the listening throng look back to the grey dawn of time. He told how the new-created world turned away from chaos. His song pleased the elegant listeners, and they followed him in their minds gladly.

The more to please his audience, the second minstrel told a merry tale of gnomes and their treasures, and of an army of green dwarves. He sang of many wondrous things, and of many a devious prank. His joking brought the house down, and set them all laughing.

And now it was the third man's turn. Gently, from the depths of his heart, he breathed a song of love and honour, and of the pain and joy of longing. Scarcely had his song begun than every face was downcast, and tears were wrung from shining eyes.

[*The last verse tells how the king awarded the victory to the third minstrel for 'he sings the most beautiful song who moves our hearts to melancholy'.*]

The author was identified by Dietrich Berke. The poem was published in a collection of 'Poems for Reading Aloud' in 1815. The last page of Schubert's autograph (Vienna, SB) is missing, but the probability is that he completed the song. It appeared first in the *Gesamtausgabe* in 1895. It has been completed and privately printed by Reinhard van Hoorickx.

The song is a curiosity. The square four-bar phrases, the studious avoidance of recitative (unless one counts the final cadence of the king's speech), the abrupt changes of rhythm and tonality, without any attempt at modulation from one section to the next, all this gives the song a very un-Schubertian air. The only precedent, of a sort, is to be found in the *Don Gayseros* songs, which rely similarly on the juxtaposition of sections in different keys and on a very simple melodic line. It may be that *Die drei Sänger* and the three *Don Gayseros* songs are all part of a deliberate attempt on Schubert's part to break away from the traditional ballad pattern and to experiment with a primitive kind of polytonality.

D. Berke, 'Zu einigen anonymen Texten Schubertscher Lieder', *Die Musik forschung*, XXII, 1969, p.485

## DIE EINSIEDELEI The Hermitage (1)
**Johann Gaudenz von Salis-Seewis**                    (?) March 1816

A major  D393  Peters VI p.14  GA XX no.198

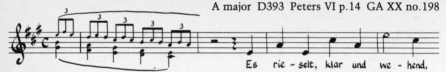

Es  rie - selt,  klar  und  we - hend,

Within the oak grove a stream runs clear. There I choose to sojourn on my lonely way. A grotto, cool and airy, serves as my chapel, my hermitage, hidden among the greenery.

Nothing disturbs the silence of the forest far and wide, save when a green woodpecker pecks and screams at the dry branches. A raven croaks on the tall spire of a mossy fir tree, and in the rocky crevice a ring-dove moans.

How the heart is uplifted in the dense confines of the wood. Its secret shade soon cheers dull melancholy. Here no officious prying eye can trace my steps: here I am free, close to nature and simplicity.

O that I might remain unfettered by the turmoil of the world, and that I could fly to you, beloved hermitage, glad to escape the din of the crowds. Here I should build a refuge for my love and me.

The poem dates from 1787. Of the six verses, Schubert uses four (1, 4, 5, 6) in this first version, and three (1, 5, 6) in the second. There is also a setting for male-voice quartet (D337). The autograph is a first draft, subtitled by Schubert *Lob der Einsamkeit* ('In Praise of Solitude'). Its whereabouts are now unknown, and there is some doubt about the date of the song. The list appended to Kreissle's biography dates it precisely – 3 May 1817 – but that may be due to confusion with the second version. The song was published in 1845 in book 38 of the *Nachlass*.

This is an attractive strophic setting, but it is easy to see why Schubert was not satisfied with it. The dancing triplets in the pianist's right hand do very well for the babbling brook in the first line of the poem, but they do not match its general mood of reflection and retirement from the world.

## DIE EINSIEDELEI (2)
**Johann Gaudenz von Salis-Seewis**                         May 1817

Etwas bewegt

A minor  D563  Peters VII p.72  GA XX no.322

Es    rie-selt, klar und  we  -  hend, ein___ Quell im  Ei - chen - wald,

For translation, see the preceding entry. The autograph (Berlin, SPK) is a first draft dated May 1817. There is a copy in the Witteczek–Spaun collection (Vienna, GdM), similarly dated. The song was first published in vol. VII of the Peters edition in 1887. In this second setting the running semiquavers are transferred to the inner parts, and the movement is more subdued, so that the song is much nearer to the mood of contented retirement.

**DIE ENTFERNTE GELIEBTE** see ALS ICH SIE ERRÖTEN SAH

# DIE ENTZÜCKUNG AN LAURA Enchanted by Laura (1)

**Friedrich von Schiller**                                    March 1816

A major D390 Not in Peters GA XX no.195

In sanfter Bewegung

sempre pp

Lau - ra, ü - ber die - se Welt zu flüch-ten wähn ich,

Laura, when your sparkling eyes meet mine, I fancy I am flying from this world to bathe in the sun of a celestial May: when my image is reflected in the soft sky-blue of your eyes, I seem to breathe ethereal airs.

I rave to hear in my intoxicated ears the sound of lyres from a distant Paradise, the sweep of harps from more congenial stars. My muse senses the idyllic hour, when from your warm voluptuous mouth the silver notes take their reluctant flight.

I see cupids flap their wings. The swaying pine trees behind you dance as though brought to life at the call of Orphean strings. When your foot trips, light as a wave, in the whirl of the dance, the poles revolve more swiftly about my head.

Your glances, when smilingly they speak of love, could kindle marble into life, and set the veins of rock throbbing. Dreams become reality here around me, if I can only read in your eyes: Laura, *my* Laura!

The poem, originally entitled *Die seligen Augenblicke* ('Happy Moments'), was written in 1781. Schubert's autograph, dated March 1816, is in private possession, and there is a copy, also dated, in the Witteczek–Spaun collection (Vienna, GdM). The song was first published in the *Gesamtausgabe* in 1895. In this first attempt Schubert is content to evoke a mood of 'dreamy rapture', as Capell calls it, with a long flowing melody accompanied by broken chords in triplets. The tune hardly ventures outside the limits of tonic and dominant, and the song makes no attempt to match the changing images of the poem.

Capell, 114

# DIE ENTZÜCKUNG AN LAURA (2)

**Friedrich von Schiller**                                    August 1817

A major D577 Not in Peters GA XX no.597

Lau - ra, Lau - ra, ü - ber die - se Welt____

For translation, see the preceding entry. Two manuscript fragments survive of the second setting, in which Schubert treats the poem episodically so as to distinguish between the singing, playing and dancing of the incomparable Laura. The first (Berlin, DS) is dated August 1817; it covers the first verse and the beginning of the second. The second fragment (Vienna, SB) includes the third verse and the beginning of the fourth. The tonality moves from A to A flat, and from D flat to E. A performing edition has been edited by Reinhard van Hoorickx and published privately. It is available on record (DG 1981007).

The first two verses are set to enchanting music in this much more interesting second version. The structure is, however, unashamedly episodic, and whether Schubert could have imposed some kind of unity on the whole song if he had completed it is an open question. He seems to be aiming here at the same tone, the same mood of devotion, as characterises that fine song, the 1823 setting of Schiller's *Das Geheimnis*. The first page of the manuscript is reproduced in August Reissmann's *Franz Schubert: sein Leben und seine Werke* (Berlin, 1873).

### DIE ERDE  The Earth

**Friedrich von Matthisson**  Autumn 1817

E major  D989 (D2 579B)  Not in Peters  Not in GA

Mäßig

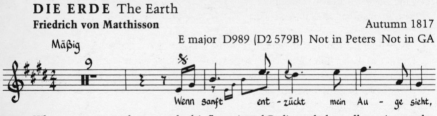

Wenn sanft ent - zückt mein Au - ge sieht,

When my enraptured eyes see the fair flowering of God's earth, how all creation nestles at her bountiful breast; how she loves all her children, and gives nourishment to each;
  and with the unfailing strength of youth brings forth and cherishes and creates growth;
    then I feel a heartfelt desire to sing the praises of him whose wonderful omnipotence made this vast and beautiful world.

The poem, originally entitled *Die schöne Erde*, dates from 1778. Schubert used a shortened and revised version published in Vienna in 1811 in an anthology for young girls called *Wilhelmine*. He set the first three of the five verses. A complete copy of the song was discovered only in 1969 in the archives of the Gesellschaft der Musikfreunde, Vienna, but its existence has long been known. A fragmentary autograph containing the last seven bars has been missing since 1906. It was part of a much larger manuscript containing several songs dating from September and October 1817. The song was published, together with the companion piece *Vollendung*, in 1970 by Bärenreiter, edited by Christa Landon. *Die Erde* is a cheerful song, with something of the innocent gaiety of *Seligkeit*.

  C. Landon, 'Neue Schubert-Funde', *ÖMZ*, XXIV, 1969, p.299, trans. in *MR*, XXXI, 1970, p.200.

### DIE ERSCHEINUNG  The Apparition

**Ludwig Kosegarten**  7 July 1815

E major  D229  Peters IV p.117  GA XX no.92

Lieblich

Ich lag auf grü-nen Mat - ten, an kla - rer___ Quel - len___ Rand.

I lay in green meadows by the clear brook's side. The shade of alders cooled my burning cheeks. I thought of this and that, and dreamed, with gentle melancholy, of many a good and lovely thing, which this world cannot give.

  And lo! From the grove there rose a maiden, clear as day, with a white veil wound round her nut-brown hair. Her shining eyes were heavenly blue, and tears of sadness glistened like pearls of dew on her eyelashes.

  A sad smile hovered over her sweet lips. She shook and trembled. I thought her tear-filled eyes, her love-lorn gaze, were bent on me. Who was so deluded, who was so happy, as I?

  I started up to embrace her, but ah, she turned away. I saw her quickly grow pale, and her look was troubled. She gazed at me so fervently. With pensive dignity she pointed up towards heaven, and vanished.

  Farewell, farewell, you vision! Farewell, I know you well. And I know what your gesture means, as indeed I should. Though we are parted now, we are united by a fairer bond. Love has its home not here below, but up above.

The poem dates from July 1787. Schubert's first draft, now in the University of Texas, is entitled *Erinnerung: Die Erscheinung*. A fair copy is now missing, but there is a copy, dated 7 July 1815, in the Witteczek–Spaun collection (Vienna, GdM). The song was published by Sauer and Leidesdorf on 11 December 1824 in an 'Album Musicale', and republished as op.108 no.3 in January 1829 under the title *Erinnerung* ('Recollection'). It is so titled also in the Peters edition.

This tuneful strophic song is perhaps more interesting as the prototype of *Die Forelle* than for its own sake. The tune, the rhythm and the harmony all remind us of the later masterpiece, and the upward tenor phrase in bar 2 is particularly significant. The setting of the two poems is similar, and the verse form is the same; Schubert may well have linked the two poems unconsciously.

## DIE ERSTE LIEBE First Love

**Johann Georg Fellinger**

12 April 1815

C major D182 Peters V p.202 GA XX no.61

First love fills the heart with longing for an unknown realm of the spirit. The soul teeters on the brink of life, and sweet melancholy finds release in tears.

Then intimations of beauty are awakened, you see the goddess robed in light. The easy bonds of faith coalesce, and the days slip by to the music of love.

Her image only do you see reflected, that of the beloved who has you in thrall. She alone inhabits the mansions of your being.

From the golden rim of heaven she smiles down upon you, when the silent stars hang in the sky; exultantly you cry to the whole world: She is mine!

The poem was written in 1812 and published in a periodical called *Selam* in 1814. The autograph is lost, but there are two copies in the Witteczek–Spaun collection (Vienna, GdM), both dated 12 April 1815. One of the copies is in A flat, but an annotation explains that the original key was C. The song was published – in the key of B flat major – in book 35 of the *Nachlass* in 1842. The Peters edition prints this version, whereas the *Gesamtausgabe* reverts to the original key.

Though it is not, strictly speaking, a love song, the eighteen-year-old Schubert makes *Die erste Liebe* sound like one, and a remarkable one at that, for the composition seems to have all the freedom and assurance of his mature through-composed style. It escapes not only from the formal limitations of the strophe, but from those of the four-bar phrase as well. With complete equality between voice and piano, and complete freedom of melodic and tonal invention, each phrase grows out of the preceding one. A close examination reveals that the whole song is built on a few short motifs – the rising third, the appoggiatura, the little dotted figure which the pianist inherits from the singer ('Da wacht es auf') and which becomes a significant (and prophetic) figure in its own right – all of which enables Schubert to build an impressive climax at the final words – 'She is mine!' *Die erste Liebe* is in its cumulative power one of the most predictive of the purely lyrical songs of 1815; the variety of accompaniment figures used – right- and left-hand triplets, broken chords, repeated chords, dotted rhythms against triplet rhythms, and so on – is striking.

## DIE ERWARTUNG Expectation

**Friedrich von Schiller**                                             May 1816

B flat major  D159  Peters III p.84  GA XX no.46  NSA IV vol.7 pp.141, 153

Did I not hear the wicket-gate? Was that the creak of the bolt? No, it was the sighing
of the wind in the poplars. Leafy canopy, adorn yourself, for you are to receive the
one radiant in grace. Branches, make a shady bower, to enfold her secretly in sweet
night; and all you caressing airs, be watchful, frolic and play about her rosy cheeks
when her tender foot, with light step, bears its fair burden to the throne of love.

Hush! What is that rustling in the hedge, scurrying in haste?

No, only a startled bird scared out of the bush.

Put out the light of day! Come, pensive night, with your sweet silence. Spread
your purple veil about us, enfold us in your secret arms. The bliss of love shuns
the listening ear, and the immodest witness of the light. Only in Hesperus, the silent
one with steadfast gaze, may it confide. Was that a distant call, like soft whispering
voices? No, it is the swan drawing circles on the silver surface of the lake.

Flowing harmonies sound in my ear, the spring murmurs pleasantly; the
flowers droop beneath the kiss of evening, and all creatures join in love. The grape
beckons, the swelling peach waits to be enjoyed, luscious as it listens there behind
the leaves. The air, spice-scented, drinks up the ardour of my burning cheek.

Do I hear footsteps? Something rustling along the leafy path?

A fruit, heavy with its own ripeness, fell there.

The burning eye of day sinks in sweet death, its colours fade. The flower-cups
which shun its heat boldly open in the gentle dusk. The quiet moon lifts its radiant
face. The world dissolves into silent massive shapes. By that magic the girdle is
untied, and beauty stands before me in its nakedness.

Did I not see something white glimmering there? Gleaming like a silken robe?
No, it is the shimmer of the willows against the dark yew trees.

O yearning heart, pleasure yourself no more, toying with sweet images in vain.
The arm that would embrace her embraces the air. No phantom happiness can cool
this breast. Lead my love here to me! Let me touch her tender hand, or even the
shadow of her garment's hem, and the hollow dream will come to life.

And softly, as from the heavenly heights, the happy hour arrives. So had she
come, unseen, and wakened her love with kisses.

The poem was written in 1799, and the beloved so urgently awaited was Charlotte von
Lengefeld, whom Schiller married in 1790. Schubert's song was modelled on the setting
by Zumsteeg, published in 1800. The cantata form, with alternating recitative and arioso
passages, suits the poem. Schubert took it over from Zumsteeg, and adopted a similar
layout, but his version shows a wider rhythmic and dynamic range, and much more
independent use of the pianoforte.

There are two versions. The surviving autograph, in the Bodmer Library, Geneva,
is a first draft dated May 1816. In this first version there is an opening section in B flat
and substantial sections in E. The final sections are in C and, finally, G. Towards the
end of his life Schubert prepared a new version for publication, revising the final sections
so that the piece ends, as it began, in B flat. This version was published by M. J. Leidesdorf
as op.116 in April 1829, and dedicated by Schubert before his death to Joseph Hüttenbrenner.
Both versions are published in the *Neue Ausgabe*, which also prints Zumsteeg's setting
in the appendix.

The opening pages are full of good music, and the lover's uncertain moods, with their undercurrent of excitement, are admirably caught. But once again the problem of giving unity and cumulative effect to the solo cantata form seems to defeat Schubert. That arises partly from the form itself, and it is significant that in his final version Schubert attempted to reduce the tonal diffuseness of the original. But the real trouble is that the song gets less interesting as it goes along. About halfway through Schubert's invention seems to flag; it is the last sections which make the least impression.

Capell, 90; Fischer-Dieskau, 140

## DIE FORELLE The Trout

**Christian Friedrich Schubart**                              (?) Early 1817

D flat major  D550  Peters I p.197  GA XX no.327(a), (b), (c) and (d)
NSA IV vol.2 pp.194, 202, 198, 109, 206

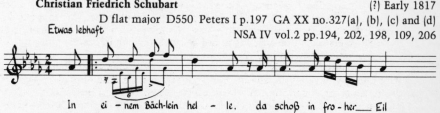

In a sparkling stream the playful trout darted about happily and swift as an arrow. I stood on the bank and watched contentedly as the frisky little fish swam in the clear brook.

A fisherman also stood on the bank with his rod and coldly watched as the fish wound to and fro. So long as the water stays clear, I thought, he will never catch the trout with his line.

But in the end the thief lost patience. He treacherously muddied the stream, and before I realised what was happening the rod jerked, and the little fish was writhing on it. My blood was stirred as I beheld the victim of deceit.

The poem was published in 1782. Schubert omitted that last of the four verses, which pointedly advises young girls to be on their guard against young men with rods. Schubert's first draft is lost, and the song cannot be precisely dated. Since the earliest copies date from the spring of 1817, however, it cannot be later than that, and the immediate popularity of the song suggests that it is unlikely to be much earlier.

There are many variant versions, but the differences are minor, and concerned for the most part with the tempo indication and the prelude–postlude. The first draft had no introduction, though the shape of the familiar introduction is already adumbrated in a seven-bar postlude, which would doubtless have been used in practice as prelude also. This first version, marked 'Mässig', is preserved in copies in the Stadler, Ebner and Schindler collections (Lund, UB). In May or June 1817 Schubert made a copy for Franz Kandler's album, marked 'Nicht zu geschwind'; and on 21 February 1818 in Anselm Hüttenbrenner's rooms he wrote another (*Etwas geschwind*) with a message for Anselm's brother Josef. This last is the famous manuscript which had the ink sprinkled on it instead of the sand. It is reproduced in Walter Dahm's biography of the composer (*Schubert*, Berlin, 1912).

On 9 December 1820 the song appeared as a supplement to the *ZfK*. Schubert wrote out a fair copy for the printer which is now in private possession in Portugal. It has no tempo indication, no prelude and a slightly shorter postlude. Finally in October 1821 he made another fair copy, now in Washington (LC), which is reproduced in the *Neue Ausgabe*. It has the only authentic version of the prelude. The song was republished several times as op.32 by Diabelli between January 1825 and 1829, and for the last of these publications Diabelli added his own version of the prelude. Not surprisingly, it differs very little from Schubert's own. The tempo indication is *Etwas lebhaft*. This is the version printed in the Peters edition and as the last of the four versions in the *Gesamtausgabe*. Schubert used the tune of the song as the theme for the set of variations that forms the fourth movement of his Piano Quintet (D667; the 'Trout'), an indication that by 1819 the song was already widely known.

Even without the smug moral, the sentimental verses are feeble enough; yet Schubert turns them into one of the greatest, and perhaps the best loved, of his songs. Its greatness is compounded of two aspects of his genius: his instinctive feeling for folksong melody gives the basic strophe its rounded inevitability, while the pictorial quality of the piano writing gives it its irresistible vivacity. As has been noted, the musical germ-cell of *Die Forelle* had appeared in July 1815 in *Die Erscheinung* (D229), and it was to reappear, in all its formal perfection, in the theme of the 'Trout' variations. But the special treatment given to the third verse gives the song an added dimension, and makes it something more than a perfectly balanced strophic song.

Capell, 135–6; Fischer-Dieskau, 107

## DIE FRÖHLICHKEIT Cheerfulness

**Martin Josef Prandstetter**                                      22 August 1815

E major D262 Not in Peters GA XX no.134

Lebhaft

The man whose blood runs lightly through his veins is rich; neither hope nor fear hold him in their golden chains.

For cheerfulness with its magic wand guides him through a long life to a gentle death.

At peace with all men, loving them as brothers, he never feels in his heart the bright flame of revenge.

It is the countless bonds of friendship which sustain him; therefore he does not hate his enemies, and never even knows them.

Wherever he turns his cheerful gaze he sees only beauty and goodness; everything is well, deserving of love, and glad as he is.

For him the world becomes a paradise in the sunshine. The stream is clear, the fountain pure, and its murmur sweet.

The flowering landscape delights him with its ever-changing face, and for him alone blessed nature never grows old.

If I were rich as Croesus, and powerful too, if I had golden ingots huge as mountains,

if I were master of all that men can see from the North Sea to the Black Sea, and if I had not a cheerful disposition, sadly I should hang my head and think myself a poor wight, and speak to Dame Fortune thus:

O goddess, if you value my wellbeing, hear me! Take back all these things, but give me a light heart instead!

For gladness makes men rich and free, and rarely is a man lucky enough, whoever he may be, to hold it fast.

The autograph, dated 22 August 1815, has been missing since 1920. There is a copy dated August 1815 in the Witteczek–Spaun collection (Vienna, GdM). The song remained unpublished until it appeared in the *Gesamtausgabe* in 1895. A routine strophic setting, lively and pleasant, but not able to sustain the song through twelve verses.

# DIE FRÜHE LIEBE Young Love
**Ludwig Hölty**

May 1816

E major  D430  Not in Peters  GA XX no.222

Schon im bun-ten kna-ben-klei-de pfleg-ten hüb-sche Mäg-de-lein

Even when I wore a boy's bright clothes I used to feast my eyes on pretty girls rather than on a doll or a ball.

I forgot birds' nests, and threw my hobbyhorse on the grass, whenever a pretty girl sat beside my sister under a tree.

The sprightly lass delighted me, with her rosy cheeks, her mouth, her brow, and her blonde curls.

I used to gaze at her shawl and bodice, as she leaned back against a tree; then I would stretch out on the grass close to the hem of her gown.

The poem, originally entitled *Minnehuldigung* ('Homage to Love'), was written in February 1773. Schubert omitted the last verse. The autograph, in private possession, is dated May 1816. A different version in D, marked 'Heiter' and with a four-bar introduction, is preserved in a copy in the Witteczek–Spaun collection (Vienna, GdM); this remains unpublished. The E major version appeared first in 1895, in the *Gesamtausgabe*. Schubert's strophic setting is pretty and slight, like the verses.

# DIE FRÜHEN GRÄBER Untimely Dead
**Friedrich Gottlieb Klopstock**

14 September 1815

A minor  D290  Peters V p.162  GA XX no.144

Etwas geschwind

Will-kom-men, o sil-ber-ner Mond,schöner, stil-ler Ge-fähr - - te der Nacht!

Welcome, silver moon, fair silent consort of the night. You fly? Haste not away, stay, friend of remembrance. See, she stays; only the clouds move on.

May's awakening is even lovelier than the summer night, when the bright dew drips from the locks of the morning, as it rises red behind the hill.

And you, nobler youths, already your monuments are overgrown with gloomy moss. Oh, how happy I was when I could still, with you, watch the day break, and the stars gleam!

The poem was written in 1764. The autograph (Vienna, GdM) is marked 'Mässig' and dated 14 September 1815. The surviving fragment of a fair copy (New York, PML) gives only the last four bars and the text of verses 2 and 3. There are copies in the Witteczek–Spaun (GdM), Stadler and Ebner (Lund, UB) collections, all marked 'Etwas geschwind'. When the song was published in book 28 of the *Nachlass* in 1837 Diabelli transposed it to G minor and wrote a spurious four-bar prelude. He seems also to have tampered with Schubert's tonality by making the cadence at the end of the first couplet end on the minor chord, thus entirely destroying the tonal ambiguity Schubert gives to the song. This 'diabolic' version is followed in the Peters edition. The *Gesamtausgabe* follows the original autograph.

Gluck's C major setting is perhaps nearer in spirit to Klopstock than Schubert's is, but this plaintive A minor setting, with its idiomatic shift into B major at the halfway mark, deserves to stand beside it.

## DIE GEBÜSCHE The Thicket
**Friedrich von Schlegel**                                        January 1819

G major D646 Peters VII p.3 GA XX no.350

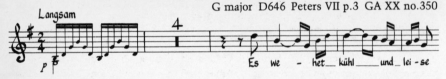

The breeze blows cool and soft over the dark fields. Only the heavens smile, from a thousand bright eyes.

One soul alone moves through the raging sea, and in the murmured words that whisper through the leaves.

Thus wave echoes wave, where spirits mourn in secret. Thus words follow words, where is the breath of life.

For him who listens inwardly, one faint sound echoes through all the sounds of this earth's motley dream.

The poem comes from part II of the sequence called *Abendröte*. Schubert seems to have come across this collection at the beginning of 1819 and to have started with the poems in part II, moving on to some of the poems in part I a year later. The autograph of *Die Gebüsche* (in private possession) is dated January 1819. There is a copy in the Witteczek–Spaun collection (Vienna, GdM). The song did not appear until 1885, in vol. VII of the Peters edition.

It seems appropriate that the year 1819 should begin with *Die Gebüsche*, for it is a characteristically 'Romantic' poem in both form and substance. Indeed, the final quatrain often serves as a summing-up of the Romantic doctrine of the unity of nature, and of its underlying euphony, as the 'voice of God'. Schumann used it, for instance, as the motto for his C major Fantasia op.17. The song looks forward, too, with its on-running, through-composed form, the forward movements sustained by a process of continuous modulation. It is no coincidence that the song seems to foreshadow the third of the op.90 Impromptus, for the rapprochement between the emotional world of the songs and Schubert's keyboard manner is one of the distinguishing marks of his middle years. *Die Gebüsche* is not among the greatest songs, but it deserves to be better known than it is.

Einstein, 187

## DIE GEFANGENEN SÄNGER The Captive Songsters
**August Wilhelm von Schlegel**                                   January 1821

G major D712 Peters V p.193 GA XX no.389

Do you hear the nightingales' song echoing through the grove? See, sweet May is here. Every lover woos his mate; every melting sound proclaims what bliss there is in love.

Those others, who live captive behind the bars of their cages, listen to the song outside. They would gladly fly off to freedom, to join in the joy of spring and love; but ah, they are closely confined.

And now from these tormented souls the song bursts out of their urgent throats in force; and instead of echoing through the swaying trees it rebounds from the hard stone prison walls.

So the soul of man, held captive in this valley of earth, is troubled to hear the songs of nobler brothers, and vainly seeks to enlarge the boundaries of this earthly existence to those of the serene heavens. And this he calls Poetry.

Yet, if he appear to dedicate his songs of praise in verse, as from a heart intoxicated with life, yet the tender heart feels that his joy flowers from the root of deepest suffering.

The poem was written in 1810. Schubert's first draft (Vienna, SB) is written in pencil on the back of sketches for the Credo of the Mass no.5 in A flat. The song is sketched out for sixty-one bars on two staves, without title or text, and without tempo indication. The first complete draft, dated January 1821, also without marking, is in New York (PML). Two copies in the Witteczek–Spaun collection (Vienna, GdM) are similarly dated; one is marked 'Lieblich, klagend'. The song was published in June 1842 as no.2 of book 33 of the *Nachlass*, where the marking is *Mässig*.

Schlegel's caged birds are not, as has been supposed, the victims of Metternich's secret police, for the poem dates from 1810, when liberal hopes were high. It is an expression of Romantic neo-Platonism, of the longing of the artist for the ideal world beyond his reach. Romantic longing (*Sehnsucht*) is a kind of philosophical balancing act; the artist is forever poised between two worlds, the harsh reality of here and now, and the ideal beauty of the beyond. In Schubert's tonality the musical equivalent of this two-eyed stance is of course the major–minor alternation. So here the basic idea of the song hinges on G major/G minor, as the concluding bars make clear. But before that point is reached the song has gone through a whole series of melodic and tonal adventures which take it from G major to B flat minor and back again. This delightful song is in fact a most interesting translation of a philosophical poem into musical terms.

Capell, 169; Fischer-Dieskau, 296-7

## DIE GESTIRNE The Constellations
**Friedrich Gottlieb Klopstock**        June 1816

F major D444 Peters V p.35 GA XX no.229

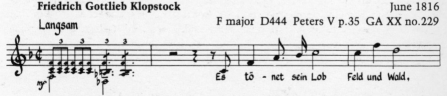

Field and forest, valley and mountain sing his praise; the shore resounds, the ocean's hollow roar thunders the praise of the Infinite One, of his glory and perfection, in nature's hymn of thanksgiving.

The poem was written in 1764. There are fifteen verses, but Schubert wrote out only the first below the stave. The repeat marks at the end of the song may or may not mean that he intended the singer to decide for himself how many to sing. The autograph (Berlin, SPK) is a first draft, dated June 1816. The song was published in 1831 in book 10 of the *Nachlass* (*Geistliche Lieder* no.2). Friedländer in the Peters edition prints a selection of five verses (nos.1, 3, 6, 10 and 14). The *Gesamtausgabe* prints them all. The two-bar introduction is interesting as an early example of the tonic–German sixth–tonic sequence as a musical image of the remote and infinite. But there is no double-bar line and Schubert can hardly have meant it to be played before each verse.

## DIE GÖTTER GRIECHENLANDS The Gods of Greece
**Friedrich von Schiller**                                               November 1819

A minor  D677  Peters VI p.30  GA XX no.371(a) and (b)

Beauteous world, where art thou? Return again, fair springtime of nature. But ah, your fabled dream lives on only in the enchanted realm of song. The fields, deserted, mourn; no god appears before my eyes. Of all that vivid image of life only the shadows have survived.

Schiller's ode was written in 1788. Schubert used the later, and shorter, version, and set only one of the sixteen verses, the twelfth. His autograph (Vienna, SB) is headed 'Strophe von Schiller', and dated November 1819. There are two versions on the same manuscript, the second superimposed on the first by means of pencilled corrections. The main differences are that the piano link between the first (A major) section and the A minor section is shortened by one bar, and the ambiguity of the final cadence is resolved on the tonic, in the second version. Both versions are published in the *Gesamtausgabe*. Contemporary copies carry the title *12te Strophe des Schiller'schen Gedichtes: Die Götter Griechenlands*; but there is no generally acceptable title, and the song is often referred to simply by its first line, 'Schöne Welt, wo bist du?' The song was published in book 42 of the *Nachlass* (1848), under the title *Fragment aus dem Gedichte: Die Götter Griechenlands*.

Schiller's great poem is both an ode to the glory of Greece and a lament for that lost paradise of the Romantic imagination. Significantly, it is the second aspect that captures Schubert's attention. Of the sixteen verses he chooses to set only one, that which most eloquently expresses the sense of loss; and by repeating the opening lines at the end he gives the song a musical shape and emphasises its nostalgic appeal.

Though it is not among the greatest of Schubert's songs, *Schöne Welt, wo bist du!* is a *locus classicus* for those tonal ambiguities which for Schubert are associated with the key of A minor. The open octave E's reach out like unanswered questions, an eloquent symbol of *Sehnsucht*, significantly left unresolved in the first draft. The close thematic links with the A minor String Quartet op.29 are so obviously marked that there must have been some conscious association in the composer's mind. A certain affinity of mood between the song and the Violin Sonata in A of August 1817 (D574) is less obvious. There is a family likeness about Schubert's A minor themes: something very like the tune to which the key words – 'Schöne Welt, wo bist du' – are set appears at bar 45 of *Leichenfantasie* as early as 1811; and there are close parallels with the setting of Werner's *Morgenlied* in 1820.

Capell, 158; Einstein, 190

## DIE HERBSTNACHT Autumn Night
**Johann Gaudenz von Salis-Seewis**                                          March 1816

F major  D404  Peters VII p.12  GA XX no.200

Greetings to you, Melancholy, with the soft strains of the harp! Nymph, you quench the sacred spring from which our tears flow. At your touch a soft shiver runs through me, and your twilight glow glimmers on the path of destiny.

You cause joy to weep, and sorrow to smile, so that grief and pleasure intermingle. You brighten clouded skies with evening sunshine, and hang lamps in tombs and garlands on the tombstone.

The poem, written in the 1790s, has six more verses in the same vein. It was entitled *Die Wehmut* ('Melancholy'). But Schubert's title was as above. His autograph, in the Curtis Institute of Music, Philadelphia, is a first draft, dated March 1816. A fair copy, also entitled *Die Herbstnacht*, is dated April 1816 (Vienna, SB). There are two copies in the Witteczek–Spaun collection (Vienna, GdM), one of them headed 'Wehmut'. The song is supposed by Deutsch to have been published by C. A. Spina in 1860, but no copy has been found. It appeared under the title *Die Wehmut* in vol. VII of the Peters edition in 1885. This edition prints only the first and last verses. The *Gesamtausgabe* prints them all.

The shift into A flat in line 3, and the minor inflection of line 6, give the song a characteristically Schubertian tone, but only, so to speak, within eighteenth-century terms of reference. There is no hint of the personal feeling which informs a song like *An den Mond in einer Herbstnacht* two years later.


**DIE HOFFNUNG** see HOFFNUNG (Schiller)


## DIE JUNGE NONNE The Young Nun

**Jacob Nicolaus Craigher**                                    1824/early 1825

Mäßig                    F minor  D828  Peters I p.201  GA XX no.469

Wie braust durch die Wip - fel der heu-len-de Sturm!

How the raging storm howls amid the treetops. The rafters groan, the house trembles, the thunder rolls, the lightning flashes! And the night is dark as the tomb. Still, still –

So too it lately raged in me. Life raged, as the storm does now. My limbs trembled as now the house. Love blazed, as now the lightning flash. And my heart was dark as the tomb.

Now, wild and mighty storm, rage on! There is peace and tranquillity in my heart. The loving bride awaits the groom, cleansed in the proving fire, vowed to eternal love.

With longing eyes I am waiting, my Saviour. Come, heavenly bridegroom, claim your bride. Free the soul from its earthly bonds.

Hark! The bell tolls peacefully from the tower. Its sweet sound calls me irresistibly to the eternal heights. Halleluja!

The poem was written in 1823 but was not published until 1828. Like the other Craigher settings, it was given to Schubert in manuscript. The dramatic situation is something of a Romantic cliché (cf. Tennyson's *St Agnes Eve*, 1831, and Keats's *Eve of St Agnes*), but the conscious desire for death as a refuge from the storms of life was a sentiment familiar enough in Schubert's circle. Schubert's autograph has not survived, and the date of the song cannot be determined with certainty. It cannot be earlier than 1823 or later than February 1825, for on 3 March 1825 Sophie Müller reported in her journal that she sang it to Schubert and Vogl (*Docs*. no.535). She refers to it as 'a new song', but she may have meant only that it was new to her. The catalogue of the Witteczek–Spaun collection (Vienna, GdM) dates the song 1825.

*Die junge Nonne* was published by A. W. Pennauer in July 1825 as op.43 no.1. The edition was corrupt, as Franz Hüter, Pennauer's manager, admitted in a letter to Schubert (*Docs*. no.573). He claimed that the mistakes had been corrected, but there is still doubt about Schubert's intentions. (See Mandyczewski's comments in the *Revisionsbericht* to the *Gesamtausgabe*.) It seems likely, for instance, that in bars 16 and 39 the octave B sharp in the pianist's left hand should be B natural, to conform to the vocal line in bars 18 and 40.

This wonderful song represents Schubert's art as a songwriter at its peak. It seems to have been conceived in a single moment of illumination, so complete and intangible is its unity of mood and form. A whole dramatic scena of ninety-four bars is built upon a single short motif. As Capell perceptively puts it, 'the sense of grandeur is created by the strength of the first F minor theme, and by the symphonic breadth of its treatment'. That theme is itself a marvellous example of Schubert's power of tonal analogy, concentrating as it does in one unified motif the howling wind, the booming thunder, and the tolling bell.

But *Die junge Nonne* is much more than a fine piece of nocturnal scene-painting. First and foremost it is a dramatic scena. The physical background is distanced (as it is, for instance, in *Im Dorfe* and *Der Doppelgänger*). The storm rages on to the end, but the dynamic level hardly rises above *pp*; the switch into the major mode at 'Nun tobe, du wilder gewaltger Sturm', and the changes in dynamic level towards the end reflect, not any abatement of the storm, but a change of psychological stance as the protagonist finds reassurance in her faith. Everything is heard and seen through the mind of the singer. It would be difficult to find a song which, in its dramatic power, psychological depth and feeling for the poetry of nature, better sums up the achievement of early Romantic song.

Capell, 207–8; Fischer-Dieskau, 205–6

## DIE KNABENZEIT Boyhood
**Ludwig Hölty**

13 May 1816
A major D400 Not in Peters GA XX no.219

How happy is the boy whose coat still trails about his shoulders. He never rails at the evil times, and is always merry and content.

The soldier's wooden sword is now his joy, the spinning-top, and the hobby-horse, on which he sits like a lord.

And when he throws the gaily striped ball up into the blue sky he pays no heed to the scented flowers, or the lark, or the nightingale.

Nothing in all the wide world makes his cheerful face cloud over, unless his ball should fall into the water, or his sword break.

Just run and play the livelong day, my boy, through the garden and over the meadows, chasing the butterflies.

Soon, your happy days done, you will be sweating within the narrow walls of the classroom, learning the dry-as-dust Latin of stuffy old Cicero!

The poem was written in 1771. Schubert's autograph (LC) is a first draft on an MS dated 13 May 1816. The first four bars of the voice line have been revised on the draft, but for some reason Mandyczewski chose to disregard this alteration, preferring to regard it as the beginning of an entirely new version, and printed the original melody line in the *Gesamtausgabe* (see *Revisionsbericht*). The revised version (as above) is given also in D2. There is no tempo indication, but a brisk pace and a lively manner are demanded by the charming verses and by Schubert's carefree setting, one of the best of his essays in the simple folksong manner.

### DIE KRÄHE see WINTERREISE no.15

### DIE LAUBE The Arbour
**Ludwig Hölty**                  17 June 1815

A flat major D214 Peters VI p.98 GA XX no.81

Never shall I forget you, cool green shade, where my love used often to sit, rejoicing in the spring.
> My nerves will quiver at the thrill, when I see you in bloom, see her image float toward me, her divine presence hover over me.
> In the moonlit night, full of tears, in the grey witching hour I shall go trembling to meet you and see many ghosts.
> Oh, I shall lose myself in many dreams of heaven until, trembling with rapture, I coo to my sweet dove whose image sways before me.
> When I stumble on the path of virtue and earthly delight ensnares me, then let the thought flash through me, of what I once saw in you.
> And as virtue streams down upon me from God's clear heaven I shall flee from earthly turmoil and take up my pilgrim's staff again.

The poem was written in April 1773. Schubert's autograph is lost, but there is a copy in the Witteczek–Spaun collection (GdM) dated 17 June 1815. The song was published by C. A. Spina in 1866 as no.2 of 'Six Songs ... by Franz Schubert' (op.172). Schubert groups the verses in pairs and his strophe has two distinct but complementary halves, the first sad and reflective, the second more animated and passionate. In key, mood and movement *Die Laube* bears a strong resemblance to *Erster Verlust*, written a fortnight later, and although it does not have the emotional resonance of that famous song, it deserves to be better known.

### DIE LIEBE Love
**Johann Wolfgang von Goethe**           3 June 1815

B flat major D210 Peters II p.236 GA XX no.78

Joyful or woeful, lost in thought;
Longing, languishing, never free from pain;
In seventh heaven of delight, or sunk in mortal despair;
Only the loving soul is truly happy.

The words come from Act III Scene 2 of *Egmont*, where they are sung by Clara, Count Egmont's lover. But the immediate source for Schubert may well have been Reichardt's setting of the words, which was published in 1804, and which has the same title. Schubert's autograph (GdM) is a first draft, headed 'Die Liebe' and dated 3 June 1815. Stadler's copy (Lund, UB) has the same title, but a copy in the Witteczek–Spaun collection (GdM) is headed 'Clärchens Lied'. The song was published under the title *Clärchens Lied aus Egmont von Göthe* in book 30 of the *Nachlass* (1838).

Beethoven's fine setting has tended to overshadow Schubert's, but the whole conception is different. Beethoven's scena, with its rapid changes of mood and pace, extracts every ounce of dramatic point from every line, with the help of an extensive repeat. His version is uncompromisingly diatonic. Schubert's is equally revealing in a quite different way. His setting is purely lyrical and confines itself to the inner drama. As an expression of deep emotion it achieves its effect by a startlingly 'Romantic' use of chromaticism. The diminished sevenths and German sixths which in the classical musical language had a primarily structural function are here made to carry a weight of personal emotion and an emphasis which is Schumannesque.

> Capell, 101

## DIE LIEBE Love
**Gottlieb von Leon**

January 1817
G major D522 Not in Peters GA XX no.291

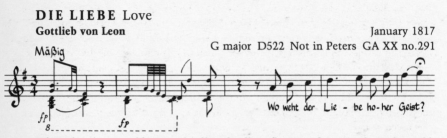

Where does love's noble spirit dwell? It dwells in flower and tree, in the wide world; it dwells where the buds burst open and flowers unfold.

Where does love's noble spirit dwell? It dwells in the glow of evening, and in the constellations; wherever the bees and cockchafers hum and the turtle-doves murmur.

Where does love's noble spirit dwell? In joy and sorrow in every mother's heart; it dwells with the young nightingales, when their sweet songs ring out.

Where does love's noble spirit dwell? In water, fire, and air, and in the fragrance of morning. It dwells wherever life stirs, wherever even one heart beats.

The autograph is missing, but a copy in the Witteczek–Spaun collection (GdM) is dated January 1817. The song first appeared in the *Gesamtausgabe* in 1895.

The harmonic sequences of *Die Liebe* hardly move outside the primary relations of G major, yet the song carries a considerable weight of emotion. Of particular interest is the rhythmical freedom of the last four bars: the singer converts two 3/4 bars to one 3/2 bar, and the postlude is then foreshortened to lead back to the prelude. The influence of Beethoven, who was to play so important a role in the piano sonatas of 1817, seem already discernible here at the beginning of the year.

**DIE LIEBE FARBE** see DIE SCHÖNE MÜLLERIN no.16

# DIE LIEBE HAT GELOGEN Love has Played me False

**August Graf von Platen** March/April 1822

C minor D751 Peters II p.60 GA XX no.410

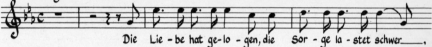

Die Lie-be hat ge-lo-gen, die Sor-ge la-stet schwer____,

Love has played me false. Sorrow oppresses me. I am betrayed, betrayed, by all about me.
>Always the hot tears run down my cheeks. Poor heart, beat no more, beat no more.
>Love has played me false. Sorrow oppresses me. I am betrayed, betrayed, by all about me.

The poem consists of two four-line verses. Schubert repeated the first at the end. The autograph is missing, and there are no known contemporary copies. The date of the song can, however, be deduced from the circumstances. Schubert was introduced to Platen's poetry by his friend Franz Bruchmann, who met the poet at Erlangen in January 1821. In September 1821 Bruchmann sent Platen copies of Schubert's Goethe songs (*Docs.* no.252), adding that he had not been able to hand over Platen's own poem to the composer, because Schubert was away from Vienna. On 17 April 1822 he wrote again, enclosing Schubert's setting (*Docs.* no.284). The only song to which these letters could apply is *Die Liebe hat gelogen*, and since Bruchmann would be likely to send Schubert's song to his friend as soon as it became available, it is fairly safe to assume that it was written shortly before the date of the second letter. In August 1823 the song was published by Sauer and Leidesdorf as op.23 no.1. In this first edition, and subsequent reprintings, the last chord of bar 11 is that of A minor. In the *Gesamtausgabe*, however, the phrase ends, more convincingly, on the major chord, and the analogy with the preceding phrases is preserved.

Platen's poetry is concerned with formal perfection; the emotion is contained within its meticulous craftmanship. Schubert's two settings have an epigrammatic perfection also, but what surprises us is their emotional intensity. There is nothing quite like it until we come to *Winterreise*. Indeed, *Die Liebe hat gelogen* seems to combine the funereal solemnity of *Das Wirtshaus* with the tortured rejection of *Einsamkeit*. The final cry of anguish inevitably recalls the end of the latter song.

The song is a miniature masterpiece, on which Schubert with unerring instinct imposes an ABA form. The significance of the crotchet–quaver–quaver rhythm in the outer sections is highlighted by the wide separation of voice and piano; in the middle section however the movement changes to a syncopated figure which moves chromatically upwards to a climax. The final cry reverts to the major. Capell is right to invoke the name of Wolf in his discussion of the Platen songs; the comparison is more apt for this song than for the companion piece *Du liebst mich nicht*.

Capell, 180; Fischer-Dieskau, 155-6

## DIE LIEBENDE SCHREIBT The Love Letter

**Johann Wolfgang von Goethe**                                         October 1819

Mäßig, zart

B flat  D673  Peters VI p.85  GA XX no.369

One glance from your eyes into mine; one kiss from your mouth upon mine; who, with a certain pledge of these, as I have, can find joy in aught else, however agreeable it may seem?

Far from you, estranged from those I love, my thoughts range far and wide; and always return to that one unique hour. Then I begin to weep.

Suddenly my tears are dried: he loves indeed, I think, here in this silence; oh, should you not reach out, then, toward me far away?

Listen for the murmur of this love-message. In your will lies all my earthly happiness. give me a sign!

The poem is one of a series of sonnets written in 1807, inspired by Goethe's romantic feelings for Minna Herzlieb. Most of the sonnets, like this one, express the emotions of a young girl in love. The autograph is missing. The catalogue of the Witteczek–Spaun collection (Vienna, GdM) dates the song October 1819. It is not entirely clear what the original key was. There is a copy in the Witteczek–Spaun collection in A major, and the song appears in that key also in C. A. Spina's publication (as op.165 no.1) in 1863, which had been engraved many years earlier. The first publication, however, was in June 1832 as a supplement to the *ZfK*, and there the song is in B flat.

The song fails to capture either the poignancy of the situation or the psychological subtlety of the poem. Schubert seems content to find a mood of devotion – significantly, the song bears a strong resemblance to the first setting of Schiller's *Die Entzückung an Laura* of March 1816 – and express it in the regular melodic phrases and flowing triplets. But it can be argued that a young woman's changeable moods in love are not tragic, and the modulation to F major at the words 'Then I begin to weep' has exactly the right suggestion of utter dejection soon to be vanquished. The song hardly deserves the muted response it has evoked from the commentators.

Capell, 154; Einstein, 192; Fischer-Dieskau, 130

## DIE LIEBESGÖTTER The Gods of Love

**Johann Peter Uz**                                                          June 1816

Zart

C major  D446  Peters VII p.98  GA XX no.231

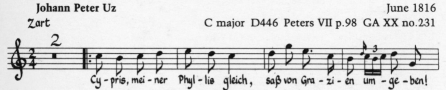

Cypris, like my Phyllis, sat surrounded by graces; I saw her happy kingdom, her wine had befuddled me. A sacred myrtle grove, darkened by secret shadows, was where the goddess dwelt, and the gods of love made sport.

Under cover of the green bushes, in the distant brushwood, there I saw them trip most gladly. Many, light of foot, fled the restraint of tear-stained fetters, fluttered from kiss to kiss and from blondes to brunettes.

The poem was written in March 1744. There are five verses, all printed in the *Gesamtausgabe*. But Friedländer in the Peters edition includes only the first and the fourth, as above. Schubert's autograph is missing, but there is a copy in the Witteczek–Spaun collection (Vienna, GdM) dated June 1816. The song first appeared in vol. VII of the Peters edition in 1887.

Einstein dismisses the poem as 'Anacreontic doggerel, full of pastoral conceits', which is fair enough, though brusque. There is nothing parodistic, however, about Schubert's vivacious strophic setting, so full of high spirits that the postlude breaks into a dance. The instruction *Zart* suggests that the pace should be *allegretto* rather than *allegro*.

### DIE MACHT DER AUGEN see L'INCANTO DEGLI OCCHI

### DIE MACHT DER LIEBE The Power of Love
**Johann Nepomuk von Kalchberg**                                         15 October 1815

B flat major D308  Not in Peters  GA XX no.156

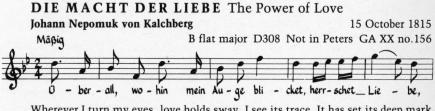

Wherever I turn my eyes, love holds sway, I see its trace. It has set its deep mark on every shrub and meadow-flower. Its breath fulfils, inspires, rejuvenates and adorns all that nature's ceaseless toil creates. All earth, all heaven, every creature lives only through love, made happy by its power.

The poem appeared as a sonnet in *Selam* in 1814. Schubert set only the first quatrain, altering every line and changing the rhythm so that it becomes trochaic rather than iambic. Whether he was taking ruthless liberties with the text, or was working from another, possibly manuscript, version is not clear. The autograph, now in ÖNB, Vienna, is a first draft dated 15 October 1815. On it Schubert has noted 'Dazu eine Strophe' ('One more verse'). But the second quatrain requires even more radical revision than the first if it is to fit the tune, though Mandyczewski in the *Gesamtausgabe* makes the attempt. The best solution is to sing one verse only. The song first appeared in the *Gesamtausgabe* in 1895.

*Die Macht der Liebe* is one of eight songs written on 15 October 1815, and it looks as though Schubert did not really give himself time to consider the difficulties involved in setting a sonnet before embarking on this one. There is no way in which the rest of the poem can be made to fit the strophe.

### DIE MAINACHT May Night
**Ludwig Hölty**                                                          17 May 1815

D minor D194  Not in Peters  GA XX no.70

When the silvery moon gleams through the shrubbery, pouring its slumbrous light across the grass, and the nightingale sings, sadly I wander from bush to bush.

Then I call you blessed, fluting nightingale, because your darling shares your nest, and gives her tuneful mate a thousand loving kisses.

Concealed in the foliage, a pair of doves coo for me in ecstasy; but I turn away in search of deeper shade, and a solitary tear falls.

O smiling image, that lights up my soul like the dawn, when shall I find you on earth? And the solitary tear trickles more warmly down my cheek.

The poem dates from 1774. The autograph is a first draft (Vienna, SB) dated 17 May 1815. The song was first published in 1894, in the *Gesamtausgabe*.

Comparisons with Brahm's splendid setting written some fifty years later are not really very apposite. Much more to the point is the gulf that seems to separate this essentially eighteenth-century setting from another Hölty 'nightingale piece' written only a few days later. *Die Mainacht* is faithful to the undercurrent of *Frühromantik* feeling implicit in the poem, but its regular structure and emotional restraint, the purely supportive role of the piano, and its strict observance of what might be called the Weimar rules for strophic song, all place it firmly in Schubert's early pre-Romantic phase. Yet *An die Nachtigall* (D196), a setting of a similar poem written just five days later, inhabits a different world, in which passionate personal feeling is not merely implicit, but explicit in the structure and style of the song.

## DIE MÄNNER SIND MÉCHANT Men are up to no good!

**Johann Gabriel Seidl**                                     (?) Summer 1828

*Etwas langsam*                 A minor  D866 no.3  Peters IV p.88  GA XX no.510

Du sag - test mir es, Mut - ter: Er ist ein Springinsfeld!

You warned me, mother: he is a young reprobate! I would not believe you, until I tormented myself sick. Yes, now I see he really is, I had simply misjudged him. You warned me, mother: 'Men are up to no good'.

Yesterday as dusk fell, in the wood outside the village I heard a sound: 'Good evening!' and another, 'Many thanks!' I crept up and listened, then stood as though spellbound. There he was with somebody else. – 'Men are up to no good!'

Oh, mother, what torture! I must speak out, I must! It did not stop at whispering. It did not stop at compliments. It went from greetings to kissing, and from kissing to holding hands, and from holding hands – oh, mother dear! – 'Men are up to no good!'

This is the third of 'Four Refrain Songs', published by Thaddäus Weigl in August 1828 as op.95. O. E. Deutsch gave the songs an earlier date (1826), but the autograph (Vienna, MGV) links them with a sketch for the Piano Sonata in C minor D958, and they belong to 1828. It may have been Weigl's idea to harness Schubert's genius to Seidl's light satirical verse. The two were on friendly terms, and Schubert probably worked from a manuscript copy of the verses. The songs were published as op.95 and dedicated by Schubert to the author 'in most friendly fashion'. A 'refrain song' is so called because the motto phrase is repeated at the end of each verse, usually in a new context.

Op.95 seems to have been a conscious attempt on the part of Schubert and his publisher to meet public taste halfway. But the tone of *Die Männer sind méchant* is by no means comic. It does not entirely match the selfconsciously arch manner of the verses, and the direction (*Etwas langsam*) rules out any attempt to represent the girl's predicament as an occasion for merriment. The song seems to have been conceived in the spirit of light opera, serious but not tragic.

# DIE MONDNACHT The Moonlit Night

**Ludwig Kosegarten**                                    25 July 1815
F sharp major  D238  Not in Peters  GA XX no.102

Look, the moonbeams touch the meadow and the bushes with silver, the brook ripples and glistens. The rays stream down, spots of light cascade from the gently stirring leaves, and the dewy landscape gleams and shimmers. The mountain tops are luminous as they grow dim; the topmost branches of the poplar trees glow.

The bright spaces are alive with whispering voices and hovering dreams, that speak intimately to me. Bliss that stirs my memory, joy that brings me sweet forebodings, tell me, where do you blossom and come to fulfilment? Break not my heart with mighty longing; soothing tears, quench my sorrow.

How shall I find relief from torment? Where, oh where, is there a loving soul to calm sweet pain? Each absorbed in the other, quite lost, enraptured, till every empty space is filled – such a being, I fancy, would cool my longing, and quench my grief with exquisite tears.

I know but one, ah, one alone; I know only you, O perfect one, who understands the heart's sorrow. Embracing you, by you embraced, one with you, closely united – spare, oh spare me, sunk in bliss. Heaven and earth vanish before my love-intoxicated eyes.

The first draft (in private possession) is on the same sheet as *Abends unter der Linde*, which is dated 25 July 1815. There is an autograph fair copy in the Fitzwilliam Museum, Cambridge, and two copies, both dated 25 July 1815, in the Witteczek–Spaun collection (Vienna, GdM). The song was first published in 1894 in the *Gesamtausgabe*.

This, the finest of the Kosegarten songs, makes nonsense of our neat chronological categories. Heard with the innocent ear, it might suggest Schumann or even Richard Strauss, so expressively does it capture the mood of rapture and *Innigkeit*. The steady build-up of the climax, and the heart-easing appoggiatura with which the song ends, seem to herald a whole century of Romantic song. Astonishingly, the song had to wait until the end of that century for publication. Like some other rhapsodic songs (*An die Nachtigall*, for instance) the song begins in the subdominant.

Einstein, 47–8

# DIE MUTTER ERDE Mother Earth

**Friedrich Leopold, Graf zu Stolberg-Stolberg**                April 1823
A minor  D788  Peters V p.164  GA XX no.427

Life's day is heavy and oppressive; death breathes light and cool, floating us gently down into the quiet grave like withered leaves.

The moon shines, the dew falls on the grave as on the flowery field. But the tears of friends are lit as they fall by the gleam of tender hope.

We are all gathered up, great and small, into the lap of Mother Earth. Oh, if we would but look her in the face, we should not fear to rest in her bosom.

The poem, entitled simply *Lied*, was written in 1780. Schubert's first draft (Vienna, SB) is in A minor and is headed 'Lied von Stolberg'. It lacks the last four bars and is dated April 1823. There is a complete copy in G minor in the Witteczek–Spaun collection (Vienna, GdM), and an autograph copy of the voice part only, in A flat minor, in the University Library, Hamburg. The song was published in June 1838 in book 29 of the *Nachlass*. The key is G minor and the title *Die Mutter Erde*. It may have been Diabelli's own idea to give the song a more convenient and more easily identified title, though one of the two copies in the Witteczek–Spaun collection is headed 'Lied, oder Die Mutter Erde'. It seems clear that Schubert did not use it.

The note of solemnity and resignation which characterises this lovely song must owe something to Schubert's circumstances when it was composed, for in April 1823 his illness was approaching its first and most serious crisis. Schubert's attitude to death had never been morbid or purely sentimental; here it achieves a kind of personal serenity. The composer, like the poet, was looking death in the face. It is in keeping with this mood that the middle section of the song, with its accented sixths and sevenths and stately movement built on the tonic arpeggio, recalls the Andante of the Piano Sonata in A major (D664). The song deserves to be much better known. Its sentiments were echoed by Schubert in a well-known letter to his father (*Docs*. no.572).

Capell, 185


## DIE NACHT The Night

**James Macpherson (Ossian)**                                    February 1817

G minor D534 Peters IV p.162 GA XX no.305

Machpherson's original text, with his introductory note, is to be found in a footnote to *Croma*:

Those extempore compositions were in great repute among succeeding bards ... The translator has met with only one poem of this sort, which he thinks worthy of being preserved. It is a thousand years later than Ossian ... The story of it is this: Five bards, passing the night in the house of a chief, who was a poet himself, went severally to make their observations on, and returned with a description of, night.

*First bard*: Night is dull and dark. The clouds rest on the hills. No star with green trembling beam; no moon looks from the sky. I hear the blast in the wood; but I hear it distant far. The stream of the valley murmurs; but its murmur is sullen and sad. From the tree at the grave of the dead the long-howling owl is heard. I see a dim form on the plain! It is a ghost! It fades, it flies. Some funeral shall pass this way: the meteor marks the path.

The distant dog is howling from the hut of the hill. The stag lies on the mountain moss; the hind is at his side. She hears the wind in his branchy horns. She starts, but lies again ... Dark, panting, trembling, sad, the traveller has lost his way. Through shrubs, through thorns he goes, along the gurgling rill. He fears the rock and the fen. He fears the ghost of night. The old tree groans to the blast; the falling branch resounds. The wind drives the withered burrs, clung together, along the grass. It is the light tread of a ghost! He trembles amidst the night. Dark, dusty, howling is night, cloudy, windy, and full of ghosts! The dead are abroad! My friends, receive me from the night.

*The chief*: Let clouds rest on the hills: spirits fly, and travellers fear. Let the winds of the woods arise, the sounding storms descend. Roar streams and windows flap, and green-winged meteors fly!

Rise the pale moon from behind her hills, or enclose her head in clouds! Night is alike to me, blue, stormy, or gloomy the sky. Night flies before the beam, when it is poured on the hill. The young day returns from his clouds, but we return no more.

Where are the chiefs of old? Where our kings of mighty name? The fields of their battles are silent. Scarce their mossy tombs remain. We shall also be forgot. This lofty house shall fall. Our sons shall not behold the ruins in grass. They shall ask of the aged, 'Where stood the walls of our fathers?'

Raise the song and strike the harp; send round the shells of joy. Suspend a hundred tapers on high. Youth and maids begin the dance. Let some grey bard be near me to tell the deeds of other times; of kings renowned in our land, of chiefs we behold no more. Thus let the night pass until morning shall appear in our halls. Then let the bow be at hand, the dogs, the youths of the chase. We shall ascend the hill with day, and awake the deer.

See OSSIAN SONGS. Schubert used the translation by Edmund, Baron von Harold. But the published editions, based on Diabelli's version, are all corrupt (see below). Schubert's autograph was discovered in the 1960s in Budapest (HNL). It is a first draft dated February 1817. It ends at bar 206, that is, before the concluding section in 6/8 time marked 'Feurig'. This is an arrangement of the song *Jagdlied* ('Hunting Song') D521, appended by Diabelli in a misguided attempt to give *Die Nacht* a suitably rousing finale. The song was published as book 1 of the *Nachlass* in July 1830. Not content with giving the song an entirely spurious conclusion, Diabelli did not scruple to alter the text, and even the notes, as he thought fit. This corrupt and trivialised version is followed both in the *Gesamtausgabe* and in the Peters edition.

*Die Nacht* is Schubert's last and most interesting attempt to exploit the popular appeal of the Ossian myths. The early sections are wonderfully atmospheric: the kal-eidoscopic key changes, the subtle interplay of voice and piano, the oppressively 'dark' themes with their stepwise-moving thirds and sixths, make the first half of the song an impressive tone poem. The mood and the idiom look forward to the sacred drama *Lazarus* of 1820. But once again the musical interest falls away in the concluding pages. The dance theme (2/4 *Munter*) sounds merely trivial, while the horn fanfares in the postlude are perfunctory. Schubert's failure to bring the song to a satisfactory conclusion means that it is never performed. But nobody seems to have thought of performing only the first half, which contains almost all of the best music, and which ends (in G major) at bar 100.

I Kecskemti, 'Eine wieder aufgetauchte Eigenschrift Schuberts', ÖMZ, XXIII, 1968, p.70

## DIE NACHT The Night

**Johann Peter Uz**

(?) June 1816

A flat major D358 Peters VI p.40 GA XX no.235

Night, you disturb us not. See, we are drinking in the shrubbery, and a fresh breeze springs up to cool our wine. Night! Mother of kindly darkness, secret sharer in our sweet cares, who has cheated vigilance with many a hidden kiss; you alone know what rapture possesses me when, clasped to my lover's breast, I listen among the dewy flowers. Whisper to her, gently swaying trees, whisper to her when all is still; as the hot flood comes welling up, whisper me into dreams of bliss.

Schubert's autograph (Lund, UB) has been mutilated; how and when is not known. The signature and part of the first five bars have been cut away. The song cannot be precisely dated, but on the other side of the sheet is another Uz setting (D363), and this is attributed to 1816 in the catalogue of the Witteczek–Spaun collection (Vienna, GdM). *Die Nacht* was published in book 44 of the *Nachlass* in June 1849.

Schubert's solemn processional chant seems oddly out of keeping with the scarcely suppressed excitement and the conspiratorial mood of the poem. Even stranger is the close resemblance to a quite different song, *Abschied (nach eine Wallfahrtsarie)*, written in September 1816, for the two poems have nothing in common.

### DIE NEBENSONNEN see WINTERREISE no.23

## DIE NONNE The Nun

**Ludwig Hölty**                                                    29 May/16 June 1815

Erzählend, mäßig          A flat major D208, 212  Not in Peters  GA XX no.77

[*Synopsis*] Once long ago in Italy a fair young nun, Belinda, was wooed ardently by a knight. He swore 'by the image of the Virgin, and by her Jesus child' that he would love her until death. Beguiled, she renounced her vows, risking eternal damnation to become his paramour. She left cell and cloister, only to discover that man is fickle. Tiring of his lover, he pursued a life of pleasure with other women, drinking and roistering and boasting of his conquests.

At last the nun, her Latin temperament inflamed, began to think of nothing but revenge, and she hired a band of assassins to murder him. His black soul departed to hell and his bleeding body was thrown into a vault. At nightfall the nun fled to the village chapel, taking the body of the dead knight with her, cut out his false heart and trampled it under foot.

Legend has it that her ghost, in its blood-stained shroud, rises from the grave at midnight, weeping and wailing and carrying a bleeding heart, which she raises three times to heaven, then dashes to the ground. At daybreak, when the cock crows, she vanishes.

The village watchman has often seen her as she shakes the blood from her veil and rolls her eyes in rage.

The poem dates from 1773. There are two versions. The autograph first draft, which has been divided into two sections, is dated 29 May 1815; both parts are in Vienna (the first in SB, the rest in ÖNB). The second version (Vienna, SB) is dated 16 June 1815. There is a copy in the Witteczek–Spaun collection (Vienna, GdM). *Die Nonne* was first published in the *Gesamtausgabe* in 1894. Extensive extracts from the first version are included in the *Revisionsbericht*.

Hölty's exercise in the macabre is remarkable for its early date. Schubert's setting now seems no more than an interesting curiosity. It begins well, as though telling a story (the marking is *Erzählend*), but the horrors are faintly comic: when, for example, the nun stamps the heart of her faithless lover under foot, Schubert obliges with a series of *sforzando* descending chords. The last three verses are set to a 6/8 tune in F minor, in ballad style.

## DIE PERLE The Pearl

**Johann Georg Jacobi**  August 1816

Schreitend  D minor D466 Not in Peters GA XX no.248

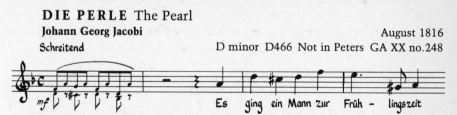

A man went forth at springtime, ranging far and wide through forest and field, past birch and beech and alder. He did not see the green trees in the May sunlight, nor the flowers beneath them. He was looking for his pearl.

His pearl was all his worldly wealth. To find it he had sailed the seas and suffered much. He had hoped it would be a consolation to him for life. He cherished it in his heart, and guarded it from many a thief.

Now he sought it with sighs and groans. Men showed him the sparkling brook with its golden loach, but the sunlit stream and the dancing loach meant nothing to him. His quest was for his pearl.

And so it will always be; he will find no joy in life, no longer watch the dawn in the crimson sky. Uphill and down he must fare, until he finds it.

Poor pilgrim! Like him, I go forth in springtime, past birch and beech and alder. I do not see the glory of Maytime. But ah, what I lack is more than a pearl.

What I lack, what I have lost, what was all my worldly wealth, is the love of a faithful heart. In vain I wander up and down; but one day I shall find a cool grave, and all my sorrows will be over.

Schubert's autograph (Paris Conservatoire) is a first draft dated August 1816. There is a dated copy also in the Witteczek–Spaun collection (Vienna, GdM). The song was published in 1872 by J.P. Gotthard as no.31 of 'Forty Songs'.

The thematic germ is a combination of the familiar drop from tonic minor to dominant major and the pacing rhythm associated with *An die Freunde* and *Winterreise*; in short, Schubert treats the poem as an expression of *Sehnsucht*, of a longing to be satisfied only in death. For the purposes of the song, what matters is the last two verses, and if this finely crafted strophic song is to be shortened, they at least should always be included.

App.IV; Capell, 118; Fischer-Dieskau, 76; Porter, 117–18

## DIE POST see WINTERREISE no.13

## DIE ROSE The Rose

**Friedrich von Schlegel**  (?) March 1820

Mäßig, zart  G major D745 Peters II p.140 GA XX no.408(a) and (b)

The lovely warmth tempted me to venture into the light; but fierce heat burned there, which I must ever rue.

In the mild bright days I could blossom a long time; now I must soon wither, my life renounced already.

The dawn came; I plucked up courage, and the bud, in which all my charms lay concealed, opened. I could graciously scent the air, and wear my crown.

But then the sun grew too hot; for that I must lay a complaint against it. What good is the cool evening, I must sadly ask. It can no longer save me, or dispel my grief.

The sunset glow has paled; soon the cold air will nip me. Though I die, I wished to tell of my short young life.

The poem is no.7 of part I of the cycle *Abendröte*, written 1800–1. Schubert's autograph, in F major, formed part of the Spaun–Cornaro collection (Vienna, privately owned). There is a fair copy (Vienna, SB) also in F, without tempo indication and with the text written below the stave in another hand. The fair copy in G, which was presumably made for the first edition, has been lost. None of the surviving manuscripts is dated, and there is doubt about the song's provenance. There seems to be no evidence for the date usually given — 1822 — other than the fact that the song was published in May of that year. It is much more likely, however, that the poems from part I of *Abendröte* were set at the same time, for that was Schubert's usual way of working. Three of them belong with reasonable certainty to March 1820, and it seems probable that *Die Rose* does too. The song first appeared as a supplement to the *ZfK* on 7 May 1822, in G major, and was reprinted by Diabelli in May 1827 as op.73. The *Gesamtausgabe* prints both versions.

*Die Rose* is a jewel of a song, as perfect in form and as delicate in expression as its subject; like the rose, it can best speak for itself. But it also speaks in defence of transposition. G major suits a light soprano voice better than F, in which the song was written, and there is little doubt that Schubert thought so too, since he agreed to its publication in that key.

Capell, 177–8; Einstein, 253

## DIE SCHATTEN The Shades
**Friedrich von Matthisson** 12 April 1813

A major D50 Not in Peters GA XX no.8 NSA IV vol.6 p.68

Friends, whose graves are already overgrown with moss! When the full moon rises over the wood your shades float up from the still shore of Lethe.

My blessing on you, ever memorable friend! You above all — honest Bonnet! — who spelled out for me so many mysteries in the book of life.

My craft would long ago have foundered in the seething breakers, or been dashed to pieces on the reef, if you had not protected me against the storm like a guardian angel.

To see again one's loved ones, under the light of the golden stars of our homeland — O heavenly longing of the impoverished soul languishing in the grave!

The poem was written after the death of Matthisson's friend Charles Bonnet (1720–93), the Swiss teacher and scientist. Schubert's autograph (Lund, UB) is dated at the end 12 April 1813. There is a copy in the Witteczek–Spaun collection (Vienna, GdM) in F major. The song was first published in 1894 in the *Gesamtausgabe*.

*Die Schatten* is a new beginning with Matthisson, for the two earlier settings of *Der Geistertanz* are no more than attempts to treat the poem in the Zumsteeg manner.

Here, by contrast, is the long, smooth melodic line, faithfully moulded to the words, and the supportive accompaniment, which Schubert had practised under Salieri's supervision. And how skilfully it is managed! The irregular verse form, with its short fourth line, is accommodated by the simple expedient of extending the third phrase of the strophe, and the melodic phrases are shaped even to take account of the commas in verse 3. There is no depth of feeling in the song, however. It seems a little cheerful even for Matthisson's rather formal tribute to his friend; rather like an exercise for Salieri, as in a sense it is.

### DIE SCHIFFENDE The Boatwoman
**Ludwig Hölty** (D2 990D)

A Schubert song with this title is listed by Kreissle among 'songs not yet published'. The Hölty poem certainly exists, but no trace of a Schubert setting has so far been found.

### DIE SCHLACHT The Battle
**Friedrich von Schiller**

Schubert made two attempts to set this poem, first as a solo song (D249) in August 1815 and as a cantata for soloists, choir and piano (D387) in March 1816. Neither progressed beyond a first unfinished sketch. The marchlike theme was the same in both settings, and Schubert finally used this tune as the first of a set of four-handed marches – *Trois marches héroïques* op.27 (D602) – probably written at Zseliz in 1818.

### DIE SCHÖNE MÜLLERIN The Maid of the Mill
**Wilhelm Müller** 1823
D795 Peters I pp.4–53 GA XX nos.433–52 NSA IV vol.2

The song cycle by Wilhelm Müller was published at Dessau in 1821, but it had its origin in a party game played by a group of young Berlin intellectuals some years earlier. The circumstances are thus described in the critical notes to the collected edition of Müller's poems (ed. J. T. Hatfield, Berlin, 1906): 'Towards the end of 1816 a circle of gifted young men and women meeting in the house of the Privy Councillor von Stägemann, who cultivated the "old German" spirit with an almost religious zeal, organised a party game as a kind of literary entertainment. This took place perhaps in imitation of Paisiello's much-loved opera *La Molinara*, but above all under the influence of Goethe's mill-romances (especially *The Journeyman and the Mill-stream*). These romances look back to folksong, and they first appeared in Schiller's *Musenalmanach* for the year 1799.'

The game took the form of an elaborate charade, in which each player assumed a particular role and was expected to write and speak his own part, in verse. As we have seen, it made a conscious appeal to the fashionable enthusiasm for 'folk' subjects, and based itself on the characters of a traditional popular myth; but at the same time the players cultivated a certain ironic detachment, analogous in some ways perhaps to the attitude of a modern intellectual circle to Victorian popular art. These literary societies were a regular feature of the society of that time. Indeed, the reading parties which were held every week during 1821 and 1822 by the Schubert circle had much in common with the group to which Müller belonged, and they masqueraded under assumed names in just the same way.

In 1818 some of the songs which originated at the Berlin meetings were published in settings composed by Ludwig Berger, another member of the group. Wilhelm Müller, who played the part of the young miller (naturally enough) and was the only practising writer in the circle, had more ambitious ideas. Over the next few years he added to his own stock of poems until he was able to publish them as a complete cycle of twenty-three poems. They appeared in 1821 as part I of a volume to which Müller gave the disarming title 'Seventy-seven Poems from the Posthumous Papers of a Travelling Horn-player'. The cycle bore the subtitle 'To be read in winter', and Müller added a prologue and an epilogue in rhymed couplets, in which he poked gentle fun at the current fashion for rustic balladry.

There is some evidence that Schubert had been searching for some time for just such a text. Given his admiration for Beethoven, the appearance of *An die ferne Geliebte* in 1816 must have alerted him to the possibilities of the song cycle, and in the intervening years he had experimented with sequences by Friedrich von Schlegel (*Abendröte*) and Johann Mayrhofer (*Heliopolis*) without success. But neither of these poets had Müller's gift for song – that is, for strong, simple verse forms which meet the composer halfway; nor did their sequences offer a dramatic situation and a narrative thread.

At any rate, Schubert seized on the poems eagerly and adapted them to his own purposes, which were not by any means identical with Müller's. First, he discarded the prologue and epilogue, for he did not intend to adopt Müller's stance of ironic detachment. Instead, he saw the story as a folk myth of universal significance (what I have elsewhere called 'a parable of the doom that waits on innocence in an evil world'), which deserved to be treated seriously. Secondly, he rejected three of the poems in Müller's cycle, either because they were too long, or because they did not make an indispensable contribution. For his intention was not to follow Beethoven in linking the songs together to form a continuous whole, but to aim at a larger unity, in which each song would be complete in itself, and yet also an essential part of the whole.

The fair copy of the complete cycle, made for the printer, is missing, and the detailed chronology of the work is not clear. The main facts to be taken into account are these: (1) A first draft of *Eifersucht und Stolz*, no.15, dated October 1823, has survived (Vienna, GdM). (2) In a letter to Schober of 30 November 1823 Schubert wrote: 'I have composed nothing since the opera except a few mill-songs. The mill-songs will appear in four books, with vignettes by Schwind.' The opera referred to is *Fierabras*, the score of which was completed on 2 October. (3) There is a well-documented tradition, vouched for by Spaun (*Memoirs* p.367) and confirmed by Schober and others (*Memoirs* p.266), that Schubert composed some of the songs while under treatment in hospital, but when that was, and where, is not known. Towards the end of July he left Vienna for a working holiday in Upper Austria and did not return until mid-September. This seems more likely to have been after his stay in hospital than before; and indeed, there is a conspicuous gap in the record – no documented visits or engagements, no dated autographs – for June and most of July, which may conceal the crisis of the disease. It seems significant, in particular, that work on the full score of *Fierabras*, which was proceeding at a remarkable pace at the end of May, came to a full stop on 7 June, when the third act was begun, so that the final act was not completed until the end of September. Walther Dürr, however, argues for a later date (October) for Schubert's stay in hospital (see the introduction to vol.2 of the NSA edition of the songs); on general grounds this seems less likely. (4) The casual reference to 'a few mill-songs' in the letter to Schober suggests that the latter was aware at least of the existence of the project. But Schubert had not seen Schober since he left Vienna for Upper Austria, for Schober himself had left Vienna in August to live in Breslau. (5) Franz von Hartmann mentions 'the *Müllerlieder*' among the songs performed by Schubert and Vogl on a visit to his family on 28 July 1823 (*Memoirs* p.273). While his reminiscences were written down towards the end of his life, and long after the event, they were based on contemporary journals.

The most likely hypothesis, on this evidence, is that the hospital treatment took place in June or July and that the cycle was begun then. During his holiday Schubert worked at the opera score (*Docs.* no.174), and he took up the song cycle again only after that was finished at the beginning of October. The first draft of the complete cycle was completed in November.

*Die schöne Müllerin* was published as op.25 in five books – not four, as Schubert anticipated – by Sauer and Leidesdorf. The dedication was to Karl, Baron von Schönstein, an amateur baritone of some distinction and a great admirer of Schubert's songs. The first two books came out in February and March 1824, but Leidesdorf was dilatory over the rest, which finally appeared in August. By that time Schubert was living at Zseliz with the Esterházy family and in no position to supervise the operation, so that the final stages were entrusted to Ferdinand Schubert. This first edition is full of errors, and Schubert's intentions are not always clear. As a result there are many disputed readings in the score, some of which are noted in the following pages. Schönstein's own manuscript copy of the complete cycle has disappeared; but autograph copies of nos.7, 8 and 9, made for Schönstein, probably at Zseliz, and transposed down to suit his voice, have survived. In 1830, Diabelli, having acquired the rights to the cycle, published a much revised second edition, which is thought to incorporate the many changes and embellishments made by Michael Vogl and Schönstein himself in their performances of the songs. This edition has a vignette of the maid of the mill on the title page, but it is not by Schwind, who never produced the illustrations for the cycle that Schubert had hoped for.

Finally, some necessarily brief critical observations: (1) Müller's contribution to Schubert's achievement has never been fully recognised, except by Capell, and it is now fashionable to discount it. But Müller is a better poet than is usually allowed, and he gave Schubert exactly what he wanted. He wrote 'for the voice', and his songs directly inspired the two great masterpieces. (2) These should be seen as complementary. *Die schöne Müllerin* has in recent times been somewhat overshadowed by the popularity of *Winterreise*, perhaps because the unrelieved pessimism of the later cycle has matched the mood of the time. But the earlier cycle better sustains the level of inspiration throughout the work. (3) It is not, as is sometimes alleged, a reversion to older and simpler verse forms. True, there are several strophic songs in it; but the strophic song is not 'simple' (*Ungeduld* is as much a masterpiece as *Der Neugierige*). And for variety of form and subtlety of expression the cycle has never been surpassed; witness *Wohin?*, *Tränenregen*, *Pause*, *Trockne Blumen*.

Capell, 188–97; W. Dürr, Introduction to NSA IV vol.2; Feil; Moore, 3–72; J. Reed, '*Die schöne Müllerin* reconsidered', *M and L*, LIX, October 1978

(1) **DAS WANDERN** A-Roving                                             B flat major

A-roving is the miller's joy. A sorry miller he would be who never felt the urge, to go a-roving.

It was the water taught us this. It never rests, by day or night, always intent, to go a-roving.

We see it in the mill-wheels too. They never rest. All day they turn and never tire, the mill-wheels.

The very stones, for all their weight, join in the merry dance. They would go faster if they could, the mill-stones.

To go a-roving is my joy. Dear master and dear mistress mine, let me go on my way in peace, a-roving!

Müller's title for this poem was *Wanderschaft* ('Wanderings').

The most extended strophic songs in the cycle are the first and the last, each with five verses. Here the effect is to establish the association with folksong at the very beginning, as though to distance the events of the cycle from real life. The young miller sets out on his travels with a spring in his step, and the sky seems to be unclouded. The brisk, steady movement is the essence of the song; it acts as a point of reference throughout the cycle. And it is worth noting that although it embodies the idea of a walking pace with the precision we expect from Schubert, it is not merely an imitation of that pace; for at two beats to the bar it is too slow to walk to, and at four beats too fast. The symmetrical four-bar patterns are also more complicated than they seem. The stresses vary from bar to bar, so that the stress at the beginning of bar 2 is the strongest of the first two bars, while the heaviest accent of all in the four-bar prelude falls at the beginning of bar 4. The rhythmical counterpoint is designed to suggest the idea of the mill's unceasing chatter, without monotony.

(2) **WOHIN?** Where to?                                            G major

I heard a little stream babbling down to the valley from its source among the rocks, so clear and strangely bright. I don't know what came over me, or who put the idea into my head, but I too had to head down the valley with my wanderer's staff.

Always on and down, and always following the stream, which babbled on, ever more clear and bright.

Is this my way then? Streamlet, tell me, where are we going? You have quite fuddled my wits with your murmuring. But why am I talking about murmuring? That cannot be the murmur of the stream. It is the water-nymphs singing, as they dance in a round down below.

Let them sing, wanderer; let the brook murmur on, and follow it cheerfully. Mill-wheels turn beside every clear stream.

*Wohin?* introduces us to the other protagonist in the story, the mill-stream, which holds within itself the key to the solution of the drama. Müller's words hint at tragic possibilities, especially at the mention of the water-nymphs dancing *tief unten* ('far below') and the stress given to the word *hinunter* at the beginning, but Schubert's music flows unconcernedly along in this loveliest of all his stream-songs.

The song is a seamless robe, and it defies analysis. The first two pages have the feel of a strophic song; and it is easy to identify a roughly tripartite form, the outer sections in the tonic, and the middle section moving towards the dominant by way of E minor, and back again. But the song flows on as uninterruptedly as the stream. Everything grows from the initial keyboard figure and the opening melodic sentence. The mill-stream holds the secret of the young miller's fate, and its music is to sound throughout the cycle, as the long-held D at the end of the song suggests.

(3) **HALT!** Halt!                                                                C major

I see a mill gleaming among the alders. The sound of its wheel rises above the singing and murmuring water.

O, welcome; welcome, sweet song of the mill! How friendly the house looks, how its windows shine!

And how brightly the sun sheds its light from the sky! Now, you dear little mill-stream, is *that* what you meant to say?

*Wohin!* is a favourite with recitalists as a separate song; its greatness is beyond challenge. *Halt!*, on the other hand, seems to belong entirely within the cycle, though it has the same on-running style and freedom of form. Both songs gain, however, from being heard in context, for the musical and psychological links between these first four songs are very close.

*Halt!* is built on the twin motifs presented in the prelude: the *sforzando* arpeggio figure which traverses a sixth up and down again, which symbolises the clack of the mill-wheel, and the flowing semiquavers in the pianist's right hand. The leaping phrases on the repeated words 'wie helle vom Himmel sie scheint' are the climax of the song, and there is a touch of foreboding in the last line, 'is *that* what you meant...?'

(4) **DANKSAGUNG AN DEN BACH** Expression of Thanks to the Mill-stream

G major

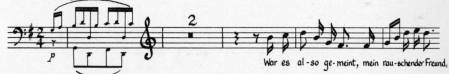

Is *that* what you meant, my babbling friend! Your singing and rippling, is that what they meant?

'To the maid of the mill' — That was the message, am I not right? 'To the maid of the mill.'

Did she send you? Or have you bewitched me? Though I would dearly like to know whether she sent you.

However it was, I accept my fate. I have found what I was looking for, be that as it may.

I asked for work, and I now have enough both for hands and for heart — enough and to spare!

A change of pace, and of mood, Up to this point the young miller has been presented as eager, even lighthearted, and outward-looking. Here the movement is slowed for the first time (*Etwas langsam*) and the drama turns inward. The song links up with *Wohin!* and *Der Müller und der Bach* — all in G major — to form a trilogy which holds the key to the drama. The young man's fate lies in the hands of the mill-stream, not the miller's daughter. It is the human situation which is at issue in Schubert's cycle, not a rustic romance in fancy dress.

By analogy with bar 7, the singer's third quaver in bar 35 should be G, not F sharp.

(5) **AM FEIERABEND** After Work                                                    A minor

If only I had a thousand arms to work with! If only I could drive the rushing mill-wheels, whirl through the woods like the wind, and turn every millstone! Then the fair maid of the mill would see how much I loved her.

But my arm, alas, is so weak. This lifting, carrying, cutting and hammering, why, any apprentice could do it as well as I.

And there I sit in a circle with them all, in the cool quiet hour when work is done; and the master says to us: 'I was pleased with your work today,' and the fair maid bids us all goodnight.

The first four songs have set the scene – the young miller, the mill-stream, the mill and the maid. *Am Feierabend* involves us more deeply in the psychological drama. Yet the beginning of the song suggests that, like *Halt!*, it will present another picture of the busy mill, so aptly do the percussive quaver chords and the on-running semiquavers portray its noisy beams and wheels. This time, however, Schubert has a different purpose in mind, and the break in the rhythm at bar 46 calls our attention to the inner dream. This quasi-recitative middle section conveys exactly the casual matter-of-factness of the miller's commendation and the girl's goodnight. Schubert then repeats the first verse, so as to emphasise the contrast between the busy workaday world of the mill and the young man's aspirations. At the end the rushing wheels sound only fitfully and menacingly.

(6) **DER NEUGIERIGE** The Questioner                                               B major

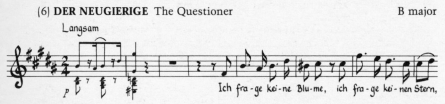

I ask no flower, I ask no star; none of them can tell me what I would so dearly like to know.

And then, I am no gardener; the stars are too remote; so I shall ask the mill-stream if my heart deceived me.

Brook of my love, how mute you are today! I only want to know one thing, a single word, one way or the other.

One little word is 'yes', the other 'no'; these two words hold all the world for me.

O brook of my love, how strange you are. I shall tell no-one else. Tell me, does she love me?

The problem of reconciling the dramatic force of recitative with the unity of mood of the true lied had occupied Schubert since his earliest years. In *Erlkönig*, and Schmidt's *Wanderer*, he had shown early in his career how the solo cantata could be revivified by giving it the organic unity of the lyric. But the reverse problem, how to bring the dramatic force of recitative within the compass of the lied, was to take him longer.

In *Der Neugierige* that problem is triumphantly solved. In the opening B major sections the singer seems to be communing with himself; the music has the flow, the *Innigkeit*, of a serenade to the mill-stream. But suddenly, át verse 4, we switch into close-up. The even flow of semiquavers is arrested; the focus is changed; we hear a kind of musical direct speech as the accompaniment slips up a semitone into G major (the flattened sixth again) and there follows a magical passage in a different rhythm (actually 2/4, though it is still notated in 3/4) which sharply delineates the young man's bewilderment and uncertainty. But though this passage is, in a sense, an interruption, it remains firmly within the lyrical context of the song. The song is a wonderful demonstration of Schubert's power to give psychological depth and perspective to the lied.

Here follows in Müller's original cycle a poem called *Das Mühlenleben* ('The Life of the Mill'), which Schubert omitted. Its length (eleven verses) disqualified it, and it adds little to what has gone before.

(7) **UNGEDULD** Impatience A major

I would like to carve it on every tree, engrave it on every stone; I would like to sow it in every newly dug plot with cress-seed, which would soon let the secret out; I would like to inscribe it on every sheet of paper: Yours is my heart, and ever shall be yours.

    I would like to train a young starling to speak the words loud and clear, in my own voice, from the fullness of my own passionate heart. Then his song would ring out at her window. Yours is my heart, and ever shall be yours.

    I would like to whisper it into the morning breeze, to waft it through the rustling wood. Let it shine from every flower! Let the scent carry it to her from near and far! Stream – can you drive nothing but mill-wheels? Yours is my heart, and ever shall be yours.

    I thought it must have shown in my eyes, that everyone would see it burning in my cheeks; that it could be read on my silent lips, that every breath would declare it plainly. But she notices nothing of all these anxious urges: Yours is my heart, and ever shall be yours.

An autograph fair copy, transposed to F major, until recently in private possession in Vienna, is now missing. It was made for Schönstein, probably at Zseliz in 1824.

*Ungeduld* is the first genuinely strophic song in the cycle after *Das Wandern*, and perhaps the best-known of them all. But so far from being a return to a more primitive design, it is in its way as much a miracle of subtle form as *Der Neugierige*. The young man's impatient ardour is expressed by a sort of rhythmic dislocation, so that the voice seems always to be a beat ahead of the piano. (This can in fact be easily demonstrated by omitting the third beat of the accompaniment in bar 9, when the harmonic arrival points will coincide, though the song will lose its dramatic urgency.) This sense that voice and piano are out of phase persists until the climax of the verse, when the rhythmic ambiguity is resolved, voice and piano join forces, and the clinching phrase – *Dein ist mein Herz* – is given an emphasis that makes it every tenor's joy and pride.

(8) **MORGENGRUSS** Morning Greeting                                                      C major

Mäßig

Gu-ten Mor - gen, schö-ne Mül - le - rin,

Good morning, lovely miller's maid! Why do you quickly turn your head away, as though something was wrong? Does my greeting so displease you? Does my glance so disturb you? Then I must go away again.

O let me just stand far off and gaze up at your window from quite a distance! Fair little head, come forth! You blue stars of the morning, peep out from your round sockets!

Eyes heavy with sleep, flowers bedimmed with dew, why do you shrink from the sun? Has the night been so kind, that you close up and droop and weep for its quiet bliss?

Shake off the veil of dreams, and rise up fresh and free to God's bright morning! The lark is trilling in the sky, and from the depths of the heart love summons away care and sorrow.

Schönstein's autograph copy is in A major. There are a number of variant readings, of which the most important are in bar 3, where the top line is in dotted rhythm, and bars 8 and 15, where the singer is given a quaver rest before the final quaver. The song is as fresh as the morning itself. The passing shadows are wonderfully suggested in the descending bass line of bars 12–15, and in the yearning appoggiaturas at bars 20 and 39.

(9) **DES MÜLLERS BLUMEN** The Miller's Flowers

A major D795 (9) Peters I p.24 GA XX no.441

Mäßig

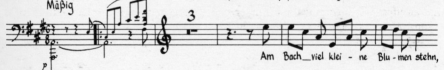

Am Bach_viel klei - ne Blu-men stehn,

By the stream grow many tiny flowers, peeping from clear blue eyes. The mill-stream is the miller's friend, and my love's eyes are bright blue, so these are the flowers for me.

I will plant the flowers close beneath her window. There you shall call to her when all is still, when she lies down to sleep; you know what I want to say.

And when she shuts her eyes and rests in sweet sleep, then whisper dreamlike in her ear: 'Forget – forget me not!' That's what I mean to say.

And when in the morning she opens the shutters, then you must gaze up at her with loving glances. The dew in your eyes, that will be the tears which I would weep over you.

Schönstein's autograph copy is in G major. At the end there is a note in Schubert's hand: 'The accompaniment of this song can conveniently be played an octave higher.' Evidently he was not particular about such things. However, nobody dares to act on the suggestion nowadays, perhaps because the modern piano is better equipped to supply the warm legato tone the piece requires than the pianos of Schubert's day.

Here again, the song's simple harmonic structure and the beautifully shaped vocal line give it the flavour of folksong. Yet the five-line verse might seem difficult to set. By repeating the last line, Schubert gives himself room for the *Nachgesang*, and at the same time puts the emphasis where it properly belongs.

(10) **TRÄNENREGEN** Shower of Tears A major

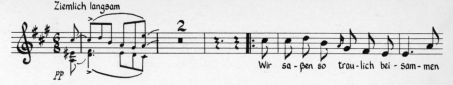

So quietly we sat together beneath the alders' shade; so quietly we looked down together, into the murmuring stream. The moon had come out too, and the stars, and they looked down so quietly, reflected in the silver surface of the water.

It was not the moon or the starlight I was looking at. I gazed only at her reflection, and at her eyes.

I watched them nod and glance toward me from the happy stream; the blue flowers on the bank nodded and glanced at her.

And the whole sky, sunk beneath the stream, seemed to want to draw me down into its depths.

And the stream rippled merrily over the clouds and the stars, and its singing and babbling summoned me: 'Come, follow me!'

Then my tears welled up, and the image became blurred. She said: 'It's coming on to rain. Goodbye, I'm going home.'

Schubert ignores the deliberate anti-climax of the last couplet, which reminds us that Heine was a great admirer of Müller. Instead of lowering the emotional temperature, as Müller had done, he raises it, enriching the harmony with major–minor alternations, and veering off into the remote key of C major. The effect is magical, but not at all what Müller intended.

This wonderful modified strophic song ends on a note of tender uncertainty. Mathematically speaking it completes the first half of the cycle, but it does not bring it to an effective climax, and there is much to be said for ending the first half with the next song, *Mein*, as Capell long ago suggested (p.195).

(11) **MEIN** Mine D major

Mill-stream, peace to your babbling! Mill-wheels, cease your rumbling! All you sprightly birds of the forest, big and small, an end to your singing!

Through the woods, in and out, one rhyme alone shall sound today: My sweetheart, the maid of the mill, is mine. Mine!

Spring, are these all the flowers you have? Sun, can't you shine more brightly? Ah, then with that happy word of mine I must be all alone, not understood anywhere in the wide world!

There are three points in the cycle where the music sounds a note of joy, of love self-fulfilled and triumphant; three points at which the singer must give full rein to the voice. One is *Ungeduld* ('Dein ist mein Herz!'), the others *Mein* and the last verse of *Trockne Blumen* ('Der Mai ist kommen, der Winter ist aus!'). These three songs, in a sense, convey the essence of the cycle, its passion and its Romantic pessimism.

*Mein* is thus a climax and a turning-point. Here at last the doubts and difficulties of the first half of the cycle are, momentarily, resolved. Schubert's ABA form, with the middle section in the flattened sixth B flat, enables him to repeat the first two verses, and so to build the final climax on the all-important line – 'Die geliebte Müllerin ist mein, ist mein!'

(12) **PAUSE** Pause                                                                  B flat major

I have hung up my lute on the wall, and have tied a green ribbon around it. I cannot sing any more, for my heart is too full, I don't know how to force it into rhyme. I could express in playful song even the burning pangs of my longing, and as I complained so sweetly and tenderly, I still thought my sorrow was a burden. Ah, how great my load of happiness must be, if no earthly music can contain it!

Rest on this nail, then, dear lute. And if a breath of air moves over the strings, or a bee brushes you with its wings, then I shall feel fearful, and shudder. Why did I let the ribbon hang so far down? Often it trails across the strings with a sighing sound. Is it the echo of my love's torment, or the prelude to new songs?

Of the last five songs, three are strophic, and the other two (*Tränenregen* and *Mein*) are based at least on an easily identified strophe, with accompaniments that are supportive rather than entirely independent. But here is a very different conception. The major role is given to the piano, and the strumming motif given out in the prelude occupies the foreground, while the young miller communes with himself in a kind of free descant. Voice and piano are distanced, one from the other, the latter sharply focussed and insistent, the voice detached and reflective. Here is a superb example of that psychological depth which we noticed in *Der Neugierige*, and which looks forward to the greatness of *Im Dorfe* and *Der Doppelgänger*. It derives essentially from the ability to present two musical ideas in counterpoint.

When the strumming stops, as it does in bar 63, and the piano resumes a more supportive role, the words themselves come into sharper focus, and the unanswered question ('Is it the echo of my love's torment?') hangs on the air in the remote key of F flat before slipping back to the home key – a magical end to the most subtle and inspired song in the cycle.

(13) **MIT DEM GRÜNEN LAUTENBANDE** Verses to Accompany the Green Ribbon                                                          B flat major

'What a pity that the beautiful green ribbon should fade here on the wall – I am so fond of green!'

So you said to me today, my love; and I have untied it and send it to you at once. Now enjoy its greenness!

Though your lover is dressed all in white, yet green should have its reward, and I too am fond of it. For our love is evergreen and hope blossoms green far away; that's why we are so fond of it.

Now plait the green ribbon nicely in your hair, for you are so fond of green. Then I shall know where hope lives on, and where love reigns; then I shall really love green.

The held tonic chord at the beginning seems to have no thematic significance and sounds like an intrusion. It is often omitted in performance. This has the additional advantage that it makes the girl's opening remark – 'Schad um das schöne grüne Band ...' – follow directly from the question with which *Pause* ends, 'Is it to be the prelude to new songs?'

The somewhat mannered formality of the title (and of others too – *Pause*, for instance, and *Danksagung an den Bach*, and *Tränenregen*) reflects Müller's ambiguous attitude towards the folk tradition. While taking full advantage of that tradition he is anxious to maintain a standpoint of ironic detachment. Significantly perhaps, *Mit dem grünen Lautenbande*, with its simple form and harmonic structure, and supportive accompaniment, gets as close to the pure folksong as any song in the cycle.

(14) **DER JÄGER** The Huntsman            C minor

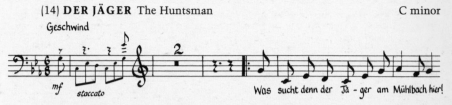

What is the huntsman doing here by the mill-stream? Stay where you belong, proud hunter! Here is no game for you to hunt, only a tame young deer, for me. And if you wish to see that gentle deer, then leave your rifle behind in the wood, leave your baying hounds at home, stop sounding your horn, and shave the rough hairs from your chin; or the deer will take fright and hide in the garden.

But it would be better to stay in the forest and leave mills and millers alone. What use are fishes among the green branches, what can the squirrel want in a blue pond? So stay in the greenwood, proud hunter, and leave me alone with my three mill-wheels. And if you want to please my girl, I'll tell you, my friend, what is troubling her heart: the wild boars, they come out of the forest at night, and break into her cabbage-patch, trampling and rooting about in the field: shoot the wild boars, you brave huntsman!

The appearance of the huntsman on the scene rudely interrupts the internal drama, serving as a brutal reminder of external reality. Significantly, he does not speak for himself; we hear of him only through the words of the young miller. But it is the huntsman, and the vaguely sinister threat he poses whose character is symbolised in the song itself, with its crude energy, square phrases and jackboot rhythms. It is unlike any other song in the cycle. It is true, in one sense, that the internal drama would be complete without it, in that the seeds of the final tragedy lie within the mind of the protagonists. But *Der Jäger* represents an essential element in the allegory, as a symbol of the inevitable hostility of events.

There is also another purpose at work. The last two songs have brought the drama almost to a standstill. *Der Jäger* sets everything in motion again, so that events move on swiftly to the appointed end.

## (15) **EIFERSUCHT UND STOLZ** Jealousy and Pride    G minor

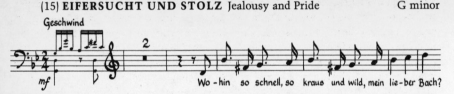

Wo-hin so schnell, so kraus und wild, mein lie-ber Bach?

Whither away so fast, ruffled and wild, beloved stream? Do you angrily pursue your bold fellow-huntsman? Turn back; turn back and first chide the miller's maid for her wanton flightiness. Did you not see her standing at the gate last night, craning her neck to watch the high road? When the happy huntsman returns from his kill, no modest girl puts her head out of the window. Go and tell her so, mill-stream, but say nothing, do you hear, about my sad looks. Tell her: He cut himself a reed-pipe from my bank and plays lovely songs and dances for the children. Tell her!

In *Der Jäger* events are looked at from the outside; it is a narrator's song, and the words do not seem to belong to the miller himself. Here in the following song the emotions are once again personalised, and the music has the gait and inflection of direct speech; we are looking at events through the eyes of the young miller. None the less, the two songs belong together, both in the minor key, both quick, passionate and doom-laden. Together they form a kind of dark interlude between no. 13 ('Nun habe das Grüne gern') and no. 16 ('Mein Schatz hat Grün so gern').

The pianist's running semiquavers are a kind of angry minor version of the brook music in *Das Wandern* and *Wohin?* But as the words tell of the huntsman returning from the hunt they give way to staccato chords, with hunting calls in the voice line, full of sharpness and menace. Again, the singer is heard 'in close-up', as the music assumes the intermittent phrasing of direct speech. Yet the changes of mood and focus are all subsumed within the formal unity of the song.

In bars 77 and 83 the singer's dotted crotchet should probably be E, as in Friedländer's edition, not D.

## (16) **DIE LIEBE FARBE** The Favourite Colour    B minor

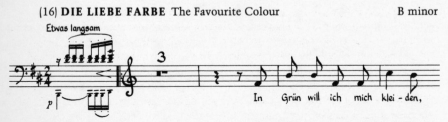

In Grün will ich mich klei-den,

I shall dress all in green, the green of weeping willows: my love is so fond of green. I shall seek out a cypress grove, a heath full of green rosemary: my love is so fond of green.

The merry hunt is up! Away over heath and hedge! My love is so fond of hunting. The game I hunt is Death; the field I call 'Love's Anguish'; my love is so fond of hunting.

Dig me a grave in the sward, cover me with green turf: my love is so fond of green. No black cross, no gay flowers – everything green, green all around: my love is so fond of green.

Before *Die liebe Farbe* Müller inserted a song called *Erster Schmerz, letzter Scherz* ('First Sorrow, Last Laugh'), which Schubert rejected. It has ten verses, and adds little to the development of the drama.

Here, for the first time in the cycle, we hear the insistent tonality of B minor, which almost always with Schubert is associated with a tragic sense of loss and disorientation. And as so often, the glimpse of the major in bars 19 and 20 serves only to intensify the pathos. Here for the first time also the consummation which has been implicit in the cycle from the beginning finds overt expression: 'The game I hunt is Death; the field I call "Love's Anguish" '. The F sharps beat incessantly through the song like a funeral march. But the funeral is to be a celebration of Romantic love and longing, as the words of the first verse make clear. And Schubert will later, in *Trockne Blumen*, give it the appropriate note of triumph.

(17) **DIE BÖSE FARBE** The Hateful Colour  B major

I would travel far away into the wide world, if only it were not so green out there in the woods and fields.

    I would pluck the green leaves from every bough; I would weep the green grass pale as death with my tears.

    O green, you hateful colour, why are you always there, looking at me so proudly, so boldly, so spitefully; at me, a poor white miller?

    I would lie at her door in storm and rain and snow, and softly sing day and night the one little word: farewell.

    Hark: when the hunting horn winds through the wood I hear the sound of her window; and though it is not for me she looks out, yet I can look in at her.

    O, untie the green ribbon from your brow, and give me your hand in token of farewell.

The contrast in mood between this song and the previous one is strongly marked, though there are obvious structural links – the key and the shape of the melody, for instance, and in particular the repeated triplets on B and F sharp in the accompaniment. The contrast between the two owes more to Schubert than to Müller, however. So far as the poems are concerned the titles seem to be intended to show the miller's instability, for they are alike in their tone of pessimism and self-pity. Schubert's aim in emphasising the differences is clear enough. *Die böse Farbe* serves the same purpose, at the same point in the cycle, as *Muth* in *Winterreise*, that is, it provides for a change of mood, a point of contrast, before the dénouement of the drama. Without it, the last five songs of the cycle would all sound the same note of passivity and pathos.

    The leaping tune on which the song is based (exceptionally marked *f*, and the piano *ff*) is full of vigour and resolution, though it is a resolution born of desperation, as the pianist's ominous triplet chords tell us. As the song proceeds the listener is increasingly aware of the undercurrent of disquiet. The middle section, with its repeated single notes, inevitably recalls the repeated F sharps of *Die liebe Farbe*, and the cry of anguish in the closing bars, as the harmonic base moves up from B minor to C major and the singer from F sharp to G, makes it clear that the protagonist in the drama is near the end of his tether.

    Here follows in Müller's cycle the third poem which Schubert omitted. It is called *Blümlein Vergissmein* ('The Forget-me Flower') and has eight verses. The tone is similar to the foregoing poems, and Schubert had already set a forget-me-not poem in no.9. Its inclusion might also have weakened the effect of the following song.

(18) **TROCKNE BLUMEN** Withered Flowers

E minor

All the flowers which she gave me shall be laid in the grave with me. How sadly they look at me, as though they knew what was happening to me.

How faded they are, how pale; and how is it they are so wet?

Alas, tears do not bring back the green of May, nor can they make a dead love bloom again.

And spring will come, and winter will pass, and the flowers will spring up in the grass.

And flowers will lie on my grave, all the flowers which she gave me. And when she wanders by the graveside, and thinks in her heart, 'He was true to me!' then all you flowers, come out, come out! The spring has come, and winter is over!

The note of triumphant fulfilment sounds only twice in the cycle: first in *Mein*, when the young miller for the moment believes that his love is understood and returned, and again in this song, at the words: 'The spring has come, and winter is over!' And between these two points the whole work is, in a philosophical sense, suspended. For *Die schöne Müllerin* is not a sort of pastoral love story. It is a parable on a favourite Romantic theme, the belief that a true and pure ideal love can never find its fulfilment on earth. It is about Romantic longing which is its own reward, because it can only be satisfied in death. The young miller's love finds its fulfilment only when his love thinks in her heart 'He was true to me'. Then, at last, spring has come.

*Trockne Blumen* is thus the true climax of the whole work. Schubert gives to its closing couplet all the emotional emphasis he can. And he does so by a process of rhythmic elaboration, so that within one unifying *Bewegung* the music moves from the deadness of winter, in the bare opening minor chords, to a wonderful burgeoning.

(19) **DER MÜLLER UND DER BACH** The Miller and the Stream

G minor/major

*The Miller*: When a constant heart is lost in love, then do the lilies wither in their beds; then the full moon must hide behind the clouds, lest mortals should see her tears. Then the angels cover their eyes, and sobbing sing the soul to rest.

*The Stream*: And when love struggles free from sorrow, a new star twinkles in the sky. Three roses bloom, half red and half white, and nevermore fade on their thorny stem. And the angels cut off their wings, and come down to earth each morning.

*The Miller*: Ah streamlet, dear streamlet, you mean so well. But mill-stream, do you know the ways of love? Ah there, down there, is cool repose. Mill-stream, dear mill-stream, sing on, sing on!

We have taken our leave of the miller's daughter, but the story cannot end here. Schubert and Müller have to show events in their cosmic perspective, to return to the mood of irony and restraint after the passionate involvement of *Trockne Blumen*. So we take up again the unfinished business between the young miller and the brook, and true protagonists, which began with *Wohin!* and continued with *Danksagung an den Bach*. We return to G major/minor, so often associated by Schubert with death and dissolution; to the ambiguities of the young miller's attitude towards his fate, and to Schubert's infinitely subtle sense of melodic and harmonic variation within a broadly ternary form.

(20) **DES BACHES WIEGENLIED** The Brook's Lullaby        E major

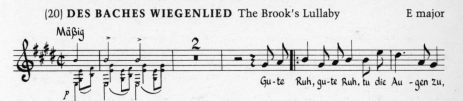

Rest! Rest! Close your eyes! Wanderer, weary wanderer, now you are at home. Here is constancy and truth; you shall lie by my side until all streams are swallowed up in the sea.

Your bed will be cool, your pillow soft, in the crystal blue of your little room. Come, come, whatever can rock him, rock and cradle my boy for me!

When a hunting horn sounds from the greenwood, I will rush and roar about you. Little blue flowers, do not look in, for you bring bad dreams to my sleeping boy.

Keep away, wicked girl, keep away from the path by the mill, lest your shadow should wake him. Throw me down your scarf so fine, that I may cover his eyes.

Goodnight, goodnight, till all things wake, sleep out your joy, sleep out your sorrow! The full moon climbs, the mists recede, and how spacious the heaven up there above!

The last song is a *Nachgesang*, an epilogue. The miller has found 'constancy and truth' at last, in death; the brook's lullaby has the sweetness of fulfilment. This conclusion, however Romantically orthodox, must have seemed a trifle bland even in the 1820s to sophisticated listeners. Müller was careful to dissociate himself from it in his verse epilogue, declaring that he was not to be held responsible for the brook's 'watery funeral oration'. Schubert seems to have had no such reservations. He lavishes on the song the loveliest of his cradle music. It is true, however, that the strophic form itself is a kind of distancing, enabling him to frame the song within the context of the folksong tradition.

There is a significant contrast here with the end of *Winterreise*, which moves steadily towards isolation and alienation rather than death, and culminates in a song which faces reality with a bleak stoic resolution. *Des Baches Wiegenlied* moves gently forward at the same pace and *Bewegung* for some 120 bars, and so long a strophic song runs a certain risk of monotony. But the secret of the song's greatness is the shape of the strophe, which culminates at bar 16 in a rocking motif first given out by the piano. This seems to embody the identity of singer and stream, and is wonderfully enhanced by the flattened sixth at bar 19. The music is so enchanting that we return to the beginning of each verse with a fresh sense of anticipation.

## DIE SOMMERNACHT The Summer Night
**Friedrich Gottlieb Klopstock**        14 September 1815

C major D289 Not in Peters GA XX no.143(a) and (b)

When the light of the moon streams down over the woods, and the scent of the lime trees is borne on the cool breezes; then my mind is overcast by thoughts of the grave of my beloved; only that do I see in the dusky forest, and no fragrance reaches me from the blossom.

With you, O souls of the departed, I enjoyed it once! How the scented cool breezes played about us then; O beautiful nature, how you were transfigured by the moon!

The poem was written in July 1766, after the death of the poet's wife. There are two versions of the song, the first marked 'Nicht zu langsam' and the second 'Langsam, feierlich'. The only significant difference otherwise is that in the second version bars 19 and 20 are telescoped in a single bar, and the verbal repeat is cut. Schubert's first draft, dated 14 September 1815, is in Berlin (SPK). The revised version survives only in contemporary copies, of which there are several. Both versions were first published in the *Gesamtausgabe* in 1895. Like the earlier Matthisson song, *Trost, An Elisa* (q.v.), *Die Sommernacht* is written entirely in recitative, except for a brief arioso passage at the end. It does not match the earlier song, however, in expressiveness and purity of style.

Einstein, 111

**DIE SONNE STEIGT** see KLAGE

## DIE SPINNERIN The Spinster
**Johann Wolfgang von Goethe**                                         August 1815

B minor  D247  Peters IV p.151  GA XX no.119

As I sat quietly spinning, on and on without stopping, a handsome young man came up to me at the distaff.

He paid me the compliments there were to pay – what was the harm in that? – He praised my flaxen hair, and the flaxen thread.

But he would not be satisfied with that, and let things be. And so the thread which I had held so long snapped in two.

And the distaff-weight went on working, and I finished many a stint. But ah! I could no longer boast about them.

When I took my work to the weaver I felt something stir, and my poor heart beat faster.

Now in the heat of the sun I bring it to be bleached, bending painfully over the nearest pool.

What I span so quiet and fine in my little workroom will in the end – how can it be otherwise? – come into the light of day.

Schubert's first draft is lost, but the fair copy made for Goethe survives in Berlin (DS). The song is dated August 1815 in the catalogue of the Witteczek–Spaun collection (Vienna, GdM). It appeared in June 1829 as op.118 no.6, published by Josef Czerny.

*Die Spinnerin* might be quoted as a triumphant vindication of Goethe's views on the supremacy of the strophic song, so aptly does the music match the verses, and so successful is it in catching the spirit of folksong. The running semiquavers are reminiscent of *Gretchen am Spinnrade*. The simple harmonic structure of the song is pure folksong, but not the conscious artistry. The song is at once playful and serious, compassionate yet unsentimental, with an undercurrent of tragedy.

Einstein, 111; Fischer-Dieskau, 53

**DIE STADT** see HEINE SONGS no.4

## DIE STERBENDE The Dying Maid

**Friedrich von Matthisson**

(?) May 1815

A flat major D186 Not in Peters GA XX no.65

Heil! dies ist die letz-te Zäh-re, die der Mü-den Aug ent-fällt!

Hail! This is the last tear to fall from her tired eyes. Already shadows fall upon the
world she knows. The dream of life has lightly fled like vanishing spring mists, and
already seraphim are weaving the flowers of paradise for her garland.

There are two more verses, which Schubert did not set. The poem, written in 1780, had
earlier appeared under the title *Die sterbende Elisa*. This Elisa (cf. *Trost, an Elisa*) was
betrothed to the poet's friend Rosenfeld, and died of a broken heart after his untimely
death. The autograph, in private possession, contains also *Naturgenuss* and the first setting
of *Stimme der Liebe*. The date on the manuscript is said to be May 1815, but it has also
been read as May 1816. The first page of *Die Sterbende* has been cancelled, and Schubert's
dissatisfaction with it is not difficult to understand. The rather dull hymnlike setting seems
bland and featureless. The song was first published in 1894 in the *Gesamtausgabe*, where
all three verses are set out.

R. van Hoorickx, 'Thematic catalogue of Schubert's works: new additions,
corrections and notes', *Revue belge de musicologie*, XXVIII–XXX, 1974–6, p.156

## DIE STERNE The Stars

**Johann Georg Fellinger**

6 April 1815

A flat major D176 Not in Peters GA XX no.57

*Lieblich, ziemlich langsam*

Was fun-kelt ihr so mild mich an, ihr Ster-ne hold___ und hehr___!

Why do you twinkle so tenderly at me, you stars, lovely and sublime? What do you
do on your dark journey across the blue ocean of the heavens? You look down so
kindly upon me from east and west, from north and south, like the eyes of God.

And everywhere you shine upon me with a soft dusky light. The sun rises in
the morning, and yet you do not leave me. Scarcely does evening darken than you
shine in my face again, so gentle and loving.

Welcome then, welcome, pale tranquil friends, wandering like luminous
spirits across your spacious realm. And ah, perhaps a noble friend, untimely dead,
salutes me from among you.

Perhaps one day bright Sirius will be my home, when this wormlike body must
cast its skin; perhaps, when this weak mould must break, the soul will rise like
a spark and reach Uranus!

Only continue to smile! Beckon me in silence toward you. The great Earth
Mother guides me according to her grand plan. The end of the world does not trouble
me, if only I can find my loved ones all united there.

The poem was written in 1812 and published in 1814 in the periodical *Selam*, where
Schubert presumably found it. Only the first verse is written out on Schubert's autograph,
which is in private possession, but there are repeat signs at the end. The copy in the
Witteczek–Spaun collection (Vienna, GdM) is dated 6 April 1815, and there is also a copy

in the Stadler collection (Lund, UB). The song was published in 1872 by J. P. Gotthard, as no.30 of 'Forty Songs'. It is a slight but charming strophic song, which seems to have escaped notice. The repeated octave and arpeggio figures in the pianist's right hand are Schubert's twinkling stars, and the mood of tenderness and wonder is admirably caught.

### DIE STERNE The Stars

**Ludwig Kosegarten**                              19 October 1815

B flat major  D313  Not in Peters  GA XX no.160

How good it is to be in the warm dark night, when God's stars twinkle in their solemn splendour. Come forth, Ida, and let us look up in wonder.

See how Lyra shimmers and Aquila glows. Corona gleams and Gemma sparkles. The bright watchers beckon and the golden chariots shine, and Cygnus swims proudly in the blue ocean.

O stars, witnesses and messengers from a better world, you calm the tumult that fills our breast. I look up to your bright spheres and thoughts of greater pleasure quiet my angry heart.

O Ida, when melancholy dims your soft eye, when the world fills your cup with bitterness, go out into the darkness, look at the twinkling stars; your pain will ease, your heart will beat more freely.

And when in the dust your spirit sickens, when your belief in God and the future wavers, look up at those far-off eternal stars, and believe in God.

[*The poem has three more verses*.]

Schubert's autograph, in private possession, is a first draft dated 19 October 1815. There is a fair copy in the Houghton Library, Harvard University, and a dated copy in the Witteczek–Spaun collection (Vienna, GdM). The song was first published in the *Gesamtausgabe* in 1895. The regular phrases and hymnlike movement of this strophic setting give the song a quasi-religious feeling. Neither the sentiments nor the music will sustain eight verses.

### DIE STERNE The Stars

**Karl Gottfried von Leitner**                              January 1828

E flat major  D939  Peters II p.182  GA XX no.552

How brightly the stars shine through the night! They have often aroused me from slumber. But I do not reproach the bright creatures for that; for silently they do us many a good service.

They wander like angels high above, lighting the pilgrim through heath and wood. They hover like messengers of love, and often bear kisses far across the sea.

Their gentle gaze rests on the sufferer's face, and they dry up his tears with their silvery light. And kindly, consolingly, they point beyond the grave, beyond the blue sky with fingers of gold.

Blessings upon you, shining throng! Long may you shine on me with your warm clear light. And if one day I fall in love, look kindly on the bond; may your gleam be a blessing upon us.

The poem was written in 1819. Schubert's patron and hostess, Marie Pachler, had drawn his attention to Leitner's poems during his stay in Graz in September 1827. Schubert's autograph is dated January 1828 and is now in the Třeboň Archive at the Státní Archív, Jindřichův Hradec, Czechoslovakia. The song was first published by the Lithographic Institute in Vienna, which was managed by Schober, in July 1828, as No.1 of four songs dedicated by Schubert to Karoline, Princess von Kinsky 'in deepest respect'. In February 1829 the publication was reissued by Diabelli as op.96. *Die Sterne* was sung by Michael Vogl at Schubert's public concert on 26 March 1828.

The song is a fine example of Schubert's mature mastery of the modified strophic song, which might also be said to be through-composed, in the sense that every verse is modified in its second half to match the text. Leitner's dactylic rhythm is preserved, and indeed becomes the integrating factor in the whole song, which sustains the crotchet–quaver–quaver rhythm through every one of its 188 bars. But Leitner's eight verses are regrouped into four with longer lines. All the verses begin and end in the tonic, so creating a sense of timeless stability. But the middle section of each ranges widely over the 'circle of thirds', to C major, C flat major, G major and C major again. So Schubert manages to suggest infinite space and variety within the stable tonal universe.

It is perhaps worth noting that the basic rhythm is a kind of 'twinkling' version of the slow march which, in *Der Tod und das Mädchen* and elsewhere, serves as Schubert's death, or fate, motif. Like the Impromptus, the song seems to grow inevitably from the opening phrase, conveying as it develops a sense of spontaneity; like them, it combines a single rhythmic pulse with the greatest tonal freedom and melodic invention.

Capell, 246; Einstein, 352; Fischer-Dieskau, 273

## DIE STERNE The Stars
**Friedrich von Schlegel**                                                    (?) 1819 or 1820

*Langsam*                              A flat major D684 Peters VI p.58 GA XX no.378

You wonder, O man, what our sacred beams signify. If only you followed the heavenly signs, you would understand better how friendly we shine, how mortal suffering would fade away. Then love would flow for ever from heavenly vessels, all would breathe deep the pure azure air, the light blue sea would encompass the meadows, and stars would twinkle in our native valleys.

We all spring from the same divine origin. Is not all being united in one choir? Now that the gates of heaven all stand open, what profit lies in dread despair? O, if you had already pierced to the depth of things, you would see the stars whirling about your head; and the waves playing innocently about your heart, untouched by the storms of life.

The poem comes from part II of the cycle called *Abendröte* (1800–1). Schubert's autograph is missing, and the only documentary evidence for the date of the song comes from the catalogue of the Witteczek–Spaun collection (Vienna, GdM), which assigns it to 1820. But this is by no means incontrovertible; and since it is clear that Schubert worked on part II of the cycle at the beginning of 1819 (cf. D652 and D646, which can be precisely dated) it may well be that *Die Sterne* belongs to the same period. There is a copy in the Witteczek–Spaun collection that differs in some respects from the published version. The song was published in 1850, in book 48 of the *Nachlass*. The source was probably an autograph manuscript, now lost.

The *Gesamtausgabe* has repeat marks at the end and prints both verses. Friedländer in the Peters edition prints only one verse, while Capell in the course of an enthusiastic note on the song confesses that 'the poet has really nothing to add in the second [verse]'. This is difficult to accept, for the comforting assurances of the first verse are dependent on the philosophical doctrine of the unity of man and nature, which is explicitly asserted in the second. The *maestoso* theme with which this fine song begins seems to be Schubert's tonal image for the sense of awe felt in the presence of nature; there is a similar passage at bars 21–31 of Schober's *Todesmusik*. The song moves on from awe to a kind of subdued rapture, expressed in long, arching cantilena phrases. *Die Sterne* is among the best of the *Abendröte* songs.

Capell, 166

## DIE STERNENNÄCHTE Starry Nights

**Johann Mayrhofer**                                                      October 1819

Sanft                                  D flat  D670  Peters VI p.88  GA XX no.366

In mond-er-hell-ten Näch-ten   mit dem Geschick zu rech-ten

On moonlit nights this heart has learnt not to remonstrate with fate. The starry heavens lap me in peace. And then I think, here down below flowers also grow; and my mute, sad gaze turns to the stars' eternal course with renewed strength.

With them too hearts bleed, and pain torments, but they shine serenely on. So I cheerfully conclude that our little earth, so full of dissonance and deceit, itself shines brightly in this diadem of light. 'Tis distance makes the stars so.

The poem's title is *Sternennächte*, as is Schubert's title on the original autograph; the article was inserted on publication. There are two versions of the song, which derive from the autograph and from the first edition. The surviving autograph is in D flat major, and is dated October 1819. There is no tempo indication, the small notes in bar 38 are missing, and there is a different, rather weaker, version of bars 34 and 35. This manuscript has been split up; the first 28 bars are now in Berlin (SPK), the rest in the Paris Conservatoire. The copy in the Witteczek–Spaun collection (Vienna, GdM) may well be based on an autograph fair copy. It is in B flat and carries the marking *Sanft*, and it provided the source for the first edition in 1862, when the song was published by C. A. Spina as op.165 no.2. The Peters edition follows the published version, while Mandyczewski in the *Gesamtausgabe* prefers to keep to the original key, though he takes over some details from the published version.

There is no good reason to despise the B flat version, in which the tessitura lies more comfortably for the voice. This gently flowing serenade to the stars is one of the finest of the Mayrhofer settings; the simplicity of its ABA form, and the perfection of the melodic line, match the serenity of the poet's mood.

Capell, 161; Einstein, 191–2

## DIE STERNENWELTEN Starry Worlds
**Johann Georg Fellinger**                                   15 October 1815

Langsam, feierlich                          F major D307 Not in Peters GA XX no.155

O - ben_ dre - hen sich die gro - ßen un - be-konn-ten Wel — ten dort,

Great unknown worlds circle there far above, bathed in sunlight, revolving in their courses. The countless army of stars ranges itself cosily around; smilingly they gaze from the distance and spread God's glory far and wide.

A band of light runs down through the far blue heaven, and the power of God guides the stars in their courses; everything is rounded off, everything cradled in light and fire, and this great universe proclaims the hand of a mighty artist.

Creator, those starry hordes show forth thy majesty! Only he whose spirit turns toward you can count himself blessed. He will sing praises only to thee, dwelling beyond the spheres, moving joyfully through the worlds, drinking pure angel songs.

The verses are a translation of a poem by the Slovene poet Urban Jarnik. They appeared in the periodical *Selam* in 1814. Schochow prints all three verses and the Slovene original. Schubert's autograph (in ÖNB, Vienna) has the first verse written out under the stave and a note – '2 more verses' – with repeat marks at the end. It is a first draft dated 15 October 1815. There is a dated copy also in the Witteczek–Spaun collection (Vienna, GdM). The *Gesamtausgabe* inconsistently shows the repeat marks but prints only the first verse. The song was first published in 1895 in the *Gesamtausgabe*.

'Slow and solemn' is Schubert's instruction, and the song does convey, within its short span, a sense of grandeur. There is an impressive climax at the end of the fourth line, and another at the sixth, where there is an unexpected sequence of chords, falling from F major through E flat to D. But the mediocre verses can hardly justify a repeat.

## DIE TAUBENPOST The Pigeon Post
**Johann Gabriel Seidl**                                      October 1828

G major D957 no.14 (D2 965A) Peters I p.166 GA XX no.567

Ziemlich langsam

Ich hab ei - ne Brief-taub in mei - nem Sold,

I have a carrier-pigeon in my pay, devoted and true. She never flies short of the goal, or overflies the mark.

I send her out a thousand times a day on patrol, over many a favourite spot till she reaches my darling's house.

There she peeps secretly in at the window, observing every look and step, conveys my greetings cheerfully, and brings hers back to me.

No longer need I write a note; even my tears I can entrust to her. She will certainly not miscarry them, for she serves me eagerly.

Day and night, dreaming or awake, it is all the same to her; as long as she can range and roam, she is more than happy.

She never tires or flags; for her the route seems always new. She needs no bribe or reward, so faithful is this pigeon to me.

That's why I cherish her in my heart so dearly, sure of the fairest prize. Her name is – Longing: Do you know her? The messenger of faithfulness.

The poem does not appear in the two-volume edition of Seidl's work published in 1826; presumably Schubert set it from a manuscript copy. There is a rough sketch, on two staves, in Vienna (SB). The first complete draft (New York, PML) is dated October 1828. It follows on from the end of the Rellstab and Heine songs. *Die Taubenpost* was appended by Tobias Haslinger to the collection of Rellstab and Heine songs that he published in the spring of 1829 under the title *Schwanengesang*. This was not in accordance with Schubert's intentions or wishes, and there is no stylistic or other good reason for associating it with the two groups. The first performance was given by Michael Vogl at a private concert arranged by Anna Fröhlich on 30 January 1829.

Schubert's last song turns its back on adventures of the soul. In keeping with Seidl's verses, which are as simple and conventional as a keepsake, the song dances along, all sweetness and good humour. It is entirely right that his last word on the song should reflect the sheer goodness and happiness that lie at the centre of his art, and that it should reveal his mastery of the modified strophic song at its best. The seven verses of the poem are organised in three strophes and a coda. The structure is the one he had himself evolved, an integrating piano figure and a basic tune, both submitted to a programme of tonal and melodic variation so as to give point to every line. How enchantingly, too, does Schubert linger over the climax, at the words, 'Her name is – Longing: do you know her?' The song serves as a kind of epigraph on his own life and art.

Capell, 257–8; Fischer-Dieskau, 282–3

## DIE TÄUSCHUNG Illusion

**Ludwig Kosegarten**                                                        7 July 1815

E major  D230  Peters VI p.93  GA XX no.93

In the alder grove and the pine wood, by the light of sun, and moon, and stars, a smiling vision surrounds me. In its smile the dusk grows bright, and the wilderness turns to paradise.

I open my longing arms to it, and strive to press it fondly to my breast. I grasp at it, and snatch the empty air as it swims away out of sight like a wraith of mist.

O haste away! I shall follow you. Bliss is not here, but with you. Tell me where I may lay hold upon you, that I may never, never leave you but, free from pain, may embrace and be embraced by you always.

The poem was written in 1787. It has six verses, all printed in the *Gesamtausgabe*. But only verses 1, 4 and 6 (as above) appear in the Peters edition. The first draft, in private possession, is dated 7 July 1815. There is an autograph fair copy in Vienna (SB) and a dated copy also in the Witteczek–Spaun collection (Vienna, GdM). The song appeared in May 1855 as a supplement to Zellner's *Blätter für Musik Theater Kunst*, I, no.29. In June 1862 it was reissued by C. A. Spina as op.165 no.4.

*Die Täuschung* is sweetly tuneful, and grateful to the hands and the voice, attractive music for domestic consumption but little more. There is no hint here of the poignancy of *Irrlicht* or *Täuschung*.

## DIE UNTERSCHEIDUNG The Distinction

**Johann Gabriel Seidl**

(?) Summer 1828

G major D866 no.1 Peters IV p.83 GA XX no.508

Mäßig

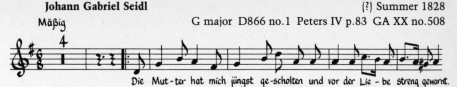

Die Mut-ter hat mich jüngst ge-scholten und vor der Lie - be streng gewarnt.

Mother scolded me lately, and warned me strongly against love. 'Every woman',
she said, 'pays its price, and once you're caught all is lost.' So in my opinion it's
best for us not to speak of it again. Of course I am still yours for ever – But Hans!
I can't *love* you!

Above all, Hans, don't ever forget that you must love only me. Let my smile
be always your delight, and every other smile a bore. Yes, to please Mother I will
be true to both of you, and always try to please you – But Hans! I can't *love* you!

Whenever we make holiday my greatest pleasure will be to wear your spray
of spring offerings in my bodice as decoration. And then, when the dancing starts,
and you have your duty dance with Gretchen – that's only fair – I shall even be
jealous. But Hans! I can't *love* you!

And when in the cool of the evening we rest, tenderly excited, keep your hand
on my breast, and feel how my heart beats! And if you intend to teach me, with
your kisses, what your eyes silently say to me, even that I won't deny you. But Hans!
I can't *love* you!

The song is the first of 'Four Refrain Songs', published by Thaddäus Weigl in August 1828
as op.95. The autograph is in Vienna (MGV). See note on *Die Männer sind méchant*. The
four 'Refrain Songs' are all written in the spirit of light opera, and this one particularly
so. The decorative 'woodwind phrases' in the pianist's right hand seem to call for
orchestration; the unexpected modulation to B flat in the middle of each verse, and the
interrupted cadence before the last line, are in the same operatic tradition. Indeed, in form
and spirit, not to mention the key, the song is faintly reminiscent of Lieschen's aria, *Der
Vater mag wohl immer*, in Act I of *Die Zwillingsbrüder*.

## DIE VERFEHLTE STUNDE The Hour that Failed

**August Wilhelm von Schlegel**

April 1816

F minor D409 Not in Peters GA XX no.206

Unruhig

Quä - lend un - ge -still - tes Seh-nen pocht mir in em-pör-ter Brust.

Restless longing beats furiously in my tormented breast. Love, you could capture
my soul and my senses with your flattery; does your magic delude me with dreams
of short-lived pleasure, only to waken in tears? One thing alone can still my longing
– to be intoxicated with tears of joy, to lean on my beloved's breast, locked in his
arms, his lips pressed to mine.

Ah, I gave him no warning, hardly knew myself beforehand. And now I tremble
so anxiously. Will my beloved come? The hour is quiet and auspicious. No eaves-
dropper threatens our secret understanding. One thing alone can still my longing
– to lean on my beloved's breast in happy communion, locked in his arms, his lips
pressed to mine.

When I hear quiet footsteps I think: ah, here he is! His feelings must have told
him that the hour of bliss has come, the time to exchange our joys freely; but it
is half gone already, in misunderstanding. One thing alone can still my longing – to

lean on my beloved's breast in rapture, locked in his arms, his lips pressed to mine.

I hoped that the joy of song would perhaps relieve my longing, that sweet melodies would cool the fire of raging desire. But the song escaped from the depths of my heart like a groan, and died in tears. One thing alone can still my longing – to lean on my beloved's breast, drunk with sweet tears, locked in his arms, his lips pressed to mine.

The poem was written in 1791. The first draft, dated April 1816, is in the Ikutoku Kai Foundation, Tokyo. The fair copy, also dated April 1816, is in Berlin (DS). There are two copies in the Witteczek–Spaun collection (Vienna, GdM) one in D minor with a note to the effect that the original key is F minor. The song was first published in 1872 by J. P. Gotthard, as no.26 of 'Forty Songs'.

The febrile emotionalism of the verses does not tell in the song's favour, but that does not excuse its neglect. Schubert's strophic setting is divided into two contrasted halves, the first moving at a slow harmonic speed from F minor to E flat major in a way that recalls the beginning of *Hektors Abschied* and points forward to the great duet Fantasie in F minor. The passionate undertow is reflected in the singer's descending triplets from a top A flat. The second half moves quickly and at a much brisker harmonic speed. At the climax – 'One thing alone can still my longing' – Schubert achieves a fine cadence, pivoting on the seventh chord on F flat, first moving to C flat and then to A flat major. The song deserves to be rescued from oblivion.

Capell, 125; Einstein, 135

## DIE VIER WELTALTER The Four Ages of the World
**Friedrich von Schiller**                                    (?) March 1816

G major  D391  Peters IV p.130  GA XX no.196

Behaglich

Wohl per – let im Gla - se der  pur - pur - ne Wein, wohl glän - zen die Au - gen der Gä - ste;

The red wine sparkles in the glass; the guests' eyes shine. The minstrel appears and steps forward. To the good things he brings the final touch; for without the sound of the lyre even a banquet of the gods serves only common appetites.

The poem, written in January 1802, has eleven more verses. Schubert wrote out only the first and put repeat marks at the end, leaving the singer to solve the problem of how many to sing. Both the *Gesamtausgabe* and the Peters edition print all twelve verses; and since the poem presents a kind of summary of the history of the arts from the pastoral age through the heroic and the classic to the Christian, it can hardly be shortened without damage. The autograph is missing, and the date is not certain. That usually given is quoted from the catalogue of the Witteczek–Spaun collection (Vienna, GdM). The song was published by Josef Czerny in February 1829 as op.111 no.3.

Schubert's jolly little tune in 6/8 tempo might go down well at many banquets, especially at the end, but as a vehicle for Schiller's elevated sentiments it seems quite unsuitable. Maybe Schubert did not bother to read beyond the first verse.

# DIE VÖGEL The Birds
**Friedrich von Schlegel**

March 1820

A major D691 Peters VI p.104 GA XX no.373

Lieblich

*How lovely it is to soar and to sing, to look down on the earth from brilliant skies. Men are foolish; they can't fly. They bewail their plight, but we fly up to the heavens.*

*The huntsman whose fruit we pecked wants to kill us, but we have to mock him, and take our plunder.*

The poem comes from part I of the cycle called *Abendröte*, written 1800–1. Schubert's autograph is a fair copy (Vienna, SB), marked 'Lieblich'. The date March 1820 has been added in another hand. There are two copies, similarly dated and marked, in the Witteczek–Spaun collection (Vienna, GdM). The song was first published in 1866 by C. A. Spina, as no.6 of 'Six Songs'. The tempo indication *Allegretto* in the Peters edition seems to be editorial. At this stage in his career Schubert rarely used Italian for tempo markings.

The most popular, and perhaps the most perfect in its simplicity, of the *Abendröte* songs, and a splendid vehicle for the light soprano voice. Its popularity perhaps owes something to the fact that it is short enough to provide the perfect encore.

**DIE VOLLENDUNG** see VOLLENDUNG

# DIE WALLFAHRT The Pilgrimage
**Friedrich Rückert**

(?) 1822–3

F minor D2 778A (not in D)  Not in Peters  Not in GA

Mäßig

*My tears instituted the pilgrimage in penitential robe to the temple of Beauty; but they are buried in a waste of burning sand, never having arrived to worship.*

The existence of the song was unsuspected until July 1968, when a manuscript copy of it was discovered by Reinhard van Hoorickx among papers in the possession of the Cornaro family, which is related to Schubert's friend Josef von Spaun. The authorship of the text was established by Walther Dürr. The lines are to be found in the first edition of Rückert's *Östliche Rosen* ('Oriental Roses'), first published in 1822 or perhaps late 1821. *Die Wallfahrt* was published privately in 1968 by Reinhard van Hoorickx and reprinted by Bärenreiter (Kassel, 1969) in *Ausgewählte Lieder*, edited by Walther Dürr.

The song, written for bass voice, is a solemn chant against F minor harmonies which move towards A flat and G flat major at the climax. It is authentic Schubert, though it lacks the striking originality of the other Rückert songs.

**DIE WEHMUT** (Salis-Seewis) see DIE HERBSTNACHT

**DIE WETTERFAHNE** see WINTERREISE no.2

## DIE WOLKENBRAUT The Bride from the Clouds
**Franz von Schober**                                       D683

In the 1865 edition of Schober's poems the text appears with a note, 'Composed by F. Schubert'. So it was, for Troila's aria at the beginning of Act II of *Alfonso und Estrella*. It was not at first realised that Schober had abstracted the poem from the opera libretto, and some commentators assumed that a separate setting must exist. But no such song has been found, nor is it likely to be. The poem is a typically Schoberesque fancy about a huntsman who is lured to his death by a beautiful maiden who materialises from the clouds.

**DIE ZÜRNENDE DIANA** see DER ZÜRNENDEN DIANA

## DITHYRAMBE Dithyramb
**Friedrich von Schiller**                                         (?) 1824

*Geschwind, feurig*                   A major   D801   Peters II p.128   GA XX no.457

Nim - mer, das glaub mir, er - schei - nen die Göt - ter,

Never, I believe, do the gods appear singly. No sooner is jolly Bacchus there than Cupid comes too, the smiling boy; and the splendid Phoebus joins in. As they approach, all the immortals, the temples of the earth are filled with gods.

Tell me, how can this earthborn mortal entertain the heavenly choir? Ye gods, grant me the gift of immortal life. What can a mere mortal give you? Lift me up to Olympus! Give me the cup filled with nectar; for joy dwells only in the hall of Jupiter.

Pass him the goblet, Hebe! Just one more cup, for the poet. Moisten his eyes with the dew of heaven, that he may not behold the Styx, the hateful shore; that he may think himself one of us. The heavenly spring gushes and foams; the heart grows tranquil, the eye grows bright.

The poem, originally entitled *Der Besuch* ('The Visit'), was written in 1796 and published in the *Musenalmanach* for 1797. But Schubert used a later, slightly different version. The autograph, undated, is in the Schiller archive at Marbach am Neckar. The song was published in June 1826 by Cappi and Czerny as op.60 no.2, and this printed version shows minor differences and one significant change from the autograph: the postlude lengthened. This clearly represents Schubert's second thoughts, and since the first edition must have been based on his own fair copy, it should surely take precedence over the autograph. Mandyczewski in the *Gesamtausgabe*, however, prefers to follow the autograph. Friedländer in the Peters edition gives the later version.

The song is usually ascribed to 1824, but there is no decisive evidence. It is written for bass voice, possibly for Count Esterházy, Schubert's patron, during his residence in Zseliz during that year. There is a much earlier setting (D47) for mixed chorus and male soloists, but this seems never to have been completed. *Dithyrambe* was given its first public performance at a concert of the Gesellschaft der Musikfreunde on 20 November 1828, the day after Schubert's death.

This last of the Schiller songs is the most uninhibited, and the most irresistible, of them all. Schubert takes his cue from the priority given to Bacchus in the poet's parade of the gods and writes a 'sublimation of a students' song', to borrow Capell's phrase. There is a certain irony in the fact that Schubert, who had always shown deference towards

Schiller's great reputation, here in a strophic setting does less than justice towards the poem; yet *Dithyrambe* is perhaps the only one of the Schiller settings which may be said to belong among the best-known and best-loved Schubert songs. It calls for a strong and flexible baritone, for the weight of the accompaniment makes difficulties for the singer.

Capell, 203–4; Fischer-Dieskau, 189–90

## DON GAYSEROS I

**Friedrich de la Motte Fouqué**                                              (?) End of 1815

Mäßig                    F major D93 no.1 Not in Peters GA XX no.13 NSA IV vol.7 p.167

Don Gay - se - ros, Don Gay - se - ros, wun - der - li - cher, schö - ner Rit - ter,

'Don Gayseros, knight so strange and fair, you have enticed me from my stronghold with your pleas. The forest and the evening light are in league with you, and lure us on. Tell me now, charmer, whither shall we go?'

'Donna Clara, you are the mistress, I the servant. You set the course, I follow. Sweet commander, pray give your orders.'

'Good, so let us go to the cross down below the cliff there; let us go to the chapel, homewards beside the meadow.'

'Ah, why to the chapel and the cross?'

'Why do you argue now? I thought you were my servant.'

'Yes, mistress, I will follow in your footsteps just as you say.' And they wandered on together, talking of love.

'Don Gayseros, here we are at the cross. Have you not bowed your head before the Lord, like other Christians?'

'Donna Clara, how can I look at anything other than your tender hands toying with the flowers?'

'Don Gayseros, could you not reply then, when the pious monk greeted you with ''God's peace be with you''?'

'Donna Clara, will I ever be permitted to hear the one sound on earth I long for, as you whisper ''I love you''?'

'Don Gayseros, look, the stoup of holy water sparkles in front of the chapel. Come and do as I do, beloved.'

'Donna Clara, I must be quite blind, for when I look in your eyes I lose myself completely!'

'Don Gayseros, come, do as I do, dip your right hand in the water, and make the sign of the cross upon your forehead.'

But Don Gayseros, horrified, kept silent, and fled. Donna Clara timidly took her way with faltering steps back to her castle.

The texts of the three *Don Gayseros* songs all come from the novel *Der Zauberring* ('The Magic Ring'), published in 1812. In chapter 19 a Spaniard, Don Hernandez, is asked by his host Herr Folko to speak of his homeland. He replies that he would rather sing about it, and taking up his lute he sings these ballads. The episode reflects the revival of interest in Spanish culture, and in the Catholic faith, during the Romantic period.

The autograph (Berlin, DS) is a first draft without title or date. The second song breaks off abruptly, and there is probably a page missing. The songs were first published in the *Gesamtausgabe* in 1894. Nothing is known of the provenance of the cycle. The foursquare phrases, supportive accompaniments and kaleidoscopic key-scheme seem to mark them off from the rest of Schubert's work, and their authenticity has often been doubted. The date is also an open question. On stylistic grounds they were thought to be a very early work, and Deutsch tentatively suggests 1814. But Robert Winter, after an examination of the manuscript paper, gives a much later date, between February 1816 and June 1817 (*MT*,CXIX, 1978, p.500).

It is not quite true, as Einstein asserts, that 'the cycle stands like a foreign body among the rest of the songs'. The setting of Friedrich Bobrik's *Die drei Sänger*, which is firmly dated 23 December 1815, adopts a very similar style of procedure, a further reason for regarding the cycle as later than was previously thought. None the less, there is something undeniably strange and experimental about the *Don Gayseros* songs, and especially the first one. Walther Dürr, in the preface to vol.7 of the *Neue Ausgabe* edition of the songs, argues persuasively that they represent an attempt to give to the strophic treatment of the ballad a sense of development and climax through key-changes alone. There must be some conscious intention, for instance, in the extraordinary key sequence of no.1, which proceeds by way of the subdominant in two great arcs: F–B flat –E flat–A flat–D flat, descending in thirds through B and G to C–F–B flat–E flat–A flat.

Such an experiment necessarily excludes the use of recitative, which appears only in the third of the songs, and then in a somewhat etiolated form. It also by implication excludes the use of normal modulation, since that would lessen the listener's sense of mounting tension. Yet it seems strange indeed that Schubert should embark on such an experiment some months after composing *Erlkönig*.

Einstein, 66

## DON GAYSEROS II (Nächtens klang die süsse Laute)

**Friedrich de la Motte Fouqué** (?) End of 1815

F major D93 no.2 Not in Peters GA XX no.14 NSA IV vol.7 p.173

Näch - tens klang die sü – ße Lau - te

By night, as so often, sweet sounds were heard, and the handsome knight sang as he always sang.

The window opened, and Donna Clara looked down, but fearfully her gaze swept the dewy darkness.

But instead of sweet love-talk and honeyed words, she loudly conjured him: 'Say, who are you, dark lover? Say, by your love and mine, and for the peace of your soul, are you Christian, are you Spaniard? Do you stand within the bonds of the church?'

'Mistress, in truth you shall discover. Ah, I am no Spaniard, nor am I of your church. Mistress, I am a Moorish king, burning with love for you. I am rich and powerful, and equally brave. The gardens of Granada bloom red, the towers of the Alhambra are golden, the Moors await their queen – fly with me through the dewy dusk.'

'Begone, false ravager of souls; begone, Satan!' She tried to cry for help, but before she had spoken the word 'Satan' it died in her mouth.

Her fair body held powerless in dark coils he bore her to his charger, and out swiftly into the night.

See *Don Gayseros I*. The pattern is similar to that of the first song, but the tunes have a more attractive Schubertian lilt to them. The key-scheme moves upwards from F major through G to A flat, D flat and G flat, then after an interlude in B minor it moves abruptly towards the climax in C major. The song sounds incomplete, but the marchlike postlude may be intended to lead directly into the third song. There is a strong resemblance between this song and the Ariette from *Claudine von Villa Bella* ('Hin und wieder fliegen die Pfeile') of July 1815.

## DON GAYSEROS III (An dem jungen Morgenhimmel)
**Friedrich de la Motte Fouqué**
(C major) E flat major  D93 no.3  Not in Peters  GA XX no.15  NSA IV vol.7 p.177

The bright sun shines in the morning sky, but blood is spilt on the grass, and a riderless horse trots nervously in a circle.

A mounted knight stands motionless. Moorish king, you have been slain by the two brave brothers who witnessed your bold abduction in the forest. Donna Clara kneels by the corpse, her golden hair hanging loose, now recognising without shame how dear the dead man was to her.

Her brothers plead, the priests admonish; only one thing is clear to her. The sun sets, the stars come out, the eagle soars up and down. All earthly things change; she alone is constant.

At length the faithful brothers build a chapel for her there, and an altar. Now she spends her life in prayer; day after day, year by year, she offers herself as a sacrifice for the soul of her beloved.

See *Don Gayseros I*. Schubert's interest in the experiment, and his invention, seem to be fading in this last song. He sets the first ten lines in conventional recitative in E flat major, then changes to a march tune in A minor – marked 'Quite fast but determined'. This does not seem very appropriate to Clara's remorseful mood, and the song returns to E flat for a triumphant conclusion. Is this, one wonders, supposed to celebrate the triumph of virtue?

## DRANG IN DIE FERNE  The Urge to Roam
**Karl Gottfried von Leitner**                                    Before March 1823
Etwas geschwind ♩. = 76                    A minor  D770  Peters II p.136  GA XX no.424

Father, you don't believe what it means to me, to see the clouds or stand beside the stream.

The golden clouds, the green waves drift gently by, lingering in the sunshine, but not by the flowers.

They linger but never stay still, moving on as though they knew of some better land that no sailor ever discovered.

Ah, from cloud and stream my young blood has caught the secret urge to storm through the world.

The rocky valleys of home are too confined – no room there for my yearning dreams.

Father and mother, do not be angry; let me go, for I must firmly kiss you goodbye.

I love you, but a wild urge drives me on through the forest, far from home.

Don't be anxious! Wherever my lonely path may lead me, the moon and stars will still light my way.

Everywhere the earth is vaulted o'er by the blue shield with which God protects the whole world.

And even if I never return to you, my loved ones, you must think that, happy at last, I have found a fairer land.

The poem was written in 1821 and published, with Schubert's music, as a supplement to the *Zfk* on 25 March 1823. The autograph is missing, but it is clear from the circumstances of the publication that Schubert set the poem at the request of the editor, Johann Schickh, so that it must have been composed shortly before it appeared. In March 1827 the song was republished by Diabelli as op.71.

*Drang in die Ferne* is the first of the extended modified strophic songs of Schubert's maturity, the precursor, at least so far as form is concerned, of *An mein Herz, Im Frühling, Der Wanderer an den Mond* and many others. It is the pianist who sets and controls the integrating lilt, giving the song its unity of mood and movement. But within this unity there is the greatest freedom of tonal and melodic variation. Everything grows from the initial bars. The verses are grouped, and since the third group begins in the relative major and ends in the tonic major, the song assumes an overall ternary form. The major–minor alternations which are used so effectively in the last verse as a symbol of *Sehnsucht* remind us that this song is roughly contemporary with *Die schöne Müllerin*.

Capell, 183; Fischer-Dieskau, 254

## DU BIST DIE RUH You are Rest and Peace
**Friedrich Rückert** 1823

E flat major D776 Peters I p.212 GA XX no.454

You are my rest, and gentle peace; you are my longing, and yet you still it.
Full of joy and grief, I consecrate my eyes and heart to you as a dwelling place.
Come in to me, and silently close the doors behind you.
Drive all other cares from my breast. Let my heart be filled with your joy.
The temple of my eyes is lit only by your radiance. O, fill it wholly!

The poem was written 1819–20 and published in *Östliche Rosen* ('Oriental Roses'), dated 1822 (although it may have appeared late in 1821). The poems in this collection were originally untitled, and Schubert made up his own titles. In later editions, however, this one was headed 'Kehr ein bei mir' ('Come in to me'), the first line of the third verse. The autograph has not survived, but there is a copy in Anton Schindler's songbook (Lund, UB). The song is dated 1823 in the catalogue of the Witteczek–Spaun collection (Vienna, GdM). *Du bist die Ruh* was published in September 1826 by Sauer and Leidesdorf as no.3 of 'Four Songs by Rückert and Graf Platen'.

There is no trace of sensual feeling in Schubert's justly famous setting of Rückert's love poem; in its purity of sentiment and perfection of form it becomes an expression of religious devotion. Rightly so, one feels; for Schubert, as for the young miller in the song cycle, a true and unselfish love was itself an expression of longing for an ideal world. Schubert's mastery of the *Abgesang* or 'after-strain' was never better illustrated than in this song, not only in the basic strophe itself, which is a perfect model of the medieval

Bar, but also in the modification of that strophe in the final verse. Like so many of the greatest of his songs, this one is outwardly simple, yet full of the most illuminating detail.

In the first edition the singer's note in bar 70 is F flat. In the *Gesamtausgabe* Mandyczewski rejected this as a misprint, and substituted D flat, by analogy with bar 56. But the melodic variation is here surely part of Schubert's intention – compare bars 20 and 43 – and the F flat heightens the climax. Friedländer in the Peters edition prefers to follow the original edition.

Capell, 201–2; Fischer-Dieskau, 196–7

## DU LIEBST MICH NICHT You Love me Not

**August Graf von Platen**                                                   1822

Mäßig                    A minor  D756  Peters II p.120  GA XX no.409(a) and (b)

My heart is broken: you love me not. You have shown me plainly that you love me not. Though I have come to you begging and wooing, devoted, you love me not. You have told me in so many words, all too plainly, you love me not.
So, I must forgo the stars, the moon and the sun. You love me not.
What does it mean to me that the rose blooms, and the jasmine, and the narcissus? You love me not.

The poem was published at Erlangen in 1821 in a volume entitled *Ghaselen*. (A *ghazal* is an oriental verse form.) Schubert's first draft appears to have been in G sharp minor, the only example of this key in the songs. There is an autograph copy of the song in that key, dated July 1822, in the convent at Kremsmünster, Upper Austria. A copy of the same version, transposed to A minor, is in Vienna (SB). Schubert appears to have revised the song before it was published in September 1826 by Sauer and Leidesdorf as op.59 no.1. Here the dynamic markings are different, the postlude is shortened, and the key is A minor. The *Gesamtausgabe* prints both versions.

On the strength of the fair copy the song is usually assigned to July 1822. But it may well, like the companion piece *Die Liebe hat gelogen*, have been written earlier in the year.

It may seem strange at first sight that *Du liebst mich nicht* has the same key, the same texture and the same basic rhythm as *Abendstern* (D806) and moves at much the same pace, for Mayrhofer's poem is about steadfastness in love. But Schubert's purpose, doubtless not consciously conceived, is quite plain. Here too the background idea is that of steadfastness; but whereas in *Abendstern* it is reinforced by the stable tonality and unvarying rhythm, here the background rhythm (dotted crotchet followed by three quavers) is disturbed both by the misplaced accents (bars 8, 12 etc.) and by restless, continuous and abrupt changes of tonality in such a way as to suggest a kind of derangement, a world turned upside down. That the rhythm itself held some special association with love in Schubert's mind is suggested by the use of it also in *Suleika I* and in *Fülle der Liebe*. Here it assumes a tortured intensity, symbolic perhaps of the obsessive love that can never be cast aside.

Capell, 179

# EDONE

**Friedrich Gottlieb Klopstock**

June 1816

C minor D445 Peters V p.161 GA XX no.230

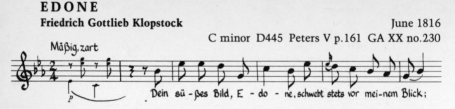

*Dein sü - ßes Bild, E - do - ne, schwebt stets vor mei-nem Blick;*

Your sweet image, Edone, ever floats before my eyes; but it is blurred by tears, because it is not you.

When the evening light pales, and when the moon shines bright, I see it and I weep, because it is not you.

By the flowers in yonder valley which I wish I could describe for her, and by these myrtle stems that I would like to plait for her, I conjure you forth, phantom! Transform yourself, and become Edone.

The poem was written in 1767. The autographs are in C minor, one in Vienna (GdM) and one in the Therese Grob songbook (see GROB). But there must also have been a fair copy in B minor, for it is referred to on a copy in the Witteczek–Spaun collection (Vienna, GdM). This B minor version was presumably the source for the first edition. *Edone* was first published in 1837 in book 28 of the *Nachlass*. Friedländer in the Peters edition follows this (B minor) version, but the *Gesamtausgabe* prints only the C minor version.

The fact that the song took pride of place in the collection of songs which Schubert copied out for Therese Grob in November 1816 suggests that it was associated in his mind with his love for her. The beautiful tune is one of the best examples of the 'woodwind' type of melody – sweet, plaintive, and evocative – which appears for the first time in the compositions of 1816. *Der Leidende* (May 1816) is another example, and so is the middle section of the slow movement of the Symphony no.4 (the 'Tragic'), written in spring 1816. It strikes a note of sweet resignation, as though Schubert, in parting from Therese, recognised that he was turning his back on a part of himself.

Capell, 119

**EDWARD** see EINE ALTSCHOTTISCHE BALLADE

**EIFERSUCHT UND STOLZ** see DIE SCHÖNE MÜLLERIN no.15

# EINE ALTSCHOTTISCHE BALLADE Old Scottish Ballad

**Percy's 'Reliques' trans. J.G. Herder**

September 1827

G minor D923 Peters VI p.94 GA XX no.545(a) and (b)

*Etwas geschwind*      Weibliche Stimme

*Dein Schwert, wie ist's von Blut so rot, E - duard, E - duard!*

The version published in Bishop Percy's *Reliques of Ancient English Poetry*, with spelling anglicised, runs:

'Why does your brand so drop wi' blood,
Edward, Edward?

Why does your brand so drop wi' blood,
And why so sad gang ye, O?'
'O, I have killed my hawk so good,
Mother, mother,
O I have killed my hawk so good,
And I had no more but he, O.'

'Your hawk's blood was never so red,
Edward, Edward:
Your hawk's blood was never so red,
My dear son I tell thee, O.'
'O, I have killed my red-roan steed,
Mother, mother!
O, I have killed my red-roan steed,
That erst was so fair and free, O.'

'Your steed was old, and ye have got more,
Edward, Edward:
Your steed was old, and ye have got more,
Some other dole ye dree, O!'
'O, I have killed my father dear,
Mother, mother;
O, I have killed my father dear,
Alas, and woe is me, O!'

'And what penance will ye dree for that,
Edward, Edward?
And what penance will ye dree for that,
My dear son, now tell me, O.'
'I'll set my feet in yonder boat,
Mother, mother:
I'll set my feet in yonder boat,
And I'll fare over the sea, O.'

'And what will ye do with your towers and your hall,
Edward, Edward?
And what will ye do with your towers and your hall,
That were so fair to see, O?'
'I'll let them stand till they down fall,
Mother, mother:
I'll let them stand till they down fall,
For here never more may I be, O.'

'And what will ye leave to your bairns and your wife,
Edward, Edward?
And what will ye leave to your bairns and your wife,
When ye gang o'er the sea, O?'
'The world's room, let them beg thro' life,
Mother, mother:
The world's room, let them beg thro' life,
For them never more will I see, O.'

'And what will ye leave to your own mother dear,
Edward, Edward?
And what will ye leave to your own mother dear,
My dear son, now tell me, O.'
'The curse of hell from me shall she bear,
Mother, mother!
The curse of hell from me shall she bear,
Such counsels she gave to me, O.'

Percy's *Reliques* were published in 1765 and attracted enormous interest in the ancient ballad literature both in Britain and in Germany. Herder's translation first appeared in 1773, in his *Von deutschen Art und Kunst*. Schubert's setting was written during his stay in Graz in September 1827.

There are three versions: (1) The autograph of the shortest, and probably the earliest, version has not survived, but there is a copy in the Witteczek–Spaun collection (Vienna, GdM) entitled 'Alt schottische Ballade' and dated 'Graz in September 1827'. It runs to twenty-four bars, has no piano prelude and is written for solo voice. This version (D923A, D2 923 no.2) is published in the *Gesamtausgabe* as no.545(a).

(2) The autograph of a slightly longer version with four-bar prelude, written as a duet for male and female voice, is in New York (PML). It follows on from *Heimliches Lieben* (D922), which is dated September 1827. This version (D923, D2 923 no.1) was published by C.A. Spina as op.165 no.5 in August 1863 and was republished in the *Gesamtausgabe* as no.545(b) and also in the Peters edition.

(3) A still longer version was discovered in Budapest (HNL) in 1969. It is written as a duet, and is marked 'Etwas geschwind'. This version was published in Budapest in 1971, with a facsimile of the autograph.

Schubert's original intention was to publish the song as part of op.106 early in 1828, but he withdrew it and replaced it with *An Sylvia*. It seems likely that the third version was prepared for this opus but never used. It must have found its way to Budapest with Schober, who lived there while acting as secretary to Liszt. It was Frau Pachler who drew Schubert's attention to the ballad (*Memoirs* p.300), and according to Jenger (*Docs.* no.1088) it was composed in her house. This helps to account for the somewhat bland and emasculated setting. The tale of passion and violence, so beautifully told, is reduced to the scale of a drawing-room ballad. Loewe's dramatic setting is much closer to the spirit of the verses.

> M.J.E. Brown, 'New light on some Schubert songs', *MMR*, LXXXIV, 1955, pp. 260–4; Capell, 243–4; Fischer-Dieskau, 249; I. Kecskeméti, 'Neu entdeckte Schubert-Autographe', *ÖMZ*, XXIV, 1969, pp.564–8

**EINE LEICHENPHANTASIE** see LEICHENFANTASIE

**EIN FRÄULEIN SCHAUT VOM HOHEN THURM** see BALLADE

**EIN LIED** (Ich bin vergnügt) see ZUFRIEDENHEIT

## EINSAMKEIT Solitude

**Johann Mayrhofer**                                        July 1818

Langsam                    B flat major  D620  Peters V p.175  GA XX no.339

'Give me my fill of solitude.' The gothic abbey stands in the valley, offering peace and asylum to the weary, but the young man in his cloistered cell is still tormented by worldly thoughts. He tries to stem the torrent, but his peace of mind is swept away.

'Give me my fill of activity.' In the teeming noisy world bright lights tempt the waverer, and riches. Dances and plays take the place of the green countryside. But amid the splendours he grows sad and mute, longing for the innocence and security of his youth.

'Give me the pleasure of good fellowship.' Friends round the table raise their voices in song, and friendship eases the way along the steep ascent of life. But when friends part it is all over with his peace. Filled with longing he turns his gaze towards heaven, where the star of love is shining. Love calls from the air and the flowers, and he responds in his inmost being.

'Give me my fill of bliss.' Now he walks by her side in silent communion, as if on air. Even in the desert, her eyes will shine for him. But the tombs of his ancestors, the trophies of war and victory, give him no rest. He mounts his horse, and rides into battle.

'Give me my fill of gloom.' The dead lie still. Fathers fail to return home, and a very different army comes back. Now he thinks of the defenders of the fatherland as murderers, nourishing the noble flower of freedom with human blood. And he curses empty fame, exchanging noisy tumult for the calm and cool of the greenwood.

'Give me the dedication of solitude.' The sun pierces the darkness of the pines, and the cuckoo calls from the thicket. Whatever he desired and loved, whatever brought him pleasure or pain, now passes by in gentle enthusiasm in the evening of life. The young man's longing for solitude has become the old man's lot. Life, though hard and difficult, leads finally to happiness.

The poem (here somewhat reduced) is a kind of verse treatment of the 'seven ages of man' theme. The song was written at Zseliz during Schubert's residence there in 1818 as tutor to the Esterházy family. The original autograph has not survived, but there is a copy in Franz Schober's lieder album (Dresden, SLB) dated 'Zseliz, July–August 1818'. In a letter to Schober dated 3 August 1818 (see *Docs*. no.129), Schubert wrote that he was well and 'composing like a god', adding that 'Mayrhofer's *Einsamkeit* is finished, and I believe it to be the best thing I have done, for I was without a care.' An autograph fair copy, dated June 1822 (Washington, LC) has twelve bars which do not appear in Schober's copy. A copy in the Witteczek–Spaun collection (Vienna, GdM), also dated June 1822, is evidently taken from this later autograph, which provided the source for the first and subsequent editions. The song was published in June 1840 as book 32 of the *Nachlass*.

*Einsamkeit* is not, as is sometimes suggested, the fulfilment of what Schubert had tried to achieve in the Ossian ballads or the dramatic cantatas modelled on Zumsteeg. Nor was he entirely wrong in regarding it as the best thing he had done, for it was unlike anything he had done before, and the freedom and fluency of the writing do mark the inception of a new phase in the development of his art. All the circumstances suggest that the work was a special project. The length of the poem, its schematic form, the somewhat grandiose nature of the unifying theme (not particularly typical of Mayrhofer), all suggest it was written specially for Schubert and probably at his request. And that Schubert had high hopes of it, and took the poem in manuscript to Zseliz with the special intention of giving it his whole attention, is clear enough from his own comments.

The brief recitative passages are not independent, as they would be in a dramatic cantata, but are closely integrated within the lyrical structure. In effect they are limited to the declamatory line which introduces each of the main sections. Essentially the work consists of six songs linked together to provide a varied panorama of life. There is only one work which could have provided the model and the incentive for it, and that had been written by Beethoven two years earlier. Can it be pure coincidence that *An die ferne Geliebte* also has six sections, and that it returns at the end to the opening theme? It is inconceivable that Schubert, whose preoccupation with Beethoven's work throughout 1817 is proved by his piano sonatas, should not have known the song cycle.

*Einsamkeit* should thus be regarded, not as the last solo cantata, but as the first song cycle. It is full of fine music, and is perfectly performable. Why then is it ignored? Primarily because of the abstract nature of the theme and the poverty of the text, which is Mayrhofer at his most mediocre. The ideas are too grand and impersonal for the particularity and sensuousness of Schubert's genius. Significantly, it is the scene-painting of the last verses, when the cuckoo calls from the peaceful thicket, that calls forth the best music of the work. Even so, the neglect of this song is not to be excused; it is much too fine, and too important as an expression of Schubert's art, to be ignored.

Capell, 140–1; Einstein, 183–4; Fischer-Dieskau, 109–10

**EINSAMKEIT** (Müller) see WINTERREISE no.12

**ELLENS GESANG** Ellen's Song I (Raste Krieger, Krieg ist aus)
**Sir Walter Scott trans. Adam Storck**                                      Spring 1825

D flat major D837 Peters III p.16 GA XX no.471

The original song, from the first canto of Scott's *Lady of the Lake*, runs as follows:

> Soldier, rest! thy warfare o'er,
> Sleep the sleep that knows not breaking:
> Dream of battled fields no more,
> Days of danger, nights of waking.
> In our isle's enchanted hall,
> Hands unseen thy couch are strewing,
> Fairy strains of music fall,
> Every sense in slumber dewing.
>
> Soldier rest! thy warfare o'er,
> Dream of fighting fields no more:
> Sleep the sleep that knows not breaking,
> Morn of toil, nor night of waking.
>
> No rude sound shall reach thine ear,
> Armour's clang, or war-steed champing,
> Trump nor pibroch summon here
> Mustering clan or squadron tramping.
> Yet the lark's shrill fife may come
> At the daybreak from the fallow,
> And the bittern sound his drum,
> Booming from the sedgy shallow.
> Ruder sounds shall none be near,
> Guards nor wanders challenge here,
> Here's no war-steed's neigh and champing,
> Shouting clans, or squadrons stamping.

*The Lady of the Lake*, a narrative poem in six cantos, was published in 1810 and was enthusiastically received both at home and abroad. It did much to boost Scott's growing fame in Europe. The German translation, by Adam Storck, appeared in 1819. Schubert set seven of the thirteen songs which are embodied in the narrative, five of them for solo voice. This one is prefaced with the lines: 'She sung, and still a harp unseen/Filled up the symphony between.'

Schubert's plan, as he explained in a letter to his parents (*Docs*. no.572), was to publish the songs with both German and English words, in the hope that Scott's enormous prestige would do something to make his own name better known outside Austria. This hope was not fulfilled, though the plan was carried out, at least to the extent that all but one of the songs were published with both German and English text below the stave. Schubert seems to have underestimated the difficulties involved, however. Storck's text does not exactly match the metrical scheme of the original, so that some adjustments to the vocal line have to be made when the songs are sung in English. Moreover, the translation of *Raste Krieger*, for instance, is eight lines longer than the English original. This has the incidental advantage that it enables Schubert to repeat the first four lines at the end, which suits the musical form admirably. Not surprisingly, the words fit more easily in the German version, though it is still quite possible to sing the three Ellen songs, at any rate, in English.

The autograph is lost, and precise dates for all the songs cannot be given. However, they were begun in April 1825; two of them are so dated in the catalogue of the Witteczek–Spaun collection (Vienna, GdM). And since they were performed at Gmunden while Schubert and Vogl were staying there in June and early July in that year (*Docs*. nos.572 and 574) they must have been finished before then. The *Lady of the Lake* songs were published by Artaria in April 1826 in two books as op.52. The dedication was to Sofie, Countess Weissenwolf of Steyregg, whom Schubert described in his letter home as 'a great admirer of my humble self'.

Schubert's literary enthusiasms often called out the best in him, and Scott had been one of them for several years (*Docs*. no.374). There is nothing profound about the Ellen songs, but they seem to breathe the very air of Romantic historicism. It is true, as Capell observes, that he takes liberties with the sense of the poem, turning briefly to the martial stamp of the horses in the second episode; but this can easily be forgiven, since it sets off the more effectively the tranquillity of the sudden switch to C major.

The harplike motif in the accompaniment of the outer sections was perhaps suggested by Scott's introductory lines quoted above, though Schubert had used the same idea before in an epic context, in *Hermann und Thusnelda*, as long ago as 1815. There is nothing in those early epic pieces, however, to match the subtle grasp of tonality which Schubert could command in 1825. The tonality of *Raste Krieger* centres on D flat major and its enharmonic neighbour C sharp minor. There are brief excursions to keys within the 'circle of thirds', to A, C and B flat major, and the effect is to establish a cluster of mainly semitonal relationships similar to those he was to exploit in the *Momens musicais* and other works of his last years.

Capell, 209; Einstein, 301

**ELLENS GESANG** II (Jäger, ruhe von der Jagd)
**Sir Walter Scott trans. Adam Storck**                                     Spring 1825
E flat major D838 Peters III p.22 GA XX no.472

Huntsman, rest! thy chase is done,
While our slumbrous spells assail ye,
Dream not, with the rising sun,
Bugles here shall sound reveille.
Sleep! the deer is in his den;
Sleep! thy hounds are by thee lying;
Sleep! nor dream in yonder glen,
How thy gallant steed lay dying.
Huntsman, rest; thy chase is done,
Think not of the rising sun,
For at dawning to assail ye,
Here no bugles sound reveille.

In Scott's poem this song immediately follows the preceding one, at the end of the first canto. See *Ellens Gesang I*.

The music of this second song is even more atmospheric than the first. The simple horn calls given out in the first four bars, and so wonderfully distributed between the treble and bass voices in bars 3 and 4, evoke the primitive pageantry of the scene, but recollected in tranquillity. They also define the song; Schubert needs only one more tune, that given out at the words 'Bugles here shall sound reveille', to act as climax and to make the effect of the modulation to A flat and later to C flat. Unfortunately the English words do not fit easily in the middle section.

At Linz in July 1825 the *Lady of the Lake* songs made a great impression. Writing to his brother-in-law, Schubert's friend Josef von Spaun, on 27 July, Anton Ottenwalt wrote: 'The most generally appealing, by the loveliness of its melody and its rocking horn music, is 'Huntsman, rest'. My dear fellow, how we wished each time that you could hear it!' (*Docs.* no.574).

## ELLENS GESANG III (Ave Maria)

**Sir Walter Scott trans. Adam Storck**
April 1825

B flat major D839 Peters I p.206 GA XX no.474

Sehr langsam

A – ve Ma-ri – a! Jung – – frau mild,
A – ve Ma-ri – a! mai – – den mild!

Ave Maria! Maiden mild!
Listen to a maiden's prayer!
Thou canst hear though from the wild,
Thou canst save amid despair.
Safe may we sleep beneath thy care,
Though banished, outcast, and reviled –
Maiden, hear a maiden's prayer;
Mother, hear a suppliant child.

Ave Maria! undefiled!
The flinty couch we now must share
Shall seem with down of eider piled,
If thy protection hover there.
The murky cavern's heavy air
Shall breathe of balm if thou hast smiled;
Then, Maiden! hear a maiden's prayer,
Mother list a suppliant child!

Ave Maria! stainless styled!
Foul demons of the earth and air,
From this their wonted haunt exiled,
Shall flee before thy presence fair.
We bow us to our lot of care,
Beneath thy guidance reconciled;
Hear for a maid a maiden's prayer,
And for a father hear a child!
Ave Maria!

As the chieftain Roderick Dhu summons the clansmen to defend their land against the royal forces, Ellen prays to the Virgin. The song comes from the closing pages of Canto III of *The Lady of the Lake*. See *Ellens Gesang I*.

The song is dated April 1825 in the catalogue of the Witteczek–Spaun collection (Vienna, GdM). It seems to have been a great success from the start. In a letter to his parents written from Steyr on 25 July 1825 (*Docs.* no.572), Schubert wrote: 'It seems to touch all hearts, and inspires a feeling of devotion. I believe the reason is that I never force myself to be devout, and never compose hymns or prayers of that sort except when the mood takes me; but then it is usually the right and true devotion.'

The greatness of the song has survived countless 'arrangements'. Its secret is the feeling of security and adoration suggested by the long-breathed legato line against the piano's harplike figure. Capell's suggestion that the accompaniment figure might owe something to Bach's 'Bell' Cantata is interesting, and not impossible. We know, at any rate, that Schubert had been studying the 'well-tempered Clavier' in the previous year. But he had used similar figures before: there is a curious pre-echo of the piano interludes, for instance, in *Die Nonne* (bars 33–40), written in the early summer of 1815. (There may even be some subconscious verbal association here). The emotion is secular and aesthetic rather than religious; there is even something operatic about that wonderfully shaped melodic line.

Capell, 210–11; Einstein, 302; Fischer-Dieskau, 212

## ELYSIUM
**Friedrich von Schiller** | September 1817

Nicht zu langsam | E major D584 Peters IV p.215 GA XX no.329

Vor - ü - ber die stöh - nende Kla - ge!

No more complaining! The revelry of Elysium drowns every groan. Elysian life floats onward in eternal bliss, a singing stream flowing through laughing meadows.

Eternal May, young and gentle, animates the landscape; the hours fly past in golden dreams; the soul expands in infinite space, here reality rends the veil.

Unending joy pervades the heart. Here grief and sorrowing have no name, and gentle rapture seems like pain.

Here the pilgrim stretches his burning weary limbs in the whispering shade, laying down his burden for ever. The reaper lets his sickle fall, and lulled to sleep by quivering harps sees visions of freshly mown crops.

He whose standard held firm in the thunderstorm, about whose ears murderous shouts burst, and at whose passage mountains quaked, sleeps gently here by the murmuring stream which runs playfully over the silvery pebbles. The wild clash of spears is stilled for him.

Here faithful couples embrace on the smooth green sward, gently caressed by the soft west wind. Here love is crowned; safe from the harsh stroke of death, it celebrates an everlasting wedding feast.

The poem dates from 1781 or earlier. The autograph (Vienna, SB) is an incomplete first draft, with the first nineteen bars missing. The adjacent songs on this manuscript are dated September 1817. The song was published in 1830 as book 6 of the *Nachlass*.

Schubert had been familiar with the poem since his schooldays, having set five of the six verses as separate exercises for Salieri in April–May 1813. These early efforts (D51, 53, 54, 57, 58, 60) were all partsongs for male voices, and this final setting owes nothing, musically speaking, to them, unless one regards the superficial resemblance in the setting of the words 'Here the pilgrim stretches ...' (both are in 6/8 time and similar in movement) as significant.

*Elysium* is usually compared, to its disadvantage, with the powerful setting of *Gruppe aus dem Tartarus* written in the same month, perhaps somewhat unfairly since the poem is a succession of vignettes that lend themselves to Schubert's tone-painting. The opening pages are lovely; thereafter the changes of mood, tempo and key become a little artificial. Thus the weary pilgrim and the weary reaper are delineated in two sharply contrasted sections, and the valiant standard-bearer in a veritable thunderstorm. It may also be objected that the serene mood of the last verse is not faithfully represented in the extended *Ganymed*-like peroration. However, Schubert is less concerned with the overall tone of the poem than with the opportunities it presents for a rhetorical cantata. Schiller seems to be for Schubert essentially a 'public' poet. *Elysium*, and the final setting of *Sehnsucht*, represent this public Schiller style at its best. The curious self-quotation at the end of the first section (cf. bars 31–3 and the concluding bars of the first movement of the Piano Sonata D459) seems to have no special significance.

    Capell, 130–1; Fischer-Dieskau, 100

## EMMA see AN EMMA

## ENTRA L'UOMO ALLOR CHE NASCE Abraham's Aria
from *Isaac*

**Pietro Metastasio**                                                 Autumn 1812

Andante con moto                   G major  D33 no.1  Not in Peters  Not in GA

As soon as he is born man enters upon a sea of so much pain that he is accustomed from the cradle to bear all suffering. So rarely does good fortune come upon him, so rare is joy, that he is never prepared to experience the surprise of happiness.

Metastasio's oratorio libretto dates from 1740. In September and October 1812 Schubert made several settings of the text under Salieri's supervision. Only this one is for solo voice. There are five others, for two, three or four voices. The autograph of all of them, with Salieri's corrections, is in Vienna (SB). It is dated September 1812 at the end of no.4 and October 1812 at the end of no.6. The songs were published in the supplement to Alfred Orel's *Der junge Schubert* (Vienna, 1940/R1977). A performing version of this one was prepared and privately printed by Reinhard van Hoorickx and has been recorded (DG 1981007).

## ENTZÜCKUNG Rapture

**Friedrich von Matthisson**                                    April 1816

Nicht zu geschwind                 C major D413 Not in Peters GA XX no.211

Tag voll__ Him — — mel, da aus Lau - ras Bli - cken mir

Heaven-filled day! When Laura's gaze brought love's most holy rapture to my enchanted soul! And carried away by her magic, I sank upon my fair one's trembling breast, with passionate kisses.

     I saw the clouds rimmed with deeper gold; each tiny leaf seemed to whisper: 'Ever, ever thine!'

     I shall scarce be happier in the myrtle groves of Eden, scarce more giddy with joy, after I have shed this mortal coil of dust.

Schubert repeats the first three lines at the end of the song. The autograph, in private possession, is dated April 1816, and there is a similarly dated copy in the Witteczek–Spaun collection (Vienna, GdM). The song was first published in the *Gesamtausgabe* in 1895.

    On the whole the later Matthisson settings makes less impression than the early ones. *Entzückung* is a case in point. It has a clear structure and builds up a powerful climax at the words 'Ever, ever thine!', an interesting instance of the emotive use of the flattened sixth. The brief recitative sounds like a reversion to earlier habits, however; the thing is entirely musical and well crafted, but it lacks conviction and subjective involvement.

## ENTZÜCKUNG AN LAURA see DIE ENTZÜCKUNG AN LAURA

## EPISTEL: MUSIKALISCHER SCHWANK Epistle: A Musical Prank

**Matthäus von Collin**                                    January 1822

C minor D749 Peters VI p.47 GA XX no.588

Allegro furioso                          Recit.

ᵇ Und nim - mer schreibst du?

*Recitativo:* Don't you ever write, then? Are you lost to us for ever, struck dumb? Perhaps because you have found new friends? Or did you become a judge, sitting at your grand desk sighing with boredom over your files, to cut yourself off from all jollity?

     No need, it's just us. Only we have had to suffer this silence, this dumb forgetfulness. Not one single line for the poor and needy! Everyone has not been thus neglected; for some the letters come flooding in; you must have measured them by the yard. But from us, you barbarian, you've turned your heart away!

     *Aria:* Bitter lamentations rise boldly from our angry hearts and, borne on melodious wings, dare to fly to that distant ear. To all his protests simply say: 'Though we are forgotten, we still fondly remember the good fellow.'

Collin's mock-serious letter was addressed to his cousin Josef von Spaun, who had left Vienna in September 1821 to take up a post in the public service in his home town, Linz. Schubert set the verses as a skit on the Italian operatic manner, which was then all the rage in Vienna.

The autograph, now in WSLB, Vienna, is a first draft headed as above and dated January 1822. This was the source used by Diabelli when the song was published in January 1850 as book 46 of the *Nachlass*. There is also a copy in the Witteczek–Spaun collection (Vienna, GdM), which may have been made from an autograph fair copy made for Spaun. It is headed 'Sendschreiben an –'. A second fair copy, made for Collin, was in existence in 1950 in Los Angeles. This is thought to have been the authority for the version published in the *Gesamtausgabe*, which has two bars – 18 and 19 – not included in the earlier editions. The Peters edition also has a modified vocal line in bars 98 and 99, to avoid the top C's of the original.

This delicious parody of a bravura recitative and aria in the approved Rossini style makes a magnificent party piece for any artist who can cope with its difficulty. All that is required are a powerful flexible voice with a wide range of dynamic and expression and a tessitura extending over two octaves.

**ERINNERUNG** Kosegarten see DIE ERSCHEINUNG

**ERINNERUNG** Matthisson see TODTENOPFER

## ERINNERUNGEN Memories
**Friedrich von Matthisson**                                            September 1814

B flat major D98  Not in Peters  GA XX no.24  NSA IV vol.7 pp.167, 8

By the lake shore, on mild moonlit nights, I think only of you. The stars spell out your name in gold.

The wilderness glows with unaccustomed brightness, full of you. Your image looks from every leaf, from every shady stream.

I gladly wait, dear gracious one, as you float down from the hill; lightly you pass by, like a roseleaf on the wings of the breeze.

There by the little hut in the evening glow I used to plait evergreens and fresh flowers in your bonnet.

As we watched the glow-worms dancing like fairies among the rocks, you cried out in wonderment: oh, how beautiful!

Wherever I look, wherever I turn, I always see the meadows where once we watched the mountain snow touched with crimson.

In the grove by the shore the nightingale's melting May song sighed forth; and there, with soulful gaze, I begged you: Remember me!

The poem dates from 1792. There are two versions. The first draft (Vienna, SB) is incomplete, breaking off after twenty-eight bars. An adjacent song is dated September 1814. The autograph fair copy, now missing, was formerly in Berlin (DS). It was dated 29 September 1814. There is a copy in the Witteczek–Spaun collection (Vienna, GdM) which may have provided the source for the first edition, in the *Gesamtausgabe* (1894).

The structure is typical of the mixture of lyrical and declamatory elements found in the early Matthisson songs. The first three and the last two verses are set strophically, to a gentle reflective tune. The fourth and fifth verses are a mixture of recitative and arioso, which leads to a fine climax at the words 'Oh, how beautiful!' Here the music veers away unexpectedly into the flattened sixth, before leading back to the tonic and the main tune. The evocative pastoral mood has something of *Erlafsee* about it, and since both songs have a lakeside setting, there may be some verbal association present. *Erinnerungen* is a very Schubertian song, which deserves to be better known.

## **ERLAFSEE** Lake Erlaf

**Johann Mayrhofer**                                                   September 1817

F major D586 Peters II p.19 GA XX no.331 NSA IV vol.1 p.78

Ziemlich langsam

I am so happy, yet so sad, by the quiet Erlafsee. A blessed silence in the pine trees; motionless the blue depths; only the cloud shadows drift across the smooth mirror of the lake. Fresh breezes gently ruffle the water; and the sun's golden corona grows pale. I am so happy, yet so sad, by the quiet Erlafsee.

Schubert chose to set only fourteen of the thirty-six lines of Mayrhofer's poem, and repeated the first two at the end. The complete poem is reprinted in the *Revisionsbericht*, and in Schochow (p.343). The autograph (Vienna, SB) is a first draft dated September 1817. An incomplete fair copy, consisting of the first fifty-three bars and the postlude, is in private hands, and the missing bars from this autograph exist in a copy in Vienna (MGV). *Erlafsee* was the first Schubert song to appear in print. It was published, under the title *Am Erlafsee*, on 6 February 1818 in a supplement to Franz Sartori's annual *Mahlerisches Taschenbuch* ('Pictorial Pocket-book'). A copper engraving of Lake Erlaf was also included in the supplement. In May 1822 the song was reissued by Cappi and Diabelli under the title *Erlafsee* as no.3 of op.8, which was dedicated by Schubert to Johann Karl, Count Esterhazy, 'with great respect'.

   Once seized of a creative idea, Schubert's way with a text can be ruthless. Mayrhofer's poem is arranged in alternating stanzas, the odd-numbered ones purely atmospheric and impressionistic, and even ones reflective and allegorical. Schubert entirely discards the latter, so depriving the poem of the philosophical dimension which the poet doubtless regarded as an essential part of it. But Schubert's concern is with a mood and a visual image, not with the intellectual antecedents, and the song is an overwhelming justification of his procedure. Here the essentially pictorial qualities of his musical language are wonderfully demonstrated, though within the constraints of the classical language itself. The unity of mood is complete, the simplicity of the melodic and harmonic structure impressive, yet how rich and varied are the symbolic associations. The inflection at the words 'so weh'', the melismatic turns of the melody at 'Schweigen' and 'fliehen', the way the repeated chords at bars 15 and 16 convey musically all that the word 'regungslos' means; the way the 'tonic–antitonic–tonic' figure is adapted in the middle section to suggest the troubled surface of the lake ruffled by the wind; all these make the song a kind of *locus classicus* for students of Schubert's musical language. The song encapsulates the essence of Romantic *Sehnsucht*: 'So wohl, so weh'' (So happy, yet so sad).

## ERLKÖNIG The Erlking

**Johann Wolfgang von Goethe**  October 1815

G minor D328 Peters I p.170 GA XX no.178(a), (b), (c) and (d)

NSA IV vol.1 pp.173, 180, 187, 3

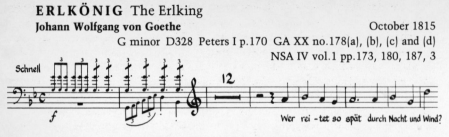

Who rides so late through the stormy night? It is the father with his child. He clasps the boy safely in his arms and keeps him warm.

'Why do you hide your face in fear, my son?' 'Father, can you not see the Erlking there, with his crown and tail?' 'It is only the mist, my son.'

'Come, sweet child, come with me. I'll play wonderful games with you. Many a gay flower grows on the shore, and my mother has many a golden gown.'

'Father, my father, do you not hear the Erlking whispering promises in my ear?' 'There, there, my child, keep calm: it is the wind rustling the dry leaves.'

'Don't you want to come with me, my dainty boy? My daughters shall wait upon you. My daughters lead the nightly dance, and they will rock, and dance, and sing you to sleep.'

'Father, father, can't you see the Erlking's daughters out there in the gloomy dusk?' 'I can see quite clearly, my son. It's only the old grey willow trees.'

'I love you, I'm fascinated by your beauty; and if you resist, I'll take you by force.' 'Father, father, now he's taking hold of me! The Erlking has hurt me!'

The father shudders, and rides on fast, holding the moaning child in his arms. Distressed, summoning up his courage, he reaches home; but in his arms the child lay dead.

The song comes from the opening scene of *Die Fischerin*, a Singspiel written in 1782. The stage direction reads: 'Scattered fishermen's huts stand by a stream under tall alder trees. It is night, and silent. Cooking pots stand on a small fire. Nets and fishing tackle everywhere about. Dortchen (as she works) sings.' The song is written in strict ballad measure, and is, as Goethe once put it, the sort of song 'the singer knows by heart, and turns to in any and every situation. These can and must have only strictly regular tunes, which everybody can easily remember.' For the first production of *Die Fischerin*, in Weimar in 1782, Corona Schröter, who played Dortchen, composed just such a melody as Goethe asked for, a simple strophic setting which proved entirely satisfactory on the stage. Of the forty or so other settings of the text mentioned in Friedländer, the most important are those by Reichardt (strophic, 1794) and by Löwe (1817).

Much academic ink has been spilt over the origins of the word *Erlkönig*, which is said to be a mistranslation of the Danish *ellerkonge* ('king of the elves'). But it was Herder who invented the word; he seems to have set the fashion in his *Erlkönigs Tochter* (1779), a translation of a Danish ballad, and there are close resemblances between his poem and Goethe's.

The song cannot be exactly dated, but it belongs to the autumn of 1815, and almost certainly to October. The most important witness is Stadler, who says it was written 'in his [Schubert's] parents' house in the late autumn of 1815' (*Memoirs* p.146). Stadler adds that when he returned to Vienna at the end of October the song was already written (*Memoirs* p.151). The famous account by Spaun of finding Schubert one afternoon in the throes of composition, which suggests that the song was written in November in one inspired rush of pen on to paper (*Memoirs* p.131), can be discounted as a misunderstanding of the situation.

There are four versions: (1) The original autograph is missing, but there are copies in the Witteczek–Spaun collection (Vienna, GdM) and the Ebner collection (Lund, UB). (2) The fair copy made for Goethe in 1816 (Berlin, DS) has a simplified accompaniment in duple quavers, not triplets. Schubert himself is said to have used this easier version. (3) A fair copy made to send to the publishers Breitkopf and Härtel in Leipzig in 1817. This was returned by accident to a Dresden composer named Franz Schubert, who angrily disclaimed any responsibility for the piece. (*Docs.* no. 102) It is now in New York (PML). (4) The fair copy made for the publishers in 1821 is now lost. It appeared on commission from Cappi and Diabelli as Schubert's op. 1 in March 1821. Of the six hundred signed copies on sale, more than three hundred were sold before October 1822.

Vol. 1 of the *Neue Ausgabe* contains all four versions, as does the *Gesamtausgabe* in the order 1, 3, 2, 4.

*Erlkönig* made an instant impression within the Schubert circle, but all Spaun's efforts to get it published in 1817 came to nothing. Finally, and largely because of the efforts of Leopold von Sonnleithner, the song launched Schubert on the road to fame. On 1 December 1820 it was sung by August von Gymnich at one of the musical receptions held at the house of Leopold's father Ignaz; it made such an impression that the performance was repeated on 25 January at one of the regular evening concerts of the Musikverein (GdM). An even more prestigious success was scored on 7 March 1821, at a charity concert organised by the Society of Ladies of the Nobility in the Imperial Opera House, when the performers were Vogl and Anselm Hüttenbrenner. Throughout the nineteenth century its popularity grew. More recently critics have tended to dismiss the ballad as a piece of bogus scaremongering, while recognising the power of the music. The often quoted criticism, that Schubert makes the Erlking too charming and seductive, has its origin probably in Friedländer's comments: 'The eighteen-year-old Schubert does not reflect the acerbity of the ballad, turns the alders of the Danish forest into a fragrant orange grove, and the raw November night into a mild August evening, and clothes the nordic hobgoblin in charming sensuality.' But, as Capell justly observes, the seductive charm is in the text.

The repeated quaver octaves which give the song its daemonic drive and cumulative power are not new. They had been used in Schubert's earliest essays in the macabre, in *Des Mädchens Klage* and *Der Taucher*, for instance, and the triplet rhythm had been adumbrated in *Der Geistertanz*. What made these elements fuse at a new creative level, and made the masterpiece possible, was Goethe's poem. Hitherto Schubert had attempted to reconcile arioso and recitative in the ballad by modifying conventional practice. Here the solution is radical. The poem is constructed almost entirely in direct speech. The composer is forced to find some way to accommodate these bloodcurdling phrases within the compass of an organically unified song. Not only do the driving quavers solve that problem; they give to the end of the song, when at last the irresistible forward drive comes to a halt on a 6–3 chord, *pp*. and we hear for the first time the unaccompanied voice in recitative, an unprecedented dramatic force. Recitative has become not an embellishment or an expedient, but a consummation.

Brown, *CB*, 45–7; M.J.E. Brown, 'The Therese Grob collection of songs by Schubert', *M and L*, XLIX, 1968, pp. 122–34; Capell, 107–12; Einstein, 112–14; Friedländer, II, 184; Stein, 64; Sternfeld, 127–9

## ERNTELIED Harvest Song

**Ludwig Hölty**                                                      May 1816

Mäßig                                        E major D434 Peters VI p.60 GA XX no.226

Si - cheln schal-len,  Äh  –  ren  fal - len   un  –  ter  Si  –  chel - schall;

The ears of corn fall to the sound of sickles; blue flowers tremble on the girls' bonnets. Joy is everywhere.

Maidens sing to the sound of the sickle; till the moonlight gleams on the stubble fields, they sing the harvest song.

Everything that has a voice leaps up and sings. Master and man drink from the same cup at the harvest-home.

Then every man teases and fondles his sweetheart. When the tankards are empty away they go, singing and shouting for joy!

The poem, written in 1773, has five verses, of which Schubert omitted the fourth. The autograph is lost, but a copy in the Witteczek–Spaun collection (Vienna, GdM) is dated May 1816. The song was published in 1850 in book 48 of the *Nachlass*. The four-bar prelude, which does not appear in Witteczek's copy, may well be spurious. It is omitted in the *Gesamtausgabe*, but Friedländer in the Peters edition follows the first edition.

*Erntelied* is one of a cheerful group of 'songs of the season', all to Hölty texts, and all in simple strophic style. This one makes a lively companion piece to the more reflective *Herbstlied* (D502), written a few months later.

## ERSTARRUNG see WINTERREISE no.4

## ERSTER VERLUST First Loss

**Johann Wolfgang von Goethe**                                    5 July 1815

F minor D226 Peters II p.11 GA XX no.89 NSA IV vol.1 p.44

Sehr langsam, wehmütig (M.M. ♩ = 54)

Ach,  wer bringt die   schö   –  nen__ Ta - ge,   je - ne Ta-ge der  er - sten__ Lie - be,

Oh, who will bring back the happy days, those days of first love. Oh, who will bring back but one hour of that sweet time!

In my loneliness I nurse my wound, and with sorrowing ever renewed, I mourn my lost happiness.

Oh, who will bring back the happy days, who will bring that sweet time back!

The poem was written in 1785, for the Singspiel *Die ungleichen Hausgenossen* ('The Unlike Lodgers'), and published separately in 1789. The original autograph is lost, but there is a copy in the library of the Seitenstetten Benedictine Monastery in Austria. The fair copy made for Goethe in 1816 is in Berlin (DS). Here the time signature is 2/2. The song was published with four other Goethe settings as op.5 in July 1821 (Cappi and Diabelli on commission) and dedicated by Schubert to Anton Salieri. This published version, which differs in some details from the extant autograph, must be assumed to represent Schubert's final intentions.

The words seem to be no more than a personal lament for lost happiness, but in the hands of the eighteen-year-old composer they encompass that universal sense of loss that accompanies the passing of the years. The ambiguous sense of mingled joy and grief finds a kind of analogue in the tonal structure of the song, which has, so to speak, two centres, F minor and its relative major A flat. It is this which gives it its strength and its reticence and distinguishes it from other settings like Mendelssohn's, which has the sweetness but not the strength.

Capell, 52, 102; Einstein, 109

**ERWARTUNG** see DIE ERWARTUNG

**ES IST SO ANGENEHM** see LIED

# EVANGELIUM JOHANNIS The Gospel according to St John
**Bible** Spring 1818
E major  D607  Not in Peters  Not in GA

In der Zeit sprach der Herr Je - sus zu den Scharen der Ju - den:

The words come from *John* vi.53–8. In the Authorised Version these read:

Then Jesus said unto them, Verily, verily, I say unto you, Except ye eat the flesh of the Son of man, and drink his blood, ye have no life in you.
    Whoso eateth my flesh, and drinketh my blood, hath eternal life; and I will raise him up at the last day.
For my flesh is meat indeed, and my blood is drink indeed.
He that eateth my flesh, and drinketh my blood, dwelleth in me, and I in him.
    As the living Father hath sent me, and I live by the Father; so he that eateth me, even he shall live by me.
    This is that bread which came down from heaven: not as your fathers did eat manna, and are dead: he that eateth of this bread shall live for ever.

This is Schubert's only setting for solo voice and piano of a prose text. His version begins with an interpolated sentence: 'In those days the Lord Jesus spoke to the crowd of Jews' and continues with the third verse ('For my flesh is meat indeed'). According to Anselm Hüttenbrenner (*Memoirs* p.184), Schubert tried his hand at setting a prose text at Anselm's suggestion.

    The autograph, a first draft, consists of two leaves and is written for solo soprano with a figured bass. The first leaf, containing the first thirty-three bars, is in the BL, London. On the other side the *Trauerwalzer* (D365 no.2) has been written out, with a dedication to Ignaz Assmayer, and dated March 1818. The second sheet, containing the last twenty-four bars, is in Vienna (SB). Anselm Hüttenbrenner's copy of this second sheet has also survived, with his own completion of the accompaniment and a note which reads: 'Composed by Franz Schubert, Vienna 1818'. A facsimile of the first part and of Anselm's copy appeared in Richard Heuberger's *Franz Schubert* (Vienna, 1902).

    According to Deutsch the German text is based on Martin Luther's translation, but this can hardly have been Schubert's source. I am indebted to Reinhard van Hoorickx (who has edited and privately published a realisation of the song) for the information that the complete text, including the introductory sentence, which does not come from the Gospel, is contained in the Gospel pericope for the Mass for the Feast of Corpus Christi. The music is obviously an attempt to realise the prose rhythms of the text, and the simple stepwise melody centred on G sharp suggests that it may have been intended for liturgical use.

## FAHRT ZUM HADES Passage to Hades

**Johann Mayrhofer**                                     January 1817

D minor D526 Peters V p.94 GA XX no.297

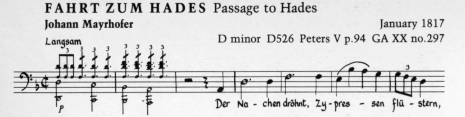

The boat creaks, the cypresses whisper – listen, the spirits interpose their chilling cries. Soon now I shall be at the shore, the dark shore, far from the lovely world.

There neither stars nor sun shine, no song is heard, no friend is found. Accept, O distant earth, the last tears shed by these weary eyes of mine.

Already I see the pale Danaides, and curse-laden Tantalus; the ancient river of Lethe murmurs, heavy with death, of oblivion.

Oblivion is a double death, I say. To lose that which took all my strength to win, and struggle to win again – When, oh when will these torments end?

The boat creaks, the cypresses whisper – listen, the spirits interpose their chilling cries. Soon now I shall be at the shore, the dark shore, far from the lovely world.

The autograph disappeared about 1865. There are however various copies, with minor differences; the one in Stadler's song album (Lund, UB) was made in 1817. The song is dated January 1817 in the catalogue of the Witteczek–Spaun collection (Vienna, GdM). It was published in book 18 of the *Nachlass* in July 1832.

A neglected masterpiece. It is sometimes compared to its disadvantage with *Gruppe aus dem Tartarus* (Capell, 136), but unfairly, for it is no Rembrandtesque *tableau vivant*, like that song, but a dramatic aria of solemn grandeur, tragic in tone and classical in its combination of deep feeling and formal restraint. The opening and closing music (Schubert repeats Mayrhofer's first verse at the end) establish the tone and the unity of the song. The theme is a combination of two of Schubert's favourite doom motifs, the repeated quaver triplets in the pianist's right hand, and the strong descending bass line. On the final page the theme is wonderfully extended and modified to carry the emotional weight of the whole song.

If the formal beauty and simplicity recalls Gluck (Schubert can hardly not have had Orpheus in mind), the wide-ranging tonality is pure Schubert. The pathos of verses 3 and 4 is wonderfully caught as the music moves from B flat minor to D flat minor and then to a heartrendingly eloquent brief recitative and arioso. The song was originally written for bass voice. It belongs among the greatest of the Mayrhofer songs of death, saluting the last enemy with a grave beauty.

Fischer-Dieskau, 96–7

**FELS AUF FELSEN HINGEWÄLTZET** see AUS 'HELIOPOLIS' II

**FERNE VON DER GROSSEN STADT** see LIED

### FISCHERLIED Fisherman's Song (1)

**Johann Gaudenz von Salis-Seewis**

(?) 1816

D major D351 Not in Peters GA XX no.204

Das Fi - scher - ge - wer - be gibt rü - sti - gen___ Mut,

The fisherman's trade makes us lusty; we inherit the wealth of the waters. We dig up no treasures, plough no fields, but gather the harvest in our nets, and haul in money.

We raise the oyster-baskets along the reed-fringed stream, and rest in the locks sorting our catch. Golden willows shade the mossy roof; we sleep on mats in the cool chamber beneath.

The Lord whose lightnings flash in the midnight storm protects us and knows our needs. Both the grassy hillock in the churchyard and the grave in the deep waters rest under the wings of the Eternal Father.

The poem, written in 1791, has eight verses, of which the first two and the last are here translated. The autograph (Stockholm, SMf) is undated, but there is little doubt that this first version belongs, like almost all the Salis settings, to 1816. Schubert's repeat marks at the end of the page leave the singer free to sing as many verses as he wishes. The song was published in the *Gesamtausgabe* in 1895. There is also a setting for male-voice quartet (D364). The stamping rhythm, and the tra-la-la refrain at the end, suggest that Schubert had some kind of convivial occasion in mind.

### FISCHERLIED (2)

**Johann Gaudenz von Salis-Seewis**

May 1817

F major D562 Not in Peters GA XX no.321

Mäßig, ruhig

Das Fi - sche - ge - wer - be gibt rü - sti - gen Mut!

For translation, see the preceding entry. The autograph of this second version (Berlin, SPK) is a first draft dated May 1817, and comprehensively cancelled. There is a copy, similarly dated, in the Witteczek–Spaun collection (Vienna, GdM). The song first appeared in the *Gesamtausgabe* in 1895.

The mood of this second setting offers a strong contrast to the first. The marking is *Mässig, ruhig*, and the scene appears to have changed, so that the singer is no longer celebrating with convivial companions, but enjoying his solitude by the river bank. The song is also something of a curiosity, in that it begins firmly in the dominant C major and ends equally firmly in F, with a bridge between the two halves in A flat major.

### FISCHERWEISE Fisherman's Ditty

**Franz Xaver von Schlechta**

(?) March 1826

Etwas geschwind

D major D881 Peters II p.186 GA XX no.495(a) and (b)

Den___ Fi - scher fech-ten___ Sor - gen und _ Gram und Leid nicht an;

The fisherman is not troubled by cares and sorrows; merrily he unties his boat at dawn. Around him the forests, fields and stream are peaceful still; with his song he wakes the golden sun.

As he labours he sings from a cheerful heart; his work gives him strength, the strength of happiness. Soon a colourful throng is seen in the depths, splashing through the sky reflected in the water.

But he who casts a net there needs good clear eyes; he must be as buoyant and as free as the waves; over there on the bridge the shepherdess is fishing – sly minx, you can stop playing your tricks, this is one fish you won't take in!

Schubert set the poem from a manuscript copy. It has seven verses; Schubert omitted the fifth, and grouped the remainder in three strophes. The first draft, marked 'Ziemlich bewegt', was part of a sheaf of papers which originally contained four songs (D878–81). The first page is dated March 1826. This manuscript is now divided up and spread about the globe; the sheet containing the draft of *Fischerweise* is in Vienna (SB). It is printed in the *Gesamtausgabe* as no.495(a). The fair copy, marked 'Etwas geschwind' and with other minor variants, was discovered in 1969 in Budapest (HNL). It was made for the printer, probably early in 1828, and originally belonged to Franz von Schober. The song was published, originally without opus number, in the summer of 1828 by the Lithographic Institute of Vienna, of which Schober was the manager, and dedicated to Karoline, Princess Kinsky. (See *Docs.* no.1119 for her letter of thanks.) Later (March 1829) the group of four songs was reissued by Diabelli as op.96.

*Fischerweise* was sung by Vogl at Schubert's concert on 26 March 1828. It should be added that the attribution of the song to 1826 is by no means certain. The Vienna autograph is annotated in Ferdinand Schubert's hand with a much earlier date – January 1817 – and the strength and pure linearity of the vocal line, and the mainly supportive nature of the accompaniment, are quite consistent with this. On the other hand the song is attributed to March 1826 in the catalogue of the Witteczek–Spaun collection (Vienna, GdM), and the fact that *An Sylvia* was written only four months later proves that Schubert's genius for the superbly simple and shapely tune was still as infallible as ever.

It is difficult to say which is the more to be wondered at, the perfection of the musical strophe, with its delicious clinching final refrain so beautifully enhanced by the canonic imitation in the accompaniment, or the skill with which this basic strophe is adapted to the words, particularly in the last verse, where the words 'sly minx' are deliberately held back so that they take on the character almost of a spoken aside. Schubert's mastery of the modified strophic form is characteristic of his later years, and for this reason also 1826 is the more likely date for this altogether delightful song.

Capell, 214; Einstein, 304; Fischer-Dieskau, 239; F. Racek, 'Von den Schubert handschriften der Stadtbibliothek', *Festschrift zum hundertjährigen Bestehen der Wiener Stadtbibliothek, 1856–1956*, Vienna, 1956, p.100

# FLORIO

**Christian Wilhelm von Schütz**                    September 1825

E major  D857 no.1 (D2 857 no.2)  Peters III p.132  GA XX no.483

*Florio (stepping forward):* Now that the shadows are slipping down, and the breezes blow soft, let the sighs from my heart vibrate the trusty strings, lamenting that they die a bitter death with me, unless she who handed me the cup of poisoned sherbet relents and cures me.

First with sounds as soft as flutes she poured pain into my veins; the victim wanted only to see her, but now her charm will kill him. Night, come and wind me in your darkness. In you I will seek the peace that I need.

The text comes from Act III Scene 6 of Schütz's play *Lacrimas*, which was edited by A. W. von Schlegel and published in Berlin in 1803. In this first edition the author was not identified, and the mistake probably led Schubert himself to attribute the poem to Schlegel. The autograph has not survived, but when the song came to be published with its companion piece *Delphine* after his death, they appeared as *Zwey Scenen aus dem Schauspiele 'Lacrimas' von A. W. Schlegel*, op.124 (A. W. Pennauer, October 1829). The date of the song is not absolutely certain, but it is given in the catalogue of the Witteczek–Spaun collection (Vienna, GdM) as September 1825. During that month Schubert was still on holiday in Upper Austria.

Florio's song is not often sung, and it is sometimes misunderstood. Fisher-Dieskau calls it 'a dancing serenade', implying that it should be sung at a brisk *allegretto*. But the marking is *Langsam*, and the song should proceed at a leisurely, contemplative pace, so that the movement of the inner parts can make its effect. The rhythmical strumming of the strings in the accompaniment, and the high tessitura, which calls for a controlled legato at *mezza voce* level, can then suggest the stillness of the night.

Capell, 218; Fischer-Dieskau, 220

## FRAGMENT AUS DEM AESCHYLUS Fragment from Aeschylus

**Johann Mayrhofer** June 1816

A flat major D450 Peters V p.78 GA XX no.236(a) and (b)

Thus the man who of his own accord is honourable will not be unhappy, he can never sink totally into misery. But when the storm seizes the sails on the shattered mast the wicked evil-doer is forced under the current of time.

He calls, and is heard by no ear, battles without hope in the centre of the whirlpool. And now the deity laughs at the evil man, and watches him, his pride gone, caught in the toils of necessity. In vain he flees one range of cliffs – on the opposite one his fortune is shattered, and he sinks unlamented.

The text is a translation in free verse of a passage for Chorus from the *Eumenides* (lines 540–55). It was not included in the collected editions of Mayrhofer's poems. Schubert's setting is for solo voice. There are two versions. The first draft, now in ÖNB, Vienna, is entitled *Aus dem Aeschylus* and dated June 1816. The fair copy (Paris Conservatoire) is slightly longer, with an extended climax. Both versions are printed in the *Gesamtausgabe*. There are several contemporary copies, including one transposed to F, with the voice part in the bass clef. The longer version was published in book 14 of the *Nachlass*, in January 1832.

This impressive dramatic scena was the only song from Schubert's early years to be included in the programme of his public concert on 26 March 1828. Perhaps the choice was Vogl's, for in spite of the piercing discords at bars 28 and 29 ('Er ruft, er ruft') both the form and the idiom are classical, and the familiar death motifs (the tremolando chords, the descending bass chromatic line at bars 18–20, the insistent triplet E flat quavers) are all contained within a form which sounds more like Gluck than the new opera.

## FRAGMENT AUS DIE GÖTTER GRIECHENLANDS  see DIE GÖTTER GRIECHENLANDS

## FREIWILLIGES VERSINKEN  Free Fall
**Johann Mayrhofer**                                                    (?) 1817

D minor  D700  Peters V p.47  GA XX no.384

Whither, O Helios?
    Into the waters I plunge my flames, in the certainty that I can bless the earth with new warmth when I will. I take nothing, accustomed only to giving; as prodigal as my life, my departure is surrounded with golden magnificence. When night approaches, I take my leave like a lord.
    How pale the moon is, how wan the stars, as long as I move in power; only when I lay aside my crown do they win fire and radiance.

The sun-god Helios, who dies daily to give life, is for Mayrhofer an image of the poet. For the poet also lives in two worlds, and his longing for the secret ideal world which he serves is also a kind of daily death. Life itself is only a pale reflection of this ideal world revealed in nature, and the poet's purpose is to remind us of this, and to express the unappeasable longing in our hearts for a happier land. Mayrhofer's Platonic idealism was thus both the expression of a deeply rooted pessimism, and a defence of the life devoted to art. Schubert, too, was deeply moved by these ideas and by the symbolic power of the Greek myths which meant so much to his friend. They inspired some of his greatest songs, including this one, and the much later setting of *Auflösung*, on the same theme.

The autograph is missing, and the date of the song is uncertain. Most of the Mayrhofer songs on classical themes belong to 1817, but the Witteczek–Spaun catalogue (Vienna, GdM) dates three of them, including this one, September 1820. The internal evidence points strongly to 1817, for the combination of sublimity and bold mastery of tonal procedures links the song with other masterpieces of the same year like *Gruppe aus dem Tartarus* and *An dem Tod*. The probability is that Witteczek was misled by the date of a later fair copy, as he certainly was in the case of *Orest auf Tauris*.

The song was published in book 11 of the *Nachlass*, in April 1831. The version printed there is followed in the *Gesamtausgabe*. Later editions of the publication, however, show significant changes in the voice part in bar 4 and in bars 29 and 30; this revised version is accepted by Friedländer in the Peters edition. But it is not at all clear whether these alterations were purely editiorial and designed to make the song less difficult to sing, or whether Diabelli had access to a copy which has since been lost.

The creative mastery of the twenty-year-old Schubert seems to defy chronology. There is a Miltonic majesty about this song, and the musical language is far in advance of its time. As Einstein remarks, if we were to come across it as the work of an anonymous composer we should be inclined to ascribe it to 1900 rather than to 1817.

The opening bars, their chromatically descending chords balanced by the rising crotchets and the vibrant trills, are perhaps the most powerful of all versions of Schubert's 'death and dissolution' motif. But the music depicts for us not only the departing glory of the sun, but also the pale beauty of the rising moon, in the complementary rising figure at bars 27–8, and in the postlude. Framed by these two evocative images, the great downward leaps and whispered cadences of the voice part have a power and dignity that Schubert was not to surpass until he came to write *Der Doppelgänger* many years later.

Capell, 163–4; Einstein, 192–3; Fischer-Dieskau, 97

## FREUDE DER KINDERJAHRE Joy of Childhood
**Friedrich von Köpken**                                                  July 1816

C major D455 Peters VII p.84 GA XX no.240

Pleasure which in early spring plaited flowers for my hair! See, decorated with your coronets I wander, holding hands with you. Even the buds I saw in my childhood bloom again in my mind, and in the dusk of evening they shine with the brilliance of morning.

The poem has five verses. Schubert wrote out only the first, with repeat marks at the end. When the song was first published in the Peters edition in 1887, Friedländer printed two verses, the second being contributed by Max Kalbeck. The *Gesamtausgabe* prints five verses, but they do not correspond with the full version of the text printed in Schochow. The autograph is a first draft dated July 1816 (Sibley Music Library, University of Rochester, NY, and there is a copy, similarly dated, in the Witteczek–Spaun collection (Vienna, GdM). The song was transposed to A major in the published version. The strophic setting is tuneful but slight.

## FRÖHLICHES SCHEIDEN A Cheerful Parting
**Karl Gottfried von Leitner**                                           Autumn 1827

F major D896 Not in Peters Not in GA

I can depart happy, I would never have expected it; usually separation brings sorrow, but I can depart happy; she cried to see me go.

How can I bear this rapture locked in my silent breast? It almost stifles me. How can I bear this rapture? She cried to see me go.

O mountains, lakes and meadows, and the moon that shines on her, I will trust you with my secret, you mountains, lakes and meadows. She cried to see me go.

And if I die abroad I shall not be afraid of that beshrouded sleep, for if I die abroad she will cry to find me gone.

The poem, written in 1821, is a 'refrain song', like Seidl's *Vier Refrain Lieder*, which Schubert also set. The autograph (Vienna, SB) is an incomplete sketch consisting of the voice line and indications of the piano accompaniment. There are two other incomplete sketches with texts by Leitner in the same manuscript. The precise date of the sketch is not known; almost certainly, however, it belongs to the months following Schubert's return from Graz in September 1827. A facsimile of the first page of the autograph appears in Richard Heuberger's *Franz Schubert* (Berlin, 3rd edition 1920).

A tuneful lighthearted song in Schubert's modified strophic manner. It has been edited for performance and published privately by Reinhard von Hoorickx.

> M. J. E. Brown, 'Some unpublished Schubert songs and song fragments', *MR*, XV, 1954, p.93

## FROHSINN Gaiety

**Ignaz Franz Castelli**                                   January 1817

Lebhaft                     F major D520 Peters VI p.44 GA XX no.289

Ich bin von lo-cke-rem Schla - ge, ge - niess oh-ne Trübsinn die Welt,

I am one of the sprightly sort and enjoy the world without melancholy. No pain or anxiety bothers me. My gaiety adds spice to life; I have chosen it as my shield.

Schochow (pp. 54–6) gives the full text of a poem nine stanzas long. Only the first verse appeared in the almanac *Selam* for 1813, where Schubert almost certainly found it. The authorship of the text was established by Berke.

There are two versions. The surviving autograph (Vienna, GdM) is dated January 1817 and marked 'Heiter'. Only one verse is written out under the stave, but there are repeat marks. There is no piano introduction, but a copy in the Witteczek–Spaun collection (GdM), also thus dated, has the three-bar prelude, presumably authentic, which is printed in the *Gesamtausgabe*. The published version, which first appeared in book 45 of the *Nachlass* in January 1850, has an improved vocal line and a quite different piano introduction, probably by Diabelli. It is marked 'Lebhaft' and has three verses, of which the second and third are spurious. This version is followed by Friedländer in the Peters edition. The song is not much more than an attractive trifle; it has something of the carefree charm of *Seligkeit*.

> D. Berke, 'Zu einigen anonymen Texten Schubertscher Lieder', *Die Musik-forschung*, XXII, 1969, p.485

## FRÜHLINGSGLAUBE Faith in Spring

**Ludwig Uhland**                                       September 1820

A flat major D686 Peters I p.194 GA XX no.380(a) and (b) NSA IV vol.1 p.141

Ziemlich langsam

pp                     Die lin - den Lüf - te sind__er - wacht,

The gentle breezes are awake, they rustle and stir night and day. O fresh fragrance, new sounds! Now, poor heart, never fear, now everything, everything will change.

With every day the world is lovelier. We feel that anything might yet happen. There is no end to the blossom. Now, poor heart, forget your torment; now everything, everything will change.

The poem, one of a series of *Frühlingslieder*, was written in March 1812 and published in 1820.

Four different autographs are known, and they present an interesting picture of the evolution of the final version. (1) The first draft in B flat major, dated September 1820, was discovered in the Vatican Library in 1960. There is no tempo indication. The piano introduction starts with a half-bar, and the dotted rhythm in the right hand is maintained in bars 2 and 5. This first version is reprinted in NSA IV vol.1 p.252.

(2) Another copy in B flat, dated 1820 and marked 'Mässig', is in the Bayerische Staatsbibliothek, Munich. Here again the prelude starts with a half-bar, but the dotted rhythm in bars 2 and 5 has become even semiquavers. There is a copy of this version in the Spaun–Cornaro collection, privately owned in Vienna. It is reprinted in NSA IV vol.1 p.256.

(3) Another copy in B flat, *Mässig*, once belonged to Ferdinand Schubert and is now in Berlin (DS). This has the piano introduction in its familiar form. It is dated 1820 in Ferdinand's hand. See GA no.380(a).

(4) The fair copy made for the printer, transposed to A flat major, was auctioned in Paris in 1881 but is now missing. The tempo indication is *Ziemlich langsam*, and there are decorations in the melodic line. According to Kreissle and Friedländer this copy was dated November 1822, and the same date is given in the catalogue of the Witteczek–Spaun collection (Vienna, GdM). Doubtless it was made for Sauer and Leidesdorf, who published the song as op.20 no.2 in April 1823. Schubert's letter to Josef Hüttenbrenner of 31 October 1822 (*Docs.* no.322) clearly refers to these negotiations for publication. The opus was dedicated by Schubert to Justine von Bruchmann.

This famous song owes its popularity in part to the poem, for the sentiments are universal, even if the verses lack distinction. Schubert's counterpointed rhythms in the piano accompaniment, seeming to symbolise on the one hand the fecundity of nature and on the other the persistence of human faith and hope, never fail in their effect. (This is one of the occasions when the dotted rhythms should not be assimilated to the triplets.) *Frühlingsglaube* has neither the passionate lucidity of, say, the Claudius songs, nor the lyrical flow of later masterpieces like *Das Lied im Grünen*, but as an expression of the renewal of human hope it is unsurpassed.

Capell, 168–9; Einstein, 193; Fischer-Dieskau, 138

## FRÜHLINGSLIED Spring Song
**Ludwig Hölty**

13 May 1816

G major D398 Peters VII p.89 GA XX no.217

The sky is blue, the valley green, and the lilies of the valley are in flower amongst the cowslips. The meadows, already bright, with every day become more colourful.
So, if May delights you, come and see the beauties of nature, and the fatherly goodness of God who created this magnificence, both the tree and its blossoms.

The poem, originally entitled *Mailied*, was written in 1773. The autograph (Washington, LC) is a first draft dated 13 May 1816. The song was first published in vol.VII of the Peters edition (1887). Schubert also set the poem as a partsong for male voices (D243).

The charm of these Hölty settings lies in their spontaneity, purity of style and natural feeling. But they also anticipate many of the features of Schubert's mature song style, as here the echo-phrases in the accompaniment, the running semiquavers and the repeat of the last line.

**FRÜHLINGSLIED** Spring Song
**Aaron Pollak** (?) Spring 1827

A flat major D919 Not in Peters GA XXI no.36(b)

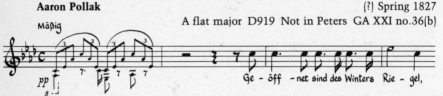

Winter's bolts are undone, its silver veil has vanished. The mirrors of the water shine bright, the lark soars high; the chorus of joy resounds as if awakened by the edict of the old king.

Spring hovers over the fields, and the breeze blows gently; the sweetness of the myriad flowers rises into the azure air. Smiling nature receives us, miraculously transfigured.

The sylphs are decked with gold, and Flora's realm blooms lovelier than ever. Everywhere there is joy and peace. The grove is crowned with leaves, the sweet cry of Eros rings out, bringing happiness to all who have feelings.

So welcome the spring, the ornament of the world, whose gentle kiss brightens and sanctifies the rosy path of life, and who leads us to the heights of pleasure, filling every heart with bliss.

An air of mystery surrounds this song, which is an arrangement for solo voice and piano of the male-voice quartet (D914) on the same text. Nothing is known of the author, or of Schubert's source. It is assumed that the quartet was commissioned by Tobias Haslinger for a planned collection of partsongs, *Die deutschen Minnesänger*, which appeared in October 1827. This was cleared by the censor on 2 June but for some reason was not included in the collection. There is no surviving autograph of the version for solo voice and piano. The only source is a copy found among the papers of a certain Rudolph Weinwurm in the 1890s. Until then the existence of the song was not suspected, and this explains why it does not appear in the collected editions, nor in the main series of the *Gesamtausgabe*. (It is included, however, in the supplementary volume.) The manuscript copy is now in Vienna (MGV).

The piano accompaniment is idiomatic Schubert and must, one feels, be authentic. Perhaps this was one reason for the rejection of the song by Haslinger, since the other two partsongs Schubert provided (D893, 901) were unaccompanied. The copy made for Weinwurm may not be altogether reliable. The pianist's left hand chord at the end of bar 35, for instance, should surely conform to the same pattern as in the first-time bar at the end of the section. The solo song remains almost completely unknown, though it has recently been recorded in a collection of little-known Schubert songs edited by Reinhard van Hoorickx (DG 1981007). It retains something of the feel and texture of Schubert's best partsongs, but it is a fine song in its own right, and would be well worth the attention of a lyric tenor or soprano in search of unfamiliar Schubert. It has, indeed, something of the lyrical flow of *Der Hirt auf dem Felsen*.

**FRÜHLINGSSEHNSUCHT** see RELLSTAB SONGS no.3

**FRÜHLINGSTRAUM** see WINTERREISE no.11

## FÜLLE DER LIEBE Unbounded Love

**Friedrich von Schlegel**                                                      August 1825

A flat major  D854  Peters III p.193  GA XX no.480

Nicht zu langsam

Ein sehnend Stre-ben theilt mir das Herz, bis al-les Le-ben sich löst in Schmerz.

My heart is split by longing; my whole existence dissolves in pain.
> My young mind awoke to a sorrow which love has perfected. Its noble flames aroused me; the path led to God.
> The strong, clear, everlasting fire drove all before it. What we desired, our good intentions, all our shared experiences, are reconciled now.
> When we parted my heart was crushed with the deep anguish of love.
> In the depths of my soul an image dwells; my mortal wound will never be assuaged.
> Many thousands of tears I shed in my eternal longing to be with her in the grave.
> My spirit flounders in waves of love until, swept away, my heart breaks.
> A star visited me from paradise; soon we shall escape there together.
> When this child of heaven shines on me here my eyes are still a little moist. I am under a spell which commands me utterly.
> As if, wedded in spirit, we were in a region where soul passes into soul.
> Even though my heart is broken I will consider its pain a blessing.

The poem comes from *Romanzen und Lieder*, published in 1809. The autograph (Berlin, SPK) is a first draft, dated August 1825 and marked 'Etwas geschwind'. There is a copy in the Witteczek–Spaun collection (Vienna, GdM). The song was first published in September 1830 as a supplement to the *ZfK*. In October 1835 Diabelli republished it in book 25 of the *Nachlass*. The published version is marked 'Nicht zu langsam' and is presumably based on a lost fair copy.

*Fülle der Liebe* belongs, like the D major Piano Sonata (D850), to August 1825 and may well have been written at Gastein, as the sonata was. The affinity between the song and the Andante con moto of the sonata has often been noticed. but the mood of the song is less contemplative and more assertive than that of the Andante; it seems to borrow something also from the defiant dotted rhythms of the sonata's Scherzo. The combination of ostinato rhythms with a wide-ranging tonal exploration is typical of Schubert's style at this time. Here the basic rhythm – a dotted crotchet followed by three quavers – is the unifying element, symbolising perhaps the strength and security of a full and un-qualified love; and with it is associated the tonality of A flat, against which is asserted, sometimes within the space of a few bars, the keys of F, C and E major. The serenity of A major is reserved for the passage which describes the lovers united in paradise. But the tonal instability returns at bars 90–7 for the last verse. Twice the music veers away in the direction of A major, only to be dragged back to the tonic. The song seems to have been written in a state of barely controlled excitement and exultation, as though something of the sublimity of the 'Great' C major still clung to it.

Capell, 217–18; Einstein, 305–6

## FURCHT DER GELIEBTEN The Lover's Fear

**Friedrich Gottlieb Klopstock**                    12 September 1815

A flat major D285  Peters VII p.24  GA XX no.138(a) and (b)

Cidli, you weep, and I sleep safely where the path creeps onwards, losing itself in the sand; even when the quiet night covers it with its shadow I sleep safely.

Where it ends, where the river becomes the sea, I float over the waters which move more gently; for he who accompanies me, the God, bids them be calm. Do not weep, Cidli.

The poem, also called *An Cidli*, was written in autumn 1752. Cidli was the poet's nickname for Meta Moller, whom he married in 1754. An incomplete autograph sketch entitled *An Cidli*, with the voice part written out in full but no text, and only indications of the accompaniment, is now in private possession, but there is a copy in Berlin (SPK). A later autograph is headed 'Furcht der Geliebten' and dated 12 September 1815. A slightly different version, however, is published in the Peters edition and appears in various contemporary copies. The *Gesamtausgabe* includes both variants. All three 'Cidli' songs are devotional in tone, but this one, with its 'walking bass' episodes, is perhaps the most liturgical in style, and the least attractive in terms of melody.

## GANYMED

**Johann Wolfgang von Goethe**                    March 1817

A flat major D544  Peters I p.244  GA XX no.311  NSA IV vol.1 p.132

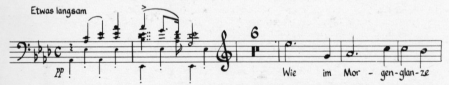

When, beloved spring, you shed your light upon me in the radiance of the morning, the sacred sense of your eternal warmth, infinite beauty, fills my heart with myriad thoughts of love. Oh, could I but hold you in my arms! I lie languishing on your breast; the flowers, the meadow, pierce to my heart.

O lovely breeze of morning, you slake the burning thirst within me. The sweet song of the nightingale is borne upon it from the misty valley.

I come, I come! But whither, oh whither? Upward, upward is our striving. The clouds sail down, yielding before the desires of love.

I come, I come, up to your bosom, embracing and embraced, all-loving Father.

The poem, which dates from 1774, expresses in its purest form the pantheism of Goethe's early nature poetry. In the legend Ganymede, a beautiful Phrygian youth, was carried up to heaven by an eagle at the command of Zeus, to become the cup-bearer of the gods. In Goethe's poem the myth is seen as the embodiment of his belief in the unity and goodness of nature, and of its power to draw man to itself.

The autograph, dated March 1817, has been missing since 1928. The marking is *Etwas langsam*. There are copies, marked 'Etwas geschwind' and in *alla breve* time, one of which belonged to Spaun and one to Josef Hüttenbrenner. The song was published as op.19 no.3 in June 1825 by Diabelli and dedicated (without permission) by Schubert to the poet. This published version is marked 'Etwas langsam'.

The sensuous immediacy of the poem is matched by the remarkable particularity of the musical language, which proceeds by a series of tonal images to re-create the serenity of the morning, the impulse of desire, the gentle life of the morning breeze, and the call of the nightingale. Yet the poem's unity of thought and emotion is preserved. The song seems to move upwards into the clear air above as the pulse quickens, and the tonality changes from A flat to G flat and to E major, and lastly to F major for the final apotheosis. These very Schubertian procedures reflect the movement of thought in the poem from sensuous delight to a kind of mystical rapture. There is no better example than *Ganymede* of the new intellectual depth and creative power which characterise the songs of 1817. From the cool freshness of the opening bars to the long arching line of the singer's final phrase, the song gathers strength and conviction.

Capell, 132–3; Fischer-Dieskau, 89–90; Stein, 66–7

## GEBET WÄHREND DER SCHLACHT Prayer during Battle
**Theodor Körner**                                                        March 1815

B flat major D171 Peters II p.214 GA XX no.55

Father, I cry to thee as the thunderous roar of battle engulfs me. Lord of battles, I cry to thee. Father, lead me on!

Father, lead me on to victory, to death. Father, I submit to thy will. Lead me wherever thou wilt.

God, I acknowledge thee, in the rustle of autumn leaves, as in the press of battle. Source of all grace, bestow thy blessing upon me.

Father, bless me, into thy hands I commit my life. Take it, as once thou gavest it. Bless me in life and in death. Father, I praise thee.

We fight not for the riches of this world, but to preserve thy holy name with the sword. So, dying, or victorious, I praise thee. I surrender myself to thee.

If the thunder of death greets me, and my veins flow with blood, to thee, my God, I surrender myself. Father, I cry to thee.

The poem was written in 1813, the year of liberation. Körner was the Rupert Brooke of Schubert's generation, who volunteered with enthusiasm to serve against Napoleon and died at Gadebusch in August 1813. The poem appeared in 1814, in *Leyer und Schwert* ('Lyre and Sword').

Schubert's autograph, in the Houghton Library at Harvard University, is dated 12 March 1815 and is in B flat major. The printed versions are in G major and show other differences. According to a note on a copy in the Witteczek–Spaun collection (Vienna, GdM), these changes emanate from Michael Vogl. The song appeared in 1831 as no.7 of *Geistliche Lieder* (*Nachlass* book 10).

The form is unusual, a strophic song preceded by an arioso and brief recitative. As an accompaniment to the first verse Schubert provides a battle scene of orchestral richness, in which the chromatic writing, low trills and sweeping scale pasages recall other famous 'death songs'. (The diminished fourths in bar 7 even have a hint of *Der Atlas* about them.) The remaining five verses are set to the same melody against a background of repeated chords. The tune itself has a simple dignity and nobility suggestive of the priestly music in *Die Zauberflöte*, but after the excitement of the opening scene it is difficult to avoid a sense of anticlimax.

**GEFRORNE TRÄNEN** see WINTERREISE no.3

## GEHEIMES A Secret
**Johann Wolfgang von Goethe**                     March 1821

E flat major D719  Peters I p.232  GA XX no.392  NSA IV vol.1 p.118

Everyone wonders about my darling's meaningful glances, but I, in the secret, know very well what they mean. That is: *this* is the one I love, and not that one or the other one.

So no more wondering, no more wishing, good people. Indeed, she does cast mighty powerful glances about her, but she only wants to give him a foretaste of the next sweet meeting.

The poem, written in August 1814, appeared in the *West-Östlichen Divan* in 1819 under the title *Glückliches Geheimes*. There is a copy of it in Schubert's own hand, now in the Goethe Museum, Dusseldorf. The autograph (ÖNL) is a first draft dated March 1821. The song was published as op.14 no.2 in December 1822 by Cappi and Diabelli. According to Franz von Hartmann, Moritz von Schwind designed a vignette for the first edition which incorporated a portrait of his own girlfriend Anna Hönig. The sketch was not used and is now lost.

The miracle of this famous song is the way the trochaic rhythm, combined with the short uneven phrases, manage to convey musically the idea of complicity. The effect is reinforced by the pauses, and by the sudden drop into the minor mode (*ppp*), suggesting an undercurrent of emotion in the formal gathering, a kind of secret drama. It is noteworthy that the setting of Schiller's *Das Geheimnis* makes use of a similar 'tiptoeing' movement.

Capell, 155–6; Fischer-Dieskau, 145; Stein, 75

## GEHEIMNIS A Secret
**Johann Mayrhofer**                     October 1816

Mäßig geschwind                     B flat major  D491  Peters VII p.46  GA XX no.269

Tell me, who teaches you to sing such tender, flattering songs? They charm a heaven out of our troubled times. Before, the landscape lay veiled in mist; but you sing – and the sun shines and spring is near.

Your gaze turns away from the reed-crowned ancient emptying his urn. You see only the water flowing through the meadow. So it is with the singer. He too sings and marvels at the wonders God secretly prepares, as you do.

The poem, which Schubert must have set from a manuscript copy, is subtitled 'To F. Schubert'. The autograph is lost, but a copy in the Witteczek–Spaun collection (Vienna,

GdM) is dated October 1816. It was about this time that Schubert moved out of the schoolhouse into the inner city, which may have brought him into closer touch with Mayrhofer. O.E. Deutsch supposes, without offering any evidence, that the poem was written during Mayrhofer's holiday in Lower Austria in September 1816. The song first appeared in vol.VII of the Peters edition in 1887.

Schubert doubtless felt under some obligation to return Mayrhofer's compliment by setting the verses to music, and it is true, as Fischer-Dieskau suggests, that there is a conventional touch in the piano writing on the last page. But the switch to D flat major at the end of the first verse, and even more the enharmonic change from A flat to E major in the second, are pure Schubert. The second verse seems to imply that Schubert did not share Mayrhofer's preoccupation with classical themes, which may well have been true in 1816. But a year later he could hardly have written in those terms.

Fischer-Dieskau, 82

## GEIST DER LIEBE Spirit of Love
**Ludwig Kosegarten**

15 July 1815

E major  D233  Peters IV p.144  GA XX no.96

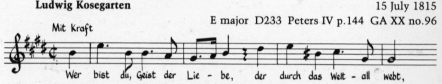

Wer bist du, Geist der Lie - be, der durch das Welt - all webt,

Spirit of love, that holds the universe together, who are you? You make the earth fruitful, and animate the atom; bind the elements together, and fashion the planets. You rejoice with the angelic harps and lisp with the suckling babe.

Only he is good and noble, whose bow is bent by you. Only he is great and godlike, whom you inspire to act like a man. His work lasts like the pyramids; his word is a strong command. He laughs at hell, and scorns death.

The poem dates from 1787. There are four verses, of which the first and last are translated. The autograph (in private possession) is a fair copy. There is a copy in the Ebner collection (Lund, UB). The date derives from the catalogue of the Witteczek–Spaun collection (Vienna, GdM). The song was published as op.118 no.1 by Josef Czerny in June 1829.

Schubert marks the strophic setting 'Mit Kraft', taking his cue presumably from the last verse, and writes a bold marching tune. But the sentiments are commonplace, and the music does not do very much to reconcile us to them.

## GEIST DER LIEBE Spirit of Love
**Friedrich von Matthisson**

April 1816

G major  D414  Not in Peters  GA XX no.212

Der___ A - bend schleiert Flur und_ Hain in trau-lich hol -de Dämmrung ein;

Evening enfolds meadow and grove closely in friendly dusk; the star of Venus, queen of love, shines forth behind the moving clouds of gold.

The waves murmur lullabies, the whispering trees sing evensong; the spring breeze frolics among the meadow grass, tenderly caressing.

The spirit of love strives to weave its spell wherever the pulse of life beats; in the flood, where wave follows wave, in the wood, where leaf cleaves to leaf.

Spirit of love, lead the young lover to his chosen bride. One loving glance from her bright eyes will fill the world with heavenly light.

The poem dates from 1776–7. The autograph is a first draft (in private possession) in a manuscript containing three Matthisson settings and dated April 1816. There is a copy in the Witteczek–Spaun collection (Vienna, GdM). Schubert set the same text as a male-voice quartet in January 1822 (D747).

The simple setting in Schubert's folksong manner has something of the tone and movement of *Heidenröslein* about it, but it lacks the compelling shape of that much greater song. Reinhard van Hoorickx points out that Schubert used the same tune for the Romance in Act I of *Die Burgschaft*, begun in May 1816 (*MQ*, LX, 1974, p.381).

### GEISTERNÄHE Empathy
**Friedrich von Matthisson**          April 1814

E flat major  D100  Not in Peters  GA XX no.17  NSA IV vol.7 p.14

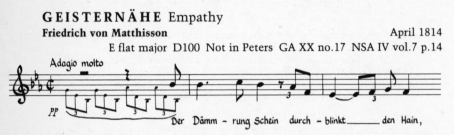

The dusky light glimmers through the grove; here, by the murmuring waterfall, I think only of you, for you are all to me.

Your bewitching image appears, beloved, to your far-distant friend as sweet and gentle as the evening star in the golden glow of twilight.

He longs for you always, as he does here; his thoughts cling to you lovingly, and as firmly as the ivy to the tree.

Does the breath of evening bring to you too faint intimations, a foretaste of reunion?

It is he, sweet child, who gently casts the silvery veil of darkness about your head, and ruffles your curly hair.

Often you hear him passing in the silent night, like sad melodies on muted strings.

Though unfettered, yet he will faithfully devote himself wholly and only to you, and watch over you wherever you are.

This fine early song had to wait until 1894 for publication, when it appeared in the *Gesamtausgabe*. The autograph has not survived, and the only source for the published version is a copy in the Witteczek–Spaun collection (Vienna, GdM), dated April 1814.

The first of Schubert's long series of nocturnes, *Geisternähe* is an important and predictive song. The key, and the broken chords, may be regarded as conventional (did Schubert, one wonders, know Mozart's *Abendempfindung*?); but the form is not. It is a subtle combination of strophic and recitative elements within a single mood, arranged in such a way that the seven short-lined verses of the poem take on the basically ABA form of a through-composed song. The echo phrases in the accompaniment, the alternation of tonic and German sixth, the accented diminished seventh at the climax, and the way the singer's last phrase is extended to give full effect to the word 'umschweben' – all this is strongly suggestive of the mature Schubert. So too is the way the melodic line is modified to suit the sense, so that it intones in the rhythm of speech the question the poet puts directly to the beloved; and so also is the way the piano triplets are suspended for the crucial fifth verse, so that the 'direct speech' of the lover can make its effect as a kind of reflective recitative, without breaking the mood or the lyrical flow of the song.

Schubert is here reaching out towards that combination of lyrical and declamatory elements which was to prove such a remarkable feature of the song cycles.

Einstein, 67

## GEISTES-GRUSS Ghostly Greeting
**Johann Wolfgang von Goethe**                                                  (?) 1815

E major D142 Peters IV p.82 GA XX no.174(a), (b), (c) and (d)

High on the ancient tower stands the noble spirit of the hero, and bids the passing ship God speed.

'See, these sinews were once so strong, this untamed heart so steadfast, these limbs full of knightly vigour, and the cup brimming over.

'For half my life I sallied forth, in peace the other half stretched out. And you, little ship of mankind, sail onward, ever onward!'

The poem was written on 18 July 1774, on Goethe's Lahn and Rhein journey with Lavater. The latter noted in his diary: 'Wonderful old castle Lahneck gleaming down on the Lahn. Goethe dictated.' The Faustian sentiments owed something to the landscape, which reminded Goethe of his own youth.

There are several different versions of the song, but only the last shows substantial changes. The earliest draft survives only in a copy made for Stadler (Lund, UB). It is not dated but was probably made in 1815. It is in E flat major and appears in the *Gesamtausgabe* as no.174(a). Early in 1816 Schubert made a copy to be sent to Goethe, softening the transition to the G flat major section (GA 174(b) ). In 1818, while at Zseliz, he made a copy for the bass singer Johann Karl Count Esterházy, transposing the song to D major/F major, and other autograph copies are to be found in the Goethe Museum at Weimar and in the Fitzwilliam Museum, Cambridge. In 1828 Schubert revised the song for publication, transposing it to E major/G major, adding a three-bar introduction of tremolo chords and extending the recitative. This more elaborate version appeared in July 1828 as op.87 (later corrected to 92) no.3 from Leidesdorf and in subsequent editions.

Goethe here adopts the ballad form to embody the optimistic message of his beneficent ghost, which is like enough to his own. Schubert's setting matches the epic tone of the opening, and gives to the second half a kind of resigned nobility with gathering emotional effect. (The tone of this second half is not unlike that of *Wanderers Nachtlied*, with its somewhat similar repetition.) It is a pity that the 1828 version is the only one which is readily available; the extended recitative with its accompaniment of tremolos in the bass adds a Romantic frisson of mystery to the song, but it may be doubted whether it adds anything of substance to the original conception.

Capell, 103

## GEISTLICHE LIEDER 'Spiritual Songs'

This was the general title given by Diabelli to book 10 of the *Nachlass*, which he published in April 1831. The collection included the following songs, on which see individual entries: *Dem Unendlichen* (Klopstock)

*Die Gestirne* (Klopstock)
*Das Marienbild* (Schreiber)
*Vom Mitleiden Mariä* (Friedrich von Schlegel)
*Litanei (Am Tage aller Seelen)* (Jacobi)
*Pax vobiscum* (Schober)
*Gebet während der Schlacht* (Körner)
*Himmelsfunken* (Silbert)

## GENÜGSAMKEIT Contentment

**Franz von Schober**                                             (?) 1815

C sharp minor  D143  Peters IV p.122  GA XX no.181  NSA IV vol.7 p.88

Dort ra-get ein Berg aus den Wol-ken hehr, ihn er-reicht wohl mein ei-lender Schritt.

There a mountain peak soars high above the clouds; as my hastening steps draw
near new peaks appear, more and more of them, urging me on in my eagerness.

Spurred on by the tremulous rosy light from the calm clear blue of the sky,
he finds that it was not the mountains, but only his own inner longing.

But now he can never turn back, though the land is bleak and flat. Gods, give
me the shelter of a hut in the valley, and peaceful good fortune.

The verses do not appear in the collected edition of Schober's poems, and there seems
something odd about them. Some editions print the first verse in inverted commas, but
this only highlights the awkwardness of the change to the third person in the next verse.

No autograph of the song has survived, and no contemporary copy. There is no firm
evidence as to the date. It was published by Diabelli in July 1829 as op.109 no.2. The restless
forward drive of Schubert's 6/8 setting makes it clear that it is the young man's state of
mind which interests him, not the pious sentiments of the last verse. The introductory
chords, and possibly also the five-bar postlude and interlude, were added by Diabelli when
the song was published.

## GESANG AN DIE HARMONIE see AN DIE HARMONIE

## GESANG (AN SYLVIA) see AN SYLVIA

## GESANG DER GEISTER ÜBER DEN WASSERN Song of the Spirits over the Waters

**Johann Wolfgang von Goethe**                         September 1816

G major  D484  Not in Peters  GA XX no.594

dann zur Tie-fe nie-der,                    Ra-gen Klippen dem Sturz entge-gen,

The soul of man is like the water; it comes from heaven, it rises to heaven, and down
again to the earth must it come, ever changing.

When the clear stream gushes from the steep cliff-face it breaks up into clouds of spray like a soft veil on the smooth rock, seething as it hisses down into the depths below.

The cliffs loom up against the fall, which foams angrily as it descends step by step into the abyss.

On the level plain it steals along the valley, and the face of the stars is mirrored on the smooth surface of the lake.

The wind is the wave's tender lover, and mingles enthusiastically with the foaming billows.

Soul of mankind, how like the water! Fate of mankind, how like the wind!

The poem was written in October 1779, after a visit to the Staubbach at Lauterbrunnen. Frau von Stein, to whom it was sent, seems to have read it as a kind of confession of faith in the transmigration of souls, but there is no need to press the analogy so far. The image of the river is used simply for the soul's relationship with heaven and with fate. But the emphasis in this poem is on man fulfilling his destiny in accordance with the inexorable laws of nature. It seems to have had a great appeal for Schubert, who set it four times between 1816 and 1821, moved perhaps not so much by the parable itself (though the 'river of life' analogy is present in many of his songs) as by the opportunity it offered for tonal images of the moving water. This setting, the first, is the only one intended for solo voice.

The autograph (Vienna, SB) is incomplete, consisting of sixty-four bars from the middle of the song. There is little doubt that it was originally complete. The opening and closing sections may have been detached in the course of making the later settings. On the same manuscript are songs dating from September 1816. The descending chromatic figure which dominates the section marked 'Geschwind' ('The cliffs loom up against the fall') is used to good effect in the final settings for male voices and orchestra. The whole composition seems to have been ambitiously conceived from the first, but this draft makes unrealistic demands on a single voice, calling for a range which extends from E below middle C to G above the stave. It may be that Schubert realised that the scale of the work he had in mind called for more flexible forces. The song has been edited, completed and privately printed by Reinhard van Hoorickx.

## GESANG DER NORNA Norna's Song
**Sir Walter Scott trans. S.H. Spiker**                                    Early 1825

F minor D831 Peters IV p.66 GA XX no.542

Schubert's text is a translation of a song to be found in chapter 19 of Scott's novel *The Pirate*. In the original it runs:

> For leagues along the watery way,
> Through gulf and stream my course has been;
> The billows know my runic lay
> And smooth their crests to silent green.

> The billows know my runic lay,
> The gulf grows smooth, the stream is still:
> The human hearts, more wild than they,
> Know but the rule of wayward will.

One hour is mine in all the year,
To tell my woes – and one alone;
When gleams this magic lamp, 'tis here;
When dies the mystic light 'tis gone.

Daughters of northern Magnus, hail!
The lamp is lit, the flame is clear,
To you I come to tell my tale,
Awake, arise, my tale to hear!

*The Pirate* appeared in a German translation in 1822, a year after its first publication. Norna, the mother of Clement Cleveland, the pirate, is subject to a curse which allows her only one hour each year in which to lament her woes.

The autograph has not survived, and there is some doubt about the date of the song. The catalogue of the Witteczek–Spaun collection (Vienna, GdM) attributes it to 1827. However, Sophie Müller recorded in her diary that Schubert and Vogl visited her on 1 March 1825, bringing with them 'new songs from *The Pirate*'. This can only refer to Norna's song. It was therefore one of the earliest of the Scott songs to be composed.

In March 1828 Diabelli published *Gesang der Norna*, together with another Scott song, the *Lied der Anne Lyle*, as op.85. The English words were not included, although that had at one time been Schubert's intention. With some adaptation they can be made to fit the tune. The song is rarely sung. Yet it has more Scottish feeling and Romantic atmosphere than the other Scott settings. The heavy 6/8 movement, with its staccato chords (the dots in bar 1 are surely meant to apply throughout) and accented first beats, suggest the surge of the boat under the thrust of the oars; while the prevailing F minor tonality seems to veil the simply structured tune in Celtic mists. There is also in bar 4 the only Schubertian example of the famous 'Scotch snap', as the accent over the fifth quaver makes clear. The song calls for a dark-toned mezzo or contralto voice.

Capell, 243

**GESÄNGE DES HARFNERS** see HARFENSPIELER

## GLAUBE, HOFFNUNG UND LIEBE Faith, Hope and Love
**Christoph Kuffner**                                          August 1828
E flat major D955 Peters II p.190 GA XX no.462

Faith, hope, love – hold fast to these three; you will never be untrue to yourself, and your skies will never be clouded.

Have faith in God and in your own heart. Faith flies heavenwards. God dwells in your own heart, even more than in the starry firmament. Though the world, and men, may lie, the heart can never deceive.

Rest your hopes upon eternity, and better times here below. Hope burns with a bright light along the path of duty. Hope on, but make no demands. Slowly the first light leads to dawn.

Let your love be generous, steadfast and pure, for without love you are but a stone. Love will refine your feelings, and lead you to your goal. Life can only be happily fulfilled in the warm glow of love.

If you would ever be true to yourself, then hold fast to these three, so your skies will never be clouded: faith, hope, love.

It can hardly be coincidence that in August 1828 Schubert set two texts based on the famous passage from Paul's letter to the Corinthians (i.13). One was a commissioned work, a setting of a poem specially written by J. A. F. Reil for the dedication of the recast bell of the Church of the Holy Trinity at Alsergrund. Schubert wrote a short choral work in his best Haydn manner for this occasion, scoring it for a quartet of male voices, chorus, and orchestra. It is an effective piece, but it is worlds away from the Schubert of the String Quintet and the last piano sonatas.

The autograph of this solo song (Vienna, ÖNB) is dated August 1828, and the song was published by Diabelli in October as op.97. It was the last of Schubert's songs to be published in his lifetime, and the speed with which Diabelli brought it out suggests that some topical interest attached to it. This time the idiom is genuinely Schubertian and wonderfully attuned to the seriousness of the text. The outer sections, in 3/4 time, have an aphoristic simplicity, but the three six-line verses which intervene are set strophically, to themes which are related both melodically and tonally (being based on the relation between E flat major and G flat and C flat) to the music which frames the song. The tonality, the long suspensions at the cadences, and the sober gait give the song a sort of Brahmsian seriousness and mellowness, so that one is bound to wonder whether Schubert's preoccupation with the first and last things at this time had any connection with his awareness of his own precarious state of health. How deeply moving is that final alternation between G flat and E flat in the closing bars. The more familiar one becomes with this fine song the more impressive it seems.

## GONDELFAHRER Barcarolle
**Johann Mayrhofer**

March 1824
C major D808 Not in Peters GA XX no.461

The moon and stars dance like fugitive spirits: who would be held captive for ever by earthly cares!

Now my boat can drift in the moonbeams, and free of all restraint rocks on the bosom of the sea.

From the tower of St Mark's tolls out the sentence of midnight. Everyone sleeps in peace; only the boatman wakes.

The song is mentioned in a letter from Schwind to Schober of 6 March 1824 (*Docs.* no.441). The text had been published earlier that year. The autograph (Berlin, DS) is dated March 1824. The version for male-voice quartet (D809) also belongs to this month. *Gondelfahrer* was published by J. P. Gotthard in 1872, as no.2 of 'Forty Songs'.

Schubert's love of the particular, his genius for the translation of sensuous impressions into music, ensured that the midnight tolling of St Mark's would figure prominently in the song, and not surprisingly the bell tolls twelve times on his favourite flattened sixth. (The same effect is used in the quartet setting.) This very Schubertian relationship between C and A flat major is the tonal basis of the song, as the prelude and postlude make clear.

**GOSPEL ACCORDING TO ST JOHN** see EVANGELIUM JOHANNIS

## GOTT IM FRÜHLINGE God in Springtime
**Johann Peter Uz**                                                    June 1816

E major  D448  Peters VII p.94  GA XX no.233

In sei-nem schimmern-den Ge-wand hast du den Früh-ling uns ge-sandt,

You have sent us Spring in his shimmering mantle, a garland of roses wound about his head. Already he is here, sweetly smiling, led by the hours to his throne of flowers, O God.

    The hedgerows bloom as he passes; the meadows are fresh and green; trees again give shade. The west wind blows caressingly, on dewy pinions, and birds sing merrily.

    Like the sweet notes of the birds, my song also shall soar up to the God of nature, for I am transported with delight. I wish to sing praises to the Lord, who has made me what I am.

The poem dates from February 1763. There are seven verses, but Schubert set only the first three. The first draft (New York, PML) is dated June 1816 and marked 'Mässig'. Later in the year Schubert made a copy for Therese Grob's songbook (see GROB), marked 'Langsam mit Gefühl'. This second version, slightly shorter, was edited and privately printed by Reinhard van Hoorickx. There is a copy of the original version in the Witteczek–Spaun collection (Vienna, GdM). The song was first published in 1887, in vol.VII of the Peters collected edition. This follows the original version.

    A captivating song, and predictive, with its unifying accompaniment figure, and masterly adaptation of the strophe in the second verse to give an ABA form. But the movement needs to be light and brisk (Schubert's first thoughts on this subject seem better than his second).

    Capell, 115–16; Fischer-Dieskau, 72

## GRABLIED Funeral Song
**Josef Kenner**                                                    24 June 1815

F minor  D218  Peters VI p.34  GA XX no.84

Er fiel den Tod fürs Va-ter-land, den sü - ßen der Be-frei - ungs-schlacht;

He fell for the fatherland, a sweet death in the fight for freedom. We bury him with loyal hands, deep in the dark peace of the grave.

    There may your shattered heart, once so full of hope, find rest with the flowers which we scatter on the silent grave, as the violets bloom in March.

The poem was written in July 1813, when enthusiasm for the war against Napoleon was at its height. It has six verses, of which two are given. The song was composed two years later, however. It calls to mind the fate of Theodor Körner, a popular hero known to Schubert, who died on active service in August 1813. The autograph, in private possession, is a first draft dated 24 June 1815. The song was published in book 42 of the *Nachlass*, in 1848. Diabelli added the three-bar prelude. There is a dated copy of the song in the Witteczek–Spaun collection (Vienna, GdM).

The descending chromatic themes that feature so frequently in association with death are prominent in this hymnlike tribute, and the effect is heightened by the contrast between the lightness of the third line ('Wir graben ihn') and the low and heavy chording of the postlude, a musical equivalent of the descent into the grave.

## GRABLIED AUF EINEN SOLDATEN Epitaph for a Soldier
**Christian Friedrich Schubart** July 1816

C minor D454 Not in Peters GA XX no.239(a)

Farewell, brave warrior, we consign you to your rest. Heavy with grief, with weapons lowered, we stand silent by your bier.

You were a true patriot, and you have fought the good fight. Your noble heart never, in the press of battle, shrank from the bullet and the sword.

You were a Christian soldier too, saying little and doing much, pious and true to fatherland and to your prince.

The poet's title is *Todtenmarsch*. There are eight verses, of which the first three are translated. The autograph, in the Sibley Library, University of Rochester, NY, is a first draft dated July 1816. It has been sadly damaged and mutilated. There is a copy, similarly dated, in the Witteczek–Spaun collection (Vienna, GdM). Schubert's title is as above. The unison opening, and the extended postlude, enhance the solemn style of this funeral march, which is not unlike the previous song in tone.

## GRABLIED FÜR DIE MUTTER A Mother's Funeral Song
**Author unknown** June 1818

B minor D616 Peters V p.170 GA XX no.338

Breathe more gently, evening breeze; mourn more softly, Philomel; a fair, angelic soul sleeps in this grave.

The father stands pale and silent with his son by the sad graveside; the glory of their lives has suddenly vanished with her death.

They weep by the grave. But their tears of love will be transfigured like pearls when the angel calls.

Josef von Streinsberg, a schoolfriend of Schubert and later a member of the circle, stated that the song was written on the occasion of his mother's death in 1818 (*Memoirs* p.167). The author of the lines has never been identified.

The autograph, a first draft dated June 1818, is in Vienna (SB). There is a dated copy in the Witteczek–Spaun collection (Vienna, GdM). The song was published in book 30 of the *Nachlass*, in 1839.

The strong sense of personal involvement in the song has led some commentators (including Fischer-Dieskau) to assume that it is autobiographical. But why Schubert's love for his own mother should find expression in this way six years after her death is not explained. It is more likely that Streinsberg is right; he may even have written the verses himself, and since he was closely associated with the Schubert circle the sincerity of the song does not need any further explanation. *Grablied für die Mutter* is full of echoes and pre-echoes. The B minor/major tonality, and the opening phrase, recall Schubert's earliest death motifs, moving from tonic minor to dominant. Bars 14–17, with their isolated chords and reminiscence of the *Wanderer* theme, look forward as well as backward; while the drop of a diminished fourth in bar 1 and elsewhere anticipates the B minor Symphony. This fine song deserves to be better known.

Fischer-Dieskau, 111; Porter, 104

# GREISENGESANG A Song of Old Age

**Friedrich Rückert**

(?) Autumn 1822

B minor D778 Peters II p.124 GA XX no.456

*Der Frost hat mir be-rei-fet des___ Hau-ses Dach;*

The roof of my house is rimed with frost, but I keep warm in the living-room.
Winter has whitened the top of my head, but the blood flows red in my heart.
The flush of youth in my cheeks has gone, the roses are all vanished, one after another.
Where are they now? Deep in my heart, where they bloom as before, on demand.
Have the sources of joy in life run dry? A quiet stream of pleasure still flows in my breast.
Are all the nightingales silent? Here, in the silence, one still sings for me.
She sings: 'Master of the house, lock your door, lest the world's chill wind should invade the parlour.
Shut out the harsh breath of reality, and give house-room only to the fragrance of dreams!'

The text comes from *Östliche Rosen* ('Oriental Roses'), published early in 1822, or possibly at the end of 1821. In this first edition the poems were untitled, and Schubert chose his own. In the later collected edition of the poems, however, this one was called *Vom künftigen Alter* (possibly, 'A Prospect of Old Age'). Schubert omitted the last two verses, which speak of the consolations of art in old age. He adapted the poem to his own mood and circumstances, grouping eight of the short stanzas into two long ones.

The Rückert songs cannot be precisely dated, though one (D741) was almost certainly composed before the autumn of 1822. In June 1823 Anton von Spaun reported (*Docs.* no.364) that he had heard Vogl sing *Greisengesang* at St Florian. The first draft (Berlin, SPK) is undated, as is a fair copy in Vienna (SB). There is a copy in the Spaun–Cornaro collection (privately owned in Vienna). The fair copy, marked 'Massig', is written for bass voice and shows some elaboration of the vocal line, so it may have been made for Vogl. The song was published in June 1826 as op.60 no.1 by Cappi and Czerny. The marking here is *Mässig langsam*.

It is remarkable that the tragic tone of the song is not really in keeping with the nostalgic, slightly ironic mood of the verses. The old gentleman looks back on the storms of youth with detachment, and finds much to console him in the pleasures of art. But

Schubert chose to omit the most consolatory verses, and his song, with its continuous sounding of the tonality of B minor/major, its melismatic voice line, and the plunging octaves in the accompaniment, sounds a note of defiance rather than complacence. Indeed, the tonal sequence in the introduction, and the scalewise descent of the voice line at the end of the strophe, have more than a hint of Schubert's familiar 'death motifs'. The song might fit into *Winterreise* well enough.

Capell, 202–3; Fischer-Dieskau, 184–5

# GRENZEN DER MENSCHHEIT Human Limitations
**Johann Wolfgang von Goethe**                                         March 1821

E major  D716  Peters III p.144  GA XX no.393

When the ancient of days, the heavenly Father, with a cool gesture scatters his beneficent thunderbolts over the earth from the rolling clouds, I kiss the hem of his garment, and my faithful heart is full of childlike awe.

For no man should measure himself against the gods. If he reaches up till his head touches the stars, then his uncertain feet lose their hold, and he becomes the plaything of the winds and the clouds.

But if he stands fast with sturdy limbs on the solid lasting earth he cannot reach up even to compare himself with the oak or the vine.

What distinguishes gods from men? Before them many waves flow on, an endless stream; but as for us, the wave lifts us up, and swallows us, and we sink.

Our life is bounded in a little ring, and one generation follows another, forming links in the unending chain of existence.

The poem dates from the period 1775–80. It is some years later than *Prometheus*, which represents the opposite, more humanistic, pole of Goethe's thought on the subject. The autograph, in private possession, is a first draft dated March 1821 and marked 'Nicht ganz langsam'. There are copies in the Witteczek–Spaun collection (Vienna, GdM) and in Schindler's song album (Lund, UB), marked 'Massig und ernst'. The song was written for bass voice. It was published in January 1832 in book 14 of the *Nachlass*, with the voice line written in the treble clef.

The most remarkable thing about the song is that it pierces to the heart of Goethe's intellectual concept, an acknowledgment of man's insignificance before the power of the gods, and matches the poem with music of comparable grandeur and sublimity. It does this by concentrating on the most intellectual aspect of music, its harmonic base, and unifies the song, not with any pictorial image (though the listener is at liberty to hear the distant rumbling of the thunderstorm in the opening bars if he wishes), but with an iambic phrase which moves up from the tonic to the subdominant and back again. The diatonic simplicity of this motif, a symbol of the unchanging and unchangeable infinite, is contrasted, as so often with Schubert, with passages that range adventurously into remote tonal regions, command of the tonal universe being here analogous with command of the real one. The result is a song of Wagnerian proportions, which can be realised only by a bass of majestic quality and range.

In one sense it can never be realised. If the song is to be criticised it is because Schubert's concept seems here to range beyond the means at his disposal. This is true not only in the sense that the orchestral sonorities disregard the limitations of the piano, and the vocal line the limitations of the human voice. There is in the idea of the song a Romantic sublimity which defies complete success in performance. It must be partly for this reason that the song has never achieved popularity.

Capell, 152−4; Einstein, 217−18; Fischer-Dieskau, 143−4

**GRETCHEN AM DOM** see SZENE AUS FAUST

## GRETCHEN AM SPINNRADE Gretchen at the Spinning-wheel
**Johann Wolfgang von Goethe**                                    19 October 1814

D minor D118  Peters I p.176  GA XX no.31  NSA IV vol.1 p.10

My heart is heavy, my peace is gone; never, never again shall I find it.
When he is not here life is like the grave; the whole world is embittered.
My poor head is in a whirl, my poor wits distracted.
If I look out of the window, or leave the house, it is only in the hope of seeing him.
His proud bearing, his noble figure, the smile on his lips, the power of his glance;
The bewitching flow of his discourse, the touch of his hand, and − ah, his kiss!
My heart yearns for him. Oh, if my arms could enfold him, and hold him.
And kiss him as I desire, I should drown in his kisses.
My heart is heavy, my peace is gone.

The text comes from part I of *Faust*, where it forms a whole scene, headed 'Gretchens Stube' ('Gretchen's Room'). The stage direction reads: 'Gretchen, alone at her spinning-wheel'. The scene forms part of the original sketches for the drama − the so-called *Urfaust* − and dates from the years 17.74−5. Unlike *Erlkönig* and *Der König in Thule*, the words are not intended to be sung on the stage. In the original conception of the drama it is clear that Gretchen's agitation and foreboding derive from the fact that she has already surrendered to Faust's love; she foresees her own tragedy as the forsaken mother of his child. In the printed version of the drama the sequence of events is changed, and it is possible to interpret the scene as the 'innocent' Gretchen's expression of an all-consuming passion which can never be fulfilled. To some extent this later conception weakens the dramatic impact of the scene, though it makes little difference to the emotional content of Schubert's song.

The autograph (Vienna, SB) is a fair copy dated 19 October 1814. The copy made for Goethe in 1816 (Berlin, DS) is now incomplete, consisting of only the first sixteen bars. There are copies in the Stadler and Ebner collections (Lund, UB) and in Schober's *Liederalbum* (Dresden, SLB). The song was published by Cappi and Diabelli on commission as op.2 in April 1821 and was dedicated by Schubert to Count Moritz von Fries.

What is it, then, that distinguishes *Gretchen* from its predecessors? Not the principle of faithfulness to the text, as has sometimes been claimed. That was the rallying-cry of the Weimar circle, and Goethe would certainly have condemned *Gretchen* (as he condemned all through-composed songs) and disapproved of Schubert's musically essential repetition of the opening words at the end of the song. It is not true, either, that Schubert's earlier songs 'give no hint of the miracle of *Gretchen*' (Craig Bell, p.15). His use of the accompaniment figure as a unifying element is much earlier, and so is his instinctive tendency to reconcile the dramatic and lyrical aspects of the lied. When we analyse the greatness of *Gretchen*, and try to account for the enormous – possibly exaggerated – importance it has assumed in the history books, it all boils down to one thing, the revolutionary nature of the unifying figure itself.

That figure is not simply a keyboard formula like the spread chords which link the supportive accompaniment of *Der Jüngling am Bache* and many other songs; it is a musical metaphor, a tonal analogue if you will, which embodies in itself the sense, the movement and the form of the song. For the songwriter, movement is form; the image of the spinning-wheel *is* the song, at least in the sense that it provides the medium through which the changing emotions of the words are conveyed. This single stroke of genius disposes of old problems and establishes a new relationship between text and music. The many attempts, in the Matthisson songs of 1814, to reconcile song and declamation, aria and recitative, are here superseded. The unifying power of that image is so strong, the forward thrust so powerful, that its suspension at the words 'Ah, sein Küss!' is more moving than any declamation could possibly be. Similarly, the contrast between the incidental pictorial image, with its centrifugal effect on the unity of the song, and the mood-defining unifying figure is here irrelevant, for the figure of the turning wheel is both at once. *Gretchen* established the independence of the lied as a musical form once and for all, using the poem as a pretext for a song, just as the opera composer uses the libretto as a pretext for an opera. In so doing, of course, Schubert was not rejecting the principle of faithfulness to the text, but showing how it could be realised at a higher musical level.

It is fair enough therefore to say, as Richard Heuberger does (*Franz Schubert*, Berlin, 1902), that with *Gretchen* Schubert created 'something new, of unprecedented power, the first composition in a hitherto unknown form, the first modern German song'.

Capell, 84–6; Einstein, 104–5; Fischer-Dieskau, 35–6; Stein, 71–2

## GRETCHENS BITTE  Gretchen's Prayer
**Johann Wolfgang von Goethe**                                   May 1817

B flat minor  D564  Peters V p.166  GA XX no.596

Look down, mother of sorrows, look graciously upon me in my need.
    The sword in your heart, racked by a thousand torments, you look up to your Son as he dies.
    You raise your eyes to the Father, a sigh rises up for His agony, and your own.
    Who can feel, as I feel the ache in my bones? Only you can know the anguish of my poor heart, its fears and longings.
    Wherever I go, what woe, what woe, beats here in my breast. No sooner alone than I weep, I weep, and my heart breaks.
[*The poem has three more verses.*]

The scene, the eighteenth in part I of *Faust*, forms part of the original sketches for the drama, the so-called *Urfaust*. Goethe's title is *Zwinger* ('The Ramparts') and the stage direction reads: 'In a niche in the wall an image of the Mater Dolorosa. Jugs full of flowers in front. Gretchen is putting fresh flowers in the jugs.'

Schubert's setting is conceived as an extended scena but is left unfinished. The first two verses (B flat minor, *Sehr langsam*) have an accompaniment of sobbing semiquavers, leading to an A major section for verses 3 and 4. At the words 'my heart breaks', the song modulates to C major. At this point it breaks off, though the key signature indicates that the next section was to be in A flat.

The autograph, now in the Goethe Museum at Frankfurt am Main, is dated May 1817 and headed 'Gretchen'. There is a copy in the Witteczek–Spaun collection (Vienna, GdM), entitled 'Gretchen im Zwinger'. The song was published in book 29 of the *Nachlass* in June 1838, under the title *Gretchens Bitte*. Diabelli simply added a concluding chord in C major. The text, in this first edition, was unaccountably attributed to Stolberg.

The song, what survives of it, is of fine quality, and it is tempting to speculate about the reasons for Schubert's failing to finish it. The operatic quality of his unfinished *Faust* pieces suggests that he may have cherished an ambition to write an opera based on the drama; but he was not ready for that in 1817, and in the final (C major) cadences one can almost sense the feeling of uncertainty about what happens next. Various attempts have been made to complete the song, among others by Benjamin Britten, Ivor Keys and Reinhard van Hoorickx.

Capell, 133–4; Einstein, 165

## GROB

Therese Grob (1798–1875) was Schubert's first love. The affair seems to have started in 1814, possibly at the time of the performance of Schubert's first Mass (in F, D105), in which Therese sang the soprano solos. Schubert's poverty and uncertain prospects ruled out any serious engagement, and when he left home in the autumn of 1816 it was all over, though the Schubert family continued to maintain close links with their neighbours the Grobs. Therese married Johann Bergmann, a master baker, in 1820.

The Therese Grob song album was assembled and given to Therese probably in November 1816, possibly as a birthday present (her birthday was on 16 November). It consists of seventeen songs in manuscript, including three (marked with asterisks) that appear nowhere else:

*Edone* D445, fair copy in Schubert's hand
*Klage* (*Nimmer trag' ich länger*) D512 (D2 Anhang I 28), not in Schubert's hand, authenticity doubtful
*An die Natur* D372, autograph fair copy, transposed to A major
*Pflügerlied* D392, autograph fair copy
*Klage* (= *Der Leidende*) D432, autograph fair copy
*Gott im Frühlinge* D448, autograph fair copy
*Lied von Salis* (= *Ins stille Land*) D403, autograph fair copy
*Der Herbstabend* D405, autograph fair copy
*Am Grabe Anselmos* D504, autograph fair copy
*Andenken* D99, autograph fair copy
*Am Tage aller Seelen* (*Litanei*) D343, autograph fair copy
*Lied aus der Ferne* D107, autograph fair copy

*Zufriedenheit* (2) D501, autograph fair copy
*Klage* ( = *Klage an den Mond*) D436, autograph fair copy
\**Mailied* D503, autograph, unpublished
*Trauer der Liebe* D465, autograph fair copy
\**Am ersten Maimorgen* D344, autograph, unpublished

Therese later had the collection of manuscripts bound under the title: 'Songs, in manuscript, by Franz Schubert, which I alone possess'. The volume passed to her nephew, and remained in the family for many years. Recently it passed into the possession of the Wilhelm family, of Bottmingen bei Basel.

> M. J. E. Brown, 'The Therese Grob collection of songs by Schubert', *M and L*, XLIX, 1968, pp.122–34; R. van Hoorickx, 'Schubert songs and song fragments not included in the collected edition', *MR*, XXXVIII, 1977, pp.

## GRUPPE AUS DEM TARTARUS Scene from Hades (1)
**Friedrich von Schiller**                                    March 1816

C minor  D396  Not in Peters  Not in GA  NSA IV vol.2 p.171

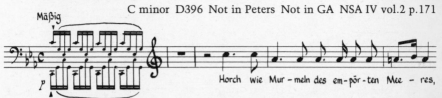

Hark! Like a murmur of the angry sea, like a brook sobbing through the hollow places in the rocks, there rises from the depths a low groan, heavy, empty, tortured.

Pain distorts their features, their open mouths transfixed with curses. Their eyes are hollow, as they look anxiously for the bridge over Cocytus, scanning the mournful course of the river as they weep.

Fearfully, softly they ask each other whether the end is yet in sight. Eternity spreads its encircling wings about them; Saturn's scythe is riven in two.

The poem dates from about 1781, and was published in the 'Anthology from the Year 1782'. The title suggests that it is conceived as the poetic equivalent of a *tableau vivant*.

This first setting is fourteen bars long, covering the first five lines of the poem. The autograph, dated march 1816, is in the Newberry Library, Chicago. It finishes at the bottom of a page, so that it is at least possible that the song was completed and that the second sheet has been lost. But more likely Schubert's own poetic insight warned him that he was not yet ready to match the Rembrandtesque richness of the poem in music. The song remained unpublished until it was included in vol.2 of the *Neue Ausgabe*. A version which continues the song for six more bars and ends in C minor was made by Reinhard van Hoorickx in 1964.

The first verse is set to a flowing melodic line (*Mässig*). The tonality moves from C minor, G flat major and F flat major to B flat major to an accompaniment of broken chords.

> M. J. E. Brown, 'Some unpublished Schubert songs and song fragments', *MR*, XV, 1954, pp.93–102

# GRUPPE AUS DEM TARTARUS (2)

**Friedrich von Schiller**                                    September 1817

C minor D583  Peters II p.61  GA XX no.328  NSA IV vol.2 p.13

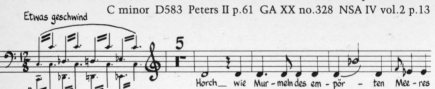

For translation, see the preceding entry. The autograph is lost, and there are no contemporary copies. The catalogue of the Witteczek–Spaun collection (Vienna, GdM), however, dates the song September 1817, which saw also the setting of Schiller's Elysium. *Gruppe aus dem Tartarus* was published by Sauer and Leidesdorf in October 1823 as op.24 no.1. The song was first performed in public by Josef Preisinger at a Music Society concert on 8 March 1821.

Nothing more clearly demonstrates the widening of Schubert's intellectual horizon in his twentieth year than the contrast between this tremendous setting and the one written eighteen months earlier. Schubert's tonal imagination, his ability to find the precise musical figure for a precise poetic image, which had already found the definitive equivalent for Gretchen's spinning-wheel and the Erlking's night ride, here finds music to match the Miltonic grandeur of Schiller's more abstract tableau. The song, as Fischer-Dieskau observes, is 'far removed from the conventional lied, even Schubert's own. The voice no longer has a "song melody", the action is depicted more by the harmonic and rhythmic audacities of the piano than by the melody.'

The upward chromatic movement which symbolises the groans of the damned rising up from Hades underlies the whole song, but the contrasted sections bring to it an astonishing variety of rhythmic and dynamic expression. Only once, at the word 'Ewigkeit', does the music emerge into the clear light of C major, and the effect, after all the tortured chromaticism, is electrifying. The postlude confirms the image by reversing it, sinking down through two octaves before the piece comes to a close on the chord of C minor (*pp*). So the cries of the damned fall silent beneath the engulfing waves of eternity. The song was published with the melodic line in the treble clef, though it is clearly intended for a bass voice. Schubert's imagination here transcends the means at his disposal, so that the song's greatness of conception is difficult to realise fully in performance.

Capell, 130; Fischer-Dieskau, 99–100

## GUARDA, CHE BIANCA LUNA see VIER CANZONEN no.2

## GUTE NACHT see WINTERREISE no.1

# HAGARS KLAGE Hagar's Lament

**Clemens August Schücking**                                    March 1811

C minor D5  Not in Peters  GA XX no.1  NSA IV vol.6 p.3

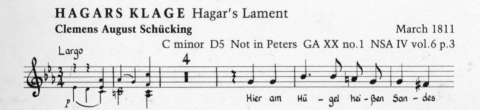

[*Synopsis*] Here I sit in the wilderness beside my dying child. His eyes fixed on his afflicted mother, he languishes for water. If it would quench your thirst I would fight the lioness for her milk, or suck water from the desert. But alas, I must watch you die. No, I must turn away, lest I reproach God in my despair.

I open my parched lips in this last prayer. 'Look down upon us, Jehovah, have pity on this child. Was he not born of Abraham, who wept for joy at his birth? His father asked your blessing on his head.

'If I have sinned, I deserve punishment, but the boy has done nothing, that he should share in my suffering. Would I had died in Syria, the unborn child under my heart. But a stranger bade me return to Abraham, who now cruelly rejects us. Was that stranger not an angel of the Lord, who prophesied that Ishmael would be great, and his seed would multiply?' Here now we lie dying, and our bodies will rot like those of outcasts. Cry to heaven, my poor boy. Lord God, scorn not his innocent plea!

The story of Hagar and Ishmael is told in *Genesis* xxi. Schücking's poem was published in the Göttingen *Musenalmanach* for 1781. Schubert's source, however, was almost certainly Zumsteeg's setting of the text, which he took as a model. This appeared in 1797; it is reprinted in the appendix to vol. 6 of the *Neue Ausgabe*. The poem has nineteen verses, but these are grouped in both Schubert's version and Zumsteeg's to provide a succession of contrasted sections, in varying tempi and styles.

The autograph, in private possession, is incomplete, breaking off at bar 193, at the end of the section marked 'Geschwind'. This first part of the song follows Zumsteeg closely, as the tempo indications indicate. The autograph also contains a cancelled earlier sketch of the Adagio section, bars 194–204. There is a copy of the complete song in the Witteczek–Spaun collection (Vienna, GdM), on which is inscribed: 'Schubert's first song composition, written in the *Konvikt* at the age of fourteen, 30 March 1811.' This served as the source for the first publication, in the *Gesamtausgabe* in 1894.

*Hagars Klage* is the earliest of Schubert's songs to have survived complete, though it is almost certain that other, less ambitious, song compositions must have preceded it. Spaun tells us that Schubert 'wanted to modernise Zumsteeg's song form' (*Memoirs* p. 127), and we can see what he meant. For the first 200 bars the song follows the layout and markings of Zumsteeg's setting closely, and Schubert's opening theme is clearly modelled on Zumsteeg's. Thereafter Schubert breaks the song up into shorter sections and begins to exploit the dramatic potential of the story on his own account. The descending bass octaves of what was to become a familiar Schubert death theme are heard at bars 217–28 ('And then may death come quickly!'). It is superficial therefore simply to write off *Hagars Klage* and its companion pieces as a false start. The form was valid enough in its day as a kind of home opera; and Schubert was right to begin with it because it offered growth points for the sort of song he was destined to write. There is ample evidence, even in *Hagars Klage*, that he was fully equipped to take advantage of them.

App. IV; Capell, 30, 70; Einstein, 43–4; Fischer-Dieskau, 18; Schnapper, 83

**HALT!** see DIE SCHÖNE MÜLLERIN no. 3

## HÄNFLINGS LIEBESWERBUNG The Linnet's Wooing

**Friedrich Kind**                                                    April 1817

A major  D552  Peters IV p.12  GA XX no.316  NSA IV vol.1 pp.260, 145

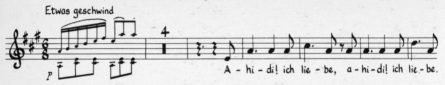

A - hi - di! ich lie - be, a - hi - di! ich lie - be.

Tra-la-la, I am in love. The sun's smile is gentle, the west wind blows tender, the spring waters ripple, the flowers scent the air. Tra-la-la, I am in love.

I love you, my darling, your soft silken feathers, your little eyes shining. Loveliest of sisters! Tra-la-la, I am in love.

See how the flowers greet one another, tenderly nodding. See how the ivy entwines the oak tree, with loving embraces. Will you not love me? Tra-la-la, I am in love.

These embarrassingly arch verses are the only ones of Friedrich Kind, the librettist of *Der Freischütz*, that Schubert set. The autograph (Vienna, SB) is dated April 1817 and marked 'Lieblich'. The song was published by Sauer and Leidesdorf as op.20 no.3 in April 1823. This published version is marked 'Etwas geschwind', and it is followed by Friedländer and Mandyczewski. Both versions are included in the *Neue Ausgabe*.

The song is in much the same vein as *Seligkeit*, and the accompaniment has the same Ländler-like lilt and melodic pattern. Indeed, Schubert used it also as the third of his *Drei Deutsche für Klavier* (D972 no.3), which was probably written about the same time. But which came first, song or dance, it is impossible to say. *Hanflings Liebeswerbung* is as fresh and innocent as a daisy.

## HARFENSPIELER The Harper's Songs, from *Wilhelm Meister*

**Johann Wolfgang von Goethe**

There is a good case for grouping these three songs together as a kind of miniature song cycle. The figure of the blind Harper is for Schubert a prototype of the Wanderer. He submits to his destiny with humility and courage, accepting his grievous isolation with a quiet dignity; and the unity of the songs is emphasised not only by the identity of key (A minor), but by the generally melancholy mood also. The songs were written as a group in September 1816, revised in 1822 and published as op.12 in December 1822 by Cappi and Diabelli.

However, the very uniformity of mood means that the songs are rarely performed together. Moreover each of them has a complicated history of its own, involving several different versions; they are therefore discussed individually under their first lines, which is how they are usually identified:

*Wer sich der Einsamkeit ergibt*
*Wer nie sein Brot mit Tränen ass*
*An die Türen will ich schleichen*

This is the order in which they finally appeared in 1822. In Schubert's autograph of September 1816, now split up, the second and third songs are reversed. Goethe's order in *Wilhelm Meister* is different again.

## HARK, HARK, THE LARK see STÄNDCHEN

# HEIDENRÖSLEIN The Wild Rose

**Johann Wolfgang von Goethe** 19 August 1815

G major D257 Peters I p.182 GA XX no.114 NSA IV vol.1 p.24

Sah ein Knab ein Rös - lein__ stehn, Rös - lein auf der Hei - den

A boy espied a wild rose growing in the heather, so young and morning-fair. He ran fast and looked close, with great joy. Wild rose, wild rose, wild rose red, growing in the heather!

Said the boy, 'I shall pluck you, little rose, wild rose in the heather!' Said the rose, 'Then I shall prick you, so that you will never forget me. I won't put up with it.' Wild rose, wild rose, wild rose red, growing in the heather!

And the rough boy plucked the little rose in the heather. The rose pricked him in self-defence. But her oh's and ah's were all in vain; she had to put up with it after all. Wild rose, wild rose, wild rose red, growing in the heather!

A German folksong about a wild rose can be traced back to the sixteenth century, and the precise relationship between the folksong, Herder's version written in 1771 and Goethe's definitive version, also written in 1771 and first published under its familiar title in 1789, is now impossible to determine, though much academic ink has been spilt in arguing the matter. The most probable explanation is that Goethe drew Herder's attention to the traditional children's song *Es sah ein Knab' ein Röslein stehen* about 1771 and that they both then produced a 'parody' of the song, Herder adopting a moralistic tone, and Goethe reverting to the sturdier tradition of folksong, complete with sexual overtones. What is clear is that Goethe's accomplished exercise in the vernacular style has become a folksong by adoption. Curiously enough, the 6/8 tune to which it is sung in Germany also has the status of a folktune, though it was composed by Heinrich Werner and first published in 1829. It is a derivative of Schubert's setting.

The first draft (Lund, UB) is dated 19 August 1815. The fair copy made for Goethe is in Berlin (DS). The song was published in May 1821 by Cappi and Diabelli on commissions as op.3 no.3, together with three other Goethe settings, and dedicated by Schubert to Ignaz von Mosel 'with great respect'.

The contrast between this original folktune, perfect in its melodic shape and in its kinship with the text, and the setting of Goethe's *Das Veilchen* which Mozart had written thirty years earlier, says a great deal both about the revolution in poetic feeling which had taken place in the meantime and about Schubert's instinctive feeling for folksong. *Das Veilchen* is a fine song, but it is still essentially operatic; its simplicity is the mannered simplicity of the *grande dame*, there is never the remotest possibility that it could have been adopted into the vigorous and anonymous world of popular song as a genuine piece of folk art. But Schubert, here and in *Am Brunnen vor dem Tore* (from *Der Lindenbaum*), has achieved a kind of honorary membership of the circle of anonymous composers.

The five Goethe songs which Schubert wrote on 19 August 1815 provide us with an interesting glimpse of the indiscriminate procedure of genius. One (*An den Mond*) is well wide of the mark, three are what might be called good routine Schubert, and one – *Heidenröslein* – is a masterpiece.

Capell, 103–4; Einstein, 110; Fischer-Dieskau, 62–3.

## HEIMLICHES LIEBEN Secret Love

**Karoline Louise von Klenke**

September 1827

B flat major D922 Peters IV p.104 GA XX no.544

When I feel the touch of your lips, desire threatens to ravish my soul; a nameless trembling stirs deep within my breast.

My eyes flame, blushes suffuse my cheeks, my heart beats with an unfamiliar yearning. My thoughts, confused, come stammering from my lips, scarce to be controlled. At such a moment the thread of life hangs from your soft lips, tender as the rose; enfolded in your beloved arms, I wish almost to die.

Oh, that I cannot escape from life, my soul absorbed in yours; that our lips, aflame with longing, must part! Oh that my being may not dissolve in kisses, my lips pressed so close to yours; and to your heart, which may never dare to beat aloud for me.

The text was given to Schubert during his stay in Graz in September 1827 by his hostess Marie Pachler, to whom the song was dedicated on its publication early in the following year. For many years the erotic verses were attributed to Karl Gottfried von Leitner, another of Marie's favourite authors; the true story was revealed only in the 1870s by Marie's son Faust (*Memoirs* pp.198–9). The author was the mother of Helmina von Chézy, who wrote the libretto of *Euryanthe* and of *Rosamunde*. The original title was *An Myrtill*, and the first line read 'Myrtill, wenn deine Lippen mich berühren'. Marie received the poem in manuscript from her old friend Julius Schneller, a professor of philosophy who had been forced to leave Graz because of his liberal views. According to Faust Pachler, it was Schneller who changed the first line.

Schubert's first draft (New York, PML) is headed 'Graz September 1827'. A fair copy made for the printer, marked 'Massig', is in Budapest (HNL). The song was published early in 1828 with two Leitner settings and *An Sylvia*, and dedicated to Marie Pachler. The publisher was the Lithographic Institute of Vienna, of which Schubert's friend Schober was at that time manager. The group of songs was later republished as op.106.

This modified strophic song makes a fine vehicle for a strong lyric soprano. The triplets in the pianist's right hand flow along smoothly, and the voice floats serenely above, the chromatic progressions suggesting, rather than expressing, strong feeling. It is beautiful, and even moving, but it has to be admitted that von Klenke's Sapphic ode has had the raw passion drained out of it. Schubert was made much of in the drawing rooms of Graz, and it is not surprising perhaps that the songs he wrote there seem to be tinged with *Gemütlichkeit*.

Capell, 244–5; Fischer-Dieskau, 249–50

## HEINE SONGS

**Heinrich Heine**

1827–8

The six Heine songs were published after Schubert's death by Tobias Haslinger with the Rellstab settings under the general title *Schwanengesang* ('Swan Song'). The title, invented by Haslinger himself, was intended to convey the idea that the publication represented 'the last blossoming of his [Schubert's] noble art'. But the two groups should properly be treated separately. It is true that the autograph, now in New York (PML), includes all thirteen songs, but it may well have been a collection made from earlier drafts at Haslinger's suggestion, and in response to his proposal to publish the two groups together.

There is no lack of evidence that the Heine songs originated much earlier than August 1828, the date on the front page of the autograph. The texts are all taken from a sequence of poems called *Die Heimkehr* ('The Homecoming'), written in 1823–4 and first published in part I of the *Reisebilder* ('Travel Scenes') in Hamburg in May 1826. This was probably Schubert's source. The poems were republished in 1827 in the much more comprehensive collection called the *Buch der Lieder*. The amateur singer Karl von Schönstein said many years later (in 1875; see *Memoirs* pp.332–4) that he found this book in Schubert's possession some years before his death, with the pages turned down to mark the poems he intended to set. It would not be surprising if Schönstein's memory was confused about the precise sequence of events; even when challenged however he continued to assert that the Heine songs were written long before August 1828. Heine did not give titles to the individual poems in his sequence. The titles in the songs are Schubert's own.

We know from Franz von Hartmann's diary (*Docs*. no.1000) that part II of the *Reisebilder* was read and discussed by the Schubert circle when the reading parties were resumed in January 1828, and this led O. E. Deutsch to assume that the Heine songs were sketched then. But the reading parties seem to have been concerned only with the prose section called *Ideen* ('Notions'). Schubert's acquaintance with the poems could easily have begun much earlier. As late as 2 October 1828 (and therefore after the surviving autograph had been written), Schubert wrote to the Leipzig publisher Probst (*Docs*. no.1152) mentioning the Heine songs as among his works available for publication. It is reasonable to assume, therefore, that the two groups originated at different times and in different ways, and that Schubert's intention was to publish them separately if he could find a publisher to accept them.

For what it is worth, the internal evidence points in the same direction. There is no real unity of theme or consistency of mood in *Schwanengesang*. The Heine songs do have a vague continuity of theme, though it is obscured by the fact that Schubert's order is different from Heine's, and their mood of bitter irony and tragic alienation is much closer to *Winterreise* than it is to the Rellstab songs. In a real sense the Heine songs begin where *Winterreise* leaves off, and the aphoristic power which is so remarkable a feature of *Der Leiermann* finds its natural sequel in *Der Atlas* and *Der Doppelgänger*. For that reason, if for no other, the chronology of the Heine songs is a matter of great critical importance. To suppose that they were begun in August 1828 runs counter to much of the evidence. It is more probable that the autograph represents the final stage of a creative process which began much earlier.

A month after the composer's death his brother Ferdinand handed over the thirteen songs by Heine and Rellstab to Haslinger in exchange for a fee of 290 florins. It is possible that this was in accordance with terms agreed with Schubert before his death. Haslinger's intention was to publish them in four books, but in the end they appeared (May 1829) in two books which did not even recognise the integrity of the separate groups. Vol. I contained the first six Rellstab songs, vol. II the last Rellstab song, the six Heine songs, and the Seidl setting *Die Taubenpost*. This last song, written in October 1828, has no connection with the others whatsoever; it is included only to make good Haslinger's claim that his publication included the 'last blossomings' of Schubert's art.

There remains a final problem of baffling complexity. O. E. Deutsch asserts, in the original edition of the thematic catalogue, that 'in October 1828 Schubert planned to publish the Heine songs, selected and their order altered, separately'. He gives no authority for this statement, and it may be no more than an over-confident construction put on a remark of Spaun's in his memoir of the composer (*Docs.* p.875), that the last songs were to be dedicated to his friends and published by Haslinger. If the order of the Heine songs *was* changed, it is much more likely that the published order is the revised version, and that Schubert altered his original draft at Haslinger's suggestion or request, than that the published order represents his first draft. For it was Schubert's practice to respect the poet's sequence wherever that was practicable, and this the familiar order signally fails to do; moreover, as Harry Goldschmidt has persuasively argued, if the songs are rearranged in Heine's order (that is, 3, 5, 4, 6, 2, 1) they make better sense both musically and as an implied narrative. Once again, it looks as though Schubert's original intentions have been frustrated and obscured by the harsh necessity of finding a publisher.

The significance of the Heine songs can hardly be overestimated. Two works set the tone for the final creative phase of Schubert's life, *Winterreise* and the Heine songs. The continuity of theme is plain. Heine himself acknowledged his debt to Müller, sharpening the cutting edge of Müller's irony as the alienated Wanderer becomes the embittered artist at war with a philistine society. The emotional intensity of the Heine songs prove that for Schubert too this theme struck home.

> H. Goldschmidt, 'Welches war die ursprüngliche Reihenfolge in Schuberts Heine-Lieder?', *Deutsches Jahrbuch der Musikwissenschaft 1972*, pp.52–61; J. Kerman, 'A romantic detail in Schubert's *Schwanengesang*', MQ, XLVIII, 1962, p.36; Moore; H. Schenker, 'Ihr Bild', *Der Tonwille*, I, Vienna and Leipzig, 1921

**(1) DER ATLAS** Atlas      G minor  D957 no.8  Peters I p.151  GA XX no.561

I am the unhappy Atlas, who must bear the whole world of sorrows. I bear the unbearable, and my heart threatens to break in my body.

You, proud heart, have willed it so. You meant to be happy, endlessly happy, or endlessly wretched: and now, proud heart, you are wretched.

Atlas led the Titans in war against Zeus; when they were defeated Atlas was given an exemplary punishment and made to carry the sky on his shoulders. He is the archetypal figure of the man who dares, and suffers. Here the idea of alienation takes on a symphonic grandeur. The insistent tonality of G minor, framed by the hammer-blows in the bass – G, B flat, F sharp, G – strikes with the inexorable finality of fate itself. Those four notes are nearly akin to the germ-cell of *Der Doppelgänger* also and, with the first interval changed from a minor to a major third, form the harmonic basis of the middle section of *Der Atlas*. It is easy to see that the opening bars of *Ihr Bild* provide us with a kind of melodic version of the theme. It pervades the Heine songs like a musical image of the force of destiny. The wide dynamic range (*pp* to *fff*) reinforces the intensity of feeling of the song. It calls for a voice of quite exceptional power and range.

Capell, 252; Fischer-Dieskau, 280

(2) **IHR BILD** Her Likeness     B flat minor D957 no.9 Peters I p.154
                                  GA XX no.562

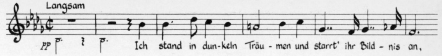

I stood in sombre reverie, gazing at her likeness, and mysteriously those beloved features began to come alive.

A smile played wondrously about her lips, and her eyes sparkled as though with wistful tears.

The tears flowed down my cheeks too ... Ah, I cannot believe that I have lost you!

Nowhere is the sadness of lost happiness expressed with more epigrammatic force than in this wonderful song. Its thirty-six bars distil the essence of the bitter poem with an exactness that defies analysis, though it is not difficult to isolate aspects of its greatness: the alternation of bare unison phrases, for instance, always with Schubert an image of loneliness and deprivation, with echoing homophonic phrases, as though to convey the contrast between bleak reality and the memory of happier days: the mysteriously heart-easing effect of the simple modulation to G flat major at the words 'A smile played wondrously about her lips': and the runic precision of the bare B flats (*pp*) at the beginning, which Heinrich Schenker, in a famous essay, took to be a tonal analogue for the act of staring (*Der Tonwille*, I, 1921). It might be remorse, however, or simply the act of introspection. All one can say is that the song proves Mendelssohn's point, when he protested that music cannot be paraphrased in words because it is a more precise emotional language in its own right. The three-bar postlude, which says something about the irrevocability of the past, has the same overwhelming inevitability.

The Heine songs, as has been said, set the tone for the music of Schubert's last year. The affinity of mood between *Ihr Bild* and the B flat Piano Sonata D960 is especially noticeable in the link phrases at bars 5–7 and 28–30, while the stepwise descending unison phrases and answering cadences hint at the Trio of the C major Quintet.

Capell, 252–3; Fischer-Dieskau, 280

(3) **DAS FISCHERMÄDCHEN** The Fisher Maiden     A flat major
                                                D957 no.10 Peters I p.156 GA XX no.563

Lovely fisher maiden, row your boat ashore. Come and sit beside me, and hand in hand we will murmur love-talk.

Lay your little head on my heart, and don't be too frightened. Every day you put your trust in the raging sea and are not afraid.

My heart is just like the sea. It storms, and ebbs and flows, and in its depths lies many a lovely pearl.

*Das Fischermädchen* is a charming barcarolle, without the emotional intensity or the psychological depth of the other Heine songs. It can be argued, indeed, that it misses the ironic tone of the poem, which surely carries the implication that a simple uncomplicated love like that of the fisher girl is beyond the reach of a disenchanted poet. Schubert's 6/8 rhythm and regular phrases announce, however, that he is writing a quite different sort of song, in its own way quite as successful as the others; and that he is more interested in the carefree life of the fisher girl than in the reflections of the poet.

Capell, 252; Fischer-Dieskau, 280–1

(4) **DIE STADT** The Town                    C minor  D957 no.11  Peters I p.159
                                                                 GA XX no.564

On the far horizon the towers of the town appear like a misty vision, shrouded in the dusk of evening.

A moist wind ruffles the grey surface of the water; with a mournful stroke the boatman rows my boat.

Once more the sun rises sparkling from the earth, to show me that place where I lost my love.

The impressionist brilliance of *Die Stadt* seems to mark the beginning of a new phase in Schubert's development as a pictorial composer. Like the other Heine songs (and even more like *Im Dorfe*) it is a study in alienation, but it looks outward, at the visual scene, rather than inward. The despair of the observer–narrator is implied rather than expressed. The bare octaves of the opening are a colder, open-air version of the first two bars of *Ihr Bild*, and soon the diminished sevenths are swirling about our heads, while the dotted rhythms convey the laboured weariness of the journey. In the end we are left alone with the swirling gusts, and a single low C on the piano. The unity of mood and economy of means in this extraordinary song seem far in advance of its time. It should be noted that the tempo indication is *Mässig geschwind*. The instruction *leise* ('in an undertone'?) applies to the first two verses.

Capell, 253–4; Fischer-Dieskau, 281

(5) **AM MEER** By the Sea                    C major  D957 no.12  Peters I p.162
                                                                 GA XX no.565

The wide sea sparkled in the sun's last rays, as we sat by the lonely fisherman's house, silent and alone. The mist lifted, and the water rose; the gull flew to and fro. From your loving eyes the tears came falling.

I watched them fall on your hand, and sank upon my knee. From your white hand I drank away those tears. Since that same hour my body is consumed, and my soul expires with longing. That unhappy woman has poisoned me with her tears.

*Am Meer* is, in a sense, Schubert's farewell to the strophic song. The melodic line is pure Schubert, and so is the way the accompaniment circles round the mediant. But here they take on an epigrammatic intensity. Significantly, the song is framed within a repeated statement of one of Schubert's favourite motifs in a concentrated, elliptical form – the alternation of tonic and German sixth. This figure, which he inherited as an orchestral formula from the language of classical music, is here invested with atmospheric feeling, so that it conjures up the whole sad, misty seascape. It is the visual sharpness of Schubert's imagination which impresses here, as in *Die Stadt*. The tremolando chords convey the threatening murmur of the rising waters.

Heine's four verses are grouped in pairs. The strophe has two distinct halves, the first diatonic, almost serene, the second chromatic, and disturbed. The melodic line is adjusted to suit the words, but otherwise the effect is entirely strophic. Schubert makes no attempt to match the bitterness of the last line, so that the ironic reversal of feeling at the end of the poem is lost. But to do so would have put the unity of mood of the song at risk, something which the mature Schubert never does.

Not without reason, Capell calls this 'the most difficult song in Schubert'. It demands exceptional breath control within a high tessitura, and at a slow pace. In the second half of each strophe the forward momentum must be sustained without an obtrusive beat.

Capell, 255; Fischer-Dieskau, 281

## (6) **DER DOPPELGÄNGER** The Ghostly Double      B minor D957 no.13

Peters I p.164 GA XX no.566

The night is still, the streets are hushed; within this house my love once dwelt. She left the town long ago, but the house still stands, in the very same place.

    A man is standing there too, and looking up, wringing his hands in pain. I shudder when I see his face – the figure revealed in the moonlight is my own.

    You ghostly double, pale companion, why do you mock the pain of love which tormented me in this very place, many a night in days gone by?

Schubert's lifelong concern to reconcile recitative and 'pure song', to give to the lied the dramatic force of opera, is here fulfilled. *Der Doppelgänger* is neither song nor recitative, but lyrical declamation. In a short lifetime Schubert had taken the lied on a journey from Zumsteeg to Hugo Wolf. The song is a kind of passacaglia on the four-note theme set out in the opening bars. Its key (B minor) and the affinity with the theme of the first movement of the 'Unfinished' Symphony, and still more with the Agnus Dei of the E flat Mass written in June 1828, give a tragic significance to the song which goes beyond the disenchantment of the verses, so that the weight of emotion conveyed by this wonderful song is almost oppressive. Perhaps Schubert did, after all, have some premonition of his approaching end.

Capell, 255–7; Fischer-Dieskau, 281–2

## **HEISS MICH NICHT REDEN** Bid me not speak (1)

**Johann Wolfgang von Goethe**      April 1821

B minor D726 Not in Peters GA XX no.394

Bid me not speak, bid me be silent, for my duty is to guard my secret. Fain would I reveal to you my whole heart, but fate wills otherwise.

    The sun in his appointed course dispels the dark, and night must turn to day.

The hard rock is riven to the heart, and spills its hidden springs ungrudgingly upon the earth.

Every human soul seeks peace in the arms of a friend, for there the heart can pour forth all its woes. But my lips, alas, are sealed by a vow, and only a god can open them.

The date of the poem is uncertain. Most authorities attribute it to the Weimar years before the Italian journey; others regard it as a product of the 1790s. The fact that Goethe seemed to find some difficulty in fitting it into the story of *Wilhelm Meister*, in spite of its obvious connection with Mignon, and finally appended it somewhat uneasily to the end of book 5, may suggest that it is earlier than the main narrative. There is no suggestion in the book that the words are to be sung.

The autograph of this first version (Vienna, SB) is headed simply 'Mignon. Göthe.' and dated April 1821. The song was published by J. P. Gotthard in 1870 and dedicated by the publisher to Fräulein Helene Magnus. The rhythm is a familiar image of death though here it seems to signify rather the death-in-life which was Mignon's tragic destiny. It is a pity that this fine song has been eclipsed by the later and much greater setting, for it catches the simple pathos for the verses perfectly with its B minor–major modulations, though it lacks the breadth and variety of the second version.

Capell, 156–7; Einstein, 218

## HEISS MICH NICHT REDEN (2)

**J. W. von Goethe**

(?) January 1826

E minor D877 no.2 Peters II p.130 GA XX no.489

For translation, see the preceding entry. The song was published as op.62 no.2, together with three other 'Songs from *Wilhelm Meister* by Goethe', by Diabelli in March 1827 and dedicated by Schubert to Mathilde, Princess Schwarzenberg. But it is not certain that the four songs were written at the same time. A manuscript in Vienna (SB) contains sketches for the first three songs, and a sketch for the second version of the fugue Cum Sancto Spiritu from the A flat Mass. The complete autograph of the four songs, the first one dated January 1826, is now divided; the first five sheets are in Dresden (SLB) and the sixth in Vienna (SB).

This, the greatest of the Mignon songs, has an operatic richness and variety. In the space of forty-two bars we move from the measured pathos of the opening (which retains the rhythm of the earlier setting) to the flowing C major four-bar phrases of the middle section, to a restatement in the major of the first theme, and finally to the eloquence of the declamatory final lines. And yet each of these separately identifiable sections is contained within the song's organic unity, and each seems equally to reflect the pathos of the innocent girl's fate. The song thus mirrors in a wonderful way the movement of thought in the poem: first, a simple statement of Mignon's mysterious fate; then her mind turns to the world of nature and the world of men, as the phrases flow more easily and openly; finally, as the tragic contrast with her own position impresses itself on the mind, the declamatory phrases take on a dignified grandeur.

Capell, 220

## HEKTORS ABSCHIED Hector's Farewell

**Friedrich von Schiller**

19 October 1815

Langsam        F minor D312 Peters IV p.53 GA XX no.159(a) and (b)

Andromache: Will sich Hek - tor e - wig von mir wen - den,

*Andromache:* Will Hector ever turn away from me, while Achilles' arrogant hands make fearful sacrifice for Patroclus? Who will teach your son to throw the javelin and venerate the gods, when the dark underworld engulfs you?

    *Hector:* Dear wife, weep not. My ardent heart longs for battle. These arms will protect Troy. I fall fighting for the sacred home of the gods and descend to the Stygian stream as the saviour of my fatherland.

    *Andromache:* Never more shall I hear the clash of arms. The sword will lie useless in the hall. Priam's heroic race will be destroyed. You will go where never light of day appears, where sad Cocytus weeps through the drear wastelands. Your love will drown in the waters of Lethe.

    *Hector:* In Lethe's still stream I shall drown all my longing and all my thoughts, but not my love. Hark, the wild tumult rages at the walls. Gird on my sword. Cease lamenting. Hector's love will not in Lethe die.

The poem dates from about 1777. The autograph, in the Paris Conservatoire, is dated 19 October 1815. The song was first published in April 1826 as op.58 no.1 (originally op.56) by Thaddäus Weigl in a revised version, which was presumably based on Schubert's fair copy. Both versions are published in the *Gesamtausgabe*. Copies made for Stadler and Ebner are now in Lund (UB).

    This elaborate dramatic scena for tenor and soprano voices is one of eight songs dated 19 October 1815, but one does not have to believe that the autograph written out on that day was a first draft in the literal sense. There is no question that Andromache's plight inspired the more eloquent music. Her lyrical pleas are in F minor and A minor, while Hector's responses, in F and A flat major, seem conventional by comparison. Like so many of Schubert's early attempts at the extended scena, the piece does not quite live up to its first promise. There is a curious resemblance between the opening F minor section and the main theme of the F minor Fantasie for piano duet.

## HELIOPOLIS see AUS 'HELIOPOLIS'

## HERBST Autumn

**Ludwig Rellstab**

April 1828

Mäßig      E minor D945 Not in Peters GA XX no.589

Es rau - schen die Win-de so herbstlich und kalt,

The autumn winds blow cold, the fields are bare, and leafless the trees. You blossoming meadows, you sunlit green! Thus do the flowers of life wither away.

    The storm clouds are gathering, dark and grey. The stars in the blue heaven are gone. Ah, as the stars vanish from the sky, so does hope fade from life.

    You spring days, crowned with roses, when I pressed my love to my heart! Chill winds, blow on across the hillside. So do the roses of love die.

Rellstab's poems had been published in 1827. But there is no reason to doubt Schindler's story that he passed on manuscript copies of Rellstab poems which he found in Beethoven's *Nachlass* to Schubert (*Memoirs*, pp.303, 319). The song came to light only in the 1890s, when the autograph was discovered in the album of Heinrich Panofka, a professional violinist and an acquaintance of Schubert in the last years of his life. It is now in the Kongelige Bibliotek, Copenhagen. The song is inscribed 'Zur freundlichen Erinnerung', signed and dated April 1828. Brahms's copy of the song is now in Vienna (GdM). His own song *Herbstgefühl* is somewhat similar in mood, but it was written long before the discovery of Schubert's.

This fine song remains virtually unknown, simply because it is at present available only in the *Gesamtausgabe*. It does not seem to fall below the standard of the other Rellstab settings, which were included in *Schwanengesang*, and it is not clear why Schubert excluded it from that collection. But it does share the key, and the bleak mood, of *Aufenthalt*, and there is a certain similarity in the piano writing, so he may have felt that to include it would upset the diversity in unity of the group. Whatever the reason, it is high time *Herbst* was taken into general circulation, for it is a splendidly atmospheric song.

Fischer-Dieskau, 274–5

## HERBSTLIED Song of Autumn
**Johann Gaudenz von Salis-Seewis**                    November 1816

G major  D502  Not in Peters  GA XX no.282

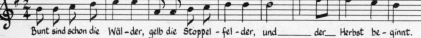

Bunt sind schon die Wäl-der, gelb die Stoppel-fel-der, und___ der___ Herbst be-ginnt.

The woods are already bright with colour, the stubble-fields are golden, and autumn has come. Red leaves fall, grey mists swirl, and chiller blows the wind.

How purple shines the plump grape among the vine's foliage! The peaches, streaked with red and white, ripen on the terraces.

See how the maid deftly fills her basket with ripe plums and pears. Look, another carries her golden quinces, lightfooted, to the house.

Nimbly the young men dance and the maidens sing. All is merry and bright. Coloured ribbons on straw hats move among the tall vines.

Fiddles and flutes make music in the glow of evening, and by the light of the moon. The young vine-dressers beckon to each other to join in the old German round-dance.

The poem dates from 1782. The autograph is lost, but a copy (in F major) in the Witteczek–Spaun collection (Vienna, GdM) is dated November 1816. The song was first published in 1872 by J. P. Gotthard as no.24 of 'Forty Songs'. A simple setting in Schubert's folksong manner, livelier, and less deeply felt, than the setting of the same poet's *Der Herbstabend* which Schubert had made earlier in the year.

## HERMANN UND THUSNELDA Hermann and Thusnelda
**Friedrich Gottlieb Klopstock**                    27 October 1815

E flat major  D322  Peters V p.154  GA XX no.169

Ha,    dort kömmt er,  mit Schweiß, mit Rö-mer-blut,

*Thusnelda:* Lo, there he comes, stained with sweat, with Roman blood, and with the dust of battle. Never did Hermann look so fair, nor shone his eyes so bright. Come, I tremble with desire. Give me the eagle and the dripping sword. Come, breathe and rest here in my embrace from the fearful battle. Rest, let me wipe the sweat from your brow, the blood from your cheek. How your cheek glows! Hermann, never has Thusnelda loved you so, even when your sun-tanned arm embraced me fiercely in the shadow of the oaktree. As I fled I stood firm, sensing that immortality which now is yours. Make it known in every grove, that Augustus is now in fear, as he drinks nectar with his gods, and that Hermann is more immortal than he!

*Hermann:* Why do you twine your fingers in my hair? Does not my father lie dead and silent before us? Oh, if only Augustus had led his armies, he would now lie bloodier there!

*Thusnelda:* Let me raise your drooping locks, Hermann, that they may droop menacingly over the victor's wreath. Siegmar is with the gods! You must succeed him, and mourn him not.

The poem, dating from 1752, reflects Klopstock's interest in early German history. Hermann der Cherusker, earlier known as Arminius, served in the Roman army, but on returning to his homeland led a revolt against the Roman forces. His wife Thusnelda was captured by Germanicus and taken to Rome. It is noteworthy that this interest in 'bard poetry', with its epic tone and legendary background, predates Ossian in Germany.

The autograph (Vienna, SB) is a first draft, dated 27 October 1815. There is a fair copy, differing only in minor details, in New York (PML) and copies in the Witteczek–Spaun (Vienna, GdM), Stadler and Ebner collections (Lund, UB). The song was published in April 1837 in book 28 of the *Nachlass*.

The song, like the poem, leads nowhere, and the end comes as an anticlimax. But it is interesting as a source for Schubert's epic style, later to blossom in the Walter Scott songs. Here the opening march theme sets the tone, and the D flat major section, with its harplike accompaniment, is much the most attractive part of the song. Evidently Schubert thought so too, for he used it in the setting of Scott's *Warrior rest, thy warfare o'er* ten years later.

**HERRN JOSEF SPAUN** see EPISTEL: MUSIKALISCHER SCHWANK

## HIMMELSFUNKEN Glimpses of Heaven
**Johann Petrus Silbert**                                                    February 1819

G major D651 Peters II p.218 GA XX no.169

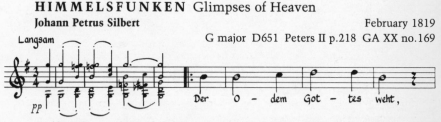

God breathes, and quietly longing awakes. The enraptured heart swoons in aching wonder.

The heavy bonds of earth dissolve in air. Weeping sacred tears, we long for the heavenly land.

How the mighty heart is lifted up into the blue. Ah, what makes that sweet anguish pass so tenderly away?

O rapture! Gentle as the celestial dew, God's greeting beckons us from the azure sky on high!

And the orphaned heart, hearing the quiet call, yearns for its home, and for the Father, its creator.

The poem was published in a collection called 'The Holy Lyre' in 1819. The autograph is missing. The only other Silbert setting, however, is dated February 1819, and the catalogue of the Witteczek–Spaun collection (Vienna, GdM) gives this one the same date. A copy made for Ferdinand Schubert is in B major. The song was published in 1831 in book 10 of the *Nachlass* (*Geistliche Lieder*, no.8).

The poets of the 1819 songs – Friedrich von Schlegel, Schiller, Mayrhofer, Novalis, Silbert – all bear witness to Schubert's growing interest in transcendental modes of thought. *Himmelsfunken* is a slow dance in 3/4 time rather than a hymn, and it may be compared with the setting of Mayrhofer's *Die Sternennächte* later in this same year. The unvaried gentle movement, the bold modulations (especially the sudden side-step into the flattened sixth at bar 11) and the moving inner parts in the accompaniment are thoroughly Schubertian. The song is predictive, presenting not merely new modes of thought, but a musical language which bears little relation with that of the nature songs of 1816, and which looks forward to the masterpieces of his full maturity.

Einstein, 189

### HIN UND WIEDER FLIEGEN PFEILE  To and fro the arrows fly

**Johann Wolfgang von Goethe**                              End of July 1815

Allegretto                      F major  D239 no.3  Peters VII p.16  GA XV vol.7 no.11

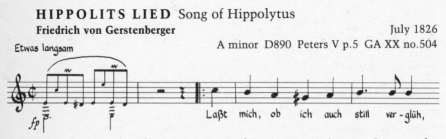

Hin und wie – der flie-gen die Pfei-le,

To and fro the arrows fly, love's light arrows from the slender golden bow. Maidens, are you not smitten? It is just chance, pure chance.

Why does he fly so fast? He would vanquish that maid there, already he has passed by. The carefree heart remains unscathed, but take heed! He will come back.

This is the third number from Schubert's setting of Goethe's three-act Singspiel *Claudine von Villa Bella*, of which only the first act has survived. The autograph is in Vienna (GdM). Strictly speaking, this delightful song has no place in a study of Schubert's lieder; it is included here only because it is sometimes sung in recitals and can be found in the Peters edition of the songs.

### HIPPOLITS LIED  Song of Hippolytus

**Friedrich von Gerstenberger**                              July 1826

Etwas langsam                      A minor  D890  Peters V p.5  GA XX no.504

Laßt mich, ob ich auch still ver - glüh,

Let me be, even if in silence I am consumed. Leave me to go in peace. Late or early, she is ever there before my eyes.

Why do you bid me be at peace? She took my peace from me; and wherever she is, either here or there, I must be.

Be not angry with this poor heart. It has only one fault, that it must beat faithfully till it breaks, and has made no secret of that.

Leave me, my thoughts are only of her and in her; without her I shall never know bliss.

Whether in life or death, in heaven or here on earth, in joy or in the anguish of parting, I belong only to her.

Hippolytus was the son of Theseus and Hippolyta, and was loved by his stepmother Phaedra. He was the subject of a play by Euripides. The poem was used by Johanna Schopenhauer, the mother of the philosopher, in her novel *Gabriele* published in 1821. But the real author was another member of the Weimar literary circle, Friedrich von Gerstenberg. None the less, the poem is attributed to Johanna in the Peters edition, and often elsewhere. The autograph is contained in a small notebook (Vienna, SB) dated at the beginning 'Währing, July 1826'. It contains also Schubert's three Shakespeare settings. The song was published in book 7 of the *Nachlass* in November 1830.

The plaintive melody, moving stepwise between G sharp and E, and the bare A minor harmonies, give the song an affinity of mood with the final setting of *Nur wer die Sehnsucht kennt* (D877 no.4) and with *Der Leiermann*. For Schubert Hippolytus is, like Mignon and the outcast protagonist of *Winterreise*, an outsider whose only refuge is in isolation. The bleakness of the unvaried two-bar phrases is almost oppressive. The gait, and the repeated crotchets at the beginning of the second and fourth verses, anticipate *Der Wegweiser*.

## HOCHZEITLIED Wedding Song

**Johann Georg Jacobi**                                             August 1816

Lebhaft, herzlich                     E flat major  D463  Not in Peters  GA XX no.245

I will sing you a song in the old strain, such as our fathers used to sing, but to the lover ever new.

In happy times it brings great joy, comforts in time of grief. 'Nothing shall part two loving hearts, nothing shall part them but death.

'Man shall protect his mate to his life's end in newness of heart, and sacrifice all his wealth and his life for the sake of his wife.

'She alone is his one desire in all the world, and he willingly earns her kiss by the sweat of his brow.

'When the lark sings in the field, then his wife laughs in joy; and even when the ground is covered with thorns she makes his work seem light.

'And doubly pleasant is his rest, every meal refreshes. On her breast his cares are soothed, and even death is eased.

'Then he feels his cold hand pressed in hers, as he goes from her arms to his new home.'

The autograph is lost, but the song almost certainly belongs, like the other Jacobi settings, to August or September 1816. The copy in the Witteczek–Spaun collection (Vienna, GdM) is dated August 1816. Schubert probably used the Vienna edition of the poems, which came out in 1816. The first publication of the song was in the *Gesamtausgabe* in 1895. A charming little strophic song which moves to the dominant and back again in regular four-bar phrases, as happy and innocent as the verses.

## HOFFNUNG Hope
**Johann Wolfgang von Goethe**  (?) October 1819

Langsam  F major D295 Peters VII p.62 GA XX no.175

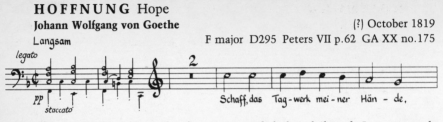

Schaff, das Tag-werk mei-ner Hän-de,

Grant, O Fortune, that my hands may accomplish their daily task. Let me not, oh let me not grow weary!

These are not empty dreams; these trees, now mere saplings, will one day be fruitful, and give shade.

The poem may date from November 1776. The date of the song is uncertain. There are two autographs, neither dated. One, in F major, assumed to be the earlier, is now in Berlin (SPK). A fair copy in E major, marked 'Mässig', is in Washington (LC). The song has usually been attributed either to 1815 or 1816. But its association with the second version of *An den Mond* in the earlier autograph, and examination of the paper used in this manuscript, suggest a much later date, possibly the autumn of 1819. The song was first published by J. P. Gotthard in 1872, as no.14 of 'Forty Songs'.

Goethe's prayer is set as a solemn hymn, with a marching bass. It is a reversion to the devotional style of *Die Betende*, yet the well-prepared tonal points of arrival, and the rising vocal line at the close, are strangely moving.

R. Winter, 'Schubert's undated works: a new chronology', *MT*, CXIX, 1978, p.500

## HOFFNUNG Hope (1)
**Friedrich von Schiller**  7 August 1815

Etwas geschwind  G flat major D251 Not in Peters GA XX no.106

Es re-den und träu-men die Men-schen viel von bes-sern künfti-gen Ta - gen;

Men talk and dream of happier days to come. They run after the happy end, the golden age! The world grows old, and young again, but man goes on hoping for better things.

Hope leads us into life, it hovers about the carefree boy. Its magic glow inspires the youth. Nor is it buried with the old man in the grave. For though his tired life is closed there, yet on the grave he plants the seed of hope.

Hope is no empty, flattering illusion, a figment of the fool's imaginings. Loudly it proclaims itself in the hearts of men. We are born for better things; and the inner voice does not deceive the hopeful heart.

The poem dates from 1797. The autograph, in private possession, is dated 7 August 1815. The copy in the Witteczek–Spaun collection (Vienna, GdM) is similarly dated. The song was first published in 1872 by J. P. Gotthard, as no.23 of 'Forty Songs'. Hope comes naturally to the young, and this first version misses the obstinate humanity of Schiller's poem. The words are set to a pretty tune, but it is too slight for the occasion.

# HOFFNUNG (2)

**Friedrich von Schiller**                                                      (?) 1817

Etwas geschwind

B flat major  D637  Peters IV p.75  GA XX no.358

For translation, see the preceding entry. The date of the song is uncertain. No autograph or dated copy has survived. It may belong with the third setting of Schiller's *Der Jüngling am Bache* (April 1819), with which it was published; but it could well be earlier. The song was published by A. W. Pennauer in August 1827 as no.2 of op.87. There the title is *Die Hoffnung*, but Schubert's title, and Schiller's, was *Hoffnung*.

Capell, in a rare misjudgment, says that this 'racy little song ... makes the effect of the wilder kind of drinking song'. But the song has a kind of split personality. Played loud, fast, and *con brio*, it can be made to sound like a rollicking party piece. But if *etwas geschwind* is taken as equivalent to *allegretto*, and the *piano* marking is observed, it has an altogether more gracious character, a reflective tenderness entirely in keeping with the text. It is supremely important to find the right *Bewegung*. Once that problem is solved, the essence of the song is seen to be the way it leads gently forward to the repeat of the final phrase. The rhythmic freedom of this repetition embodies in an indefinable way the invincible persistence of human aspirations. In the *Gesamtausgabe* Mandyczewski altered the melody line in bar 9, by analogy with bar 5. But the melodic variation seems entirely in character.

Capell, 157–8; Fischer-Dieskau, 41

# HULDIGUNG Homage

**Ludwig Kosegarten**                                                      27 July 1815

E major  D240  Not in Peters  GA XX no.103

Etwas geschwind

Ganz__ ver-lo-ren, ganz__ ver-sun-ken  in___ dein An-schaun_, Lieb-lin-gin,

Lost in contemplation of you, my darling, trembling with joy, drunk with love, my spirit yearns for you. Nothing can I do, or think, or write – nothing fills my heart but your dear image.

Sweet and pure you are, beloved, chaste as snow, unadorned red rose, spotless lily, gracious anemone; beauty's prize and crown, you know that I am wholly yours to command.

Gracious lady, to you have I surrendered soul and body, heart and mind. Without you life would be death, but by your side death would be a gain. Sweeter by far to be your slave than to wear golden crowns. Better to dedicate myself to your service than to rule the world.

The poem, which was entitled *Minnesang* ('Love Song'), has six more verses. Schubert's autograph, dated 27 July 1815, and entitled *Huldigung*, is now in Berlin (DS). Of two autograph copies known to exist, one is now in ÖNB, Vienna. The autograph has repeat marks at the end. The *Gesamtausgabe* prints all the verses.

The song bubbles with happiness. The tonal structure is perfectly conventional, yet there is something peculiarly satisfying about the way the tune, having arrived at the dominant, gestures towards the subdominant and the dominant again before it returns to the security of the tonic.

# HYMNE I Hymn I

**Novalis**

May 1819

A minor D659 Not in Peters GA XX no.360

Mit Andacht

We - ni - ge wis - sen das Ge - heim - nis der Lie - be,

Few know love's secret, its voraciousness, its endless thirst. The divine meaning of the Last Supper is a riddle for the earthbound mind. But he who has drawn the breath of life from the passionate lips of the beloved, or felt his heart melt in trembling waves in love's sacred fire, or scanned the heavens, measuring their unfathomable depths, we will eat of his body and drink of his blood eternally.

For who has guessed the noble purpose of man's body? Who can say that he understands the blood? One day all will be one body; one body, the blessed couple swim in celestial blood.

O that the ocean might turn red, and the rock spring up as fragrant flesh! Never does the sweet meal end, never is love satisfied; never can it possess the beloved inwardly and utterly. In embraces ever more tender the beloved is transformed, ever more closely and more inwardly possessed.

Thirstier, hungrier grows the heart, as more passionate desire pulses through the soul; and so the pleasure of love endures for ever and ever. If only the sobersides were once to taste it, then, forsaking all else, they would sit with us at the table of desire, which is never empty. They too would acknowledge the infinite fullness of love, and glory in the nourishment of body and blood.

The poem, written in 1799, is no.14 of the *Geistliche Lieder* ('Spiritual Songs') published by Tieck in 1802. Schubert set four of these spiritual songs, all of them contained on one autograph now in the Bodmer Library, Geneva. It is dated May 1819. There are copies in the Witteczek–Spaun collection (Vienna, GdM), where *Hymne I* is in F sharp minor. All four 'Hymns' were first published by J. P. Gotthard in 1872, as nos. 37–40 of 'Forty Songs'. None of them is included in the Peters edition.

Schubert encountered the work of Novalis in his twenty-second year, when his natural sympathy for transcendental modes of thought was taking a religious turn, probably because of his involvement with Franz von Bruchmann and his circle. But the mystical blend of eucharistic thought and sensuous (even erotic) experience seems to have struck only a superficial chord in Schubert's mind. It is sometimes said, and with justification, that Schubert had a different style for each of the poets he set. But it is not true of the Novalis settings, which lack homogeneity. This first one sounds like a pale reflection of his early cantata style. The long reflective opening (both parts repeated) leads to a majestic declamation of the words 'all will be one body', which narrowly escapes mere pomposity. The song comes to a brisk conclusion, but for once Schubert seems uncertain of the proper tone for the words he was setting.

Capell, 159; Einstein, 190–1; Fischer-Dieskau, 124–5, 127

# HYMNE II Hymn II

**Novalis**

May 1819

B flat minor D660 Not in Peters GA XX no.361

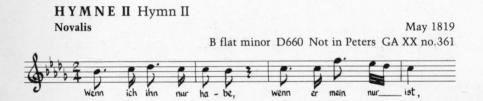

Wenn ich ihn nur ha - be, wenn er mein nur___ ist,

If only I have him, if he is only mine, if my heart is faithful unto the grave; then I will know no suffering, feel nought but devotion, love and joy.

    If only I have him, then gladly will I forsake all else, to follow my Lord with my pilgrim's staff, loyal only to him, quietly letting the others roam the wide, bright, busy streets.

    If only I have him, then joyfully will I go to sleep. His heart's flow will always be a sweet comfort to me, softening and pervading all things with gentle constraint.

    If only I have him, the world is mine. Blissful as a cherub holding the Virgin's veil, lost in contemplation, nothing in the world can make me fearful.

    Wherever I have him, there is my home, and every gift falls into my hand like an inheritance: in his followers I find my long-lost brethren again.

See the preceding entry. The poem is no.5 of the 'Spiritual Songs', and the autograph is headed 'Novalis V'. The second, third and fourth of the Novalis *Hymne* abandon the cerebral tone of the first, and the through-composed form, and rely upon simple strophic settings expressing a kind of childlike trust and faith, most successfully perhaps in this second song, which moves gracefully from minor to major.

    Capell, 159

## HYMNE III Hymn III
**Novalis**

                                      May 1819

B flat minor D661 Not in Peters GA XX no.362

If all things should prove false, yet will I stay faithful to you; lest gratitude on the earth should be thought dead and gone. For my sake sorrow engulfed you; for me you died in pain; therefore I gladly give you my heart for ever.

    Often must I shed bitter tears that you are dead; and that many who were dear to you have long forgotten you. Inspired only by love you have done so much, and yet now you are gone, no one thinks about it.

    Full of true love, you always stand by every man, and if no one stayed beside you, then would you still be faithful; the truest love triumphs, and at the last men feel it so, and weep bitterly, clinging to you like a child at its mother's knee.

    I have known you; O leave me not, let me be inwardly close to you for ever. Some day my brethren will once again look toward heaven, and sink down in love, and be gathered to your heart.

See *Hymne I*. The poem is no.6 in the 'Spiritual Songs', and the autograph is headed simply 'VI'. There are copies of this – and of the other – songs in the Witteczek–Spaun collection (Vienna, GdM) and in the monasteries at Kremsmünster and Seitenstetten. The strophic setting is a companion piece to *Hymne II*, in the same key and rhythm, and with the same tonal and melodic pattern.

## HYMNE IV Hymn IV
**Novalis**

                                      May 1819

A major D 662 Not in Peters GA XX no.363

I tell everyone that he lives and is risen, that he is in our midst and is ever with us.

I tell everyone, and everyone straightway tells his friends, that the new kingdom of heaven will soon be at hand.

Now, for the first time, the world to our new sense seems like home. Enraptured, men receive a new life from his hand.

Gone is the fear of death, sunk in the ocean depths, and everyone can look to the future, exalted and light of heart.

The gloomy path he trod leads on to heaven; and those who follow his teaching will also come to the house of the Father.

Now none shall weep on earth, when a loved one's eyes are closed. This grief is sweetened by the hope of reunion, soon or late.

After every good deed, another burns brightly, for the seed will blossom splendidly in lovelier lands.

He lives, and will be with us when all else is gone. Let us then celebrate this day the world's rebirth.

See *Hymne I*. The poem is no.9 of the 'Spiritual Songs', and the autograph is headed simply 'IX'. It is curious that the longing for death, the Romantic *Sehnsucht*, to which Schubert responded so often in the poetry of Mayrhofer, Müller, Schulze and others, fails to move him in the same way when it finds expression in Novalis. The middle section of this strophic setting moves characteristically to the flattened sixth, but the song does not carry any great weight of emotion, either secular or spiritual.

**HYMNE AN DIE JUNGFRAU** see ELLENS GESANG III

**ICH SASS IN EINER TEMPELHALLE** see LEBENSTRAUM

## IDENS NACHTGESANG Ida's Song to the Night
**Ludwig Kosegarten**        7 July 1815

B flat major D227 Peters VII p.22 GA XX no.90

Hear, Night, what Ida confides in you, who, surfeited with day, flies to your arms. Stars, as you look down kindly and lovingly upon me, hearken tenderly to Ida's song.

O night, and stars, listen! I have found him, whose image I have long carried in my heart; whom I dreamed of in tender hours, for whom my heart beat with longing.

The poem, entitled *Agnes Nachtgesang*, has six verses of which the first two are translated. Schubert changed the title, altering the lady's name to Ida (genitive form *Idens*). He made the same change in two other Kosegarten poems, presumably for reasons of euphony.

The autograph (London, BL) is dated 7 July 1815. Only the first verse is written beneath the stave, but there are repeat marks at the end. There is a copy, similarly dated, in the Witteczek–Spaun collection (Vienna, GdM). An autograph fair copy is now in ÖNB, Vienna. The song was first published in vol. VII of the Peters edition (1885). The autograph has an introductory chord of B flat major. The first edition, however, has an introductory chord of D minor, and different dynamic markings.

The song is full of poetic feeling, though the musical language is classical. The lines, of uneven length, are moulded into a single flowing strophe, which builds up to a moving climax at the final phrase.

# IDENS SCHWANENLIED Ida's Swan-song

**Ludwig Kosegarten**  19 October 1815

F minor D317 Not in Peters GA XX no.164

Traurig

Wie___ schaust du aus dem Ne - bel - flor, o Son - ne, bleich und mü - de!

Sun, how pale and tired, and veiled in mist, you gaze on me! The hoarse chorus of crickets churrs to my swan-song.

Departing nature whispers a sad farewell. Shrubs, trees and meadows stand forlorn and chill.

Leafless the alder grove, the grey garden desolate, where he and I once kept out anxious tryst in the moonlight.

The poem, entitled by Kosegarten simply *Schwanenlied*, has seventeen verses. Schubert's first draft, dated 19 October 1815, now in LC, Washington DC. A fair copy, with slightly longer postlude, is at Yale University. There is a dated copy in the Witteczek–Spaun collection (Vienna, GdM). The song first appeared in the *Gesamtausgabe* in 1895. The elegiac tune is contained within the limits of the classical language; but in the F minor cadences, and the chromatic sequence of the middle phrase, Schubert seems to be searching for ways of extending its expressive limits.

**IHR BILD** see HEINE SONGS no.2

# IHR GRAB Her Grave

**Karl August Engelhardt**  (?) End of 1822

E flat major D736 Peters VI p.8 GA XX no.402

Sehr langsam

pp

Dort ist ihr Grab, die einst im Schmelz der Ju - gend glüh - te;

There is her grave, who once glowed with the fire of youth; there she was struck down, there, the fairest blossom on the tree of life.

There is her grave – there she sleeps under that linden tree. Ah, never again shall I find the consolation she gave me.

There is her grave – she came from heaven, and she made the earth a heaven for me in my happiness. There she sank down.

There is her grave, and there in those quiet vaults, by her side, will I joyfully lay down my pilgrim's staff.

The poem appeared, not altogether appropriately one might think, in the 'Pocket-book of Sociable Pleasures' for 1822, an annual published in Leipzig and Vienna. Almost certainly this was Schubert's source. The autograph, in the Spaun–Cornaro collection (privately owned in Vienna), has been mutilated, so that the date is no longer readable. Sophie Müller noted in her diary (*Docs.* no.537) that Vogl sang the song at her house in March 1825, but there is no reason to suppose that it had only recently been composed. More probably it belongs to the second half of 1822. It was published in book 36 of the *Nachlass* in 1842.

*Ihr Grab* is reminiscent, in its dignity and compassion, of two Claudius songs written six years earlier, *Am Grabe Anselmos* and *Bei dem Grabe meines Vaters*. The key is the same, and there is a similar combination of a strong diatonic vocal line with flat side harmonies and chromatic inflections. All three songs 'speak' in the same way, as though the current of emotion runs deep, but is firmly controlled. In *Ihr Grab*, however, the weight of feeling is nearer the surface, and at the climax – 'There she sank down' – it threatens to interrupt the song. But the music recovers its poise as it returns to the opening phrase, and the song ends on a note of diatonic reassurance.

Capell, 173–4; Fischer-Dieskau, 206–7

## IL MODO DI PRENDER MOGLIE The Way to Choose a Wife
**Author unknown**                                                                1827

C major D902 no.3 Peters VI p.157 GA XX no.581

Come on! Let's not think about it. Courage, let's have done with it. If I have to take a wife, I know very well why. I do it for the money, I do it to pay my debts. I don't hesitate to say so, again and again.

Of all the ways of choosing a wife in the world I don't know a happier one than mine. One marries for love, another out of respect, another takes advice, another from a sense of duty, another for a whim. Isn't that the truth, yes or no?

Well, why shouldn't I take a little wife as a remedy for all my troubles? I say it again. I do it for the money. So many people do it. I do it too.

In September 1827 Tobias Haslinger announced the publication of 'Three Songs for Bass Voice'. The songs were settings of Italian words with German translations, and the texts were attributed to Metastasio. In fact, however, only the first two are by Metastasio; the author of this third one has never been traced. Schubert dedicated the songs, published as op.83, to the famous bass singer of the Italian opera, Luigi Lablache. Spaun tells us (*Memoirs* pp.135–6) that Schubert was much taken with Lablache, and that the two got on well together. The three songs are all in the Italian operatic style, and it may be that Lablache had a hand in choosing the texts. The autograph fair copy of this song, together with drafts of the other two, is in London (BL). See the following entry. This *buffo* aria, very much in the Figaro manner, confirms Spaun's statement that Schubert was captivated by Rossini's *Barbiere di Siviglia*. Indeed, there is a suggestion of the *Largo al factotum* about it. Schubert's brilliance as a musical impersonator is astounding; these exercises 'in the Italian style' must have been written about the same time as the *Momens musicals* and the op.90 Impromptus.

Capell, 226; Fischer-Dieskau, 259

## IL TRADITOR DELUSO The Traitor Outwitted
**Pietro Metastasio**                                                              1827

E minor D902 no.2 Peters VI p.150 GA XX no.580

*Recit:* Alas, what unknown power inspires these voices? I tremble. A cold sweat breaks out upon by breast. I must flee, but whither? Who will show me the way? Oh God, what do I hear? What has happened? Where am I?

    *Aria:* Ha, the air sparkles and flashes. The earth quakes. Deep night surrounds me with horror. What fearful creatures surround me! What wild terror I feel in my breast!

See the preceding entry. The text comes from part II of the sacred drama *Gioas re di Giuda* ('Joab, King of Judah'). The song was published as op.83 no.2, with Italian and German words. The manuscript in the British Library contains only the voice line of no.2 with German text. A sketch in Vienna (SB) is fully worked for the first sixty-four bars, thereafter only the voice line in the bass clef, with Italian words. A sketch of the voice line in the treble clef (D2 990F), formerly in private possession, is missing.

This splendid operatic recitative and *da capo* aria is the most impressive of the three songs of op.83. The opening recitative is full of dramatic tension, and the aria works with cumulative effect. The unexpected shift from E minor to C minor at bar 60, and from B minor to G minor at bar 78, is a particularly effective, and Schubertian, touch. One is reminded of the tonal juxtapositions at the beginning of the Sanctus in the E flat Mass of 1828.

    For op.83 no.1 see *L'Incanto degli occhi.*

    Capell, 226; Fischer-Dieskau, 259


## IM ABENDROT Sunset Glow

**Karl Lappe**                                                    (?) January 1825

A flat major D799 Peters II p.219 GA XX no.463

How lovely, Father, is your world, radiant with golden light! When your glory descends, to paint the dust with splendour; when the red glow from the clouds sinks down silently to touch my window.

    Could I complain, or be fainthearted? Could I be false to you, or to myself? No, for here in my heart I hold your heaven already, and this heart, before it breaks, still drinks in the fire and the light.

Schubert's source for the text is not known; the collected poems of Karl Lappe were not published until 1836. The first draft has not survived, but there is a copy in the Witteczek–Spaun collection (Vienna, GdM), dated 1824 and marked 'Very slow, with sustaining pedal'. Another copy of the same version, in 4/4 time, is in the Schindler collection (Lund, UB). A fair copy, dated February 1825, *alla breve*, marked 'Langsam, feierlich', is in New York (PML); the marking *con pedale* appears below the stave. The first edition (in book 20 of the *Nachlass*, 1833) is marked 'Sehr langsam' and follows the first draft. While there is no certainty about it, it seems likely that the song was written at the same time as *Der Einsame*, that is, early in 1825.

    This, the most famous of all Schubert's sunset pieces, is also the simplest in its tonal and melodic structure: no German sixths or diminished sevenths here. The song is, essentially, a continuous sounding of the tonality of A flat major, the inner parts moving only to give fresh emphasis to the return to the tonic. And the brief excursion into the dominant and subdominant in the second half ('Könnt ich klagen') etc.) also serves only to prepare us for the last line, where the long-held A flat major chord seems to stretch on into infinity on the word 'Licht'.

Yet it is the Schubertian inflections which give the song its unique appeal: the unexpected G (instead of A flat) in the alto voice at the first chord of bar 4, for instance, and the similarly unexpected C (instead of B flat) on the first beat of bar 13; or one could point to the way the voice line clings to the mediant. Schubert's tonal adventurousness is often remarked upon, but his ability to give to the most familiar chord sequences a new inflection and an altogether new expressive power is less often noticed. There is no better example of this power than *Im Abendrot*, which seems to incorporate in its thirty-six bars a whole new world of Romantic feeling.

Capell invokes Wordsworth: 'quiet as a nun, breathless with adoration', but the singer would be ill-advised to take this last phrase literally! The song calls for a pure legato line, at a controlled *mezza voce*, and superb breath control. Incidentally, this is one of the very few occasions when Schubert actually specifies the use of the sustaining pedal.

Capell, 205–6; Fischer-Dieskau, 236

**IM DORFE** see WINTERREISE no.17

## IM FREIEN In the Open
**Johann Gabriel Seidl**                                                                March 1826

Mäßig, mit Innigkeit                     E flat major D880 Peters III p.39 GA XX no.494

Drau-ßen in der___ wei-ten Nacht steh ich wie-der___ nun,

Again I stand outside in the vastness of the night; the bright splendour of the stars gives no peace to my heart!
    A thousand arms beckon me, sweetly enticing. A thousand voices call: 'Greetings to you, you dreamer!'
    And oh, I know what draws me, what calls me, like a friendly word, a song hovering in the air.
    Do you see the cottage there, sleeping in the moonlight? From its shining windows loving eyes look out!
    Do you see there the house by the stream, lit up by the moon? My dearest friend sleeps under its snug roof.
    Do you see that tree, gleaming with silvery leaves? Oh, how often did my heart swell there in happier days.
    Every tiny place that waves to me is dear to my heart, and wherever the light of the moon falls, a treasured memory entices.
    So everything here commands my affection, and draws me, like the call of a dear love.

The poem was published in 1826, in a sequence called *Lieder der Nacht* ('Poems of Night'). The first draft (Vienna, SB), is dated March 1826 and marked 'Mässig'. The fair copy made for the printer is now in the Kolbenheyer Gesellschaft, Nürnberg. The song was published by Tobias Haslinger in May 1827 with two other Siedl songs as op.80 no.3. This opus was dedicated by Schubert to Josef Witteczek.

It is a characteristic of the songs of the middle 1820s, and particularly of the Seidl and Schulze settings, that the accompaniments take on the idiomatic quality of an independent piano piece. *Im Freien* is a good example. The pianist's dancing semi-quavers define and control the song, giving to the accompaniment the flavour of a piano impromptu. The voice line is complementary, though it often does no more than double the top line of the piano.

Schubert's imagination is caught by the sphinx-like remoteness of the stars, rather than by the sense of homecoming which pervades Seidl's poem, so that many features of the song – the running-on chords, the tune that reaches up and circles round before settling again on the tonic, the pervasive sense of a quiet dance – recall other nightscapes: *Der Winterabend*, for instance, and *Der liebliche Stern*. In the closing pages of this extended song the piano part reaches up into the higher range of the instrument, unusually for Schubert, and this enhances the feeling of remoteness. In spite of the piano figure which runs throughout the song, Schubert's infinite capacity for melodic and harmonic variation keeps the interest alive to the end. No two verses, no two phrases, are exactly alike.

Capell, 221–2; Fischer-Dieskau, 246

## IM FRÜHLING In Springtime

**Ernst Schulze**                                                                                     March 1826

Andante                                             G major D882 Peters II p.227 GA XX no.497

Still sitz ich an des Hü-gels Hang, der Him-mel ist_so_klar,

Silent I sit on the hillside. The sky is so clear. The breeze frolics in the green vale where once, at the first gleam of spring, I was, oh, so happy. Where I used to walk so close by her side, and see the bright blue of the heavens mirrored in the depths of the dark mountain stream, and she was part of that heaven.

See, the spring colours already peep out from the buds and flowers. Not all the flowers are the same to me; I like best to pluck them from the same stems as she did. For everything is just as it was then, the flowers, the fields; the sun shines no less brightly, the blue image of the sky ripples, just as friendly, along the stream.

Only will and whim change, and pleasure and strife. The happiness of love passes away, leaving only love itself and, alas, sorrow. O if I could only be the bird, there on the meadow-steep! Then I would rest here on this bough, singing a sweet song about her all summer long.

Like the other Schulze texts, the poem comes from his *Poetisches Tagebuch* ('Verse Journal'), where it is headed 'Am 31sten März 1815'. The song title is Schubert's. The first draft, in the Paris Conservatoire, is dated March 1826, and marked 'Langsam'. The fair copy made for the printer, presumably marked 'Andante', is missing. The song was first published on 16 September 1828 as a supplement to the *ZfK*. At the end of the year it appeared as the first of 'Four Songs' (op.101) from Probst of Leipzig, and in 1835 it was included in book 25 of the *Nachlass*.

It is significant that Schubert's greatest spring songs (and there is none greater than this one) do not adopt the rhapsodic tone of voice of the later Romantics, but speak with a sort of lazy contentment. The music of this wonderful song seems to dawdle, dragging its feet as only Schubert's music can; it is as though the burden of time itself has been lifted. The poem is reflective, nostalgic even, and that suits Schubert's mood too. Happiness quickly passes, says the poet, and the music turns to G minor. But it is like the shadow of a passing cloud on a sunny day. The music murmurs on to the end (*ppp*), pausing momentarily, for the third time, on the words 'den ganzen Sommer lang'.

Structurally the song is a triumph. It has often been pointed out that the accompaniment is a set of variations on the tune with which it begins, on a down-beat.

Yet the interest is evenly shared between piano and voice. The singer begins with a tune of his own (on an up-beat), which provides the perfect foil to the other, and the dialogue between the two is conducted with such striking skill and invention that the listener is continually delighted. The six verses are grouped in pairs, the second of each pair starting on the second half of a phrase, so that the song moves continuously forward.

Capell, 216–17; Einstein, 328–9; Fischer-Dieskau, 228

## IM HAINE In the Wood

**Franz von Bruchmann**                                         (?) 1822

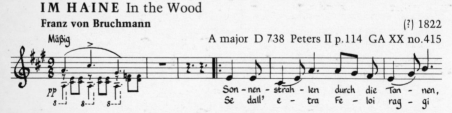

Sunbeams, slanting through the fir trees, dispel all our grief, leaving only peace in our hearts.
   The quiet sighing of the warm breeze, the delicate scents that float down from the murmuring branches, pervade the whole landscape.
   If only shady trees, shimmering sunlight and greenwood paths were to flower and flourish about us for ever, effacing every trace of woe!

The autograph is missing, and there is no evidence as to the date of composition. But Schubert must have set the song from Bruchmann's manuscript, for his poems were never published, so it seems likely that it belongs, like other Bruchmann settings, to the winter of 1822–3, when relations between the two were closest. *Im Haine* was published in July 1826 by A. W. Pennauer as op.56 no.3 and dedicated by Schubert to Karl Pinterics. In the second edition an Italian translation of the text, probably by Jacob Craigher, was added.
   The lilting 9/8 rhythm is irresistible, and Schubert seems reluctant to let the tune end. Having reached bar 11, where lesser mortals might be tempted to stop, he repeats the second half of the strophe with a slightly different shape and finally adds a three-bar coda.

Capell, 175–6

## IM KALTEN, RAUHEN NORDEN see AUS 'HELIOPOLIS' I

## IM WALDE In the Forest

**Friedrich von Schlegel**                                    December 1820

E major  D 708  Peters III p.159  GA XX no.388

The roar of the wind, like the wings of God, deep in the cool depths of the forest night. As the hero springs to horse, so do men's thoughts leap up. As the old pine trees moan, so do our spirits soar.
   Glorious is the fiery light in the red dawn, or the flashes lightening the earth, often pregnant with death. Quickly the flame flickers and flares, as though summoned to God.

Always the murmur of the gentle springs charms sorrow from the flowers; yet sadness beats enticingly against our hearts in mild waves. The Spirit to which we are attracted by those waves dwells far off.

The urge to escape life's bonds, the struggle of the strong, untamed life force, are stilled by the breath of the Spirit, and turned to fullness of love. We feel the creative breath permeate our souls.

The roar of the wind, like the wings of God, deep in the darkness of the forest night! Freed from all fetters, the power of thought soars aloft. Unafraid, we hear the song of the spirits borne on the wind.

The poem, written about 1802, is a good example of romantic nature-worship. Nature is visible Spirit; spirit is invisible nature; poetry is the Infinite, finitely described. But it is the external, sensory aspect of the subject which attracts Schubert's attention, rather than the philosophical.

The autograph (Vienna, GdM) is a first draft dated December 1820. There are copies in the Witteczek–Spaun (GdM) and Spaun–Cornaro (Vienna, privately owned) collections. The key and title are as above. But when the song came to be published in 1832 (book 16 of the *Nachlass*) it appeared under the title *Waldesnacht*, in E flat. These changes were made by Diabelli, presumably to distinguish the song from Schulze's *Im Walde*, which had been published in 1828. The Peters edition follows this first publication, and a comparison with the *Gesamtausgabe* shows that four bars are omitted following bar 180. Considerable changes were made also in the text.

December 1820 seems to mark some kind of creative peak for Schubert, for it produced a series of works of Promethean energy and grandeur, the *Quartettsatz* in C minor, the setting of Psalm 23 for female voices, the setting of Goethe's *Gesang der Geister über den Wassern* in its most ambitious form, *Der zürnenden Diana*, and *Im Walde* itself, a monumental song whose grandeur of scale and conception threatens to outrun the means at the composer's disposal.

The spirit of the song is Wagnerian – this is Schubert's 'Forest Murmurs' – and so too is the melodic line, full of octave leaps and arpeggio sequences. So too is the slow harmonic speed, combined with the irresistible rush of the piano semiquavers, and the wide dynamic range. The song sweeps on for 214 bars without a break, though ternary form is suggested by a middle section (*pp*) in C major, Schubert's favourite key of the flattened sixth. The torrent of energy which was later to flow through the 'Great' C major Symphony is here foreshadowed.

Capell, 166–7; Einstein, 216; Fischer-Dieskau, 123–4

# IM WALDE In the Forest
**Ernst Schulze**                                                                      (?) March 1825

B flat minor D834 Peters III p.57 GA XX no.476

I wander over hill and dale, and over the green heather; and my anguish travels with me, and never leaves my side. And even if I were to sail across the wide sea, it would follow me there.

Many flowers bloom in the meadow that I have not noticed; for I see but one flower wherever I go. Often I have stooped towards it, and yet I have never plucked it.

The bees hum in the grass and hang from the blossoms. My eyes grow dim and fill with tears; I can't help it. So did I never hang from her sweet lips, so red and soft.

Far and near the birds sing sweetly on the bough. Fain would I join in their song, but I must, alas, keep silent. For every man must bear the pleasure and pain of love alone.

I watch the clouds sailing across the sky on swift wings; the rippling wave must ever ebb and flow. But when the wind dies, the clouds and the waves still play.

I wander to and fro, through foul and fair weather; yet nevermore can I find again the longing and the torment of love. When will the wanderer find rest again?

In Schulze's *Poetisches Tagebuch* ('Verse Journal') the verses are headed 'Im Walde hinter Falkenhagen den 22sten Julius 1814'. Falkenhagen is a village near Göttingen. Schubert's title is *Im Walde*. The autograph has not survived, and there is some uncertainty about the date. The catalogue of the Witteczek–Spaun collection (Vienna, GdM) says March 1825; the copy is in G minor. The song was published with another Schulze setting, *Auf der Brücke*, which also belongs to 1825, as op.90 in May 1828. However, the two songs were published by J. A. Kienreich of Graz, who claimed that they were written during Schubert's visit to Graz in September 1827. Almost certainly the truth is that Schubert wrote out fair copies for the printer at that time, in different keys. *Im Walde* was published in B flat minor, and this version has been followed by Friedländer and Mandyczewski. Diabelli republished the songs as op.93 in 1835 in the original keys.

It has often been noted that the Schulze songs anticipate *Winterreise*. The sense of alienation and rejection is the same, and the obsessive rhythms are often similar. Here the driving triplets in the pianist's left hand inevitably call *Erstarrung* to mind. The song is basically strophic, but Schubert cleverly counters the risk of monotony by using a double strophe, the first in the tonic minor, the second in the dominant, and reversing the order for verses 4 and 5. Verses 1, 3, 4 and 6 are thus virtually identical, while verses 2 and 5 are in F major. It is significant that the idea of the wanderer's headlong flight dominates the song, so that the insistent triplets do not pause for breath even at the thought of his lover's kiss.

Capell, 215; Fischer-Dieskau, 225–6

**IMPROMPTU** see NUR WER DIE LIEBE KENNT

**IN DER FERNE** see RELLSTAB SONGS no.6

## IN DER MITTERNACHT At Midnight

**Johann Georg Jacobi**                                                                August 1816

Sehr langsam                             E flat major D464 Not in Peters GA XX no.246

To - des - stil - le deckt___ das Tal bei des   Mon - des - fal - bem_ Strahl;

Deathly silence shrouds the valley by the half-light of the moon. Winds whisper, dull and fearful, as the night-watchman calls.

Here in my anxious heart it sounds softer and duller, dimming the gleam of hope, as the clouds veil the moon.

Clouds, obscure the light ever more fully! I want to hide the deep, deep pain of my heart from him.

My lips must not speak his name, nor tears make him known; one day he will lie beside me in the cold grave.

O for the long, lovely night, when earthly love never charms, when faith betrayed never plaits its crown of thorns.

The gentle hand of death will lead the way home; there love is free from pain, and happy I shall be.

The autograph, dated August 1816, is in private possession. There is a dated copy in the Witteczek–Spaun collection (Vienna, GdM). Surprisingly, the song was not published until 1895, in the *Gesamtausgabe*. The neglect of this fine song is difficult to explain. The unison opening in the relative minor, broadening out into the tonic, anticipates many later and greater songs; and the gently moving semiquavers in the pianist's right hand from bar 4 onwards stir the song into life as the poem speaks of the whispering winds of the night. The tone of stillness and serenity recalls that of the settings of Goethe's *Wandrers Nachtlieder*.

## INS STILLE LAND To the Land of Peace

**Johann Gaudenz von Salis-Seewis** March 1816

Mäßig, mit Sehnsucht    A minor D403 Peters VI p.25 GA XX no.201(a) and (b)

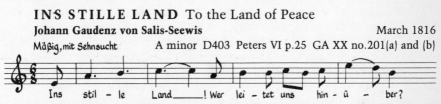

To the land of peace! Who will lead us thither? The evening sky already grows cloudy and dull, and the shore ever more strewn with wreckage. Who will lead us gently over, ah, over to the land of peace?

To the land of peace! To the free and open spaces which ennoble; where the tender morning dreams of men's pure hearts give pledge of the life to come. He who has fought the good fight carries with him the seeds of hope into the land of peace.

O land of peace, the land for all who are storm-tossed: which beckons us with torch held aloft, the gentlest harbinger of fate, and leads us over into the land of the mighty dead, the land of peace.

The poem, entitled simply *Lied*, dates from 1800–6. There are four variant autographs: the first draft (Berlin, SPK) is in G minor, *Mässig*, dated 27 March 1816 and headed simply 'Lied. Salis'. There is no prelude. A fair copy in A minor (Vienna, SB), also without prelude, but revised, is dated April 1816. There are several contemporary copies of this version, which presumably represents Schubert's final thoughts. A copy in the Therese Grob song album (see GROB) is dated March 1816, though it may have been made later in the year. It has a two-bar prelude, presumably authentic, in A minor, and is marked 'Langsam mit Sehnsucht'. Finally, a copy made in August 1823 for the album of an unknown friend has a three-bar introduction.

The song was published in 1845 in book 39 of the *Nachlass*. The source for this first edition was Ferdinand Schubert's copy of the first draft, but the publisher gave the song its familiar title, and added the four-bar introduction. The *Gesamtausgabe* prints the first two versions. The later ones have appeared only in privately printed editions.

The song evidently had a great vogue among Schubert's friends, and it is not surprising that he used it again, in a revised form, for the final setting of *Nur wer die Sehnsucht kennt* in 1826. But the introduction of a disturbed middle section in that later setting to match the shape of Mignon's song is often felt to destroy the simplicity and unity of the original tune. It is a song of haunting beauty, characteristically poised between sweetness and sadness, between sorrow and hope, and the C sharp in the second bar, on the word 'Land', is a wonderful example of Schubert's ability to transform a familiar sequence with an unexpected inflection. Schubert's own introduction consisted only of the tonic arpeggio, sounded twice.

Capell, 117

## IPHIGENIA
**Johann Mayrhofer**                                                     July 1817

G flat major  D573  Peters IV p.97  GA XX no.325

Does then no flower from the land of Hellas bloom on the shore of Tauris? Does no gentle breeze blow like a blessing from the beloved fields where I played with my sisters? Ah, my life is consumed.

Sadly I wander through the grove with faltering steps. I cherish no hope – none – that I shall see my native land again. My soft entreaties are drowned by the great waves of the sea, as they break against the cold cliffs.

Goddess who rescued me and imprisoned me in this wilderness, save me once more. Have mercy, let me rejoin my own people; grant, O goddess, that I may appear in the hall of the great king.

Iphigenia, daughter of Agamemnon and Clytemnestra, was to be sacrificed to appease the wrath of Diana when the Greeks were detained by contrary winds on their way to Troy. But the goddess carried her away to Tauris and entrusted her with the care of the temple. The legend was a favourite dramatic and operatic subject. Spaun tells us (*Memoirs* pp.21, 129) that Schubert was deeply moved as a youth by Gluck's *Iphigenie auf Tauris*, and Goethe's play on the subject (1779) may also have been in his mind.

The autograph, in private possession, is dated July 1817. The key is G flat major and the marking *Nicht zu langsam*. A copy in the Spaun–Cornaro collection (Vienna, privately owned) is in E flat major, and one in Schindler's album (Lund, UB) in F, annotated 'transposed from G flat major'. The song was published in July 1829 in F as op.98 no.3 by Diabelli. The original key calls for a high soprano voice and suits the song better.

*Iphigenia* is an operatic aria of grave beauty, classical in its poise and restraint, yet deeply felt, like the music of Schubert's beloved Gluck. For most of its length it adopts the tone and the form of accompanied recitative, but wonderfully varied to match the words. The accompaniment, too, sounds like a piano reduction of an orchestral score. Not until the closing section, where the singer turns to make her appeal to the goddess, do the phrases take on a regular metrical form, and the simplicity and nobility of those final bars are deeply moving.

Capell, 137

## IRDISCHES GLÜCK Earthly Happiness
**Johann Gabriel Seidl**                                              (?) Summer 1828

D minor/major  D866 no.4  Peters IV p.91  GA XX no.511

So many people look on the wide world with gloomy faces, and grumble. The wonderful stage of life tempts them in vain. But I know better how to help myself; far from hiding my face from joy, I relish every moment. And that is happiness indeed.

Many a heart have I wooed, though success was short-lived. For folly often spoiled all that my light heart had won. And so I escaped the net. For since no fancy held me prisoner, so I had none to flee. And that is happiness indeed.

No laurels ever crowned my head, no glorious halo shines about it. Yet my life is not in vain, for quiet thanks are also a reward! He who, far from audacious flights, is content with the peaceful pleasures of the country, does not have to worry about his safety. And that is happiness indeed.

And when one day the solemn call comes to summon me, as it summons all, then I shall freely take my leave, bidding the lovely world farewell. Maybe, after all, true friends will be there at the end, to grasp my hand and bless me with a kindly look. And that, brothers, is happiness indeed.

This is the last of the 'Four Refrain Songs', published by Thaddäus Weigl in August 1828 as op.95. The last line of each verse provides the refrain. No autograph or copy of this one has survived, and the date is not certain. But like the rest of the group, it probably belongs to the last summer of Schubert's life.

Schubert sets the verses to a strophe in two halves, alternating a sturdy but unexciting march tune in D minor with a more cheerful, cheeky tune in the major. The moral of the verses is that it is a mistake to expect too much of life, and the music is obviously intended to be light and sociable. But truth to tell, it is also, for Schubert, a little dull and monotonous.

**IRRLICHT** see WINTERREISE no.9

# JAGDLIED Hunting Song

**Zacharias Werner**                                                         January 1817

F major D521 Not in Peters GA XX no.290

Tara, tara! We are coming home, bringing the trophies of our hunt. Night is falling, so we keep watch; for light has power over darkness. Tara, tara! Up, up! Fan the fire into a blaze.

Tara, tara! We drink in a circle, mocking the darkness of night. Man in his strength and pride happily mocks pain and laughs at death. Tara, tara! Up, up! The fire is blazing.

The poem occurs at the end of Act I of Werner's play *Wanda, Königin der Samarten*, a 'romantic tragedy with songs' published in Vienna in 1816. The verses are headed 'Chorus of Knights and Horsemen', and Schubert's setting also is clearly intended as a unison song for male chorus. The autograph (Vienna, GdM) is dated January 1817 and written on two staves only. There is no introduction, but a copy in the Witteczek–Spaun collection (Vienna, GdM), also dated, has the four-bar postlude also as introduction.

The direction is *Feurig* and the song needs a chorus of strong male voices to do it justice. Schubert's changes of pace and dynamic exploit all the dramatic possibilities in the text. The song has, however, achieved a certain notoriety, because it was adapted, probably by Leopold von Sonnleithner, to serve as the final section of the unfinished Ossian song *Die Nacht*, when that song was published in the first book of the *Nachlass*.

**JÄGER, RUHE VON DER JAGD**  see ELLENS GESANG II

## JÄGERS ABENDLIED Huntsman's Serenade (1)
**Johann Wolfgang von Goethe**                                     20 June 1815

F major  D215  Not in Peters  Not in GA  NSA IV vol.1 p.198

Sehr langsam

Im  Fel - de schleich____ ich still  und wild,  ge - spannt__mein Feu - er - rohr,

Through the fields I slink, quiet and fierce, with my flintlock cocked; your sweet
image hovers brightly before me.

You too are probably wandering, quiet and gentle, through the fields and the
familiar valley. Oh, does my fast fading image not appear to you at all?

The image of the man who travels through the world ill-humoured and peevish,
who roams east and west because he must leave you.

When I think of you it is as if I were gazing into the moon. A peaceful,
inexplicable tranquillity descends on me.

The poem was written in Weimar towards the end of 1775 and reflects the persistence
of Goethe's feelings for Lili Schönemann, from whom he parted in September of that year.
The title, therefore (originally *Jägers Nachtlied*), and the first verse are not to be taken
at face value. It is more a love poem than a huntsman's song. The autograph of this first
setting, formerly in the family of Schubert's half-brother Andreas, is lost, but a copy made
in 1906 is now in Berlin (SPK). It is dated 20 June 1815. The song was first published by
Eusebius Mandyczewski in *Die Musik*, VI/7, 1907, suppl. pp.2–3.

The mood of the song is one of stillness and reconciliation, somewhat akin to that
of the two *Wandrers Nachtlieder*. As in those songs, the almost static harmonies at the
beginning move gently forward from bar 5, when the triplet rhythm is established. But
the poetic feeling of those later songs is missing in this first attempt.

## JÄGERS ABENDLIED (2)
**Johann Wolfgang von Goethe**                                        Early 1816

D flat major  D368  Peters I p.228  GA XX no.262  NSA IV vol.1 p.25

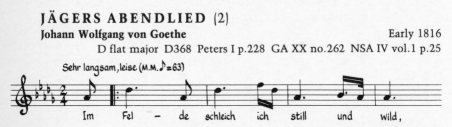

Sehr langsam, leise (M.M. ♪=63)

Im  Fel  –  de  schleich  ich  still  und  wild,

For translation, see the preceding entry. Schubert's first draft has not survived, but the
fair copy made for Goethe early in 1816 is now in Berlin (DS). This omits the third verse,
as also does the first edition. The copies made for Stadler and Ebner (Lund, UB), however,
which may go back to the first draft, include all four verses. A different version is preserved
in the copy in theWitteczek–Spaun collection (Vienna, GdM), in which various embellishments to the vocal line have been added by J. M. Vogl. This is printed in vol.1(b) of the
*Neue Ausgabe*. The song was first published in 1821 as op.3 no.3 by Cappi and Diabelli.

Goethe wanted a distinction to be made between the energetic tone of the first and
third verses and the gentler feelings of the second and fourth. Schubert's instinct tells
him to disregard this, and he is right, both because such a contrast can hardly be accommodated in a strophic setting, and because Goethe was, when all is said and done, content

to be parted from his Lili. The 'tranquil peace' of the last verse is, in fact, the key to the mood of the poem, and of the song. Even the sliding sixths and thirds, so often thought to be inspired by the figure of the huntsman 'slinking' through the forest in line 1, serve only, in their musical context, to reinforce the diatonic shapeliness of the tune.

Capell, 123; Fischer-Dieskau, 80

## JÄGERS LIEBESLIED Huntsman's Love Song

**Franz von Schober**                                                     February 1827

Mäßig geschwind                    D major  D909  Peters III p.70  GA XX no.515

Ich  schieß  den Hirsch im  grü-nen Forst,

I shoot the stag in the green forest and the roe in the quiet valley, the eagle in its eyrie on the cliffs and the duck on the lake. No place affords protection when my gun is aimed; and yet I too, hard as I am, have felt love.

I have often worked in bitter weather, on stormy winter nights, and covered in frost and snow made my bed on stones. I sleep as softly on stones as on down, immune to the north wind; yet my rough breast has known love's delicate dream.

The savage hawk was my companion, the wolf my battle-mate. My day began with the baying of hounds, and my night with carousing. A twig of fir was the flower in my sweaty cap; and yet love struck my fierce hunter's heart.

O shepherd on the soft moss, playing with flowers, who knows whether you feel the passion of love so hotly and strongly as I do? Every night the great brightness hovers over the dark forest bathed in moonlight, majestic beyond the skill of a master to paint it.

And when she gazes down upon me, her glance piercing me, I understand what happens to the wild animals as they flee from my gun. I feel terror, joined with supreme happiness, as if my best friend were folding me in his arms.

Schubert set the poem from Schober's manuscript. His fair copy looks like one made for the printer; it is dated February 1827. This lends support to O. E. Deutsch's assertion (in D1) that the song first appeared as a supplement to the *ZfK* on 23 June 1827. But D2 makes no mention of this. In the summer of 1828 it was published as no.2 of 'Four Songs' by the Lithographic Institute of Vienna, of which Schober was manager. The volume was dedicated by Schubert to Karoline, Princess Kinsky (see *Docs.* no.1119). It was later (March 1829) reissued by Diabelli as op.96. The autograph fair copy is included in a bound volume of Schubert songs which once belonged to Schober and is now in Dresden (SLB).

Capell's dismissal of the song as insignificant seems harsh. The D major − B flat major alternations are charming, and the echo effects too. And if there is nothing very subtle about the song, that applies with equal force to the poem.

Capell, 225

## JOHANNA SEBUS

**Johann Wolfgang von Goethe**                                          April 1821

                    D minor  D728  Not in Peters  GA XX no.601

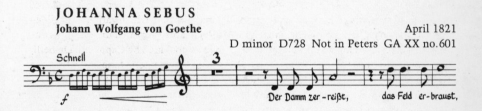

Der Damm zer-reißt,          das Feld er-braust,

The dam bursts, the fields send up a roar, the waves lap, the plain howls. 'I'll carry you, mother, through the flood; it's not yet very high, I'll be able to wade.' 'Don't forget us in our need, the poor weak woman who shares your house, and my three young children ... Are you leaving us behind?' She is already carrying her mother through the water. 'Make for the hill over there, and wait. I'll soon be back, and we'll all be safe. It's still dry on the hill, and it's only a few steps away. But take my goat along with you.'

The dam crumbles, the fields send up a roar, the billows rage, the plain howls. She sets her mother on the firm land, pretty Susie, and turns back to the flood. 'Where, where are you going? The distance has grown; the water is deep on either side. Are you going to dare to plunge into it?' 'They must and they shall be saved!'

Goethe's full title is self-explanatory: 'Johanna Sebus. In memory of the virtuous and beautiful seventeen-year-old girl from the village of Brienen who, on 13 January 1809, during the freezing of the Rhine and the great collapse of the dam at Cleverham, died while bringing succour.' Schubert's setting breaks off barely halfway through the poem. The four remaining verses tell how Johanna returned to save her neighbours, but perished in the attempt. The autograph (Vienna, SB) is dated April 1821. The first publication was in 1895, in the *Gesamtausgabe*. A performing version was completed and privately printed by Reinhard van Hoorickx in 1961.

On 7 March 1821 *Erlkönig* made a sensational success on its first public performance in the Kärntnertor Theatre by Michael Vogl. It can hardly be a coincidence that during the ensuing weeks Schubert began two more settings of words on heroic themes by Goethe – this one and *Mahomets Gesang* – and left both unfinished. The two songs are similar in style and conception, each attempts to build up the cumulative tension which the piano triplets so effectively convey in *Erlkönig*, by means of running semi-quavers in the pianist's right hand; but here the continuous scalic passages fail to impress. The truth seems to be that Schubert had ceased to respond to tales of heroism of this rather naive kind. For where the subject touched his imagination – as in the contemporary *Suleika* songs, for instance – the running semiquavers worked for him to wonderful effect.

## JULIUS AN THEONE Julius to Theone
**Friedrich von Matthisson**                                      30 April 1816

G minor D419 Not in Peters GA XX no.215

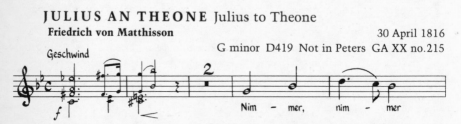

Never, never can I confess, sweet enchantress, what my heart felt when first I pressed your hand. My sighs, the concealed supplications I send up in my solitude, will be swept away by the storm, and my tears will trickle unseen down your picture, until the grave calls me to its silent darkness.

Ah! You gazed into my face so unaffectedly, so full of angelic sweetness, without any idea how your beauty triumphed. O Theone! Did you not see my anxious loving glance hanging on your glances? Did the flush on my cheeks not betray the lost peace of my hopeless heart?

If only oceans had separated us after that first gentle touch of our hands. Shuddering, I totter now on the brink of a sheer abyss, where despair lies in wait, dry-eyed, on a bed of thorns with diamond chains. Ah, to rescue me, fair enemy of my peace of mind, hand me the cup of forgetfulness.

The mysterious characters whose unconsummated passions are celebrated in these conventional verses belong, not to the world of classical mythology, but to an unfinished novel. In the 1787 edition of Matthisson's poetry they were entitled *Theon and Lyda*, and a note in the 1811 edition reads: 'From an unfinished romance'. The autograph, formerly in private possession in Vienna, has disappeared. It was dated 30 April 1816. There is a copy, similarly dated, in the Witteczek–Spaun collection (Vienna, GdM). The first publication was in 1895, in the *Gesamtausgabe*.

The song is an eighteenth-century operatic aria masquerading as a lied, owing something perhaps to Schubert's new enthusiasm for Mozart. The piece is well structured, with a middle section in E flat and a concluding section in 3/4 time marked 'Mässig'. It is, moreover, highly rewarding for the singer. Yet Schubert's imagination does not seem to be involved so much as his inborn musicality. There is something almost as conventional about the modulations as there is about the poet's sentiments.

## KAISER MAXIMILIAN AUF DER MARTINSWAND
Emperor Maximilian on Martinscliff
**Heinrich von Collin** (?) 1818

B flat major  D2 990A  Not in Peters  Not in GA

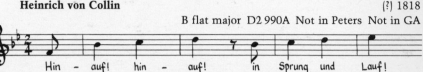

The text consists of a long narrative of twenty-six verses, which is thus summarised by Reinhard van Hoorickx ('Schubert songs and song fragments not included in the collected edition', *MR*, XXXVIII, 1977, p.274): 'It relates the story of Emperor Maximilian I, who loves hunting, not least in very dangerous places. So one day he climbs the Martinswand, the "steepest cliff in all the world". While climbing, he stumbles and falls on a prominent rock, from where he can neither climb higher nor get down. He is noticed by some shepherds and hunters, but nobody seems able to help him. Then the Emperor succeeds in throwing down a note, asking for a priest to give him a last blessing before he dies. The priest comes and the people pray, and suddenly a young man stands before the Emperor and shows him a way of escape which he had not noticed before. When he is finally safe the young man disappears, and the Emperor realises that God has sent an angel to save his life.'

The autograph (Vienna, SB) has no text, but the strophe is written out on two staves, with repeat marks at the end. It is headed 'Kaiser Maximilian auf der Martinswand in Tyrol. 1490'. In 1853 Schubert's brother Ferdinand published a school songbook called *Der kleine Sänger* ('The Young Singer'), in which several of Schubert's songs appeared (without acknowledgment) arranged as vocal duets with bass accompaniment. During the years 1816–18 Franz wrote various pieces for his brother to use in his work as a teacher at the Imperial Orphanage, and this is almost certainly one of them. The voice line of Ferdinand's arrangement is identical with the top line of Franz's piano sketch. The style is deliberately simple and unsophisticated. See also *Der Graf von Habsburg*. The song has been edited and privately published by Reinhard van Hoorickx.

**KEHR EIN BEI MIR** see DU BIST DIE RUH

## KENNST DU DAS LAND? Do you know the land?

**Johann Wolfgang von Goethe**                                          23 October 1815

A major D321 Peters II p.221 GA XX no.168

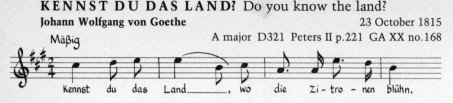

Kennst du das Land____, wo die Zi-tro-nen blühn,

Do you know the land where lemon trees blossom and golden oranges glow amidst the dark foliage? A gentle wind drifts from the blue sky; the myrtle stands silent, the bay tree tall: do you know it perhaps? There, oh there I long to go, with you, my beloved!

Do you know the house? On pillars its roof rests; the hall gleams, the chamber shimmers, and marble statues stand and gaze at me: what have they done to you, poor child? You know the place perhaps? There, oh there I long to go, with you, my guardian!

Do you know the mountain, and the cloudy paths leading up to it? The mule seeks its way through the mists; the ancient brood of the dragon dwells in its caves; the cliff falls, and over it the water. Do you know it? There, oh there, lies our way. O father, let us go!

See MIGNON'S SONGS. The song is placed at the beginning of book 3 of Goethe's novel, *Wilhelm Meister*. Its date is not certain, but since it is also included in the first draft of the novel, it must predate the Italian journey. The three verses of the famous lyric provide us with three clues to the mystery of Mignon's past history, the first giving recollections of her childhood in Italy, the second of the villa where she was brought up, and the third of the dangerous journey over the Alps to Germany. They also tell us of the strange relationship between the homeless child and Wilhelm, whom she addresses first as lover, then as protector and father. However, the song also transcends its context in the novel, and becomes an expression of Romantic longing for the south and the sun. Significantly, it echoes closely some lines from *The Seasons*, by James Thomson (see 'Summer', 663ff).

In the novel Wilhelm, who has been searching for Mignon, hears her singing outside his door. She enters, and sings the song in her native Italian. Her manner of singing it is described in detail: 'She began each verse in a solemn, grand manner, as if she wanted to draw attention to something special, or recite something important. At the third line the song became darker and sadder. To the question, "Do you know it perhaps?", she gave a mysterious, thoughtful expression, and there was an irresistible yearning in the phrase "There, oh there!". And she knew how to vary the phrase "Let us go!" at each repetition, so that it sounded at first pleading and urgent, and then persuasive and promising.' This description has been quoted because it obviously influenced Beethoven's famous setting, which in turn influenced Schubert's. None the less, Goethe disapproved of Beethoven's setting. Speaking to the composer Tomaschek in 1822 he said: 'I cannot understand how Beethoven and Spohr could have so completely misunderstood the song as to set each verse to a different melody ... By her very nature, Mignon can sing only a song, not an aria.'

The autograph of Schubert's song, dated 23 October 1815, is in private possession. A fair copy made for the Goethe collection in May 1816 is in the Paris Conservatoire. There are copies in the Witteczek–Spaun collection (Vienna, GdM) and in those of Stadler and Ebner (Lund, UB). It was first published in December 1832 in book 20 of the *Nachlass*. This first edition, which transposed the song to F major, is followed by Friedländer in the Peters edition.

Schubert adopts the key, as well as the ground plan, of Beethoven's setting, but his is a fine song in its own right; and there are moments, notably in the bars leading up to the wistful question 'Kennst du es wohl?', when it seems closer to the spirit of the lyric than any other setting. But it has to be admitted that the galloping triplets in the pianist's right hand tend to sound over-urgent after the restraint of the opening, so that the song does not quite achieve the unity and dignity of Beethoven's. It may be significant that Schubert, always sensitive about comparisons with his great contemporary, did not publish the song in his own lifetime.

Capell, 99–100; Einstein, 114–15; Fischer-Dieskau, 54; Stein, 79

**KLAGE** Lament (Die Sonne steigt)

**Friedrich von Matthisson**      April 1816

C major   D415   Not in Peters   GA XX no.213

The sun rises, the sun sinks, the changeful disc of the moon gleams, the golden dance of the stars is shot through with the blue of the sky: But the light of the sun, the smiling face of the moon, the silent and sublime dance of the stars no longer irradiate my heart with exaltation.

The meadow blossoms, the verdant bushes resound with spring melodies, the stream meanders down to the wooded valley in the glow of the sunset: But the song of the woods, the myriad coloured flowers of the meadows, the alder-fringed stream in the twilight no longer uplift my soul as they used to.

The poem was originally called *Liebespein* ('Anguish of Love'). In the 1811 edition of Matthisson's poems, which Schubert appears to have used, it is called *Klage*, and a fifth verse is added. But since Schubert grouped the verses in pairs in his strophic setting, this final verse had to be discarded. The autograph, a first draft dated April 1816, is in private possession. The song has been crossed out in pencil. The accompaniment for the last seven bars is written in the margin below. The song was first published in 1895, in the *Gesamtausgabe*.

It is not difficult to understand why Schubert was dissatisfied with the song. It is in two halves, the first part 3/4 *Ruhig*, the second part (for verses 2 and 4) 4/4 *Ziemlich geschwind*; but nowhere does it touch the sense of bereavement which lies at the heart of the poem.

**KLAGE** Lament (Nimmer länger trag' ich)

**Author unknown**      (?) 1817

G minor   D512 (D2 Anhang I 28)   Not in Peters   Not in GA

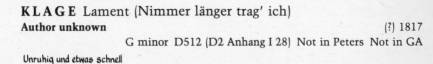

For translation, see *Der Leidende*. In the Therese Grob songbook (see GROB) there are two settings of this text, which is attributed to Hölty, though it is not included among his works. One (D432) is undoubtedly by Schubert. There are two versions, both in

B minor, and Schubert's original title was *Der Leidende* (q.v.). The other is also called *Klage*, though the word order in the first line is different. It is thought to have been added to the collection at some time after it was given to Therese (November 1816) and before it was bound. It is unlikely that this song is by Schubert, both because the script is not his and because he had already included one setting of the text in the collection, so it is hard to see why he should have included another.

R. van Hoorickx, 'Schubert songs and song fragments not included in the collected edition', *MR*, XXXVIII, 1977, pp.270–1

## KLAGE Lament (Trauer umfliesst mein Leben)

**Author unknown** (?) January 1816

Langsam B minor D292, 371 Not in Peters GA XX no.185(a) and (b)

Trau-er um-fließt mein Le - ben, hoff - nungs - los mein Stre - ben,

My life is steeped in sadness, my efforts are in vain; in tremulous passion my life runs away from me; oh, I can bear it no longer!

My feelings are a tumult of sorrow and anguish; no breezes can cool the fever born of nameless terrors: oh, I can bear it no longer!

Only death, far distant, can cure such a visitation of torment. When the gates open for me I shall be cured. Oh, I can bear it no longer!

The author has not been identified; the text, like that of the previous entry, has been attributed to Hölty. The date of the song is not certain. There are two autographs. The first (D292) is an untitled and undated sketch, without text. On the back of the sheet are the last twenty-six bars of *Shilrik und Vinvela* (D293), written in September 1815. This sketch is in Vienna (SB). The later autograph (D371), in private possession, is complete except for bars 13–20 and belongs to a sheaf of papers which also contained several songs written in May 1816, including both versions of the somewhat similar *Der Leidende*, the text of which has also been attributed to Hölty. A copy in the Witteczek–Spaun collection (Vienna, GdM; complete) is headed 'Klage no.II by Hölty' and dated January 1816. The song was published in October 1872 by J. P. Gotthard as no.21 of 'Forty Songs'.

The association with *Der Leidende* – same key, similar text, same manuscript and the same air of hopeless misery – is too close to be accidental. May 1816 seems to have been a bad month for Schubert, perhaps because it was about this time that his love affair with Therese Grob came to its unhappy climax. There is no mistaking the depth of feeling in the song. One feels that the tragic role the key of B minor was to play in Schubert's mature work is here clearly adumbrated.

## KLAGE AN DEN MOND Lament to the Moon

**Ludwig Hölty** 12 May 1816

Mäßig F major/D minor D436–7 Peters VI p.62 GA XX no.216

Dein Sil -ber schien durch Ei - chengrün, das küh -lung gab, auf mich her-ab

Your silver beams, O moon, shone through the cool green of the oak trees on the happy boy that I was, and shed peace upon me.

When your light breaks through the window it sheds no peace on the young man I am: it sees my cheeks pale, and my eyes wet with tears.

Soon, dear friend, ah soon your silver rays will shine on the gravestone that hides my ashes, the ashes of the young man.

The poem, originally entitled *An den Mond*, was written in February 1773. In later editions it was called simply *Klage*, which was also Schubert's title. *Klage an den Mond* appears first in the Peters edition, and may have been used by Friedländer to avoid confusion with other songs. There are two versions. The original autograph has not survived, but there are copies in the Witteczek–Spaun (Vienna, GdM), Stadler and Ebner (both Lund, UB) collections, the first of these dated 12 May 1816. A fair copy in the Therese Grob songbook (see GROB), entitled *Klage* and dated 1816, differs in some details. The song was published in book 48 of the *Nachlass* in 1850. This published version, entitled *Klage*, has a two-bar prelude which does not appear elsewhere, and is probably spurious.

The third verse, with its reminder of mortality, brings an ordinary song to sudden glory. The eloquent pause at bar 22, and the sudden shift to D minor; the repeated staccato A's in the pianist's right hand; and we are brought to the edge of the infinite. This anticipates the very similar effect in the setting of Claudius's *An die Nachtigall*, written a few months later.

## KLAGE DER CERES Ceres' Lament

**Friedrich von Schiller**                                November 1815–June 1816

G major D323, 991 Not in Peters GA XX no.172

Has gentle spring appeared? Has the earth become young again? The sunny hills grow green, and the crust of ice snaps. From the blue mirror of the rivers Zeus laughs unclouded; the Zephyrs' wings beat softly, and the young shoots break into bud. Birdsong awakens in the grove, and the Oread speaks: your flowers return, but your daughter does not.

Ah, how long have I been wandering through the world's plain in search of her! Titan, I sent your rays of light to track down my darling but none has yet brought me news of her sweet presence, and day, which discovers all, has not discovered my lost daughter. Have you, Zeus, abducted her from me? Has Pluto, touched by her charm, taken her down to the black rivers of Orcus?

Who will bear tidings of my sorrow to the dark shore? The boat continually pulls away from the land, but it only accepts shades. The fields of night are closed to the eyes of the immortals, and as long as the Styx has flowed it has carried no living thing. A thousand paths lead downwards but none leads back up to the daylight. There is no witness to describe the daughter's tears to her anxious mother.

Mortal mothers, born of the line of Pyrrha, may follow their beloved children through the flames of the grave; only those who live in Jove's house never approach the dark shore; your strict hands, O Fates, spare none but the immortals. Cast me from the golden hall of heaven into the night of nights! Do not respect the rights of the goddess – alas, they are the torment of the mother!

Where she sits, sadly enthroned with her gloomy husband, I would descend, treading softly with the soft shadows before the queen. Ah, her tear-filled eyes seek vainly for the golden light and, wandering to distant spheres, do not fall upon her mother – until her joy discloses her and bosom is pressed against bosom, rousing even rough Orcus to tears of pity.

Idle wishes! Vain laments! The sturdy chariot of the day rolls calmly on its even course; the decision of Zeus stands for ever. He has turned his head away from those dark and miserable regions. Torn from me one night, she remains for ever lost, until the waves of the black river glow with the colours of dawn, and Iris draws her radiant bow right through the heart of hell.

Is nothing of her left to me? No sweet souvenir to prove that, although parted, we still love one another? No trace of the beloved hand? Is there no love bond between mother and child? No contract entered into between the living and the dead? No, she has not entirely left me! No, we are not completely parted! For the immortal gods have granted us a language!

When the children of the spring die, when leaves and flowers wither in the cold breath of the north wind, and the sad bushes stand bare, I take from Vertumnis's cornucopia the seeds of life and sacrifice the golden grain to the Styx. Mourning, I plant it in the ground, laying it on the heart of my child, so that it becomes a language expressing my love and my anguish.

When the measured dance of the hours brings back the happy spring again what was dead is reborn in the life-giving rays of the sun; seeds which appeared to have perished in the cold womb of the earth struggle gaily up into the cheerful realms of colour. While the stems hasten skywards the roots shyly seek the dark: in their cultivation the powers of the Styx and of the air are equally divided.

They belong half to the regions of the dead, and half to those of the living – ah, as messengers they are dear to me, sweet voices from Cocytus! Although it holds her prisoner in its terrible gorge her gracious mouth speaks to me through the young spring shoots, telling me that, though far from the golden daylight, where the sad shades wander, a breast still beats with love, and hearts still glow with tenderness.

So let me greet you, children of the spring meadows: your cups shall run over with the pure dew of nectar. I shall bathe you in sunbeams, paint your petals with the rainbow's beautiful colours like the face of Aurora. In the joyous splendour of spring and in the faded coronet of autumn my joy and my anguish are visible to those with eyes to see them.

When Proserpine (Persephone) was carried away by Pluto to become queen of the underworld, her mother Ceres (Demeter) was so inconsolable that Zeus finally allowed Proserpine to spend six months of each year on earth and the remainder with Pluto. Ceres' lament for her daughter in Schiller's fine poem is a re-creation of this myth of the seasons.

Schubert began work on the song in November 1815, set it aside, presumably for the Mass no.3 in B flat which was started on 11 November, and took it up again in June the following year. All the relevant autographs are in Vienna (SB): (1) A fair copy of the first 142 bars, dated 9 November 1815. There are copies of this manuscript in the Witteczek–Spaun collection (Vienna, GdM), and in Franziska Tremier's song album (Vienna, SB). (2) Two drafts of bars 143–203. (3) A manuscript containing bars 143 to the end, annotated in another hand 'Fortsetzung zur Klage der Ceres' and dated June 1816. Another leaf, listed separately as D991 in Deutsch's thematic catalogue, seems to have been lost. These manuscripts provided the source for the only publication of the song, in the *Gesamtausgabe* in 1895. Mandyczewski's comments on the alterations and corrections are to be found in the *Revisionsbericht*.

*Klage der Ceres* is one of Schubert's last essays in the solo cantata form on the Zumsteeg model; and if it is true, as Mandyczewski suggests, that he intended to produce a revised version of the whole work but never got round to it, that in itself is some evidence that his interest in the form was waning. Commentators have, understandably, cold-shouldered the piece, in terms which make one wonder whether they have actually looked at it; 'the date could never have been guessed' (Capell, p.90); 'like a five-finger exercise' (Fischer-Dieskau, p.41). This is far wide of the mark, for however outmoded the form, the writing is remarkable for its variety of mood and invention, and particularly for the freedom and boldness of modulation. When, in verse 5, Ceres descends to Hades in search of her lost daughter, a dramatic sequence climaxes in a declamatory passage in which the tonalities of A major and F major are violently juxtaposed. In the hands of a dramatic soprano prepared to accept the conventions of the form, the piece would, one suspects, surprise its detractors.

## KLAGE UM ALI BEY Lament for Ali Bey

**Matthias Claudius**                                                  (?) 1815/1816

E flat minor D2 496A  Not in Peters  GA XViii no.6  NSA IV vol.7 p.84

Leave me, leave me to lament! I shall no more be joyful. Abu Dahab has slain Ali and his host!

Such a brave and cheerful warrior there will never be again. He was victorious over all, hacked everything into little pieces!

He followed the path of war, despising wine and women, and was always the darling of the newspapers.

But now he has fallen. Would that he had not! Ah, of all the Beys, among all of them there was no Bey like him.

Everyone in Syria is saying: 'What a pity that he fell!' and throughout Egypt men and crocodiles mourn.

Daher imagines with a shudder his friend's head on show in the harem, and cries his eyes out.

Claudius's ironic verses celebrate a minor sensation of the year 1773. Ali Bey, an Egyptian prince, was murdered by his favourite Abu Dahab. Daher was Ali's Syrian ally. Just to make his satirical intentions plain, the poet added the words 'Da capo' at the end.

No autograph has survived, and the date of composition is not certain. The copies in the Witteczek–Spaun collection (Vienna, GdM) preserve the song in two forms: as a male-voice trio (TTB, D140), unaccompanied, and as a solo song with piano accompaniment (D2 496A). The block harmonies, and the detailed expression marks, which would be most unusual in a solo song for Schubert, strongly suggest that the piece was originally written as a trio, and that the piano reduction was written out later, possibly simply for rehearsal purposes. The trio is dated 1815 in the catalogue of the Witteczek–Spaun collection. One of the two copies of the solo song, however, is annotated: 'Composed in 1816. Copied from the manuscript.' When Diabelli published the song in book 45 of the *Nachlass* (1848) he published it as a trio for female voices, adding the piano accompaniment and a prelude and postlude of his own. The solo song version first appeared in the *Neue Ausgabe*.

Schubert has done his best to enter into the spirit of the verses. The tone is excessively lugubrious, and the intention is clearly parodistic.

## KLAGLIED Lament
**Johann Friedrich Rochlitz**                                                    1812

G minor D23  Peters IV p.160  GA XX no.6  NSA IV vol.6 p.56

Langsam, mit Ausdruck

Mei-ne_ Ruh ist da - hin,

My peace is lost, joy has left me; in the rustling of the wind, in the murmuring of
the stream, I, trembling, hear nothing but lamentation.

His flattering words and the press of his hands, his hot desire and his glowing
kisses; alas, that I did not resist.

When I see him from a distance I long to draw him to me, but as soon as he
sees me and approaches me I want to escape to my grave.

Ah, if once, only once I could see him happy here on my beating heart, on
my languishing breast, I could die with a smile.

The verses, clearly influenced by the famous scene in *Faust*, appeared in 1805 in a collection
called *Glycine*. The autograph (Vienna, SB) is a corrected draft in G minor. There are several
contemporary copies. Most of them give the date of the song as 1812, and two of them
refer to it as 'Schuberts erstes Lied'. There are differences in the melodic line at the
beginning, and minor ones elsewhere; these are shown in the *Neue Ausgabe*. *Klaglied* was
published by Josef Czerny in November 1830, in a set of three songs later given the opus
number 131.

Schubert's friends believed that *Klaglied* was Schubert's first true lied, though
Mandyczewski in the *Gesamtausgabe* gives pride of place to *Der Jüngling am Bache*.
Almost certainly there were earlier attempts, but *Klaglied*, probably written in the first
half of 1812, remains the first complete strophic song to have survived.

The contrast presented by this accomplished, stylistically assured song in comparison with the brilliantly uneven and episodic cantata-like settings of 1811 is astonishing.
How natural and Schubertian are the pulsing semiquaver chords from bar 12 onwards (bars
9–13 are a curious pre-echo of a phrase from the Andante of the Piano Trio in B flat op.99)
and the interrupted cadence before the clinching repeat of the last line. This, Schubert's
first lied, already lays claim to the song as an independent musical form. Schubert set
only the first verse. The tune fits the remaining verses with difficulty.

Capell, 80; Einstein, 48–9; Fischer-Dieskau, 18–19

**KLÄRCHENS LIED** see DIE LIEBE (Goethe)

## KOLMAS KLAGE Colma's Lament
**James Macpherson (Ossian)**                                          22 June 1815

C minor D217  Peters II p.207  GA XX no.83

Ziemlich langsam

Rund um      mich Nacht, ich irr' al - lein, ver - lo - ren am stür- mischen Hü – gel;

The episode comes from the *Songs of Selma* (1760). Schubert used a verse translation by an unknown hand. The corresponding passages in Macpherson's text are as follows:

It is night; I am alone, forlorn on the hill of storms. The wind is heard in the mountain. The torrent pours down the rock. No hut receives me from the rain; forlorn on the hill of winds!

Rise, moon, from behind the clouds. Stars of the night arise. Lead me, some light, to the place, where my love rests from the chase alone. With thee I would fly, from my father; with thee, from my brother of pride. Rise, moon, from behind the clouds!

Cease a little while, O wind! Stream, be thou silent awhile! Let my wanderer hear me. Salgar, it is Colma who calls! Here is the tree, and the rock. Why delayest thou thy coming? Cease a little while, O wind.

Lo, the calm moon comes forth. The flood is bright in the vale. The rocks are grey on the steep. I see him not on the brow. His dogs come not before him, with tidings of his near approach. Here I must sit alone.

Who lie on the heath beside me? Are they my love and my brother? To Colma they give no reply. Their swords are red from the fight. O my brother, why hast thou slain my Salgar? O Salgar, why hast thou slain my brother?

Oh, from the rock on the hill, from the top of the windy steep, speak, ye ghosts of the dead! Speak, I will not be afraid. Whither are ye gone to rest? In what cave of the hill shall I find the departed? No feeble voice is on the gale; no answer half-drowned in the storm!

Here shall I rest with my friends, by the stream of the sounding rock. When night comes on the hill, when the loud winds arise, my ghost shall stand in the blast, and mourn the death of my friends.

See OSSIAN SONGS. Schubert's setting is in three sections, each strophic: the first three verses 4/4 in C minor, *Ziemlich langsam*, the next two in A flat major 6/8, *Etwas langsam*, and the last two in F minor 2/4, *Langsam trauernd*. The autograph (Vienna, GdM) is a draft of the first section, containing the first seventeen bars and the text of the next two verses, dated 22 June 1815. The manuscript of the remainder, formerly in private possession, is missing, but there is a copy of it in Berlin (SPK). Schubert's instructions on the first manuscript are that the second verse 'will be sung throughout somewhat softer', and the third 'so much the stormier'. The song was published in book 2 of the *Nachlass* in July 1830.

*Kolmas Klage* is the first of the Ossian settings, and the most impressive. It has the unity of mood of the true ballad, within a narrow tonal range, it dispenses with recitative, and the piece has a misty grandeur which shows how precisely Schubert could identify and characterise the literary quality of his authors. The pity is that the text does not provide him with the cumulative tension which he was later to find in *Erlkönig*, so that the last section is the weakest. But the opening is superb; dark and oracular, moving at the slowest possible harmonic speed, it has the evocative splendour of a Bruckner symphony.

Capell, 93

**KRIEGERS AHNUNG** see RELLSTAB SONGS no.2

## LA PASTORELLA AL PRATO The Shepherdess in the Meadow

**Carlo Goldoni**

January 1817

G major D528 Not in Peters GA XX no.574

The shepherdess in the meadow tends her flock, the little lambs by her side as she sings, free from care.

So long as she is able to please her shepherd, the fair shepherdess will always be content.

The verses come from Act II of Goldoni's drama *Il Filosofo di campagna*, set to music by Galuppi and produced at Venice in 1754. Goldoni wrote librettos for all the best stage composers of his day, including Salieri, Schubert's teacher; almost certainly Schubert set the text at Salieri's suggestion, first as a male-voice quartet (D513) and then as a solo song. The autograph (Berlin, SPK) is a first draft headed *Ariette* (a short light aria) and dated January 1817. There is a dated copy in the Witteczek–Spaun collection (Vienna, GdM). The song was first published in 1872 as no.19 of 'Forty Songs' by J.P. Gotthard.

In November and December 1816 Vienna had had its first taste of the new Italian opera of Rossini, an experience which soon went to the head of the Viennese. Schubert himself was much taken with the zest and tunefulnes of the new style, and it is interesting to find him, doubtless very conscious of his new freelance status at the beginning of 1817, practising his operatic skills. *La Pastorella al prato* is a delicious exercise in the bel canto style.

## LABETRANK DER LIEBE The Cordial of Love

**Joseph Ludwig Stoll**

15 October 1815

F major D302 Not in Peters GA XX no.150

When my sick soul floats amid the harmony of soft chords, and the sweet tears of melancholy evaporate under your warm glance, I sink speechless on the gentle rise and fall of your bosom; heavenly melodies sound, and earth's shadows flee.

So, sunk in Eden, exchanging love for love, and murmuring kisses, drunk with delight, as if surrounded by rustling seraphim; you offer me, in the guise of an angel, a cordial warm as love, just as my yearning soul was sinking back into the foul dust of the plains.

Schubert's source was probably the annual publication *Selam*, in which these verses appeared in 1814. The autograph, now in ÖNB, Vienna, is dated 15 October 1815. The fair copy is in Washington (LC). There is a dated copy in the Witteczek–Spaun collection (Vienna, GdM). The song was first published in the *Gesamtausgabe* in 1895.

*Labetrank der Liebe* is ignored by the commentators, yet there is a purer vein of poetry in it than in many better-known songs. The sense of innocence, of dedication, of *Innigkeit*, which is so perfectly caught in the opening bars, mark the song off from its neighbours, and prefigure later 'songs of innocence' like *Du bist die Ruh* and *Litanei*. But there the melody is more self-contained; here the equality of voice and piano, their identity rather, in the expression of a single idea, is complete.

## LACHEN UND WEINEN Laughter and Tears

**Friedrich Rückert**                                                                (?) 1822–3

A flat major  D777  Peters II p.122  GA XX no.455

In love, laughter and tears depend at different times on so many different causes. In the morning I was laughing with joy; and why now in the glimmer of evening I am weeping I scarcely know myself.

In love, laughter and tears depend at different times on so many different causes. In the evening I was weeping with pain, and now I ask my heart how it can wake in the morning laughing.

The poem comes from the collection called *Östliche Rosen* ('Oriental Roses'), published at the end of 1821 or early 1822. In later editions the title *Lachens und Weinens Grund* ('The Cause of Laughter and Tears') was added. Schubert's title is as above. The autograph has not survived, and the Rückert songs cannot be exactly dated. It seems likely that they were all written in the summer of 1822, or during the ensuing winter. *Lachen und Weinen* was published in September 1826 as op.59 no.4 by Sauer and Leidesdorf.

Schubert's genius for musical characterising is splendidly illustrated in this justly popular song. The suggestion of adolescent flightiness in the prelude and postlude is unmistakable, and the 'laughter and tears' syndrome is perfectly caught in the major–minor changes. It is not, however, a purely lighthearted piece. Schubert, who 'knew nothing but the rapture and the poignancy of first sensations', as Capell puts it, knew the reality of a young girl's tears. Witness the way the running crotchets and quavers falter and die, as the sustained minor harmonies weep at the words 'bei des Abendes Scheine'. The miracle is that the music is a complete portrait, and no caricature.

Capell, 202; Fischer-Dieskau, 197

**LACRIMAS** see DELPHINE and FLORIO

**'LADY OF THE LAKE' SONGS** see ELLENS GESANG I–III

## LAMBERTINE

**Josef Ludwig Stoll**                                                        12 October 1815

E flat major  D301  Peters VI p.5  GA XX no.149

Oh, how sweet the bliss of the love which fills my heart! But ah, with how cruel a pain hopelessness invades me.

He does not love me, he does not love me; without him all pleasure in life is gone. I am born only for sorrow, pain racks my breast.

But no, I will not go on complaining comfortless. Fate still allows me to see him, and if I may not tell him of my love, I can yet be satisfied with the sight of him.

His image is a comfort in my silent woe. I have set it up here as a source of pleasure. This will delight me until the everlasting sleep relieves my weary heart.

Schubert's source for the text is not known. The autograph (Washington, LC) is dated 12 October 1815, and there is a dated copy in the Witteczek–Spaun collection (Vienna, GdM). The song was published in book 36 of the *Nachlass*, in June 1842.

*Lambertine* is ignored by the commentators. Yet as an example of Schubert's facility in the style of a Haydn canzonet (that is, in the drawing-room song in an operatic manner) it is full of interest and charm. Schubert sets the song in a series of related sections, rather than strophically, and its classical restraint and articulate manner anticipate the great songs of 1817 like *Iphigenia* and *Memnon*. It is a whole world away from the subjectivity of Platen's *Du liebst mich nicht*, yet equally impressive in its way.

## LAURA AM KLAVIER Laura at the Piano
**Friedrich von Schiller**                                      March 1816

A major  D388  Not in Peters  GA XX no.193(a) and (b)

When your fingers command the strings, Laura, I stand there either mindless as a statue, or quite forgetful of my body. You have the power of life or death; as mighty as Philadelphia, claiming the sympathy of countless souls.

Out of reverence the breezes rustle more softly whilst listening to you; all beings with ears stop in their orbits to take in the sweet delight, enraptured by the song. Enchantress, you hold them in thrall with music, as you do me with your eyes.

A wealth of harmonies, sensual and vehement, bursts from the strings like newborn seraphim from their heaven. As the suns shone out of darkness, when they escaped from the titanic arms of Chaos, driven out by the tempest of creation, so the magic power of music streams forth.

Now silver-piping flutes ripple sweetly as if over smooth pebbles; now the music has the sonorous magnificence of the thunder's diapason; now it rages down as the rushing torrents tumble and foam from the rocks; now it is like the sweet sound of the seductive breezes wafting their soft flatteries through the poplar woods –

And now it is heavier, dark with melancholy, like Cocytus dragging tear-filled waves through the dead wastes filled with fearful night-whisperings and the howls of lost souls.

Say, girl – I'm asking, so tell me: are you in league with the gods? Be truthful now: is this the language they speak in Paradise?

The poem is one of the so-called 'Laura odes', a set of six poems of tormented love published by Schiller anonymously in the 'Anthology for the year 1782'. (The topical allusion in the first verse has nothing to do with America, but refers to a famous conjuror called Philadelphia who performed before Frederick the Great.)

There are two widely differing versions. The first is in E major, though it ranges through remote keys to end in B flat major. The final bars of this version survive on a manuscript in Vienna (SB), linked with the beginning of a draft of *Des Mädchens Klage* which is dated March 1816. There is a complete copy in the Witteczek–Spaun collection

(Vienna, GdM). The autograph of the second version is missing, but there are copies originally belonging to Ferdinand Schubert, dated March 1816, and to Stadler and to Ebner (both Lund, UB). This version is in A major throughout, and longer by some twenty bars. Both versions are included in the *Gesamtausgabe*.

If *Laura am Klavier* is not a very good song, it is certainly a very interesting one. It has been pointed out that Laura's music, which Schubert is bold enough to include as a sort of extended prelude and postlude, bears little resemblance to the *Sturm und Drang* music suggested by Schiller's exuberant rhetoric. Instead of sensuous harmonies, bursting vehemently from the strings like angels from heaven, we find ourselves in an eighteen-century drawing-room listening to a Mozart piano sonata, or at any rate to music of such suave good manners and polite restraint that it might be a Mozart sonata. Nor is there any attempt (except, in a halfhearted way, in the first version) to respond to the wild succession of nature images in verse 4. Instead, all is order and symmetry. Schubert seems to be under the spell, not of Schiller's verse, but of Mozart's music.

The song was first conceived as a solo cantata, with recitative and no single tonal centre. The second version is a big improvement on the first, not simply because the idea of the song, as a kind of duet between Laura and the poet, is more fully worked out, but more importantly because it has a single tonal centre and is much more tightly organised.

Capell, 113–14; Fischer-Dieskau, 70–1

## LEBENSLIED Song of Life
**Friedrich von Matthisson**                                        December 1816

Mäßig geschwind                    C major D508 Peters VI p.16 GA XX no.284

Kom - men und Schei - den, Su - chen und___ Mei - den,

Arrival and departure, search and avoidance, fear and hope, doubt and supposition, poverty and plenty, desolation and splendour, alternate on earth like dusk and darkness.

Vainly here below you strive for peace. Will-o'-the-wisps beckon, but like the furrows cut by the skimming boat, the enchanted illusions vanish.

Let faith bravely raise its eyes from the dust to the skies bright with stars: there an immortal bond links truth, peace, union, permanence.

Favourable currents carry the virtuous and the brave safely to harbour. To the noble mind life closes like a sweetly dying song.

Let it be our aim and our endeavour manfully to suffer, vigorously to reject, boldly to despise, conscious of a pure will within our iron breast.

The poem dates from 1786; there are five verses, of which the Peters edition prints only the first, third and last. The autograph (Vienna, GdM) is dated December 1816 and annotated 'In the house of Herr von Schober'. There is a copy in the Witteczek–Spaun collection (GdM). The song was published in book 38 of the *Nachlass* (1845). Albert Stadler mentions a setting of this text for male-voice trio (*Memoirs*, p.147), but no such autograph has come to light.

Schubert's strophic setting matches both the sadness and the resolution of the poem. The opening descending C major sentence leads to a strong answering unison phrase; then the shadows gather as the tonality sinks down to E flat before we return to the tonic. This sequence is beautifully echoed in the piano interludes. This, the last complete Matthisson setting, is one of the best of them.

## LEBENSMELODIEN Melodies of Life

**August Wilhelm von Schlegel**                                       March 1816

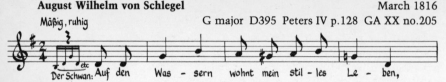

G major  D395  Peters IV p.128  GA XX no.205

*The Swan:* On the waters my quiet life is passed, drawing equal circles which float away to nothing. And in the damp mirror the curve of my neck and my figure are ever-present.

*The Eagle:* I have my home in the jagged cliffs, I rush on the eddies of the storm, confident in the power of my beating wings when hunting, battling ,seizing.

*The Swan:* Often, filled with strange insight, I watch the stars in the deep-vaulted firmament of the flood, and I am drawn by deep-moving desires from my home waters to a heavenly country.

*The Eagle:* Joyously, from my first youth, I turned my wings towards the immortal sun; I cannot accustom myself to the dust; I am related to the gods.

*The Doves:* In the shade of the myrtles, wife true to husband, we flutter and exchange long kisses. We seek and wander, find and coo, languish and lurk; what desire, what pleasure!

We draw the chariot of Venus, billing in our flight. The gold of the sun borders our blue wings, How they flutter when she smiles at us! Easy success, a charming reward!

The poem, written in 1797, consists of seventeen verses, fourteen of them a 'dialogue' between the swan and the eagle, followed by three verses from the doves. The autograph has not survived, and there are no copies. The date derives from an entry in the catalogue of the Witteczek–Spaun collection (Vienna, GdM). The song was published by Josef Czerny in February 1829 as op.111 no.2. This first edition gave only one verse from each of the dramatis personae. A wider selection is given above. The *Gesamtausgabe* prints all seventeen verses.

Schubert set the verses of each 'speaker' to a different strophe; the Swan is in G major, *Mässig ruhig*, the Eagle in C minor, *Geschwind*, and the Doves in E flat major, *Lieblich*. Since the autograph is missing there is no way of telling how many verses Schubert meant to be sung. Nor is it easy to see why he should have decided to set this long and rather tedious poem in the first place. Certainly there is nothing in the music to suggest that he was moved or excited by it.

## LEBENSMUT Courage

**Ludwig Rellstab**                                                    (?) 1827

B flat major  D937  Peters VII p.58  GA XX no.602

Courage boils in the quick blood; the sparkling fountain of life flows bright as silver. But before the hour flies, before the spirit loses its fire, draw courage from the clear waters.

Dare to take the bold leap; he who hesitates is lost: fortune rises and falls fast, the moment is yours. He who dares not leap will not enjoy the sweetness of the fruit. Ah, if you are chasing fortune, dare to take the bold leap.

Boldly embrace death when his powerful command touches you. Take your full glass and knock it against his hourglass; the brotherhood of death unlocks the prison of life. A new dawn shines; embrace death with courage!

See RELLSTAB SONGS. The autograph (Vienna, GdM) is a first draft, untitled and undated, together with two other drafts of Rellstab songs. It is sometimes described as a fragment, but misleadingly, for the draft is complete on three staves to the end of the strophe, and only the *Nachspiel* remains to be added. A copy in the Witteczek–Spaun collection (GdM) is headed 'Lebensmut', and is similarly incomplete. When the song was published in 1872 by J.P. Gotthard, as no.17 of 'Forty Songs', the publisher sensibly repeated the four-bar prelude at the end, and added the tempo indication *Geschwind*. Friedländer in the Peters edition followed suit, printing all three verses.

There seems little doubt that Schubert originally intended *Lebensmut* to be included with the group of Rellstab settings later published in *Schwanengesang*. Whether he withdrew it, and why, or whether the decision was Haslinger's, is not clear; but whatever the reason the fact is regrettable, for *Lebensmut* is a fine song which would have enriched the collection.

There are certain superficial resemblances to the setting of Schulze's verses with the same title: the key, for instance, the pace, and the arpeggio-based figures in both the accompaniment and the melody. Schubert's marking for the Schulze song – *Nicht zu schwind, doch kräftig* – would also suit this one very well. Schubert's rejection of the song, if that is what it was, may owe something to the fact that it misses the mood and sense of the final verse.

Capell, 69, 247

# LEBENSMUT Courage

**Ernst Schulze**

March 1826

Ziemlich geschwind, doch kräftig      B flat major D883 Peters V p.80 GA XX no.498

Oh, how powerfully my youth surges through my mind and heart! I feel everything is glowing and ardent, pleasure and pain are doubly intense. In vain I seek to tame the spirits of my active breast; they govern me at will, for sorrow or pleasure.

Blaze high, my mighty love, and higher still! Break open, blossoms of desire! What if my heart is stained with blood, or succumbs to sudden pain: I would rather be totally ruined than live only half a life.

This hesitation, this longing which vainly swells my breast, these sighs and tears held prisoner by pride, this painful, idle wrestling, this struggle without strength, without hope, without achievement; this has drained the marrow from my bones.

No, let the quick keen battle cry wake my sleeping mind! Long I dreamed, long I rested, and resigned myself to my chains. Here there is neither hell nor heaven, neither frost nor fire. On towards the hostile tumult, and boldly beyond it through the flood!

So that once again the waves of desire, daring, anger, love, good and evil beat upon me in the wild sea of life, and I, with the cheerful strength born of experience, steer my little boat, bravely battling with the current that seeks to carry me away.

The poem, from the *Poetisches Tagebuch* ('Verse Journal'), is headed 'Am 1sten April 1815'. Schubert's title is as above. The autograph, formerly in the possession of Josef von

Gahy, is missing. A copy in the Witteczek–Spaun collection (Vienna, GdM) is dated March 1826. The song was published in 1832 in book 17 of the *Nachlass*.

The many links between the Schulze songs and *Winterreise* have often been noticed, and *Lebensmut* is a kind of preview of *Mut*. But it is not so great a song. The main theme catches well enough the undaunted spirit of the poem, but the song lacks the subtle and continuous melodic and harmonic variation which makes the best of the Schulze songs such a delight; and in spite of the switch into the minor for verse 3, it is difficult to sustain the interest to the end.

Capell, 217

## LEBENSTRAUM Dream of Life

**Gabriele von Baumberg**                                                      (?) 1809 or early 1810

Andante                          C major  D39  Not in Peters  Not in GA  NSA IV vol.6 p.171

In the soft evening light I sat at the entrance to a temple in the grove of the muses.

This is the beginning of a long allegorical poem, consisting of 221 lines, which prefaced a volume of poems by Gabriele von Baumberg published in Vienna in 1805. Schubert's incomplete setting of it, written probably in his thirteenth year, was almost certainly his first serious attempt at song-writing. The autograph, undated and untitled, has been split up into three sections. The first (to bar 140) is in the Paris Conservatoire. The notes are complete on three staves, but only the first two lines of verse are written out. A second sheet, in private possession, continues the setting to bar 226. A third sheet was discovered in Vienna (MGV) in 1968. These sketches overlap and the song seems to be complete, at least in conception, though Schubert never made a finished draft. Nowhere on the manuscript is the name of the author mentioned, and the song was earlier identified by the first line ('Ich sass an einer Tempelhalle'). The author was identified by Heinz Sichrovsky of Vienna.

There are close thematic links between this song and another very early Schubert manuscript, the song (without text) in G minor (D2 1A) which seems to be even earlier. This sketch, which breaks off after 394 bars, is similar in style and structure to *Lebenstraum* and may have been inspired by the same text. It also is published in the appendix to vol.6 of the *Neue Ausgabe*.

It seems somehow typical of Schubert that his first effort as a songwriter should be, not a modest strophic setting, but an extended cantata. Juvenile and unsophisticated as it is, the song gives only a hint of the pictorial composer, and the great melodist, who was to come.

M.J.E. Brown, 'Schubert: discoveries of the last decade', *MQ*, XLVII, 1961, pp.296–7; R. van Hoorickx, 'Schubert's reminiscences of his own works', *MQ*, LX, 1974, pp.373–4; R. van Hoorickx, 'Schubert: songs and song fragments not included in the collected edition', *MR*, XXXVIII, 1977, pp.281–2, and XXXIX, 1978, p.95; C. Landon, 'Neue Schubert-Funde', *ÖMZ*, XXIV, 1969, trans. as 'New Schubert finds', *MR*, XXXI, 1970, p.216.

## LEBEWOHL see ABSCHIED VON EINEM FREUNDE

# LEICHENFANTASIE Funereal Phantasy

**Friedrich von Schiller**                                                                         1811

Adagio                    D minor D7 Not in Peters GA XX no.3 NSA IV vol.6 p.22

Mit er - storb - nem Scheinen steht der Mond auf to - ten - stil - len Hai - nen,

The moon shines palely over the death-still grove, the night spirit sighs through the air; clouds of mist shiver, the wan stars gleam mournfully like lanterns in a vault. Like ghosts, silent, hollow, gaunt, a procession moves in black funeral pomp towards the graveyard, masked by the chilling veil of the burial night.

Who is it that, trembling on his stick, with gloomy down-sunk glance, his existence one long cry of anguish, tormented by his iron fate, totters behind the silent pallbearers? Did the word 'Father!' fall from the youth's lips? Damp shudders of fear shake his bones, molten with grief; his silvery hair stands on end.

His burning wound is torn apart by the hellish anguish of his soul. 'Father!' came from the youth's lips, and the father's heart has whispered 'Son!' Ice-cold, ice-cold he lies there in his shroud, and your dream, once so sweet and golden, has become a curse upon you, father. Ice-cold, ice-cold he lies here in his shroud, your bliss and your paradise!

Gentle, as if caressed by heavenly breezes, and wreathed with the heavenly scent of roses, like Flora's son leaping over the flowery fields released from Aurora's embrace, he flew across the smiling meadows reflected in the silver stream; flames of desire were kindled by his kisses as he chased after the maidens in the glow of love.

Boldly he sprang amongst the throng of humanity like a young roe in the mountains; his desires circled the heavens cloud-high like an eagle. As proud as wild foam-flecked horses tossing their manes in the storm, or rearing at the touch of the reins, he trod before slaves and princes.

His life passed serene as a spring day, flowed over him in the glow of Hesperus; he drowned his sorrows in the gold of the vine, and hopped his cares away in the whirl of the dance. Worlds lay asleep in the splendid youth – ah, if he had only matured into the man! Rejoice, father, in splendid youth, when once the latent germ has ripened!

But no – Listen, father, the churchyard gate rumbles, and the iron hinges creak open – how horrible it is in the vault. But no – let your tears fall! Go, fair youth, follow the path of the sun towards perfection and, released from sorrow, quench your noble thirst blissfully in the peace of Valhalla!

To see him again – ah, heavenly thought! – to see him again at the gates of Eden! Listen, the coffin sinks with an uneven rumble, the straps screech upwards, whining. When we rolled about drunkenly together our lips were silent, but our eyes spoke – Wait, wait! When we quarrelled ... But the tears fell the more warmly afterwards.

The moon shines palely over the death-still grove; the night spirit sighs through the air; clouds of mist shiver, the wan stars gleam mournfully like lanterns in a vault. The clods form a mound, thudding onto the coffin. Oh, for one more glimpse of the world's treasure! The bolts of the grave close tight for ever. The clods form a mound, thudding heavier and heavier upon the coffin. The grave never gives back its own.

The poem, written in 1780, was occasioned by the death of Schiller's friend August von Hoven. It has the macabre clarity of a Caspar Friedrich moonscape, yet the rhetoric also conveys a passionate sense of loss. The author's title is *Eine Leichenphantasie*; Schubert's is as above. There are only minor changes in the text. The autograph (Vienna, SB) is undated. It belongs however to the earliest group of surviving Schubert songs, written in 1811. At bar 203 it borrows a theme from a sketch for the Fantasie in G for piano duet, which probably belongs to 1810. Parts of the song were used by Schubert's brother

Ferdinand for his 'Pastoral Mass' of 1833. The song was first published in the *Gesamtausgabe* in 1894.

*Leichenfantasie* is the most interesting of Schubert's early attempts to improve on Zumsteeg. For one thing it does not fade away at the end. For that, and for the nicely contrasted 'flashback' scenes in the middle, Schiller must take some of the credit: his poem has shape and variety. Moreover, he inspired Schubert to write the most vivid and arresting music of his early years. The opening page of the song is wonderful, and so is the setting of the final verse. Significantly, this song affords us the first glimpse of those recurrent motifs of death and desolation which outline the course of his genius: the chromatically descending bass, the staccato chord groups, the piercing minor seconds, the harmonic movement from tonic minor to dominant – all this holds the seed from which greater songs were to grow.

Capell, 79; Einstein, 44–5; Fischer-Dieskau, 19; Schnapper, 116–25

## LEIDEN DER TRENNUNG Sorrows of Parting

**Heinrich von Collin**                                                    December 1816

*Etwas langsam*                         G minor  D509  Not in Peters  GA XX no.285

The wave separates from the sea, and sighs its way through the flowers in the valley;
whether cradled in the spring, or confined in the well, it feels nothing but torment.
    Whether in the whispering spring, in the murmuring stream, or in the well-chamber, the wave longs
    to be back in the sea from whence it came, from which it took its life, and from which, tired of wandering, it hopes for sweet rest and peace.

The poem is a free translation of Arbace's aria from Act III of Metastasio's *Artaserse*. There are two autographs, both dated December 1816. The first draft (New York, Public Library) breaks off at bar .18. The fair copy (Vienna, GdM) is also incomplete, consisting of the first eight bars only. It bears the inscription 'In Herr von Schober's house'. There are two copies (complete) of this final version, one in the Witteczek–Spaun collection (GdM) and one in Stadler's song album (Lund, UB), which provided the source for the published version. The first draft begins in 2/4 time, but Schubert changed the signature to common time. The fair copy is *alla breve*. The song was first published by J. P. Gotthard in 1872 as no.32 of 'Forty Songs'.

Schubert's uncertainty about the time signature is interesting, in view of the metrical irregularity of the poem. The first verse is anapaestic, the second dactylic and the third iambic. Yet the song moves smoothly and seamlessly in the flowing eight quavers to a bar; and by running verses 2 and 3 together he builds the climax by a process of melodic extension. The song rests finally in the security of the relative major, like the river returning to the sea. The singer's opening phrase is accompanied by a version of the familiar harmonic descent from tonic minor to dominant which is so closely associated in Schubert's work with *Sehnsucht*. There is a perfection of form nd expression in this fine song which reminds us of Schubert's enthusiasm for Mozart in this his twentieth year.

Capell, 126; Fischer-Dieskau, 88

**LETZTE HOFFNUNG** see WINTERREISE no.16

## LIANE
**Johann Mayrhofer**

October 1815
C major D298 Not in Peters GA XX no.170

'Have you seen Liane?' 'I saw her go towards the pond.' Through bushes and hedgerows he runs and comes to her favourite place.

The linden stretches its green net, the brook babbles among the rose bushes; the golden sun gilds the leaves, and everything is alight with joy.

Liane glides in a boat beside her tame swans; she plays her lute and sings a song about the happy love blossoming in her heart.

The little ship drifts where it will. Her head sinks and meditates about him – who is in the bushes, and very soon will fold her in his arms.

The autograph, dated October 1815, was auctioned in Vienna in 1934. It is now in the GdM, Vienna. There is a copy, similarly dated, in the Witteczek–Spaun collection (Vienna, GdM). The song was published in the *Gesamtausgabe* in 1895. The pianist's right-hand triplets, idly rocking between tonic and dominant, the simple tonal relationships and the slow harmonic speed point forward to later boating songs like *Der Fischer* and *Am Flusse*. But the song does not rank among the best Mayrhofer settings.

## LICHT UND LIEBE Light and Love
**Matthäus von Collin**

(?) 1822
G major D352 Not in Peters GA XX no.286

*A song in the distance. Man's voice:* Love is a sweet light. As the earth strives for the sun, and for those bright stars in the broad blue firmament, so the heart strives for the bliss of love, for it is a sweet light.

*Woman's voice:* Look, how the bright stars twinkle high above in silent celebration. The dim dark veils of melancholy flee from the earth. Woe is me! How heavy I feel in my heart, which once blossomed in joy and now, deprived of love, is desolate.

*Both voices:* Love is a sweet light. As the earth strives for the sun, and for those bright stars in the broad blue firmament, so the heart strives for the bliss of love; love is a sweet light.

The text comes from Act IV of Collin's tragedy *Der Tod Friedrichs des Streitbaren* ('The Death of Duke Frederick the Valiant'), published in 1813. As Frederick reflects on his past happiness, he hears voices echoing through the wood. (His own asides are not set by Schubert.) The piece is a duet for tenor and soprano, with piano accompaniment.

The autograph has not survived, and there is no clue to the date of composition. O. E. Deutsch suggested 1816, but offered no evidence in support. A later date is much more likely. Schubert came into contact with Collin through his friend Josef von Spaun (who was Collin's cousin) about 1820, and all the other Collin settings date from 1822 or 1823. Moreover, the operatic feeling is much more characteristic of 1822 than 1816. The song was published in book 41 of the *Nachlass*, about 1847. This first publication included a four-bar introduction, almost certainly spurious.

This lovely duet has the grace and assurance of the best music in Schubert's mature operas. How well the undercurrent of disquiet is conveyed in the middle section, and how naturally it breaks into recitative at the words 'Wehe mir!' The imitative phrases in the *da capo* section, and the cadential phrases in the coda, renew the listener's pleasure in the opening music by presenting it in a new light.

## LIEB MINNA Sweet Minna
**Albert Stadler**

2 July 1815

F minor  D222  Peters VII p.31  GA XX no.86

'A sultry breeze is wafted across to me, causing the flower at my breast to fade. Ah, where do you tarry, William my dear, delight of my soul? I am for ever weeping, but you never appear. Perhaps you are already asleep in the earth's cool womb; do you still think of me, under the moss?'

Minna wept, gradually the colour left her lips and her cheeks. William had marched off in the ranks to a soldier's death. From that moment no news came. Minna thinks: you have probably been asleep a long while in the cool earth, under the moss.

The poor darling sits nursing her grief, watching the golden stars go by, and the moon casts sympathetic glances on her. Listen, the evening breezes blow across to her from the heights: your sweetheart is waiting for you there, by the cliff.

Pale and anxious, Minna hurries across the plain in the glittering moonlight; but she does not find her William, she finds only his grave. 'Soon I shall be over there with you, dearest, if from the cool earth you say to me: I am thinking of you, Minna, under the moss.'

And thousands of flowers spring courteously from the grave. Minna recognises this testimony of love; she makes a little bed upon them. 'Soon I shall be over there with you, dearest.' She lies down upon the flowers, and finds her William again.

The autograph is a first draft, dated 2 July 1815 and headed 'Lieb Minna. Stadler. Romanze'. There is a dated copy also in the Witteczek–Spaun collection (Vienna, GdM), and others in the Stadler and Ebner collections (Lund, UB). The song was first published in 1875, in vol. VII of the Peters edition.

The simple strophic setting, the F minor tonality and the minimal accompaniment match the 'primitive' nature of Stadler's verses admirably. Moreover, the strophe is cleverly constructed so that it may end happily either in the dominant C major or in the relative major A flat. This enables Schubert to preserve the continuity and avoid too monotonous an effect by ending the two middle verses in A flat. The instruction *Sehr langsam, schmerzlich*, may be interpreted with discretion. The tone of sweet melancholy does not need to be stressed.

## LIEBE SCHWÄRMT AUF ALLEN WEGEN Love
wanders along every path

**Johann Wolfgang von Goethe**                                            July–August 1815

D major  D239 no.6  Peters I p.258  GA XV 7 no.6

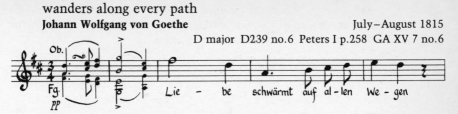

Love wanders along every path; fidelity lives alone. Love comes running up to you; fidelity has to be searched out.

The song comes from the surviving act of Schubert's Singspiel *Claudine von Villa Bella*, and strictly speaking has no place in this book. But it has found its way into the Peters collected edition of the songs (where it is transposed to C major) and is occasionally included in recitals. In the score of the opera (Vienna, GdM) the number is headed 'Ariette' and is sung by Claudine.

**LIEBESBOTSCHAFT** see RELLSTAB SONGS no.1

## LIEBESLAUSCHEN The Serenade

**Franz Xaver von Schlechta**                                            September 1820

A major  D698  Peters III p.151  GA XX no.381

A knight stands below me in the clear moonlight, and sings to his zither a song of the torment of true love:
    'Breeze, spread your blue wings and gently carry my message; call her with soft music to this little window.
    'Tell her that, from the cover of the leaves, a familiar sound sighs forth; tell her that someone is still awake, and that the night is cool and safe.
    'Tell her how the waves of moonlight breaks against her window; tell her how the forest and the fountain whisper secretly of love!
    'Let the sweet light of your image shine through the trees, that image which is woven into my dreams and my waking hours.'
    But the soft melody could not have reached the ears of his beloved. The singer swung himself softly up to her window.
    And once up there the knight pulled a posy from his breast and bound it to the lattice and sighed: 'Bloom in joy!
    'And if she asks who brought you, flowers, tell her who it was.' A voice below softly laughed: 'Your knight, Liebemund!'

The text of the song makes up the second part of a poem in two parts, the first called 'The Knight', and the second 'The Lady'. The piece was inspired by a genre painting by Ludwig Schnorr von Carolsfeld, which is reproduced in *Franz Schubert: sein Leben in Bildern* (Munich, 1913, ed. O. E. Deutsch), p.192. The painting is in the ducal museum at Gotha. Both Schlechta and Schnorr were members of the Schubert circle, and the song was almost certainly written from a manuscript copy, though both poem and illustration were published in a Vienna periodical in 1821.

The autograph (Vienna, SB) is entitled *Des Fräuleins Liebeslauschen*, and dated September 1820. The text has been altered at many points by another hand, possibly Schlechta's. The fifth verse of Schubert's text does not appear in the published version of the poem. A copy of the song in Franziska Tremier's song album (Vienna, SB) is transposed to G major. *Liebeslauschen* was published (under that title) in January 1832 in book 15 of the *Nachlass*.

The quavers flow on gently but insistently, the tonality returns inexorably to A major, and the four-bar echo phrase in the accompaniment, which leans towards the subdominant before returning to the tonic, has an almost hypnotic effect. There is a risk that the pervasive mediant tonalities will begin to cloy, but Schubert seems well aware of it. The subtle rhythmic and tonal variations in the vocal line enliven the song until verse 8, where he surprises us with a sudden switch to a brisk 6/8 Allegretto. The three last verses are all given individual treatment, though the tonal pattern is sustained.

> Capell, 168; A. Orel: 'Der ursprüngliche Text zu Schuberts Liebeslauschen', *Festschrift Johannes Biehle*, Leipzig, 1930

## LIEBESRAUSCH Love's Ecstasy (1)

**Theodor Körner**

March 1815

G major D164 Not in Peters Not in GA

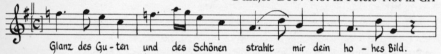

Glanz des Gu-ten und des Schönen strahlt mir dein ho-hes Bild.

For you, maiden, my tremulous heart beats, full of love and fidelity. In you, in you, my striving ends, for you are my fairest ambition. Your name alone has filled my bold breast with holy music; your noble image shines with the brightness of beauty and goodness.

Love sprouts from tender seeds, and its blooms never fade. You, maiden, live in my dreams with heavenly harmonies. Inspiration fills me with ecstasy; boldly I strike the strings, and all my finest songs name you alone.

My heaven glows in your eyes; my paradise is at your breast. Ah, how lovely and sweet are the charms with which you are decked! My breast swells with pleasure and pain. I have only one desire, only one thought in my heart: my eternal longing for you!

The autograph (New York, PML) is a fragment consisting of the last four bars of the strophe and a two-bar postlude. The whole page has been cancelled. On the reverse is another Körner song, *Das war ich* (1) (D174), dated 26 March 1815. A facsimile of this fragmentary setting was published in the first number of *Musik aus aller Welt* (Vienna, January 1929), edited by O. E. Deutsch.

The beginning of the song has been imaginatively reconstructed by Reinhard van Hoorickx and the completed version privately published. This version has been recorded as one of several 'Unknown Schubert Songs' (DR 1981007). This shows conclusively, not only that the first version was quite distinct from the second, more familiar, one, but that it is also a most attractive song in its own right.

## LIEBESRAUSCH (2)

**Theodor Körner**                                                  8 April 1815

Langsam                              G major  D 179  Not in Peters  GA XX no.59

Dir, Mäd - chen, schlägt mit  lei - sem Be - ben

For translation, see the preceding entry. The autograph, now in the Erasmus–Haus, Basel, is a first draft dated 8 April 1815. There is a dated copy in the Witteczek–Spaun collection (Vienna, GdM). The song was first published in 1872 by J. P. Gotthard as no.29 of 'Forty Songs'.

*Liebesrausch*, like *Als ich sie erröten sah* written two months earlier, has the manner and the movement of the true love song, and it is tempting to suggest that the freshness and spontaneity of these early love songs owes something to Schubert's personal circumstances – for was this not the springtime of his own love for Therese Grob? Quite new is the way the song is written for the voice, the phrases beautifully moulded to the compass of the voice and to the words. It has, too, a tonal freedom which enhances its spontaneity, swinging away into B flat (the flattened third) at the shorter third line and back again to the tonic, then feinting in the direction of the dominant before reaching a climax on B major.

The accompaniment, superficially a simple affair of supportive chords repeated in triplets, shows Schubert's subtle mastery of moving inner parts, which provide a concealed counterpoint to the tune. *Liebesrausch* is something of an unknown gem, and it is ignored by the commentators. But it foreshadows the lyrical perfection of some of Schubert's best-known masterpieces.

## LIEBESTÄNDELEI Flirtation

**Theodor Körner**                                                 26 May 1815

Etwas geschwind                      E flat major D206  Not in Peters  GA XX no.75

Sü - ßes  Lieb - chen, komm__ zu__ mir!  tau - send Küs - se geb_ich__ dir.

Sweet darling, come to me! I will give you a thousand kisses. See me here at your feet. Girl, the warmth of your lips gives me strength and courage. Let me kiss you!

Girl, don't blush! Even if your mother did forbid it, are you to miss all the pleasures? Only on your lover's breast does life's best leasure flower. Let me kiss you!

Darling, why do you put on airs? Listen, and kiss me. Don't you want to know about love? Isn't your little heart beating with pleasure and pain? Let me kiss you!

See, your resistance does you no good! Already I have done my duty as a singer and snatched the first kiss from you! And now, warm with love, you sink willingly into my arms, and let yourself be kissed!

The autograph (Washington, LC) is a first draft dated 26 May 1815. There is a dated copy in the Witteczek–Spaun collection (Vienna, GdM). The song was first published in 1872 by J. P. Gotthard as no.11 of 'Forty Songs'.

Playful hesitation surrenders to boldness! The music mirrors the mood, demanding a firm *allargando* before the pause at bar 7, and again before the final bar. The middle erotic verses are effectively distanced by the purely eighteenth-century manner, playful but uninvolved.

# LIEBHABER IN ALLEN GESTALTEN A Lover in Many Shapes

**Johann Wolfgang von Goethe** May 1817

Etwas lebhaft A major D558 Peters VII p.97 GA XX no.120

I wish I were a fish, so nimble and so fresh. If you came to catch me, I would not fail to take the bait. I wish I were a fish, so nimble and so fresh.

I wish I were a horse, then you would value me. Oh, if I were a coach, I could carry you in comfort! I wish I were a horse, then you would value me.

I wish I were gold, always at your service. If you bought something I would come running back to you. I wish I were gold, always at your service.

But I am as I am, so you'll just have to accept me! If you want a better man you will have to have him made to measure. I am as I am, so you'll just have to accept me.

The poem, written in the summer of 1810, has nine verses, of which Schubert set the first three and the last. Friedländer in Peters vol.VII prints only verses 1, 3 and 9. The autograph, in the Paris Conservatoire, is dated May 1817. There is a copy in Stadler's song album (Lund, UB). The first publication was in 1887, in vol.VII of the Peters edition.

A delightful song, which surprises by its simplicity and its humour. The exchange of witticisms between voice and piano in the closing bars is perfect.

# LIED (Brüder, schrecklich brennt die Träne)

**Author unknown** February 1817

G minor D535 Not in Peters GA XX no.585

Brothers, the tears of deserving poverty burn terribly; does this distressing scene find no friend amongst us?

A prey to despair, she wrings her pale hands. Come now, lighten her existence with your compassionate sympathy.

The song is one of the occasional pieces written for Schubert's brother Ferdinand, who held a teaching post at the Vienna Orphanage from 1816 onwards. Neither the occasion nor the author of the words (possibly Ferdinand himself?) is known. The autograph (Vienna, SB) is headed simply 'Lied', and dated February 1817.

The piece is scored for soprano solo and a small orchestra of oboes, bassoons, horns and strings. In later years Ferdinand arranged it as a vocal duet with piano accompaniment and published it as his own composition in a collection of songs for school use called 'The Young Singer' (1853). This version was entitled 'Song of the Poor Schoolchildren addressed to their Patrons and Benefactors'. The original version was first published in the *Gesamtausgabe* in 1895. The piece is written in the hymnlike Haydnesque manner which Schubert thought appropriate for these charitable occasions.

**LIED** (Des Lebens Tag ist schwer) see DIE MUTTER ERDE

## LIED (Es ist so angenehm)

**(?) Friedrich von Schiller**

6 September 1815

G major D284 Not in Peters GA XX no.137

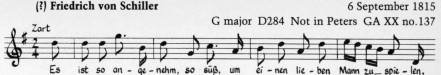

Es ist so an-ge-nehm, so süß, um ei-nen lie-ben Mann zu_ spie-len,

It is so very pleasant and sweet to dally with the man one loves; ravishing, like paradise, to feel his fiery kisses.

Now I know what my pair of doves were saying as they softly cooed, and what the hosts of nightingales lamented so tenderly in their songs.

Now I know what oppressed my overflowing heart during the long, long nights; now I know what the sweet pain was which so often filled my breast with sighs.

And why no flower pleased me, why May never smiled for me, why the chorus of birdsong fanned no pleasure within me.

The whole world seemed sad to me before I knew the beauty of desire. Now I possess what I for so long lacked. Envy me, nature! I am in love!

The poem first appeared, anonymously, four years after Schiller's death, in a 'Ladies' Pocket-book' published in Tübingen. Its attribution to Schiller is very doubtful, and it does not appear in collected editions of his work. O. E. Deutsch suggested that the real author may have been Schiller's patroness Karoline von Wolzogen.

The autograph, in private possession, is dated 6 September 1815, and there is a dated copy in the Witteczek–Spaun collection (Vienna, GdM). The song was first published in the *Gesamtausgabe* in 1895. It is a graceful and lighthearted strophic setting in the vernacular style.

## LIED (Ferne von der grossen Stadt)

**Karoline Pichler**

September 1816

E major D483 Not in Peters GA XX no.265

Fer-ne von der gro-ßen Stadt, nimm mich auf in dei-ne Stil-le,

Far from the great city, receive me into your silence, O valley decked by nature with the riches of spring; where no noise, no tumult shortens my slumbers and serene skies smile ceaselessly on the happy plain.

Here, undisturbed, I will taste the joys of peace; here where trees shelter me and the linden scatters its fragrance. This spring will be my mirror, the young clover my parquet flooring, and the newly grassed hill my green sofa.

And in the end when the north wind rages through the leafless forests and mountains of snow lie heaped on the frozen fields, then friends will shorten the winter nights for me by the hearth until, decked with fresh green, the new spring wakens afresh.

The text forms the concluding section of Pichler's idyll *Der Sommerabend* ('The Summer Evening'), a poem in praise of the joys of the countryside, addressed 'To my friend Fräulein Josepha von Ravenet'. There are eight verses, of which the first two and the last are given above. The autograph, in private possession, is a first draft dated September 1816, untitled. There are several contemporary copies, including one in the Witteczek–Spaun collection (Vienna, GdM), also dated, and entitled *Lied*. This provided the source for the first publication, in the *Gesamtausgabe* in 1895.

The key, the movement and the ceremonial manner are reminiscent of the setting of Schiller's 'Ode to Joy' (D189) for solo voice and chorus, and this song may possibly have been written with the same forces in mind, and for some special occasion. The simple strophic setting is pleasing but of no great significance, unless one counts the allusion to Haydn's 'Emperor's Hymn' in the closing bars and the postlude as significant.

**LIED** (Ins stille Land)  see INS STILLE LAND

## LIED (Mutter geht durch ihre Kammern)
**Friedrich de la Motte Fouqué**                              15 January 1816
G minor  D373  Not in Peters  GA XX no.184

Mother goes through her rooms, filling and emptying the cupboards, seeking she knows not what; lamenting, she finds nothing but an empty house.

An empty house! What sad words for someone who once dandled there a darling child in the daytime, and gently rocked it to sleep at night.

The beech trees will grow green again, the light of the sun will return, but you can stop looking, Mother; your darling will not come back.

And when the evening breezes blow and the father returns home to the hearth, he is moved by something akin to a smile, which gives way at once to tears.

Father knows that in his rooms all will be as still as death; he will hear only the moans of the pale mother, no little child will chuckle at him.

The text comes from Fouqué's Romantic fairy tale *Undine*, published in 1811. E. T. A. Hoffmann based an opera on the tale in this same year, 1816. The autograph (Vienna, SB) is an untitled and undated first draft. Associated with it on the same manuscript is *An die Natur*, which is dated 15 January 1816. The first publication was in the *Gesamtausgabe* in 1895. The simple strophic setting has the pathetic air of a minor mode folksong.

**LIED** Zufriedenheit  see ZUFRIEDENHEIT

**LIED AN DEN TOD** see AN DEN TOD

## LIED AUS DER FERNE  Song from Afar
**Friedrich von Matthisson**                                    July 1814
E major  D107  Not in Peters  GA XX no.21  NSA IV vol.7 pp.26, 29

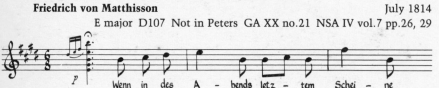

When, in the last glimmer of dusk, as you sit on the grass in the oak grove, a smiling figure passes you with a wave of greeting, that is the faithful ghost of your friend, promising you joy and peace.

When in the dim moonlight your dreams of love become sweeter, and a melodious rustling is heard in the broom bushes and the pine trees, and your bosom swells with anticipation, it is my ghost that hovers round you.

If, while lost in blissful recollection of the magic domain of the past, you feel a soft, incorporeal touch, like the kiss of Zephyr on your lips and hands, and if the unsteady candlelight flickers: that is my ghost, oh never doubt it!

If, in the silver starlight, in your secret closet, you hear as soft as aeolian harps in the distance the password: For ever thine! Then sleep sweetly, for it is my ghost promising you joy and peace.

The poem dates from 1811. Schubert set all four verses, and there are two versions. The autograph of the first, in E major and marked 'Allegretto', is lost, but there are copies in the Witteczek–Spaun collection (Vienna, GdM), one dated July 1814, and in Stadler's song album (Lund, UB). In this version verses 2 and 3 are given a slightly more elaborate accompaniment. A fair copy in the song album of Therese Grob (see GROB) is in D major, marked 'Etwas geschwind'. The *Gesamtausgabe* (1894) prints only the E major version; the *Neue Ausgabe* includes both. The strophic setting trips along gracefully, but too lightheartedly for this ghost-haunted poem.

## LIED DER ABWESENHEIT see LIED IN DER ABWESENHEIT

## LIED DER ANNE LYLE Anne Lyle's Song

**Andrew MacDonald, Sir Walter Scott** (?) Early 1825

C minor D830 Peters IV p.63 GA XX no.541

Wärst du bei mir im Le - bens - tal____,

In chapter XXI of Scott's novel *The Legend of Montrose* the song is sung by the heroine, Annot Lyle. The author introduces it thus: 'A little Gaelic song in which she expressed her feelings has been translated by the ingenious and unfortunate M'Donald, and we gladly transcribe the lines here.' The reference is to the comedy *Love and Loyalty* by Andrew MacDonald. In the original the lines run:

Wert thou, like me, in life's low vale,
With thee how blest, that lot I share;
With thee I'd fly wherever gale
Could waft, or bounding galley bear.
But parted by severe decree,
Far different must our fortunes prove;
May thine be joy – enough for me
To weep and pray for him I love.

The pangs this foolish heart must feel,
When hope shall be for ever flown,
No sullen murmur shall reveal,
No selfish murmurs ever own.
Nor will I through life's weary years,
Like a pale drooping mourner move,
While I can think my secret tears
May wound the heart of him I love.

Schubert set the song in German, though it is not clear whose translation he used. O. E. Deutsch (*Thematic Catalogue*) cites Sofie May, but her translation, if it ever existed, has not been traced. The autograph is missing, and the date of composition is not altogether certain. The song was published, together with *Gesang der Norna*, as op.85 by Diabelli in March 1828. The catalogue of the Witteczek–Spaun collection (Vienna, GdM) gives

1827 as the date of both songs, but wrongly. *Gesang der Norna* (q.v.) certainly belongs to the beginning of 1825, and probably the companion piece also.

An ostinato rhythm of a martial kind seems to be an essential ingredient in Schubert's Scott songs, and he provides one even when, as here, there is no warrant for it in the text. The insistent crotchet–quaver–quaver beat is here given a percussive quality by the staccato bass line and the strong accents, as though to suggest the beat of war drums. The effect might be monotonous, but for the fact that the unexpected modulations keep the listener alert and interested. The mingled grief and pride in love are touchingly expressed by the minor–major changes.

It is important that the dynamic level nowhere rises above a *mezzoforte*, for the undertones of war are just that; they exist in Anne's mind. The mood is introspective and the general level varies from *p* to *pp*. The song can, with difficulty, be sung to the English words, but it suits the German words much better. Einstein points to an affinity of mood, key and rhythm with the Andante of the E flat Piano Trio.

Capell, 243; Einstein, 351

**LIED DER DELPHINE** see DELPHINE

**LIED DER DIDONE** see DIDO ABBANDONATA

## LIED DER LIEBE Song of Love

**Friedrich von Matthisson**                                                July 1814

Allegretto        B flat major  D109  Not in Peters  GA XX no.23  NSA IV vol.7 p.33

Durch Fich-ten am Hü-gel, durch Er-len am Bach,

Through the fir trees on the hill, through the alders by the stream, your image, beloved, follows me. It greets me with a smile of love, it greets me with a smile of peace, in the friendly glimmer of the moon.

In the brightness of morning your lovely figure appears from the rose bushes in the garden; it floats, like an elysian shadow, from the purple mists over the mountains.

In dreams I have often seen you, the most beautiful of fairies, seated in splendour on a golden throne; and often I have glimpsed you transported to high Olympus as Hebe among the gods.

I hear, like the music of the spheres, your heavenly name resounding from the valleys and from the heights; I imagine the fragrance clinging to the blossoms to be vibrant with your melodious voice.

At the holy hour of midnight my prophetic spirit crosses the regions of the upper air; there, beloved, a country beckons us where lovers are for ever reunited.

Joy vanishes, no sorrow lasts, the years rush away in the current of time; the sun will die, the earth pass away, but love shall last for ever and ever.

The poem dates from 1792–3. Schubert's autograph is lost, but there is a copy in the Witteczek–Spaun collection (Vienna, GdM) dated July 1814. The first publication was in 1894, in the *Gesamtausgabe*. Schubert's habit of combining a strophic form with an element of declamation leads him here to set the fifth verse, with its suggestion of spookery, to a solemn recitative in the relative minor. The strophe itself is pleasantly tuneful and the elaboration of the accompaniment in the last verse admirable, but the contrast with verse 5 is too sharp for comfort.

**LIED DER MIGNON** see MIGNON'S SONGS

# LIED DES GEFANGENEN JÄGERS Lay of the
Imprisoned Huntsman

**Sir Walter Scott trans. Adam Storck**                                    April 1825

D minor D843 Peters II p.106 GA XX no.475

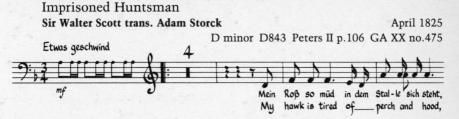

The song comes towards the end of *The Lady of the Lake*, Canto VI stanza 24, where Ellen overhears her lover, Malcolm Graeme, singing it from the turret of the castle where he is held captive. In the original it runs:

> My hawk is tired of perch and hood,
> My idle greyhound loathes his food,
> My horse is weary of his stall,
> And I am sick of captive thrall.
> I wish I were, as I have been,
> Hunting the hart in forest green,
> With bended bow and bloodhound free.
> For that's the life is meet for me.
>
> I hate to learn the ebb of time,
> From yon dull steeple's drowsy chime,
> Or mark it as the sunbeams crawl,
> Inch after inch, along the wall.
> The lark was wont my matins ring;
> The sable rook my vespers sing;
> Those towers, although a king's they be,
> Have not a hall of joy for me.
>
> No more a dawning morn I rise,
> And sun myself in Ellen's eyes,
> Drive the fleet deer the forest through,
> And homeward wend with evening dew;
> A blithesome welcome blithely meet,
> And lay my trophies at her feet,
> While fled the eve on wing of glee –
> That life is lost to love and me!

Schubert's autograph is lost. In the catalogue of the Witteczek–Spaun collection (Vienna, GdM) the song is dated April 1825. The *Lady of the Lake* songs were first published as op.52 by Matthias Artaria in April 1826 and dedicated by Schubert to Sofie, Countess von Weissenwolf. The English version was printed separately, presumably because it requires so much alteration to the melody. The first public performance was at a concert of the Gesellschaft der Musikfreunde by Johann Schoberlechner on 8 February 1827.

The brisk polonaise rhythm turns Scott's iambic tetrameters into galloping anapaests, and this, combined with the regular strophic form, does not at first sight seem suitable for what the poem calls a 'heart-sick lay'. But Schubert's purpose presumably is to emphasise Graeme's unbroken spirit. The song is a fine vehicle for a dark, incisive baritone voice, and the minor to major shift in the middle of each stanza adds interest to a song which is sometimes felt to be lacking in variety of tone and colour. The dramatic setting for the song, and the basic concept, are much the same as in Anne Lyle's song, but this one does not have the same tonal freedom.

Capell, 212; Einstein, 301–2; Fischer-Dieskau, 212–13

## LIED DES ORPHEUS (ALS ER IN DIE HÖLLE GING)
Orpheus's Song, as he Journeyed to Hell

**Johann Georg Jacobi**                                    September 1816

G flat major D474 Peters V p.98 GA XX no.250(a) and (b)

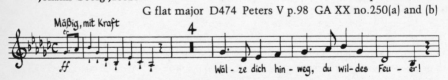

Wäl - ze dich hin - weg, du wil - des Feu - er!

Roll back, raging fire! These strings have been crowned by a god, one who commands all monsters, and perhaps hell itself.

His right hand tuned my strings: flee, fearful shadows! And you, whimpering inhabitants of this darkness, listen to my song.

Of the earth, where the sun shines, and of the tranquil moon; where dew spangles the young moss, where song dwells in the green fields;

From the dear homeland of mankind, where the skies once smiled on you, I am drawn by strong ties, I am drawn downwards by love itself.

My lament is heard in your lament; fortune has fled this place, but remember those days, look back at that world!

If you embraced there even one sufferer, oh, then feel once more what desire is; and may the moment in which you felt compassion for it relieve this long torment.

Oh, I see tears flow! Through the darkness a ray of hope breaks now; the kindly gods will not allow you to make atonement for ever!

The gods who created the earth for you will call you out of the blackest night to the pastures of the blessed, where virtue sits smiling among the roses.

The poem dates from about 1770. There are two versions of the song. The autograph of the first version, dated September 1816, is in Vienna (SB). It is entitled as above, in 4/4 time, and the final section is in D major. The last leaf is missing, but there is a complete copy in the Stadler collection (Lund, UB). The revised version survives only in a copy in the Witteczek–Spaun collection (Vienna, GdM). It is in *alla breve* time, headed simply 'Orpheus', and the final section is in B flat major. The *Gesamtausgabe* prints both versions, but Friedländer in the Peters edition only the more practicable later version. This latter was first published in book 19 of the *Nachlass* (announced October 1832).

There is a Mozartian strength and humanity, a classical grandeur of conception, in this splendid dramatic scena. The legend of Orpheus seems to have had a special appeal for Schubert (see Sams), and the orchestral richness of his invention in this song makes it one of the greatest of the year 1816. His intention in revising the song was clearly to bring it within the normal range of the baritone voice, and in this respect the familiar version is preferable. But there is a price to pay. In purely musical terms the original version is better, because the climax is more impressive, and the transition from the A major middle section more smoothly achieved; it may still be recommended to any singer able to encompass a range of more than two octaves, from A flat below the stave to A natural above it – and to do so, moreover, while getting faster and faster from bar 74 onwards.

Capell, 118; Einstein, 134; Fischer-Dieskau, 75; E. Sams, 'Notes on a magic flute: the origins of the Schubertian lied', *MT*, CXIX, 1978, p.947.

# LIED EINES KINDES A Child's Song

**Author unknown**

November 1817

B flat major D596 Not in Peters GA XX no.598

*I feel only joy, I hear only love, I so fortunate a child at my happy games.*
*Over there my good father, here my dear mother, and around them us children.*

The song is a fragment, breaking off after twenty-four bars. The autograph is lost, but there is a copy in the Witteczek–Spaun collection (Vienna, GdM) dated November 1817, and this provided the source of the (1894) publication in the *Gesamtausgabe*. The song has been completed and privately printed by Reinhard van Hoorickx.

*Lied eines Kindes* is attractive in its simple nursery-song style. It breaks off at the third line of the second verse, and it is not known how many verses there were originally.

# LIED EINES KRIEGERS Soldier's Song

**Author unknown**

31 December 1824

A major D822 Peters V p.204 GA XX no.464

*Solo:* The finest emblems of proud manhood are flame, thunder and the strength of the oak. But speak no more of the play of steel and the gleam of weapons; everlasting peace has come our way, and the power of the fist has been pledged to sleep.
*Chorus:* Everlasting peace has come our way, and the power of the fist has been pledged to sleep.
*Solo:* Not long ago we wielded the sword and fought boldly for life or death; but now the days of high battle have ended, and what remains to us of those days is over; soon, alas, it will be nothing but a legend.
*Chorus:* What remains to us of those days is over; soon, alas, it will be nothing but a legend.

The author of these pedestrian lines has never been identified. The autograph, formerly in private possession in Paris, is missing. The original title was *Reiterlied* ('Trooper's Song'), but this was cancelled and the above title inserted. The voice line was written in the bass clef and was complete, but the accompaniment was written out in full only for the first forty-five bars. A copy in the Witteczek–Spaun collection (Vienna, GdM) has the voice line in the treble clef and the tempo indication *Lebhaft*. It differs from the autograph in other details and may well be based on a lost fair copy. The song was first published in book 35 of the *Nachlass* in June 1842. This edition and the *Gesamtausgabe* follow the Witteczek copy, with the voice written in the treble clef. A rather different version was published about 1847 in book 41 of the *Nachlass*, which is closer to the fragmentary autograph.

The stiff and amateurish verses, the easy chorus part, the celebratory style and the date all suggest that this is an occasional piece, commissioned for some new year's eve reunion. There is no doubt that it was written for solo bass voice and men's chorus in unison, with piano accompaniment.

A. Orel, 'Die authentische Fassung von Schuberts "Lied eines Kriegers"' *Archiv für Musikwissenschaft*, II, 1937, pp.285–98

## LIED EINES SCHIFFERS AN DIE DIOSKUREN
Boatman's Song to the Dioskuri
**Johann Mayrhofer** (?) 1822

A flat major D360 Peters III p.32 GA XX no.268

Dioscuri, twin stars, shining on my boat, your mildness and your wakefulness calm me on the sea.

> The man who, full of confidence, meets the storm without fear feels doubly strong and blessed when you shine upon him.

> This oar with which I drive a path through the waves of the sea I shall, once safely home, hang on the pillars of your temple.

The poem, entitled *Schiffers Nachtlied*, was first published in 1824. Schubert's autograph is lost, and the date of the song is not certain. The catalogue of the Witteczek–Spaun collection (Vienna, GdM) enters it under 1816. However, Schubert must have worked from Mayrhofer's manuscript, or from a copy of it, and there is in Vienna (SB) a Mayrhofer manuscript dated September and October 1821, which includes this poem together with the *Heliopolis* poems and *Nachtviolen*, set by Schubert in April 1822. The Spaun copy is entitled simply *Dioskuren*. The song was published under the full title above in November 1826 as op.65 no.1 by Cappi and Czerny.

> The combination of hymnlike simplicity and subtlety is common enough in Schubert's middle years (cf. for instance *Nachtviolen* and the setting of Senn's *Schwanengesang*), and 1822 seems a much more suitable date than 1816. Essentially the song is a continuous statement of the tonality of A flat major, often for Schubert a symbol of serenity and security; the menace of the sea is subtly suggested by the arpeggio bass and the displaced accents in the postlude. As an effective mood-piece the song is perhaps the best-known of all the Mayrhofer settings.

> Capell, 127

## LIED IN DER ABWESENHEIT
**Friedrich Leopold, Graf zu Stolberg-Stolberg** Song of Absence April 1816

B minor D416 Not in Peters Not in GA

Ah, my heart is heavy! I wander sadly here and there. I search for peace and, finding none, go to the window and weep.

> If you were sitting in my lap all my cares would leave me, and from your blue eyes I would draw love and delight!

> If only, sweet child, I could fly swiftly to be with you! If only I could embrace you for ever and hang on your lips!

The poem dates from 1775. The autograph, dated April 1816, is in private possession. The second sheet has been lost, and the concluding bars are missing. However, five bars to complete the piece were supplied by Eusebius Mandyczewski, and it was published as a supplement to *Moderne Welt* (Vienna), edited by O. E. Deutsch, in December 1925. The song has been recorded in a collection of 'Unknown Schubert Songs' edited by Reinhard van Hoorickx (DG 1981007).

Schubert's failure to complete the song has deprived us of a minor masterpiece. The first verse is set to a sweetly plaintive tune reminiscent of other B minor settings of 1816 like *Der Leidende* and Holty's *Klage*. The second verse, in G major, is beautifully contrasted and sets up an expectation of a return to B minor which Mandyczewski's conclusion fails to satisfy. Other attempts to complete the song, by van Hoorickx and Karl Pils, are more successful in recognising the suggestion of tripartite form in the surviving fragment.

**LIED NACH DEM FALLE NATHOS** see OSSIANS LIED NACH DEM FALLE NATHOS

## LIEDESEND Song's End

**Johann Mayrhofer**                                                                                   September 1816

C minor  D473  Peters V p.139  GA XX no.249(a) and (b)

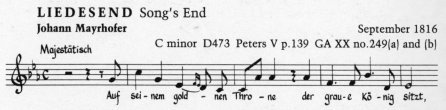

On his golden throne the grey king sits, and stares into the sun that gleams red in the west.

The bard strokes the harp, a song of victory resounds; but high seriousness resists sharply the triumphant sound.

Now he plays sweet tunes, appealing to the heart; to see whether he can soften the king by gentle means.

His efforts are in vain, the power of song is exhausted; the storm clouds of care gather on the king's brow.

The bard, embittered, strikes the harp in two: the cry of the silver strings vibrates through the air.

Yet, though all tremble, the ruler is not angry; the light of mercy shines upon his countenance.

'You must not accuse me of lack of sensibility; in months of May long gone how much pleasure you have given me.

'How you increased every joy which fate offered! Your playing restored to me what the gods had denied.

'But now the magic of your song slips away from my cold heart, and mortality and the grave tread closer and closer.'

There are two versions. The autograph of the first, dated September 1816, has the voice line of the concluding (3/4 *Ernst*) section in the bass clef. The fair copy, similarly dated, has the voice line in the treble clef throughout, and an altered and extended postlude. Both autographs are in Vienna (SB), and both versions are included in the *Gesamtausgabe*. There is a copy in the Witteczek–Spaun collection (Vienna, GdM) of the revised version, which was first published in book 23 of the *Nachlass* (1833). Friedländer in the Peters edition prints the second version but arbitrarily shortens the postlude.

The piece is usually damned with faint praise. The poem does no more than colour a conventional ballad situation with Mayrhofer's habitual pessimism, and the song's episodic form is against it. Yet Schubert's invention is astonishingly free and economical. Every verse is characterised individually. The tonal scheme is, even for Schubert, adventurous. As a sort of home-made Ossian ballad (note the grey stepwise consecutive tenths at the end, very reminiscent of *Die Nacht*) *Liedesend* is worth an occasional performance.

Porter, 127

## LILLA AN DIE MORGENRÖTE  Lilla to the Dawn
**Author unknown**                                    25 August 1815

D major  D273  Not in Peters  GA XX no.130

How beautiful you are, O golden dawn; how splendid you are! The shepherd's flute celebrates his gratitude to you with a festive melody.

The chorus of the woods greets you, lark and nightingale sing sweetly, and round about from hill and valley the echoes of joy reverberate.

The autograph, in private possession, is dated 25 August 1815, and there is a dated copy in the Witteczek–Spaun collection (Vienna, GdM). The song was first published in the *Gesamtausgabe* in 1895. A pretty and unpretentious song; the simple marchlike accompaniment nicely suggests the shepherds' flutes (two of them, apparently) and the fluting birds.

## L'INCANTO DEGLI OCCHI  The Enchantment of Eyes
**Pietro Metastasio**                                     1827

C major  D902 no.1  Peters VI p.146  GA XX no.579

On you, dear eyes, depends my whole life. You are my gods, and my destiny. At your will my mood changes.

If you shine with happiness you fill me with daring. When the clouds gather you make me tremble.

On you, dear eyes, depends my whole life. You are my gods and my destiny. At your will my mood changes.

The text comes from Metastasio's opera *Attilio Regolo*, written in 1740. The song is the first of 'Three Songs for Bass Voice', announced by Tobias Haslinger in September 1827, and dedicated to Luigi Lablache, the celebrated bass singer of Barbaja's company at the Kärntnertor Theatre. The songs were written in the Italian style and designed to cash in on the popularity of the Italian opera in Vienna. See notes on *Il Modo di prender moglie* and *Il Traditor deluso*.

The three songs were published as op.83 in three parts, with both Italian and German words. This one is sometimes referred to by its German title, *Die Macht der Augen*. The autograph fair copy is in London (BL), together with the first draft of the other two. The catalogue of the Witteczek–Spaun collection gives the date of the songs as 1827. It is to be noted, however, that the preliminary sketches for the melody of this and the companion songs may be much earlier than 1827. See D2 990E and 990F, which leave open the possibility that Schubert worked up the songs from much earlier exercises in the Italian style.

It is a proof of the universal nature of Schubert's genius that he could so easily slip into the Italian operatic manner, even in a year which produced *Winterreise* and the *Momens musicals*. There is, to be sure, something academic about this song; the melodic line falls into familiar patterns, and the purely supportive accompaniment sounds faintly anachronistic, though not more so than in *Der Hirt auf dem Felsen*. It is easy to believe that Schubert was fascinated by 'the sweetness and range of Lablache's voice, and the ease with which he could alter his register' (Einstein, 346), for only a singer who aspires to the same strength and flexibility will be able to do justice to this fine song.

## LITANEI (AUF DAS FEST ALLER SEELEN)
Litany for the Feast of All Souls
**Johann Georg Jacobi**                                      August 1816

E flat major D343 Peters II p.212 GA XX no.342

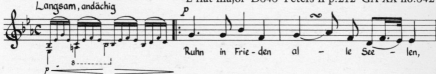

May all souls rest in peace, those who have finished their fearful agony, those who have completed a sweet dream; those who have departed the world weary of life, and those who were scarcely born. May all souls rest in peace!

   The souls of girls in love, who, abandoned by faithless lovers, shed countless tears and rejected the blind world. May all who have departed, may all souls rest in peace!

   And those who never smiled at the sun, and lay awake on beds of thorn under the moon, so that one day they might see God face to face in the pure light of heaven – may all who have departed, may all souls rest in peace!

The poem has nine verses. Schubert's autograph has the first verse written below the stave, and repeat marks at the end. The first edition, and following that the Peters edition, prints verses 1, 3 and 6, which are translated above. The *Gesamtausgabe* prints all the verses, but the mood of compassionate devotion is too intense to be sustained for more than two or three verses.

   The only surviving autograph is that included in the Therese Grob song album (see GROB). The direction here is *Langsam mit Andacht*, and there is no piano prelude. The song is entitled *Am Tage aller Seelen*. The song was published in 1831 in book 10 of the *Nachlass* (*Geistliche Lieder* no.5). *Litanei* is given the full title above, and a one-bar piano introduction which may be spurious, though it seems likely that the edition was based on a lost fair copy. The song is dated August 1816 in the catalogue of the Witteczek–Spaun collection (Vienna, GdM). The later date often quoted – August 1818 – is a mistake.

   The song's magic lies in its freshness and depth of feeling, and it defies analysis. As with many of Schubert's most popular songs, the feeling is strongly homophonic, but strengthened by the tension between the firm bass line and the melody. The chromatic descending bass line in bars 4 and 5 is particular effective, and is echoed by the pianist's right hand in bars 7 and 8. The postlude, rising and falling in a great arch, sounds like a sigh of consolation. It may not be irrelevant to recall that Schubert noted in his diary in June 1816 his own thoughts about his dead mother, during a walk through the Währing cemetery (see *Docs.* no.87).

   App. IV; Capell, 117–18; Fischer-Dieskau, 75–6

## LOB DER TRÄNEN In Praise of Tears

**August Wilhelm von Schlegel** (?) 1818

D major D711 Peters I p.187 GA XX no.294 NSA IV vol.1 pp.100, 229

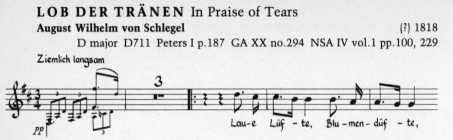

Gentle breezes, the scent of flowers, full of spring and youthful desire: sipping kisses from fresh lips, nestling against a soft breast: then stealing the nectar from the grapes; dances and games and jests: what the senses alone can achieve, ah, does it ever satisfy the heart?

When damp eyes glisten with the mild dew of melancholy, then the fields of heaven, mirrored there, lie open to the gaze. How invigorating, to see every wild passion extinguished on the instant! As flowers are by rain, so is the tired spirit revived.

Prometheus did not force our clay to live with sweet water, but with his tears; so with longing and with pain are we at home. To earthbound senses these springs rise bitterly, but they penetrate beyond our limits to the ocean of love.

Eternal longing flowed in tears and surrounded the lifeless world, which now for ever holds this symbol of mercy in its watery embrace. If man is to rid himself of earth's dust he must be united through tears with the holy source of those waters.

The poem dates from 1807. The surviving autograph, undated and untitled, is in Vienna (SB). The tempo indication is *Andante*. At the bottom of the page Schubert has scribbled in pencil: 'Spaun! Don't forget Gahy and the Rondo'. This may refer to a forthcoming performance of the Rondo in D major ('Notre amitié est invariable', D608), written in January 1818. Schubert was away in Zseliz from July to November of that year. There are several contemporary copies, one dated 1819. The most likely hypothesis is that the song dates from the first half of 1818.

A fair copy made for the printer, probably in 1821, is lost, and this may account for the fact that the catalogue of the Witteczek–Spaun collection (Vienna, GdM) mistakenly attributes the song to 1821. *Lob der Tränen* was published as op.13 no.2 in December 1822 and dedicated to Josef von Spaun (Cappi and Diabelli on commission). The tempo marking here is *Ziemlich langsam*.

The song's Viennese lilt catches the mood of the poem, with its sentimental mixture of sweetness and tears. It is not only a question of 3/4 time, and the pianist's right-hand triplets, but more particularly of the ambiguity of the singer's dotted quavers against the piano's triplets. This would pose no problems for Vogl, who would recognise it as reserving to the singer the rubato necessary to his art. One suspects that he would have given the dotted notes their full value in the first half of the strophe, but that from bar 14 onwards, where the accompaniment turns to repeated chords, he would have assimilated the semiquavers to the final note of the triplet.

Capell, 143; Fischer-Dieskau, 67

## LOB DES TOKAYERS In Praise of Tokay

**Gabriele von Baumberg**　　　　　　　　　　　　　　　August 1815

*Nicht zu geschwind, doch lebhaft*　　　B flat major　D248　Peters IV p.148　GA XX no.135

O exquisite Tokay, O royal wine! Thou tunest my lute to rare rhyming. With a bliss of which I have too long been deprived, and newly revived joy, thou warmest my half-frozen heart like the sun. Thou tunest my lute to rare rhyming, O exquisite Tokay, O royal wine!

O exquisite Tokay, O royal wine, thou drivest strength and fire through my marrow and my bones. I feel new life sparkling in my veins as thy nectar grapes warm my breast. Thou drivest strength and fire through my marrow and my bones, O exquisite Tokay, O royal wine!

O exquisite Tokay, O royal wine: to thee this song is dedicated as dissipator of sorrows! In melancholy moods thou lendest wings to my blood; thou gives boldness to the coy, whether blonde or brunette. To thee this song is dedicated as dissipator of sorrows, O exquisite Tokay, O royal wine!

The autograph is lost, and the only evidence as to the date comes from the catalogue of the Witteczek–Spaun collection (Vienna, GdM); however, four other Baumberg settings can be certainly attributed to August 1815, so there is little doubt about it. The song was published by Josef Czerny as op.118 no.4 in June 1829. *Lob des Tokayers* is a lively drinking song set to a rousing march tune.

## LODAS GESPENST Loda's Ghost

**James Macpherson (Ossian)**　　　　　　　　　　　　17 January 1816

　　　　G minor　D150　Peters IV p.181　GA XX no.44　NSA IV vol.7 p.105

The original text, from Macpherson's prose poem *Carric-Thura*, runs as follows:

The wan, cold moon rose in the east. Sleep descended on the youths. Their blue helmets glitter to the beam; the fading fire decays. But sleep did not rest on the king; he rose in the midst of his arms, and slowly ascended the hill, to behold the flame of Sarno's tower.

The flame was dim and distant; the moon hid her red face in the east. A blast came from the mountain, on its wings was the spirit of Loda. He came to his place in his terrors, and shook his dusky spear. His eyes appear like flames in his dark face; his voice is like distant thunder. Fingal advanced his spear in night, and raised his voice on high.

'Son of night, retire: call thy winds, and fly! Why dost thou come to my presence, with thy shadowy arms? Do I fear thy gloomy form, spirit of dismal Loda? Weak is thy shield of clouds; feeble is that meteor, thy sword! The blast rolls them together; and thou thyself are lost. Fly from my presence, son of night; call thy winds and fly!'

'Dost thou force me from my place?' replied the hollow voice. 'The people bend before me. I turn the battle in the field of the brave. I look on the nations and they vanish; my nostrils pour the blast of death. I come abroad on the winds: the tempests are before my face. But my dwelling is calm, above the clouds; the fields of my rest are pleasant.'

'Dwell in thy pleasant fields,' said the king; let Comhal's son be forgot. Do my steps ascend, from my hills, into thy peaceful plains? Do I meet thee, with a spear, on thy cloud, spirit of dismal Loda? Why then dost thou frown on me? Why shake thine airy spear? Thou frownest in vain: I never fled from the mighty in war. And shall the sons of the wind frighten the king of Morven? No: he knows the weakness of their arms.'

'Fly to thy land,' replied the form: 'Receive the wind, and fly! The blasts are in the hollow of my hand: the course of the storm is mine. The king of Sora is my son, he bends at the stone of my power. His battle is around Carric-Thura, and he will prevail! Fly to thy land, son of Comhal, or feel my flaming wrath!'

He lifted high his shadowy spear! He bent forward his dreadful height. Fingal, advancing, drew his sword, the blade of dark brown Luno. The gleaming path of the steel winds through the gloomy ghost. The form fell shapeless into air, like a column of smoke, which the staff of the boy disturbs, as it rises from the half-extinguished furnace.

The spirit of Loda shrieked as, rolled into himself, he rose on the wind. Inistore shook at the sound. The waves heard it on the deep. They stopped in their course with fear; the friends of Fingal started at once, and took their heavy spears. They missed the king; they rose in rage; all their arms resound!

The moon came forth in the east. Fingal returned in the gleam of his arms. The joy of his youth was great, their souls settled, as a sea from a storm. Ullin raised the song of gladness. The hills of Inistore rejoiced. The flame of the oak arose; and the tales of heroes are told.

See OSSIAN SONGS. The German text is from the translation by Edmund von Harold. Schubert followed it closely, but numerous alterations were made in the first edition. The autograph, in the Paris Conservatoire, is a first draft dated 17 January 1816. There is a copy in Stadler's song album (Lund, UB). It seems that the putative earlier autograph of August 1815 mentioned by Deutsch (*Thematic Catalogue*) does not exist.

The song was published as book 3 of the *Nachlass* in July 1830, but the edition was corrupt: Diabelli took it upon himself to rewrite the text, cancel Schubert's five-bar postlude, and add a final section consisting of forty-six bars from Schubert's male-voice trio *Punschlied* (D277). His collaborator in this piece of editorial vandalism was Leopold von Sonnleithner, who lived to regret the part he played in it. (See *Memoirs* pp.441–2).

Fischer-Dieskau praises the artistry of *Lodas Gespenst*, 'with its virtuoso declamation and characterisation', but his is a lone voice. 'Long and inferior' is Capell's verdict, and it is true that the music nowhere seizes the imagination like the beginning of *Kolmas Klage* or parts of *Die Nacht*. Yet the song is remarkable for the proto-Wagnerian quality of the writing and of the central conception. In spite of Macpherson's pasteboard prose, the encounter between Fingal and Loda's spirit has a certain grandeur, which Capell compares to the confrontation between Siegfried and Wotan in Act III of *Siegfried*; and as for the writing, the story is told almost entirely in accompanied recitative, with the piano playing the part of linking narrator.

Capell, 93; Fischer-Dieskau, 55

# LORMA (1)

**James Macpherson (Ossian)**

28 November 1815

A minor D327 Not in Peters Not in GA

Lor - ma saß in der Hal - le von Al - do,

Schubert made two attempts to set a passage from Ossian's prose poem *The Battle of Lora* but completed neither. It is not clear how long a work he planned. The text of that part of the poem he actually set runs, in the original, as follows:

Lorma sat in Aldo's hall. She sat at the light of a flaming oak. The night came down, but he did not return. The soul of Lorma is sad!

'What detains thee, hunter of Cona? Thou didst promise to return. Has the deer been distant far? Do the dark winds sigh round thee on the heath? I am in the land of strangers. Who is my friend but Aldo? Come from thy sounding hills, O my best beloved!'

Her eyes are turned towards the gate. She listens to the rustling blast. She thinks it is Aldo's tread. Joy rises in her face! But sorrow returns again, like a thin cloud on the moon.

See OSSIAN SONGS. The autograph of this first setting, in private possession, is dated 28 November 1815. It breaks off at the words, 'She listens to the rustling blast'. A further six bars were identified by Maurice Brown on the back of a manuscript dating from July 1817 (Brown, *CB*, 66). A facsimile of the autograph was privately published by Walter Schutz of Stuttgart to mark the centenary of Schubert's death. The song has been completed and privately published by Reinhard van Hoorickx.

M. J. E. Brown, 'Some unpublished Schubert songs and song fragments', *MR*, XV, 1954, p.93; R. van Hoorickx, 'Schubert songs and song fragments not included in the collected edition', *MR*, XXXVIII, 1977, p.285

## LORMA (2)
**James Macpherson (Ossian)**

10 February 1816
A minor D376 Not in Peters GA XX no.592

For text, see the preceding entry. The autograph of this second setting, dated 10 February 1816, is in Vienna (SB). It is written on both sides of a sheet, and finishes at the bottom of the page with a modulation to E flat major in the middle of a recitative. The song was first published in the *Gesamtausgabe* in 1895. The second attempt breaks off after fifty-two bars. The opening recitative in A minor is expressive (*Traurig, langsam*), and the C minor arioso which follows has an accompaniment in consecutive sixths reminiscent of *Die Nacht*. But Schubert seems to have lost interest in the song.

## LUISENS ANTWORT Louisa's Answer
**Ludwig Kosegarten**

19 October 1815
B flat minor D319 Not in Peters GA XX no.166

God's angels weep when lovers part: how shall I be able to live, beloved, without you? Dead to all joys I shall henceforth live in sorrow, and never, William, never shall Louisa forget you.

How could I forget you? Wherever I turn, dear friend, wherever I cast my eyes, your image shines on me. With drunken rapture I see it watching me. No never, William, never will Louisa forget you.

At the fearful hour of midnight I would cast a radiance about your bed, and murmur softly in your ear: 'I am Louisa: Louisa cannot hate you, Louisa cannot leave you, Louisa comes to bless you, and still loves you up above.'

The poem was intended as a companion piece to Klamer Schmidt's *Trennungslied*, which Mozart set in 1787 (K519). This famous poem, very characteristic of the 'age of sentiment', begins in the same way: 'God's angels weep when lovers part. How shall I be able to live without you, maiden? A stranger to every joy, henceforth I shall live in sorrow. And you? And you? Louisa will forget me, perhaps for ever, perhaps for ever.' Kosegarten's poem was an attempt to present the other side of the coin. It consists of nineteen verses, of which the first two and the last are translated. (It may be remembered that Schubert also set a more lighthearted treatment of the same human situation in Leitner's *Fröhliches Scheiden*, D896).

The autograph (Vienna, SB) is dated 19 October 1815. There is also a fair copy, now in private possession. There is a dated copy in the Witteczek–Spaun collection (Vienna, GdM). The song first appeared in the *Gesamtausgabe* in 1895.

*Luisens Antwort*, one of the best of the Kosegarten settings, has a strong affinity with Mozart's setting fo Schmidt's poem, even to the shape of the melodic line. But in Mozart's song a continual flow of new ideas gives an individual colour to the treatment of the last three verses. It is a salutary exercise, especially for believers in the theory that Schubert 'invented' the lied, to compare the two songs in detail.

## MAHOMETS GESANG Mahomet's Song (1)

**Johann Wolfgang von Goethe**                                    March 1817

E major  D549  Not in Peters  GA XX no.595

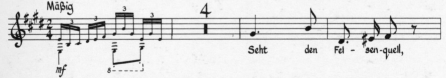

Look at the spring among the rocks, joyful and bright as a star's twinkle; benevolent deities above the clouds nourished its youth in the bushes between the crags.

With the spriteliness of a boy it dances from the clouds down upon the marble rocks, and rebounds exulting to the sky.

Through channels among the peaks it chases after coloured pebbles, and with the precocious step of a leader carries its brother streams along with it.

Down in the valley flowers spring up in its footprints, and the meadows draw their life from its breath.

But the shadowy valley cannot detain it, nor the flowers embracing its knees and making eyes at it; winding like a snake it rushes towards the plain.

Streams cling to it sociably. Now, bright as silver, it enters the plain, and the plain too is bright, and the rivers of the plain and the mountain streamlets greet it with jubilation, crying: Brother, brother, take your brothers with you!

The poem is part of a projected dramatic poem on the subject of Mahomet, dating from 1772–3. Schubert made two attempts to set it, but neither is complete. The autograph of this first attempt, dated March 1817, is in Vienna (SB). It covers the first thirty-five lines of the poem (about half of the whole) and breaks off at the bottom of a page after

114 bars. It is possible, therefore, that the continuation has been lost. The fragment was first published in the *Gesamtausgabe* in 1895.

There are strong resemblances between this poem and Goethe's *Gesang der Geister über den Wassern*, and it is significant that Schubert worked at both texts in March 1817 (D538 and 549) and again (D714 and 721) four years later. Even in March 1817 he seems to have had in mind a brilliant large-scale work, suitable for public performance, which would link his name with Goethe's. The ambition was finally to be realised with the performance of the *Gesang der Geister* with orchestral accompaniment at the concert of 7 March 1821. He seems, however, to have realised that the time was not ripe for such a venture in 1817. The 'river of life' theme was of course a familiar convention; it is interesting that Schubert's treatment of it here is much more brilliant and detached, less emotionally involved, than in the settings of Mayrhofer poems on the same theme.

## MAHOMETS GESANG (2)

**Johann Wolfgang von Goethe** March 1821

C sharp minor D721 Not in Peters GA XX no.600

For translation, see the preceding entry. This second setting is written for bass voice, and gets only as far as line 12 (thirty-nine bars) before breaking off. The rushing semiquavers in unison octaves are intended as a more orchestral, more impressionistic, treatment of the text, a display piece for Vogl, perhaps; but Schubert must have realised that this rather empty idea could never suffice for the whole song.

## MAILIED May Song

**Ludwig Hölty** November 1816

G major D503 Not in Peters Not in GA

The meadow turns greener, and the sky blue; the swallows return, and the little birds warble their first songs in the grove.

Since the arrival of spring the breath of love blows from the blossoming bushes; it rules the green world, painting the flowers with many colours and the mouths of the girls red.

Brothers, kiss them, for the years pass quickly! No one can deny you a respectful kiss! Kiss them, brothers, since they are kissable!

See, the dove is cooing; see, the dove in billing with his dear little mate. You too, like the dove, must take a wife and be merry!

The poem dates from 1773, and has four verses. Schubert wrote out the first verse under the stave, and put repeat marks at the end. There are two earlier settings of the same text, one for male-voice trio (D129) and one as a duet for two voices or two horns (D199). The only surviving autograph is a fair copy in the Therese Grob songbook (see GROB), dated November 1816. This was privately printed and published by Reinhard van Hoorickx. The songbook contains the text of all four verses, though the last three are written out separately, and have been detached from the music.

There is a similarity between the three settings. All are in 6/8 time, and begin in much the same way, but this version for solo voice is the most attractive of the three. The music is as sweet as a May morning.

> M. J. E. Brown, 'Some unpublished Schubert songs and song fragments', *MR*, XV, 1954, p.96; R. van Hoorickx, 'Schubert songs and song fragments not included in the collected edition', *MR*, XXXVIII, 1977, p.271

## MARIE Mary
**Novalis**

(?) May 1819

D major D658 Not in Peters GA XX no.364

I see you in a thousand pictures, Mary, sweetly depicted; but none of them shows you as my soul has glimpsed you. I only know that since that moment the tumult of the world blows over me like a dream, and an indescribably sweet heaven is ever present in my mind.

The poem was written in 1799 and published by Tieck in *Geistliche Lieder* ('Spiritual Songs') in 1802. It is addressed to the Virgin Mary, but may be coloured also by the poet's feelings for Sophie von Kühn, his betrothed, whose early death in 1797 became a deeply religious experience for him. The autograph, undated, is in private possession. There is no direct evidence as to the date, but it is usually assumed that it belongs, like several other Novalis settings, to May 1819. The first publication was in the *Gesamtausgabe* in 1895.

Schubert sets the two verses in one continuous strophe, which has the simple piety and sincerity of the *Hymnen* II and III, but adds a sweetness of its own. The song is flawless, and the only surprising thing is that it remained unknown until 1895. Alone of the Novalis settings, *Marie* may claim to be completely successful as a song, and to achieve an expressive unity of text and music. It is true, as Capell suggests, that there is nothing of the 'spiritual song' about it; but the identification of human love and religious experience is an important part of Novalis's own mysticism.

> Capell, 159; Fischer-Dieskau, 126–7

## MEERES STILLE Calm Sea (1)
**Johann Wolfgang von Goethe**

20 June 1815

C major D2 215A Not in Peters Not in GA NSA IV vol.1 p.197

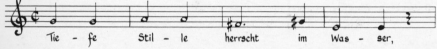

Deep silence rules the waters; the sea rests motionless, and the boatman gazes anxiously round him at the glassy surface of the ocean.

No wind from any quarter: the silence of death – fearful! In the whole vast expanse of water no wave rises.

The poem, with its companion piece *Glückliche Fahrt* ('Prosperous Voyage'), first appeared in 1796 in Schiller's *Musenalmanach*. They relate to an episode during Goethe's Italian tour, when in 1787 he crossed by boat from Naples to Sicily and experienced for the first time the wonder and the perils of the sea at first hand. On the voyage the ship encountered head-winds, a flat calm and a violent storm, and it is said that the lives of the travellers were in some danger. The poems may have been written at any time between 1787 and 1795.

The autograph of the first setting is in two sections, the first containing the first thirty bars and the second the remaining five bars. Both parts are in private possession, but there are copies of both in Berlin (SPK). The song was written out on the reverse of *Jägers Abendlied* (I), which is dated 20 June 1815. The song was first published in 1952 by O.E. Deutsch in the *Schweizerische Musikzeitung*, XCII, p.447.

This first setting is obviously very close in conception to the second, but it would be a mistake to regard it as merely a preliminary sketch. It can be argued, indeed, that it is more successful than the second version in conveying the undercurrent of fear and anxiety which undoubtedly is in the poem, especially in the setting of lines 3 and 4. Here the chromatic upward movement of the bass, and the melodic line, hint at a well-known passage from *Gruppe aus dem Tartarus*, bars 21–30.

> M.J.E. Brown, 'Some unpublished Schubert songs and song fragments', *MR*, XV, 1954, pp.84–5

## MEERES STILLE (2)

**Johann Wolfgang von Goethe**                                        21 June 1815

C major D216 Peters II p.3 GA XX no.82 NSA IV vol.1 p.23

For translation, see the preceding entry. There are two autographs, a first draft dated 21 June 1815 (Vienna, GdM) and a fair copy made for Goethe early in 1816 (Berlin, DS). The song was published by Diabelli on commission as op.3 no.2 in May 1821 and dedicated to Ignaz von Mosel.

The visual and pictorial nature of Schubert's imagination is splendidly illustrated in this boldly conceived song. Compared with Reichardt's original setting, which has a certain serenity of an entirely eighteenth-century kind, and Beethoven's powerful four-part setting, Schubert's is frankly impressionistic. He turns the glassy calm of the waters into music which scarcely moves, and which never rises above the level of *pp*. The thirty-two arpeggio chords of which the accompaniment consists succeed each other so slowly as to convey the effect of total calm, but a sinister calm, as the strangely disquieting modulations make clear.

> Capell, 101–2; Fischer-Dieskau, 52

**MEIN** see DIE SCHÖNE MÜLLERIN no.11

## MEIN FINDEN My Find
### C. Heine

A song with this title is recorded by Kreissle in the list of unpublished songs appended to his biography of Schubert (1865) and listed as no.30 in the appendix to the revised edition of the Deutsch thematic catalogue, under 'Doubtful and Unauthentic Works'. No poem with this title has been discovered, and the entry is almost certainly due to confusion with *Mein Frieden*. See the following entry.

## MEIN FRIEDEN My Peace
### C. Heine

Date unknown

E flat major  Not in D  Not in Peters  Not in GA

Fer - ne,   fer - ne   flam-men hel - le   Ster - ne

Far away, far away the bright stars blaze, they sink and reappear, they gaze down upon me like friends; from the far blue distance the stars just shine.

Far away, far away the bright stars blaze, they never come down to me, they never restore peace; from the far blue distance the stars just shine.

Far away, far away the bright stars blaze, their twinkling becomes ever brighter, they are beckoning me up to them; peace is not far away, it dwells on those stars.

A song with this title and text, engraved on a single sheet, was discovered among a collection of Schubertiana in the monastery of Seitenstetten, Lower Austria. At the bottom of the sheet is the signature of Father Leopold Puschl (1802–74), an enthusiastic collector of Schubert first editions and copies, and the date 25 September 1848. This discovery was made by Ignaz Weinmann. The sheet is headed: '*Mein Frieden*/Gedicht von C. Heine/componiert von Franz Schubert.'

Reinhard van Hoorickx has linked this song with the entry in Kreissle's appendix referred to in the preceding entry, and it seems highly likely, in view of the author's name and the similarity of the titles, that Kreissle's *Mein Finden* was simply a misreading of *Mein Frieden*. But its authenticity is highly doubtful. The source of the text has not been found, nor has the author been certainly identified. The song has been privately published, in facsimile, by Van Hoorickx, with an explanatory note.

R. van Hoorickx, 'A Schubert song rediscovered', *MT*, CXXI, 1980, p.97

## MEIN GRUSS AN DEN MAI My Greeting to May
### Johann Gottfried Kumpf

15 October 1815

Fröhlich

B flat major  D305  Not in Peters  GA XX no.153

Sei   mir - ge - grüßt, o  Mai___, mit dei - nem Blü - ten-him-mel

O May, with your heaven of blossoms, your spring, your oceans of pleasure, I salute you! O happy throng of waking creatures surrounding me, I salute you!

Your divine breath streams through the dull grey air, and mountain, valley and meadow quickly grow green. Sweet-smelling breezes blow softly, caressingly; the clear blue of the air laughs aloud.

> O May, with your oceans of pleasure, your joy, your flowery splendour, I salute
> you! Lovely youth, dry every tear, and brighten the dark night of fate.

The poem was published in 1814 in the periodical *Selam*, under Kumpf's pseudonym
Ermin. It has nine verses, of which the first two and the last are given above. The autograph,
now in ÖNB, Vienna, is dated 15 October 1815. There is a dated copy in the Witteczek–
Spaun collection (Vienna, GdM). Schubert wrote out only the first verse under the stave,
but added 'Dazu 8 Strophen' ('eight more verses'). The song was first published in the
*Gesamtausgabe* in 1895.

Much of the charm of this unpretentious but delightful little song derives from the
piano interludes. The prelude anticipates the voice, and the postlude improvises on the
singer's last phrase, while in the middle, between lines 2 and 3, the piano interposes a
dance of its own devising.

# MEMNON
**Johann Mayrhofer**                                    March 1817

D flat major  D541  Peters III p.4  GA XX no.308  NSA IV vol.1 p.46

Inured to eternal silence and sorrow, only once during the day may I speak; at the
moment when Aurora's lovely purple beams break through the night-born walls
of mist.

To the ears of men it is music. Because I voice my lament in melody, and in
the fervour of composition refine its harshness, they suppose my blossoming joyful.

Me – clutched at by the arms of death, snakes writhing in the depths of my
heart, nourished by the anguish of my thoughts; and almost maddened with restless
desire.

To be united with you, goddess of the dawn, and far from this vain existence
to shine down from spheres of noble liberty and pure love, as a pale silent star.

Memnon, Prince of the Ethiopians, was the son of Eos, the Dawn. He went to the assistance
of his uncle Priam, and was slain by Achilles. 'The Greeks used to call the statue of
Amenophis, in Thebes, the statue of Memnon. This image, when first struck by the rays
of the rising sun, is said to have produced a sound like the plucking of a chord. Poetically,
when Eos kisses her son at daybreak, the hero acknowledges this salutation with a musical
murmur' (*Brewer's Dictionary of Phrase and Fable*). For Mayrhofer the legend symbolises
the unhappy situation of the poet in an unsympathetic world, whose longing to be
translated to a better world of love and liberty is turned into songs of enchantment.

The autograph (Vienna, SB) is dated March 1817. The song was published as op.6
no.1 by Cappi and Diabelli on commission in August 1821 and dedicated by Schubert to
Michael Vogl.

It has truthfully been said that Schubert has a different style for every poet; for the
more philosophical expressions of Mayrhofer's sombre but genuine poetic gift he reserves
a nobility of utterance which compares only with the greatest Goethe songs. The slow
and majestic pulse of the piano introduction sets the tone and pace for the whole song;
and the repeated octaves in triplets toll like a bell through it. But within this unity each

verse is given its own characteristic form of expression: the first sad and brooding, the second more lyrical, as the poet speaks of the nature of his art, the third full of passionate protest, and the fourth noble and enraptured as the triplet chords are linked in a broad flowing melody and the pulse which at the beginning sounded like a funeral march becomes a song of triumph. So the theme which lies at the heart of the poem – that the poet's vision is a vision of eternity, that his sadness and his suffering are transfigured in his art – is reflected in the form of the song.

Capell, 21, 137–8; Fischer-Dieskau, 95

## MIGNON'S SONGS

Mignon first appears in book 2 of Goethe's novel *Wilhelm Meister*, where she is discovered by Wilhelm in a travelling circus. He buys her freedom from a troupe of tight-rope dancers and she attaches herself to him with submissive obedience and secret love. An air of mystery surrounds the pathetic child, and her tragic history is not revealed until the end of the novel, when she dies. The daughter of the blind Harper by his sister Sperata, she is taken as a child from her demented mother and brought up by good foster parents who lived by the lakeside. Here her adventurous spirit expresses itself in a passion for climbing and roaming over the countryside. One day she fails to return from her wanderings, and when her hat is found floating on the water it is assumed that she has had an accident on the rocks and been drowned.

In fact Mignon has been kidnapped by a troupe of acrobats and is taken to Germany, where Wilhelm releases her. The four songs which she sings in the novel are among Goethe's most justly famous lyrics. There are no titles, so they are usually referred to by the first line, though Schubert sometimes headed his settings 'Mignon', or 'Lied der Mignon', or 'Mignons Gesang'. The songs are here discussed individually under their first lines:

*Kennst du das Land* (D321)
*Heiss mich nicht reden* (D726 and D877 no.2)
*Nur wer die Sehnsucht kennt* (D310, D359, D481, D877 no.1 and D877 no.4)
*So lasst mich scheinen* (D469, D727 and D877 no.3)

## MINNELIED Love Song
**Ludwig Hölty**                                              May 1816

E major  D429  Peters VII p.10  GA XX no.221

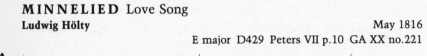
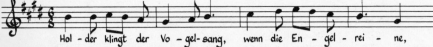

When the pure angel who has taken possession of my youthful heart wanders through the grove, even the birdsong sounds lovelier.

Valley and meadow bloom redder, the turf grows greener where her hands have gathered the red and blue flowers.

Without her everything is dead; flowers and herbs hang their heads, and the spring sunset seems neither beautiful nor serene to me.

Sweet, lovely lady, don't ever leave me; then my heart, like this meadow, shall bloom with bliss.

The poem dates from 1773. The autograph, dated May 1816, is in private possession. There is a dated copy in the Witteczek–Spaun collection (Vienna, GdM). The song was first published in 1885, in vol. VII of the Peters edition.

Brahms's famous setting (op.71 no.5) has, so to speak, laid claim to the verses, and Schubert's is lightweight by comparison. But the comparison itself is illuminating, for Schubert treats the poem simply as the pre-Romantic text it is, uncomplicated by layers of Romantic feeling. For Brahms, sixty years later, this is impossible. His version, marked 'Sehr innig', is essentially a Romantic document, for Schubert himself and Schumann interposed themselves between him and the poet.

### MINNESANG see HULDIGUNG

## MINONA Minona, or The Mastiff's Message
**Friedrich Anton Bertrand**                                   8 February 1815
A minor D152 Not in Peters GA XX no.40 NSA IV vol.7 p.124

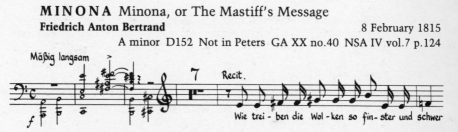

How dark and heavy the clouds are, racing across the sweet face of the sun! How the raindrops rattle on windows and rooftops! How violently the wind rages out there, as if spirits were engaged in a battle!

And strange! Suddenly the contenders rest, as if their battle had been stopped dead by the grave. And a cold and desolate wind blows chill over the heath and the forest from the shimmering crag.

O Edgar, where is your whizzing arrow? Where your fluttering mane of hair? Where your wheeling charger? Where are the black mastiffs panting at your side? Up there on the crag, where are you seeking out game to bring back to me? Your beloved expects you.

Your fearful bride, young man, hears your return in every sound, she awaits you with such longing; she thinks the love-knot broken, she imagines your hunting clothes stained with blood – for the dead never love us!

Their love song still echoes like the ripple of harps along the close-cropped hill. What use is that? The night stars already twinkle down upon the bed of earth, where the lovers lie in an iron sleep.

So she laments; and a soft tapping is heard outside, and an eager, fearful, deep whine. Horror-struck she staggers to the door: the finest of the mastiffs, her favourite, cowers before the expectant girl.

Not as yesterday, a messenger of love, did it leap up at her, demanding caresses. Scarcely raising its sad eyes from the ground it slinks to the door and back again to indicate its terrible message.

Poor Minona follows in silence, ashen-faced, as if summoned before the high court. How darkly the stars shine. She follows through swamps, through the heath and the valley, to the foot of the shimmering crag.

'Where, O shimmering crag, does death lie in wait? Where does the sleeper slumber, red with blood?' It was true: the love-knot was broken; a murderous arrow, loosed by an evil hand, had pierced his breast.

With a cry of fear she draws near and recognises her father's bow lying there. 'Father, O Father, may God forgive you! How terribly and with what evil mockery you have today carried out your threat of revenge.

But am I now to leave this place, crushed? He looks so enticing, so sweet and handsome as he sleeps. The iron knot is tied for ever now, and the spirits of our ancestors in misty garments strike up on silver harps.'

And suddenly, with desperate haste, she tears the fatal arrow from her lover's wound; wavering between joy and pain she thrusts it hurriedly into her snow-white bosom, and sinks down beside the shimmering crag.

Of this ballad one can only say that its naivety rivals that of a second-grade 'Lassie' feature film; and perhaps it should be judged by the same critical standards. It was printed in the 1808 'Pocket-book of Sociable Pleasures', published by Becker of Leipzig. Schubert's first draft, dated 8 February 1815 both at the beginning and the end, is in Vienna (GdM). There is an autograph fair copy (Vienna, SB) and a dated copy in the Witteczek–Spaun collection (GdM). The song first appeared in the *Gesamtausgabe* in 1894.

*Minona* shows Schubert's early conception of the ballad in its loosest and, to modern ears, least attractive dress. The story is told for the most part in recitative; not until verse 6 is there any extended arioso passage; and frequent changes of key and pace preclude any unity of mood or cumulative effect. Even the opportunities for scene-painting, like the pattering raindrops at bar 13, are not seized on with Schubert's usual skill and enthusiasm.

**MIO BEN RICORDATI** see VIER CANZONEN no.4

## MISERO PARGOLETTO Unhappy Child
**Pietro Metastasio**                                                    1812/1813
    G minor D42  Not in Peters  GA XX no.570  NSA IV vol.6 pp.60, 180, 181

Unhappy child, you do not know your fate. Ah, never tell him who his father was.
   O God, how everything was changed in a moment! You were my delight, now I fear for you.

The text is part of Timante's aria from Act III Scene 5 of *Demofoonte* (1733). There is little doubt that it was chosen by Salieri and given to Schubert as an exercise. Stadler dates Schubert's regular lessons with Salieri 1812–14 (*Memoirs* p.145), and this setting may well belong, like the similar exercises D76 and D78, to the autumn of 1813. The autograph, undated, is now in the BL, London. There are two incomplete sketches for a first version, and a second version written out complete on three staves, on the manuscript. All three are printed in the *Neue Ausgabe*.

Salieri was a staunch supporter of what might be called the Gluck–Metastasio tradition, as represented in Gluck's Italian operas, and an opponent of Mozart's attempts to modernise the *opera seria*. The fact that Schubert served his operatic apprenticeship under Salieri was of great importance in moulding his style. The model for this shapely *da capo* aria is clearly Gluck.

**MIT DEM GRÜNEN LAUTENBANDE** see DIE SCHÖNE MÜLLERIN no.13

**MORGENGRUSS** see DIE SCHÖNE MÜLLERIN no.8

## **MORGENLIED** Morning Song
**Author unknown**

24 February 1816
C major D381 Not in Peters GA XX no.189

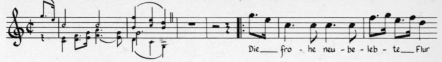

Die___ fro - he neu - be - leb - te___ Flur

The waking plain sings joyful thanks to its Creator. O Lord and Father of nature let my song also be to thee.

    Thou givest many pleasures to those who know how to enjoy them. May this, O Father, be always my aim when I am happy.

    I can still take pleasure in life in this beautiful world; my heart shall be consecrated to those who know how to keep it so.

    Then, when I am tired and death beckons me to a better world, I shall be greeted by a yet more beautiful dawn at the resurrection.

The autograph, a first draft dated 24 February 1816, is in the PM Library, NY. There is a copy in Vienna (SB), formerly in the collection of Schubert's nephew, Eduard Schneider. The song was first published in the *Gesamtausgabe* in 1895. There is a Papageno-like lilt to this happy little song, and a Mozartian sweetness in the postlude.

## **MORGENLIED** Morning Song
**Friedrich Leopold Graf zu Stolberg-Stolberg**

24 August 1815
F major D266 Not in Peters GA XX no.126

Lieblich

Will - kom - men, ro - tes Mor - gen-licht!

Welcome, red glow of morning! My spirit greets you, breaking through the wrappings of sleep to praise its Creator.

    Welcome, golden morning light, which already greets the mountains and will soon be kissing the little flowers by the stream in the valley.

    O sun, be for me the image of God, daily renewed, ever noble and ever mild, giving pleasure to the whole world!

The poem dates from 1793. There are eleven verses, of which only the first three are translated. The autograph, a first draft dated 24 August 1815, is in London (BL). There is a dated copy in the Witteczek–Spaun collection (Vienna, GdM). The first publication was in the *Gesamtausgabe* in 1895. A happy, lighthearted strophic setting in a brisk 6/8 measure, in the traditional vernacular style.

## **MORGENLIED** Morning Song
**Zacharias Werner**

1820
A minor/major D685 Peters II p.4 GA XX no.379 NSA IV vol.1 p.30

Ziemlich langsam (M.M. ♩ =63)

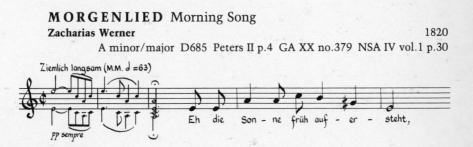

Eh die Son - ne früh auf - er - steht,

Before the sun rises in the morning, when the red flags of dawn wave up and down over the misty sea, marching ahead with gleaming spear; little birds flutter to and fro, singing gaily here and there a song of jubilation.

What makes you all so happy, little birds, in the warm sunshine? 'We are happy because we are alive, and because we are airy fellows. In our good old fashion we flutter through the bushes caressed by the sweet morning breeze, and the sun is enjoying itself too.'

Why do you little birds sit crouching dumbly in your mossy nests under the roof? 'We sit here because the sun is not looking at us; night has already dowsed it in the waves. The moon alone, with its sweet beams, the sweet reflection of the sun, saves us from the dark, so that we remain happy and tranquil.'

O time of youth, cool morning hour when with hearts wide open and waking senses we took pleasure in the freshness of life, how you have fled away. Away! We old ones sit crouching in our nests. But the sweet reflection of our youth, when we rejoiced in the rosiness of the dawn, remains with us even in old age – a tranquil, sensible happiness!

The text comes from part I of Werner's drama *Die Söhne des Thales* ('The Sons of the Valley'), which was published in 1803. The autograph (Vienna, GdM) is headed 'Morgenlied von Werner', and has a note in Schubert's hand at the end: 'NB I recommend this song very specially to the singer P and the pianist St!! 1820'. The initials stand for Pepi (Josefine) von Koller, whom Schubert had met at Steyr in 1819, and for his old friend Albert Stadler. Evidently the autograph was sent to Steyr, probably by the hand of Michael Vogl when he took his annual holiday in Steyr in the summer of 1820. The manuscript remained there until 1880, when it passed to Brahms. Schubert's fair copy, which he must have made for the printer, is lost. *Morgenlied* was published by Cappi and Diabelli at op.4 no.2 in May 1821 and dedicated by Schubert to Johann Ladislaus Pyrker, the Patriarch of Venice.

The poem's Wordsworthian message suggests to Schubert the symbolism of A minor/major; the sharp distinction between the two in this song emphasises the contrast between the joy of the innocent eye of childhood and the occluded vision of age. There are obvious reminiscences of *Schöne Welt, wo bist du*, as the opening bars make clear.

Capell, 168; Einstein, 190


**MUT** see WINTERREISE no.22


**MUTTER GEHT DURCH IHRE KAMMERN** see LIED


## NACH EINEM GEWITTER After a Storm
**Johann Mayrhofer**                                           May 1817

Mäßig                               F major D561 Not in Peters GA XX no.320

Pearls glisten on the flowers. Philomel's plaintive song pours forth. More bravely now the dark alders shoot up into the pure air.

A warm glow returns to the pallid valley; birds bathe their plumage in the fragrance of flowers.

When the storm in the heart is over, God slants his bow across, and his golden image shimmers more clearly on the peaceful waves.

The autograph is lost, but there are two dated copies in the Witteczek–Spaun collection (Vienna, GdM). The song was first published in 1872, as no.5 of 'Forty Songs', by J.P. Gotthard. The unaffected simplicity of the song presents such a striking contrast to the sublimity of the Mayrhofer dramatic monologues, or even to the shadowed melancholy of *Trost* and *Erlafsee*, that Capell appears to doubt its authenticity, but without any reason or excuse. The strophic setting is all innocence and freshness, not unlike the Stolberg *Morgenlied* in mood and tone.

> Capell, 139

## NACH OSTEN! To the East

This is the original title of a song by August Heinrich von Weyrauch, with words by Karl Friedrich Gottlob Wetzel. Published in 1824, it was later attributed to Schubert and republished under the title ADIEU ('Lebe wohl!') with a different text. The song is included in the Peters edition, vol.VI p.130.

## NACHT UND TRÄUME Night and Dreams

**Matthäus von Collin** (?) 1822

B major  D827  Peters II p.97  GA XX no.470  NSA IV vol.2 pp.184, 267

You sink down, holy night, and dreams too float down, like moonlight through space, into the silent hearts of men.
    With delight they listen, crying out when day wakes: Come back, holy night! Sweet dreams, come back, come back again!

The autograph is missing, and the date of the song cannot be precisely determined. However, it must have been written before June 1823, for Spaun reported hearing the song sung at St Florian before then (*Docs.* no.364). It probably belongs, like *Wehmut* and *Der Zwerg*, also by Collin, to the winter of 1822–3. Schubert must have set the poem from manuscript, for it was not published until 1827.

    The song was published as op.43 no.2 in July 1825 by A.W. Pennauer, with the text mistakenly attributed to Schiller; this can only have been due to the carelessness of the publisher. A slightly different version is preserved in a copy belonging to the Spaun family and marked 'Langsam, Sempre legato'. Both versions are published in the *Neue Ausgabe*.

    The discovery of the unconscious, and the preoccupation with night, with mystery and with dreams to which it led, is here celebrated in the most Romantic song Schubert wrote. Here is the musical equivalent of the gibbous moons and moon-haunted landscapes which permeated the imagination of Samuel Palmer and Caspar Friedrich, the first deeply felt expression in music of that sense of mystery and the infinite which *heilige Nacht* conjured up in the breast of every Romantic.

    The structure of the song depends upon the relationship between the tonic in the outer sections and the flattened sixth, G major, for the beginning of the second verse. The postlude rests upon another favourite Schubert tonal symbol of mystery and transcendence. The long, slow legato line makes cruel demands on the singer, especially since the only dynamic marking is *pp*. Schubert's original marking, *Langsam*, is more practicable than *Sehr langsam*, and however slowly the song is sung, the pulse should still be discernible.

Capell, 208–9; Fischer-Dieskau, 219–20

**NÄCHTENS KLANG DIE SÜSSE LAUTE** see DON GAYSEROS II

**NACHTGESANG** Song of Night
**Johann Wolfgang von Goethe**                                    30 November 1814
A flat major  D119  Peters VI p.56  GA XX no.32  NSA IV vol.7 p.55

O____! gib  vom wei - chen Pfüh - le,  träu - mend, ein  halb____ Ge - hör.

O lend from your soft pillow, dreaming, half an ear! Sleep to the music of my lute: what more can you desire?

 As I pluck the strings, the host of stars blesses eternal longings. Sleep, sleep! What more can you desire?

 These eternal longings lift me far above the turmoil of the world. Sleep, sleep! What more can you desire?

 You detach me from the turmoil of the world only too well, banishing me by this coolness. Sleep, sleep! What more can you desire?

 You banish me with this coolness; give ear only in your dream. Ah, sleep on your soft pillow! What more can you desire?

The poem, first published in the *Musenalmanach* for 1804, is a good example of Goethe's habit of fitting new words to old tunes. In this case the model was Reichardt's setting of the Italian folksong *Tu sei quel dolce fuoco*. Goethe's parody was then in its turn set by Zelter, and the catchy last line invited imitation by later poets. There are five verses, of which the Peters edition prints only the first three.

 The original autograph was divided into two sections, but both parts are now missing. The fair copy made for Goethe in 1816 is now in the Paris Conservatoire. The song was written in A flat major. But when it came to be published in 1850 (*Nachlass*, book 47 no.4) it was transposed to G major and given a spurious introduction and postlude. The Peters edition follows this first publication. The *Gesamtausgabe* gives the song as Schubert wrote it.

 The mood of contemplative detachment is achieved in part by the broad flowing melody, ending *sehnsuchtvoll* on the mediant, and partly by the separation of the tune, which does not fall below A, from the accompaniment which for the most part remains below C. The key to this mood seems to be the third verse: 'These eternal longings lift me far above the turmoil of the world'. The effect is much closer to the poem than, for instance, Zelter's tuneful and attractive setting. Diabelli's introduction and postlude tend to prettify the song.

Capell, 86; Einstein, 105

## NACHTGESANG Song of Night

**Ludwig Kosegarten**                                          19 October 1815

E flat major D314 Peters VII p.88 GA XX no.161

Deep peace descends upon the world. Brown mists veil wood and field. Sad, pale and tired, all living things nod off to sleep, and ineffable peace is wafted round all being.

Wakeful sorrow, leave me a little while; golden slumber, fold me in your wings. Dry my tears with the hem of your veil, and cheat my longing, friend, with your fairest dream!

Blue distance high above me raised, sacred stars in your lofty majesty, tell me, you silent ones: is it more peaceful with you than in this mutinous kingdom of vanities?

The poem, written in 1787, has three verses, but the Peters edition prints only two. The autograph, now in the LC, Washington DC, is a first draft dated 19 October 1815. There is a fair copy in the Houghton Library at Harvard University and a dated copy in the Witteczek–Spaun collection (Vienna, GdM). The song was first published in 1887, in vol. VII of the Peters edition.

*Nachtgesang* is a solemn hymn to holy night, entirely homophonic and traditional in idiom, but by no means lacking in romantic feeling, as is evidenced by the unexpected shift to D flat in bar 14 and the diminished fourths in bars 9–11. The intensity is not sustained, however, in the closing bars and the postlude.

Capell, 95; Fischer-Dieskau, 57

## NACHTHYMNE Hymn to the Night

**Novalis**                                                   January 1820

D major D687 Not in Peters GA XX no.372

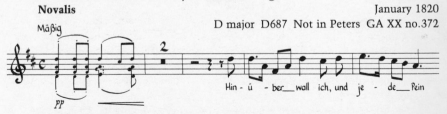

I float away, and all pain becomes a stab of delight. In a little while I am free, lying enraptured in the bosom of love.

Eternal life surges powerfully through me. I look down upon you from above; your radiance fades on yonder hill; a cool shadow crowns it.

O draw me in, beloved, with your power, that I may fall asleep and love.

I feel the rejuvenating current of death, my blood is changed to fragrant air.

By day I live in faith and courage; and at night I die in the holy fire.

The poem was written in 1797 and prefaced with a prose poem in praise of night, which Schubert omits. The title is *Hymne an die Nacht*.

The autograph, entitled *Nachthymne* and dated January 1820, is in Vienna (GdM). There is no tempo indication. A dated copy in the Witteczek–Spaun collection (GdM) has the indication *Mässig*. The song was published by J. P. Gotthard in 1872 as no.4 of 'Forty Songs'. In this edition it was transposed to C major, and the direction *Mässig* was added.

Like the first *Hymne* of Novalis, *Nachthymne* is an extended composition in sections, aiming at cumulative effect. The setting of the first verse has an arresting simplicity and sweetness, floating timelessly between tonic and dominant as though to suggest the suspension of time. The repeated semiquaver chords and the chromatically descending tonality convey the presence of death in the middle section. The final transfiguration, however, comes almost as an anticlimax, for the triplet figures in the pianist's right hand suggest the serenity of *Abendbilder* rather than 'the holy fire'. Schubert responds to the sweetness to Novalis's mysticism, but he misses the visionary fierceness and ecstasy.

Capell, 159–60; Fischer-Dieskau, 132

## NACHTSTÜCK Nocturne

**Johann Mayrhofer**                                                   October 1819

C minor/major  D672  Peters II p.82  GA XX no.368  NSA IV vol.2 pp.125, 225

When the mist creeps over the mountains and Luna battles against the clouds, the old man takes up his harp and steps towards the wood, singing softly:
   'Holy Night, soon it will be accomplished. Soon I shall sleep the long sleep which frees from all affliction.'
   Then the green trees rustle. The trembling blades of grass whisper: 'Sleep well, good old man. We will cover your resting-place.' And many a bird sings sweetly: 'Oh, let him rest in his grassy tomb!'
   The old man listens, and keeps silent. Death has beckoned to him.

Schubert's first draft, in C sharp minor/major, dated October 1819, is in Vienna (GdM). It differs in some details from the printed version. The fair copy made for the printer is missing. Presumably it was in C minor/major and represented the composer's final intentions. The *Neue Ausgabe* prints both versions, the *Gesamtausgabe* only that in C sharp. The song was published as op.36 no.2 by Cappi in February 1825 and dedicated by Schubert to Katharina von Lászny, née Buchweiser, the opera singer.

Mayrhofer's short poem is transformed into an extended tone poem with a fluency and assurance that are new. The words of the old man are repeated unchanged. The repetitions here and elsewhere are made to serve the music, which reflects contrasted aspects of Schubert's ballad style. The introductory bars are a wonderful nocturne, polyphonic in style, like the introduction to a Mozart string quartet, yet embodying one of Schubert's own characteristic motifs, the descending chromatic line from C to G in the pianist's left hand, which identifies the song as a 'welcome death' piece. There follows an extended arioso to a harplike accompaniment, strongly reminiscent of *Dem Unendlichen*, for the old man's greeting to the night. The final section combines a piece of Schubertian scene-painting with a tonal descent from E flat through D flat to C major, as death slowly takes the old man to itself. The marking at bar 18 for the pianist is *mit gehobener Dämpfung* ('with the dampers lifted'). Schubert's pedal markings are rare, and this one suggests that the sustaining pedal was reserved for the effect of a blended, slightly blurred tone.

The link with *Dem Unendlichen*, no less than the music itself, shows clearly enough the concept of death as a triumphant flight into eternity, as a kind of cosmic release, which was later to find expression in the song cycles, and in songs like *Der Sieg* and *Auflösung*.

Capell, 161; Einstein, 191; Fischer-Dieskau, 205

## NACHTVIOLEN Dame's Violets

**Johann Mayrhofer** April 1822

Langsam C major D752 Peters VII p.60 GA XX no.403

Nacht - vi - o - len, Nacht - vi - o - len!

Dame's violets, dark, soulful eyes, how blessed it is to immerse myself in your velvety blue!

Green leaves strive cheerfully to deck you out brightly, but stern and silent you look out upon the mild spring air.

You have pierced my faithful heart with your lofty glances of melancholy; and now in silent nights our sacred union flowers.

Schubert cut three of the poem's fifteen lines and reduced its four verses to three. In bar 21 the correct reading is 'hellen', not 'helfen', as in Peters. The autograph, undated, is on two separate sheets: the first, containing the first 25 bars, is in the Udbye collection in Oslo; the second, with the remaining bars, is in Vienna (ÖNB). A copy in the Witteczek–Spaun collection (Vienna, GdM) is dated April 1822. The song was published in 1872 by J.P. Gotthard as no.20 of 'Forty Songs', in the key of A flat. A note on the copy in the Witteczek–Spaun collection indicates that this was the original key, but no manuscript in that key has survived.

A 'masterpiece of mysterious intimacy', says Einstein, and certainly there is something magical about Schubert's ability to invest a simple harmonic sequence with overtones of yearning tenderness, and to clothe the syllables of the word *Nachtviolen* with music that sounds so inevitable. But his most potent magic is reserved for the third verse. It is possible to find the sweetness of the opening theme a little cloying, but when at the words 'und nun blüht in stummen Nächten' it is combined with a counter-melody in the voice which moves in contrary motion, all such reservations vanish.

Capell, 177; Einstein, 252–3; Fischer-Dieskau, 149–50; Porter, 123–4

## NÄHE DES GELIEBTEN Nearness of the Beloved

**Johann Wolfgang von Goethe** 27 February 1815

G flat major D162 Peters I p.243 GA XX no.49 NSA IV vol.1 p.40

Ich den - ke dein, wenn mir der Son - ne Schimmer

cresc.

When the shimmer of the sun gleams from the sea, I think of you; when the glimmer of the moon is reflected in the streams, I think of you.

When the dust rises along the distant road, I see you; in the dead of night, when the traveller trembles on the narrow bridge.

When the waves surge with a dull roar, I hear you; often I go into the silent grove and listen, when all is still.

However far away you may be, I am beside you, and you are near me! The sun sets; soon the stars will shine forth for me. If only you were here!

The history of the poem illustrates very vividly the close relationship between poetry and song in the eighteenth century. It is based on some verses by Friederike Brun (née Münter), which Goethe heard sung at a party in 1796 in a setting by Zelter. He was much taken with the tune, and decided to write some verses of his own to fit it, based on the same idea and the same metrical pattern. These were published in Schiller's *Musenalmanach* for that year. In its turn Goethe's verses became the model for many similar efforts.

There are two drafts. The first version (Berlin, SPK) is in 6/8 time. It has been crossed out and the words *Gilt nicht* ('Won't do') written in the margin. The second autograph, dated like the first 27 February 1815, is in private possession, and is written in 12/8 time. The fair copy, made for Goethe in 1816, is in Berlin (DS). The song was published as op.5 no.2 in July 1821 by Cappi and Diabelli on commission and dedicated by Schubert to Anton Salieri. Both versions are published in the *Gesamtausgabe* and the *Neue Ausgabe*.

*Nähe des Geliebten* is the first strophic song of Schubert's that presents itself as an unassailable masterpiece. It divides into two perfectly balanced halves, the first like a cry of joy, which falls an octave from the top G flat; the second half too falls an octave, but more introspectively, as though reflecting upon the happiness of love. This perfection of form and expression was not achieved without trouble, as a comparison between the two versions shows. The notational change emphasises the broad sweep of the melody; in the first version the singer holds the D flat on to the end of the song, but in the second the drop to the tonic balances the end of the first phrase.

Above all it is the complete integration of piano and voice which strikes the listener as new. The entry of the voice is beautifully prepared by the mounting tension of the introductory bars. How much the song would lose without the off-key beginning which climbs chromatically towards the tonic! The brief glimpse of the relative minor in the second half adds reassurance to the final cadence, and the tonal stability of the postlude anchors the song in the tonic before the upward climb starts again. The song is as great an achievement, in its way, as *Gretchen*.

Capell, 100–1; Einstein, 109; Fischer-Dieskau, 41–2

## NAMENSTAGLIED Name-day Song

**Albert Stadler**                                                                      March 1820

A major D695 Not in Peters GA XX no.587

Father, grant me this hour, and listen to a song from my lips. I thank you for granting my request to sing today, for you have generously prepared the way yourself.

Oh, let me kiss your hand. See, the tears of gratitude flow! For you have given me more than song: a fine life, and I thank you with childlike joy for life's happiness.

Heaven bless the man we revere. Sun of happiness, shine upon him. May his cup of joy overflow. Let a garland of glorious flowers be offered him.

With moist eyes I pray that God may ever preserve your garlanded head. You must receive another decoration too; this one is blue and gold, and speaks for everyone: Forget me not!

In 1858 Stadler wrote (*Memoirs*, p.149): 'In 1820, at my written request, Schubert was good enough to set to music a poem for Fräulein Josefine von Koller, in honour of her father's name day on 19 March, which she sang with as much feeling as had gone into its composition.' The autograph, untitled, is in London (BL). Schubert wrote out the second verse at the bottom and added a note: 'Stadler is to copy out the voice-part and add this for the repeat.' The song was first published in the *Gesamtausgabe* in 1895.

Schubert had met Josefine von Koller, a talented amateur musician, and her family during his stay in Steyr in the summer of 1819, and treasured happy memories of their music-making together. The song is tuneful and workmanlike rather than distinguished, but characteristic enough to immortalise Stadler's pedestrian verses.

## NATURGENUSS Enjoyment of Nature
**Friedrich von Matthisson**                                      (?) May 1815
B flat major  D188  Peters VII p.86  GA XX no.64

In the glow of evening the brook flows through the purple-bright meadows. The poplar, turning green, gently whispers as it waves above them.

The spirit of the Lord breathes in the spring breeze. Look! Near and far nature rising from the dead; young things in profusion, a sea of beauty, and joyous rapture everywhere!

I look close and I look away, and my thoughts soar higher and higher. Splendour, and gold, and glory are only the tinsel which decks out the shrine of nature!

Whoever understands your love-music is surrounded by intimations of heaven; pressed close to the heart of mother nature, he will be charmed away to heaven itself!

The autograph, dated May 1815, has been split up. Most of it is in Vienna (SB), but the last bar and the last three verses are on another sheet, in private hands. Schubert also set the text as a male-voice quartet (D422). There is a copy in the Witteczek–Spaun collection (Vienna, GdM) dated May 1816, but that may be a mistake. The song first appeared in vol. VII of the Peters edition in 1887. For a discussion of its date see van Hoorickx. The best of the purely strophic settings of Matthisson, this delightful song matches the simple piety of the verses.

R. van Hoorickx, 'Thematic catalogue of Schubert's works: new additions, corrections and notes', *Revue belge de musicologie*, XXVIII–XXX, 1974–6, p.156

## NIMMER TRAG' ICH LÄNGER see KLAGE

## NON T'ACCOSTARE ALL'URNA see VIER CANZONEN no.1

## NORMANS GESANG Norman's Song
**Sir Walter Scott trans. Adam Storck**                           April 1825
C minor  D846  Peters II p.99  GA XX no.473

Die Nacht bricht bald her-ein, dann leg ich mich zur Ruh,

The song comes from canto III of Scott's narrative poem *The Lady of the Lake*. Norman, heir of Armandave, has to leave his new bride to answer the clansmen's summons to battle. As he rides across country he 'bursts into voluntary song':

> The heath this day must be my bed
> The bracken curtain for my head,
> My lullaby the warder's tread,
> Far, far from love, and thee, Mary.
>
> Tomorrow eve, more stilly laid
> My couch may be my bloody plaid,
> My vesper song thy wail, sweet maid!
> It will not waken me, Mary!
>
> I may not, dare not, fancy now
> The grief that clouds thy lovely brow,
> I dare not think upon thy vow
> And all it promised me, Mary.
>
> No fond regret must Norman know:
> When bursts Clan Alpine on the foe,
> His heart must be like bended bow,
> His foot like arrow free, Mary.
>
> A time will come with feeling fraught,
> For if I fall in battle fought,
> Thy hapless lover's dying thought
> Shall be a thought on thee, Mary.
>
> And if returned from conquered foes,
> How blithely will the evening close,
> How sweet the linnet sing repose
> To my young bride and me, Mary!

Schubert used the translation published in 1819, which changes Scott's iambic tetrameters into galloping hexameters. Unlike the other songs from this work, this one cannot be sung to the English words. The autograph is missing, and the date is not quite certain. The catalogue of the Witteczek–Spaun collection (Vienna, GdM) gives 4 April 1825, but the figure 4 may be a reference to the month. All the solo songs from Scott's poem were written before the summer of 1825 (*Docs.* no.574), and *Normans Gesang* was probably one of the first to be written. The song was published as op.52 no.5 in April 1826 by Artaria and dedicated by Schubert to Sophie, Countess Weissenwolf.

The objectivity of Scott's historical romanticism proved a strong stimulus for Schubert, and led him to adopt powerful rhythms which unify the songs, even though some of the intellectual content may be lost. So here it is the insistent rhythm of the galloping horse which dominates the song, even to the extent of overshadowing Norman's train of thought, though it is true that the modulation to C major for the last verse follows the sense nicely.

Schubert's double strophe, the first in C minor and the sequel in the dominant G major, enables him to avoid a sense of monotony. The tempo indication is *Geschwind*. But a letter of Anton Ottenwalt to Spaun (*Docs.* no.574) suggests that Schubert and Vogl did not always perform it that way. He writes: 'Schubert himself regards this as the best of the Scott songs. Vogl himself interprets it heavily (a syllable, often a word, to each note) but splendidly.'

Capell, 211; Fischer-Dieskau, 221

# NUR WER DIE LIEBE KENNT Only he who knows love
**Zacharias Werner**                                                      (?) 1817

A flat major  D2 513A  Not in Peters  Not in GA

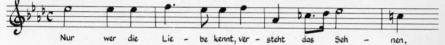

Only the lover understands the longing ever to hold fast to the beloved, and drain
the draught of life from his loving glance.
 Only he knows the aching happiness of longing to dissolve into a flood of tears,
and find fulfilment in the sea of love.

The poem has thirteen lines, but Schubert's unfinished sketch breaks off after six. The
author was identified by Dietrich Berke. The verses were published in the periodical *Die
Harfe* in 1815, under the title *Impromptu: in Tharants Ruinen geschrieben*. They are clearly
modelled on Goethe's famous lyric *Nur wer die Sehnsucht kennt*; such 'parodies' were
a characteristic of the age, and did not imply any satirical intent.
 Schubert's autograph (Vienna, SB) is undated. The first twelve bars are complete,
and the melody is sketched for eleven more bars. The whole is crossed out. The date of
this fragment is highly conjectural. A performing version has been completed and published
by Reinhard van Hoorickx (*Mitteilungen des Steirischen Tonkünstlerbundes*, July 1974).

# NUR WER DIE SEHNSUCHT KENNT Only he who
knows what longing is (1)
**Johann Wolfgang von Goethe**                              18 October 1815

A flat major  D310  Not in Peters  GA XX no.158(a) and (b)

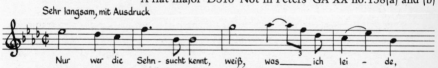

Only he who knows what longing is knows what I suffer. Alone, cut off from every
joy, I search the sky in that direction. Ah, he who loves and knows me is far away.
 My head swims, my vitals burn. Only he who knows what longing is knows
what I suffer.

See MIGNON'S SONGS. The famous lyric expresses not only Goethe's own longing for
Italy, but that vague and indefinable search for a world better and nobler than the real
one which gave the Romantic movement its characteristic mode of expression. It was
written in June 1785. In the final version of *Wilhelm Meister* it appears at the end of book 4,
chapter 11, where it is sung as 'an irregular duet' by Mignon and the Harper; in an earlier
version, however, it is sung as a solo by Mignon. In neither case is its connection with
the story very close or clear. Neither Mignon nor the Harper has a lover far away. The
song is best regarded as an expression of that generalised feeling of nostalgia which belonged
both to the characters in the story and to the age in which they lived.
 The song presents special difficulties for the composer. It was written originally
as one stanza, but the sense suggests two, or even three, sections. Reichardt's melody,
which was published in the 1795 edition of *Wilhelm Meister*, is a strophic setting with
two verses. Beethoven made four attempts to set the song, three strophic and one through-
composed, without achieving a definitive setting, and some fifty other composers have
met a similar lack of success. Only Tchaikovsky's setting (op.6 no.6, *None but the lonely
heart*) is really widely known and loved.

Schubert set the poem six times, once as a duet, once as a quintet for male voices, and four times as a solo song. His titles vary, sometimes *Mignon* or *Mignons Gesang* or *Die Sehnsucht*, sometimes *Lied der Mignon*. For the sake of consistency the various solo versions are here listed under the first line.

There are two versions of this first setting, the first in A flat major and the second in F. Both autographs survive, dated 18 October 1815, in private hands. The fair copy made for Goethe in 1816 is in the Paris Conservatoire. The tessitura in the second version is more manageable, but the other changes are of questionable value. Both versions were published for the first time in the *Gesamtausgabe* in 1895.

Schubert's solution for the basic problem, how to reconcile simplicity of form with the expressive demands of 'Es schwindet mir, es brennt mein Eingeweide', is to treat the line as a kind of emotional storm which interrupts the smooth flow of the lyric. This first version has a dignity and restraint which the later ones lack, and the contrast between the outer sections and the inner is not too marked.

## NUR WER DIE SEHNSUCHT KENNT (2)
**Johann Wolfgang von Goethe**  1816

D minor D359 Not in Peters GA XX no.260

For translation, see the preceding entry. The autograph of this second setting is missing, and it cannot be precisely dated. There is a copy in the Witteczek–Spaun collection (Vienna, GdM), in the catalogue of which it is dated 1816. The song was first published in 1872 as no.13 of 'Forty Songs' by J.P. Gotthard.

This setting is in 6/8 time, and in a minor key. The staccato chords at bar 17 express the singer's growing agitation and make a more successful transition to the stormy middle section. But on the whole this is the least memorable of Schubert's settings.

## NUR WER DIE SEHNSUCHT KENNT (3)
**Johann Wolfgang von Goethe**  September 1816

A minor D481 Not in Peters GA XX no.259

For translation, see *Nur wer die Sehnsucht kennt (1)*. The autograph, entitled *Sehnsucht. Mignon* and dated September 1816, is in the Paris Conservatoire. There is no tempo indication. There is a copy in the Witteczek–Spaun collection (Vienna, GdM), headed 'Mignons Gesang aus Wilhelm Meister'. The autograph version ends in A minor, but the copy ends in A major, and this is followed by the *Gesamtausgabe* in which the song first appeared in 1895.

This minor key version in 2/4 time preserves the unity of mood. A sense of agitation is achieved for the fifth line without interrupting the repeated semiquavers chords in the pianist's right hand, and the extended postlude adds an attractive comment of its own to the melody.

## NUR WER DIE SEHNSUCHT KENNT (4)

**Johann Wolfgang von Goethe**                                              January 1826

A minor D877 no.4 Peters I p.214 GA XX no.491

For translation, see *Nur wer die Sehnsucht kennt* (1). Schubert's op.62, 'Songs from *Wilhelm Meister* by Goethe', was advertised by Diabelli in March 1826. It included two settings of *Nur wer die Sehnsucht kennt*, one as a duet for soprano and baritone, and this one for solo voice. The opus was dedicated to Princess Mathilde zu Schwarzenberg. Two other Mignon sings made up the opus.

The autograph of the complete opus is on six sheets, the first five of which (in Dresden, SLB) include the first three numbers. The first sheet is dated January 1826. The last sheet, containing the fourth song, is in Vienna (SB). However, expert opinion supports the view that all six sheets originally belonged to one manuscript, which has been divided. While the date of the song is to a certain extent conjectural, it seems likely that Schubert (or his publisher) wanted a solo version of the text to complete the opus, and that Schubert, not altogether satisfied with any of his early attempts, wrote another.

Schubert used a revised version of an old song, *Ins stille Land* (D403), written ten years earlier. This is a marvellously evocative tune which matches the innocence and pathos of Mignon's situation very well. This is the best of the solo settings, and probably the best-known of all, Tchaikovsky's alone excepted. The variety of mood and expression which Schubert can explore in the space of forty-six bars is astonishing, yet the consistent flow of the melody can still, in a sympathetic performance, be preserved.

## NUR WER DIE SEHNSUCHT KENNT (5)

**Johann Wolfgang von Goethe**                                              January 1826

B minor D877 no.1 Not in Peters GA XX no.488

For translation, see *Nur wer die Sehnsucht kennt* (1). This, the only one of Schubert's six settings which follows the scene in Goethe's novel in setting the text as a duet between Mignon and the Harper, is arguably the finest. There is an operatic richness in the writing that distinguishes it from all the earlier versions, and the key is B minor, Schubert's key of loneliness and alienation. The melodic flow is unbroken, the texture seamless, yet the music responds to every nuance in the words. If the song were more readily available it would become a favourite for duettists.

Capell, 219–20; Einstein, 306–7; Stein, 78–9

# O QUELL, WAS STRÖMST DU RASCH UND WILD
Fountain, why do you flow so fast?

**Ernst Schulze**                                                    (?) March 1826

G major D874 Not in Peters Not in GA

*The Flower:* Fountain, why do you flow so fast and so wild, churning up the silver sand and, veiled by light foam, overflowing on to the green bank? Fountain, ripple smooth and bright so that I, radiant with delicate dewdrops, may see my trembling image reflected in you.

*The Fountain:* Flower, can I be calm when your image is mirrored in me, and the strange torments of love now hold me back, now lend me wings? So I soar uncertainly, and try, with languish and longing, to embrace your tender cup.

*The Flower:* Fountain, I am much too far away, you can never rise to my height; but my starry blossom shall tremble amiably on your serene surface. So ripple on peacefully! It is sweet to bear without complaining the chaste image of your beloved upon your breast.

*The Fountain:* Flower, counsel and comfort are easy, but it is difficult to be ardent without hope; even if my kisses do not reach you I shall still have to go on trying. Let but one petal fall into my turbulent depths, then will I run quietly by.

Schulze's symbolic dialogue between Love and Life comes from his *Poetisches Tagebuch* 'Verse Journal' and is headed 'Am 8sten Januar 1814. Schubert's sketch, unfinished and untitled, is written on the last sheet of a manuscript which contains another Schulze song, *Tiefes Leid*. Witteczek dates these two songs January 1826, but this may be a misunderstanding of the title Schubert gives to the latter song (*Im Jänner 1817 Schulze*). The order of the song on the autographs suggests that they belong rather to March 1826 (see van Hoorickx).

The sketch contains a four-bar introduction and fourteen bars of melody, with scanty indications of the accompaniment. It has been completed for performance purposes and privately printed by Reinhard van Hoorickx (1959) under the title *Die Blume und der Quell*. It has an attractive on-running accompaniment, like a 'brook song', but Schubert wrote only one verse, so it is not clear how he would have dealt with the dialogue.

> R. van Hoorickx, 'Schubert songs and song fragments not included in the collected edition', *MR*, XXXVIII, 1977, p.287

## OREST AUF TAURIS Orestes on Tauris

**Johann Mayrhofer**                                                    March 1817

C minor D548 Peters V p.40 GA XX no.382

Is this Tauris? Where Pythius promised to allay the anger of the Furies? Alas, the snake-haired sisters pursue me here from Greece! Rough island, you announce no blessings: the golden fruit of Ceres does not sprout here. No vines bloom; the singers of the air avoid this bay, as the ships do.

Art does not pile these stones into buildings; the poverty of the Scythians allows them only tents; beneath unbending crags and untamed forests life is lonely and full of terrors. 'But here', so the holy decree was made known to the suppliant, 'Diana the huntress shall lift the curse on me and my ancestors.'

Mayrhofer's title is *Der landende Orest* ('Orestes Disembarking'). To escape the Furies, Orestes was ordered by the priestess at Delphi to sail through the Black Sea to Tauris and bring back the image of Artemis from the temple.

The autograph, formerly in private possession, now in the ÖNB, Vienna. It is headed as above and dated March 1817. (The date given in the catalogue of the Witteczek–Spaun collection (Vienna, GdM) – September 1820 – is an error, though it may well be that Schubert made a fair copy at that time.) The song was published in book 11 of the *Nachlass* in 1831. The accompaniment for the phrase beginning at bar 43 is here set an octave higher than in the autograph.

Schubert's two Orestes songs are splendid fragments from an unwritten opera on the theme. In the space of fifty-four bars *Orest auf Tauris* ranges widely over the hero's emotions, and over the keys. Starting in E flat and ending in D major, the song occupies the middle ground between recitative and aria, moving with remarkable rhythmic and tonal freedom, yet never losing the tone of dignity and humanity. Doubtless the poem reminded Schubert of his early enthusiasm for Vogl's portrayal of the role. It strengthens one's conviction that he might have written a great *opera seria*.

Capell, 162; Fischer-Dieskau, 199

## ORPHEUS, ALS ER IN DIE HÖLLE GING see LIED DES ORPHEUS

## OSSIAN SONGS

Ossian is the latinised form of Oisin, a legendary Gaelic warrior and bard. He was the son of Finn (or Fingal), a King Arthur-like figure in Irish mythology supposed to belong to the third century AD. In 1760 James Macpherson, a young Highland schoolmaster with literary ambitions, published *Fragments of Ancient Poetry collected in the Highlands of Scotland and translated from the Gaelic or Erse Language*, which purported to be based on the authentic writings of Ossian. These made a literary sensation and, encouraged by their success, Macpherson soon produced two long prose narratives, *Fingal* (1762) and *Temora* (1763), as further examples of the long-lost Ossianic literature. These works were widely denounced as forgeries, especially by that enemy of cant Samuel Johnson. How far Macpherson drew upon an existing oral tradition, and how far he simply adapted Irish myths to his own purposes, has never been established.

In an age which was in the process of rediscovering the appeal of the remote and primitive, however, these epic tales with their misty background and Gothic vocabulary made an instant appeal. They were especially popular in Germany, where Herder welcomed them with open arms. Between 1760 and 1770 at least ten German translations of Ossian appeared, and for fifty years and more the Ossianic literature set a fashion of irresistible appeal to young and romantically minded artists. Its influence can be seen not only in Schubert's settings of Ossian but in the ballads of his contemporaries, like Josef Kenner and Johann Mayrhofer (not to mention greater names like Goethe and Schiller), all of them full of ruined castles on storm-girt cliffs, mossy banks and cloudy seas.

For most of the songs Schubert used a translation by Edmund von Harold published in Mannheim in 1782. His Ossian songs date mostly from 1815. The last was written in February 1817. They were published in 1830 in the first five books of the *Nachlass*.

For the individual entries, see under the following titles: .

*Lodas Gespenst* D150
*Kolmas Klage* D217
*Ossians Lied nach dem Falle Nathos* D278
*Das Mädchen von Inistore* D281
*Cronnan* D282
*Shilrik und Vinvela* D293
*Lorma* D327, 376
*Der Tod Oscars* D375
*Die Nacht* D534

It is noteworthy that Schubert's 'Ossian style' can be sharply differentiated from the heroic style of his settings of Mayrhofer's classical poems. If one compares *Das Mädchen von Inistore* with *Iphigenia*, or *Kolmas Klage* with *Der entsühnte Orest*, for instance, it can easily be seen how much nearer the former are to the folksong and the Romantic ballad, how much more operatic are the latter.

## OSSIANS LIED NACH DEM FALLE NATHOS Ossian's Song after the Death of Nathos

**James Macpherson (Ossian)**                    1815 (? September)

E major  D278  Peters IV p.200  GA XX no.147

The text comes from *Dar-Thula*. In the original the passage runs:

I touched the harp before the king; the sound was mournful and low. 'Bend forward from your clouds,' I said, 'ghosts of my fathers, bend. Lay by the red terror of your course. Receive the falling chief; whether he comes from a distant land, or rises from the rolling sea. Let his robe of mist be near; his spear that is formed of a cloud. Place an half-extinguished meteor by his side, in the form of the hero's sword. And oh, let his countenance be lovely, that his friends may delight in his presence. Bend from your clouds,' I said, 'ghosts of my fathers, bend!'
Such was my song, in Selma, to the lightly-trembling harp.

Schubert used the translation by Edmund von Harold. His title is a little misleading, since in Macpherson's version the song precedes the death of the hero. Fingal hears the ominous sound of the harp in the mountain wind, mournful and low, and says, 'I hear the sound of death on the harp. Ossian, touch the trembling string.'

The first draft (Vienna, SB) breaks off after twenty-nine bars. The published versions derive from a slightly different second version preserved in the Stadler and Ebner collections (Lund, UB). The first draft is quoted in the *Revisionsbericht* volume of the *Gesamtausgabe*. The song was published in book 4 of the *Nachlass* in July 1830.

Like *Das Mädchen von Inistore*, *Ossians Lied* is a song rather than a ballad, a simple hymnlike expression of grief. In contrast with the strictly homophonic outer sections, the middle section has converging chromatic sequences suggesting emotional disturbance.

**PAUSE** see DIE SCHÖNE MÜLLERIN no.12

## PAX VOBISCUM Peace be with you

**Franz von Schober**                                                    April 1817

Mit heiliger Rührung                    F major D551 Peters II p.213 GA XX no.315

„Der Frie - de sei mit euch!" das war dein Abschieds - se - gen.

'Peace be with you!' – that was your parting blessing. And so, surrounded by the
prayers of the faithful, kindled by the light of the victorious godhead, you soared
to the eternal homeland. And peace entered their true hearts, and rewarded them
in their greatest anguish, and strengthened them in their martyrs' death. I believe
in you, Almighty God!

Peace be with you! So sweetly smiles the first flower of spring when, decked
with charms, it unfurls in the sanctuary of creation. Who could remain untouched
by peace when earth and sky are renewed, and life is reborn after the death of winter?
In you I hope, all-powerful God!

Peace be with you! you cry every evening in the rosy glow of sunset, when
all creatures go happy to rest after the hot travail of the day; and mountain, valley,
river, and ocean wave, veiled by soft mists, are beautiful in the wild glow. I love
you, dear God!

In the collected edition of Schober's poems verses 2 and 3 are reversed. All three verses
are printed in the published versions of the song, though Schubert wrote out only the first
on his autograph, and put no repeat marks at the end. The autograph (Vienna, SB) is dated
April 1817. There is no introductory chord and the marking is *Ruhig*. The song was
published in 1831 in book 10 of the *Nachlass* (*Geistliche Lieder* no.6). The marking is
*Mit heiliger Rührung* ('With sacred feeling').

At the request of Schubert's family, Schober wrote new words to the tune for
performance at Schubert's funeral on 21 November 1828. On this occasion the song was
arranged for choir and wind instruments, and conducted, by Johann Baptist Gänsbacher
(see *Docs*. App. no.4 p.826). The square phrases and block harmonies suggest conventional
piety rather than genuine feeling. It seems ironical that this undistinguished song was
the only one heard at Schubert's funeral.

## PENSA, CHE QUESTO ISTANTE Remember that this fateful moment

**Pietro Metastasio**                                                September 1813

D major D76 Peters VI p.180 GA XX no.571 NSA IV vol.6 pp.76, 184

Andante maestoso

Pen - sa che que - sto i - stan-te

Remember that this fateful moment decides whether today Alcide is reborn for a
future time.

Remember that you are a man, a son of Jove, and that your reward will depend,
not on counsel, but on your own merit.

The text, presumably chosen by Salieri, is that of Fronimo's aria from the first scene of
*Alcide al bivio* ('Hercules at the Crossroads'). The manuscript (Vienna, SB) contains the
first draft of *Pensa*, dated 7 September 1813, a sketch of the cantata (D80) written for

Schubert's father's name day, and the revised version of *Pensa*, dated 13 September 1813. Both versions are headed 'Aria'. The song was published by J. P. Gotthard in 1871 as no.5 of '5 Canti'. The *Neue Ausgabe* prints both versions.

*Pensa* was written as an exercise under Salieri's direction, and shows how quick and versatile was Schubert's sense of style. Here he is, at sixteen, using the long-breathed legato line and the formalised accompaniment typical of Salieri himself and of Salieri's revered Gluck.

### PFLICHT UND LIEBE Duty and Love
**Friedrich Wilhelm Gotter**                                          August 1816

C minor D467 Peters VII p.37 GA XX no.593

Young friend, who always grieves for me, when you sigh you do not sigh alone, unpitied; when your soul is seared by pain my calm expression is feigned. I will not, must not understand the tearful supplication in your eyes; but do not be angry! My duty forbids me to confess what I feel.

Friend, turn your eyes elsewhere. Find your pleasure in nature, which has always smiled on you. Ah, it will make me happy if only it makes you happy. Dear friend, be comforted! See, greeted with songs of joy, the sun rises! Yesterday it sank beclouded; today it appears in full radiance.

Where Schubert found the poem is not known; in August 1816, when his love affair with Therese Grob was drifting to its unhappy end, its relevance to his own situation would have been only too plain. There are six verses, of which Schubert omitted the third and fourth. The remainder are combined in two strophes.

The autograph, in private possession, is dated August 1816. The last bar and the postlude are missing, but the song was completed by Max Friedländer and published by him in vol. VII of the Peters edition in 1885. The minor mode, the tonal sequences, and the 'gait' of the voiceline give the song an emotional affinity with *Luisens Antwort* and with that song's unacknowledged model, Mozart's *Lied der Trennung*; but it is less successful.

### PFLÜGERLIED Ploughman's Song
**Johann Gaudenz von Salis-Seewis**                                    March 1816

C major D392 Not in Peters GA XX no.197

Hard-working and stouthearted we plough the fields, singing as we go. Carefully we part the loose clods, the grave of our seed.

Driving up and down we cut the furrows, our backs always turned to what we have achieved. Dig deep, O plough-share, dig deep! Outside the heat is oppressive, down in the earth it is cool.

There are eight verses, of which only the first two are translated. The first draft, in private possession, has no tempo indication and no postlude. Its present whereabouts are unknown. There is a fair copy, marked 'Mässig', in the Therese Grob song album (see GROB) and a copy in the Witteczek–Spaun collection (Vienna, GdM) dated March 1816. Copies in the Stadler and Ebner collections (Lund, UB) are marked 'Ruhig'. The song first appeared in the *Gesamtausgabe* in 1895. It is a simple strophic setting of no great significance.

## PHIDILE
**Matthias Claudius**                                                    November 1816

G flat major  D500  Not in Peters  GA XX no.279

I was only sixteen summers old, simply an innocent, and knew nothing but our forest, its flowers, grass and herbs.

Then a young stranger came along; I had not asked him to come, and did not know where he came from. He came, and spoke of love.

He had beautiful long hair flowing round his neck; and such a neck as that I had never seen before.

His friendly eyes, as blue and clear as the sky, seemed to be pleading for something; such blue and friendly eyes I had never seen before.

And his face, like milk and blood! I had never seen one like it and what he said was very fine too, except that I could not understand it.

He followed me everywhere, and pressed my hands, and kept saying 'oh' and 'alas', and quickly kissing them.

One day I gave him a friendly look and asked him what he meant; then this handsome young man fell on my neck and wept.

No one had ever done that to me before, but I did not find it unpleasant, and my two eyes sank down to my bosom.

I did not say a single word to suggest that I took it amiss; not one – and he fled away. If only he would come back!

The subtitle adds a touch of drama to the story: 'When she had retired to her room after the wedding'. The poem first appeared in print in 1770 and quickly became popular. Deutsch, in the thematic catalogue, records a tradition that Schubert's mother used often to sing the song in an earlier setting, possibly that of Josef Anton Steffan, but he does not quote any authority. The autograph is missing, but there are two copies in the Witteczek–Spaun collection (Vienna, GdM), one of them dated November 1816. The first publication was in the *Gesamtausgabe* in 1895.

The tune has the simplicity and inevitability of a folksong, and the marking is 'Innocent'. The emotion is restrained, but plainly to be felt, so that it is difficult to avoid speculating about the circumstances in which this charming song was written. It was probably in November 1816 that Schubert assembled a group of songs for Therese Grob, his first love, and about this time too that they parted company.

## PHILOKTET (Philoctetes)
**Johann Mayrhofer**

March 1817

B minor D540 Peters V p.45 GA XX no.307

Da sitz ich oh - ne Bogen und starre in den Sand.

I sit here without my bow, staring into the sand. What did I do to you, Ulysses, to make you take it from me?

The weapon which was the messenger of death to the Trojans, and which provided me with sustenance on this barren isle.

Flocks of birds whirr over my grey head. I reach for my bow – in vain; it has been stolen.

The brown stag leaps out of the thick bushes; I stretch my empty hands up to Nemesis.

O cunning king, fear the vengeful eyes of the goddess! Have mercy – return me my bow.

After Achilles' death, Calchas prophesied that Troy could never be taken except with the magic bow and arrows of Heracles. Odysseus (Ulysses) was therefore despatched to Lemnos to steal them from Philoctetes. The autograph (Vienna, SB) is an incomplete first draft consisting of the first thirty-seven bars and dated March 1817. When Diabelli published the song in book 11 of the *Nachlass* (April 1831) he used a fair copy, which has been lost.

Another fragment from Schubert's unwritten *opera seria* on a classical theme. This one begins off-key, with an arresting little motif which seems to symbolise Philoctetes' anger at the injustice done to him. The bold B minor theme with which the singer begins is a remarkable version of Schubert's favourite tonal image of fate/death, plunging down from B minor to the dominant F sharp major. Lacking the lyrical splendour of *Memnon*, and the dramatic power of the Orestes songs, this one seems to need a full dramatic context to make its proper effect.

Capell, 137

## PILGERWEISE Pilgrim's Song
**Franz von Schober**

April 1823

F sharp minor D789 Peters III p.175 GA XX no.429

Ich bin ein Wal - ler auf_____ der Er - de

I am a pilgrim on the earth, moving silently from house to house; oh, offer me the gifts of love with a friendly gesture!

With open, sympathetic glances, and with a warm clasp of the hand, you can refresh this poor heart, freeing it from long oppression.

But do not think that I shall reward you, or repay you with service in return; I shall only strew blue flowers over your threshold;

and sing a quiet song to my zither, which gasps out a stammering sigh, and which may well sound to you like tinsel dross, like a worthless plaything.

To me it sounds sweet, I cannot do without it, and to every pilgrim it is of worth. But you, of course, you cannot know what makes him happy, who is content with little.

Your pleasure is in luxury, and a thousand diversions are to hand; day after day your treasury of love is increased.

But for me, as I struggle on with my tough pilgrim's staff, one thread after another breaks in the insubstantial fabric of happiness.

So I can only live from moment to moment, on charity. Oh, give it without reproach, for your pleasure, and my happiness.

I am a pilgrim on the earth, moving silently from house to house; oh, offer me the gifts of love with a friendly gesture.

Schober's sentimental verses sound like a piece of special pleading for the right of the artist to live his own life. The autograph (Vienna, SB) is in F sharp minor and is dated April 1823, and there is a dated copy in the Witteczek–Spaun collection (Vienna, GdM). Another copy is in D minor, and when the song came to be published in book 18 of the *Nachlass* (July 1832) it appeared in E minor. Friedländer followed the first edition in the Peters volume, but the *Gesamtausgabe* reverts to the autograph.

The often noted resemblance to Mendelssohn's op.30 no.6, the Song without Words subtitled 'Venetian Gondolier's Song', is almost certainly fortuitous. Schubert's own use of a very similar theme in the same key and movement in the Andantino of his A major Piano Sonata D959 is, however, much more significant. The volcanic eruption which takes place in the middle of that movement suggests that the theme may have had tragic associations for Schubert.

In the central sections the switch to G major and a variation in the piano figuration lightens the mood, but it is not easy to keep the interest alive to the end of this rather sombre song. The truth is that the verses are pedestrian in more senses than one, and there is nothing in them to arouse Schubert's pictorial imagination, whatever relevance they may have had to his condition.

Capell, 185–6; Einstein, 326–7; Fischer-Dieskau, 173

## PROMETHEUS
**Johann Wolfgang von Goethe**                                    October 1819

B flat major  D674  Peters III p.212  GA XX no.370

Cover your heaven, Zeus, with cloudy vapours and, like a boy beheading thistles, practise on oak trees and mountain tops; yet you will have to leave my world standing, and my hut, which you did not build, and my hearth, whose warmth you envy me.

I know of nothing poorer under the sun than you gods! Wretchedly you feed your majesty on the tithes of sacrifice and the breath of prayer, and would famish, if children and beggars were not optimistic fools.

When I was a child and knew nothing, I turned my bewildered eyes to the sun, as if beyond it there were an ear to listen to my complaint, a heart like mine to take pity on distress.

Who helped me against the presumption of the Titans? Who preserved me from death and slavery? Sacred and glowing heart, did you not achieve it all on your own? Yet, in your youthful goodness, did you not swell with false gratitude to the sleeping god up there for your deliverance?

> I honour you? For what? Have you ever relieved the sufferings of the oppressed? Have you ever quenched the tears of the careworn? And have not all-powerful Time and everlasting Fate, to which I and you are subject, forged me into a man?
>
> Did you imagine perhaps that I would hate life, and flee to the desert, because not all my flowery dreams bore fruit?
>
> Here I sit, forming men in my image, a race that shall suffer, weep, enjoy, and be happy, as I am, and that shall take no notice of you, as I do!

In the Napoleonic era the Prometheus myth embodied the hopes and aspirations of an enlightened and revolutionary age. For Goethe, for Beethoven and Schubert, Prometheus is not the tortured hero of Shelley's poem, defiant under senseless tyranny, but the Hero as Artist–Creator (as Carlyle might have put it), confident in the power of his own mind and spirit, who can afford to turn away from the gods with indifference, even contempt.

In 1773 Goethe wrote the first two acts of a Prometheus drama, but he left it unfinished, possibly because the humanist conception of an invincible Prometheus did not leave much room for conflict. The poem was written in the autumn of 1774 as a dramatic monologue intended – so Goethe many years later asserted – to open the third act. But it seems likely that the poem marked, not the continuation of the drama, but its final abandonment; that it was an attempt to salvage at least the creative cell of the drama in permanent form. It is significant that *Ganymed*, a poem which expresses adoration of the gods rather than contempt, also belongs to 1774, an early example of that creative polarity which seems to guide Goethe's development. The poem represents, not Goethe's personal views, but one aspect of his complex attitude towards the problem of man and destiny, expressed in dramatic form.

The song was written for bass voice. The autograph (Vienna, GdM) is dated October 1819, but there is no tempo indication. A copy in the Witteczek–Spaun collection (GdM), however, is marked 'Kräftig'. When the song was published in book 47 of the *Nachlass* (early 1850), the voice line appeared in the treble clef, and with the editorial marking *Allegro*. As usual, the Peters edition follows that version.

The short unison motif with which the song opens, and which symbolises the majestic power of Prometheus (Diabelli's *Allegro* marking is misleading), is Wagnerian in form and scale; so too is the tonal freedom with which Schubert allows the song to develop, and the contrast between the chromaticism and atonality of the middle sections and the bold diatonic C major of the last verse 'Here I sit, forming men in my own image'. In this dramatic scena he has matched Goethe's poem with music of equal power. He has also explored the dramatic limit of the lied, within a few years of its emergence. Even in the arioso sections there are no concessions to 'pure song'; the vocal line is fierce, angular and fragmented. The effect is admittedly episodic, but magnificent.

> Capell, 149–52; Einstein, 192; Fischer-Dieskau, 130–1; G. Mackworth-Young, 'Goethe's "Prometheus" and its settings by Schubert and Wolf', *PRMA*, LXXIX, 1952–3, p.53; A. Robertson, 'The songs', *Symposium*, 165; Stein, 65–6

**PSALM 13** see DER 13. PSALM (entry following DER PILGRIM)

# PUNSCHLIED (IM NORDEN ZU SINGEN) Drinking
Song (to be sung in the north)
**Friedrich von Schiller**                                    18 August 1815
B flat major  D253  Peters VII p.93  GA XX no.110

Auf der Ber - ge frei - en Hö - hen, in  der  Mit - tags son - ne  Schein,

On the free heights of the mountains, in the light of the noontide sun, and by the
power of its hot beams, nature engenders the golden wine.

Sparkling like the son of Phoebus, like a fiery fountain of light, it gushes
bubbling from the barrel, crimson and bright as crystal.

Giving pleasure to all the senses, and pouring the balm of hope and renewed
pleasure in life into every apprehensive heart.

The poem, which dates from 1803, has twelve verses, all printed in the *Gesamtausgabe*.
It is not to be confused with another Schiller poem with the same title, which Schubert
set as a male-voice trio (D277). The first, third and fourth verses, which appear in the
Peters edition, are translated above.

The autograph is now missing, but there are two copies in the Witteczek–Spaun
collection (Vienna, GdM), both dated 18 August 1815 and annotated 'Can also be sung
as a duet without accompaniment'. Both duet parts are written in the top stave. The
*Gesamtausgabe* assumes that the piece was written as a vocal duet, and that the piano
accompaniment is optional. There is nothing in this spirited drinking song, with its simple
harmonic structure and purely supportive accompaniment, to suggest that it was intended
as a solo song.

# QUELL'INNOCENTE FIGLIO The Innocent Son
**Pietro Metastasio**                                            (?) Autumn 1812
F major  D17 no.1  Not in Peters  Not in GA

Quell' in - no - cen - te  fi - glio, do - no del Ciel si___ra - ro

God demands from you your innocent son, most rare gift of heaven, the son so dear
to you. He requires his father, who gave him life, to shed his blood before his own
eyes.

The text comes from the oratorio *Isacco* (1740). Schubert set it several times in the autumn
of 1812 as an exercise for Salieri. This is the only setting for solo voice. The autograph
is in Vienna (SB) and shows many corrections by Salieri. Only the melody line is given.
The song was published by Alfred Orel in *Der junge Schubert* (Vienna, 1940/R1977). A
performing version, with added piano accompaniment, has been published privately by
Reinhard van Hoorickx.

This is perhaps the most interesting of Schubert's early exercises, because of the
strong resemblance to *Der Jüngling am Bache* in movement, key and melodic inflection.
His first setting of this Schiller poem, sometimes regarded as the earliest Schubert song,
belongs to September 1812.

**RAST** see WINTERREISE no.10

**RASTE KRIEGER, KRIEG IST AUS** see ELLENS GESANG I

## RASTLOSE LIEBE Love without Respite
**Johann Wolfgang von Goethe**                                    19 May 1815

E major  D138  Peters I p.222  GA XX no.177  NSA IV vol.1 pp.35, 208

'Gainst snow, 'gainst rain, 'gainst wind, through the boiling mists of the ravines
– on, on! without stop or stay!
    Rather would I battle my way through sorrow than suffer so much joy. This
attraction of one heart to another, ah, in how strange a manner it becomes pain.
    How – shall I escape? Flee further into the forest? All in vain! Love, thou art
the crown of life, happiness without peace.

The poem was written on 6 May 1776 at Ilmenau in the Thuringian Forest, a few months
after Goethe had moved to Weimar and met Charlotte von Stein. Two days before there
had been a heavy snowstorm. The *rastlose Liebe* is certainly his love for Charlotte; the
poem reflects conflicting aspects of this disturbing experience. According to Bauernfeld
(*Memoirs* p.31) the poem made an instant impression on Schubert. Capell goes so far as
to say that he was 'transported into a kind of ecstasy', but the authority for this and similar
statements elsewhere is not clear.

    The autograph in the city archive at Linz is dated 19 May 1815 and marked 'Schnell,
mit Leidenschaft'. The metronome marking is crotchet = 152. There is a fair copy in the
first songbook made for Goethe, now in Berlin (DS). Another autograph, transposed to
D major, is dated May 1821. There are various copies. The song was published by Cappi
and Diabelli as op.5 no.1 in July 1821, dedicated to Anton Salieri. The *Neue Ausgabe*
includes both versions.

    *Rastlose Liebe* was one of the first Schubert songs to win public acclaim. He recorded
in his diary (*Docs.* no.86) that he sang it at a musical party in June 1816, adding that its
great success owed a good deal to Goethe's poem. The lover's impetuosity is splendidly
suggested by the rushing semiquavers, and the third verse builds up to a fine climax. The
more reflective second verse presents a problem – how to change the tone without losing
the song's impetus. Schubert solves this beautifully, by a modulation to G major and by
slowing the pianist's right hand from semiquavers to triplet quavers. But it has to be
admitted that many Schubert lovers find it hard to put the song among the best Goethe
settings. The square melodic phrases lack charm.

    Capell, 106; Craig Bell, 24; W. Dürr, 'Beobachtungen am Linzer Autograph von
    Schuberts "Rastlose Liebe"', *Historisches Jahrbuch der Stadt Linz 1970*;
    Einstein, 116; Fischer-Dieskau, 68–70

**REITERLIED** see LIED EINES KRIEGERS

# RELLSTAB SONGS
## Ludwig Rellstab

1827–8

Seven of the ten poems by Ludwig Rellstab (1799–1860) which Schubert set were included in the compilation *Schwanengesang* published by Tobias Haslinger in the spring of 1829. It is proper to treat them as a group because the evidence suggests that the composer planned to publish them together. The autograph (New York, PML) includes all seven written out one after the other, the top page being dated August 1828. It does not necessarily follow, however, that all the songs were written in that month. The collected edition of the poems had appeared in 1827. But Schubert's source was more likely the manuscript copies which Anton Schindler, according to his own account (*Memoirs* p.319), handed over to Schubert from Beethoven's *Nachlass* during the summer of 1827. Schindler is by no means always a trustworthy witness, but Rellstab himself confirmed the story (*Memoirs* p.303). It seems likely therefore that some at least of the Rellstab songs were written in 1827, and the autograph of August 1828 was to that extent a compilation and a fair copy.

The three Rellstab songs which were not included in the final group, at any rate, were certainly written before August. *Herbst* (q.v.) is firmly dated April 1828, and *Lebensmut* and *Auf dem Strom* also belong to the spring of the year. These three songs are listed separately under their titles.

It has been said that Schubert had a different style for every poet he set, and the truth of the observation can be seen in the *Schwanengesang* collection. The Rellstab songs are more lyrical and expansive than the Heine set, and lack the aphoristic sharpness and economy of the latter. It is another good reason for treating them as separate groups.

## (1) **LIEBESBOTSCHAFT** Love's Message

G major  D959 no.1  Peters I p.122  GA XX no.554

Ziemlich langsam

Rau - schen-des Bäch - lein, so  sil - bern und hell,

Rushing streamlet, silvery bright, are you hastening to my beloved with such cheerful speed? Ah, friendly streamlet, be my messenger, and bring her greetings from her distant lover.

Revive, streamlet, with your refreshing waters, all the carefully tended flowers in her garden, which she wears with such grace on her bosom, and her roses with crimson glow.

When, sunk in dreams of me, her head nods as she sits on the bank, comfort my sweetheart with your friendly glance, for her lover will soon return.

When the sun sinks and the sky reddens, lull my darling to sleep; murmur peacefully to her, and whisper dreams of love.

The last of Schubert's 'brook songs', and as perfect in its quiet lyricism as any of them, *Liebesbotschaft* might serve as a model for his mature on-running modified strophic style. The rippling acompaniment figure unifies the song, while the ternary form is based on the tonal structure. The first two verses, grouped together, and the last are set to the same tune, which does not stray far from the ambience of the tonic; verse 3 begins in A minor and wanders further afield to B major and related keys. The only dynamic markings are *p* and *pp*, and the crescendos and diminuendos are to be observed within that range.

Capell, 248

### (2) **KRIEGERS AHNUNG** Warrior's Premonition

C minor  D957 no.2  Peters I p.126  GA XX no.555

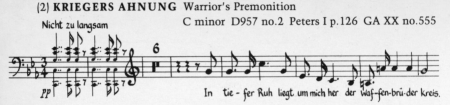

In tie-fer Ruh liegt um mich her der Waf-fen-brü-der kreis.

My comrades at arms lie round me in a peaceful circle; my heart is anxious and heavy, and hot with longing.

How often I have dreamt sweet dreams on her warm breast! How cheery the warmth of the stove seemed when she was in my arms.

Here where the sombre glow of the flames plays only on weapons the heart feels its solitude; a tear of melancholy wells up.

Be not comfortless, my heart. There are many battles yet to come. Soon I shall rest well and sleep fast. Sweetheart, goodnight!

*Kriegers Ahnung* is unique among the Rellstab songs – indeed among the songs of Schubert's final years – in adopting a sectional structure. The four short verses are treated individually, the first in C minor (3/4), the next two in A flat major, with excursions to F sharp minor and F minor (4/4 *Etwas schneller*), and the last verse in C major (6/8 *Geschwind unruhig*). The soldier's final farewell is repeated at the end to the doom-laden music of the opening bars, to confirm the air of foreboding which informs the whole song. But the song represents a return to Schubert's earlier practice in ballads like Schmidt's *Wanderer* and Ossian's *Kolmas Klage*.

For some critics this method puts the principle of unity of mood at risk; the contrast between the tragic weight of the first verse and the lyrical second section is too sharp for comfort. But the momentary dream of happiness, and the rocking figure with which it is associated, seem natural enough; the section builds up to a fateful climax as the insistent C sharp quavers on the piano threaten, and 'a tear of melancholy wells up'. Moreover, Schubert is at pains to keep the piece in touch with the tonal centre of C minor/major. Even the lyrical section in A flat major, it is interesting to note, is annotated in three flats to avoid a change of key signature. As for the double-dotted, heavily accented figure which frames the song, it is perhaps the most eloquent variation on an expressive motif which appears both early (in *Leichenfantasie*, for instance) and late (in *Rast* and *Gefrorne Tränen*). The isolated, accented chord-groups strike the imagination like a muffled drum-beat.

Capell, 249

### (3) **FRÜHLINGSSEHNSUCHT** Spring Longing

B flat major  D957 no.3  Peters I p.131  GA XX no.556

Säu - seln - der Lüf - te  we - hen so  mild,

Murmuring breezes gently blow, exhaling the scent of flowers, and welcoming me with their blissful breath. What have you done to my beating heart? It longs to follow your airy flight. Whither?

The cheerful silver streamlets splash down into the valley. Earth and sky are mirrored there. Why does my longing, languishing mind draw me down with them?

The friendly sun brings the dazzle of gold, the bliss of hope. It beams so comforting a welcome from the deep blue of the sky, and yet fills my eyes with tears. Why?

The forests and hills are crowned with green; the snow of blossom glitters and gleams; everything surges towards the bridal light. Seeds swell, buds burst; they have discovered what they need. And you?

Ceaseless longing, an unfulfilled heart, tears, complaints and pain! I too am conscious of swelling impulses. Who will appease my urgent desire? Only you can liberate the spring in my heart, only you!

If the Heine songs seem to begin, emotionally speaking, at the point where *Winterreise* ends, the tone and texture of the Rellstab songs frequently remind us rather of *Die schöne Müllerin*. Most of all perhaps this one, where the strophic form is so beautifully matched with the words, where the eager on-running 6/8 movement is so magically held in suspense for the lover's yearning self-questioning at the end of the strophe, and where the move into the minor for the last verse recalls the heartache of *Tränenregen*.

### (4) **STÄNDCHEN** Serenade

D minor D957 no.4 Peters I p.135 GA XX no.557

Softly my songs plead through the night to you; down to the silent grove, my darling, come to me!

The slender tree-tops rustle and whisper in the moonlight; do not be afraid, sweetheart, of being heard by anyone.

Do you hear the nightingales? Ah, they are pleading with you: their songs of sweet lament plead for me.

They understand the soul's longing, know the pain of loving, and their silvery notes touch every tender heart.

Let your heart too be moved, my darling, hear me! Trembling I wait for you. Come and make me happy!

This celebrated song is perhaps the best-known serenade in music. With its staccato right-hand chords (the staccato dots appear only in the four-bar introduction, but they are surely meant to apply throughout), its echo phrases, and an irresistible tune shaped to the ebb and flow of the voice, it is a kind of sublimation of the mandoline serenade from *Don Giovanni*. Its formal perfection does not need analysis, but the way the lover's passion swells up at the end in a phrase which echoes the concluding bars of the strophe, and then declines to a whisper of desire, is as purely sensuous a moment as can be found in all Schubert.

### (5) **AUFENTHALT** Resting Place

E minor D957 no.5 Peters I p.138 GA XX no.558

Rushing stream, raging forest, unyielding rock – these are my resting place.
As wave follows wave, so do the tears flow ever anew.
As the high tree-tops bend and stir, so does my heart beat ceaselessly.
Like the age-old rock in the earth, my pain stays ever the same.
Rushing stream, raging forest, unyielding rock – these are my resting place.

Once again the image of the Wanderer, the outcast, inspires in Schubert one of his finest songs. *Aufenthalt* has the inner compulsion, the restless movement, of the Schulze songs, but with a difference. For there is a certain dignity, a composure even, about the song. The protagonist is still a fugitive from life and society, but he is better able to see his own situation with detachment. The headlong flight has become an orderly retreat, stiffened with stoic resolve.

Here the dotted rhythms of the voice line are meant to be heard against, not with, the pianist's triplets. In that way they contribute to the inner tension, as well as reflecting the speech rhythm more effectively. The five verses are grouped effectively in a basically ternary form, with a middle section in the relative major.

(6) **IN DER FERNE** Far Away

Ziemlich langsam

B minor  D957 no.6  Peters I p.142  GA XX no.559

We - he dem Flie - . hen-den, Welt hin-aus  Zie - henden!

Woe to the fugitive, world-forsaker, travelling among strangers, forgetful of home, hating the earth, abandoning friends: no blessing follows him on his way.
      The yearning heart, the weeping eye, endless longing drawing him home, sighing, lamenting, the evening star twinkling and hopelessly sinking.
      Murmuring breezes, curling wavelets, fleeting sunbeams nowhere lingering, you broke my faithful heart with pain. I, the fugitive, the world-forsaker, greet you!

Rellstab's verbal assault, piling phrase on phrase, is far removed from Müller's transparent manner, but the theme might be straight out of *Winterreise*: the disorientation of the wanderer, the curse that rests on the head of the fugitive from home and homeland. In another mood this theme might have sparked off in Schubert a non-stop piece like Schulze's *Im Walde*, but here it is the sense of loneliness, of alienation that possesses him, rather than the idea of flight; he turns instinctively to B minor, and to the mood of *Einsamkeit*.

*In der Ferne* is the most deeply felt of the Rellstab songs, as *Der Doppelgänger* is the most deeply felt of the Heine songs; both are songs of the outcast, songs of alienation akin to madness. And there is something inherently tragic in the solemn alternation of tonic and dominant, and in the obsession with the rise and fall of a semitone which is given such emphasis in the six-bar prelude that it has three quite distinct rhythmic values in that space: the octaves in the pianist's right hand extend over two bars each, the thirds in bars 2 and 4 receive added emphasis from the preceding semiquavers, while the final cadence is extended to two bars. This feature is immediately echoed in the voice line at bar 9.

There is a certain indefinable strangeness about the song which can be felt in the uncomfortable but oddly moving harmonic sequence in bars 17–22. The rhythmic irregularities of the middle section, the persistent juxtaposition of three against four, is sometimes described as an attempt to portray the 'murmuring breezes, curling wavelets, fleeting sunbeams' of the poem. Schubert could do this sort of thing as well as anyone when he wished, but here the effect is rather to produce a sort of rhythmical disorientation analogous perhaps with the wanderer's distraught frame of mind. The emphatic reaffirmation of B minor in the closing bars is like a final slamming of the door against the fugitive.

(7) **ABSCHIED** Farewell

E flat major D957 no.7 Peters I p.146 GA XX no.560

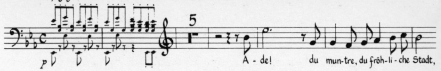

Farewell, lively cheerful town; my horse stands ready. Take this, my last farewell. Never have you seen me sad, nor shall you now at parting. Adieu!

Farewell, trees and gardens. Along the silver stream I ride. My farewell song echoes round the countryside. You have never heard a sad song, nor shall you now. Adieu!

Farewell, warmhearted maidens. You look out from your houses bowered in flowers with tempting roguish eyes. I greet you as before, and turn my head, but not my horse. Adieu!

Farewell, dear sun, as you sink to rest. Now come the stars in twinkling, shimmering gold. How fond I am of you, little stars in heaven; though we travel the world far and wide, you serve always as faithful guides. Adieu!

Farewell, little window gleaming bright, shining so cosily with your faint light, and inviting us so kindly inside. Ah, I have passed you by so many times; could this be the last? Adieu!

Farewell stars, veil your light. You countless stars cannot make up for the loss of that little window's fading light. If I may not linger, but must ride on, what use are you to me, however faithfully you follow. Stars, veil your light! Adieu!

Schubert's motor images are analogues, not imitations. The young man who takes his leave in this song is obviously moving off at a brisk trot. But it would be just as difficult to trot in time to this music as to gallop to that of *Normans Gesang*, or to walk to the steady pacing quavers of *Gute Nacht*. It is the *idea* of the trotting horse which is so precisely conveyed by the insistent staccato quavers and the jog-trot bass, and a very infectious idea it is, like many of Schubert's *moto perpetuo* rhythms (*Auf der Brucke*, for instance, another riding song) and likely to keep one awake at night if it stays in the mind.

What is remarkable is that the listener's interest is sustained over nearly 170 bars without rhythmic change or relief. But although the character of the song does not change, the notes do, constantly, and so does the tonality. This 'strophic' setting is not based on a single tune; it is made up like a mosaic of two-bar phrases which are constantly varied and reassembled. Even the refrain – 'Ade!' – is sung in seven different registers in the course of the song. Above all it is the tonal scheme which keeps us constantly on the alert. Every verse begins and ends in E flat major, but the middle verses explore A flat and D flat also, while the last verse quickly moves to E flat minor and C flat (the flattened sixth again) before returning to the tonic.

## RITTER TOGGENBURG The Knight of Toggenburg
**Friedrich von Schiller**                                   13 March 1816

E flat major D397 Peters V p.103 GA XX no.191

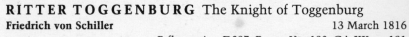

'Sir Knight, this heart of mine dedicates a true, sisterly love to you; ask no other kind of love, for that pains me. Calmly I wish to see you appear, and calmly go again; I do not understand the silent tears in your eyes.'

And he listened with silent grief, tore himself away with a bleeding heart, pressed her violently in his arms, leapt on to his charger, and sent word to all his men in the country of Switzerland. To the holy sepulchre they went on pilgrimage, the cross on their breasts.

Great deeds were carried out at their hands, the plumes of their helmets flew among the enemy hosts, and the name of Toggenburg struck terror into the Mussulman. Yet his heart cannot be healed of its sorrow.

When he had borne it for a year he could bear it no longer. Finding no peace he left his army, and seeing a ship on the shore at Joppa, with the wind filling its sails, he sailed home to that dear land where she draws breath.

And the pilgrim knocked at the gate of her castle. Alas, as it opened the words came like a thunderclap: 'She whom you seek wears the veil; she is the bride of heaven; yesterday was the solemn day which united her with God.'

Then he left the castle of his fathers for ever, looking neither at his weapons nor at his faithful horse. He went down from the Toggenburg unrecognised, his noble limbs covered in a hair shirt.

And built himself a hut in the neighbourhood where the convent stood amid dark linden trees; from the first light of morning until the dusk of evening he sat there alone, waiting, with silent hope in his face.

He gazed across at the convent; for hours he gazed at the window of his beloved, until the window rattled, and his darling appeared; until her dear form leant out over the valley, calm, and gentle as an angel.

Then he lay down happy and slept comforted, looking forward to when it would be morning again. And so he sat for many days, for many long years, waiting without sorrow or complaint for the rattle of the window.

Waiting until his darling appeared, until her dear form leant out over the valley, calm, and gentle as an angel. And there, one morning, he sat, a corpse, his pale silent face still gazing up at the window.

The poem dates from 1797. The autograph, which belongs to the Deutsche Grammophon Gesellschaft, Hamburg, contains both a full sketch for the song and a fair copy, both dated 13 March 1816. There is also a dated copy in the Witteczek–Spaun collection (Vienna, GdM). The song was first published in book 19 of the *Nachlass*, in October 1832.

It is closely modelled on Zumsteeg's setting of the same text, even to the formal layout. The first five verses are set to an on-running homophonic style, rather like a pilgrim's chant; at this point Schubert, like Zumsteeg, switches to a strophic setting for the next four verses, reserving the last verse for special treatment. There are two different versions, one in F, ending in E flat minor, as in the GA, the other in E flat, ending in A flat major, as in Peters. This latter version is possibly based on a lost fair copy.

Schubert's enthusiasm for these tales of the cloister and the crusade may be excused as an aberration of the age. The style he considers suitable for them – something between a monkish march and a sentimental hymn – is not, however, conducive to great music. *Ritter Toggenburg* is a curious reversion to early habits in its cantata-like shapelessness. The solemn mode was to be used much later, in *Der Kreuzzug*, for instance.

# ROMANZE Romance *(Der Vollmond strahlt)*
**Helmina von Chézy**                                                  December 1823
                                              F Minor D797 no.3b Peters I p.230

[see Addendum p.482]

## **ROMANZE** Romance
**Ignaz Franz Castelli**

Early 1823
F minor D787 no.2 Peters VI p.127

This lovely song resembles Rosamunde's song (*Der Vollmund strahlt*) and is sometimes sung as a solo song, though strictly speaking it has no place in this book. It comes from the one-act Singspiel *Die Verschworenen*.

## **ROMANZE** Romance
**Friedrich von Matthisson**

September 1814
G minor D114 Not in Peters GA XX no.27 NSA IV vol.7 pp.36, 42

In the dark tower on the sea-shore a maiden lamented. Wind and wave roared and howled above her cries of distress.

Rosalia of Montanvert was praised by many a troubadour, and by a whole host of knights, as the crown of nature.

:But before her heart had felt the power of sweet love her father fell in battle by the Saracen shore.

Her uncle, a knight called Manfry, became her guardian; his heart, hard as flint, laughed at the thought of the lady's wealth and possessions.

Soon the sad tidings spread through the land: 'Death's dark night has claimed Rose Montanvert!'

The black flag of death waved on high over the lady's castle; for three days and nights the hollow death-knell sounded.

Gone for ever, dead for ever, oh, Rose Montanvert! No longer now will you relieve the widow's plight and the orphan's grief!

So from dawn to dusk, blinded by tears, old and young with one voice lamented Rose Montanvert.

Her uncle hid her in a dungeon full of the stench of decay; then her empty coffin was laid in the vault of her fathers.

The maid, in silent fear, heard the litanies of the priests; the red glow of the torches shone dimly through the prison bars.

Shuddering, she began to comprehend her fate; she became dull and heavy; in the horror of death her eyes closed. She sank down and was no more.

The ruins of that tower by the sea can still be seen today. As he approaches the traveller is seized by a strange dread.

And many a shepherd will tell you that he has often seen at night the maiden floating there, like a silver cloud.

The poem was written in 1791, a fairly typical example of the fashion for making the flesh creep with medieval horrors. Schubert's friend Kenner was so impressed that he imitated the ballad in his own poem, *Ein Fräulein schaut vom hohen Turm*, which Schubert also set (D134). In the 1811 edition the title of Matthisson's poem was given as *Das Fräulein im Thurme: Romanze*, but Schubert's title is as above. Also in this edition the lady's name was changed to Rosalia von Mortimer.

There are two complete autographs: a fair copy (Vienna, ÖNB) dated September 1814 and marked 'Ziemlich langsam'; and another fair copy (Berlin, DS) marked 'Etwas langsam' and dated 29 September 1814. There are copies of this second version in the Witteczek–Spaun collection (Vienna, GdM) and in Schindler's songbook (Lund, UB), all dated 29

September 1814. These two versions show two quite different settings of verses 10 and 11, beginning 'Das Fräulein horchte', the climax of the poem. Yet another version of this part of the song is preserved on a single sheet which is probably a part of the first draft. The *Neue Ausgabe* publishes both versions, and the fragmentary first draft in an appendix. The second version was published by Wilhelm Müller as no.4 of 'Six Previously Un-published Songs' (Berlin, 1868). It also appears in the *Gesamtausgabe*.

This is Schubert's first attempt to reduce the scale of the ballad, and to bring to it the balance of lyrical and dramatic interest that he sought in the Matthisson songs. It is evident that he took a lot of trouble over it, making several attempts to get the climax right. The song as it stands is an impressive performance, in spite of a text which seems to modern ears comically macabre. It has a stronger narrative thread, and a much more unified tonal scheme, than the earlier Zumsteeg–inspired ballads. The main burden of the story is carried by the expressive 6/8 G minor music which recurs twice; recitative is used sparingly but effectively, only for the villain's part; most remarkable of all is the thematic invention and pictorialism which Schubert brings to the hollow death-knell, and to the maiden's gruesome end.

## ROMANZE Romance
**Friedrich Leopold, Graf zu Stolberg-Stolberg**                      April 1816
E major D144 Not in Peters GA Rev. Ber., note to no.192 NSA IV vol.7 p.201

In the hall of his fathers the heroic arm of Sir Rudolph rested, Rudolph who delighted in battle, Rudolph feared by France and the Saracen hordes.

This is the first of thirteen verses of a poem which tells the story of the conflict between the noble Albrecht and the villainous Horst for the hand of the fair Agnes, Rudolph's daughter. It dates from 1774. The fragment of seven bars is written on the same sheet as *Daphne am Bache* (D411, April 1816). It was evidently the beginning of a ballad composition which Schubert never got round to writing. A performable version of the first verse was completed and privately published by Reinhard van Hoorickx.

## ROMANZE DES RICHARD LÖWENHERZ Richard the Lionheart's Song
**Sir Walter Scott trans. Karl Ludwig Müller**                      (?) March 1826
B minor/major D907 Peters III p.45 GA XX no.501

The song is sung by the king for Friar Tuck in chapter XVII of Scott's novel *Ivanhoe*. There it is entitled *The Crusader's Return*. The original runs as follows:

High deeds achieved of knightly fame,
From Palestine the champion came;
The cross upon his shoulders borne,

Battle and blast had dimmed and torn.
Each dint upon his batter'd shield
Was token of a foughten field:
And thus beneath his lady's bower,
He sung, as fell the twilight hour.

'Joy to the fair! – thy knight behold,
Returned from yonder land of gold;
No wealth he brings, nor wealth can need,
Save his good arms and battle steed;
His spurs, to dash against a foe,
His lance and sword to lay him low;
Such all the trophies of his toil,
Such – and the hope of Tekla's smile!

'Joy to the fair! whose constant knight
Her favour fired to feats of might;
Unnoted shall she not remain
Where meet the bright and noble train:
Minstrel shall sing and herald tell –
"Mark yonder maid of beauty well;
'Tis she for whose bright eyes was won
The listed field of Askalon!"

'Note well her smile! – it edged the blade
Which fifty wives to widows made.
Even vain his strength and Mahount's spell,
Iconium's turban'd Soldan fell.
Seest thou her locks, whose sunny glow
Half shows, half shades, her neck of snow?
Twines not of them one golden thread
But for its sake a Paynim bled.

'Joy to the fair! – my name unknown,
Each deed, and all its praise thine own;
Then oh, unbar this churlish gate,
The night dew falls, the hour is late.
Inured to Syria's glowing breath
I feel the north breeze chill as death;
Let grateful love quell maiden shame,
And grant him bliss who brings thee fame.'

Schubert used a translation by Karl Ludwig Müller published in 1820. It turns Scott's
iambic tetrameters into trochees, so that the song cannot be sung to the English words.

No complete autograph has survived, and the date is not certain. The catalogue of
the Witteczek–Spaun collection (Vienna, GdM) gives March 1826. Franz von Hartmann,
who heard the song sung at a Schubertiad on 12 January 1827, noted in his diary that it
was 'ganz neues' – brand new – but he surely meant only that it was quite new to him
(*Docs.* no.772). The Vienna Stadt- und Landesbibliothek has a manuscript containing a
fragmentary sketch of the song. The fair copy made for the printer is missing. The song
was published by Diabelli as op. 86 in March 1828.

The dotted-quaver rhythm persists for seven pages, with only the alternation of
minor and major tonality to provide relief. The song has something of the relentless drive
of the finales of Schubert's D minor and G major string quartets, also finished in 1826,
but it seems less appropriate here, for it does not really suit the words. Schubert is clearly
content, however, to sustain an image of pageantry and war.

**RÜCKBLICK** see WINTERREISE no.8

## RÜCKWEG The Return

**Johann Mayrhofer**                                September 1816

D minor D476 Not in Peters GA XX no.252

*Etwas geschwind*

Zum Do-naustrom, zur Kai-ser-stadt geh ich in Ban-gig-keit

Anxious and uneasy I approach the river Danube and the imperial city; for all the beauty of life I leave further and further behind me.

Gradually the mountains disappear, and with them the forests and valleys; the cowbells tinkle after us, and the chalets nod a greeting.

Why do your eyes, wet with tears, stare into the blue distance? Ah, there I lived happily, in solitude, a free man among free people.

Where love and faith still count for something, there the heart unfolds; in their beams the fruit ripens, and reaches up towards heaven.

In September 1816 Mayrhofer went on a walking holiday with his friend Hermann Watteroth. The poem seems to be occasioned by their return to Vienna; Mayrhofer's uneasiness must have been due at least partly to the increasingly illiberal political climate in Vienna, not at all the right environment for 'a free man among free people'. The poem is thus a kind of companion piece to *Abschied* D475 (q.v.). The autograph is a first draft dated September 1816. There is a copy in the Witteczek–Spaun collection (Vienna, GdM) and another in the Moravské Muzeum at Brno, marked 'Allegretto'. The song was published in 1872 by J. P. Gotthard as no.15 of 'Forty Songs'.

Schubert groups the verses in pairs and sets them to a plaintive 6/8 melody in D minor which seems too slight for the reflective character of the poem. The strophic setting can do little more than match the general tone of melancholy.

## SÄNGERS MORGENLIED Minstrel's Aubade (1)

**Theodor Körner**                                27 February 1815

G major D163 Not in Peters GA XX no.50

*Lieblich, etwas geschwind*

Sü - ßes Licht! aus gol - de - nen Pfor - ten

Sweet light, that bursts in triumph from the golden portals, scattering the night! Lovely day that is breaking! With mysterious words set to tuneful melodies I greet your rosy splendour.

Ah, love's soft breeze swells my troubled heart as gently as a familiar pain. If only I could tread those golden heights in the scent of morning. I long to soar heavenwards!

The autograph, in private possession, contains also the second draft of *Nähe des Geliebten*. It is dated 27 February 1815. The song was first published in the *Gesamtausgabe* in 1894. The poem has six verses, but the *Gesamtausgabe* prints only two for this first setting. See the following entry.

# SÄNGERS MORGENLIED (2)
**Theodor Körner**                                    1 March 1815

C major D165 Not in Peters GA XX no.51

For translation, see the preceding entry. The autograph (Berlin, DS) is dated 1 March 1815.
There is a dated copy in the Witteczek–Spaun collection (Vienna, GdM). The first
publication was in 1872 by J.P. Gotthard as no.33 of 'Forty Songs'.

*Sängers Morgenlied* is unique in one respect. Schubert's second versions of solo
settings of a text are usually closely related to the first. Once seized of the essence of a
poem, and a way of re-creating it in song, he will often make several attempts to realise
that initial concept in successive versions. But here are two quite different, indeed
contrasted versions of the text, both for solo voice, and written within days of each other:
the first a high-spirited joyful dance (*Lieblich, etwas geschwind*) and the second (*Langsam*)
quiet and reflective. It is as though Schubert deliberately set out to reflect two different
aspects of the words, the unclouded joy of the first verse, and the underlying *Sehnsucht*
of the second.


# SCHÄFERS KLAGELIED Shepherd's Lament
**Johann Wolfgang von Goethe**                        30 November 1814

C minor D121 Peters I p.225 GA XX no.34(a) and (b) NSA IV vol.1 pp.20, 194

Up there on yonder mountain I have stood a thousand times, leaning on my staff
and gazing down into the valley.
    Then I follow the grazing flock which my dog takes care of for me. I have come
down here without knowing how.
    There stands the meadow, all full of lovely flowers. I pick them without
knowing who I mean to give them to.
    And I sit out the rain, the storm and thunder under the tree. The gate over
there stays closed; but alas, it is all a dream.
    It looks like a rainbow standing over that house! But she has gone away, far
into the depths of the country.
    Far away in the country and beyond, perhaps even over the sea. Up along,
sheep, up along! Your shepherd's heart is heavy.

The poem, written in the spring of 1801, was based on a folksong which Goethe heard
at a party, *Da droben auf jenem Berge*. He was so taken with the tune that he decided
to write a folksong of his own to fit it.

    There are two versions. The autograph of the first (Vienna, ÖNB) is dated 30
November 1814. It is in C minor and has no piano introduction. There is a fair copy in
the songbook made for Goethe in 1816 (Berlin, DS). *Schäfers Klagelied* was the first
Schubert song to be sung at a public concert, by the tenor Franz Jäger on 28 February 1819.
For this first performance Schubert wrote a transposed version in E minor, and added

a four-bar prelude. The autograph of this second version is in Vienna (SB). Both versions are included in the *Gesamtausgabe* and the *Neue Ausgabe. Schäfers Klagelied* was published as op.3 no.1 in May 1821 (Cappi and Diabelli) and dedicated to Ignaz von Mosel.

One has only to compare the song with Zelter's simple strophic A minor setting to appreciate the subtlety of this through-composed version. The folksong elements are all there – the gentle 6/8 movement, the minor key, the supportive accompaniment. The structure however is cleverly varied, verses 5 and 6 repeating verses 1 and 2, but in reverse order. The middle verses are in A flat major/minor, leading to the brief storm – a sudden *forte* in C flat. Yet the unity of mood and style is never broken; even the quasi-recitative of verse 4 ('alas, it is all a dream') is beautifully integrated into the texture of the song, while providing just the right emotional climax. The song is at once the culmination and the vindication of the Matthisson settings of 1814.

Capell, 86–7; Fischer-Dieskau, 115–16; Sternfeld, 9–13

## SCHATZGRÄBERS BEGEHR The Treasure-seeker's Request

**Franz von Schober** November 1822

D minor/major D761 Peters IV p.22 GA XX no.412 NSA IV vol.2 pp.10, 189

Gehend

In the depths of the earth an old law sleeps which I am driven to track down relentlessly, and as I dig I can achieve nought else. For me too the world may spread its golden snare;
    I too may listen to the shallow chatter of the worldly-wise: 'You are wasting your strength and your time to no avail.' That shall not distract me from my labour; I go on digging furiously, now as always.
    And if I am never to be rewarded by the joy of discovery, if inspired by this hope I am only digging my own grave, still I like to climb down, for so is my longing stilled.
    So leave me in peace with my obsession! A grave is surely not too much to grant anyone, so will you not allow me one too, my friends?

The original autograph has disappeared, but a fair copy inscribed in the album of Johann von Püttlingen survives in private possession. It is dated November 1822 and marked 'In mässiger Bewegung' (*Moderato*). The published version is marked 'Gehend' ('At a walking pace') and shows other minor differences. The song was first published in August 1823 by Sauer and Leidesdorf, as op.23 no.4.

Schober's verses leave many questions unanswered. What is the 'ancient law' which lies hidden under the earth? Is it only the unattainable Schillerian Ideal, as Capell suggests? Is it perhaps Love, or Fame? And why the curiously personal and informal tone of verses 2 and 4, suggesting some topical or circumstantial meaning? Fischer-Dieskau implies that the poem is intended as a reply to Vogl, who had been sharply critical of the *Alfonso und Estrella* project. If so it is a strangely oblique one.

A consideration of the thematic material does not help much. The quavers in octaves which stalk their way through the song are a version of the familiar Schubert motif suggesting a stubborn search for the unattainable, with a hint of eccentricity or derangement. It appears as early as 1811, and later in songs on this theme like *Die Perle* and *An* die Freunde. Here it is combined with the equally familiar chromatic descending line, often used in the context of unfriendly fate and despair. The song is an oddity. It may be that some allusion is intended to Goethe's famous poem *Der Schatzgräber*, which Schubert had set in 1815, and to its 'message' that it is better to stick to one's last than aim at the stars. Vogl would no doubt have agreed; Schober's answer would appear to be, 'Ay, but a man's reach should exceed his grasp, Or what's a heaven for?'

Capell, 174; Einstein, 253; Fischer-Dieskau, 164; Porter, 118

**SCHIFFERS NACHTLIED** see LIED EINES SCHIFFERS AN DIE DIOSKUREN

## SCHIFFERS SCHEIDELIED The Sailor's Farewell

**Franz von Schober**                                                February 1827

E minor  D910  Peters III p.181  GA XX no.516

The rollers break on the beach, the wind rattles in the canvas, and murmurs among the white waves. I listen to its wild words. It is calling me away, and the dinghy, rocking impatiently, is beckoning me to the long voyage.

My way stretches far across the barren seas; you cannot come with me, my child, as you see. How easily my guiding stars may sink, how easily the wind grows to a tempest: then death threatens in a thousand shapes. How can I defy it, if I know you are in danger?

Oh, loose me from your embrace, and unlock me too from your heart. How can I tell whether I shall be successful and return home victorious? The wave that sings so enticingly now may be the very one that engulfs me.

The decision is still in your own hands; you have not yet totally committed yourself. Oh, cut your young life free quickly from my uncertain existence. Do it voluntarily, before you have to; it is easier to renounce than to suffer loss!

And let me take the tiller knowing that I am alone in the world, then my mind will not give way before the terrors of the unknown. I shall dice with horrors, and perhaps find myself suddenly at my goal.

For your image will fly at my masthead to encourage me, and lit by the lightning will lift my courage; and however fearfully the winds howl, they will not drown the sound of your voice.

If I can still see and hear you there is nothing else that I need. I shall not lack life, and I shall battle against death. How could a world seem wearisome to me which contains angels as fair as you?

You too must preserve my image and consecrate it with tears of friendship; in times of sorrow and of joy it will be your comfort and your companion. If I have lost all else you must remain my friend in the paradise of home.

And if a treacherous wave should wash my dead body back on to the flowery shore, then I shall know that there will still be one faithful pair of hands at that dear place which will not be prevented by disdain or sorrow from committing my remains to a grave.

The autograph is lost, but a copy in the Witteczek–Spaun collection (Vienna, GdM) is dated February 1827. The song was published in book 24 of the *Nachlass*, in September 1833.

*Schiffers Scheidelied* has the obsessive forward drive of the Schulze songs, and something of the majestic scale of the setting of Schlegel's *Im Walde*. But it lacks the variety and subtlety of the latter. The nine verses are distributed between two strophes, one in E minor, a little reminiscent of *Über Wildemann*, and another, more lyrical, in B major. Two verses are set to each strophe (the last verse is repeated) so that the song takes on the symmetrical form ABABA. But there is little variation in the music; it lacks that close association of tone and sense which belongs to the genuine modified strophic song. It is significant perhaps that in the only available recorded version two verses are cut. The twelve pages the song occupies in the Peters edition seem too many.

Capell, 226; Fischer-Dieskau, 245

## SCHLACHTGESANG Battle Song
**Friedrich Gottlieb Klopstock**                                     June 1816

E major D443 Not in Peters GA XX no.228

By our own strength we can do nothing unless the Almighty, who perfects all, is with us!
    In vain we are fired by courage if the victory does not come to us from him who perfects all!
    In vain our blood flows for the fatherland if we are not aided by him who perfects all!
    In vain we die the death for the fatherland if we are not aided by him who perfects all!

The poem, headed 'Schlachtlied', was written in 1767 and has fourteen verses, of which the first four are translated. The autograph, entitled *Schlachtgesang*, is dated June 1816 (Berlin, SPK). It is a draft for a male-voice chorus or partsong on two staves. Schubert returned to it many years later, in February 1827, and revised it for double chorus (D912), in which form it was performed at his public concert on 26 March 1828. Strictly speaking the song has no place among the solo songs, though it is included in series XX of the *Gesamtausgabe*.

## SCHLAFLIED Lullaby
**Johann Mayrhofer**                                               January 1817

F major D527 Peters II p.66 GA XX no.298 NSA IV vol.2 pp.20, 193

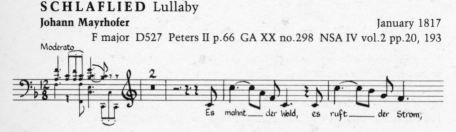

The forest calls, the river cries: 'Sweet child, come to us!' The boy approaches, full of wonder, and stays, and is cured of every pain.
    The quails' cry sounds from the bushes, the daylight plays with deceptive lights; and the damp dew from heaven glistens on the red flowers and the blue.

He lies down in the cool grass, and lets the clouds sail by. As he nestles up to his mother the god of dreams rocks him to sleep.

There are two versions of the song, one notated in 2/2 time and the other in 12/8. A fair copy of the former version, entitled *Abendlied* and marked 'Langsam', is in the Sibley Library, University of Rochester, NY. The autograph of the second (published) version is missing. The song is dated January 1817 in the catalogue of the Witteczek–Spaun collection (Vienna, GdM). There are copies of the first version, marked 'Mässig', in the Stadler and Ebner collections (Lund, UB). *Schlaflied* was first published in October 1823 by Sauer and Leidesdorf as op.24 no.2. When it was republished by Diabelli it appeared under the title *Schlummerlied*, and so it appears also in the Peters edition. The published versions are marked 'Moderato'.

In its purity of style, and perfection of form, *Schlaflied* is unsurpassed among Schubert's cradle songs. *Wiegenlied*, written two months earlier, has a marvellous tune, but its appeal is entirely melodic. Here melodic and harmonic interest is evenly distributed, while the strophe itself is perfectly balanced, the stasis of the outer sections set against the brisk harmonic pace of a middle section which moves through A major, E flat and B flat on its way back to the tonic, all in three bars. Schubert's first thoughts are here better than his second. The pulse is slow, with two beats to the bar, and the song calls for a *mezza voce*, *pp* throughout. Even the *sf* in bar 11 is no more than an accent.

**SCHÖNE WELT WO BIST DU** see DIE GÖTTER GRIECHENLANDS

**SCHWANENGESANG** Song cycle. See under RELLSTAB SONGS; HEINE SONGS; DIE TAUBENPOST

# SCHWANENGESANG Swan Song
**Ludwig Kosegarten**

19 October 1815
F minor D318 Not in Peters GA XX no.165

At last the gates stand open. At last the grave welcomes me, and after long fears and hopes I decline towards the night. Now I have completed the days of my life. After the tears of lamentation sweet peace closes my tired eyelids.

The night will not last for ever, nor this sleep. Behind the horror of the grave a new light breaks. But until that light shines on me, until the day of judgment dawns, I will go calmly into the dark, cool, silent night of sleep.

The poem, written in 1775, is an invocation to death. The first and last of its seven verses are translated. The autograph (Vienna, SB) is a first draft dated 19 October 1815. There is a fair copy in the music library of Yale University, and a dated copy in the Witteczek–Spaun collection (Vienna, GdM). The first publication was in the *Gesamtausgabe* in 1895. The conventionally solemn setting in the minor moves gently forward, like a hymn.

## SCHWANENGESANG Swan Song
**Johann Chrysostomus Senn**                                      (?) Autumn 1822

A flat  D744  Peters IV p.21  GA XX no.407  NSA IV vol.2 p.8

'How shall I express the death-feeling, the dissolution, that courses through my limbs?'
>'How can I sing the sense of life, the deliverance, that breathes upon my spirit?'
>So it lamented, so it sang, fearful of annihilation, glad of transfiguration, until life fled.
>That is the swan's song!

The poem must have been set from Senn's manuscript, or from a copy, for it was not published until 1838. In September 1822 Franz von Bruchmann met Senn at Innsbruck, where he was eking out a living in exile; almost certainly Bruchmann brought the two Senn poems which Schubert set back with him. This helps to date the songs. The autograph (Berlin, SPK) is undated. The same manuscript, however, contains a fair copy of *Aus 'Heliopolis' II*, which Witteczek assigned to April 1822. The song was published by Sauer and Leidesdorf as op.23 no.3 in August 1823. This edition 'simplified' the notation of bar 7 by dispensing with the double flats, but the *Gesamtausgabe* restored the original form.

A wonderful miniature, as epigrammatic as it is expressive. The ambivalence of the swan's death song is conveyed by the alternation of the major and minor mode in the tonic, while the tonal adventuring into the remote regions of F flat and C flat seems to symbolise a journey into the unknown. Once again we hear the 'death rhythm' of crotchet and two quavers which signals Schubert's emotional involvement with the subject, but this time the bare opening sequences convey only an ethereal sense of submission and of compassion.

## SCHWEIZERLIED Swiss Song
**Johann Wolfgang von Goethe**                                      May 1817

F major  D559  Peters VII p.36  GA XX no.121

I sat on the mountain side watching the birdies; they sang and they hopped and they built their nests.
>I stood in a garden watching the bees; they hummed and they buzzed and they built their cells.
>I walked in the meadow watching the butterflies; they sucked and they flitted and they flirted beautifully.
>And then Hansel comes along, and happily I show him what they do, and we laugh, and do the same.

Goethe's earthy little exercise in the *Des Knaben Wunderhorn* manner was written in March 1811. A translation into Devon dialect by A. H. Fox Strangways was published in *M and L*, II, July 1921. The autograph, in the Paris Conservatoire, is a first draft dated May 1817. There is a copy in the Stadler collection (Lund, UB). The song was first published in vol. VII of the Peters edition in 1885.

Schubert's 'sturdy little peasant tune' swings along between tonic and dominant, the off-beat accents in the postlude more suggestive of a peasant dance than a yodelling song. And like a true Swiss song, the accompaniment is full of horn calls. Like *Heidenröslein*, *Schweizerlied* is one of Schubert's 'unintentional folksongs', as Einstein calls them.

Capell, 104; Einstein, 111

### SCHWERTLIED Song of the Sword

**Theodor Körner**                                                   12 March 1815

C major  D170  Not in Peters  GA XX no.54

*Kräftig und stark*

Du Schwert an mei - ner Lin - ken, was soll dein heit - res Blin - ken?

O sword at my left hand, why do you gleam so brightly? Your friendly glance gives me great joy. Hurrah! Hurrah!

'I am worn by a brave knight, that is why I gleam so brightly; and I defend a free man: that is the sword's delight.' Hurrah! Hurrah!

Now let my darling sing until the bright sparks fly! The wedding morning dawns. Hurrah for the iron bride! Hurrah! Hurrah!

[At the words Hurrah! the swords are clashed.]

The poem was written a few hours before the poet's death in action against Napoleon's forces at Gadebusch on 26 August 1813. There are sixteen verses, of which the first two and the last are given. The autograph, in the Houghton Library at Harvard University, is dated 12 March 1815. The marking is *Geschwind*. The footnote 'At the words Hurrah! the swords are clashed' is Körner's; it occurs also at the end of Schubert's draft. Copies in the Witteczek–Spaun (Vienna, GdM) and the Stadler collections (Lund, UB) are marked 'Kräftig und stark', and the word 'CHOR' is added over the Hurrahs at the end. The song was first published in the appendix to August Reissman's *Franz Schubert: sein Leben und seine Werke* (Berlin, 1873). Schubert's intentions are not altogether clear, but the song appears to be written for double chorus of male voices.

### SCHWESTERGRUSS Sister's Greeting

**Franz von Bruchmann**                                               November 1822

F sharp minor/major  D762  Peters V p.135  GA XX no.413

*Langsam*

*pp*

Im Mon - den schein__ wall ich auf____ und ab____,

I wander up and down in the moonlight, seeing dead bones and the silent grave.

Something floats by in the ghostly breeze; it shivers past like a flame and a vapour.

From the swirling mists a figure rises, without sin or falsehood, and hovers past.

With blue eyes and imposing gaze, as in the fields of heaven, as in the lap of God.

A white garment clothes it, and a lily springs from its delicate hand.

She speaks to me in a ghostly whisper: 'Already I walk in the pure light.

'I see the moon and the sun at my feet, and live in bliss among the angels' kisses.

And your heart, child of man, cannot know the extent of the joy I feel.

Unless you abandon the god of this world before fearful death seizes you.'
The air resounds, the wind moans, the child of heaven calls to the stars,
And before she flees the white form is folded in fresh flowers,
She floats up in pure flame, without pain or sorrow, to the angel choir.
Night enshrouds the holy place; filled with the spirit of God I sing the Word.

The poem was written in July 1820, after the death of the poet's sister Sybilla. Bruchmann's poems were never published; Schubert must have worked from a manuscript copy. The autograph (Vienna, SB) is dated November 1822. There is a dated copy also in the Witteczek–Spaun collection (Vienna, GdM). The song was published in book 23 of the *Nachlass*, in July 1833.

*Schwestergruss* is a neglected masterpiece. What it was in Bruchmann's sentimental verses which inspired it, two years after the poem was written, we do not know. The fact that the song is contemporaneous, however, with the 'Unfinished' Symphony, with Senn's *Schwanengesang* and Schober's *Schatzgräbers Begehr*, suggests that it belongs to a time of emotional crisis, and that Schubert used an inferior poem for his own purposes, as he had often done before, in a way that is deeply revealing.

Schubert imposed his own musical structure on the thirteen short verses of the poem, dividing it into three main sections so as to establish a broadly ternary structure, which was his favourite way of organising a through-composed song. The first section, in F sharp minor, ends halfway through verse 6. The second section, lighter in tone and texture, in F sharp major, dispenses with the heavy bass line. It consists of the ghostly Sybilla's admonition. The music moves back to the minor, and the triplets switch back to the bass, as she speaks of the ominous threat of death. In the final section the octave triplets are replaced by full chords as Sybilla's ascension into heaven is described, but the powerful bass octaves return as the song comes to rest (*ppp*) in the major.

Within this structure the complex fabric of the song is woven from three significant themes, or groups of themes, with symphonic subtlety. It begins with a double statement (*pp*) in open octaves of what might be called Schubert's death motif, the long–short–short rhythm always associated with *Der Tod und das Mädchen*. At bar 3 a melodic figure is inserted below this continuing rhythm, which provides the melodic thread on which the song is woven. This figure, which has obvious affinities with the opening theme of the 'Unfinished' Symphony, divides easily into two, and gives rise to several subsidiary fragments, all operating within the compass of a fourth. It is the basis of the moving bass line which underpins the song. The third group of motifs consists of the descending chromatic line, also a death symbol for Schubert, to be seen at bars 9, 13, 15 and elsewhere. These themes are combined to provide a developing texture of wonderful richness and complexity.

Critical comment on this superb song is sometimes curiously inept. The supposed resemblance to *Erlkönig* seems entirely superficial. The ostinato triplets and the clashing minor seconds look back rather to *Leichenfantasie*, to Mayrhofer songs like *Fahrt zum Hades* and *Sehnsucht*. Much more significant, however, is the way the song looks forward to the visionary masterpieces of Schubert's last months. No Schubert lover can play this accompaniment without being reminded of the B flat piano sonata of 1828 in the texture (bars 15–21 for example) and at particular cadences, especially the valedictory cadence at bars 67–8, which plays so significant a role both in the sonata and in *Abschied von der Erde* (D829). There is, too, something ominously predictive about the long descending bass line in the closing phase of the song.

Capell, 174–5; Einstein, 253; Fischer-Dieskau, 185–6

**SEHNSUCHT (MIGNON)** see NUR WER DIE SEHNSUCHT KENNT

## SEHNSUCHT Longing

**Johann Wolfgang von Goethe**                    3 December 1814

G major  D123  Peters VI p.10  GA XX no.35  NSA IV vol.7 p.60

What tugs at my heart so and draws me out of doors? What wrenches and screws me out of house and home? Over there by the crags the clouds disperse. That's where I would like to be, that's where I would like to go!

The ravens flock together in undulating flight. I join them and follow the flock. And we soar above the mountain and its walls. She dwells below; I try to catch a glimpse of her.

There she comes, wandering along; at once I hasten, like a singing bird to the greenwood. She lingers, listening, and smiling to herself: 'He sings so sweetly, and he is singing for me.'

The setting sun gilds the mountains; the pensive beauty takes no notice. She wanders along the stream through the meadows, and the path winds darker and darker.

Suddenly I appear, a twinkling star. 'What is that shining up there, so near yet so far?' And when, astonished, you catch sight of its gleam, I shall throw myself at your feet. Then I shall be happy!

The autograph is a first draft, dated 3 December 1814. It is in G major, is marked 'Andante' and has been cancelled by the composer. This manuscript seems to have been divided into two during the 1880s, and one part, consisting of the first thirteen bars, is now missing. The remainder is in Vienna (SB). There is a fair copy made for Goethe in 1816 (also Vienna, SB) and a copy in the Witteczek–Spaun collection (Vienna, GdM), wrongly dated 1815. When the song came to be published in book 37 of the *Nachlass* (June 1842) it was transposed to F major, and it appears so also in the Peters edition. When it was reissued, however, in 1887 by Weinberger and Hofbauer, the original key was restored. The tempo indication is *Mässig*.

*Sehnsucht* is a sad miscalculation. It misses both the spirit and the lilt of Goethe's lighthearted poem and gives us a miniature solo cantata, in which there are no fewer than twelve changes of rhythm and key. On the evidence of this song one would judge that Schubert had not come across Beethoven's witty and spirited setting published in 1811.

Capell, 43, 69; Fischer-Dieskau, 37

## SEHNSUCHT Longing

**Johann Mayrhofer**                    (?) Spring 1817

C major  D516  Peters II p.22  GA XX no.386  NSA IV vol.1 p.73

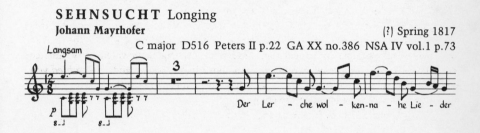

The lark's songs ring out from the clouds, chasing winter away. The earth is clad in velvet, and the blossoms form red fruit. You alone, storm-tossed soul, are barren, turned in upon yourself, devoured by deep longing even in the golden brightness of spring.

What you desire will never sprout from this earth, alien to the Ideal, which defiantly opposes its rough strength to your finest dreams. You wear yourself out wrestling with its harshness, consumed by the burning desire to migrate, like an aspiring companion of the cranes, to a milder clime.

Mayrhofer's fine poem turns characteristically from the beauty of this world to a longing for a better one. The surviving autograph (Vienna, SB) is an incomplete sketch of the voice line, undated. The song is usually attributed to 1816, but 1817 is much more likely. The pessimistic tone is unlike the 1816 songs, and the paper evidence points in the same direction. The incomplete sketch is published in the *Neue Ausgabe* and in the *Revisionsbericht*. The song was published in May 1822 as op.8 no.2 (Cappi and Diabelli) and dedicated to Johann Karl, Count Esterhazy.

Like *Auf der Donau*, the song moves from untroubled lyricism to sombre introspection. The impression of the lark ascending is enchanting, and when the tonality shifts enharmonically from A flat to E major the sturdy accompaniment hints at the rhythm of *Todesmusik* ('Release my afflicted soul from earthly strife'). The F sharp repeated octaves also speak ominously of Schubert's death motifs, but they do not toll so inexorably as in *Auf der Donau*, and in the last G major section the song seems to lose conviction.

Einstein, 193–4; Fischer-Dieskau, 204

### SEHNSUCHT Longing (1)
**Friedrich von Schiller**

15–17 April 1813

D minor D52 Not in Peters GA XX no.9

Allegretto

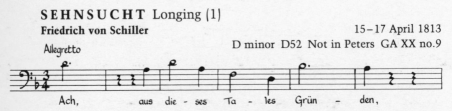

Ach, aus die - ses Ta - les Grün - den,

Ah, if only I could find the way out of the depths of this cold mist-enshrouded valley, how happy I should be! Over there I see lovely hills, eternally young, eternally green. If I had wings, if I had pinions, I would fly to the hills.

I hear music, the sweet sounds of heavenly peace, and balmy scents are carried to me on the breeze; golden fruits I see glowing enticingly through the dark foliage, and the flowers blossoming there are ravaged by no winter.

How lovely it must be to walk there in the eternal sunshine, and how refreshing the air on those mountains! But the raging torrent prevents me, that roars so angrily in my path; its waves are so high that my soul shrinks back.

I see a little boat rocking there but, alas, no ferryman. Leap in without hesitation! Its sails are full. You must believe, you must venture, for the gods give no pledges. Only a miracle can take you to that lovely land of miracles.

The poem was written in 1802. The autograph (Berlin, DS) is a first draft dated 15 April 1813 at the beginning and 17 April 1813 at the end. There is a copy in the Witteczek–Spaun collection (Vienna, GdM) and another in Berlin (SPK). The song was written for bass voice. *Sehnsucht* was published by Wilhelm Müller of Berlin in 1868 as no.1 of 'Six Previously Unpublished Songs'.

This first version is eclipsed by the brilliance of the later one. It is not that episodic treatment is doomed from the start, for the changing moods and scenes of the poem suit it. But the piece is too dependent on conventional melodic and accompaniment figures, of which the opening bars are fairly typical. The invigorating final section in F major works well; significantly, Schubert retained it when he revised the song eight years later. But even this, Edith Schnapper points out, is based on a conventional march theme.

Capell, 81; Fischer-Dieskau, 141; Schnapper, 119–20

## SEHNSUCHT (2)
**Friedrich von Schiller**                                                     (?) Beginning of 1821

B minor D636 Peters II p.86 GA XX no.357(a) and (b) NSA IV vol.2
pp.165, 250, 258

*Ziemlich geschwind*

Ach, aus die - ses Ta - les Grün - den,

For translation, see the preceding entry. The date of this second setting is not quite certain. On 8 February 1821 it was sung at an evening entertainment of the Gesellschaft der Musikfreunde by the bass singer Josef Götz (*Docs*. no.206), and Kreissle implies that it was written for that occasion. Moreover, the fragmentary first draft (London, BL) which covers only the last three stanzas, has the voice line in the bass clef. A fair copy made for the bass singer Adalbert Rotter by Schubert in 1824 is subtitled 'for a bass voice' (Washington, LC). There are contemporary copies, on the other hand, with the voice line in the treble clef. The song was published by A. W. Pennauer as op.39 in February 1826. The voice line is in the treble clef and there are other minor differences from the fair copy. The tempo indication is *Etwas geschwind*; the fair copy for Rotter has *Nicht zu schnell* (see *Docs*. nos. 465 and 501). All three versions are published in the *Neue Ausgabe*.

This fine song takes over from the earlier version the sectional plan, the wide-ranging tonality, and the theme of the irresistible final section. The structure may seem still rather loose, but the song banishes all doubts by the richness of Schubert's invention. The recitatives are jettisoned; instead, the idyllic passages of verses 2 and 3 are set to an enchantingly lyrical tune in B flat major; the raging torrent roars vividly; the interest never flags. More appealing in its variety than *Dithyrambe*, more lyrical than *Gruppe aus dem Tartarus*, *Sehnsucht* has a good claim to be recognised as Schubert's best Schiller setting. It was written as a recital piece, and should be judged as such.

Capell, 157; Einstein, 190; Fischer-Dieskau, 141

## SEHNSUCHT Longing
**Johann Gabriel Seidl**                                                             March 1826

D minor D879 Peters IV p.100 GA XX no.493

*Nicht zu geschwind*

Die Schei - be friert, der Wind ist rauh, der nächtge Himmel rein und blau.

The window-pane freezes, the wind is raw, the night sky clear and blue. I sit in my little room gazing out into the clear blueness.

Something is missing, that I know: my love is missing, my faithful companion, and when I try to look at the stars my eyes brim over.

My love, where are you, so far away, my lovely star, my treasure? You know that I love and need you – again I am close to tears.

For many a day I have been tormenting myself, because none of my songs has worked, because none could be persuaded to blow as freely as the west wind.

And now a gentle glow fills me; for behold – a song has appeared! Even though fate separates me from my darling I still feel that I can sing.

The poem was published in 1826, one of a group entitled Lieder der Nacht. The manuscript in which the autograph appeared originally contained four songs, three by Seidl and one (*Fischerweise*) by Schlechta. The first page is dated March 1826. This manuscript is now split up. The sheets containing the first seventy-one bars of *Sehnsucht* are now in Washington (LC), and the remainder in Vienna (SB). There is a copy in the Schindler collection (Lund, UB). The song was published in November 1828 by Josef Czerny as op.105 no.4.

*Sehnsucht* is without question among the greatest of the Seidl songs. It shares with other songs of 1826 a mastery of moving inner parts in the accompaniment, a complete equality of voice and piano, a wonderful economy of effect. But the tone is more sombre than the other Seidl songs; indeed, it is more sombre than the words might suggest. With the shift into D major the clouds lift a little, but the general mood is one of chastened recollection. Significantly, the thematic cell (see bars 1–5) is one more restatement of Schubert's death motif, the harmonic descent from D minor to A major underpinned by the firm chromatic bass line. The pre-echoes of *Erstarrung* are unmistakable. *Sehnsucht* might be called the first of Schubert's *Winterreise* songs.

Capell, 221; Fischer-Dieskau, 238

## SEHNSUCHT DER LIEBE Love's Longing
**Theodor Körner**                                                                8 April 1815

E minor  D180  Not in Peters  GA XX no.60

How solemnly, how tremulously, the night lies on the silent earth! How softly it rocks the soul, with all its strivings, its strength and richness, and its full life, to sweet slumber! But in my breast longing stirs with renewed pain. When in the heart all feeling slumbers, and in the soul torment and pleasure are silent, love's longing never slumbers, love's longing wakes early and late.

As gently as the chords of an Aeolian harp a soft breeze blows over me. Selene shines, gracious and friendly, and night runs its course in mild and pensive beauty. But love leads the drunken sense along bold tempestuous paths. How powerfully one's faculties are brought into play! Ah, and all peace of mind is gone; love's longing never slumbers, love's longing wakes early and late.

The world rests, scarcely breathing, in sweet holy silence; beautiful images rise from the many-coloured dance of life, and dreams come to life. But even amongst the images of dreams the painful longing assails me, shaking my heart with ruthless force from its blissful rest: love's longing never slumbers, love's longing wakes early and late.

So the circle of the hours goes by until day dawns grey in the east. Then the new-born bride of heaven rises bright and hot from the rosy portals of morning. But with the morning the longing in my heart wakes to new strength; my pain is eternally young. It torments me by day, it torments me by night. Love's longing never slumbers; love's longing wakes early and late.

The poem was published in 1815. The only surviving autograph (now in the Erasmus-Haus, Basel) is a fragment consisting of the first eight bars, dated 8 April

1815. There are, however, copies in the Witteczek–Spaun collection (Vienna, GdM) and in Stadler's song album (Lund, UB) which differ slightly in detail, and which may derive from a later fair copy – especially so since the catalogue of the Witteczek–Spaun collection dates the song July 1815. These copies are complete, and they provided the source for the *Gesamtausgabe* when the song was first published in 1894.

The contrast between the peace and serenity of nature and the unruly emotions in the lover's breast is reflected in the metrical scheme of the poem, each of the four verses consisting of a first half of slow-moving trochees and a second half of quicker dactyls. Schubert follows this plan closely, setting the first five lines of each verse to a slow, hymnlike tune marked 'Ruhig, langsam', and the remainder in 3/8 time, 'Schnell'. It works very well first time round, but four times are too many, especially since the long postlude is too conclusive to revive the listener's expectations.

## SEI MIR GEGRÜSST I Greet You
**Friedrich Rückert**                                         1822

B flat major  D741  Peters I p.190  GA XX no.400  NSA IV vol.1 p.137

O thou beloved, torn from me and from my embrace, I greet you, I kiss you! Out of reach except by my message of longing, I greet you, I kiss you!

O thou who wert given to this heart by the hand of love, thou who hast been taken from this loving breast, in a flood of tears I greet you, I kiss you!

In spite of the distance that has imposed itself like an enemy between us, and in defiance of the power of envious fate, I greet you, I kiss you!

As in love's wonderful springtime you once came to meet me with greetings and kisses, with the whole warmth of my heart I greet you, I kiss you!

One breath of love, and time and space dissolve: I am with you, you are by me. I hold you closely in my arms, I greet you, I kiss you!

The poem is a *ghazal*, an oriental love poem, in which the verses are dominated by a single rhyme or phrase. The form was first adopted by Friedrich von Schlegel, and it became fashionable in Romantic circles. Schubert's attention may have been drawn to the poem by the orientalist Hammer-Purgstall, whom he met at the house of Matthäus von Collin. It comes from a collection called *Östliche Rosen* ('Oriental Roses'), which is dated 1822, though it may have appeared at the end of 1821.

The autograph is lost, and the song cannot be precisely dated. However, Schubert's note of 31 October 1822 to Josef Hüttenbrenner (*Docs.* no.322) must refer to the songs of op.20, including this one, so that it must have been written before then. In the summer of 1822 Schubert made an agreement with the Viennese publishers Sauer and Leidesdorf whereby he would supply them with songs over a period of two years in exchange for an annual subvention. Op.20, dedicated to Frau Justine von Bruchmann, was the first fruit of this new agreement. It appeared in April 1823.

Schubert turns the oriental hyperbole and the erotic feeling of the poem into an idealised serenade. The physical passion of the verses hardly sounds in the song, for though the undertow of strong emotion does sound (*ff*) before the closing refrain of each verse, it emerges only to be quietened by the refrain itself which expresses a mood (*pp*) of selfless devotion.

The combination of a simple harmonic structure with a willingness to decorate the accompaniment wherever possible with a chromatic inflection gives the song a sensuous sweetness which can easily seem *schmalzig*. It is not so great a song as *Du bist die Ruh*, written a year later; but it has an eloquent *Innigkeit* which in a sympathetic rendering will justify Capell's use of the word 'noble'. 'Of a commonplace of sensuous experience Schubert has by force of feeling made a soaring aspiration; of a waltz, a hymn.'

The third movement of Schubert's Fantasy in C major for piano and violin op.159, written in December 1827, consists of a set of variations on the theme of this song.

Capell, 170–1; Fischer-Dieskau, 251–2

## SELIGE WELT The Blessed World
**Johann Chrysostomus Senn**                                      (?) Autumn 1822

A flat major  D743  Peters IV p.19  GA XX no.406  NSA IV vol.2 p.6

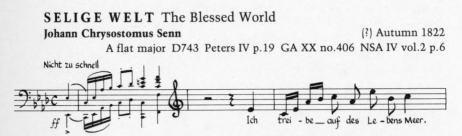

I sail the sea of life, I sit comfortably in my boat without destination or tiller, moving to and fro according to the pull of the current and the set of the wind. Folly seeks for a Blessed Isle, but there is no one such place. Have faith, and make your landing wherever the water breaks on the shore.

The poem is not included in Senn's collected works. It must have reached Schubert in manuscript, and almost certainly via Franz von Bruchmann, who visited Senn at Innsbruck early in September 1822. The autograph (Berlin, SPK) is headed 'Selige Welt. Von Senn.' but not dated. The voice line is in the bass clef, and the tempo indication is *Nicht zu schnell. Kräftig.* The song was published by Sauer and Leidesdorf in August 1823 as op.23 no.2, the voice line here in the treble clef.

Senn was banished in 1821 and eked out a living for many years in Innsbruck. A brave and honourable man, and a considerable poet, he became for the Schubert circle the type of the honest artist at war with society for conscience's sake. All the more significant then that this song has a close affinity with *Mut*, from *Winterreise*. It has the same mood of defiant resolution, the same rhythm and tempo, and a similar pattern in the accompaniment. The tonal scheme, however, is more adventurous than in *Mut*, where the second verse is in the tonic major. Here the modulation into the distant key of C flat major is splendidly effective.

Fischer-Dieskau, 157

## SELIGKEIT Bliss
**Ludwig Hölty**                                                        May 1816

Lustig                                E major  D433  Peters VII p.111  GA XX no.225

Numberless pleasures blossom in the halls of heaven for the angels and the saints, as our fathers taught us. How I would like to be there, and rejoice!

Each smiles lovingly on his heavenly bride; harp and psaltery sound and everyone dances and sings. How I would like to be there, and rejoice!

But if Laura smiles at me with a look that says I have suffered long enough, then I would rather stay here. I shall stay here with her in bliss for ever and ever!

The poem dates from 1773. The autograph, in private possession, is a first draft dated May 1816. There is a dated copy in the Witteczek–Spaun collection (Vienna, GdM). This delightful song has had a chequered history. It spent the first hundred years of its life in obscurity, and had to wait until 1895 for publication. In our century it has been taken up by sopranos as the perfect encore, and the patronage of Elisabeth Schumann in particular has made it a favourite with the public. It is now included in the last volume of the Peters edition.

The song is in 3/8 time, but it is not really a waltz, still less a Ländler, for the pace is too fast and the lilt too regular, more 6/8 than 3/4. Its popularity is easy to understand. The harmonic base is as simple as can be, and the melody is perfectly shaped – four symmetrical phrases leading back to the tonic, followed by a *Nachgesang* of three phrases. Nothing could be simpler, and nothing more difficult to encompass than its effect of effortless spontaneity.

## SELMA UND SELMAR
### Friedrich Gottlieb Klopstock
14 September 1815

F major D286 Peters V p.158 GA XX no.140(a) and (b)

Weep not, best beloved, because a sad day separates us from each other. When Hesperus smiles on you once more, blessed by fortune I shall return.

But in the dark night you climb the crags; in the treacherous darkness of night you hang above the waters! If only I could share with you the mortal danger, would I, so blessed by fortune, weep?

The poem dates from 1766. In spite of the Ossianic ring of the title, it has no connection with the royal palace of Fingal but reflects Klopstock's interest in early German legend. There are two versions, almost identical except that the second has a two-bar introduction and a different tempo indication. The autograph of the first version, marked 'Etwas langsam, innig', is lost, but there are copies in the Witteczek–Spaun (Vienna, GdM) and the Stadler (Lund, UB) collections. The autograph of the second version (Berlin, SPK) is marked 'Etwas geschwind' and dated 14 September 1815. Both versions are published in the *Gesamtausgabe*. The song (second version) was published in April 1837 in book 28 of the *Nachlass*.

Schubert's change of mind about the tempo is difficult to understand and perhaps is indicative of a lack of confidence in the song. If the solemn hymnlike setting is to carry any conviction, it would seem to demand the slower tempo.

**SENDSCHREIBEN** see EPISTEL: MUSIKALISCHER SCHWANK

**SERAFINA AN IHR KLAVIER** see AN MEIN KLAVIER

## SERBATE, O DEI CUSTODI Guard, O ye gods

**Pietro Metastasio**                                                December 1812

C major D35 no.1 (D2 35 no.3) Not in Peters Not in GA

Guard, O ye gods who watch over the fate of Rome, in Titus the Just the honour of our age. Preserve his happiness. Guard the immortal laurels on the brow of Caesar. Yours was so great a gift: may it last long. May future ages envy us because of him.

The text comes from Act I Scene 4 of *La Clemenza di Tito*, written in 1734. Schubert made several settings of it under Salieri's direction towards the end of 1812. This one, for solo tenor, was finished on 10 December. The autograph, containing two versions of the song, was dated 10 December 1812. It was destroyed in 1945. A description is given in A. Orel, *Der junge Schubert* (Vienna, 1940), and the revised version was published in an appendix to that book. The first version was arranged and privately printed by Reinhard van Hoorickx. It is a stirring *da capo* aria for which Schubert drafted the voice line, the bass and the piano prelude and postlude. A setting of the same melody for chorus (SATB) survives in Vienna (SB).


## SEUFZER The Sigh

**Ludwig Hölty**                                                      22 May 1815

G minor D198 Not in Peters GA XX no.74

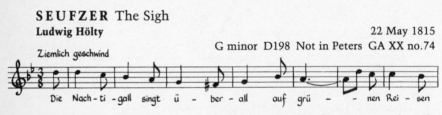

All around the nightingales on the green boughs sing their finest tunes, and woods and banks resound.

     Young couples go where the streamlet bubbles clear, and stand and listen happily to the songsters.

     But sadly on the dark path I listen to the resounding song of the nightingales; for I, alas, wander in the grove alone.

The poem, written in February 1773, was originally entitled *Die Nachtigall*, but Schubert used a revised version published in 1804. The autograph, in the Paris Conservatoire, is dated 22 May 1815. There is a dated copy in the Witteczek–Spaun collection (Vienna, GdM). The song was first published in the *Gesamtausgabe* in 1894.

*Seufzer* is one of the best of the Hölty songs, and it deserves to rank with *An die Nachtigall* as an illustration of the poetic feeling the poet's work brought out in Schubert's music. The six short lines of the stanza are linked together to form a long arching melodic statement in G minor. This is repeated in the relative major. The treatment of the third verse, with an expressive change of harmony and melodic line, brings a touch of Schubertian magic to the piece, for all the world like a poetic sigh. The song is undeservedly neglected, perhaps because it is at first glance a simple setting on a small scale.

# **SHILRIK UND VINVELA** Shilric and Vinvela

**James Macpherson (Ossian)**                    20 September 1815

B flat major  D293  Peters IV p.192  GA XX no.146

The text comes from Macpherson's prose poem *'Carric-Thura'* and in the original runs as follows:

*Vinvela*: My love is a son of the hill. He pursues the fleeing deer. His gray dogs are panting round him; his bow-string sounds in the wind. Dost thou rest by the fountain of the rock, or by the noise of the mountain stream? The rushes are nodding to the wind, the mist flies over the hill. I will approach my love unseen; I will behold him from the rock. Lovely I saw thee first by the aged oak of Branno; thou wert returning tall from the chase, the fairest among thy friends.

    *Shilric*: What voice is that I hear? that voice like the summer wind! I sit not by the nodding rushes; I hear not the sound of the rock. Afar, Vinvela, afar I go to the war of Fingal. My dogs attend me no more. No more I tread the hill. No more from on high I see thee, fair moving by the stream of the plain, bright as the bow of heaven, as the moon on the western wave.

    *Vinvela*: Then thou art gone, O Shilric! I am alone on the hill! The deer are seen on the brow; void of fear they graze along. No more they dread the wind, no more the rustling tree. The hunter is far removed; he is in the field of graves. Strangers! Sons of the waves! Spare my lovely Shilric!

    *Shilric*: If fall I must in the field, raise high my grave, Vinvela. Grey stones, and heaped up earth, shall mark me to future times. When the hunter shall sit by the mound, and produce his food at noon, 'Some warrior rests here,' he will say; and my fame shall live in his praise. Remember me, Vinvela, when low on earth I lie!

    *Vinvela*: Yes, I will remember thee; alas, my Shilric will fall! What shall I do, my love, when thou art gone for ever? Through these hills I will go at noon: I will go through the silent heath. There I will see the place of thy rest, returning from the chase. Alas, my Shilric will fall; but I will remember Shilric.

See OSSIAN SONGS. The passage is followed by two others which Schubert also set, *Cronnan* and *Lodas Gespenst*. It seems possible that Schubert thought of them as parts of a larger work based on *Carric-Thura* which never materialised. The source for the German text is not clear. According to Deutsch (*Thematic Catalogue* p.101) Schindler said that Franz von Hummelauer revised Harold's translation for Schubert.

    The autograph, dated 20 September 1815, has been divided in two. The first seven pages are in Gesellschaft der Musikfreunde, the remainder in the Stadt- und Landesbibliothek, Vienna. There is nothing either in the autograph or in the tessitura to suggest that the song was intended as a duet. The first publication was in book 4 of the *Nachlass*, in July 1830. There are minor differences between the autograph and the first edition, and it is possible the latter was based on a lost fair copy.

    *Shilric und Vinvela* lacks the atmospheric quality of *Cronnan*, and the ballad form, with its alternation of recitative and arioso, lacks conviction. Vinvela promises to remember her Shilric at the end with a vigour and tunefulness that suggests she is not altogether sorry to be rid of him.

## SIE IN JEDEM LIEDE She in Every Song
**Karl Gottfried von Leitner**                                        Autumn 1827

B flat major  D2 896A  Not in Peters  Not in GA

When, under the influence of tender feelings, I take up my harp, I think of you too, maiden, and believe me, without harps there cannot long be minstrels.

When as I sing I conjure up crofters and cells, castles and tournaments, I see you on the balcony among the ladies resplendent in their caps and ruffs.

When I praise the peaceful alpine breezes, high above the wild tumult of the valleys, you as a dairymaid fill the ravines with trills, and laugh your way out of the little wooden house.

When I sing of the lovely water-maidens alone in the moonlit sea, you are floating down there among them in the blue water, holding out your snow-white arms to me.

In the rosy land of poetry you, my love, are always close to me. Ah, only in life, harsh and dreary, does the hostile hand of fate keep us apart!

Schubert's interest in Leitner was revived by Marie Pachler during his visit to Graz in September 1827. Two of his songs were included in Schubert's op.106, published in the spring of 1828 and dedicated to Marie. Three others were left as sketches (now in Vienna, SB). The songs were sketched in Schubert's usual way, the voice line and the piano prelude and interludes written out with scanty indications of the accompaniment elsewhere. But in the case of this song no text was added. It was identified as a setting of *Sie in jedem Liede* by Reinhard van Hoorickx.

*Sie in jedem Liede* is a full-length modified strophic song in Schubert's mature manner, as expressive and constantly inventive as the best of the Leitner songs, though it is not quite so epigrammatic as *Die Sterne* nor so fluent as *Drang in die Ferne*. It is, however, made on the same pattern, unified by a continuing gait and rhythmical figure, but constantly enlivened by melodic and tonal variation; a more attractive song than either of the two which were included in op.106, and a piece of vintage Schubert which deserves a permanent place in the repertoire. The song has been completed for performance and privately published by Reinhard van Hoorickx, and recorded on DG 1981007. Intending tenors should be warned that in B flat the tessitura lies mercilessly high, with a top C in the last verse.

## SKOLIE Drinking Song
**Johann Ludwig von Deinhardstein**                         15 October 1815

B flat major  D306  Not in Peters  GA XX no.154

Let us enjoy life's blossoms in the sunshine of the May morning before their scent fades. And if it should infect the heart with torments, there is a spirit glowing in the wine-cup that can easily send them packing.

Joy kisses us; death beckons, and it is gone. Should we be afraid of death? The lips of girls breathe life: whoever sips it from them laughs at death's threats.

The poem, which does not appear in the collected volume of Deinhardstein's verse, was published in the annual *Selam* in 1814. The autograph, now in the ÖNB, Vienna, is a first draft dated 15 October 1815. There is a dated copy in the Witteczek–Spaun collection (Vienna, GdM). The first publication was in the *Gesamtausgabe* in 1895. 'Skolion' is a Greek word for a drinking song in which the cup is passed round. Schubert's setting is slight but charming, in the vernacular style.

### SKOLIE Drinking Song
**Friedrich von Matthisson**                                    December 1816

G major  D507  Not in Peters  GA XX no.283

The girls have unsealed the bottles, brothers – up, and snatch life's winged pleasures: curls, and beakers ringed with glowing roses!

Up, to drink bliss from rosy lips, and homage to the bloom of youth, before the mossy mound claims us.

The poem dates from 1791, but Schubert used the revised version published in 1794. The autograph, in the New York Public Library, is dated December 1816. The last two bars are missing. There are two dated copies in Vienna (GdM), one made by Ferdinand Schubert, and another in Berlin (SPK). The song has the characteristics of the true drinking song, hearty, noisy, tuneful but unsubtle. Einstein (p.160) says it is 'almost identical with Zumsteeg's setting of 1796'.

### SO LASST MICH SCHEINEN Such let me seem (1) and (2)
**Johann Wolfgang von Goethe**                                September 1816

A flat major  D469  Not in Peters  GA (*Rev. Ber.*, note to no.394)

NSA IV vol.3 p.254

Such let me seem till such I be. Do not take off my white dress! Soon I shall leave the fair world for that secure dwelling below.

There for a short silence I shall rest, and then I shall see with a fresh eye. I shall leave behind then this pure raiment, my girdle and my crown.

The heavenly beings there do not ask who is man or woman; no clothing, no drapery encloses the transfigured body.

True, I lived without toil and trouble; yet I had my share of anguish. Sorrow aged me too early; make me young again for ever.

The poem was written in 1796, especially for the end of *Wilhelm Meisters Lehrjahre*, where Mignon dies. When Wilhelm goes to the house of his long-lost ideal love, Natalie, in search of Mignon, he finds that she is ill. She has taken to wearing women's clothes, having been dressed up as an angel for a children's party. She begs to be allowed to keep her angel's dress on, and sings this song. Of all the Mignon lyrics this is the one most closely related to the text of the novel, and to Mignon's own enigmatic nature. Schubert found the essence of it as elusive as *Nur wer die Sehnsucht kennt* and made four attempts to set it. The first two, in September 1816, survive only as fragments.

The autograph (Vienna, SB) consists of (a) seven opening bars of a setting in A flat major, written out in the voice line and the top line of the accompaniment, and cancelled; and (b) eleven bars from the second verse of a setting in G. It is possible that this second attempt was completed, and that the remainder has been lost. Both fragments are published in the *Revisionsbericht* volume of the *Gesamtausgabe*. They have also been edited and published in a completed version by Reinhard van Hoorickx. The first sketch is headed 'Mignon. 1. Weise' (Mignon. First tune).

## SO LASST MICH SCHEINEN (3)
**Johann Wolfgang von Goethe**                                        April 1821

B minor  D727  Peters VI p.64  GA XX no.395  NSA IV vol.3 p.852

For translation, see the preceding entry. The autograph (Vienna, SB) follows on the same manuscript as the first setting of *Heiss mich nicht reden* D726, which it closely resembles in tone, tempo and tonality. The first page of this manuscript is dated April 1821. The song was first published in book 48 of the *Nachlass* in 1850.

Schubert's attempts to set the Mignon and the Harper songs from *Wilhelm Meister* in September 1816 were conditioned by the limits of the classical language which was at that time his natural mode of expression. Most of them are in A minor or A flat major, and the first two settings of *So lasst mich scheinen*, promising as they are in a Mozartian kind of way, survive only as fragments. Now, five years later, Schubert turns to the Romantic key of B minor/major as the only appropriate key for Mignon's pathetic songs; the four-bar introduction is one more variant on the familiar tonal sequence associated with death and deprivation, the shift into B major one more example of the idea of transfiguration in death. This fine song is rarely heard, because of the popularity of the 1826 setting. Yet it is nearer to the real Mignon, the dispossessed child, than the sweeter vision of heaven in that later setting.

Capell, 156–7; Einstein, 218

## SO LASST MICH SCHEINEN (4)
**Johann Wolfgang von Goethe**                                      January 1826

B major  D877 no.3  Peters II p.132  GA XX no.490

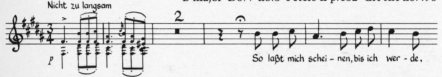

For translation, see *So lasst mich scheinen* (1) and (2). Autograph sketches exist for the first three of the Mignon songs published as op.62, including this one. As was Schubert's habit, he wrote out only the voice line in full, with the piano introduction and postlude and indications of the accompaniment where necessary. These sketches are in Vienna (SB).

A complete fair copy of all four songs of op.62 also exists on six sheets. Nos. 1–3 on five sheets are now in Dresden (SLB), but the last sheet, containing no.4, has been separated from the rest and is now in Vienna (SB). Numerous engravers' markings on this fair copy show it to have been the source of the first edition. The first page is dated January 1826. The song was published by Diabelli as op.62 no.3 in March 1827 and dedicated by Schubert to Mathilde, Countess Schwarzenberg. The changed wording of the last line of the first verse – 'in jenes dunkle Haus' for Goethe's 'in jenes feste Haus' – presumably derives from Schubert's manuscript. It is easier to sing, but damaging to the sense.

There is a sensuous richness about the B major harmonies, unrelieved in this final version by the minor–major alternations of the 1821 setting, which seems inappropriate to Mignon's childlike plea; the full chords with their moving inner parts suggest too sophisticated a sadness, especially at the passionate D minor cry of anguish in the last verse. Yet this is undeniably the most popular song of the four, the most memorable and the most organically integrated; in a word, the most Schubertian. So often in the *Wilhelm Meister* songs he appears to be composing in the shadow of Goethe's greatness; here he is composing with full confidence in his own.

Capell, 220–1

### SON FRA L'ONDE At the mercy of the waves
**Pietro Metastasio**                                          13 September 1813

C minor D78 Not in Peters GA XX no.572 NSA IV vol.6 p.150

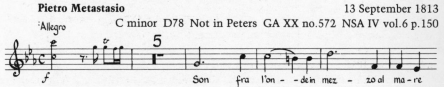

I am tossed by the waves in the midst of the sea, and by the fury of the adverse wind; one moment I hold firm and the next I tremble, caught between hope and terror.
    One moment I fear for your faith and for your life, the next I am bold; yet in boldness and in fear the anguish is the same.

The aria is sung by Venus in the first part of *Gli orti esperidi* ('The Gardens of the Hesperides', 1721). It is one of the many texts set by Schubert under Salieri's instruction. The autograph (Vienna, SB) is dated 13 September 1813. The first publication was in the *Gesamtausgabe* in 1895. Conventional as the elements of the piece are, with its insistent appoggiatures and arpeggios, the song is effectively written, and the wavelike accompaniment may perhaps be regarded as an early sample of Schubert's pictorialism.

### SONETT I Sonnet I
**Petrarch trans. August Wilhelm von Schlegel**                November 1818

B flat major D628 Not in Peters GA XX no.345

Apollo, if the sweet desire her blonde hair aroused in you on the banks of the Thessalian stream still lives, and has not sunk into oblivion in the course of the years; now, where first you, and then I, were taken captive, preserve this revered and holy plant from the frosts and mists which assail when your bright face is hidden.

And by the power of a lover's hope, which in your youth preserved you from
death, let warmth return to the air, free from the press of winter.

So that we both, in happy amazement, may see our mistress sitting on the
grass, in the shadow of her own arms.

Petrarch (1304–74), inventor of the sonnet, cultivated an ideal unattainable love for his
Laura, whom he glimpsed as a young man in a church in Avignon. Schlegel's note to his
translation explains that Petrarch often presents his Laura in the image of a laurel tree;
the poem is therefore to be interpreted allegorically as a prayer to Apollo to restore Laura
to health. The original Italian text is given in Schochow, p.572.

The autograph (Vienna, SB) is dated November 1818 and headed 'Sonett (Ms)'. There
is a dated copy in the Witteczek–Spaun collection (Vienna, GdM). The translation had
been published in 1804, but Schubert's heading suggests that he worked from a manuscript
copy, perhaps provided by one of his friends in the Bruchmann circle, or by Mayrhofer,
who also made translations of Petrarch. The first publication was in the *Gesamtausgabe*
in 1895.

Setting a sonnet to music is a notoriously difficult exercise, and Schubert had no
precedents to guide him. His solution is to treat the text rather like one of Mayrhofer's
classical monologues, that is by a combination of free moving recitative and arioso passages
which often come near to declamation. The result is pleasing and highly musicianly,
without persuading us that the composer is re-creating the essence of the poem in a song.
We move on quickly from one idea to the next, but the whole does not succeed in
impressing the listener as greater than the sum of the parts.

Capell, 145–6; Einstein, 185–6; Fischer-Dieskau, 114–5

## SONETT II Sonnet II
**Petrarch trans. August Wilhelm von Schlegel**      November 1818

G minor D629 Not in Peters GA XX no.346

Alone and pensive, limping and cramped, with slow footsteps I cover the barren
fields, searching around me for those paths where the sand is stamped by human
footprints, only so that I may avoid them.

No other defence can I find in the battle against the sharp eyes of people I meet;
for in my actions, bereft of joy, they observe from without how I fume within.

So that I now believe that the mountains and plains, the rivers and forests,
know of what stuff my life is made, though I have kept it hidden from everyone.

But I can find no path so rough and wild that the god of love does not constantly
confront me there, and talk with me, and I with him.

See the preceding entry. The autograph (Vienna, SB) is dated November 1818 and headed
'Sonett. Schlegel'. There are dated copies in the Witteczek–Spaun collection (Vienna,
GdM). The song was first published in the *Gesamtausgabe* in 1895.

Schubert's starting-point is a motor image derived from the first line. The opening
bars (marked 'Slow and slinking') paint an impressive picture of the forlorn lover slinking
away, 'limping and cramped', into the wilderness. There is more continuity of tone and
movement than in the first *Sonett*, and more unity of mood. On the whole this is perhaps
the most impressive of the three Petrarch songs.

# SONETT III Sonnet III

**Petrarch trans. J. D. Gries**

December 1818

C major D630 Not in Peters GA XX no.347

Nun - mehr, da Him-mel, Er - de schweigt und Win - de

Now that heaven and earth are silent, and winds, birds, animals are enchained by sleep, night drives the star-chariots in their orbits, and the sea sinks quietly into its depths.

Now I wake, think, glow, weep, finding only her, my sweet tormentor. War is my state, anger and discontent; but when I think of her, peace softly beckons.

So my nourishment, both sweet and bitter, flows from the living sunshine of a single fount; the same hand heals me as wounds me.

And because my torment never ends I die and rise again a thousand times each day; so far, even now, am I from being cured.

Like the previous two translations, this one appeared in Schlegel's *Blumensträusse italiänischer, spanischer, und portugiesische Poesie* (Berlin, 1804); the translator, however, was not Schlegel but Johann Diederich Gries. Schubert's autograph (Vienna, SB) is dated December 1818 and headed 'Sonett. Dante'. This mistaken attribution was repeated in the copy in the Witteczek–Spaun collection (Vienna, GdM) and followed in the *Gesamtausgabe* when the song was first published in 1895.

This is the longest and the most lyrical of the three settings. Formal recitative is abandoned, there is more repetition of the text, and the piano is freely used to prepare changes of mood. Note, for example, the expressive link between verses 1 and 2, and the sudden tightening of the rhythm at the words 'War is my state', and the descending bass line as the sea sinks down quietly into its depths. But on the whole these Petrarch songs seem to lack a personality of their own.

# SPRACHE DER LIEBE The Language of Love

**August Wilhelm von Schlegel**

April 1816

E major D410 Peters IV p.142 GA XX no.207

Laß dich mit ge - lin - den Schlä-gen rüh- ren,

Let me touch you softly, my tender lute. The evening dews have fallen, so we must speak in whispers. As your notes sound, as they breathe, lament, moan, so my heart flies on pilgrimage to my beloved, and draws from the depths of her soul all the sorrows that lay sleeping there; love thinks in sweet harmonies.

The poem, written in 1802, is prefaced by some lines of Tieck: 'Love thinks in sweet harmonies, for thoughts remain too distant. Only in music does it like to beautify all those things it intends.' Schlegel's poem, subtitled 'Second tune', has four verses, but Schubert wrote out only the first. The autograph (Vienna, SB) is dated April 1816. The song appeared as op. 115 no. 3, published by Leidesdorf in June 1829. The autograph did not come to light until 1912, too late to influence the *Gesamtausgabe*, which prints all four verses.

The song begins with quiet tenderness and grows with cumulative power to a climax; the effect is that of a single long crescendo of feeling, as the accompaniment moves from simple quavers to semiquavers, and then to repeated chords in semiquavers. The development of feeling is marked also by Schubertian modulations of striking originality, witness the sudden sideslip from C minor to A major at bar 17, and the climaxing G major chords which subside finally into the tonic.

Capell, 125–6

## STÄNDCHEN (Rellstab) see RELLSTAB SONGS no.4

## STÄNDCHEN Serenade: Hark, hark, the lark
**William Shakespeare**                                                   July 1826
C major  D889  Peters I p.234  GA XX no.503

The song comes from *Cymbeline* Act II Scene 3:

Hark, hark! the lark at heaven's gate sings,
And Phoebus 'gins arise,
His steeds to water at those springs
On chaliced flowers that lies;
And winking Mary-buds begin
To ope their golden eyes;
With everything that pretty is
My lady sweet, arise:
Arise, arise!

Schubert used the Vienna *Shakespeare-Ausgabe* of 1825, with translations by A. W. von Schlegel, Eduard von Bauernfeld and Ferdinand Mayerhofer. The song was written while Schubert was staying at Währing, then outside the city, with Schober, and the autograph is contained in a small notebook (Vienna, SB) inscribed 'Währing July 1826'. The song was published in book 7 of the *Nachlass* in October 1830. For this first edition Friedrich Reil was commissioned to write two extra verses, which appear also in the Peters edition.

Because of its irresistible lilt, this famous song is often described as a Ländler, but to do so is to ignore its essential property: it is not a dance but a song. It is inseparable from the words and belongs entirely to the voice (some would add to the soprano voice). The side-step to the flattened sixth halfway through the song, and the lovely swelling return to the tonic via a German sixth, are in a sense by now conventional procedures for Schubert; yet how wonderfully they leave us here 'surprised by joy' – only to be further surprised by the enchanting *Nachgesang*, the repeated 'Steh auf, steh auf, du süsse Maid, steh auf!' The song celebrates the universality of two of the world's greatest song-writers.

Capell, 224–5; Fischer-Dieskau, 233

## STERNENNÄCHTE see DIE STERNENNÄCHTE

# STIMME DER LIEBE The Voice of Love (1)

**Friedrich von Matthisson**                                        (?) May 1815

F major  D187  Not in Peters  GA XX no.63

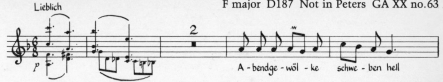

Bright evening clouds float across the crimson sky; Hesperus darts his loving glances through the blossoming linden grove, and the cricket chirps its prophetic lament amongst the grasses.

Love's joys await you! the winds whisper softly. Love's joys await you! the nightingale sings. From the high starry vault the voice of love calls down to me.

Out from the labyrinth of the plane trees fair Laura comes! Flowers spring up from her footsteps, light as air, and like the music of the spheres the sweet voice of love comes trembling to me from the roses of her lips!

The poem dates from 1777. The autograph (Vienna, SB) is dated May 1815. A copy in the Witteczek–Spaun collection (Vienna, GdM) is dated May 1816, but this is thought to be a mistake. The song was first published in the *Gesamtausgabe* in 1894. This first setting has the peaceful 6/8 lilt of a pastorale in the conventional pastoral key of F major.

R. von Hoorickx, 'Thematic catalogue of Schubert's works: new additions, corrections and notes', *Revue belge de musicologie*, XXVIII–XXX, 1974–6, p.156

# STIMME DER LIEBE (2)

**Friedrich von Matthisson**                                        29 April 1816

G major  D418  Not in Peters  GA XX no.214

For translation, see the preceding entry. The autograph is an incomplete first draft, lacking the text and part of the accompaniment, dated 29 April 1816 (New York, PML). There is a dated copy, complete, in the Witteczek–Spaun collection (Vienna, GdM). The first publication was in the *Gesamtausgabe* in 1895.

The repeated chords were to become a cliché of nineteenth-century song. Schubert had previously used them more imaginatively in *Nähe des Geliebten* and *Liebesrausch*. In combination with the plain harmonic sequences the effect here is a little static; but this second setting carries more subjective feeling than the first.

# STIMME DER LIEBE The Voice of Love

**Friedrich Leopold, Graf zu Stolberg-Stolberg**                        April 1816

D major  D412  Peters III p.200  GA XX no.210

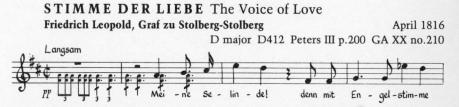

My Selinde! For love sings to me with the voice of an angel: She will be yours! She will be mine! Heaven and earth vanish! My Selinde!

> The tears of longing which trembled on my pale cheeks fall as tears of joy.
> For the heavenly voice sings to me: She will be yours! Yours!

The poem dates from 1775. The surviving autograph, in private possession, is a first draft dated April 1816. It is in E major, without tempo indication. The fair copy, presumably in D major, *Langsam*, is missing. There is a dated copy, in B flat, in the Witteczek–Spaun collection (Vienna, GdM). The song was published in D major in book 29 of the *Nachlass* (June 1838). The E major version is unpublished.

   This astonishingly predictive song is the best of several love songs written in April 1816. The repeated triplet chords are themselves a Schubert fingerprint; what is remarkable is the tonal freedom with which the long crescendo of feeling is built up. The song starts quietly; the naked thirds and the wisp of melody in the bass might almost be the beginning of a Mahler symphonic movement. But by bar 8, after an ecstatic top A flat on the word 'Deine', we are in D flat major. The relationship of D major to B flat major (tonic and flattened sixth) – that most characteristic of Schubertian tonal relationships – is basic to the song. In the second verse the tonality moves from B flat major enharmonically to B major before being wrenched back again for the final cadence. In its controlled tension and dynamic form the song has a strong affinity with *Die erste Liebe*, written a year earlier. It may – or may not – signify that the Therese Grob affair came to some sort of crisis at about this time.

   Capell, 119; Einstein, 134; Fischer-Dieskau, 68

## STROPHE VON SCHILLER see DIE GÖTTER GRIECHENLANDS

## SULEIKA I
**Marianne von Willemer rev. Johann Wolfgang von Goethe**      March 1821
   B minor/major D720 Peters II P.38 GA XX no.396 NSA IV vol.1 pp.108, 239

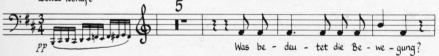

What is the meaning of this stirring? Does the east wind bring me good news? The fresh touch of its wings cools the deep wound in my heart.
   It plays gently with the dust, chasing it into puffs of cloud, and sends the happy insect people scurrying to the security of the vine-leaves.
   Mildly it tempers the heat of the sun, and cools my hot cheeks too; and in passing it kisses the grapes decking the fields and hills.
   And its soft whisper brings me a thousand greetings from my friend; before these hills grow dark I shall be greeted by a thousand kisses.
   So go on your way, wind, serving afflicted lovers. Where the high walls glow, I shall soon find my well-beloved.
   Ah, the true message from his heart, the breath of love and the renewal of life, can come to me only from his mouth, from his breath.

The three days which Goethe and Marianne von Willemer spent in Heidelberg together in September 1815 mark the climax of their brief but intense relationship. The two Suleika poems which Schubert set were written by Marianne: the first, addressed to the east wind, on her way eastward from Frankfurt to Heidelberg on 23 September, and the second, to the west wind, on her return journey. They were included in book 8 of the *West-östlicher Divan* when it was published in 1819. The title (*Divan* means simply anthology) is meant to suggest the ambiguous standpoint from which the poems are written. Goethe saw himself as a latterday Hafiz, and the *Buch Suleika*, which purports to celebrate the love of Hatem and Suleika, provided an outlet for the feelings of Goethe and Marianne. Goethe revised the poems before publication, not always to their advantage. Verse 4 originally ran:

> Und mich soll sein leises Flüstern
> Von dem Freunde lieblich grüssen;
> Eh' noch diese Hügel düstern
> Sitz ich still zu seinen Füssen.

(And its gentle whisper comes as a loving greeting from my friend; even before these hills grow dark, I shall be sitting at his feet.)

The autograph (Vienna, ÖNB) is a first draft headed 'Suleika. Göthe' and dated March 1821. The fair copy made for the first edition is lost. The song was published as op.14 no.1 by Cappi and Diabelli on commission in December 1822 and dedicated to Franz von Schober. There are minor differences between the autograph and the first edition. Both versions are included in the *Neue Ausgabe*.

Brahms thought it 'the loveliest song that has ever been written', possibly because it is more explicitly erotic than Schubert's love songs normally are, and certainly Brahms's own *Von ewiger Liebe* owes something to it. *Suleika I* is a masterpiece in which some of the basic elements of Schubert's song style come to full expression. The association of B minor/major with the pain and joy of love runs like a thread through his work from *Die Betende* to *Der Doppelgänger*. The ostinato rhythm which dominates the first five verses, like a heartbeat, is his thematic symbol for emotional disturbance, for the heartbreak of passion, as in *Der Zwerg* and *Du liebst mich nicht*, and – above all – in the B minor Symphony of 1822, the first movement of which uses the same tonality and rhythm. The final section, in which the tonality of B major is subjected to a process of 'dreamy and enthusiastic extension', as Capell puts it, carries an astonishing weight of emotion. This music seems to 'wear the lineaments of gratified desire'.

Capell, 156; Einstein, 219; Fischer-Dieskau, 144–6

## SULEIKA II

**Marianne von Willemer rev. Johann Wolfgang von Goethe**   (?) December 1824

B flat major   D717   Peters II p.68   GA XX no.397

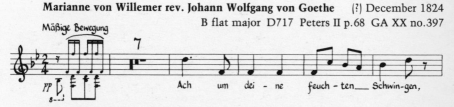

Ah, west wind, how often I envy you your damp wings, for you can take him news of what I suffer at our parting.

The movement of your wings awakes a silent longing in the breast; flowers, eyes, forests and trees dissolve in tears where you pass.

But your soft, mild breath soothes my sore eyelids; alas, I should die of sorrow if I had no hope of seeing him again.

So hasten to my love and speak softly to his heart; but conceal my sorrow from him, so that he will not be sad.

Tell him, but tell him humbly, that his love is my life, and that his presence will give me happiness in both.

See the preceding entry. Goethe and Marianne were never to meet again, though they continued to correspond until Goethe's death. The autograph is missing. There is a copy in Vienna (GdM) made for Anna Milder, the famous prima donna; this is headed 'Suleika's second song' and annotated – 'This copy Schubert sent to Milder' – by the singer's sister, the pianist Jeannette Bürde. *Suleika II* was published as op.31 by A. W. Pennauer in August 1825 and dedicated to Anna Milder.

The date of the song is not certain. It is usually assumed that it belongs, like the companion piece, to March 1821. At the end of 1824 Milder wrote to Schubert expressing admiration for his songs and promising to use her influence in Berlin on his behalf. In reply Schubert sent her the score of *Alfonso und Estrella* and a copy of *Suleika II*, which she acknowledged on 8 March 1825 (*Docs.* no.538). Milder sang the song at her concert in Berlin on 9 June 1825, with considerable success (*Docs.* nos.558, 559, 563).

The documentary evidence points strongly to the conclusion that the second Suleika song was written in response to Anna Milder's letter of December 1824 (*Docs.* no.511). If the song was written at the same time as *Suleika I*, as is commonly supposed, there seems no reason why it should not have been published along with its twin setting in December 1822. There is also a difference of tone and style between the two Suleika songs. The second is more brilliant, carries less subjective emotion, in fact is more of a 'public' work, halfway perhaps between *Suleika I* and *Der Hirt auf dem Felsen*.

Fischer-Dieskau, 145–6

## SZENE AUS FAUST Scene from *Faust*
**Johann Wolfgang von Goethe** December 1814

D126 Peters V p.108 GA XX no.37(a) and (b) NSA IV vol.7 pp.71, 196

[*Cathedral Service, organ and singing. Gretchen surrounded by a crowd. Evil Spirit behind Gretchen.*]

*Evil Spirit:* How differently you felt, Gretchen, when you used to come to the altar here still full of innocence, lisping prayers from the wrong page of your little book, your heart half full of children's games, and half of God! What are you thinking of, Gretchen? What sin lies in your heart? Are you praying for the soul of your mother, who passed over into the long, long sleep of torment because of you, and whose blood is on your hands? Does not something stir and swell already beneath your heart, a presence that fills you and it with fear and foreboding?

 *Gretchen:* Alas, alas! If I could only be free of the thoughts that come and go in my mind, against my will.

 *Choir:* Dies irae, dies illa,
    Solvet saeclum in favilla.

 *Organ:*

*Evil Spirit:* Retribution seizes you! The trump sounds! The graves quake! And your heart, fanned from an ashen peace to fiery torments, trembles!

 *Gretchen:* If only I were away from this place! The organ seems to take my breath away, and the singing to loosen my heartstrings.

 *Choir:* Judex ergo cum sedebit,
    Quidquid latet adparebit,
    Nil inultum remanebit.

 *Gretchen:* I feel trapped. The pillars in the walls imprison me! The vault bears down on me! – Air!

*Evil Spirit:* Go and hide yourself! Sin and shame will not stay hidden. Air? Light? Woe upon you!

    *Choir:* Quid sum miser tunc dicturus?
           Quem patronum rogaturus?

*Evil Spirit:* The saints turn their faces from you. The pure in heart shudder at the thought of helping you. Woe!

    *Choir:* Quid sum miser tunc dicturus?

*Gretchen:* Neighbour! – Your smelling salts! [*She falls unconscious.*]

The scene belongs to Goethe's first sketch of the drama, written before 1775. In the final version it appears as Scene 20 of part I.

Two versions of Schubert's setting survive, one (Paris Conservatoire) dated December 1814, another (in the Royal Museum of Mariemont, Belgium) dated 12 December 1814 both at the beginning and the end. An undated autograph in Berlin (DS), annotated 'Sketch for a further setting', may be later. The first version is marked 'Chorus', 'Organ', 'Trombones' at the appropriate places, proving that Schubert conceived the work as a full operatic scena for voices, chorus, and orchestra. But these markings are missing in the later version. The song was published in December 1832 in book 20 of the *Nachlass* as a solo song with piano accompaniment, though it makes little sense as such.

The concept is thoroughly dramatic, as Gounod was to prove. The force of Gretchen's accompanied recitative is heightened by the off-stage choir. Doubtless the aspirations of the seventeen-year-old composer included an opera on the Faust theme, but nothing remains to show what he might have made of it except this splendid sketch, the angels' chorus from the first scene (D440) and the unfinished sketch for the 'Gretchen im Zwinger' scene (D564).

    Fischer-Dieskau, 37; R. Winter, 'Schubert's undated works; a new chronology', MT, CXIX, 1978, p.500

# TÄGLICH ZU SINGEN A Daily Hymn
**Matthias Claudius**

February 1817
F major D533 Not in Peters GA XX no.304

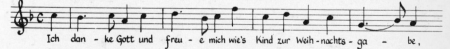

Ich dan - ke Gott und freu - e mich wie's Kind zur Weih - nachts - ga - be,

I give thanks to God, and am as happy as a child at Christmastime, because I exist. I live, and possess the fair face of humanity.

    Because I can see the sun, the mountains, and the sea, the leaves and the grasses, and can walk in the evening under the host of stars and the friendly moon.

    I give thanks to God with music of the strings that I was not born a king; I would have been much flattered, and perhaps have been spoilt.

    May God give me every day just so much as I need to live. He gives as much to the sparrows on the roof; why should he not to me?

The poem was published in 1778. It has nine verses, of which Schubert used the first two, the fourth and the last. The autograph, in the Taussig collection (Lund, UB), is a first draft dated February 1817. The song appeared in an arrangement for piano by J. P. Gotthard in 1876 under the title *Ich danke Gott*. The original version first appeared in the *Gesamtausgabe* in 1895.

    According to Fischer-Dieskau, Claudius intended the poem to be sung to the chorale *Mein erst Gefühl sei Preis und Dank* ('Let my first feeling be of praise and thanks'). Schubert preserves the archaic quality of the chorale in his setting, giving a melodic interest to each of the three parts, so that it flows gently forward, rather like the three-part counterpoint exercises he had done for Salieri in earlier days.

TÄUSCHUNG see WINTERREISE no.19

### THEKLA: EINE GEISTERSTIMME Thekla: A Phantom Voice (1)

**Friedrich von Schiller**                                22–3 August 1813

G major D73 Not in Peters GA XX no.11 NSA IV vol.4 p.230

Where am I, you ask, and where did I go when my fleeting shadow disappeared? Have I not finished, made an end? Have I not loved and lived?

Would you ask after the nightingales whose soulful melodies ravished you in the spring days? They lived only so long as they loved.

Did I find the one I had lost? Believe me, I am united with him in a place where those who have exchanged vows are never parted, and where no tears fall.

There you will find us again, when your love is as great as ours. There too is our father, cleansed of sin, no longer the victim of a bloody murder.

And he knows that he was not deceived, when he looked to the stars for help; for as you judge others, so shall you be judged, and whoever holds to this belief is close to holiness.

Up there in space every fine instinctive belief will be fulfilled. Dare to err, and to dream: often there is a higher purpose hidden in the play of children.

The poem was written in 1802, supposedly in response to complaints that the fate of Wallenstein's daughter Thekla was left unresolved at the end of Schiller's dramatic trilogy. Schubert used all six verses in this first setting. The autograph (Berlin, DS) is a first draft dated both at the beginning and the end. There is also a fair copy, dated 23 August 1813, in Stockholm (SMf). The song was published in 1868 as no.2 of 'Six Previously Unpublished Songs' by Wilhelm Müller of Berlin.

In this first version Schubert's perhaps over-respectful attitude to the poem prompts him to use alternating passages of recitative and arioso. This suits the question-and-answer form of the verses well enough but makes for a dull song, especially since the contrasted sections are under-characterised.

### THEKLA: EINE GEISTERSTIMME (2)

**Friedrich von Schiller**                                    November 1817

C minor/major D595 Peters II p.168 GA XX no.334(a) and (b)

NSA IV vol.4 pp.102, 235

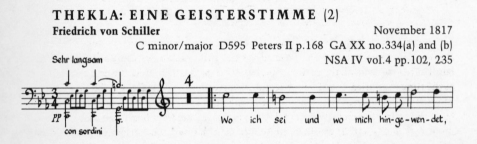

For translation, see the preceding entry. There are two versions. The first, in C sharp minor/major, is a simple strophic setting consisting of two eight-bar sentences, the second in the tonic major. There are repeat marks at the end, and the second verse is written out, but Schubert did not apparently intend all the verses to be sung. The autograph of this first version, dated November 1817, is in the Paris Conservatoire. The tempo indication, originally *Leise, von ferne*, has been altered to *Langsam, von ferne*. There are copies in the Witteczek–Spaun collection (Vienna, GdM) and in the Spaun–Cornaro collection (Vienna, privately owned), the latter in C minor/major.

The familiar version is in C minor/major, and the strophe now has a second half so that it covers two verses. The only surviving autograph of this revised version, in Washington (LC), is fragmentary, lacking the first nineteen bars, and there is no date. The marking is *Sehr langsam*, and for the pianist *con sordini*. This is the version published in December 1827 as op.88 no.2 by Thaddäus Weigl. Both versions are included in the *Gesamtausgabe*.

What a significant contrast there is between this 1817 version and the earlier one! Here the manner is purely lyrical. The alternation between recitative and arioso is discarded in favour of a simple strophic form, and the contrast between earthly cares and heavenly joys is conveyed by the tonal expedient of a shift to the major. The melody, moving by tones and semitones within a narrow range of a fourth, expresses the wraithlike image of the departed Thekla. The only dynamic markings are *pp* and *ppp*.

Capell, 131; Fischer-Dieskau, 100–1

## TIEFES LEID  Deep Sorrow

**Ernst Schulze**

December 1825/March 1826

E minor  D876  Peters III p.202  GA XX no.487

All tranquillity has forsaken me; I drift this way and that on the wild waters. There is only one place where I shall find peace, and that is the place where everything is at rest. Even if the wind whistles chill and the rain falls cold, I would rather live there than in this inconstant world.

For as dreams vanish without trace, as one follows another in swift succession, so life is a confused play of events: each one draws near, but none remains. The false hopes never fade, nor with those hopes our fears and struggles; the ones above, the ever-silent, the ever-pale, promise us nothing and deny us nothing.

My footsteps will not waken them in their lonely darkness. They do not know what I have suffered; my deep sorrow disturbs none of them. There can my soul more freely lament, with her whom I truly have loved; there will be no cold stone to tell me, alas, that my suffering grieves her.

The poem is from Schulze's *Poetisches Tagebuch* ('Verse Journal'), where it is headed simply 'Am 17ten Januar 1817', and this is the title also on Schubert's autograph. The familiar title appears on the manuscript, but not in Schubert's hand. It was probably added at the time of publication. The autograph, undated, is in the Bodleian Library at Oxford. There is a copy in the Witteczek–Spaun collection (Vienna, GdM) dated January 1826, but this is almost certainly a mistake due to confusion with Schulze's title. The song probably belongs with the bulk of the Schulze settings, written earlier in December 1825 or March 1826. *Tiefes Leid* was published in 1838 in book 30 of the *Nachlass*.

The mood of lonely defiance, of suffering beyond endurance, is very suggestive of *Die Winterreise*, and the musical links are close also, both with *Rückblick* and with *Auf dem Flusse*. But compared with them *Tiefes Leid* seems somewhat undercharacterised, and it is perhaps the least impressive of the Schulze songs.

Capell, 216; Fischer-Dieskau, 227–8

## TISCHLERLIED Carpenter's Song

**Author unknown**

25 August 1815

C major D274 Peters VI p.67 GA XX no.131

*Etwas langsam*

Mein Handwerk geht durch al - le Welt und bringt mir man-chen Ta - ler Geld,

My handiwork travels all over the world, and brings me in a mint of money, which gives me great satisfaction. Men from all walks of life need the carpenter. Even babies are rocked to rest in my handiwork.

My hard work is responsible too for the richly painted bed for the wedding night. However mean a skinflint may be, he needs a coffin at the end, and he pays well for it.

So I always keep cheerful, and whether I make a table or a cabinet I do my work well. And to those who place good long orders and always pay me in cash I am duly grateful.

The autograph is a first draft dated 25 August 1815 and marked 'Etwas langsam'; its present whereabouts are unknown. There are copies in the Witteczek–Spaun (Vienna, GdM), Stadler (Lund, UB) and Spaun–Cornaro (Vienna, privately owned) collections. The song appeared in 1850 in book 48 of the *Nachlass*, in a version marked 'Mässig'. There is also a two-bar introduction, which may well be spurious. Whether Diabelli based this version on a lost fair copy, or whether he was using his notorious 'editorial discretion', is not clear. *Tischlerlied* is an attractive little song which resembles the three-part canons and partsongs which Schubert also wrote in this summer.

## TISCHLIED Drinking Song

**Johann Wolfgang von Goethe**

15 July 1815

C major D234 Peters IV p.147 GA XX no.97

*Guter Laune*

Mich er - greift_, ich__ weiß nicht wie, himm - li-sches Be - ha - gen.

I am filled, I know not why, by a heavenly sense of comfort. Am I perhaps about to be carried up to the stars? But to tell the truth, I would rather stay here, tapping on the table to a song, with my glass of wine.

Do not be surprised, my friends, at my behaviour; truly life is best of all on the dear old earth. So I solemnly swear without danger of perjuring myself that I shall never unlawfully leave it.

But since we are all congregated here together I would have thought that the cup should ring in time with the poet's lines. Good friends are going a hundred miles or so away, so we must make haste to touch glasses while we are still all here.

The poem, written in February 1802, was a 'parody' written to fit the tune of the famous medieval drinking song *Mihi est propositum in taberna mori*. Its fame had been established by J. A. P. Schulze, who included the song in his *Lieder im Volkston* (Berlin, 1782), quoting both the Latin words and a German 'parody' by Bürger. Goethe's verses in their turn were widely imitated and frequently set to new tunes. The whole story is a classic instance of that free trade in texts and tunes which was so characteristic of the time.

Goethe's poem has eight verses, but it is not clear how many Schubert intended should be sung, or whether he cared. The Peters edition prints the first three, and the *Gesamtausgabe* eight. The first draft of the song has not survived. The fair copy made for Goethe in 1816 (Vienna, SB) is retrospectively dated 15 July 1815. The song was published in June 1829 as op.118 no.3 by Josef Czerny.

A drinking song for solo voice is a kind of contradiction in terms, and though *Tischlied* was published as a solo song, it sounds more like a rousing chorus for male voices, punctuated by hearty whacks on the table. The autograph and the first edition have different versions of the vocal line, the first edition being better adapted to the words. It is possible that Schubert provided a fair copy for the printer.

Sternfeld, 13–15, 112

## TODESMUSIK Death Music
**Franz von Schober**                                    September 1822

G major D758 Peters IV p.112 GA XX no.411

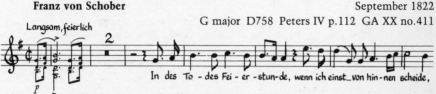

In des To - des Fei - er -stun-de, wenn ich einst von hin-nen scheide,

In the solemn hour of death, when one day I pass hence and suffer the last battle, grant, holy muse, that your tranquil songs, your pure notes, may shed their healing power one last time upon the deep death wound in my heart. Release my afflicted soul from earthly strife, and bear it aloft on wings of music to marry with the light.

Ah, the sounds will hover about me with sweet delight, and I will cast off my chains with tranquil ease. In them I shall see transfigured everything noble that once gave me joy. All the beauty that once flowered for me will appear even more glorified before me.

The music will bring to mind every star that during my short journey shed a friendly light through the darkness of doubt, every flower that decked the way; and those terrible moments when I might have bled to death in agony will resound with happiness. Everything will be bathed in glorious light. So I shall sink in bliss, gently engulfed by waves of joy.

The second and third lines ('when one day I pass hence and suffer the last battle') do not appear in the published version of the poem. Either Schubert inserted them, or Schober left them out when he prepared the poem for the printer.

The first draft, in G flat major, is dated September 1822 (Vienna, Schubert-Bund). There is a copy of this version with autographed title page (Vienna, SB) made by Ferdinand Schubert. The song was published by M. J. Leidesdorf as op.108 no.2 in January 1829. This published version is in G major and was almost certainly based on a lost fair copy. The edition was advertised as early as Easter 1828, so that it could not have been prepared without Schubert's knowledge and approval. Originally the opus was given a number (93) which had already been allocated, but this was corrected. The title page gave the title erroneously as *Todes Kuss*, but the correct title appeared at the head of the song.

Another song in praise of death, but this one begins and ends in the rhapsodic key of G major, moving in enharmonic shifts through E flat major, F sharp major and minor, and B flat major in the process. Stylistically the song is something of a pastiche; the resolute dotted theme belongs to Schubert's epic style, while the triplet chords in the final section recall the visionary climaxes of *Die Mondnacht* (D238) and *Liebesrausch*. More significant perhaps is the fact that the song has obvious affinities with the first movement of the B flat Piano Trio. The movement and layout of the accompaniment in the B flat section of the song are identical with those of the Trio, and even the triplet figure in the opening bars of the Trio seems to be anticipated in the closing bars of the song. 'Kamöne' (the 'holy muse' of verse 1) is the German form of Camena, the lyric muse.

Capell, 174; Porter, 112

**TODTENMARSCH** see GRABLIED FÜR EINEN SOLDATEN

## TODTENOPFER An Offering for the Dead
**Friedrich von Matthisson**                                                    April 1814

Andante                     E minor D101 Not in Peters GA XX no.18 NSA IV vol.7 p.18

kein Ro - - sen - schim - mer   leuch - tet dem Tag — zur Ruh,

No rosy glow lights the day to rest. The evening mist drifts up the beach, where dying breezes whistle through the dry grasses of the cliff-top.

 The autumn winds were not more melancholy when they trembled through the dead grass by the sinking mound which marks the spot where the ashes of my young lover slumber under the weeping willow.

 I shall shed tears for him when the leaves fall, and when the May buds rustle again in the grove; until at last, from a lovelier star, I shall see the friendly earth shimmering in the round dance of the universe.

The poem, written in 1793, was originally entitled *Erinnerung* ('Remembrance'), but in the 1811 edition, which probably served as Schubert's source, it was renamed *Todtenopfer*. The autograph is lost, but there appear to be two copies in the Witteczek–Spaun collection (Vienna, GdM), where both titles are found. Of the published editions, only the *Neue Ausgabe* follows the original title. The song was first published in 1894, in the *Gesamtausgabe*.

 The through-composed setting has an affecting tenderness and sincerity, suggestive almost of the later Schubert of the song cycles. The unity of the song is constantly felt, though the melodic line is always changing, and each verse is individually characterised, though the gentle lyrical flow is nowhere interrupted. The middle verse, which speaks more directly of the lover's grief, is broken up into short phrases which have the emotional force of recitative, without its disjunctive effect, while the outer verses express both the depth of the lover's grief and – in the murmuring semiquavers – the pictorial scene. *Todtenopfer* is one of the best of the early Matthisson songs, and one of the most successful in combining lyrical and declamatory elements.

Einstein, 67

# TOTENGRÄBERLIED The Grave-digger's Song
**Ludwig Hölty**                                      19 January 1813

G major D44 Not in Peters GA XX no.7 NSA IV vol.6 p.64

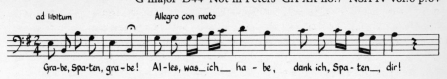

Dig, spade, dig. All I have I owe to you! All people, rich or poor, become my prize, they come to me at last!

Once this great nobleman's skull acknowledged no greeting! This bag of bones without cheeks or lips possessed gold and rank.

That hairy head, a few years ago, was as beautiful as an angel! Thousands of young sparks licked his hands, and stared themselves silly.

Dig, spade, dig: all that I have I owe to you. All people, rich or poor, become my prize, they come to me at last!

The poem dates from 1775. The autograph, untitled and dated 19 January 1813, is in the Taussig collection (Lund, UB). There is a copy in the Witteczek–Spaun collection (Vienna, GdM). The song was first published in the *Gesamtausgabe* in 1894. There is no hint of irony in this lighthearted little song, nor of those more sombre thoughts of death which recur so insistently in later songs. The most interesting feature is the curious two-bar 'digging motif' which punctuates the song and appears as an (off-key) prelude. The marking, *Ad libitum*, suggests that it may have been intended as a kind of chorus.

Capell, 80–1

# TOTENGRÄBERS HEIMWEH Grave-digger's Longing
**Jacob Nicolaus Craigher**                                      April 1825

F minor D842 Peters V p.143 GA XX no.467

O mankind, O life, to what end, to what end? Digging out, shoving in, no rest day or night! This driving and hurrying, where does it lead, ah where? 'To the grave, to the grave, deep down.'

O destiny, O sad responsibility, I can bear it no longer! When will you strike for me, O hour of rest? O death, come and close my eyes. In life all is so warm, so sultry; the grave is so peaceful, so cool! But ah, who will lay me therein? I stand alone, quite alone.

Abandoned by all, cousin only to death, I wait on the brink, with a cross in my hand, staring longingly down into the deep grave!

O home of peace, land of the blessed! My soul is bound to you with magic bonds. The everlasting light beckons me from afar: the stars disappear, my eyes grow dim. I am sinking, sinking ... You loved ones, I come, I come!

The poem was written in 1822 and appeared in the *Poetische Betrachtungen in freien Stunden*, published in 1828 under the pseudonym 'Nicolaus'. But Schubert was in close touch with Craigher in 1825, and set the verses from a manuscript copy. Craigher's title was *Gräbers Heimweh*. The comparison between life and death in the third verse recalls the opening lines of Stolberg's *Lied*, set by Schubert two years earlier under the title *Die Mutter Erde*: Life's day is hard and sultry,/Death's touch is light and cool. The autograph (Vienna, SB) is a first draft dated April 1825. There is a copy in Schindler's song album (Lund, UB). The song was published in September 1833 in book 24 of the *Nachlass*.

There is a fascinating clue to the sustained depth of feeling in this fine song in the setting of the third verse, which forms a link between the restless quaver chords of the first section, with its stepwise-moving bass, and the apocalyptic final section. At bar 40 the quaver chords subside on a long-held chord of G major (*pp*). After the pause, a quite new unison theme appears (*ppp*), which sinks down slowly through an octave and a third. This theme in descending unison octaves is of course a familiar Schubert motif for death. More remarkable is the fact that it is a straight quotation from the first movement of the Piano Sonata in A minor (D845), also written in the spring of 1825 (cf. bars 89–104).

There is a strong tradition, recorded by Kreissle and corroborated indirectly by Schwind in his letter of 14 February 1825 (*Docs.* no.528), that at the beginning of 1825 Schubert had to return to hospital for treatment; in these circumstances the direct reference to his own piano sonata must seem like a personal endorsement of the sentiments of the poet.

Capell, 206–7; Fischer-Dieskau, 228–9

# TOTENGRÄBER-WEISE Grave-digger's Air

**Franz Xaver von Schlechta**                                                     1826

F sharp minor D869 Peters III p.155 GA XX no.496

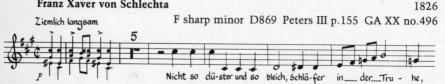

Be not so sad and pale as you sleep in your chest; under the soft light earth I lay you to rest.

Even though the body is devoured by worms and becomes the plaything of the winds, the heart, dust as it is, lives on and feels.

For the Lord sits in judgment; according to the life you have led the dreams that hover about you will be dark or bright.

Every accusing sound which charges you with causing pain will become a dagger to pierce you to the heart.

But the dewy tears of love sprinkled on your grave will take on the colour of the blue heaven, and bud and blossom.

The hero lives on in song, and to celebrate his memory a flower of fire gleams on high in the starry fields.

Sleep until the angel calls you, until the trumpet sounds, and the bodies ascend transfigured from their graves.

The autograph (Washington, LC) is a fair copy made for the printer; there are corrections to the text in a strange hand, possibly the author's. The evidence for the date of the song comes from the catalogue of the Witteczek–Spaun collection (Vienna, GdM) and from the surmise that it may well be contemporaneous with another Schlechta song, *Fischerweise*, which belongs to March 1826. The song was published in January 1832 in book 15 of the *Nachlass*.

This extraordinary song is characterised by the rigidly symmetrical structure. The thematic cell is a two-bar tolling motif (the accents over the first two bars show that the bell tolls four times in each phrase, and this applies throughout the song). The tolling note rises step by step so that the tonality is continually and inexorably changing. (The only other Schubert song to adopt this quasi-deterministic form is *Don Gayseros I*, which inhabits a quite different world.) The symmetrical phrases sound like question and answer, but the answers are never final. Side by side with this ambiguity is another. The poem hovers between the dark and the light side of death, and Schubert's song follows it, setting the more sombre verses in F sharp minor and the more comforting ones in the tonic major. At the end the bells peal softly in the major key. The 'octave higher' mark in the accompaniment to the singer's last phrase is authentic and applies to both hands.

Not surprisingly, critical comments on this highly idiomatic song differ widely. It is one of the very best of Schubert's meditations on the ever present subject of death, full of courage, sadness and a kind of solemn wonder.

Capell, 214–15; Einstein, 303–4; Fischer-Dieskau, 239; Porter, 105–6

## TOTENKRANZ FÜR EIN KIND  Wreath for a Dead Child
**Friedrich von Matthisson**                                           25 August 1815

Etwas geschwind                             G minor D275 Not in Peters GA XX no.132

Sanft wehn im Hauch der___ A - bend-luft, die___ Früh -lings-halm' auf dei - ner Gruft.

The spring grasses wave gently upon your grave in the breath of evening, as our tears of longing fall. Never, until death comes to set us free, shall your sweet memory be clouded by forgetfulness.
　　Blessed flower, scarce unfolded, to have escaped earthly pleasure, and sensual dreams, with their pain and folly! You sleep in peace; we wander anxiously through the tumult of the world, confused and unsteady, and seldom find peace.

The autograph, formerly in private hands, is now missing. It is a first draft dated 25 August 1815. There is a copy in the Witteczek–Spaun collection (Vienna, GdM). The first publication was in the *Gesamtausgabe* in 1895.

The setting of the six-line verse is unusual in that it does not consist of four symmetrical phrases followed by a *Nachgesang*. Instead, Schubert extends the strophe by an unexpected swing away into E flat major at the end of the third line, so that we do not arrive at the dominant and the concluding cadence until the final couplet. The brisk pace (*Etwas geschwind*) and the unconventional tonal scheme enable Schubert to treat the poem with unsentimental seriousness.

**TRÄNENREGEN** see DIE SCHÖNE MÜLLERIN no.10

## TRAUER DER LIEBE  Love's Lament
**Johann Georg Jacobi**                                                   August 1816

Mäßig                              A flat major D465 Peters VII p.26 GA XX no.247

Wo die Taub' in stil - len Bu - chen ih-ren Tau-ber sich___er - wählt,

Where the dove chooses her mate among the silent beech trees, where the nightingales seek one another out; where the vines intertwine in marriage and the brooks join up, I used often to go, filled with gentle melancholy, and often with anxious tears, in search of a loving heart.

Ah, there in the glimmer of dusk the dark foliage brought me quiet comfort; when the light of dawn touched the grove a sweet conviction came to me. I heard it in the winds; they whispered to me that I should seek and find, find you, my dear love!

But ah, where on this earth, dear love, did any trace of you remain? Only to angels is it given to love and to have one's love requited. In place of happiness I found sorrow; clung to that which forsook me. Peace is given to faithful hearts only yonder in paradise.

The autograph, in the Paris Conservatoire, is a first draft dated August 1816. There is a dated copy in the Wittezek–Spaun collection (Vienna, GdM), and a fair copy in the Therese Grob song album (see GROB). This last has a slightly longer postlude. A corrupt version of the song appeared in an arrangement for piano duet in 1876 (Kratochwill, Vienna), as no.5 of 'Sechs nachgelassene Lieder'. The authentic version appeared first in vol.VII of the Peters edition in 1885. The variant version in the Therese Grob album (see GROB) was published privately by Reinhard van Hoorickx in 1967. This is Schubert in his 'Magic Flute' mood, giving to the demotic style the formal perfection of a jewel.

**TRAUER UMFLIESST MEIN LEBEN** see KLAGE

## TRINKLIED Drinking Song
**Ignaz Franz Castelli**                              February 1815
                                                     D148 Peters IV p.159

A solo version of this song is included in the Peters edition, but it was written for tenor solo and male-voice chorus and, strictly speaking, has no place there.

## TRINKLIED Drinking Song
**William Shakespeare**                                  July 1826
                                     C major D888 Peters VI p.63 GA XX no.502

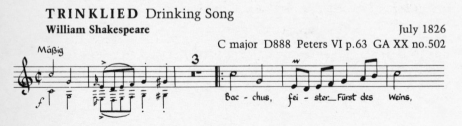

The song comes from *Antony and Cleopatra*, Act II Scene 7:

Come, thou monarch of the vine,
Plumpy Bacchus with pink eyne!
In thy vats our cares be drowned
With thy grapes our hairs be crowned;
Cup us, till the world go round,
Cup us, till the world go round!

Schubert used the Vienna *Shakespeare–Ausgabe* (1825) with translations by A. W. von Schlegel by Eduard von Bauernfeld and Ferdinand Mayerhofer. There is only one verse, but Schubert put repeat marks at the end, presumably on the principle that a good song is worth singing twice. However, when the song was published a second verse was added to the German text by Friedrich Reil, the author of *Das Lied im Grünen*. This appears in the Peters edition but not in the *Gesamtausgabe*.

The autograph (Vienna, SB) is a first draft written in a notebook dated 'Währing July 1826', which contains all three Shakespeare settings. There are dated copies in the

Witteczek–Spaun collection. Schubert stayed at Währing, then a village outside Vienna, at Schober's invitation for a few days in July 1826. The song was published in 1850 in book 48 of the *Nachlass*.

Capell finds echoes of Handel in this rollicking song, and Fischer-Dieskau suggests also Mozart for good measure. But it is not really very different from Schubert's adolescent drinking songs. The tune can be sung to the English words, though it was not written for them.

Capell, 224; Fischer-Dieskau, 233

## TRINKLIED Drinking Song
**Alois Zettler**                                               12 April 1815

Mäßig, lustig                        G major D183 Peters VII p.69 GA XX no.62

Solo: Ihr Freun - de und_ du_ gold - ner Wein, ver - sü - ßet_ mir das Le - ben;

You friends, and this golden wine, are what sweeten life for me. Without them to delight me I should never stop worrying. [*Chorus*] Without friends, without wine, I would not care to remain alive!

The man who locks away thousands in his chest, only to add more to them; the man who forgets himself and the needs of his friends may stay rich – we despise him. [*Chorus*] Without friends, without wine, I would not care to be rich!

What is a hero, without any friends? What are the great men of state? What is it to be lord of all the world? They are all in need of good advice! [*Chorus*] Without friends, without wine, I would not care even to be Emperor!

And if at some time in the future my soul has to part from my body, let me find in the shelter of the blessed angels a welcoming friend, and the juice of the vine. [*Chorus*] Otherwise, without friend and without wine, I would not care to be in heaven!

The poem appeared in the annual *Selam* in 1814. The autograph is missing. The copy in the Witteczek–Spaun collection (Vienna, GdM) is dated 12 April 1815 and headed 'Rundgesang mit Chor' (Roundelay with Chorus). The song was published in 1887, in vol. VII of the Peters edition. It is one of several rousing drinking songs written in Schubert's early years, presumably for some local *Singakademie* or musical gathering.

## TROCKNE BLUMEN see DIE SCHÖNE MÜLLERIN no.18

## TROST Consolation
**Author unknown**                                               January 1817

G sharp minor D523 Peters VII p.9 GA XX no.292

Langsam, mit schwärmerischer Sehnsucht

Nim - mer lan-ge weil ich hier, kom - me bald hin - auf_ zu dir_;

I shall not linger here much longer; soon I shall join you up there. Deeply, silently I feel in my heart that I shall not linger here much longer.

Soon I shall join you up there; pains and torments rage ceaselessly in my breast; soon I shall join you up there.

> Deeply, silently I feel it in my heart – there is a flame of hot desire which consumes me within; deeply, silently I feel it in my heart.
> I shall not linger here much longer; soon I shall join you up there. Deeply, silently I feel in my heart that I shall not be here much longer.

The autograph is lost, but there is a copy in the Witteczek–Spaun collection (Vienna, GdM) dated January 1817. The song was first published in 1885, in vol.VII of the Peters edition.

This mysterious little song attracts scant attention, yet it is strangely moving and predictive. Here for the first time in a solo song the solemn tread of death is clearly defined, two months before *Der Tod und das Mädchen*. (Significantly also, it assumes its most characteristic form at the two points – bar 7 and bar 11 – where the tonality is most emotionally charged, first at the sudden side-step from B major to G major, and again where it moves warmly towards B major.) The tempo indication is 'Slow and with passionate longing'; the simple strophic setting is completely Romantic in feeling.

### TROST Consolation

**Johann Mayrhofer**                                     October 1819

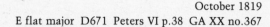

E flat major  D671  Peters VI p.38  GA XX no.367

Horn calls sadly ring out from the green night of the forest; work their powerful magic, transporting us to the realm of love.
Happy is he who has found a heart to give itself in love. For me that happiness has vanished, for my darling is in her grave.
When the sound of the horns reaches my ears from the depths of the forest I seem to find her once again, and I am drawn up towards her.
On that further shore she who gave herself to me in love will reappear. Ah, what a blissful union that will be! For me the grave holds no terrors.

The poem is not included in the collected edition of Mayrhofer's work. Verses 3 and 4 (the verses are grouped in pairs) do not appear on the autograph, but there are repeat marks at the end. The autograph (Paris Conservatoire) is dated October 1819 and the tempo indication is *Mässig*. The published version, presumably based on a fair copy, is marked 'Lebhaft'. There is a copy in the Witteczek–Spaun collection (Vienna, GdM). The song was published in June 1849 in book 44 of the *Nachlass*.

It was Mayrhofer who taught Schubert the meaning of the word 'Trost'; consolation, in nature, in song, in the evocative notes of the distant horn, lies at the centre of his poetic impulse, and this lovely song is as perfect an expression of it as the somewhat similar *Trost im Liede*. The simple horn calls are wonderfully integrated into the strophe, and the flattened seventh is used with special effect to weigh the song down towards the dark side of the poet's thought. Note also the striking series of interrupted cadences at the end of the strophe.

## **TROST, AN ELISA** Consolation, for Elisa
**Friedrich von Matthisson**                                                  1814

C major D97 Not in Peters GA XX no.19 NSA IV vol.7 p.6

Do you still rest your grief-pale cheek against this jar of ashes, weeping for the death of one who long ago was borne aloft on wings of perfection to join the jubilant choirs of seraphim?

Do you see the hand of God there in the twinkling stars, promising an end to your unquiet melancholy? Your faith will shine all the brighter, now that the spirit of your beloved soars high above the ruins of his earthly frame.

Happy, ah happy, is the dear companion for whom you long, for he is yours for ever! You, who now endure, will see again the one whom you have so long missed, and like him will find immortality.

The poem, written in 1783, was originally entitled *Die Unsterblichkeit, an Elisa*. Schubert's autograph is lost, but there is a copy in the Witteczek–Spaun collection (Vienna, GdM) dated 1814. The song was first published in the *Gesamtausgabe* in 1894.

The Matthisson songs, written very much under the influence of Salieri, are concerned with the various uses of the voice, and particularly with the relationship between recitative and pure song. *Trost, an Elisa* (and later the Klopstock song *Die Sommernacht*, which has much the same tone and content) lies at one extreme, being written almost entirely in recitative prose, broken only twice, briefly, by a few bars of regular pulse. The result is a minor masterpiece. Attracted by the somewhat operatic and conventional sentiments of the poem, Schubert models this pure and expressive song on his master Gluck (the notation should be interpreted accordingly). The wide-ranging tonality, and the independence of the vocal line, look forward to later masterpieces like *Dass sie hier gewesen* and *Letzte Hoffnung*.

Einstein, 67

## **TROST IM LIEDE** Consolation in Song
**Franz von Schober**                                                  March 1817

F major D546 Peters VI p.83 GA XX no.313

When the tempest of misfortune rages, I hold up my harp before me. The strings cannot protect me, for they are easily broken by its fury; but it strikes on the ear more gently through the gates of song.

The soft chords I hear pierce my soul, bringing a strange sense of comfort on the wings of harmony. Though lamentations escape my lips and I weep with quiet bitterness, yet I feel reconciled; so that I firmly believe that this mingled joy and pain is part of my very life.

The original autograph, now lost, is dated March 1817. The manuscript also contained another famous Schober song on the same theme (*An die Musik*) and *Der Jüngling an den Tod*. There is a copy in the Witteczek–Spaun collection (Vienna, GdM) dated 1817. A second copy has the tempo indication *Etwas bewegt*. The song first appeared as a supplement to the *ZfK* on 23 June 1827. It was published by H. A. Probst of Leipzig in December 1828 as op.101 no.3.

The song is contemporary with Schober's *An die Musik* and has perhaps been overshadowed by the enormous popularity of the latter. Yet it is just as good, though tinged with sadness. *Trost im Liede* is through-composed but monothematic, its tonality poised between F major and D minor as the poem is poised between the sorrow of misfortune and the consolation of art. The song is flawless.

Einstein, 143; Fischer-Dieskau, 83

## TROST IN TRÄNEN Consolation in Tears

**Johann Wolfgang von Goethe**                                          30 November 1814

Etwas geschwind        F major  D120  Peters II p.230  GA XX no.33  NSA IV vol.7 p.56

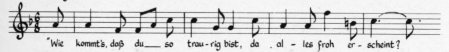

"Wie kommt's, daß du___ so trau-rig bist, da  al - les froh er - scheint?

How is it you are so sad, when all around seems cheerful? I can see from your eyes; I am sure you have been weeping.
    'And if I have been weeping to myself, the sorrow is my own; and my tears flow sweetly, easing my heart.'
    Your friends in merry mood bid you come and embrace them, and to confide in them whatever it is you have lost.
    'You rush about and make such a racket, and have no idea what it is torments me and makes me sad. No, I have not lost anything, sorely though I miss it.'
    Then pull yourself together at once: you are young, and at your age one has the strength and courage to get what one wants.
    'Ah no, I can never attain it; it is too far from me. It stands as high, and shines as bright, as that star up there.'
    One does not cry for the stars: one takes pleasure in their beauty, gazing up enraptured into the serene darkness.
    'And for many a long day I have been gazing up there enraptured; so leave me to weep my nights away, so long as I feel like weeping.'

The poem is a 'folksong parody', that is, it is based on an old folksong which had been set to a new tune by Reichardt in 1777 and then republished in 1800 to a popular Swiss folksong. Goethe's version was written in 1803 and appeared in the *Taschenbuch auf das Jahr 1804*.

The autograph, now lost, is dated 30 November 1814. The fair copy made for Goethe in 1816 is in Vienna (SB). There is also a copy in the Witteczek–Spaun collection (Vienna, GdM) dated 1815, and others in the Stadler and Ebner song albums (Lund, UB). The song was first published in book 25 of the *Nachlass*, in October 1835. There it was transposed to D major, and a spurious introductory bar was added.

The strophic setting has the schoolmasterly questions in the major, and the replies of the earnest young man who prefers weeping at the stars to aiming at them, in the minor. It is not unlike Zelter's setting, and not much more than an interesting exercise in the folksong manner.

Capell, 86; Sternfeld, 80

# ÜBER ALLEN ZAUBER Better than any Magic
**Johann Mayrhofer**
(?) Autumn 1819
G major D682 Not in Peters GA XX no.599

Sie hüpf-te mit mir auf grü-nem Plan

She skipped in front of me on the green plain, and gazed at the fading lime trees with her sad child's eyes: 'The silent arbours are leafless, autumn has stolen the flowers, autumn is good for nothing. Ah, spring is a pretty thing, a pretty thing the spring! Better than any magic − spring!'

The dainty child, I see her now, delicately formed of lilies and roses, with eyes like stars. 'When your sweet face appears like a flower before me, then − in truth I'm not afraid to say it − May can stay away. Ah love, bring colour into this sad life! Love! Better than any magic − Love!'

The autograph, untitled and undated, is in Vienna (SB). It breaks off after thirty bars, but the setting is complete except for the last line. The second verse is not written out. The song, entitled *Über allen Zauber Liebe*, was first published in the supplement to series XX of the *Gesamtausgabe* in 1895. The date is not certain, but the autograph paper is identical with that of several other Mayrhofer settings belonging to the autumn of 1819 (see Winter). The song has been completed and privately published by Reinhard van Hoorickx and is available on record (DG 1981007).

Schubert's failure to complete the song has deprived us of a little masterpiece. It strikes a note which is rare indeed in the Mayrhofer settings, that of youthful zest and unconstrained happiness; with its catchy accompaniment figure and graceful tune it is irresistible. The song changes its gait in the middle, but it can hardly have been this which caused Schubert to abandon it, for he wrote many such songs, and the dancing second half here seems exactly right.

R. Winter, 'Schubert's undated works: a new chronology', *MT*, CXIX, 1978, p.499

# ÜBER WILDEMANN Above Wildemann
**Ernst Schulze**
March 1826
D minor D884 Peters III p.80 GA XX no.500

Schnell

Die Win - de sau-sen am Tan - nen-hang,

The winds whistle across the pine slopes, the streams surge along the valley. I hurry from peak to peak through forest and snow for many a long mile.

And though life down in the open valley is already astir to meet the rays of the sun, I must go my own way with unquiet mind, preferring to look away towards winter.

In the verdant groves and flowery meads I should only suffer all the time, aware that life springs up from the very stones and, alas, that one creature only locks up her heart.

O love, O love, O breath of May! You force the young shoots to bud on tree and bush! The birds sing on the green tree-tops, the springs gush out at your touch!

Yet me you leave to wander along the rough track in the roar of the wind, beset by dark fancies. O gleam of spring, O blossoms bright, shall I never take pleasure in you again?

The poem comes from the *Poetisches Tagebuch* ('Verse Journal'), where it bears the full title *Über Wildemann: einem Bergstädtchen am Harz* ('a small town in the Harz mountains'). The date is added – 28 April 1816. A fragmentary first draft, formerly in private hands, is now missing. An autograph copy, apparently the one used for the first edition, is now in the ÖNB, Vienna (see van Hoorickx). It has the tempo indication *Nicht zu schnell*. The date is not entirely certain, but the Schulze songs belong in the main to December 1825 and March 1826. The catalogue of the Witteczek–Spaun collection (Vienna, GdM) dates the song March 1826. The song was first published by M. J. Leidesdorf as op.108 no.1 in January 1829. Earlier this opus had been announced as no.93. The tempo indication here is *Schnell*.

The galloping triplets, the spare unisons and the impetuous flight look back to an earlier Schulze song, *Im Walde*, and forward to *Erstarrung*. Like the closing pages of the 'Great' C major Symphony, the song seems to live in a world of pure rhythm. There is something demonic, Byronic even, about the protagonist of these Schulze songs. He is a close kinsman of Manfred, condemned to live on in a world to which he no longer belongs. All that remains to him is a lonely embittered defiance. The hero of *Winterreise* is of course his alter ego. So far as the unvaried rhythmic pattern permits, Schubert adapts the tonality and the dynamics to the sense. The mood softens a little for the beginning of the central verses, in D major and A major, and his skill in varying the shape of the melody without changing its character is, as always, masterly; but there is no hint of sweetness at the end ('O gleam of spring, O blossoms bright'). The angular voice line, and the relentless triplets, drive on to the end.

Capell, 216; R. van Hoorickx, 'Un manuscrit inconnu de Schubert', *Revue belge de musicologie*, XXVIII–XXX, 1974–6, pp.260–3

## UM MITTERNACHT At Midnight

**Ernst Schulze**                                                                December 1825

B flat major D862 Peters II p.162 GA XX no.499 NSA IV vol.4 pp.104, 236

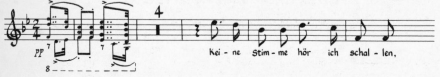

I hear no sound of voices, no footsteps on the dark path; even heaven has closed its beautiful bright eyes.

I only am awake, sweet life, gazing longingly into the night: until your star wakes in the barren distance and sheds its lovely radiance upon me.

Ah, if only I could see your dear form just once, in secret, I would gladly stand here all night in the wind and rain.

Is that you I see glimmering in the distance? Is it you gradually approaching? Ah, I hear your whispered welcome: See, my love is still awake!

Sweet words, beloved voice, which makes my heart beat faster! Your whisper has called up a thousand happy images of love.

All the stars are gleaming in their deep blue courses; the sky has cleared up there in the heavens, and also in my heart.

Blessed memory, come now and rock me gently to sleep, and in my dreams may her sweetly whispered words be oft repeated!

The poem comes from the *Poetisches Tagebuch* ('Verse Journal'). The full title is *Am 5sten März 1815: nachts um 12 Uhr*. Schubert's title is as above. The first draft, dated December 1825, has been divided into two. The first twenty-three bars of the strophic setting are in Washington (LC), and the remaining twelve bars in private hands. This draft has been cancelled by the composer, presumably when the fair copy was made. The catalogue of the Witteczek–Spaun collection (Vienna, GdM) dates the song March 1826, and this may be the date of the lost fair copy. The song was published by Thaddäus Weigl in December 1827 as op.88 no.3.

The mood of stillness and complicity is expressed by the steady tiptoeing gait reminiscent of the two settings of *Das Geheimnis*. The suppressed emotion in the mind of the wakeful lover is revealed, however, in the leap of a ninth in the melody at the end of the first half of the strophe. The verses are grouped in pairs, and the second half is cleverly varied, with a more adventurous harmonic base. Even so, it is not easy to sustain the interest third time round.

Capell, 217; Fischer-Dieskau, 227

**UNGEDULD** see DIE SCHÖNE MÜLLERIN no.7

## URANIENS FLUCHT The Flight of Urania
**Johann Mayrhofer**  April 1817

D major D554 Not in Peters GA XX no.319

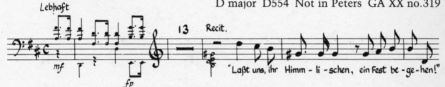

"Laßt uns, ihr Himm-li-schen, ein Fest be-ge-hen!"

'Let us, Immortals, hold a feast,' Zeus ordered; and from the underworld, from the mountains and the lakes, all climbed up to Olympus as quickly as they could.

The god of the vine left the fabled flowery banks of the Indus which he had conquered, Apollo the noble shade of Helicon, and Cypria her island home.

The naiads from their moss-rimmed streams, the dryads from the silent groves, with the ruler of the ocean waves, they all arrived at the feast in eager anticipation.

They danced the eternal changeless rounds in gorgeous apparel about our Thunderer, whose eyes were as radiant as in his youth.

He beckoned, and Hebe filled the golden bowls; he beckoned, and Ceres handed ambrosia; he beckoned, and sweet hymns of joy rang out. Everything happened just as he ordered it.

The brows and cheeks of the guests began to crimson with pleasure, and sly Eros smiled to himself: the doors opened – and walking slowly a noble woman crept softly into the company.

Surely she is of the race of the Uranides: her hair is bound with a bright crown of stars, her pale life-weary face shines with a heavenly radiance.

But her yellow hair is cropped, a shabby garment covers her chaste body. Her scarred hands show that the goddess has suffered the heavy shame of serfdom.

Jupiter scans her features. 'You are ... you are not Urania?' 'I am.' The gods stagger back from their wine jars in astonishment and cry: 'What? Urania!'

'I no longer recognise you,' said Zeus. 'Full of grace and beauty you went away to the earth. Your mission was to acquaint her sons with the Gods and to lead them to my dwelling place.

'The treasure of which Pandora once boasted was as nothing I reckon compared with the armour I gave you, the jewels my love bestowed on you.'

'The commission, lord, you gave me then, and which my own heart urged me to accept, I willingly undertook, if I may say so; but my efforts were all fruitless.

'You, O my lord, may argue it out with Fate, to which all creation is subject: man confuses good with evil, he is in thrall to lust and folly.

'For one I had to plough the fields, for another be a housekeeper, for one to rock the baby to sleep, and for another to broadcast songs of praise.

'One locked me into deep mine-shafts to dig out the jingling metal for him; another hunted me through bloody battles in search of fame – so many and varied were the torments of that wretched race.

'Even this diadem, the golden stars, which you presented me with at our parting, they would gladly have sacrificed as fuel for their fires when the winter frosts came.'

'Accursed race!' cried Zeus with angry voice, 'It shall be doomed to immediate extinction!' The cloud-capped mountain shuddered at his fury, and air and sea and land trembled far around.

With mighty force he tore the lightning from the eagle's talons; high over his head he waved the brand to burn the earth, which had so scandalously abused his darling.

He stepped forward to destroy it. His mien was even more threatening than the crimson lightning. The anxious world prepared itself for death – but the avenger's arm sank down, and he stepped back.

And bade Urania look down. In the far distance she saw a pair of lovers in a green meadow encircled by a stream; the rustic altar was decorated with her own image.

Before this the pair knelt down in sacrifice, invoking the departed goddess; and the music of their supplication flowed about the goddess like a mighty sea of harmony.

Tears filled her dark eyes, the lovers' suffering had touched her. And like a bow-string in the morning dew her displeasure relaxed.

'Forgive me,' pleaded the reconciled goddess, 'I was too quick to anger; my cult is still celebrated on the earth. Though I was scorned there, there are still pious hearts that revere my image.

'Oh, let me descend to those poor creatures to teach them your high purpose, and show them in dreams the land where the flower of perfection blooms.'

'So be it!' Zeus cried, 'I will equip you richly. Go forth, daughter, with renewed strength! And if you feel your powers failing return here to us, a citizen of heaven.

'Often shall we see you come and depart again; for longer and longer periods you will stay away, and finally your sufferings will end, and you will call the wide earth your home.

You, the patient goddess, will dwell there more highly honoured than we are ourselves. For the power in which we rejoice is finite, our thrones shall be toppled by the tempest to come. But your star shall shine on through the dark night.'

The heroine of the poem is not Urania the muse of astronomy, but Urania Aphrodite, the goddess of pure and ennobling love. Mayrhofer's purpose appears to have been to enlist the ballad form in the service of the optimistic ideas of the Enlightenment. The autograph, in the Paris Conservatoire, is a first draft dated April 1817. There are various contemporary copies, including one in the Witteczek–Spaun collection (Vienna, GdM) dated 1817 and another, in Schober's hand, in Dresden (SLB). The song was first published in the *Gesamtausgabe* in 1895.

It is a tribute to the prestige of the solo cantata that Schubert should employ it here as a vehicle for neo-classical ideas, at a time when his lyrical genius was in full flower. It is the last of his extended solo cantatas, and one of the more interesting ones, in spite of the fact that it is never sung. Recitative is used more sparingly than in his earlier essays in this style and is restricted to Zeus's more dramatic pronouncements. There is a wealth of ideas in the arioso passages, and a wide range of mood and expression; much of the song is very singable, but in the end the listener is defeated by the sheer length of the piece and by the loose episodic form. There are some sixteen changes of pace and key in the course of its 394 bars!

It is worth asking the question, however, why the best of Handel's and Haydn's solo cantatas rank among their finest works, while none of Schubert's has remained in the repertory. What one misses in the Schubert works is not only any unifying sense of tonal organisation, but also the contribution that virtuosity made to the success of the eighteenth-century cantata. It is significant that a song like *Der Hirt auf dem Felsen*, which retains some characteristics at any rate of the cantata, is partly dependent for its appeal on the virtuosity of the performers.

## VATERLANDSLIED Song of the Fatherland
**Friedrich Gottlieb Klopstock**  14 September 1815
C major D287 Not in Peters GA XX no.141(a) and (b)

Etwas geschwind, mit Feuer

Ich bin ein deut - sches___ Mäd - chen,

> I am a German girl! My eyes are blue, my glance is soft; I have a noble proud and virtuous heart.
>> I am a German girl! Anger darts from my blue eyes and from my heart I hate anyone who fails to love his fatherland.
>> I am a German girl! My virtuous, noble, proud heart beats high and loud at the sweet name of the fatherland.
>> So it will beat one day at the name of the boy who is proud as I am of his fatherland, and is virtuous, noble, and a German!

The poem, written in 1770, is subtitled 'To be sung for Johanna Elisabeth von Winthem'. There are eight verses, of which the first two and the last two are given above. Elisabeth von Winthem later became the poet's wife. There are two versions. The first draft, dated 14 September 1815, is in Berlin (SPK). The autograph of the revised version is missing, but there are copies of both in the Witteczek–Spaun collection (Vienna, GdM), and both are printed in the *Gesamtausgabe*, where the song first appeared (1895).

In its day the poem caused a considerable stir, an early indication of the emergence of nationalist feeling in Germany. Friedländer lists sixteen different settings, and quotes various imitative verses, beginning with Claudius's riposte 'Ich bin ein deutscher Jüngling, Mein Haar ist kraus, breit meine Brust' ('I am a German youth, My hair is curly and my chest is broad'). During the wars of liberation the song took on a second lease of life, and Schubert's setting doubtless owes something to this wave of patriotic feeling. The revised version of this simple strophic setting has a stronger and simpler tune, and the postlude is more effective.

Fischer-Dieskau, 47; Friedländer, II, 127–30

## VEDI QUANTO ADORO see DIDONE ABBANDONATA

## VERGEBLICHE LIEBE Love in Vain

**Josef Carl Bernard**                                    6 April 1815

C minor D177 Peters VI p.114 GA XX no.58

Yes, I know it; it is useless for my wounded heart to harbour this constant love. If only the slightest hope remained for me, then all my suffering would be richly rewarded.

But even hope is in vain – and how well I recognise her cruel game! However faithful my endeavours, the goal forever eludes me!

And yet I love, and yet I go on hoping, ever faithful, though without either love or hope. Never can I abandon this love; yet it breaks my heart in two!

The poem appeared in the annual anthology *Selam* in 1814. The autograph of the first draft, in C minor, was used as the source for the *Gesamtausgabe*, and is now in private hands. There is a copy in the Witteczek–Spaun collection (Vienna, GdM) dated 6 April 1815. The song was first published in 1867 by C. A. Spina as op.173 no.3, transposed into A minor. That version is followed by Friedländer in the Peters edition.

It is astonishing that this wonderfully expressive song has not attracted more attention, for it seems to be ten years ahead of its time, looking forward to the free speech rhythms of, say, the Platen songs. It escapes altogether from the metrical regularity of the poem, and even transcends the traditional categories of recitative and arioso, for it has the feel of an interior monologue rather than a dramatic scena, as the pauses clearly indicate. The rhythms and phrase-lengths are moulded to the individual phrases, to give the song the spontaneity of a dramatic soliloquy. It belongs with the settings of Matthisson's *Trost, an Elisa* and Klopstock's *Die Sommernacht*, early steps along the road which was to lead to *Der Doppelgänger*.

Einstein, 108

## VERGISSMEINNICHT Forget-me-not

**Franz von Schober**                                         May 1823

A flat major D792 Peters V p.112 GA XX no.430

When Spring tore himself from the breast of the blossoming earth, he took one last melancholy walk through the world that he was leaving. The brightness of the painted meadows and the green cornfields welcomed him, and the shady canopy of the dark forest rustled above his head.

There on the soft and velvety moss, half hidden by the greenery, he saw a sweet, carefree figure lying asleep. Whether it was a child still or a girl he could not tell. Short blonde threads of silken hair waved about her little round face. Her slender limbs were delicate, her figure undeveloped, and yet her bosom seemed to swell with emotion. Her cheeks beamed with a rosy warmth, her mouth smiled slyly, and through the scented veil of her eyelids the bright blue eyes peeped out roguishly. And Spring, drunk with delight and yet deeply touched, stood lost in contemplation of the sweet sight; now he was fully aware what he was leaving behind.

But the hour was pressing, he had to leave at once. Ah, he pressed a burning kiss upon her lips as he departed. And he disappeared in a scented cloud.

But the child awoke from her deep sleep, for the kiss had kindled her like a flame, as if she had been struck by lightning.

She blossomed like a flower; she stepped out of the coffin of childhood, transformed into a young woman. Her blue eyes opened, serious and loving, seeming to enquire after the happiness which she had lost without knowing it. But no one could tell her anything. They all gazed at her in wonder, and her sisters in the circle did not know what had happened to her. Alas, she did not know herself!

Tears express only their own grief, and an unfathomed longing drives them out; drives her away to try to discover the vision which lived on in her heart, pictured in her imagination, and peopling her dreams. She scrambled over cliffs, climbed up and down mountains, until she came to a river which brought her wild career to a standstill. Here the damp grass on the bank cooled her hot feet, and she saw her own image shining in the mirror of the waves. She saw there the distant blue of the skies, saw the crimson gleam of the clouds, saw the moon and all the stars, and her pain was lessened.

For she realised that she had found a soul which comprehended her innermost desires, and knew the depths of her sorrow. She was happy to build herself a quiet dwelling on this spot; she could entrust herself without fear to the gentle radiance of the waves. And her spirits revived as she murmured to the waters, as if to her visionary lover: oh, forget, forget me not!

The poem has twenty verses in ballad measure, but Schubert's through-composed setting groups them in paragraphs to suit his tonal scheme; the translation is arranged accordingly. The poem, like *Viola*, is subtitled 'A Flower Ballad'. The two songs seem to represent a conscious experiment on the part of Schubert and Schober to find a viable form for a concert piece, a kind of halfway house between the solo song and the song cycle. The autograph, dated May 1823, is in New York (PML). There are copies in the Witteczek–Spaun collection (Vienna, GdM) and in Schober's song album (Lund, UB). The song was published in book 21 of the *Nachlass*, in June 1833.

By general consent the ambitiously conceived song turns out to be a bit of a bore; but it is not altogether easy to identify the reasons. Capell, whose comments are witty and to the point, says: 'A song must in fact be short; and the smaller and daintier the theme the shorter'. But it can hardly be simply a question of length. For *Der Hirt auf dem Felsen*, which has plenty of enthusiastic devotees, is about eighty bars longer, and its text is just as pale and unsubstantial. But who bothers about the text of *Der Hirt auf dem Felsen*? The truth is perhaps that Schubert is here the victim of his own poetic sensibility. He takes Schober's weak and sentimental poem too seriously, succumbs to the preponderant tone of sweet sentiment, and ends by exhausting the listener's patience. However, there is much to interest the devoted Schubertian in the song. The central E major section is perhaps the best of it. Characteristically, the tonal scheme centres on the relationship between A flat and E major.

Einstein remarks on a curious link with the rhythm and key of the 'Unfinished' Symphony at the words 'Tränen sprechen ihren Schmerz nur aus'.

Capell, 178–9; Einstein, 253

# VERKLÄRUNG Transfiguration

**Alexander Pope trans. J. G. Herder**         4 May 1813

A minor D59 Peters V p.86 GA XX no.10 NSA IV vol.6 p.73

The text is a German translation of Alexander Pope's *The Dying Christian to his Soul*, published in 1730:

Vital spark of heavenly flame!
Quit, oh quit this mortal frame;
Trembling, hoping, lingering, flying,
Oh the pain, the bliss of dying!
Cease, fond Nature, cease thy strife,
And let me languish into life.

Hark! They whisper: Angels say,
Sister Spirit, come away.
What is this absorbs me quite,
Steals my senses, shuts my sight,
Drowns my spirits, draws my breath?
Tell me, my Soul, can this be Death?

The world recedes, it disappears!
Heaven opens on my eyes, my ears
With sounds seraphic ring:
Lend, lend your wings! I mount, I fly!
O Grave, where is thy victory?
O Death, where is thy Sting?

The translation was used by Herder in an essay entitled *How the Ancients looked at Death*, published in 1786. The translation is longer than the original, and Schubert's song cannot be sung to the English words, though parts of it (the final couplet, for instance) fit very well. The autograph is lost, but there is a copy, dated 4 May 1813, in the Witteczek–Spaun collection (Vienna, GdM) and another in the song album of Franziska Tremier (Vienna, SB). The song was first published in book 17 of the *Nachlass* in May 1832.

    *Verklärung* is no doubt a remarkable achievement for a sixteen-year-old; the classical restraint of the song matches the words, and the pulsing chords catch the mood of soaring aspiration. This is perhaps another way of saying that it lacks any sense of emotional involvement, such as one finds in later, and even in some earlier, songs about death. There is far less of Schubert in it, for instance, than there is in *Leichenfantasie*, written much earlier, and one may well question Einstein's assertion that 'even fifteen years later Schubert could not have conceived it differently'. The dramatic force of recitative in the final clinching line is undeniable, however, and a fine singer can make it sound very impressive.

    Capell, 82; Einstein, 50; Fischer-Dieskau, 24

# VERSUNKEN Lost in Love
**Johann Wolfgang von Goethe**

February 1821

A flat major  D715  Peters III p.207  GA XX no.391

Such a round head, and with such a tangle of curls! When you let me run my fingers to and fro in these abundant locks I feel full of well-being from the bottom of my heart. And when I kiss your brow, nose, eyes and mouth I am stricken afresh and ever again. Where should this five-toothed comb stop? Already it returns to your curls. Your ear joins in the game too; so tender it is in dalliance, so rich in love! But however one tousles this little head, one could wander up and down in these abundant locks for ever. Such a round head, and with such a tangle of curls!

The poem comes from the *Westöstlicher Divan*, published in 1819. Schubert omitted three lines of the poem, the tenth ('This is no mere flesh and skin') and the final couplet: 'All this, Hafiz, you also did; and now we are doing it all over again.' Instead of the final couplet he repeats the first line.

The first draft (Vienna, ÖNB) is in A flat and is dated February 1821. An autograph fair copy in F major (Vienna, SB) has a note in Schubert's hand 'Transposed July 1825'. There are dated copies in the Witteczek–Spaun collection (Vienna, GdM). The song was published in book 38 of the *Nachlass*, early in 1845.

If *Versunken* inspires respect rather than affection, it is perhaps because it misses the point of Goethe's sharply etched miniature of erotic love. Schubert's great love songs are songs of devotion, usually to a distant beloved. The nearer the beloved, the less the songs have to say. Indeed, it is difficult to think of any Schubert music (except perhaps *Suleika* I) which engages the imagination with the physical realities of love as Strauss, or Wolf understood them. So here the on-running semiquavers, the shifting tonalities and even the chromaticisms suggest impatience, emotional disturbance, excitement, but not erotic pleasure. But see Fischer-Dieskau for a different opinion.

Capell, 155; Einstein, 218–19; Fischer-Dieskau, 144–5

# VIER CANZONEN Four Canzonets
**Jacopo Vittorelli, Pietro Metastasio**

January 1820

The word 'canzonet' is of Italian origin, and in the eighteenth century it had come to mean a light song in the bel canto style, written either for performance in the drawing-room or, if included in an opera, as a lyrical interlude without dramatic importance, like Cherubino's *Voi che sapete*. The Four Canzonets were written for Franziska Roner, a musical young lady who was later to marry Schubert's friend Josef von Spaun, and may have been commissioned by her. The texts of the first two are by Jacopo Vittorelli (1749–1835) and the others by Pietro Metastasio (1698–782), but this was established only recently by the Norwegian scholar Odd Udbye. (Previously all four poems had been attributed to Metastasio.) The songs are said to have been written as practice arias for Franziska, to whom Schubert presented the autograph. It remained in the possession of the Spaun family until 1950 and is now in the library of the Wiener Schubertbund. It is dated January 1820 and contains all four songs. They do not have separate titles.

It should be remembered that in 1820 Vienna was already in the grip of enthusiasm for the Italian opera. Doubtless the ambition of every musical young lady was to sing like Colbran. But though the style is Italian, the Four Canzonets are lovely songs in their own right. They make an interesting comparison with the 'Three Songs for Bass Voice' written seven years later and dedicated to Lablache, which have more of the flavour of *opera buffa* about them. The Four Canzonets were published by J. P. Gotthard in February 1871 as nos.1–4 of '5 Canti'.

    Fischer-Dieskau, 132

(1) **NON T'ACCOSTARE ALL'URNA** Do not approach the urn

**Jacopo Vittorelli**           C major D688 no.1 Peters VI p.171 GA XX no.575

Do not approach the urn which holds my ashes; this compassionate earth is sacred to my grief. I reject your wreath of flowers. I hate your grief. What are a few tears, a few flowers, worth to the dead?
    Unkind! You should have come to my aid when my life was wasting away in pain and sighs.
    With what futile weeping do you disturb the grove. Respect a sad shade, and let it rest.

The text was a favourite with opera composers. Verdi set it as late as the 1830s.

It seems astonishing that these Italianate songs are roughly contemporary with *Nachthymne*, and with Schlegel songs like *Der Fluss* and *Der Schiffer*. For their eighteenth-century form and style completely exclude that metaphorical musical language which is the essence of his own song style. Here the tears, the flowers, evoke no Schubertian analogues. This song, it is true, sounds a bit like an exercise, but how wonderfully shapely and singable it is!

(2) **GUARDA, CHE BIANCA LUNA** How bright the moon

**Jacopo Vittorelli**           G major D688 no.2 Peters VI p.172 GA XX no.576

How bright the moon! How blue is the night! Not a breeze whispers, not a twig trembles. A solitary nightingale flits from hedge to tree, and sighing calls upon his love. She, who heard him faintly, already flies from leaf to leaf, and seems to answer, 'Do not weep, I am here'.
    What sweet feelings, what tears are there, Irene! Ah, you never learnt to answer me thus.

The bel canto style seems to demand a certain latitude in the interpretation of Schubert's dotted rhythms where they are set against the pianist's triplets. To assimilate the dotted rhythms everywhere to the triplets is to deprive the vocal line of buoyancy and rhythmic bite. So much is clear at least from the singer's opening bar. But there are occasions – in bars 24 and 26, for instance – where it seems preferable to treat the dotted quaver and semiquaver as a broken triplet. This rhythmical freedom in the vocal line is of course very Rossinian. Indeed, the whole group of songs shows how sympathetically Schubert had absorbed the Rossini style.

**(3) DA QUEL SEMBIANTE APPRESI** From that form I learnt to sigh
**Pietro Metastasio**        B flat major  D688 no.3  Peters VI p.176  GA XX no.577

From that form I learnt to sigh as a lover. For that face I shall always sigh with love. The flame which fired me with passion alone charms and pleases me. Every other is too cold to warm my heart.

The text comes from Act I of Metastasio's opera *L'Eroe Cinese* ('The Chinese Hero'). The melody seems a little bland for the lover's predicament. But again, it is grateful to the voice, and the swing away into D flat major gives it emotional force.

**(4) MIO BEN RICORDATI** If I should die, remember
**Pietro Metastasio**        B flat minor  D688 no.4  Peters VI p.178  GA XX no.578

If I should die remember, my beloved, how this faithful soul loved you. If cold ashes can love within the urn, then I shall still adore you.

The text is from Act III of *Alessandro nelle Indie* ('Alexander in the Indies'). Here again are the Rossinian sweetness and 'lift', yet the tonal scheme, with its structural change to the tonic major, is made to carry the emotional weight of the words.

## VIER REFRAIN LIEDER
**Johann Gabriel Seidl**                                      (?) Summer 1828
D866

The date of these four songs is uncertain. They were published by Thaddäus Weigl in August 1828, as op.95. A sketch of the first one, *Die Unterscheidung*, is associated with a sketch of the Finale of the C minor Piano Sonata, finished in September 1828. This could mean that Schubert worked on the Seidl songs as well as on the last piano sonatas in the summer of 1828. Equally, it could mean that both the songs and the sonatas were sketched before 1828. The four songs were written and published as a group; but they are seldom sung as such, and they are discussed here under their individual titles: *Die Unterscheidung, Bei dir allein, Die Männer sind méchant* and *Irdisches Glück*.

## VIOLA Violet

**Franz von Schober**  March 1823

A flat major D786 Peters III p.110 GA XX no.423

Schneeglöcklein, o Schneeglöcklein, in den Au-en läu-test du,

Snowdrop, snowdrop, ringing your bells in the meadows, ringing your bells in the silent grove, ring on, ring out for ever!

For you herald a happy time; spring, the bridegroom, approaches, victorious in his battle with the winter, whose icy weapons he has taken captive. So your golden clapper swings and your silver bell resounds; and your sweet scent drifts away like an enticing summons. So that the flowers in the earth rise up from their dusty beds and in honour of the bridegroom deck themselves out for the wedding feast.

Snowdrop, snowdrop, ringing your bells in the meadows, ringing your bells in the silent grove, ring the flowers out of their sleep.

Violet, tender maiden, is the first to hear the joyous sound. She rises swiftly and arrays herself carefully as a bride. She dresses herself in a green gown, puts on her velvety blue mantle, puts on her jewels of gold and her dewy diamonds. Then she hurries forth with powerful step, her faithful heart filled with the thought of her lover and glowing with the warmth of love, looking neither to one side nor the other. But a feeling of anxiety begins to agitate her breast, for everything is still so quiet, and the winds blow cold. And suddenly she stops running. Already the sun is shining on her, but she looks about her in horror – for she is quite alone.

No sisters, no bridegroom! She is too forward! Scorned!

Shuddering with embarrassment she flees as if blown away by the tempest.

She flies to a remote spot where she is hidden by grass and shade; continually she peers and listens to see whether anything rustles or moves. And insulted and disappointed she sits sobbing and weeping, lacerated by the profound fear that no one will come.

Snowdrop, snowdrop, ringing your bells in the meadows, ringing your bells in the silent grove, call her sisters to her!

The rose approaches, the lily nods, the tulip and the hyacinth swell; the bindweed comes creeping along, and the narcissus joins them.

And now when spring appears and the happy festival begins he sees them all together; but his favourite child is missing.

He sends them all out to search for the one he loves; and they arrive at the place where she is pining away.

But the sweet thing sits dumb and pale with her head bowed. Alas, the pain of her love and her sorrow has quite crushed the tender creature.

Snowdrop, snowdrop, ringing your bells in the meadows, ringing your bells in the silent grove; toll a soft requiem for Violet!

Like Schober's companion piece *Vergissmeinnicht*, the poem is subtitled 'A Flower Ballad'. There are nineteen verses in ballad measure, but the translation is arranged in paragraphs to match the sections of Schubert's through-composed version.

The manuscript in New York (PML), dated March 1823, is only partly in Schubert's hand; the notes and part of the text are in another hand. The fair copy used for the first edition is lost. There is a copy in the Spaun–Cornaro collection (Vienna, privately owned), and others in Schindler's (Lund, UB) and Franziska Tremier's (Vienna, SB) song albums. The song was published as op.123 by A. W. Pennauer in November 1830. The difference between the first edition and the autograph are listed in the *Revisionsbericht*. As usual, Friedländer in the Peters edition follows the printed version, the *Gesamtausgabe* the autograph.

*Viola* has unique claims to distinction: it is the only Schubert song to be awarded the accolade of a full-length analysis by Sir Donald Tovey. But as to whether the touch of the master sets the seal on the song's greatness, or represents the kiss of death, even informed opinions differ. Critical assessments of the song differ so widely that they cancel each other out. Tovey asserts that *Viola* is 'by far the most perfect and beautiful' of the long episodic songs, and claims that the sentimental verses 'naturally elicit a very effective musical structure'. Capell, on the other hand, dismisses the song as a curiosity. 'It is one thing to be presented with an exquisite flower; it is another to be inveigled into a tour of a horticultural show ... Here Schubert set out to tell of snowdrops and pansies on the scale of a tale of Troy.'

The song could be regarded as a conscious attempt on the part of Schubert and Schober to give to the extended episodic song a new unity and strength, and so to make it a viable concert form. The form of the poem does lend itself to musical treatment; indeed, the 'motto theme' which appears at verses 1, 5, 14 and 19 is more a musical than a literary device, though whether Schubert or Schober thought of it first it is impossible to say. On the thematic links between the sections, and on the song's structure as a whole, Tovey has said all that needs to be said. It should be added, however, that it is a classic example of that rhythmic elaboration without change of tempo (sometimes called structural acceleration) which plays so important a part in the song cycles; *Trockne Blumen* is perhaps the finest example of the device. So the structure of *Viola* resembles a great arch, proceeding from the utmost simplicity to complexity and back again.

Finally, it is impossible to miss a certain virtuosity in the piano writing, which gives to the work much the same fascination as one of the keyboard sonatas. The marvellous F minor section marked 'Geschwinder' is indeed a miniature piano sonata in itself. In short, over-sweet to the taste as it is, *Viola* makes itself indispensable to the true Schubertian by its rich variety of expression and its idiomatic inventiveness.

Capell, 178–9; Fischer-Dieskau, 172–3; A. Robertson, 'The songs', *Symposium*, 187; D. Tovey, *Chamber Music*, London, 1946/*R*1972, pp.137–41

## VOLLENDUNG Fulfilment

**Friedrich von Matthisson**                                          Autumn 1817

A major  D989 (D2 579A)  Not in Peters  Not in GA

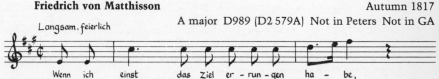

When one day I reach the haven in the fields of light of the other world, I shall bless the tears which fall upon the roses strewn on my grave.

Full of longing, with the pure joy of anticipation, as calm as the moonlit grove, and as serene as the setting sun, I shall await you, divine fulfilment.

Haste, oh haste, to wing me aloft to where the worlds turn beneath me, where palm trees are mirrored in the life-stream, where loved ones are reunited with one another.

The poem, originally entitled *Die Vollendung*, dates from 1784–5. It appeared in *Alfred: ein Lesebuch für Jüngling* (Vienna, 1812). Schubert set only the first three of the four verses. The song, mentioned by Kreissle von Hellborn in the list of songs appended to his biography of the composer, was long thought to be lost. But in 1968 a copy was discovered by Christa Landon (Vienna, MGV), together with copies of other songs dating from September and October 1817. Another copy was later discovered in Vienna (GdM). The song was edited and published, together with the companion piece *Die Erde*, by Christa Landon and Bärenreiter of Kassel in 1970.

*Vollendung* is a fine song which deserves to be rescued from oblivion. The progressive strophe moves, like the poem, from the contemplation of the joys of heaven ('slow and solemn') to rhapsodic wonder at the splendour of their fulfilment. The climax, with its pulsing triplet chords and dissolution, then re-establishment of the tonic at bar 10, is an early example of a favourite Schubert device.

> C. Landon, 'Neue Schubert-Funde', *ÖMZ*, XXIV, 1969, p.299, trans. in *MR*, XXXI, 1970, p.200

## VOM MITLEIDEN MARIÄ Mary's Compassion

**Friedrich von Schlegel**                                           December 1818

G minor  D632  Peters V p.39  GA XX no.349

As Mary stood by the cross she felt in her heart sorrow upon sorrow, pain upon pain; Christ's whole passion was imprinted on her heart.

She had to watch her son suffer on the cross, pale as death and crimsoned all over by his wounds; consider how this bitter death must have pierced her to the heart.

On Christ's head the sharp thorns stabbed, through bone and brain, through eyes and ears and brow; the thorns broke the son's head and brain, and his mother's heart.

The poem is not included in the collected edition of Schlegel's poetry, and its authenticity has been doubted. But Dietrich Berke has established that it appeared in Schlegel's *Poetisches Taschenbuch* for 1806, together with *Blanka*. The two settings appear on the same manuscript, so it seems likely that the 'Verse Pocket-book' was Schubert's source.

The autograph, dated December 1818, is in G minor. It is in private hands. A copy in Schindler's song album (Lund, UB) is transposed to F minor. The song was first published (in F minor) in 1831 in book 10 of the *Nachlass* (*Geistliche Lieder* no.4).

Schubert's attitude towards the church fell far short of his father's conventional piety. In October 1818, while he was still in residence at Zseliz, he wrote in disparaging terms to his brother Ignaz about the local priests and their hell-fire rantings (*Docs.* no.138). Yet here he is a few weeks later writing perhaps the most deeply felt of all his 'spiritual songs', writing it moreover in pure linear three-part counterpoint, almost as though he were back in the choir stalls at Lichtenthal church.

The explanation appears to be that he drew a distinction between the human tragedy which lies at the heart of the Christian mysteries, and the elaborate edifice of clerical theory and practice which had been constructed upon it. Such a distinction is implicit in his masses, and in his remarks about Ellen's song to the Virgin (*Docs.* no.572). He seems also to have drawn a distinction between the contrapuntal style appropriate for liturgical purposes and the musical language appropriate to the poetry of, say, Novalis or Mayrhofer. It is a common misconception that Schubert knew nothing of Baroque music. On the contrary, he was brought up on it. We know that he played the *Well-tempered Clavier* (see *Docs.* no.483), and there is plenty of evidence that he could write like Bach when he wanted to. (See, for instance, the Agnus Dei of his first mass.) Moreover, Salieri had given him a thorough grounding in three-part counterpoint, witness all those three-part canons which survive from the years 1813–16. Here in *Vom Mitleiden Mariä* he puts that experience to use in composing a strophic *Stabat mater*, thus setting the text apart from the Schlegel of *Abendröte*. In this he was right, for the verses belong to the years immediately preceding the poet's conversion to the Roman Catholic faith.

D. Berke, 'Zu einigen anonymen Texten Schubertscher Lieder', *Die Musik forschung*, XXII, 1969, p.485; Capell, 145; Einstein, 42, 186; Fischer-Dieskau, 120, 126

## VON IDA Ida

**Ludwig Kosegarten**

7 July 1815

F minor D228 Not in Peters GA XX no.91

Der Mor - gen blüht, der O - sten glüht; es lä - chelt aus dem dün - nen Flor

The morning blooms, there is a glow in the east; the sun smiles, weak and sickly, through a thin veil of cloud; for alas, my darling has fled!

On what plain, on what track, do you wander now so far from Ida? You, who possess my whole heart, darling of nature.

And do you hear on the morning breeze the sign which escapes from Ida's breast, the longing which languishes in her heart in the cool breath of morning?

What do you know of Ida's peace of mind, of Ida's happiness, you who took them away with you? Have you any idea of Ida's grief? Do you pray for Ida's peace?

Oh come back, come back! To your sad, forsaken love, who trembles with foreboding! Come back to your Ida.

The original title was *Von Agnes*. As in other Kosegarten settings, Schubert changed the name to Ida, probably because it is easier to sing. The first draft is in private possession. An autograph copy, formerly in Munich, is now in the University of Texas. A copy in the Witteczek–Spaun collection (Vienna, GdM) is dated 7 July 1815. Both autographs bear a note in Schubert's hand: 'N.B. If this song is sung by a tenor, the accompaniment must be played an octave lower.' The song was first published in the *Gesamtausgabe* in 1894.

This song and the preceding one are the only two written in regular three-part counterpoint. The conventional poetic diction of the poem leads Schubert to set the song in an archaic manner, which is reinforced by the modal effect of the B natural in bars 8 and 10.

## VOR MEINER WIEGE My Cradle

**Karl Gottfried von Leitner**

Autumn 1827

B minor D927 Peters IV p.109 GA XX no.547

Das al - so, das ist der en - ge Schrein,

So this is the narrow chest in which I once lay swaddled as a baby. Here I lay, feeble, helpless and dumb, shaping my lips only to cry.

My tender little hands could not hold anything, and yet I was tied up like a thief; I possessed feet, yet lay as if crippled, until mother raised me to her breast.

Then I smiled up at her as I suckled, and she sang to me of roses and angels. She sang, and rocked me to sleep as she sang, and lovingly closed my eyes with a kiss.

She spread a cool tent of shady green silk above me. When shall I find such a peaceful chamber as that again? Perhaps when the green grass covers me.

O mother, dear mother, stay with me a long while yet. Who else is there to comfort me with songs of angels? Who else is there to close my eyes with a loving kiss, for the long, last, deepest sleep?

The poem was written in 1823, but Schubert's acquaintance with it dates from his stay in Graz, Leitner's home town, in September 1827 with the Pachler family. The surviving autograph, in Budapest, (HNL), is a fair copy made for the first edition. The song was originally published as no.3 of 'Four Songs' by the Lithographic Institute of Vienna, of which Franz von Schober was manager, in the spring of 1828, and dedicated by Schubert to Marie Pachler. In February 1829 it was republished by Diabelli as op.106 no.3. (See Kecskeméti.)

Schubert's preoccupation with death in the last years of his life seems almost obsessive. Leitner's characteristically sentimental little poem makes its conventional gesture towards 'the long, last, deepest sleep' at the end. But it is this last verse which sparks off the song. Note the key – B minor; and the introduction, a version of the descending harmonic sequence from tonic minor to dominant which is Schubert's earliest and most persistent 'death motif'; note the first three bars after the introduction, which is once more the 'Wanderer' theme; note the dramatic highlighting of the words 'Perhaps when the green grass covers me', with a sudden shift from F sharp to D major, and an emphatic declamation like a huge sigh, turning that casual phrase into the key to the song's meaning.

The song might have been written for *Winterreise*. The middle section, however, a lyrical interlude for verses 3 and 4, recalls another contemporary work, the Impromptu in G flat op.90 no.3. Capell's brusque dismissal of this moving song seems to be one of his rare misjudgments.

Capell, 245; Fischer-Dieskau, 253–4; Kecskeméti, 'Neu entdeckte Schubert-Autographe', *ÖMZ*, XXIV, 1969, pp.564–8; Porter, 114–15

**WALDESNACHT** see IM WALDE (Schlegel)

**WANDRERS NACHTLIED I** Wayfarer's Night Song I
**Johann Wolfgang von Goethe** 5 July 1815
G flat major D224 Peters II p.8 GA XX no.87 NSA IV vol.1 p.34

Langsam, mit Ausdruck (M.M. ♩ = 50)

Der du von dem Him - mel bist, al - les Leid und Schmer - zen stillst,

You who are of heaven, who cures all sorrow and pain, and fills him who is doubly wretched with double rapture – Oh, I am weary of the struggle! What use is all the pain and joy? – sweet peace, come, oh come into my breast!

The poem, written in 1776 and sent to Frau von Stein, first appeared in 1780 in a religious periodical called *Christliches Magazin*. The first draft, dated 5 July 1815, is in London (BL). The fair copy made for Goethe in 1816 is in Berlin (DS). The song was published in May 1821 as op.4 no.3 (Cappi and Diabelli on commission) and dedicated by Schubert to Johann Ladislaus Pyrker.

Goethe's prayer for peace of mind is contained within one long arching sentence, which does not announce its subject until the last two lines. But Schubert rightly recognises that it is psychologically too complex to be encompassed in a single metrically regular strophe. His solution is to match the changing phases of the poet's thought with a variable pulse within a unifying mood and basic tempo. It is a method which he was to make peculiarly his own, and which consists essentially of quickening the beat while retaining the basic tempo. So the first phase (bars 1–4), which comes nearest in mood to that of a prayer, is felt as eight quavers to the bar. In bars 5 and 6 the beat quickens to four in the bar, and the repeated right-hand chords suggest the emotional stress of the weary wanderer. Finally, *etwas geschwinder*, and almost *alla breve* in feeling, comes the invocation to peace.

It may be objected that the song is more the prayer of a man already at peace with the world than that of a world-weary wanderer, and this is true. But this was not yet the time for *Winterreise*. For its date, the song is wonderfully subtle in integrating a complex mood within a mere eleven bars of music.

Capell, 102; Einstein, 110; Fischer-Dieskau, 43–4

## WANDRERS NACHTLIED II Wayfarer's Night Song II
**Johann Wolfgang von Goethe** (?) December 1822

B flat major D768 Peters I p.229 GA XX no.420

Upon all the peaks there is peace; you scarcely feel a breath stirring in the tree-tops; the little birds are silent in the forest. Wait! Soon you too will be at peace.

The poem was written on the evening of 6 September 1780, in a small shooting-box on a hill outside Ilmenau. Goethe had gone out to enjoy the sunset, and described the scene in a letter to Frau von Stein: 'Apart from the smoke rising here and there from the charcoal-kilns, the whole scene is motionless.' Shortly before his death Goethe visited the spot once more, to find the lines still written faintly on the wooden wall of the hut. In his collected works the poem appears immediately after *Wandrers Nachtlied I*, and is simply entitled *Ein Gleiches* ('The Same').

The original autograph is lost, and the date of the song is uncertain. It must have been written, however, well before July 1824, as Ferdinand Schubert's letter to his brother of 3 July 1824 (*Docs.* no.483) mentions it among a list of songs he had copied and lent to a friend. The most plausible hypothesis is that it belongs with the group of Goethe songs written in December 1822. The song first appeared as a supplement to the *ZfK* on 23 June 1827. In the summer of 1828 it was published by the Lithographic Institute of Vienna, under Schober's management, as op.96 no.3 and dedicated to the Princess von Kinsky. At the end of that year it was republished by Probst of Leipzig as part of a spurious op.101.

'In this song, if anywhere in song literature, appears the ultimate refutation of the notion that great poems should not be used as texts for art songs,' wrote Stein. *Wandrers Nachtlied* is closely modelled on the companion piece written some seven years earlier. There is the same flexible pulse within a single tone colour, the same progression from outward calm to inner peace, the same magical balance between external sensory impressions and contemplation. But it is a much greater song, because it matches the intellectual substance of Goethe's masterpiece on equal terms, finding the precise musical equivalent for the serenity of the last line in a series of simple chords, with the 'horn calls' in the pianist's right hand moving gently against the line of the voice.

The turn on the word 'balde' (bar 10) is omitted in the Peters edition, on the ground that it is a 'late embellishment'. Indeed it may owe its existence to Vogl's interpretation of the song, but it is included in the *Gesamtausgabe*.

Capell, 182–3; Einstein, 254; Fischer-Dieskau, 187–8; Stein, 93

**WASSERFLUT** see WINTERREISE no.6

**WEHMUT (Salis-Seewis)** see DIE HERBSTNACHT

# WEHMUT Melancholy
**Matthäus von Collin**                                                    (?) November 1822
                                                          D minor  D772  Peters III p.15  GA XX no.426

Wenn ich durch Wald und Flu - ren geh,

When I walk through forest and field I feel such mingled happiness and sadness in my uneasy heart; such happy sadness when I behold the meadows in the fullness of their beauty, and all the joy of spring.
For all that blows singing in the wind, all that towers up to heaven, and man himself, so fondly linked with the beauty he beholds, all shall vanish and pass away.

Like the companion piece, *Der Zwerg*, the poem was published in the annual almanach *Selam* for 1813, and this was probably Schubert's source. The poet's title was *Naturgefühl* ('Feeling for Nature'). Schubert changed it to *Wehmut – Alles vergeht*, a reminder that for the Romantics the word 'Wehmut' conveyed the sense not of a mood or a temperament, but of something inseparable from the contemplation of nature. The autograph is lost, and the date is uncertain. However, since it was published in May 1823 (by Sauer and Leidesdorf as op.22) it is likely that it was written before the end of 1822. It is likely also that it was composed at the same time as *Der Zwerg* (q.v.). The opus was dedicated to the author.

It is doubtful whether Schubert's imagination ever worked with greater assurance, with more economy of means, than it did in the autumn and winter of 1822. *Wehmut* is a splendid example. Words and music do not simply correspond, they reinforce each other; and the care with which Schubert contrived this is shown by his alterations to the text. (How much more easily the words ride on the singer's opening phrase than do Collin's original 'Wenn ich auf hohem Berge steh'.) Every phrase of the short poem is given its own definitive expression, yet the organic unity of the song is complete and unassailable. Within its thirty-nine bars Schubert contrives even to suggest a vaguely ternary structure: the opening soliloquy solemnly introspective, the tremolando–crescendo section evoking the majesty of external nature, then the long, slow descending cadence (a variant of Schubert's death motif), *wehmütig, sehnsuchtsvoll*. Not a note is out of place. In Einstein's words, 'Collin's *Wehmut* contains the whole greatness and unaffected simplicity of

Schubert in a nutshell, in its declamatory freedom, its modulations, and its harmonic symbolism ("So wohl – so weh").'

Capell, 184–5; Einstein, 255; Fischer-Dieskau, 172

**WENN ICH DICH, HOLDE, SEHE** see CAVATINE

## WER KAUFT LIEBESGÖTTER Love-gods for sale: who'll buy?

**Johann Wolfgang von Goethe**                    21 August 1815

C major  D261  Peters VI p.52  GA XX no.118

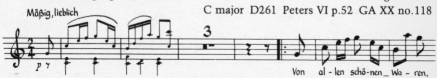

Of all the pretty wares brought here to market none will give more pleasure than those we bring you from foreign lands. O listen to our song, and look at the pretty birds: we offer them for sale.

First inspect this big one, the jolly wanton one. Lightly, merrily he hops down from tree or bush and then up to the top again. There is no need to sing his praises: just look at the chirpy bird: we offer him for sale.

Consider now this little one: he would like to look serious, and yet he is just as wanton as the big one. In secret he reveals his desire to please. This rakish little bird, we are offering him for sale.

Oh, look at the little dove, the darling little dove-wife! The girls are so dainty, so sensible and good-mannered. She likes to preen herself and to serve your love. This tender little bird, we offer her for sale.

We don't need to sing their praises; you can try them out as you like. They love anything new, but don't enquire too closely into their constancy – they all have wings. How charming the birds are. What a tempting buy!

The poem was written in 1795 as a duet for Papageno and Papagena in Goethe's sketch for a sequel to 'The Magic Flute'. The singers were intended to take alternate verses. It was published in 1796 under the title *Die Liebesgötter auf dem Markte*. The first draft, in C major, is dated 21 August 1815 (Vienna, GdM). The fair copy made for Goethe is also in Vienna (SB). There is a copy in the Witteczek–Spaun collection (GdM) in A flat. The song was first published early in 1850 in book 47 of the *Nachlass*, there transposed to A major.

Schubert's strophic setting has Papageno's melodious simplicity, and it runs along briskly in the best market manner. But it gives the singer little breathing space. Perhaps Schubert imagined the song being sung as a duet, though he gives no such indication.

Fischer-Dieskau, 45

## WER NIE SEIN BROT MIT TRÄNEN ASS Who never ate his bread with tears (1)

**Johann Wolfgang von Goethe**                    September 1816

A minor  D480 no.1 (D2 478 no.2)  Not in Peters  GA XX no.256

NSA IV vol.1 p.291

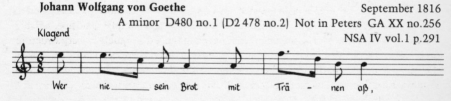

> Who never ate his bread with tears, who never spent anxious nights sitting weeping on his bed, he knows you not, you heavenly powers.
>
> You lead us into the midst of life, you allow us poor creatures to incur guilt, then you deliver us over to torment: for all guilt is avenged on earth.

See HARFENSPIELER. The song is to be found in chapter 13 (book 2) of *Wilhelm Meister*. After the blind Harper has made himself known to the troupe, Wilhelm seeks him out in a lowly inn on the outskirts of the town and, mounting the stairs to the attic, overhears the old man singing 'a few stanzas, partly singing and partly reciting them'. The song was written in 1783, and appears in the first draft of the novel.

Schubert set the text three times, twice in September 1816 and once in 1822. The autograph of this first version (Vienna, SB), is dated September 1816 and contains also a discarded sketch of the melody in the same tempo and key, reproduced in the *Revisionsbericht*. The song was first published in the *Gesamtausgabe* in 1895.

This first strophic version retains the ballad character of the verses, which Goethe describes as 'a sad, heartfelt lament'. The very simplicity of the rhythm and the tonal pattern and the texture serves to add emotional weight to the 'neapolitan' shift in bar 5. There is no repetition of the text except in the last line. Harp effects are suggested simply by the piano arpeggios in the interludes.

## WER NIE SEIN BROT MIT TRÄNEN ASS (2)
**Johann Wolfgang von Goethe**                                    September 1816

A minor  D480 no.2 (D2 478 no.2b)  Not in Peters  GA XX no.257

NSA IV vol.1 p.226

For translation, see the preceding entry. The dated autograph is in Vienna (SB). The song was first published in the *Gesamtausgabe* in 1895.

This second version moves away from the simple ballad conception to a much more elaborate and sophisticated presentation of the same basic idea. The tonality is still that of A minor, and the shape of the melodic line is the same. But the pace is brisker, the rhythm changed from 6/8 to 2/4, and the song is restructured so that the second verse is set in the tonic major and the first verse is repeated at the end, so as to give a basically ternary form to the song. Within this structure Schubert makes expressive use of moving inner parts and bold modulations. Tremolando effects and pulsating chords, suggesting emotional disturbance, replace the simple harp effects in the first version. The net result is a much more impressive, and expressive, song, but one which seems far removed from the bleak world of the Harper. It has been superseded by the final version, but it deserves an occasional hearing on its own merits.

# WER NIE SEIN BROT MIT TRÄNEN ASS (3)

**Johann Wolfgang von Goethe** Autumn 1822

A minor D480 no.3 (D2 478 no.2) Peters II p.30 GA XX no.258

NSA IV vol.1 p.89

For translation, see *Wer nie sein Brot mit Tränen ass* (1). The final version of the three *Harfenspieler* songs was published as op.12 by Cappi and Diabelli on commission in December 1822 and dedicated to Johann Nepomuk von Dankesreither, Bishop of St Pölten. The autograph fair copy made for that publication has not survived, but in a letter to Spaun written on 7 December 1822 Schubert enclosed a proof copy of the opus and made it clear that the setting of *Wer nie sein Brot* was new (*Docs.* no.328). The autograph must have been in the hands of the printer many weeks before the date of this letter, which argues that the song was composed not later than September or October 1822.

For his final, definitive version Schubert returned to the mood (and to the harp motifs) of the first setting, but he devised a more elaborate structure to reflect the emotional range of the poem, and in particular to give to the second verse separate treatment so that it sounds a note of defiance of fate and prefigures the mood of *Winterreise*. Each verse is repeated. The first moves from A minor to major, and ends in a long despairing F major cadence. When the Harper turns to his indictment of the gods for their indifference to the fate of men the sweeping arpeggios reverse the process, turning from B flat major to B flat minor. The tonality is brought back with a wrench to A minor; the opening music returns (*ppp*), and the mood changes again to a kind of abnegation. But the *sforzandi* in the postlude echo the despair and defiance of the middle section.

Capell, 120–1; Einstein, 141

# WER SICH DER EINSAMKEIT ERGIBT The man who takes to solitude (1)

**Johann Wolfgang von Goethe** 13 November 1815

A minor D325 Not in Peters GA XX no.173 NSA IV vol.1 p.220

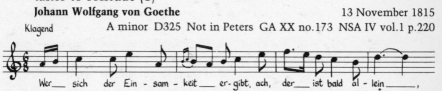

The man who takes to solitude, alas, is soon alone; each man lives, each man loves, and leaves him to his agony.

Yes, leave me to my torment! Even if I can once be in solitude, I shall not be entirely alone.

A lover steals up softly, listening to discover whether his beloved is alone. So in my loneliness misery creeps up upon me day and night; and torment in my solitude. Ah, when once I am in the solitude of the grave, then they will leave me alone.

See HARFENSPIELER. The poem was written before 1783. Like the previous song, it was sung to Wilhelm during his visit to the Harper at the inn, and is to be found in chapter 13 of book 2 of *Wilhelm Meister*. In the novel the lines are printed in two stanzas of eight lines each. In the collected poems the first stanza is divided. There are more metrical irregularities than usual. The first quatrain is in regular iambic ballad measure, but later there are shorter lines and an occasional anapaest disturbs the iambic rhythm.

The autograph of this first setting is on two separate sheets (both in Vienna, SB). The first page, containing the first thirty-one bars, is entitled *Lied aus Wilhelm Meister* and dated 13 November 1815. The bottom right-hand corner has been torn off, so that there are gaps in the manuscript. The remaining nine bars appear on the manuscript of *Hermann und Thusnelda*; they have been cancelled. The song was first published in the *Gesamtausgabe* in 1895.

This spare 6/8 A minor setting is much in the same manner as the first setting of *Wer nie sein Brot mit Tränen ass*. It is not altogether successful in imposing a sense of direction on the song, however.

## WER SICH DER EINSAMKEIT ERGIBT (2)
**Johann Wolfgang von Goethe** September 1816

A minor  D478 (D2 478 no.1)  Peters II p.27  GA XX no.254(a) and (b)

NSA IV vol.1 p.85

For translation, see the preceding entry. The original autograph, headed 'Aus Wilhelm Meister. Harfenspieler. Göthe' and dated September 1816, is in private hands. The marking is *Langsam (pp)*. The fair copy made for the printer in 1822 is lost. The published version is substantially the same as the original, but the marking is now *Sehr langsam (pp) mit der Verschiebung* ('with soft pedal'), and various embellishments are added to the vocal line, which doubtless owe something to Vogl's rendering of the song. Both versions are published in the *Gesamtausgabe* and the *Neue Ausgabe*. The song appeared in December 1822 as op.12 no.1 (Cappi and Diabelli).

There is a striking homogeneity about the Harper songs. They are all in A minor, the key of *Der Leiermann*, Schubert's key of deprivation and alienation, and the final versions of the first and third songs both move at the measured tread of the wanderer in *Winterreise*. That insistent *Bewegung* is however subtly adapted to the words. After the preludial harp-like chords the opening phrases are separated by the pauses, to give the effect almost of soliloquy. At the beginning of the second verse ('A lover steals up softly...') the stepwise bass line and the sly triplets in the piano part picture the scene. And as the tormented Harper's thoughts turn longingly towards the grave, the firm descending chromatic bass line, Schubert's constant tonal image of death, tells us what we need to know.

The three Harper songs are really too similar in tone to make a successful miniature cycle, but their relevance to the greatness of *Winterreise* is plain.

Capell, 121–2; W. Dürr, 'Schubert's songs and their poetry: reflections on poetic aspects of song composition', *Studies*, 15–20; Einstein, 141; Fischer-Dieskau, 78

For *An die Türen will ich schleichen* see p.40.

# **WIDERSCHEIN** Reflection

**Franz Xaver von Schlechta**                                    1819/1820

B flat major D639, 949 Peters III p.148 GA XX no.553

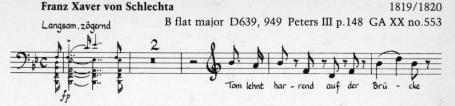

Tom lehnt har-rend auf der Brü-cke

A fisherman waits on the bridge; his lover is late. Crossly he stares into the stream, day-dreaming.

But she is lurking nearby among the elder bushes; and suddenly her image, never more faithfully portrayed, shines back from the clear water.

And he sees it! He recognises the ribbons, and the sweet apparition; and he clings to the railing, for otherwise he would be drawn down into the water!

The poem has had a chequered history, and the variant readings have been a source of confusion. The first version, published in the *ZfK* in 1818, began: 'Fischer harrt am Brückenbogen' ('The fisherman waited on the arch of the bridge'). Schubert set the text in D major (D639), and it appeared as a supplement to the Leipzig 'Pocket-book of Sociable Pleasures' in the autumn of 1820. However, very few copies of this first edition remain.

Schlechta rewrote the poem for publication in his *Dichtungen* (1824). This revised and improved version begins 'Harrt ein Fischer auf der Brücke'; only the final couplet survived unchanged from the original. In May or September 1828 Schubert made a fair copy of the song, incorporating the new text, and transposed it to B flat major (D949). This is the familiar version; but as a further complication, Schlechta made changes in the text after Schubert's death, and these were incorporated in the song when it was published in 1832 in book 15 of the *Nachlass*. The first line now ran: 'Tom lehnt harrend auf der Brücke' ('Tom leant on the bridge, waiting') and the text of the last verse reverts in part to the first version. The odd result is that the words of the song as it is usually sung do not correspond exactly with any of Schlechta's versions. The *Gesamtausgabe* restored the first line of the 1824 version because it is easier to sing. Friedländer in the Peters edition as usual follows the first edition.

The song must have been written in 1819 or early 1820. By this time Schubert had evolved a tonal language capable of evoking with extraordinary precision a visual scene or a mood. But music needs more space, or rather time, than poetry to achieve a comparable effect. Hence the generous repetitions in this song.

Here the problem is more acute, because the effect to be achieved is that of waiting, of time suspended, of expectation. In four introductory bars Schubert manages to convey all this, and also the mysterious surface of the stream, darkly and gently moving, with wonderful economy. When the singer enters we recognise the slow staccato 'tip-toeing' movement which is Schubert's musical image for the idea of complicity, of intrigue (cf. *Das Geheimnis*, *Geheimes*), while the rocking movement is sustained in the dotted phrases. When the other party to the intrigue appears on the scene the accompaniment, moving up into the treble clef, takes on a lighter, brighter texture, and the song moves into the dominant for the first time with a phrase strangely reminiscent of the first movement of the B flat Piano Sonata D960. For the last verse the accompaniment moves back to the bass and the singer's first tune returns. But Schubert has another magical trick up his sleeve. He combines the swaying triplets from verse 2 with the rocking movement from the introduction in such a way as to suggest the hypnotic spell of the moving waters, as the head of the watching lover begins to swim. *Widerschein* deserves to be much better known than it is.

Fischer-Dieskau, 139

## WIDERSPRUCH Contrariness
**Johann Gabriel Seidl**                                                    1826
D865

Schubert's autograph of this four-part male-voice chorus (Vienna, SB) is headed 'Männerchor'. It was published, however, by Josef Czerny with three solo songs (op.105, November 1828) and with the explanatory note: 'Four-part, but may be sung also with the top part only'. It is not, however, included in series XX of the *Gesamtausgabe*, and there is no reason whatever to regard it as anything other than a chorus.

## WIE ULFRU FISCHT Ulfru Fishing
**Johann Mayrhofer**                                                    January 1817
D minor D525 Peters IV p.16 GA XX no.296 NSA IV vol.1 pp.158, 269

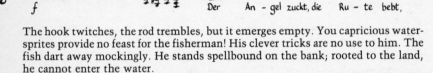

The hook twitches, the rod trembles, but it emerges empty. You capricious watersprites provide no feast for the fisherman! His clever tricks are no use to him. The fish dart away mockingly. He stands spellbound on the bank; rooted to the land, he cannot enter the water.

The smooth surface wrinkles, stirred by the scaly folk gliding about happily in the safety of its depths. The trout dart to and fro, but the fisherman's hook remains empty. They can feel what freedom is; the fisherman's age-old skill is fruitless.

The earth is wonderfully beautiful, but a safe place it is certainly not. Storms come from the icy mountain peaks; at a stroke the hail and frost destroy the golden corn, the lovely rose. But the little fish under their soft smooth roof − no storm from the land pursues them.

The autograph is lost; the evidence for the date is an entry in the catalogue of the Witteczek−Spaun collection (Vienna, GdM). A copy made for Josef Hüttenbrenner has the tempo indication *Etwas bewegt*. The song was published by Sauer and Leidesdorf in June 1823 as op.21 no.3 and dedicated to the author 'by his friend Franz Schubert'.

It is difficult to avoid invidious comparisons with a roughly contemporary song, *Die Forelle*, which it closely resembles in tone and sentiment; and both songs show Schubert's mastery in the handling of the strophic song to produce a virtual identity of words and tune. But there is something in the stolid movement of this march tune which fails to match the lighthearted tone of the verses, so that it is quite overshadowed not only by *Die Forelle* but also by the two fine songs which make up op.21. This publication was advertised as '3 Fischerlieder von Meyerhofer [sic] für den Bass'. In the Peters edition, however, the melody line is transferred to the treble clef.

# WIEDERSEHN Reunion

**August Wilhelm von Schlegel**

September 1825

G major D855 Not in Peters GA XX no.481

The sweet smile of the spring sunshine is the dawn of my hope; in the whisper of the west wind I hear the call to joy. I am coming! Over hill and vale, sweet lady of my delight, love flies to greet you on the swift wings of song.

It sends a greeting from the constant lover who, without requital, has sworn to dedicate himself to you, and to all-powerful nature. He keeps his lonely vigil watching and listening, like a sailor for the pole star, for some echo of that star to reach him through the depths of the night.

Oh, joy! I sigh with bold desire, and soon shall sigh with it on your breast, and breathe it in with your voice, pulsating with nameless bliss. You smile as my heart, embraced by your nearness, beats still more wildly, and your lips tremble with happy benevolence.

You love me, noble goddess! You love me, tender, gentle woman! It is enough. I am new-made, life floods through my soul and body. No, the blood which courses so proudly through my veins refuses to rail against the fate which tears me so swiftly from your side.

Schubert wrote out only the first of the four stanzas, but put repeat marks at the end of his strophic setting. Moreover, he added two more verses when he made a fair copy of the song. As so often, he was content to leave the matter to the discretion of the singer.

The autograph (Berlin, SPK) is part of a manuscript dated September 1825. The song must therefore have been written either at Gmunden or Steyr, and immediately after the visit to Gastein. There are dated copies in the Witteczek–Spaun collection (Vienna, GdM) and another, made by Ferdinand Schubert, in Berlin (SPK). The song was first published in 1843 as a supplement to *Lebensbilder aus Österreich* ('Scenes of Austrian Life'), an anthology edited by Andreas Schumacher. (There the text is wrongly attributed to Friedrich von Schlegel.) In 1872 it appeared as no.1 of 'Forty Songs', published by J. P. Gotthard.

The air of innocence and simple happiness may seem almost anachronistic, except that it must owe something to the memory of Schubert's revitalising experience at Gastein. The tone and form have an affinity, indeed, with the Trio of the D major Piano Sonata (D850), which was written at Gastein. Maybe Schubert's interest was concentrated on the first verse, with its 'call to joy'.

Capell, 218

# WIEGENLIED Cradle Song

**Author unknown**

November 1816

Langsam

A flat major D498 Peters II p.194 GA XX no.277

Sleep, sweet boy, your mother's hand rocks you gently; the swaying cradle straps bring you gentle peace and comfort.

Sleep in the sweet grave, still protected by your mother's arms; all her hopes, all her possessions she embraces lovingly, with the warmth of love.

Sleep on her soft lap, as the pure notes of love still hover about you; a lily, a rose – they will be your reward after sleep.

The autograph is lost, but there are contemporary copies in Stadler's song album and in Ebner's (Lund, UB). Both give the author as Claudius, and so does the first edition, published by Diabelli as op.98 (1829). Presumably this attribution derives from Schubert's autograph, but the poem is not to be found in Claudius's collected works. The date of the song, and of the companion piece *An die Nachtigall* (Claudius), is given as November 1816 in the catalogue of the Witteczek–Spaun collection (Vienna, GdM).

The song takes its place beside *An Sylvia*, *An die Musik* and *Litanei* as an example of Schubert the supreme melodist. For what gives the emotive power to this simple alternation of tonic and dominant is the perfect shape of the tune. It shares with Brahms's famous song the honour of being the best-known and the best-loved cradle song in the world. The shadow of the grave, which obtrudes here as in so many early Romantic pieces on this subject, finds no place in Schubert's music.

Capell, 120; Einstein, 161

# WIEGENLIED Cradle Song

**Theodor Körner**                                                                      15 October 1815

F major D304 Not in Peters GA XX no.152

Slumber softly! In your mother's arms you do not yet feel the torment and the joy of life. Your dreams know no sorrows; your mother's breast is your whole world.

Ah, how sweet the dreams of early hours, when we live by motherly love; my memory of them has gone; just the idea of it remains to thrill me.

Thrice may a man be so warmly cradled in love; thrice is it permitted to the happy man to believe in the higher meaning of life, as he lies in the divine arms of love.

Love blesses him first, as an infant blossoming in joy and happiness; everything greets his fresh glance with a smile; love holds him to his mother's breast.

Then when the beauty of the heavens clouds over, and the way ahead for the youth is unclear, then for the second time love takes him in her arms as his sweetheart.

But in the storm the flower-stem snaps, and in the storm a man's heart breaks: then love appears as the angel of death, and carries him in triumph up to heaven.

The autograph, now in the ÖNB, Vienna, is a first draft dated 15 October 1815. There is a dated copy also in the Witteczek–Spaun collection (Vienna, GdM). The song was first published in the *Gesamtausgabe* in 1895.

In spite of the title, the song is not a lullaby but a hymn in praise of love. And instead of the gently rocking movement of other cradle songs the tempo indication – *Langsam. Ruhig* – suggests the serenity of contemplation. The song well illustrates the purity of style and expressive grace that Schubert was able to give to the simplest diatonic sequences in his early years.

**WIEGENLIED** (Ottenwalt) see DER KNABE IN DER WIEGE

## WIEGENLIED Cradle Song

**Johann Gabriel Seidl** (?) 1826

*Langsam* A flat major D867 Peters III p.72 GA XX no.572

Wie sich der Äug-lein kind-li-cher Him-mel,

How carelessly the child's heaven shuts itself off from the slumber-laden eyes! When one day the earth tempts you back, close them thus, for heaven lies within you, joy lies without!

How your cheeks glow red with sleep! Roses from Eden have breathed on them; your cheeks are roses, your eyes the sky, bright morning, heavenly day!

How the golden curls of your hair cool the border of your glowing temple! The golden hair is beautiful, and even more beautiful the garland upon it; dream of the laurel until it blooms for you.

Dear little mouth, angels hover round you; inside is innocence, inside is love; guard them, little child, guard them faithfully; your lips are roses, your lips are warmth.

As an angel has folded your little hands, so fold them one day when you go to rest. After prayer dreams are beautiful, and the dream makes up for the awakening.

The autograph is missing, and the exact date of composition is not certain. However, Seidl's poems were published early in 1826, and the three settings which survive on dated autographs belong to March 1826. The assumption is that this one also was written either in March 1826 or in the following months. The song was published by Josef Czerny in November 1828 as op.105 no.2. Three other Seidl songs make up the opus.

There is an instructive comparison to be drawn between the famous cradle song of November 1816 (D498) and this infinitely more subtle song. The key and the tempo marking are the same, and in the first half of the strophe at any rate the tonal pattern still rests on an almost hypnotic alternation of tonic and dominant. But there the resemblance ends.

Capell, while acknowledging the 'softness and tenderness of the music', finds the song too long. Seidl's long poem, with its forty short lines and strong dactylic pattern, does present a problem, for a strophic setting is demanded (is there not something self-contradictory about a through-composed cradle song?); yet monotony has somehow to be avoided. Schubert's solution is to devise a strophe which has two contrasted halves, offering a kind of built-in relief to the prevailing mood, and then to keep the song moving along gently in four-bar phrases which match the flow of the verses, four lines to each musical phrase. Within this pattern there are subtle variations which constantly delight the listener. The insistent *alla breve* movement is enhanced by the unexpected cross-rhythm at bar 4 of the prelude and interludes, with its pre-echo of the melodic line in the pianist's right hand, while the cadential melodic phrase is given a chromatic inflection in alternate verses, so that no two adjacent verses sound exactly alike. The song is pure Schubert.

Capell, 224; Einstein, 304

**WILHELM MEISTER SONGS** see under MIGNON'S SONGS, HARFENSPIELER and individual titles.

## WILLKOMMEN UND ABSCHIED Hail and Farewell

**Johann Wolfgang von Goethe**                                December 1822

C major  D767  Peters III p.25  GA XX no.419(a) and (b)

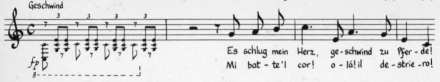

Es schlug mein Herz, ge-schwind zu Pfer-de!
Mi bat-te'l cor! o-lá! il de-strie-ro!

My heart was beating: quick, to horse! In a twinkling it was done. Evening was already cradling the earth, and night hung upon the mountains. The oak stood in its misty cloak, a towering giant, there − where darkness peeped out of the bushes with a hundred jet-black eyes.

The moon gazed piteously out of a misty bank of cloud; the winds softly flapped their wings and whistled eerily about my ears; the night created a thousand monsters, but my mood was alert and happy. What a fire was in my veins, what ardour in my heart!

I saw you, and from your sweet eyes on me flowed a gentle joy; my heart was entirely yours, and every breath I took for you. A rose-tinted springtime framed your dear features, and tenderness for me − Ye Gods, I had hoped for it, but I had not deserved it!

But ah, with the morning sun farewell began to constrict my heart. In your kisses what bliss! In your eyes what pain! I went, you stood still, looked down, and gazed after me, damp-eyed: and yet, what joy to be beloved! And to be in love, ye Gods, what joy!

The poem, written in the spring of 1771, recalls Goethe's student days in Strasbourg, and particularly his love-affair with Friederike Brion, the daughter of the pastor of Sesenheim, some thirty miles north of Strasbourg. It was published in Jacobi's periodical *Iris* in 1775.

The surviving autograph is a first draft in D major dated December 1822 (Berlin, SPK). A fair copy made for the printer, in C major, is lost. Schubert mentions the song as one of his completed compositions in a letter to Spaun of 7 December 1822 (*Docs.* no.328). The song was published by A.W. Pennauer in July 1826 as op.56 no.1 and dedicated by Schubert to Karl Pinterics. There are minor differences between the first draft and the first edition. Both versions are included in the *Gesamtausgabe*. The first edition also included a translation of the text into Italian, probably by Jacob Nicolaus Craigher.

Schubert's eager response to the motor images in a poem is the key to his creative method as a song-writer, but it has its disadvantages, as this splendid song reveals. Given the first line − 'quick, to horse!' − it was inevitable that the song should be permeated by the sound of galloping hooves. Schubert pauses only once, as the poet exclaims in incredulous joy at his undeserved good fortune, and for that break in the rhythmic pattern we are duly grateful. The song certainly matches the impetuous ardour of the poem, even if it does not do full justice to its more subtle psychological aspects; the contrast between the sinister threat of the dark night and the young man's inner excitement, for instance, and that between the unclouded joy of meeting and the uncertain pain of departure. In short, Schubert has written a fine song, even though it does not match the greatness of Goethe's poem.

Friedländer comments on the Italian manner of the final peroration. But there is something operatic about the whole song; the last verse is basically a return to the music of the second verse.

Capell, 181−2; Friedländer, II, 171

# **WINTERLIED** Song of Winter

**Ludwig Hölty**

13 May 1816

A minor D401 Not in Peters GA XX no.220

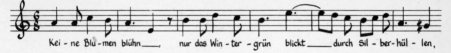

Kei - ne Blu-men blühn___, nur das Win - ter - grün blickt___ durch Sil - ber-hül - len,

No flowers bloom, only the wintergreen peeps through the silver covering; only tiny red and white flowers, blossoming out of the ice, fill the window.

Ah, no birdsong rings out with merry note, only the wintry tune of the titmouse that flits about the window chirping for food.

Love flees the grove where the little birds were wont to nest in the green shade; love flees the grove and comes indoors.

Cold January, in truth I shall not feel your frosts here among the love-games. Reign for ever, cold January!

The poem dates from 1773. The autograph (Washington, LC) is included in a manuscript dated 13 May 1816; but Schubert's 'May' is difficult to distinguish from his 'March', and Deutsch reads the earlier date. The song was first published in the *Gesamtausgabe* in 1895.

The plaintive minor 6/8 melody has a strong affinity with *Ins stille Land*, which belongs to March–April 1816, and both may be regarded as near relations of the D minor and A minor versions of *Nur wer die Sehnsucht kennt*. Both the mood and the style seem to belong especially to 1816.

# **WINTERREISE** The Winter Journey

**Wilhelm Müller**

February–October 1827

D911 Peters I pp.54–121 GA nos. 517–40 NSA IV vol.4

The text is by Wilhelm Müller, the author of *Die schöne Mullerin*, and both cycles were published under the general title of 'Seventy-seven Poems from the Posthumous Papers of a Travelling Horn-player'. Müller's title is *Die Winterreise*, but both the autograph and the first edition of Schubert's cycle omit the article.

The poems which make up the complete *Winterreise* were assembled gradually. Twelve poems were published in *Urania*, a Leipzig almanac, in 1823, and these correspond exactly with the songs in Schubert's part I, both in content and in sequence. Ten more appeared in the same year in a Breslau periodical. Finally Müller added two more, *Die Post* and *Täuschung*, and rearranged the whole cycle in a new order when it was published in 1824 in Dessau as vol.II of the 'Posthumous Papers'. This volume was dedicated 'to the master of German song Carl Maria von Weber, as a token of friendship and respect'.

Schubert's autograph, now in New York (PML), establishes beyond a doubt that the two parts of the cycle were written at different times. Part I is dated 'February 1827' at the beginning. The source was *Urania*, and Schubert wrote the word 'Finis' at the end of no.12, a clear indication that at that time he regarded these twelve songs as making up the complete cycle. It is of interest that in this first draft the last song, *Einsamkeit*, was written in D minor, the key of the opening song.

There is a publisher's copy of the autograph of part I in Vienna (SB). It is dated 1827 and has corrections in Schubert's hand. The censor's stamp on it is dated 24 October 1827. Part I was published by Haslinger in January 1828.

Part II of the autograph is a fair copy, dated October 1827, made from earlier drafts now for the most part lost. It is headed 'Continuation of *Winterreise*' and the songs are numbered 1–12. With one exception, Schubert set the additional songs in the order in which they appear in Müller's final version, as the following list makes clear:

| Schubert's order for part II | Position in Müller's cycle |
|---|---|
| 1 *Die Post* | 6 |
| 2 *Der greise Kopf* | 10 |
| 3 *Die Krähe* | 11 |
| 4 *Letzte Hoffnung* | 12 |
| 5 *Im Dorfe* | 13 |
| 6 *Der stürmische Morgen* | 14 |
| 7 *Täuschung* | 15 |
| 8 *Der Wegweiser* | 16 |
| 9 *Das Wirtshaus* | 17 |
| 10 *Mut* | 23 |
| 11 *Die Nebensonnen* | 20 |
| 12 *Der Leiermann* | 24 |

It will be noted that Schubert interchanged *Mut* and *Die Nebensonnen*, for reasons which will be discussed later. The songs were renumbered 13–24 in the first edition.

Against this background it is possible to reconstruct the probable sequence of events. Schubert came across the *Urania* publication in February 1827 (Schober said he found it in his [Schober's] library) and set the twelve poems he found there in that month. Spaun testified to his absorption in this project at about this time (*Memoirs* pp.137–8); and it was probably the first part of the cycle which he planned to introduce to his friends at Schober's on 4 March, when he failed to turn up (*Docs.* nos.819–20). Later in the year he found the complete cycle in the Dessau publication of 1824 and decided to set the additional poems. Most were probably drafted that summer, but at least one seems to have been sketched at Graz in September (see no.23). The fair copy was written out in October, but Haslinger held up publication of part II until part I was well launched. There is a well-founded tradition, vouched for by Ferdinand Schubert and Spaun (*Memoirs* pp.28 and 38) and supported by Haslinger and by Schindler, that the last work Schubert did was to correct the proofs of part II on his deathbed. Part II was published in December 1828. The opus number for the cycle was 89.

There are close links between the two song cycles, and if we are to make a proper assessment of Schubert's greatness as a song-writer they should be seen as complementary. Looked at in isolation it is possible to underrate the earlier work as no more than a charming essay in popular whimsy; and it is easy to overestimate the suicidal despair of *Winterreise*, and to ignore the stoic resolution of its end. There is a philosophical dimension to both cycles. Together they constitute the greatest achievement in the history of song; moreover they provide us with a unique insight into the development of Schubert's own mind and art.

Both works owe their existence to Müller's gift for the short evocative lyric in what might be called the sophisticated folksong tradition, and to his invention of the narrative thread. Both achieve their unity and their cumulative power by means of a subtle control – whether consciously exercised or not is beside the point – of pace, rhythm, *Bewegung* and tonality. But there are profound differences between them. The *Schöne Müllerin* cycle has a real, though shadowy, plot involving three principal characters, though we see them all through the eyes of the young miller. The listener is allowed to participate, in an oblique and allusive way, in the development of the drama, and the mood changes from eager expectation at the beginning to Romantic glorification of death as the only possible consummation at the end. *Winterreise*, on the other hand, is a wholly interior drama. There is no plot, no real change of circumstances, and little change of mood except from bitter irony to a resolute defiance. The only human figure to penetrate the closed circle of the hero's despair is the pitiable hurdy-gurdy man in the last song, and he belongs to the same tribe as the Harper in *Wilhelm Meister*. His quarrel is not with individual wrongs, but with fate itself. This gives to the protagonist of *Winterreise* a stature as a Romantic hero, as the artist figure at war with society and with fate. Significantly, the definitive tragedy has happened before the cycle opens. There is no villain in the piece except the nature of things.

This change of tone in part reflects the change in Schubert's own circumstances between 1823 and 1827. In those four years the political climate had become more illiberal, standards of taste had declined, and Schubert had been obliged to come to terms with his own chronic illness. The most perceptive comment came from Schubert's friend, the poet Mayrhofer: 'It now seems to be in order to mention two poems of Wilhelm Müller's which constitute a more extensive cycle, and permit of a more penetrating glimpse into the composer's mind. Opening with a joyful song of roaming, the mill songs depict love in its awakening, its deceptions and hopes, its delights and sorrows ... Not so with "The Winter Journey", the very choice of which shows how much more serious the composer had become. He had been long and seriously ill, had gone through shattering experiences, and life for him had shed its rosy colour; winter had come for him. The poet's irony, rooted in despair, appealed to him; he expressed it in cutting tones. I was painfully moved' (*Memoirs* p.15).

Beyond this, the protagonist in *Winterreise* is a more tragic figure than the young miller in the earlier cycle, not only because his isolation and alienation are more complete, but because he is denied the consolation of death. At the climax of *Die schöne Müllerin*, *Trockne Blumen* sounds a triumphant fanfare over the grave of the rejected lover ('Denn Blümlein alle/Heraus, heraus!/Der Mai ist kommen/Der Winter ist aus!'). At the corresponding point in *Winterreise*, however, the symbolism of *Das Wirtshaus* is unambiguous. There is to be no place for the outcast in the cool Inn of Death – 'Nun weiter denn, nur weiter,/Mein treuer Wanderstab!' Like Byron's Manfred, he is condemned to suffer without respite; unlike Wagner's hero, he is denied even the solace of redemption through love; his fate is a life in death, relieved only by the comradeship of the pathetic hurdy-gurdy man.

The organic unity of the cycle is largely a matter of tonality and *Bewegung*, though Gerald Moore, in the preface to his study of the song cycles (pp.xiii–xiv) identifies a recurrent ascending phrase. The wanderer's footsteps echo through the cycle in a variety of guises, usually in 2/4 time and in a minor key. At the other extreme the songs of derangement and alienation, like *Frühlingstraum*, *Täuschung*, *Die Nebensonnen*, *Der Leiermann*, are in triple time and take A major/minor as their tonal centre. Another group, more static and contemplative, is based upon E major/minor. But although these tonal associations play an important part in our apprehension of the work's form, they cannot easily be reduced to a rational scheme, and the fact that Schubert himself changed the key of several songs before publication makes it more difficult to find one.

There is an extensive literature, of which the following recent studies should be noted:

J. Armitage-Smith, 'Schubert's *Winterreise*, part I: the sources of the musical text', *MQ*, LX, 1974, pp.20–36; Feil; E. McKay, 'Schubert's Winterreise reconsidered', *MR*, XXXVIII, 1977, pp.94–100; Moore, 75–172

## (1) **GUTE NACHT** Good Night

D minor

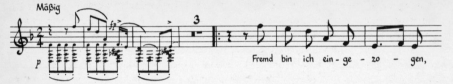

Fremd bin ich ein-ge-zo-gen,

A stranger I came, a stranger I depart. The month of May treated me kindly, with many a flowery bouquet.

The girl spoke of love, her mother of marriage even. Now the world is drear, the way covered in snow.

I cannot choose my own time to travel. I must find my own way in this darkness.

My shadow, cast by the moon, keeps me company; and on the blanched fields I seek out the deer tracks.

Why should I linger, until they drive me away? Let the stray dogs howl at their masters' gate.

Love is a happy wanderer, for God has made it so, from one to another. Good night, sweetheart.

I will not disturb your dreams. It would be a shame to spoil your rest. You shall not hear my footsteps, as I close the door softly.

As I depart I write 'Good night' on your door, so that you may see that I thought of you.

'A stranger I came, a stranger I depart.' *Gute Nacht* sets the tone for the whole cycle, and in a sense it sets the pace too. We hear the footsteps of the wanderer throughout the song. They never falter, except momentarily as the music melts into the major for the last verse, and even there there is only a suggestion of a *ritenuto*, rather than a change of pace.

The original marking on the autograph was *Mässig, in gehender Bewegung* – 'At a moderate walking pace'. Not that one could actually walk to the pace of the music; at two beats to the bar it is too slow, and at four beats too quick. But it is the notion of a steady pace which is conveyed. For the first edition Schubert deleted all but the word *Mässig*, possibly because he did not want to encourage misguided attempts to turn this into a marching song. The 'gehende Bewegung', however, runs like a linking thread through the cycle.

The verses are grouped in pairs. The switch to the major gives a magical tenderness to the last two verses, and a special pathos to the return to the minor in the postlude.

## (2) **DIE WETTERFAHNE** The Weather-vane

A minor

Der Wind_ spielt mit_ der Wet-ter-fah-ne

The wind plays with the weather-vane on my fair love's house. In my folly I thought that it mocked the wretched fugitive.

He should have noticed earlier this emblem on the house, then he would never have thought to find a faithful woman within.

Inside the house the wind plays with hearts as it does outside on the roof, though not so loudly. What do they care about my suffering? Their child is a wealthy bride.

The first song is concerned with the inner drama, the wanderer's state of mind. In *Die Wetterfahne* he pauses on his journey, and we catch a sharp glimpse of the hostile world about him. The song is first of all a marvellously original piece of tone-painting. The fitful scurrying wind, the biting cold, the empty landscape, the gyrating weather-vane are all portrayed with a kind of photographic intensity by those bare swooping unisons, wide leaps and insistent trills. The song is full of a wild impersonal energy.

Significantly, the song is more outward-looking than the poem. Schubert's ability to change the psychological point of view is the key to success in maintaining a progressive interest in the listener. Here he is content to set aside the implied self-pity of the second and third verses. Significant also is the change to the tonality of A minor, which is to be concerned throughout the cycle with the wanderer's fallible perception of external reality.

In bar 41, the better reading for the second chord is E flat in the pianist's left hand. The tempo indication on the autograph is *Ziemlich geschwind, unruhig*.

(3) **GEFRORNE TRÄNEN** Frozen Tears                                F minor

Frozen teardrops fall from my cheeks. Did I not notice then, that I have been weeping?
    Ah tears – my tears – are you so lukewarm that you can turn to ice like the cold morning dew?
    And yet you spring from the heart's source so red-hot, as though you intended to melt all the ice of winter.

In the third song the traveller stirs his frozen limbs and plods on. *Gefrorne Tränen* links with *Gute Nacht* as the second of the *gehende Lieder*. The power of the rhythmical image, the laboured alternation of tonic and dominant, the slow staccato movement and the repeated rising notes in the pianist's left hand combine to suggest an obsessive weariness and sense of effort. But the bare unisons at the close, and the open octaves at 'Ei Tränen, meine Tränen' remind us also of *Die Wetterfahne*, while the more even stresses and lyrical flow of the last verse has something of the tenderness of the last verse of *Gute Nacht*. Already Schubert begins to weave the various strands of the drama into a satisfying pattern.

(4) **ERSTARRUNG** Numbness                                      C minor

In vain I scan the snow for traces of her steps, where once we walked arm in arm over the green meadows.
    I will kiss the ground, pierce through the ice and snow with my hot tears until I see the bare earth.
    Where shall I find a flower? Where shall I find green grass? The flowers are dead, the grass looks so pale.
    Am I to take no keepsake with me then, as I go? Nothing to speak to me of her, when my grief is stilled?
    My heart is dead; within it her image stands stiff and cold. If ever my heart should thaw again, her image will melt away.

*Erstarrung* is unique in its emotional intensity and unity of mood and theme. No other song in the cycle has quite the same sense of disorientated passion and headlong flight. Its 109 bars are characterised by a single mood and a single pulse.

The unrequited passion is in the text, certainly, but the fugitive despair has an antecedent in the Schulze songs. Schulze's *Im Walde*, which Schubert set in March 1825, is also about a man who travels the world in a vain endeavour to leave the anguish in his heart behind, and it too is dominated by an obsessive pulse and by non-stop triplets. Schubert's creative imagination here seems to have been triggered by the resemblance between the two poems. The original marking for *Erstarrung* was *Nicht zu geschwind*.

### (5) **DER LINDENBAUM**  The Lime Tree                                E major

A lime tree stands by the well outside the gate; in its shade I used to dream many a sweet dream.

On its bark I carved so many words of love; I was drawn to it always both in joy and sorrow.

Today my way led past it, at dead of night; and even in the dark I closed my eyes.

And its branches rustled as though they called to me: 'Come over here, my friend, here you will find rest.'

The cold winds blew full in my face, my hat flew from my head, but I did not turn round.

Now I am many hours' journey from that place; and still I hear the rustling: 'There you would find rest!'

The song leads a double life, as an adopted folksong which every German child knows in its simple E major form, and as an art song which represents some kind of peak of the song-writer's art. Yet these two roles do not conflict. It is a proof of Schubert's greatness as an artist that the song combines the universality of folksong with the subtlety, the mastery, of the art song.

Müller's theme here, as in *Frühlingstraum*, is the conflict between dream and reality. The lime tree (the centre of village life) is the symbol of the innocence and security of childhood. So Schubert's folksong has the ease and sweetness of a dream. But his ability to change the emotional colour of a song never worked with more magical effect than it does here. The pianist's triplets, which in the prelude seem only to whisper gently like leaves in a summer breeze, are suddenly filled with menace, until in the fifth verse they howl through the song like a bitter gale.

The tempo indication on the autograph is *Mässig langsam*. In bar 45 there is a case for making the singer's quaver ('Die') E rather than F sharp (see Armitage-Smith).

(6) **WASSERFLUT** Flood                                      E minor

Many a tear has fallen from my eyes into the snow; its cold flakes greedily absorb my burning anguish.

When the grass is ready to grow a mild wind blows, and the ice breaks up into fragments and the soft snow melts.

Snow, you know about my longing, tell me – where are you going? You have only to follow my tears, and you will soon become part of the brook.

You will flow through the town with him, in and out of the busy streets; where you feel my tears burning, that will be the house of my love.

Schubert's autograph has the song in F sharp minor, and the reason for the change to E minor is not clear. It does avoid a top A for the singer in bar 27, but such a practical reason hardly applies to other changes of key. The verses are grouped in pairs, and the double strophe flows along gently like a lament, then suddenly breaks out in a cry of anguish at bar 12. The singer's final phrase sounds a note of steely defiance.

Opinions differ as to whether the dotted notes in the accompaniment should be assimilated to the triplet rhythm in the voice line. A thorough insistence on maintaining the dotted rhythm is likely to conflict with the essential smoothness and simplicity of the melody, and to sound mannered and jerky. Moreover, both the autograph and the first edition align the semiquavers with the final note of the singer's triplet; this interpretation would have been perfectly consistent with Schubert's conservative notational practice.

(7) **AUF DEM FLUSSE** On the River                           E minor

You clear wild stream, that once babbled so merrily, how still you have become. You give no parting word!

Covered with a hard unyielding crust, you lie cold and motionless, stretched out on the sand.

Upon your surface I carve with a sharp stone the name of my beloved, the hour and the day, the day of our first greeting, the day I went away. A broken ring surrounds the name and the dates.

Heart of mine, do you see your own image now in this stream? Is there a raging torrent beneath your surface too?

The mood of *Wasserflut* is already one of weariness and disenchantment. In *Auf dem Flusse* the wanderer's solitary step is renewed with a stoic resolve. It is like the beginning of a new act in the drama, after the intermissions of the last three songs. Once again we hear the 2/4 'gehende Bewegung', but the pace is slower and the mood grimmer. The original tempo indication was *Mässig*.

Under the basic pulse Schubert introduces a series of rhythmic variations by a process of filling in, so as to suggest the torrent of emotion that rages beneath the surface of the song. At first (bars 1–12) the bare rhythm is articulated in staccato quavers ('how still you have become'). But the underlying disquiet is suggested first by the magical switch into D sharp minor at bar 9, and then by a surge of semiquavers in the accompaniment. This modulation at bar 9 is also the key to the solution of a textual problem which occurs later in the song. There is a parallel sequence at bars 45–7, and the underlying harmony of bar 47 is the tonic chord of D sharp major. If so, the note F should have an accidental double sharp sign throughout this bar, in both staves (see Armitage-Smith).

(8) **RÜCKBLICK** Looking Back — G minor

The soles of my feet are burning, though I step on ice and snow: I don't mean to stop for breath until the towers are out of sight.

I was in such a hurry to be out of the town that I tripped on every stone; from every house the crows pelted my hat with snowballs and hailstones.

How differently you once received me, O city of inconstancy! At your bright windows the lark and the nightingale vied in song.

The round lime trees blossomed, the clear fountains gushed bright, and ah, two girlish eyes glowed! It was all up with you then, lad!

When I remember that day I feel like taking one last look back; I feel like stumbling back again and standing before her house.

Schubert takes his cue from the first two verses, which suggest that the wanderer is in headlong flight from the scene of his humiliation. In the prelude the quaver beats tumble over one another, and when the voice enters the piano's bass line follows a beat behind, as though unable to catch up. Moreover, the melodic shape gives the singer a 2/4 rhythm counterpointed against the pianist's 3/4 beat, giving a suggestion of disorientation to the movement. (See Feil, 44–52.)

In verse 3 the vocal line and the bass line are brought into unison in the tonic major, to achieve an effect of greater composure. Further modifications in the vocal line and the accompaniment slow the movement to a brief standstill before the close, as the singer speaks of his longing to stand once more before the house of his beloved.

It is noteworthy that the fast songs are evenly distributed throughout the cycle, in part I nos.2, 4 and this one, no.8. There is an important difference between the autograph and the first edition in the penultimate bar. In the first edition the pianist's left- and right-hand chords sound together. But the manuscript reading, with the right-hand chords struck between the quaver beats (as in the rest of the song), is much to be preferred.

(9) **IRRLICHT** Will-o'-the-Wisp — B minor

A will-o'-the-wisp lured me away deep into the mountains; How to find my way out – that does not worry me much.

I have often followed a false trail. Every path leads to the one end. Our joys and our sorrows, they are all the sport of the will-o'-the-wisp.

I pick my way calmly down through the dry bed of the mountain stream. As every river will reach the sea, so every sorrow finds its grave.

B minor is associated in Schubert's tonality with isolation, alienation and despair. But the only songs in this key in Schubert's autograph are this one and the last, *Der Leiermann*, both of them having something of the character of a grotesque dance. (The final published version presents a rather different picture.) In both the harmonic structure is of the slightest, while the 3/4 movement is so formal and deliberate that it has almost a ritualistic quality. The essence of this song is contained in the opening bars, with their question-and-answer structure, the plunge downward from tonic to dominant answered finally by a strange flick back from dominant to tonic.

This light and wayward movement is of course descriptive of the will-o'-the-wisp. But Schubert manages to adapt it to the slow pace of the bemused traveller, and at the end to give the song a steely resolve; for the lift into C major from B for the words 'Every river will reach the sea' gives to the last line an unforgettable emphasis.

The song provides a nice demonstration of the fact that Schubert's dotted notes are not always to be assimilated to the triplet rhythm in the voice. There is something symbolic about the rhythmic precision of the accompaniment set against the more lyrical line of the singer, so that it seems essential to preserve the rhythmical separation of the two in bars 13 and 35.

(10) **RAST** Rest                                    C minor

Only now, as I lie down to sleep, do I notice how tired I am. Walking kept me cheerful along the inhospitable track.

My feet did not ask to rest; it was too cold for standing about. My back did not feel its burden; the storm helped to blow me along.

I have found shelter in a charcoal-burner's little hut, but my sores smart so painfully that my limbs cannot rest.

And you too, my heart, so wild and bold in storm and strife – now, in this stillness, you feel the serpent, with its bitter sting, bestir itself.

In Schubert's autograph *Rast* is written in D minor, but it is annotated in the composer's hand: 'N.B. To be written in C minor'. There is no knowing for certain what the reasons were for this change of plan. It seems possible that he had already decided, in the interests of a cyclical tone structure, to write the last song (i.e. *Einsamkeit*) in D minor, and did not wish to weaken the effect by anticipating it. But this is conjecture.

*Rast* is a *Geh-Lied*; the steady two-in-a-bar looks back to *Gute Nacht* but is here drained of all energy. The bass line clings to C; the voice line moving painfully stepwise sounds like a tired recitative until bar 21, when it suddenly takes off on a melismatic flight which reminds us of the emotional disturbance below the surface. The emphatic repeat of this music at the end of the song leaves us in no doubt that this disturbance is associated with the sting of the serpent jealousy.

The unity of Schubert's great cycle can be evidenced in countless thematic links between songs, some obvious, some subtle, and all doubtless made with the unconscious craft of the great artist. Here it may be noticed how closely the arpeggio-based phrases remind us of the climax of *Wasserflut* (they share the same marking – *stark*); and how the bare octaves in bars 7–11 anticipate the *Langsam* section of the following song.

(11) **FRÜHLINGSTRAUM** Dream of Spring                              A major

I dreamt of bright flowers that bloom in May; I dreamt of green meadows and merry birdsong.

And when the cocks crowed my eyes opened, and all was cold and dark; and the ravens shrieked from the roof.

But who painted the flowers there on the window-pane? Would you laugh at the dreamer who saw flowers in the wintertime?

I dreamt of mutual love, of a beautiful girl, of hearts and kisses and joy and happiness.

And when the cocks crowed my heart opened; now I sit here alone and think about the dream.

I close my eyes again; my heart is still beating fast. When will the leaves on the window-pane turn green? When will I hold my darling in my arms?

*Frühlingstraum* returns to the theme of *Der Lindenbaum*, the clash of dream and reality, the conflict between life and innocence, and to a closely related key, A major. Three separate elements in the poem are identified, and the three strands are woven into a seamless texture in this supremely great song. There is first the dream world of childhood (verses 1 and 4) set to a lilting folktune which sounds like a children's dance. The crowing of the cock at dawn is a reminder of harsh reality, as the pace quickens and the tonality hurries through E minor, D major and G minor to A minor. In verses 3 and 6 the wanderer reflects upon his vanished happiness, to music which seems to embody all the broken promise of life. (There is an interesting anticipation of it in a song of 1818, *An den Mond in einer Herbstnacht*, at bar 79.) It is in this D major section also, in the repeated A's of the staccato crotchets in the bass, that we hear an ominous echo of the wanderer's plodding footsteps. The original marking was *Etwas geschwind*.

(12) **EINSAMKEIT** Loneliness                              B minor

As a dark cloud drifts through the clear sky when a faint breeze stirs in the fir tree tops –

So I take my way with dragging steps through life's bright joys, alone and friendless.

Ah, why is the air so peaceful? Why is the world so bright? While the storms were still raging I was not so wretched as this.

*Einsamkeit* was originally written in D minor, rounding off the cycle (as Schubert then thought of it) in the key in which it started. It returns also to the original gait, though at a slower pace; the steady four-quaver beat is the same as in *Gute Nacht* and the opening bars are almost identical, though the beat is shared between the pianist's two hands in *Einsamkeit*. Moreover, there is a strong resemblance between the harmonic and melodic shape of the opening phrases of the two songs. It is possible to find a reminiscence of *Gute Nacht*, and perhaps also of *Wasserflut*, in the accented appoggiaturas at bars 25 and 27.

But whereas the vocal phrases in *Gute Nacht* are regular and unbroken, in *Einsamkeit* they are broken up after the first two verses into short, emotionally charged phrases which give to the voice line the declamatory power of recitative without disturbing the lyrical flow. This is a Schubert fingerprint which belongs especially to the song cycles, and there is no more striking example of it than the last verse of this song. It gives to the last couplet an almost overwhelming pathos.

(13) **DIE POST** The Post                                                            E flat major

A posthorn sounds from the road. Why do you leap so wildly, my heart?
> The post brings no letter for you. Why then do you throb so strangely, my heart?
> Ah yes, the post comes from the town, where once I had a fond sweetheart, my heart!
> Do you want to peep in and ask how things are there, my heart?

*Die Post* is a self-contained song, which might well, one feels, have had an independent life outside the cycle, and indeed it is often sung as a recital number on its own. The second half of the strophe, which turns to the tonic minor and to D flat, enables Schubert to bring a certain *Innigkeit* to verses 2 and 4, and the effectiveness of this transition is beautifully enhanced by the pauses. But it would not be unfair to describe the song as an uncomplicated piece of tone-painting written for a robust lyrical tenor, posthorn, galloping horses and all.

However, the function of the song is to set the drama in motion again at the beginning of part II, and the sharp contrast of mood and of movement it provides does act as a foil to the sombre tone of the songs which follow.

(14) **DER GREISE KOPF** The Hoary Head                                               C minor

The frost has cast a white halo about my head. I thought I was already old, and I rejoiced.
> But soon it melted, and again my hair was black. I shudder at my youth. How distant still the grave!
> Between the sunset glow and morning light full many a head has turned grey. Who can believe it? My head has not done so, all this long journey through.

Here at the beginning of part II the continuity of the cycle is least apparent. The plodding footsteps of the wanderer are absent, and the dark despair of *Der greise Kopf* does not follow too easily after that momentary glimpse of a happier world in *Die Post*. (In Müller's final order *Die Post* took its place more naturally at no.6 and *Der greise Kopf* followed *Rückblick* at no.10.)

This and the next song, however, both in the tragic key of C minor, lead us back to the heart of the drama. In the four-bar prelude Schubert invests a familiar harmonic formula with such a weight of tragic feeling that the voice, when it enters, seems almost an irrelevance. The reason for this note of fierce desperation is soon apparent. After a cry of anguish ('I shudder at my youth') voice and piano join together in a bleak unison, ('How distant still the grave!'), and we hear the descending motif in octaves which one might call Schubert's 'Annunciation of death' theme. The song serves as a signpost, pointing to the inevitable end. Nowhere in the cycle is the expressive power of the music more concentrated.

(15) **DIE KRÄHE** The Crow                                C minor

A crow followed me out of the town and has been flying round above my head until today.

    Crow, you strange creature, don't you want to leave me? Are you thinking of preying on my corpse soon?

    Well, I have not much further to go with my pilgrim's staff. Crow, let me at last see constancy unto death.

This song too points to the inevitable end, as the wanderer looks forward to death. The crows have made a brief appearance in the cycle before, in *Rückblick*. But this one is different. It is the first living creature other than the protagonist to play a role in the drama, the first to show any interest in his misfortunes. The wanderer welcomes it as a symbol of natural feeling and, like the Ancient Mariner among the water snakes, blesses it unaware. But will its constancy last until death?

For 28 of the song's forty-three bars the accompaniment stays above middle C, and the slow-moving triplets provide a marvellously apt image of the wheeling bird. But then the quavers sink down slowly, until the postlude ends with four repeated staccato C's, which offer the suggestion of a funeral march.

(16) **LETZTE HOFFNUNG** Last Hope                          E flat major

Here and there on the trees there are still coloured leaves to be seen; and I often stand in front of the trees, lost in thought.

    I watch one of the leaves, and hang my hopes on it; if the wind plays with my leaf I tremble for all I am worth.

    Ah, and if the leaf falls to the ground my hopes are dashed with it; I myself fall to the ground and weep, weep on the grave of my hopes.

The relationship between external nature and the wanderer's inner world is the constant preoccupation of part II of the cycle. Here it is the falling leaf which stands as a symbol of his ruined hopes. But Schubert's purpose goes beyond this, to present an astonishingly original contrast between the instability of a world in which the fates play with emotions as the winds sport with the leaves, and the burning reality of his despair.

For the first twenty-eight bars the music renounces pulse, tune and tonality, all the usual marks of stability and order. The notes which make up a diminished seventh (that atonal chord) are distributed evenly between voice and piano ('here and there'). We listen in vain for a firm beat or a recognisable resolution until bar 30 ('my hopes are dashed with it'). Not until bar 36 does Schubert's purpose become plain; then we become aware of a great surge of emotion, as we hear the word 'weep' in a great arching phrase and the piano resumes its normal homophonic supportive role. Here we are back in the world we know, but a world bereft of hope.

(17) **IM DORFE** In the Village                    D major

Dogs bark, chains rattle; people are asleep in their beds, dreaming of many a thing they lack, seeking comfort in good things or bad.

And in the morning it has all melted away. Well, they have all enjoyed their share of life, and hope to find in their dreams what is still left to enjoy.

Go on barking at me, you watchdogs, give me no rest in the night hours. For me dreams are all over; why should I linger among the slumberers?

The scene is set with magical economy. The stillness of the night, the loneliness, the distant 'crumff' of the dogs, all this is conveyed in the music which frames the song. Even more remarkable is the way Schubert sets the protagonist apart from the scene, so that the voice appears to enter 'off-stage', and on a dominant harmony, just when we should least expect it. In this first section indeed voice and piano appear to be out of phase (see Feil, 34–44). If the entry of the voice is delayed by a half-bar the harmonic arrival points coincide more logically, but the effect of 'distancing' is lost.

As we have often seen, however, Schubert's ability to change the psychological focus of the song in mid-career is one of his most striking talents. In the middle verse the music assumes a more reflective tone and a comfortable gait, and we feel ourselves to be inside the minds of the sleeping villagers. The last verse is set to the original music, but with a significant difference. At the words 'Why should I linger among the slumberers?' voice and piano suddenly move together into sharp focus. The singer is now at the front of the stage, and we realise that he has found new strength to continue. These changes of focus involve changes in the *Bewegung*, so that the 12/8 time signature accommodates both a slow twelve-in-a-bar at the beginning and a brisker four-in-a-bar at the end.

(18) **DER STÜRMISCHE MORGEN** The Stormy Morning          D minor

How the storm has riven the grey canopy of the sky! The ragged clouds fly in listless strife.

And fiery flames draw off between them. Such a morning suits my mood well. My heart sees its own image painted in the sky – there is naught but winter, cold and savage.

After the troubled introspection of *Im Dorfe*, the wanderer braces himself for the final stage of his journey. *Der stürmische Morgen* is a brisk march, all energy and resolve. The only dynamic markings are *f*, *ff*, and *ffz* at the climax. Yet his new-found courage is clearly founded only on desperation. The persistent unisons between voice and piano, the wide melodic leaps, the diminished sevenths in the prelude, interlude and postlude – these are unmistakable signs of his loneliness and despair.

(19) **TÄUSCHUNG** Illusion  A major

A light dances cheerfully before me; I follow it this way and that. I am happy to follow it, though I see that it lures the wanderer astray.

Ah, anyone as miserable as I am is glad to surrender to such garish trickery; it shows him that beyond the ice, the darkness and the horror is a bright warm house, and a loved one within. Just an illusion – that is good enough for me!

In Schubert's tonal world A major stands for the dream world, as opposed to harsh reality. It is the key of *Frühlingstraum*, *Täuschung* and *Die Nebensonnen*.

Significantly, Schubert borrowed the tune for *Täuschung* from *Alfonso und Estrella*, the opera he wrote with Schober six years earlier. At the beginning of Act II Troila tells his son Alfonso the story of a huntsman lured away by a beautiful 'cloud maiden' to a castle in the depths of the mountains. But as soon as he makes to take her in his arms, she and the castle dissolve into thin air. His mind gives way, and he plunges to his death. The link with Müller's poem is obvious. In the opera the story of the young lovers ends happily, thus giving the lie to the tale. Not so in *Winterreise*.

The naive dance tune suits the context beautifully. When the singer recalls his own misery, however, the music turns to the minor, and the vocal line is broken up into Schubert's characteristic 'semi-recitative'. The final cadence is interrupted by an unexpected gesture towards F sharp minor, conveying the sense of unfulfilled longing.

(20) **DER WEGWEISER** The Signpost  G minor

So why do I avoid the paths that other travellers take, and seek out hidden ways among the snow-clad peaks?

No evil have I done, that I should shun mankind. What foolish longing drives me into the wilderness?

Signposts stand along the way, pointing toward the towns; and I wander on without respite, restless, yet seeking rest.

One signpost I see standing immovable before me. I must travel a road whence no man returns.

The 'gehende Bewegung' or walking gait which runs like a connecting thread through the cycle is much less evident in part II than in part I. But here it returns unmistakably. There is an obvious affinity with *Gute Nacht* and *Auf dem Flusse*, not only in the steady tread of the four even quavers in a bar, but also thematically. The phrase pattern is the same; the prelude can easily be seen to be a kind of melodic and harmonic paraphrase of that of *Gute Nacht*; while the short dotted rising phrase which is so marked a feature of the two earlier songs makes a striking reappearance here, in bars 16, 17 and 18, and again in bars 51, 52, 53 and 54. (See Moore, pp.xiii–xiv.)

There is also a striking parallel – both in the nature of the theme and in the way it is developed – between *Der Wegweiser* and the C minor Impromptu op.90 no.1, written at about the same time. The theme is subjected to a process of elaboration and variation, always appearing in a slightly different guise, so that the spare statement of it at the beginning leads to a progressive revelation of its potential. The song is indeed a kind of Impromptu on the theme of the 'gehende Bewegung' which plays so crucial a role in the unity of the cycle.

But the contrast between it and *Gute Nacht* is equally important. It is altogether more tragic in tone. Whereas in *Gute Nacht* the pulse never falters, here the forward movement is less insistent, and there is an ominous pause between the second and third verses. More significantly still, at the repeat of the last lines – 'I must travel a road whence no man returns' – the quaver beat resolves itself into a repeated G intoned by the singer and doubled an octave lower by the pianist; while against that monotone we hear the right-hand minims descend slowly and inexorably from F to C in what we have come to know as Schubert's 'annunciation of death' theme. Finally, the beating quavers are silent, and only the slow descent of the crotchets to the tonic G minor remains to signal the wanderer's willing acceptance of his fate. There is no more moving moment in the whole cycle.

(21) **DAS WIRTSHAUS** The Inn                                              F major

My journey has brought me to a graveyard. Here, I thought to myself, I will stay the night.

You green wreaths, you must be the signs inviting weary travellers in to the cool hospice.

Are all the rooms in this house taken then? I faint from weariness, and am wounded unto death.

Cruel hospice, do you still turn me away? On then, further still, with my trusty staff.

In psychological terms, *Das Wirtshaus* stands at the same point in the cycle as *Trockne Blumen* does in *Die schöne Müllerin*. That is, it represents the end of the 'plot'; after this comes the epilogue. And since there is no plot, in the external sense, in *Winterreise*, the symbolism of the song is inescapably clear. The wanderer is denied a place in the cool hospice of death, and is condemned to wander on entombed in his own private world of suffering and madness. But for him the tenuous distinction between illusion and reality has already broken down.

*Das Wirtshaus* is also, in a sense, the last of the *Geh-Lieder*, though the wanderer's pace is slowed to a funeral march. The liturgical associations set the song apart. The key – F major – makes its only appearance; the block harmonies and solemn hymnlike manner are reminiscent of the *Deutsche Messe* (D872) rather than of any other songs in the cycle. The last verse turns to the tonic minor, but only to return with a special irony and pathos to the major in the postlude.

(22) **MUT** Courage                                                      G minor

When the snow blows in my face I shake it off. When my heart speaks in my breast I sing loud and cheerfully.

    I don't listen to what it says to me, I have no ears; I don't hear what it is complaining about, complaining is for fools.

    I go happily into the world against the wind and weather. If there is no God to inhabit the world, then we are gods ourselves!

The song was originally written in A minor. It so appears in the autograph, and in a sketch now in private possession. The tessitura is not particularly high, but the lower key does avoid an awkward top A in bar 57. More to the point, perhaps, is the fact that Schubert, once he had decided to bring the last song down from B minor to A minor, would be anxious to avoid having the last three songs all in the tonality of A.

In Müller's final order *Mut* came immediately before *Der Leiermann*, and since this was the only change Schubert made in the poet's preferred order it is to be assumed that he had good reason for it. The most likely explanation is that he felt the violent contrast of mood between *Mut* and *Der Leiermann* would make an unsatisfactory end.

Although the time signature is 2/4, like *Der Wegweiser*, the brisk two-in-a-bar represents not a walking gait but a mood of angry defiance, a kind of philosophical protest resulting from the wanderer's rejection in the last song. 'If there is no God, then a man must shoulder the whole burden of suffering and injustice in the world himself.'

(23) **DIE NEBENSONNEN** The Phantom Suns                                  A major

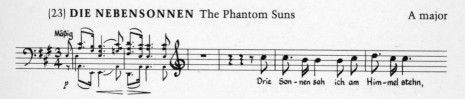

I saw three suns stand in the sky. I looked long and intently at them. And they, too, stood so fixedly there, as though loth to leave me.

    Ah, you are not *my* suns! Go and look others in the face!

    Yes, I had three suns not long ago. Now the two best have gone down. If only the third would follow them; I would fare better in the dark.

The key, A major, and the slow dancelike lilt with its characteristic dotted second beat, tell us that we are once again in the dream world, the world of lost illusions. An unnecessary mystery has been made of the first line. Fox-Strangways suggested that the three suns represent Love, Hope and Life, but this is altogether too moralistic to be convincing. The three suns are one of the wanderer's hallucinations, and we know from *Täuschung* that he willingly submitted to them. As for the two which have disappeared, they are surely the eyes of his beloved (see McKay, 97–8).

(24) **DER LEIERMANN** The Hurdy-gurdy Man    A minor

Beyond the village stands a hurdy-gurdy man, and with numbed fingers plays as best he can.

Barefoot on the ice he staggers to and fro; and his little plate always stays empty.

No one wants to listen, no one looks his way, and the dogs snarl round the old man.

And he lets it all go on as it will; he turns the handle, and the hurdy-gurdy never stops.

Strange old man, shall I go with you? Will you grind your hurdy-gurdy to my songs?

The last song, a strange valediction, lies outside the drama. Feil (p.147) compares it to Feste's song at the end of *Twelfth Night*, an ironic comment on the human condition, a poetic epilogue which reconciles us to the reality of the human tragedy. Yet in a sense it provides a wonderful summation of the whole work. Here, for the first and last time in the two cycles, the protagonist meets one of his own kind. Like the Harper in *Wilhelm Meister*, the hurdy-gurdy man is an outcast, shunned by his fellow men. The wanderer, accepting that his destiny also is alienation, not death, throws in his lot with him. Here is the Romantic vision of the artist as a stranger in society, a loner and a rebel; the Romantic protest against the inescapable terms of life.

The extraordinary song links together the various strands in the cycle, the rhythmic, the pictorial, and the declamatory. It was originally written in the key of B minor, and it has something in common with another B minor song, *Irrlicht*, in particular a curiously formal, even gait, like a grotesque dance, an economy of phrase, and a stiffness in the repetitive gestures. Only in the last verse does the voice renounce its ritualistic manner to take on the poignancy of speech itself. 'Strange old man, shall I go with you?' And in the postlude the familiar phrase rises to top A before dying away to nothing, like the ghost of the wanderer's hopes.

**WOHIN?** see DIE SCHÖNE MÜLLERIN no.2

## WOLKE UND QUELLE The Cloud and the Stream
**Karl Gottfried von Leitner**                                    (?) End of 1827

C major  D2 896B  Not in Peters  Not in GA

Auf mei - - nen hei-mi-schen Ber-gen  da sind____ die Wol-ken zu Haus,

On the mountains of my native land the clouds are at home; I have stood among them gazing into the valley. But they flew away as light and free as swans; I wanted to fly with them to the ends of the sky.

A wild instinct sent me off into distant, foreign places, but now my home country is sacred to me, and I love to stay close to it. Now I never long to be out there in the misty blue distance; now I gaze down into the narrow meadow with silent longing.

What is nodding down there by the window, blossoming like the dawn? Is it her roses by the sill, or her sweet face? Have a good journey, clouds, I shall not be going with you. But what is it beckoning me and whispering over there amongst the spring greenery?

Is it you that are whispering, O stream? Yes, yes! I shall hasten along with you, for you know the shortest way down there to her in the valley.

The autograph (Vienna, SB) is an incomplete sketch on three staves, the melody line written out complete on the top stave, but without text, and indications for the accompaniment on the other two staves, including the piano interludes and postlude. (This was Schubert's normal procedure in sketching a song.) The author and poem were identified by Reinhard van Hoorickx, who has edited and privately published the song in a completed version.

The flowing 9/8 rhythm and the arpeggio-based tune are reminiscent of *Drang in die Ferne*. Schubert intended to publish a group of Leitner songs as a tribute to Marie Pachler, his hostess at Graz during his stay there in September 1827. This one was sketched at some time between his return from Graz and the end of the year, but it was not included in the published group (op.106).

## WONNE DER WEHMUT Delight in Melancholy
**Johann Wolfgang von Goethe**                                    20 August 1815

*Etwas geschwind*                    C minor D260  Peters IV p.141  GA XX no.117

Trock - net____nicht, trock - net____nicht, Trä-nen der e - wi - gen Lie - be!

Do not dry, do not dry the tears of eternal love. Ah, how dead, how barren the world appears to those eyes which are even half dry! Do not dry, do not dry the tears of unrequited love.

The poem dates from the summer of 1775. The autograph (Vienna, GdM) is a first draft dated 20 August 1815. A fair copy made for Goethe is in Berlin (DS). The song was published by Leidesdorf in June 1829 as op.115 no.2.

The tune has neither the self-sufficiency of folksong, nor the operatic expressiveness of Beethoven's fine setting. It sounds more like a theme from a piano sonata, and that is what it eventually became; for surely here is the germ-cell of the C minor Andante of the 'Reliquie' Sonata of 1825? It is a promising idea but seems to have little relevance to the poem.

Einstein, 111

## ZUFRIEDENHEIT Contentment (1)

**Matthias Claudius**

(?) April 1816
A major D362 Not in Peters GA XX no.280

I am happy, my poem proclaims it triumphantly, and many a man with his crown and sceptre is not. And even if he is, well, so much the better; he is only what I already am.

The Sultan's pomp, the Mogul's gold, the luck of what's-his-name, who when he ruled the whole world still coveted the moon. I want none of all that. It suits me best just to smile at it.

Be content, that's my motto. What I have is enough for me. The wise man does not covet anything very much, for when a man gets what he wants he is still not satisfied.

Money and fame are brittle things, moreover. Experience shows that the strange course of events often turns little into much, and pulls the rich man up sharp.

To do right and to be kind and good is more than money and fame, so a man with friends round him will always be in good spirits. A man with pride in himself is afraid of no creature and nothing.

The poem, written in 1771, is a free paraphrase of Sir Edward Dyer's famous verses which begin 'My mind to me a kingdom is', in particular of verses 5 to the end. Dyer's poem was reprinted in Percy's *Reliques of Ancient English Poetry* (published in 1765), and this was Claudius's source.

The autograph of this first version (Vienna, SB) is headed simply 'Lied', and the date is not certain. The manuscript contains on the previous page the concluding bars of *Cronnan* (September 1815), and a sketch for the finale of the Symphony no.4 in C minor (finished 27 April 1816). On balance the later date seems more likely for the song. The song was first published in the *Gesamtausgabe* in 1895. Schubert set only the first two verses in this first, strophic version.

## ZUFRIEDENHEIT (2)

**Matthias Claudius**

November 1816
E major D501 Not in Peters GA XX no.281

For translation, see the preceding entry. The autograph of the second version is missing, but there are copies in the Witteczek–Spaun collection (Vienna, GdM), one marked 'Lebhaft', the other dated November 1816 and marked 'Massig geschwind'. The key is E major and the title simply *Lied*. There is a fair copy in G major in the Therese Grob song album (see GROB), headed 'Zufriedenheit' and marked 'Vergnügt' ('Happy'). The song was first published, in E major, in the *Gesamtausgabe* in 1895.

The pace is steadier than in the first version, but the mood is more precisely characterised. The accompaniment has more independence, and the separation of the singer's phrases gives the song a note of conscious happiness.

## ZUM PUNSCHE In Praise of Punch

**Johann Mayrhofer**                                          October 1816

D minor  D492  Peters VI p.42  GA XX no.270

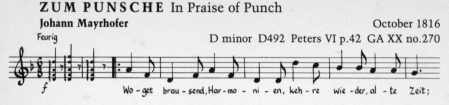

Wo-get brau-send, Har-mo - ni - en, keh-re wie-der, al - te Zeit;

Let the boisterous harmony resound; let the days of old return. Pass the cups full of punch round the merry company.

    Already the waves engulf me; I am entranced with the world. The stars beckon, the winds whisper, and my soul is enchanted.

    The cares with which life weighs us down are left on the misty shore. Strike out, like a strong swimmer, towards the high sea of peace.

    What increases the swimmer's delight is the ensuing splash; for the boon companions all follow, no one wants to be the last.

The autograph is a first draft, dated October 1816 and headed 'Zum Punsche. Chor.' (Vienna, ÖNB). A dated copy in the Witteczek–Spaun collection (Vienna, GdM) omits the word 'Chor', and has a postlude longer by one bar. The song was published in 1849 as no.3 of book 44 of the *Nachlass*.

    This, the most uninhibited of Schubert's drinking songs (direction *Feurig*), was intended as a male-voice unison chorus. The published versions for solo voice are based on Witteczek's copy, but there is no way of knowing whether this was based on an autograph fair copy or not.

## ZUR NAMENSFEIER DES HERRN ANDREAS SILLER
## For the Name Day of Herr Siller

**Author unknown**                              28 October–4 November 1813

G major  D83  Not in Peters  GA XX no.582

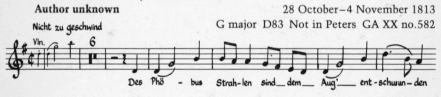

Des Phö - bus Strah-len sind__ dem__ Aug'__ ent-schwun-den

Phoebus's rays have sunk below the horizon, and now the moon illumines the festive hours of evening.

The dated autographs are in Vienna (SB). Schubert may well have been the author as well as the composer of this piece of domestic celebration. It is written for voice, violin and harp. Nothing is known of Herr Siller. Perhaps he brought his harp to the party. The song was first published in the *Gesamtausgabe* in 1895.

# II The Authors

**AESCHYLUS.** Athenian tragic poet and dramatist of the fifth century B.C. Schubert set Mayrhofer's translation of two verses from his *Eumenides* in June 1816. See MAYRHOFER, Johann Baptist.

**ANACREON.** Lyric poet of the sixth century BC whose poems celebrated the pleasures of life, especially those of love, wine, nature and friendship. His verse was imitated by many Anacreontic poets in England and Germany, especially in the eighteenth and early nineteenth centuries. Bruchmann's *An die Leyer*, which Schubert set in the winter of 1822–3, is a free translation of a poem supposedly by Anacreon. See BRUCHMANN, Franz Ritter von.

**ANONYMOUS.** Schubert drew on a large quantity of obscure and anonymous verse, some of which he found in periodicals. He also on occasion set words he had written himself. In recent years many anonymous verses have been traced to individual authors, but a number of texts still remain unattributed. The list at present includes the following:
81 Auf den Sieg der Deutschen
83 Zur Namensfeier des Herrn Andreas Siller
155 Das Bild
273 Lilla an die Morgenröte
274 Tischlerlied
292/371 Klage (Trauer umfliesst mein Leben)
381 Morgenlied
382 Abendlied
432 Der Leidende
447 An den Schlaf
498 Wiegenlied
523 Trost
535 Lied (Brüder, schrecklich brennt die Träne)
565 Der Strom
596 Lied eines Kindes
616 Grablied für die Mutter
626 Blondel zu Marien
902 no.3 Il Modo di prender moglie
    18 songs

**BAUERNFELD, Eduard von** (1802–90). Viennese poet, critic and dramatist. He was the son of a doctor, and a schoolfellow of Moritz von Schwind. He was early attracted by Schubert's songs, but although he met the composer briefly in January 1822 it was not until 1825 that he became a member of the inner circle of Schubert's friends. He wrote a libretto for Schubert in 1826 (*Der Graf von Gleichen*), but the opera was never completed. His journals and reminiscences provide a major source of information about the Schubert circle in the composer's last years.

Bauernfeld became an official of the Lottery Office in 1826, but after making a name for himself as a dramatist he left the public service and devoted himself to literature. He was one of the editors of the Vienna *Shakespeare-Ausgabe* of 1825. He was never closely involved with Schubert's song-writing, and the only surviving song to his words is disappointing.
*January 1827:*
906 Der Vater mit dem Kind
    *Lost:*
(864) (Das Totenhemdchen)
    1 song

**BAUMBERG, Gabriele von** (1775–1839). Austrian poet. Born in Vienna, the daughter of a government official, she married the Hungarian radical poet Johann Bacsanyi. In support of Napoleonic causes, and especially of the cause of Hungarian independence, Bacsanyi went to Paris in 1809 with his wife. After the war he was imprisoned as an opponent of the established regime and finally banished to Linz. There he and Gabriele lived out their last years in straitened circumstances. Her poems date from her early years and were published in 1800.

Schubert seems to have been attracted by Baumberg's verse very early in life, for the first song of which we have any record — though it is only an incomplete sketch — is to a text of hers. The other settings all date from August 1815.
*1809/1810:*
39 (2 1A) Lebenstraum
*August 1815:*
248 Lob des Tokayers
263 Cora an die Sonne
264 Der Morgenkuss
265 Abendständchen: An Lina
270 An die Sonne
    6 songs

**BERNARD, Josef Karl** (1780–1850).
Austrian journalist and critic. The editor of
various critical reviews and artistic journals
including the *ZfK*, he was well known in the
Vienna of Schubert's day. He wrote the libretto
for Conradin Kreutzer's opera *Libussa* in 1822,
to which Schubert refers in a letter to Spaun.

The only Bernard song has a dramatic power
and intensity remarkable for its early date.

*April 1815:*
177 Vergebliche Liebe
    1 song

**BERTRAND, Friedrich Anton Franz.**
Nothing certain is known about Bertrand, who
has the dubious distinction of having written
the texts for two of Schubert's longest and most
obscure songs. It seems possible that like Josef
Kenner he was a member of the Schubert circle
with an enthusiasm for ballad literature. Both
the ballads that Schubert set in 1815 are of an
embarrassing naivety.

*1815:*
152 Minona
211 Adelwold und Emma
    2 songs

**BIBLE.** Schubert wrote several songs and
partsongs inspired by the Bible. Only two,
however, are for solo voice and piano. (See R.
van Hoorickx, 'Schubert and the Bible', *MT*,
CXIX, 1978, p.953.)

*1818:*
607 Evangelium Johannis
*1819:*
663 Der 13. Psalm
The German text of *Der 13. Psalm* is by Moses
Mendelssohn.

    2 songs

**BOBRIK, Johann Friedrich Ludwig**
(1781–1844). Prussian poet and translator. He
was a legal luminary of Königsberg, who
published quantities of verse and translations in
various journals under the not very opaque
pseudonym of B-b--k. Schubert found the text
of *Die drei Sänger* in an anthology, *Dichtungen
für Kunstredner* ('Poems for Reading Aloud') in
1815. Bobrik's authorship of it was established
by Dietrich Berke. The song is an incomplete
sketch.

*December 1815:*
329 Die drei Sänger
    1 song

**BRUCHMANN, Franz, Ritter von**
(1798–1867). Austrian student of philosophy,
poet, and Redemptorist priest. In the formative
years of 1820–3, Bruchmann was the most
important link between Schubert and the circle
of Romantic poets and writers in Vienna. He
was the son of a rich merchant who kept open
house for the cultural avant garde. Friedrich
von Schlegel was a regular visitor, and although

it is not certain that Schubert and Schlegel ever
met, the composer's interest in Schlegel's
poetry must owe a great deal to Bruchmann.
Schubertiads and reading parties were held at
Bruchmann's house, and he and his sisters
Justina and Isabella played an active role in the
'brilliant life enhanced by music and poetry'
which, according to Bruchmann himself,
characterised the life of the Schubert circle in
the winter of 1822–3.

Bruchmann first studied law, but his natural
bent was towards philosophy. As a young man
he forsook his Catholic allegiance and became a
disciple of Fichte and Schelling. Like Schubert,
he supported the liberal views then current in
student circles, and when the young radical
Johann Senn was arrested in March 1820 and
banished, he and Schubert both came under
strong suspicion from the police. In December
1821 Bruchmann went to Erlangen (without
waiting for official police permission to travel) to
hear Schelling lecture. There he met Count Platen
to whose poems he introduced Schubert.

In 1823 this intellectual circle began to
break up. Schubert was ill, and Bruchmann
began to come to terms with the world. The
reading parties and the Schubertiads lost their
zest, and the circle broke up in 1825 in mutual
recrimination when Schober's engagement to
Justina von Bruchmann was broken off at her
family's insistence. Later Bruchmann rejoined
the Catholic church and in 1833 he became a
Redemptorist priest.

Bruchmann's poems were never published,
and only the five Schubert set to have
survived. All of them probably belong to the
autumn of 1822 and the following winter.

*1822–3:*
737 An die Leyer
738 Im Haine
746 Am See
762 Schwestergruss
785 Der zürnende Barde
    5 songs

**CASTELLI, Ignaz Franz** (1781–1862).
Austrian patriot, civil servant, song-writer and
dramatist. He first came into prominence
during the Napoleonic wars as a writer of
patriotic songs. After some years as a journalist
and critic he became court theatre poet in
Vienna. He wrote nearly two hundred plays,
many of them adaptations from the French. His
opera libretto *Die Verschworenen* ('Domestic
Warfare') was written as a challenge to German
composers who complained that there were no
good German libretti. Schubert accepted the
challenge in 1823, but his opera score remained
unknown and unperformed until 1861.
Castelli's *Memoirs* give a lively and amusing
account of the artistic life of Vienna in the
Metternich era.

*January 1817:*
520 Frohsinn

*(?) 1826–8:*
868 (2 990 C) Das Echo
    2 songs
Two other settings of Castelli are included in
the Peters edition, the Romance (787 no.2)
from *Die Verschworenen* and *Trinklied* (148)
for tenor solo and men's chorus. But they are
not, strictly speaking, solo songs.

**CHÉZY, Wilhelmine Christiane
von**(1783–1856). German dramatist and
novelist. Born in Berlin, she later settled in
Vienna. She wrote the libretto for Weber's
*Euryanthe* and for the musical play *Rosamunde*,
to which Schubert wrote incidental music. The
Romance from this piece is sometimes sung at
recitals, and is included in the Peters edition.
Her memoirs were published in 1858.

The text of the middle section of *Der Hirt
auf dem Felsen* (965) is her work, according to
Friedländer.

**CIBBER, Colley** (1671–1757). English
actor, poet and dramatist, Poet Laureate
1730–57. Craigher's translation of his poem
*The Blind Boy* (*Der blinde Knabe*) was set by
Schubert in 1825.

**CLAUDIUS, Matthias** (1740–1815).
German poet and journalist. A pastor's son
from Holstein, Claudius studied theology and
law before making a name for himself as editor
of the 'Wandsbeck Messenger'. With the help of
his friend Herder he later secured an administrative post, but he continued to publish
volumes of verse and prose.

Claudius played an important part in
Schubert's development as a song-writer. His
genuinely poetic treatment of the simple
pleasures of life and nature encouraged the
composer's nascent Romantic feeling in songs
like *An die Nachtigall* and *Abendlied*, where for
the first time we sense the feeling of mortality,
of the inescapable kinship of life and death.
Claudius, whose name for death was 'Friend
Hain', and whose poem *Der Tod und das
Mädchen* became so closely associated with
Schubert's genius, can be seen as an important
influence on the composer's thought.

Most of the Claudius songs date from
November 1816 and February 1817.
*End 1815/early 1816:*
344 Am ersten Maimorgen
362 Zufriedenheit (1)
    *November 1816:*
501 Zufriedenheit (2)
496 Bei dem Grabe meines Vaters
2 496A Klage um Ali Bey
497 An die Nachtigall
499 Abendlied
500 Phidile
504 Am Grabe Anselmos
    *February 1817:*
530 An eine Quelle

531 Der Tod und das Mädchen
532 Das Lied vom Reifen
533 Täglich zu singen
    13 songs

**COLLIN, Heinrich Josef, Edler von**
(1771–1811). Viennese official and dramatist.
His verse plays on classical themes, including
*Coriolan*, were played at the Burgtheater, and
his patriotic songs helped to rally public
support against Napoleon. His brother Mathäus
played a more important part in Schubert's life.
The text of *Leiden der Trennung* is a translation
from Metastasio.
*December 1816:*
509 Leiden der Trennung
    *(?) December 1818:*
2 990A Kaiser Maximilian auf der Martinswand
    2 songs

**COLLIN, Matthäus von** (1779–1824).
Viennese scholar, poet, and dramatist. After
studying law and philosophy he became
professor of philosophy at Cracow (1810) and
later in Vienna. Later still he accepted the post
of tutor to the young Duke of Reichstadt, the
son of Napoleon and the Empress Marie-Louise.
The cousin of Josef von Spaun, he was an
exponent of Romantic ideas and a link between
the Schubert circle and the group of Romantic
writers and thinkers who acknowledged the
Schlegels as leaders. He provided Schubert with
the texts for three of his most powerful and
inspired songs. These all belong to the years
1822–3, when Schubert's links with the
Viennese Romantics were closest.
*(?) 1816:*
352 Licht und Liebe (vocal duet)
    *1822–3:*
749 Epistel: Musikalischer Schwank
771 Der Zwerg
772 Wehmut
827 Nacht und Träume
    5 songs

**COWLEY, Abraham** (1618–67). English
poet and dramatist. In August 1815 Schubert
set a translation of a poem from his series
called *The Mistress*, as *Der Weiberfreund* (271).
See RATSCHKY.

**CRAIGHER, Jacob Nicolaus de Jachelutta**
(1797–1855). Italian merchant, poet and
dilettante. He was a self-made man who built
up a fortune, travelling widely and acquiring an
exceptional knowledge of European languages.
In 1820 he settled in Vienna, got to know the
Schlegel circle, and became well known in
literary circles. He came to an agreement to
provide Schubert with translations for his songs
(*Docs*. no.596) in October 1825, and the Italian
versions of three songs published in 1826–7,
*An die Leyer, Der Wachtelschlag* and *Willkommen und Abschied*, are probably by him.

He also provided the texts for three fine songs in the spring of 1825.

*1825:*
828 Die junge Nonne
842 Totengräbers Heimweh
833 Der blinde Knabe
   3 songs

**DEINHARDSTEIN, Johann Ludwig Ferdinand von** (1794–1859). Academic and critic, of Vienna. He edited the 'Yearbook of Literature' published in Vienna from 1829. The text of Schubert *Skolie* is not included in his collected works.

*October 1815:*
306 Skolie
   1 song

**EHRLICH, Bernhard Ambros.** Government official, of Prague. The text of the song quoted below was included in an anthology of 1791.

*February 1815:*
153 Als ich sie erröten sah
   1 song

**ENGELHARDT, Karl August** (1768–1834). Poet novelist and critic, of Dresden. He wrote under the pseudonym Richard Roos. Schubert's source for the text of the song *Ihr Grab* was the 'Pocket-book of Sociable Pleasures' for the year 1822.

*(?) 1822:*
736 Ihr Grab
   1 song

**ERMIN.** The pseudonym of J. G. Kumpf, q.v.

**FELLINGER, Johann Georg** (1781–1816). Austrian poet. After studying law he worked as a private tutor, then served as an infantry officer against the French. He lost an eye and was taken prisoner during the Italian campaign of 1809. Because of his disability he found it difficult to earn a living after the war, and he took his own life at the early age of thirty-five.

*April 1815:*
176 Die Sterne
182 Die erste Liebe
*October 1815:*
307 Die Sternenwelten (trans. of a Slovene poem by Urban Jarnik)
   3 songs

**FOUQUÉ, Friedrich Heinrich, Baron de la Motte** (1777–1843). German Romantic poet, novelist and dramatist. He followed a military career until his marriage in 1803, after which he settled down on his wife's estate and devoted himself to literature. From 1813 to 1815 he served with distinction against Napoleon. Through his best-known work, the Romantic fairy tale *Undine*, he influenced

many musicians and composers, but he seems to have made little impression on Schubert.

*1815:*
93 no.1 Don Gayseros I
93 no.2 Don Gayseros II
93 no.3 Don Gayseros III
*January 1816:*
373 Lied (Mutter geht durch ihre Kammern)
*April 1817:*
517 Der Schäfer und der Reiter
   5 songs

**GERSTENBERG, Georg Friedrich von** (1780–1838). Born Georg Friedrich Müller in Saxony, he later adopted his mother's name. He was a government official in Weimar and a member of the Goethe circle. Johanna Schopenhauer incorporated some of his poems in her novel *Gabriele*.

*July 1826:*
890 Hippolits Lied
   1 song

**GOETHE, Johann Wolfgang von** (1749–1832). Goethe's influence on the art of music went deeper and further than that of any other man of letters, Shakespeare alone excepted. It was part of his conscious intention to bring poetry and music into closer association, and even in his own lifetime his lyrics provided a supreme challenge to composers. But his love of folksong, his liking for traditional forms, and his antipathy towards what he regarded as the artificiality of the operatic tradition inevitably meant that his influence on the development of the lied was conservative and restrictive. The composer's task, in the view of the Weimar school, was to 'set' a poem to music, that is, to invent a musical strophe which matched the form and poetic tone of the verses, leaving the nuances of expression and the differences between stanzas to be dealt with by the performer.

The conflict between that modest view of the function of music and the claim Schubert advanced in *Gretchen am Spinnrade* – that the lied is an independent *musical* form with its own expressive rules – can be traced easily enough in Schubert's work. The point at issue was not faithfulness to the text, for many a through-composed song keeps closer to the words than a strophic song does; nor is it the case that a more sophisticated, more complex form is necessarily more expressive than a simple one, for the list of Schubert's greatest songs proves the contrary. Schubert's achievement in *Gretchen* was to demonstrate that the principle of fidelity to the text can best be realised when music is allowed to follow its own laws.

The story of Schubert's attempts to win Goethe's approval is one of disappointment and misunderstanding. The profound impression made on his friends by the first great masterpieces encouraged them to prepare an ambitious scheme to publish the songs in a series of volumes grouped under individual authors. The first two volumes were to consist of Goethe settings. Early in 1816 fair copies of selected songs were made and sent to Goethe with a suitably respectful introductory letter by Josef von Spaun (*Docs.* no.81). The songbook was sent back without acknowledgment. It probably consisted of about twenty songs. Most of the fair copies are now in Berlin (DS). Later in 1816 a second volume was prepared, but it was never sent. The collection is now divided, part being in Vienna (SB) and the rest in the Paris Conservatoire.

In 1825 Schubert made one more attempt to bring his songs to Goethe's notice. He sent the three Goethe songs which make up his op.19 to the poet, asking for permission to dedicate the opus to the author. Goethe noted the arrival of the songs in his diary, but made no reply. (See *Docs.* nos.556, 557 and 561.)

Any collection of the greatest Schubert songs must contain a high proportion of Goethe settings; and Goethe is perhaps the only author who appealed to every aspect of Schubert's genius, from the 'simple' universality of *Heiden-röslein* and *Schäfers Klagelied* to the sublimity of *Erlkönig* and *Ganymed*; from the mischievous wit of *Liebhaber in allen Gestalten* to the intellectual abstraction of *Grenzen der Menschheit*.

*1814:*
118 Gretchen am Spinnrade
119 Nachtgesang
120 Trost in Tränen
121 Schäfers Klagelied
123 Sehnsucht
126 Szene aus Faust
*1815:*
149 Der Sänger
160 Am Flusse (1)
161 An Mignon
162 Nähe des Geliebten
138 Rastlose Liebe
142 Geistes-Gruss
210 Die Liebe
215 Jägers Abendlied (1)
2 215A Meeres Stille (1)
216 Meeres Stille (2)
224 Wandrers Nachtlied I
225 Der Fischer
226 Erster Verlust
234 Tischlied
254 Der Gott und die Bajadere
255 Der Rattenfänger
256 Der Schatzgräber
257 Heidenröslein
258 Bundeslied
259 An den Mond (1)
260 Wonne der Wehmut
261 Wer kauft Liebesgötter
247 Die Spinnerin
310 Nur wer die Sehnsucht kennt (1)
321 Kennst du das Land?

328 Erlkönig
325 Wer sich der Einsamkeit ergibt (1)
*1816:*
367 Der König in Thule
368 Jägers Abendlied (2)
369 An Schwager Kronos
359 Nur wer die Sehnsucht kennt (2)
481 Nur wer die Sehnsucht kennt (3)
469 So lasst mich scheinen (1) and (2)
480 no.1 (2 478 no.2) Wer nie sein Brot (1)
480 no.2 (2 478 no.2b) Wer nie sein Brot (2)
478 (2 478 no.1) Wer sich der Einsamkeit ergibt (2)
479 (2 478 no.3) An die Türen will ich schleichen
484 Gesang der Geister über den Wassern
*1817:*
543 Auf dem See
544 Ganymed
549 Mahomets Gesang (1)
558 Liebhaber in allen Gestalten
559 Schweizerlied
560 Der Goldschmiedsgesell
564 Gretchens Bitte
*1819:*
296 An den Mond (2)
295 Hoffnung
674 Prometheus
673 Die Liebende schreibt
*1821:*
715 Versunken
716 Grenzen der Menschheit
719 Geheimes
720 Suleika I
721 Mahomets Gesang (2)
726 Heiss mich nicht reden (1)
727 So lasst mich scheinen (3)
728 Johanna Sebus
*1822:*
480 no.3 (2 478 no.2) Wer nie sein Brot (3)
764 Der Musensohn
765 An die Entfernte
766 Am Flusse (2)
767 Willkommen und Abschied
768 Wandrers Nachtlied II
(?) *1824:*
717 Suleika II
*1826:*
877 no.1 Nur wer die Sehnsucht kennt (5; duet)
877 no.2 Heiss mich nicht reden (2)
877 no.3 So lasst mich scheinen (4)
877 no.4 Nur wer die Sehnsucht kennt (4)
74 songs

**GOLDONI, Carlo** (1707–93). Venetian opera librettist. He spent the last thirty years of his life in Paris. Schubert's only Goldoni setting is of a song from *Il Filosofo di campagna* ('The Philosopher of the Countryside'), a charming exercise in the Italian style made shortly after the first visit of the Italian opera to Vienna.

*January 1817:*
528 La Pastorella al prato
1 song

**GOTTER, Friedrich Wilhelm** (1746–97). German poet and dramatist, editor of the Göttingen *Musenalmanach*.
*August 1816:*
467 Pflicht und Liebe
 1 song

**GRIES, Johann Diederich** (1775–1842). Lawyer, poet and translator, of Hamburg. He studied at Jena, and was noted for his translations from Italian and Spanish. Schubert's settings of three Petrarch sonnets were made to German texts usually ascribed to A.W. von Schlegel. But the last is certainly by Gries, and possibly the others are also.

**GRILLPARZER, Franz** (1791–1872). Austrian poet and dramatist. On his mother's side he was related to the Sonnleithner family and was therefore in close touch with the Schubert circle, though there is only one record of his actually meeting the composer. He was certainly a great admirer of Schubert's music and played an active part in promoting the plan to build a memorial to him. He himself wrote the much discussed epitaph carved on Schubert's tomb: 'The art of music here entombed a rich possession, but even fairer hopes.' His journals give a fascinating picture of the Vienna of Schubert's day, and of the political constraints under which artists were obliged to work.
*February 1819:*
653 Bertas Lied in der Nacht
 1 song

**HARDENBERG, Friedrich Leopold von.** See NOVALIS.

**HAROLD, Edmund von.** His translation of the Ossian poems, published in 1775, provided Schubert with the German text of several of his Ossian settings. Anton Holzapfel, who lent the book to Schubert in 1815 (see *Memoirs* p.308), called the translation 'old and miserable', and it is generally held to be accurate but unidiomatic.
 Not much is known about Harold, who claimed to be a baron. He was born in Limerick, and spoke Irish and English. He served as an officer in the army of the Palatinate, and in later years corresponded with Herder. (Information provided by Roger Fiske.)

**HEINE, Heinrich** (1797–1856). German poet. The son of a Düsseldorf merchant, Heine was intended for commerce, but after a disastrous venture into banking he turned to the academic world, studying at Bonn and Göttingen. His early poems appeared in various periodicals, and he learnt to rely increasingly on journalism for his living. The publication of the *Buch der Lieder* in 1827 established his literary reputation. His radical political principles were excited by the July Revolution, and he moved to Paris in 1831.
 Heine's fame has rested for the most part on

his early lyrics, many of which were set by Schubert, Schumann and many others. But the later poetry is now increasingly valued. Schubert's Heine settings come from a sequence called *Die Heimkehr*, first published in May 1826 and later incorporated into the *Buch der Lieder*. See Part I: HEINE SONGS.
*Completed August 1828:*
957 no.8 Der Atlas
957 no.9 Ihr Bild
957 no.10 Das Fischermädchen
957 no.11 Die Stadt
957 no.12 Am Meer
957 no.13 Der Doppelgänger
 6 songs

**HELL, Theodor.** The pseudonym of Karl Gottfried Winkler, q.v.

**HERDER, Johann Gottfried** (1744–1803). German poet. His enormous influence as the precursor and teacher of the Romantics doubtless helped to form Schubert's literary taste, and his enthusiasm for the Ossian ballads indirectly led Schubert to them. He was a great translator, and he provided the composer with the German texts of two songs, one at the beginning and one at the end of his career.
*May 1813:*
59 Verklärung (Pope)
*September 1827:*
923 Eine altschottische Ballade (Percy's *Reliques*)
 2 songs

**HOHLFELD, C.C.** Author of the text of a lost Schubert song, *An Gott* (863). Nothing is known about him.

**HÖLTY, Ludwig Christoph Heinrich** (1748–76). German poet. A pastor's son from Hanover, Hölty was a founder-member, as a student at Göttingen, of the Göttinger Hainbund. This group of young poets, founded in 1772, anticipated the Romantic emphasis on spontaneous feeling and opposed the artificiality of the classical style. There is an emotional ambiguity in Hölty's poetry, a bittersweet quality which in many ways resembles Schubert's own attitude to nature and love. The poignancy of sensuous experience is coloured by the awareness of death. (Hölty also died young, of tuberculosis.) This early Romantic tone is strongly marked in the best of the Hölty songs of spring 1815. A year later Schubert returned to Hölty, perhaps intending to complete a volume for the projected edition of the songs by authors, but the 1816 songs do not have the same freshness and spontaneity.
 Schubert seems to have used the edition of Hölty's works prepared by the poet's friend J.H. Voss and published in 1804, which includes many editorial 'improvements'.
*1813:*
44 Totengräberlied

*1815:*
193 An den Mond I
194 Die Mainacht
196 An die Nachtigall
197 An die Apfelbäume
198 Seufzer
201 Auf den Tod einer Nachtigall (1)
207 Der Liebende
208, 212 Die Nonne
213 Der Traum
214 Die Laube
*1816:*
398 Frühlingslied
399 Auf den Tod einer Nachtigall (2)
400 Die Knabenzeit
401 Winterlied
429 Minnelied
430 Die frühe Liebe
431 Blumenlied
433 Seligkeit
434 Erntelied
436-7 Klage an den Mond
468 An den Mond II
503 Mailied
    23 songs

**HÜTTENBRENNER, Heinrich**. Professor
of law and journalist, of Graz. He was the
youngest of three brothers who were closely
associated with Schubert. Anselm, who was a
composer, and Josef, who for several years acted
as Schubert's secretary, between them achieved
the notorious feat of hiding the existence of the
'Unfinished' Symphony from the world for
some forty years. Schubert met Heinrich while
he was at Vienna University studying law.
    *November 1820:*
702 Der Jüngling auf dem Hügel
    1 song

**JACOBI, Johann Georg** (1740–1814).
German academic, writer on the arts, and poet.
He was professor of philosophy first at Halle,
then at Freiburg. His poems were published in
Vienna in 1816, and Schubert's settings all date
from August and September of that year. The
poems are slight, but they inspired one great
song and one impressive dramatic scena, the
*Lied des Orpheus.*
    *August–September 1816:*
343 Litanei auf das Fest aller Seelen
462 An Chloen
463 Hochzeitlied
464 In der Mitternacht
465 Trauer der Liebe
466 Die Perle
474 Lied des Orpheus (als er in die Hölle ging)
    7 songs

**JARNIK, Urban**. Slovene poet, author of
the original text of *Die Sternenwelten*, which
was translated by J. G. Fellinger, q.v.

**KALCHBERG, Johann Nepomuk Ritter
von** (1765–1827). Official of Graz, supporter of
Styrian culture, and occasional poet.
    *October 1815:*
308 Die Macht der Liebe
    1 song

**KENNER, Josef** (1794–1868). Official
in the public service at Linz and occasional
poet. Kenner went from Linz to the Imperial
College in Vienna, and there met Schubert.
He studied at Vienna University but in 1816
returned to Linz to take up his appointment. He
kept in touch with the Schubert circle through
Spaun, Holzapfel and others, and probably
renewed acquaintance with the composer on
his visits to Linz. His personal memories,
written out for Luib in 1858 (*Memoirs* pp.
81–9), are noteworthy for the severity of his
judgment on Schober, whom he held responsible
for Schubert's illness. His naive verses give us
some idea of the strong appeal of sub-Ossianic
balladry of the time.
    *Early 1815:*
134 Ballade
209 Der Liedler
218 Grablied
    3 songs

**KIND, Friedrich** (1768–1843). German
poet and librettist. He was born in Leipzig
and practised law in Dresden, but from 1817
he devoted himself to letters. A prominent
member of the Dresden artistic circle, his
writings include the libretto for Weber's *Der
Freischütz.*
    *April 1817:*
552 Hänflings Liebeswerbung
    1 song

**KLENKE, Karoline Louise von**
(1754–1812). Daughter of the poet Anna Luise
Karschin, Klenke was an occasional poet and
literary figure in Berlin. The text of *Heimliches
Lieben* was for many years attributed to Karl
Gottfried von Leitner.
    *September 1827:*
922 Heimliches Lieben
    1 song

**KLOPSTOCK, Friedrich Gottlieb**
(1724–1803). German poet and dramatist. Born
near Hamburg, Klopstock spent most of his life
in that area. His declared ambition was to be a
great epic poet, like Milton, and his religious
epic *Der Messias* (1748–73) established his
reputation as a poet of great and original genius.
But it was his Odes (published 1771) which
most impressed the young Goethe and the
circle of enthusiasts who called themselves the
Göttinger Hainbund. The lyrical power and
immediacy of poems like *Die frühen Gräber*
and *Die Sommernacht* gave an example and an
impetus to the early Romantic movement. In

later years Klopstock was much occupied with political themes. Like many others, he moved from early enthusiasm for the French Revolution to final revulsion at its excesses.

Schubert's best Klopstock songs date from September and October 1815. In June 1816 he returned to the poet, but with less success.

*1815:*
280 Das Rosenband
285 Furcht der Geliebten
286 Selma und Selmar
287 Vaterlandslied
288 An Sie
289 Die Sommernacht
290 Die frühen Gräber
291 Dem Unendlichen
322 Hermann und Thusnelda
*1816:*
442 Das grosse Halleluja
443 Schlachtgesang
444 Die Gestirne
445 Edone
13 songs

**KÖPKEN, Friedrich von** (1737–1811). Lawyer, of Magdeburg.
*July 1816:*
455 Freude der Kinderjahre
1 song

**KÖRNER, Theodor** (1791–1813). Poet and patriot. Körner might be described as the Rupert Brooke of his generation. He was born in Dresden and studied law at Leipzig, but was sent down for fighting a duel. He moved to Vienna in 1811 and became resident dramatist at the Burgtheater. He met Schubert at this time through Spaun (*Memoirs* p.129) and is said to have encouraged the young composer to devote his life to the claims of art. Körner volunteered and was commissioned in March 1813. In August he died of wounds received at the skirmish of Gadebusch. His patriotic songs and poems were collected by his father and published under the title of *Leyer und Schwert* ('Lyre and Sword'). This collection made a great impression in 1814.

Schubert's Körner songs belong to February–October 1815, except for the last, and their fluent lyricism seems to mark an advance in his development. The last, *Auf der Riesenkoppe*, written three years later, is also an interesting and predictive song.

*1815:*
163 Sängers Morgenlied (1)
165 Sängers Morgenlied (2)
164 Liebesrausch (1)
179 Liebesrausch (2)
166 Amphiaraos
170 Schwertlied
171 Gebet während der Schlacht
172 Der Morgenstern
174 Das war ich (1) and (2)

180 Sehnsucht der Liebe
206 Liebeständelei
304 Wiegenlied
309 Das gestörte Glück
*1818:*
611 Auf der Riesenkoppe
14 songs

**KOSEGARTEN, Ludwig Theobul** (1758–1818). North German poet. He studied at Greifswald, Mecklenburg, and later became professor of theology there. He was a prolific writer of verse of a conventional kind. There are many differences between Schubert's texts and the published version of the poems, and Schubert's source has not been established. With the exception of the last, the Kosegarten songs belong to June–October 1815 and are strophic in form and conservative in idiom, though the best of them are deeply felt. The much later *An die untergehende Sonne* is something of a hybrid in style, and sectional in form.

*1815:*
219 Das Finden
221 Der Abend
227 Idens Nachtgesang
228 Von Ida
229 Die Erscheinung
230 Die Täuschung
231 Das Sehnen
233 Geist der Liebe
235 Abends unter der Linde (1)
237 Abends unter der Linde (2)
238 Die Mondnacht
240 Huldigung
241 Alles um Liebe
313 Die Sterne
314 Nachtgesang
315 An Rosa I
316 An Rosa II
317 Idens Schwanenlied
318 Schwanengesang
319 Luisens Antwort
*May 1817*
457 An die untergehende Sonne
21 songs

**KUFFNER, Christoph** (1780(?)–1846). Viennese court official, poet, dramatist, musician and journalist. He is the supposed author of the text of Beethoven's Choral Fantasia.
*August 1828:*
955 Glaube, Hoffnung und Liebe
1 song

**KUMPF, Johann Gottfried** (1781–1862). Doctor, and occasional poet and journalist, of Klagenfurt. He wrote under the pseudonym Ermin.
*1815:*
141 Der Mondabend
305 Mein Gruss an den Mai
2 songs

**LAPPE, Karl** (1773–1843). Schoolmaster and poet, of Pomerania. His poems were not collected and published in Schubert's lifetime. The source for the songs is not known.

*January 1825:*
799  Im Abendrot
800  Der Einsame
     2 songs

**LEITNER, Karl Gottfried von** (1800–90). Teacher and poet, of Graz. Schubert was introduced to his verses in 1822 by Johann Schickh, editor of the *ZfK*, who published the first Leitner setting as a supplement to that periodical. Leitner was highly regarded as an exponent of Styrian culture, and during Schubert's stay with the Pachler family at Graz in September 1827 he was encouraged to turn to his work again. The remaining Leitner settings all belong to the months that followed.

Leitner's verse tends to the sentimental, but the songs at their best are splendid examples of Schubert's mature song style.

*1822/1823:*
770  Drang in die Ferne
     *October 1827–January 1828:*
896  Fröhliches Scheiden
2 896A  Sie in jedem Liede
2 896B  Wolke und Quelle
926  Das Weinen
927  Vor meiner Wiege
931  Der Wallensteiner Lanzknecht beim Trunk
932  Der Kreuzzug
933  Des Fischers Liebesglück
938  Der Winterabend
939  Die Sterne
     11 songs

**LEON, Gottlieb von** (1757–1832). State official in Vienna. Schubert's source for *Die Liebe* is not known.

*January 1817:*
522  Die Liebe
     1 song

**LUBI, Michael** (1757–1808). Styrian author, whose poems were published in 1804.

*December 1814:*
122  Ammenlied
     1 song

**MACDONALD, Andrew** (1757–90). Scottish dramatist. The son of a gardener, he went to London and made a living by writing for the newspapers and the stage under the pen-name Matthew Bramble. But he fell on bad times and died of tuberculosis at an early age in extremely poor circumstances.

Scott incorporated his song *Wert thou, like me, in death's low vale* in the narrative of his novel *The Legend of Montrose*. Schubert set it to music in a German translation (as *Lied der Anne Lyle* 830) supposedly by Sophie May. The song occurs in McDonald's opera libretto *Love*

*and Loyalty*, which never reached the stage. (Information provided by Roger Fiske.)

**MACPHERSON, James** (1736–96). Scottish author and student of Gaelic mythology. In 1760 he published *Fragments of Ancient Poetry collected in the Highlands of Scotland from the Gaelic or Erse Language*. This was followed by other publications purporting to be translations from the Gaelic of an ancient bard called Ossian. The authenticity of these prose poems was widely challenged, and they are now attributed to Macpherson himself, but the hunger of the age for historical Romanticism gave them a great vogue throughout Europe, and especially in Germany, where Herder in particular did a great deal to popularise them. (See Part I: OSSIAN SONGS.)

Schubert's settings of passages from 'Ossian' in German translations by Edmund von Harold began in June 1815 and ended early in 1817.

*1815:*
217  Kolmas Klage
278  Ossians Lied nach der Falle Nathos
281  Das Mädchen von Inistore
282  Cronnan
293  Shilrik und Vinvela
327  Lorma (1)
     *1816:*
376  Lorma (2)
150  Lodas Gespenst
375  Der Tod Oscars
     *February 1817:*
534  Die Nacht
     10 songs

**MAJLÁTH, Johann, Count** (1786–1855). Hungarian poet and journalist. He had to leave the state service because of an eye injury, went to Vienna for medical treatment, and stayed there to earn a living with his pen. He was a member of the Schubert circle in the 1820s. In later years he moved to Munich. He died by his own hand, unable any longer to support himself and his daughter.

*September 1821:*
731  Der Blumen Schmerz
     1 song

**MATTHISSON, Friedrich von** (1761–1831). German poet. He was born near Magdeburg and studied at Halle and maintained himself as a private tutor, theatre director and librarian with the assistance of his patron Duke Friedrich of Württemberg. His poetry was widely read and much admired in Schubert's day for its combination of formal elegance and sentiment. He plays an important part in Schubert's development as a song-writer as the first fully contemporary poet to capture his imagination. The 1814 songs in particular are noteworthy for their varied attempts to reconcile the lyrical and dramatic elements in the lied. They also illustrate Schubert's growing understanding of the importance of the accompaniment, which is often allowed to play an independent part in the song.

*c. 1812:*
15 Der Geistertanz (1)
15 (2 15A) Der Geistertanz (2)
*1813:*
50 Die Schatten
*1814:*
95 Adelaide
97 Trost, an Elisa
98 Erinnerungen
99 Andenken
100 Geisternähe
101 Todtenopfer
102 Die Betende
107 Lied aus der Ferne
108 Der Abend
109 Lied der Liebe
114 Romanze
115 An Laura
116 Der Geistertanz (3)
*1815:*
186 Die Sterbende
187 Stimme der Liebe (1)
188 Naturgenuss
275 Totenkranz für ein Kind
*1816:*
413 Entzückung
418 Stimme der Liebe (2)
414 Geist der Liebe
415 Klage
419 Julius an Theone
507 Skolie
508 Lebenslied
*1817:*
989 (2 579A) Vollendung
989A (2 579B) Die Erde
29 songs

**MAY, Sophie**. According to Deutsch, she was the translator of Scott's novel *The Legend of Montrose*, from which Schubert took the text of *Lied der Anne Lyle* (830). But no such translation has come to light.

**MAYERHOFER, Ferdinand von Grünbühel** (1798–1869). A close friend of Eduard von Bauernfeld, Mayerhofer was a member of the Schubert circle in the 1820s and married Moritz von Schwind's girlfriend Anna Hönig. He collaborated with Bauernfeld in his work on the Vienna *Shakespeare–Ausgabe* and provided the German text for Schubert's setting of Shakespeare's *Come, thou monarch of the vine* (*Trinklied*, 888).

**MAYRHOFER, Johann Baptist** (1787–1836). Austrian poet. He came from Steyr, and went to school at Linz and St Florian. In 1810 he moved to Vienna to study law. There he renewed acquaintance with Spaun, whom he had known as a youth, and through Spaun met Schubert towards the end of

1814, when the composer set Mayrhofer's verses *Am See*.

After Schubert left home in the autumn of 1816 he was brought into much closer contact with Mayrhofer and was strongly influenced by the poet's neo-classical ideas. Mayrhofer's classicism was coloured by his own saturnine temperament and by his commitment to *Sehnsucht*. Only a Platonic belief in an ideal world ('das milde Land') could make the darkness of the real world tolerable; in this sense death was a friend to life, the only thing to give it meaning. Mayrhofer's ideas dominate Schubert's songs of 1817, and they went on to play an important part in Schubert's own thought.

Mayrhofer's melancholia was aggravated by his calling. In these early years he supported himself as a private tutor, but about 1820 he accepted a post in the Censorship Office, feeling obliged to earn his living in a way that his liberal instincts revolted against. This step may have contributed to the rift between the two young men which took place towards the end of 1820, but between 1818 and 1820 Mayrhofer was certainly the dominant influence on Schubert's development. When Mayrhofer's poems were collected and published in 1824 Schubert's name was conspicuously absent from the subscription list. He set four more Mayrhofer poems, however, two of them among the greatest. Mayrhofer was deeply moved by Schubert's early death, and afterwards wrote little. He continued to discharge his official duties conscientiously; he made an unsuccessful attempt to commit suicide in 1831 and finally succeeded in 1836.

The best Mayrhofer settings combine intellectual strength with lyrical power. They vary in style from the 'simplicity' of *Nachtviolen* and *Erlafsee* to the rugged intellectuality of *Freiwilliges Versinken* and *Der Sieg*, and there are hardly any weak songs among them. Mayrhofer's importance in Schubert's work has still not been fully appreciated.

*1814:*
124 Am See
*1815:*
298 Liane
*1816:*
450 Fragment aus dem Aeschylus
473 Liedesend
475 Abschied. Nach einer Wallfahrtsarie
476 Rückweg
477 Alte Liebe rostet nie
490 Der Hirt
491 Geheimnis
492 Zum Punsche
495 Abendlied der Fürstin
*1817:*
297 Augenlied
524 Der Alpenjäger
525 Wie Ulfru fischt
526 Fahrt zum Hades

527 Schlaflied
539 Am Strome
540 Philoktet
541 Memnon
542 Antigone und Oedip
548 Orest auf Tauris
699 Der entsühnte Orest
536 Der Schiffer
553 Auf der Donau
554 Uraniens Flucht
516 Sehnsucht
561 Nach einem Gewitter
573 Iphigenia
585 Atys
586 Erlafsee
700 Freiwilliges Versinken
  *1818:*
620 Einsamkeit
  *1819:*
654 An die Freunde
669 Beim Winde
670 Die Sternennächte
671 Trost
672 Nachtstück
682 Über allen Zauber
  *1820:*
707 Der zürnenden Diana
  *1822:*
752 Nachtviolen
753 Aus 'Heliopolis' I
754 Aus 'Heliopolis' II
360 Lied eines Schiffers an die Dioskuren
  *1824:*
805 Der Sieg
806 Abendstern
807 Auflösung
808 Gondelfahrer
  47 songs

**MENDELSSOHN, Moses** (1729–86).
Philosopher. He was a leading figure of the
Enlightenment in Germany, and grandfather of
the composer Felix Mendelssohn. Schubert
used his translation of Psalm 13 for his setting
(663) in June 1819.

**METASTASIO, Pietro** (1698–1782).
Italian poet and dramatist. He was born Antonio
Domenico Bonaventura Trapassi and renamed
by his adoptive father.

As the author of the libretti of something like
eight hundred operas he has a good claim to be
considered the most successful writer of opera
books in history. He was born in Rome, moved
to Vienna as court poet in 1730, and lived there
for the rest of his life. His reputation was at its
height when Antonio Salieri arrived in Vienna
from Venice in 1766. Salieri learnt his craft as a
stage composer from Metastasio. When Schubert
began regular lessons with Salieri in 1812 he
was given various Metastasio texts to set for
different combinations of voices, both as solos
and as concerted pieces. Many of these exercises,
with Salieri's corrections, have survived.

Schubert's close links with the central
tradition of Italian opera need to be remembered
when we consider his early enthusiasm for
Gluck, his conservative habits in the matter of
notation, and his determined attempt to make a
successful stage career. His lifelong concern
also to preserve the immediacy of recitative by
embodying a form of declamation in the lied
must owe something to his early training in the
setting of operatic texts.
  *1812:*
17 no.1 Quell'innocente figlio
33 no.1 Entra l'uomo allor che nasce
35 no.1 (2 35 no.3) Serbate, o dei custodi
  *1812/1813:*
42 Misero pargoletto [(1) and (2)]
  *1813:*
76 Pensa, che questo istante
78 Son fra l'onde
  *1816:*
510 Didone abbandonata
  *1820:*
Vier Canzonen:
688 no.3 Da quel sembiante
688 no.4 Mio ben ricordati
  *1827:*
902 no.1 L'Incanto degli occhi
902 no.2 Il Traditor deluso
  12 songs

**MIKAN, Johann Christian** (1769–1844).
Czech botanist, zoologist and occasional
versifier.
  *May 1814:*
104 Die Befreier Europas in Paris
  1 song

**MÜLLER, Georg Friedrich** Original name
of Georg Friedrich von Gerstenberg (q.v.), the
author of the text of *Hippolits Lied* (890).

**MÜLLER, Karl Ludwig Methusalem**. As
the translator of Scott's *Ivanhoe* (1820) into
German, he was responsible for the German
text of the *Romanze des Richard Löwenherz*
(907).

**MÜLLER, Wilhelm** (1794–1827). German
poet, publicist and journalist. He was born
at Dessau, studied philology and history at
Berlin and in 1813 volunteered to serve in the
Prussian army. After the war he returned to
Berlin and became a member of the circle of
young Romantics which included Arnim,
Brentano and Fouqué. His song cycle *Die
schöne Müllerin* took shape as a direct result of
a party game which originated at the house of
Councillor Friedrich von Stägemann at this
time, although it was not published until
1820. In 1817 he visited Italy in the company
of a nobleman, staying at Vienna en route.
In Vienna he met Greek exiles who kindled
his enthusiasm for the cause of Greek independence.

Returning to Dessau in 1819 he supported himself as a teacher, librarian and journalist. His two-volume 'Poems from the Posthumous Papers of a Travelling Horn-player', which includes both of the song cycles Schubert set, was published in 1824 and dedicated to Weber. He was a prolific writer of articles, reviews and essays on both aesthetic and political subjects. He died unexpectedly and in mysterious circumstances in 1827, but suspicions of his involvement in a political intrigue have never been substantiated.

Müller had a gift for fluent and evocative verse in the folksong manner, and he did a great deal to forge closer links between poetry and music. He regarded his lyrics as drafts for songs, so it is a tribute to him, rather than a criticism, that he is now best remembered as the author of the text of Schubert's great song cycles. Most of the text of *Der Hirt auf dem Felsen* comes from his poems *Der Berghirt* and *Liebesgedanken*.

*1823:*
795 *Die schöne Müllerin*
    Das Wandern
    Wohin?
    Halt!
    Danksagung an den Bach
    Am Feierabend
    Der Neugierige
    Ungeduld
    Morgengruss
    Des Müllers Blumen
    Tränenregen
    Mein
    Pause
    Mit dem grünen Lautenbande
    Der Jäger
    Eifersucht und Stolz
    Die liebe Farbe
    Die böse Farbe
    Trockne Blumen
    Der Müller und der Bach
    Des Baches Wiegenlied
*1827:*
911 *Winterreise*
    Gute Nacht
    Die Wetterfahne
    Gefrorne Tränen
    Erstarrung
    Der Lindenbaum
    Wasserflut
    Auf dem Flusse
    Rückblick
    Irrlicht
    Rast
    Frühlingstraum
    Einsamkeit
    Die Post
    Der greise Kopf
    Die Krähe
    Letzte Hoffnung
    Im Dorfe
    Der stürmische Morgen
    Täuschung

    Der Wegweiser
    Das Wirtshaus
    Mut
    Die Nebensonnen
    Der Leiermann
*October 1828:*
965 Der Hirt auf dem Felsen
    45 songs

**NOVALIS** (1772–1801). German Romantic poet. Novalis is the pseudonym of Friedrich Leopold von Hardenberg, who was born near Mansfeld. He studied at Jena, where he met Schiller, and Leipzig, where he met Friedrich von Schlegel. He became an administrator of salt mines, devoting his spare time to philosophy and poetry. He became engaged to Sophie von Kühn in 1794. In 1797 she died of tuberculosis, and this blow, combined with the death of his brother, led to a religious crisis and a turn to more mystical ways of thought. This finds expression in the *Hymnen an die Nacht* ('Hymns to the Night'), four of which Schubert set in 1819. Like Mayrhofer and many others, Novalis found his awareness of life sharpened and enriched by coming to terms with death, but his outlook is more sacramental than Mayrhofer's, so that his religious insights are given a secular, even sexual colour.

Schubert discovered Novalis at a time when he was much taken up with transcendental ways of thought; but it cannot be said that he was successful in finding the appropriate musical idiom for these rhapsodically spiritual poems. He is much more successful with the lyrical devotion of *Marie*.

*1819:*
659 Hymne I
660 Hymne II
661 Hymne III
662 Hymne IV
658 Marie
*1820:*
687 Nachthymne
    6 songs

**OSSIAN.** See MACPHERSON, James, and Part I: OSSIAN SONGS.

**OTTENWALT, Anton** (1789–1845). State official, of Linz and Vienna. He was born at Linz, was a close friend of the Spaun family, and married Marie von Spaun in 1819. He got to know Schubert through Josef von Spaun and became a leading member of what might be called the Schubert supporters' club in Linz. After the composer's death he edited Spaun's obituary essay for publication in the Linz *Bürgerblatt* (*Memoirs* pp.15–18).

Schubert seems to have set *Der Knabe in der Wiege* at Spaun's suggestion (*Docs.* no.109).

*1817:*
579 Der Knabe in der Wiege
    1 song

**PETRARCH**. (Francesco Petrarca) (1304–74). Italian poet. In 1818 Schubert set three of his sonnets (as *Sonett I–III*) in the German translation attributed to A.W. von Schlegel; the translation of no.3, however, was the work of J.D. Gries, who may also have been the translator of nos.1 and 2.

**PFEFFEL, Gottlieb Conrad** (1736–1809). German educationist and author. He founded a Protestant school in his native town, Colmar. His verse fables reflect the ideals of the French Revolution.
*December 1811:*
10 Der Vatermörder
1 song

**PICHLER, Karoline** (1769–1843). Poet, novelist and dramatist, of Vienna. She married the state servant Andreas Pichler in 1796 and they maintained a literary salon which in Schubert's day attracted all the artistic celebrities of Vienna. Schubert was a frequent visitor in the prosperous years of 1821–2. Pichler's memoirs, in four volumes (1844), give many details of Vienna's cultural life.

The two early Pichler settings date from 1816. The much more ambitious *Der Unglückliche* probably marks the beginning of Schubert's personal acquaintance with Pichler at the beginning of 1821.
*1816:*
482 Der Sänger am Felsen
483 Lied (Ferne von der grossen Stadt)
*January 1821:*
713 Der Unglückliche
3 songs

**PLATEN–HALLERMÜNDE, Karl August Graf von** (1796–1835). German poet and playwright. Born at Ansbach into an aristocratic family, he was intended for a military career. He was commissioned in 1814 but found himself unsuited to the military life and secured his release in 1818. Thereafter he travelled widely and devoted himself to poetry.

Schubert's interest in Platen's poetry came about through Franz von Bruchmann, who met the poet at Erlangen early in 1821.
*1822:*
751 Die Liebe hat gelogen
756 Du liebst mich nicht
2 songs

**PLATNER, Anton** (1787–1855). Platner was an eccentric Austrian priest and the supposed author of the text of *Die Blumensprache*, which appeared in Becker's 'Pocket-book of Sociable Pleasures' for 1805. There it is signed simply 'Pl.'
*(?) October 1817:*
519 Die Blumensprache
1 song

**POLLAK, A.** Nothing is known of him, except that his name appears on the title page of Schubert's *Frühlingslied* on the manuscript copy in Vienna (MGV).
*(?) 1827:*
919 Frühlingslied
1 song

**POPE, Alexander** (1688–1744). English poet. In May 1813 Schubert set Herder's translation of his poem *The Dying Christian to his Soul* as *Verklärung* (59).

**PRANDSTETTER, Martin Josef** (b.- Vienna 1750). The autograph of *Die Fröhlichkeit* is lost, and it is not known what Schubert's source was. Prandstetter was arrested and imprisoned in 1799 in Vienna for alleged complicity in a Jacobin plot.
*August 1815:*
262 Die Fröhlichkeit
1 song

**PRATOBEVERA, Adolf von** (1806–75). Austrian state official. He belonged to a distinguished Vienna family, several of whom were members of the Schubert circle in the 1820s. His cousin Marie recorded her memories of the composer in later life (*Memoirs* pp.297–8); one of his sisters became the wife of the Schubert biographer Kreissle von Hellborn, and another married Josef Tremier, whose collection of Schubert songs is now in Vienna (SB).

The setting of *Abschied von der Erde* was written as a melodrama for a private performance of Pratobevera's poetic drama *Der Falke* ('The Falcon') in February 1826. It is the only instance of the use of melodrama in the solo songs. (See *Docs.*, note to no.627.)
*February 1826:*
829 Abschied von der Erde
1 song

**PYRKER, Johann Ladislaus** (1772–1847). Priest, poet and dramatist. He was born in Hungary and was ordained in the Catholic Church in 1796 and held a succession of ecclesiastical appointments. He became Patriarch of Venice in 1820 and Archbishop of Erlau in 1827.

Schubert first met Pyrker in 1820 at the house of Matthäus von Collin. In the following year he dedicated his op.4 to him, a group of songs with 'Romantic' texts by Schmidt of Lübeck, Zacharias Werner and Goethe. The two met again at Gastein in August 1825. According to Schindler (*Memoirs* p.318), 'this moment was treasured by Schubert as one of the most inspiring of his life'. Both the Pyrker songs were written at that time.
*August 1825:*
851 Das Heimweh
852 Die Allmacht
2 songs

**RATSCHKY, Josef Franz von** (1757–1810). Government official, of Vienna. He knew Mozart, who set one of his Freemasons' songs, and was editor of the Vienna *Musenalmanach* in the 1770s.

The text of *Der Weiberfreund*, a translation of Abraham Cowley's poem *The Inconstant* (from a series called *The Mistress*), appeared in Becker's 'Pocket-book of Sociable Pleasures' in 1795.

*August 1815:*
271 Der Weiberfreund
 1 song

**REIL, Johann Anton Friedrich** (1773–1843). Actor and occasional poet. He came from the Rhineland but moved to Vienna in 1801 to join the Burgtheater company. He wrote plays and contributed to periodicals.

Schubert and Reil seem to have been in close touch in 1827 and 1828. Reil may have been at Dornbach in June 1827, when *Das Lied im Grünen* was written, as were the two additional verses he contributed to the translation of *Hark, hark, the lark*. In 1828 he provided the text for Schubert's male-voice quartet *Glaube, Hoffnung und Liebe* (954).

*June 1827:*
917 Das Lied im Grünen
 1 song

**REISSIG, Christian Ludwig** (1783–1822). Professional soldier and occasional poet. He was a passionate opponent of Napoleon and served as a cavalry officer in the Austrian army from 1808. His songs were published in various periodicals and were set by Beethoven, among others.

*October 1815:*
320 Der Zufriedene
 1 song

**RELLSTAB, Ludwig** (1799–1860). German poet, novelist and critic. He was born in Berlin and began his career as an artillery officer, but turned to writing. He was a promising pianist in his youth, and he was to become one of the first to practise the comparatively new profession of music critic. He visited Vienna in 1825 and met Beethoven, who toyed with the idea of collaborating with him in an opera. Rellstab was an enthusiastic supporter of German opera and viewed the Rossini craze with distaste. In 1830 he founded the weekly musical journal *Iris im Gebiete der Tonkunst*.

The chronology of the Rellstab songs is not at all clear. According to Schindler, the texts were passed on to Schubert from Beethoven's *Nachlass*. They were probably completed, in draft form at least, by March–April 1828. (See Part I: RELLSTAB SONGS.) Seven of them were included by Haslinger in his posthumous collection *Schwanengesang*.

*1827–8:*
937 Lebensmut
943 Auf dem Strom
945 Herbst
957 no.1 Liebesbotschaft
957 no.2 Kriegers Ahnung
957 no.3 Frühlingssehnsucht
957 no.4 Ständchen
957 no.5 Aufenthalt
957 no.6 In der Ferne
957 no.7 Abschied
 10 songs

**ROCHLITZ, Johann Friedrich** (1769–1842). Novelist, poet, playwright and critic of Leipzig. He founded the Leipzig *Allgemeine musikalische Zeitung* in 1798. According to his own account, Rochlitz met Schubert on his first visit to Vienna in 1822 (*Docs.* no.299). The notices of Schubert publications in the Leipzig *AMZ* were on the whole noticeably more sympathetic than the others; Rochlitz seems to have thought highly of Schubert's work. In November 1827 he wrote a long letter to the composer outlining an elaborate scheme for the setting of one of his own poems. But Schubert's reply was cool.

*Klaglied* is possibly the first genuine lied Schubert wrote.

*1812:*
23 Klaglied
*January 1827:*
904 Alinde
905 An die Laute
 3 songs

**ROOS, Richard.** Pseudonym of Karl August Engelhardt, q.v.

**RÜCKERT, Friedrich** (1788–1866). German poet. He was born at Schweinfurt and planned an academic career but abandoned a teaching post for authorship. Under the influence of Hammer-Purgstall, whom he met in Vienna in 1818, he devoted himself to the study of oriental languages and verse forms. Later he held professorial chairs at Erlangen and Berlin, but retired in 1848 to devote himself to scholarship.

The clarity, freshness and formal variety of Rückert's poetry have endeared him to Romantic composers. Schubert's Rückert songs all come from the volume called *Östliche Rosen* ('Oriental Roses'), which is dated 1822 but may have appeared in 1821; it is possible that his attention was called to it by Bruchmann, to whom Rückert would be known through his friendship with Platen, or by Hammer-Purgstall, whom Schubert must have met at Karoline Pichler's. The songs cannot be precisely dated, but they probably belong to the second half of the year 1822 and the first half of 1823.

*(?) 1822–3:*
741 Sei mir gegrüsst

775 Dass sie hier gewesen
776 Du bist die Ruh
777 Lachen und Weinen
778 Greisengesang
2 778A Die Wallfahrt
  6 songs

**SALIS-SEEWIS, Johann Gaudenz von**
(1762–1834). Swiss nobleman, government
servant and poet. He came from the canton of
Grisons and served as an officer of the Swiss
Guard in Paris before the Revolution. In 1789
he made a tour of Germany, meeting Goethe,
Schiller, Herder and others. He lived as a
civilian in Paris during the Revolution but later
returned to Switzerland to become an administrator.

He was almost the exact contemporary of
Matthisson, with whom he corresponded and
whose literary taste and style he shared.
Schubert's Salis-Seewis songs date from 1816
and 1817, but *Der Jüngling an der Quelle* is
probably some years later.

*1816:*
392 Pflügerlied
393 Die Einsiedelei (1)
394 An die Harmonie
403 Ins stille Land
404 Die Herbstnacht
405 Der Herbstabend
406 Abschied von der Harfe
502 Herbstlied
351 Fischerlied (1)
350 Der Entfernten
*1817:*
562 Fischerlied (2)
563 Die Einsiedelei (2)
*(?) 1821:*
300 Der Jüngling an der Quelle
  13 songs

**SAUTER, Samuel Friedrich** (1766–1846).
A village schoolmaster from Baden whose
unpretentious verses brought him a dubious
fame. His solid and respectable virtues were
embodied in the fictitious figure of Gottlieb
Biedermeier in the satirical pages of the Munich
*Fliegende Blätter*. Beethoven also set his poem
*Der Wachtelschlag*.
*(?) 1822:*
742 Der Wachtelschlag
  1 song

**SCHILLER, Johann Christoph Friedrich
von** (1759–1805). German poet and dramatist.
The intellectual strain in Schiller's poetry, the
emphasis on the will and the mind which can
seem somewhat dry and unattractive to modern
ears, gave him a great prestige in his own day;
and it appealed to the young Schubert, whose
interest in Schiller predates the first Goethe
song by three years. Apart from Schubert's
fashionable interest in the macabre, Schiller, as
interpreted by his friend Zumsteeg, offered an

alternative to the preoccupation with the
strophic lied characteristic of the north German
school. So Schubert started with the through-
composed *Gesang*, and only later turned to the
strophic lied.

It has been said, by Capell among others,
that Schiller's intellectuality proved inhibiting
to Schubert's lyrical inspiration. It is true that
Schubert likes to take as his starting-point a
sensuous image, a rhythm or *Bewegung*. With
Schiller he has to deal more often with an
abstract idea (*Schöne Welt, wo bist du?*) or a
state of mind (*Die Erwartung, Das Geheimnis*);
and it is significant that he made more than
one attempt to set many of the poems. The
proportion of 'once and for all' settings is lower
in the case of Schiller than for any other poet.
On the other hand, his persistence is
sometimes gloriously rewarded. *Gruppe aus
dem Tartarus* eventually inspired the masterpiece; and the final versions of *Sehnsucht* and
*Das Geheimnis* are remarkable for their psychological insight and thematic invention. But
even when the first version is a success (*Der
Jüngling am Bache*) Schubert seems reluctant to
leave well alone.

*1811:*
6 Des Mädchens Klage (1)
7 Leichenfantasie
*1812:*
30 Der Jüngling am Bache (1)
*1813:*
52 Sehnsucht (1)
73 Thekla: eine Geisterstimme (1)
77 Der Taucher
(Various settings of Schiller texts as exercises
for Salieri, March–July 1813)
*1814:*
113 An Emma
117 Das Mädchen aus der Fremde (1)
*1815:*
191 Des Mädchens Klage (2)
192 Der Jüngling am Bache (2)
195 Amalia
189 An die Freude
250 Das Geheimnis (1)
251 Hoffnung (1)
246 Die Bürgschaft
252 Das Mädchen aus der Fremde (2)
253 Punschlied
283 An den Frühling (1)
284 Lied (Es ist so angenehm)
312 Hektors Abschied
*1815/1816:*
323, 991 Klage der Ceres
*1816:*
389 Des Mädchens Klage (3)
388 Laura am Klavier
390 Die Entzückung an Laura (1)
391 Die vier Weltalter
397 Ritter Toggenburg
402 Der Flüchtling
396 Gruppe aus dem Tartarus (1)
159 Die Erwartung

*1817:*
577  Die Entzückung an Laura (2)
583  Gruppe aus dem Tartarus (2)
584  Elysium
587  An den Frühling (2)
588  Der Alpenjäger
637  (?) Hoffnung (2)
594  Der Kampf
595  Thekla: eine Geisterstimme (2)
*1818:*
990  Der Graf von Habsburg
*1819:*
638  Der Jüngling am Bache (3)
677  Die Götter Griechenlands
*1821:*
636  Sehnsucht (2)
*1823:*
793  Das Geheimnis (2)
794  Der Pilgrim
(?) *1824:*
801  Dithyrambe
44 songs

**SCHLECHTA, Franz Xaver von Wssehrd**
(1796–1875). Government servant and dilettante, of Vienna. He was a colonel's son, and first met Schubert as a fellow student at the Imperial College. He became a loyal friend and a great admirer of the composer, took part in the first performance of the cantata *Prometheus* in July 1816, and wrote a commemorative epitaph in the *ZfK* after Schubert's death. He had a distinguished career in the public service, and retired as the head of a department in the Finance Ministry.

Schlechta's occasional verses are more interesting than most, varied in mood but generally Romantic in tone. All the songs are of interest, and the later ones are particularly idiosyncratic and self-revealing.

The poems were published in 1824, but it is probable that Schubert set most of them from Schlechta's manuscripts.

*1815:*
151  Auf einen Kirchhof
*1816:*
458  Aus *Diego Manazares*: Ilmerine
*1819/1820:*
639  Widerschein
*1820:*
698  Liebeslauschen
*1825:*
832  Des Sängers Habe
*1826:*
869  Totengräber-Weise
881  Fischerweise
7 songs

**SCHLEGEL, August Wilhelm von**
(1767–1845). German Romantic poet, critic and philosopher. Schlegel came of a literary family in Hanover, studied at Göttingen, and made a living first as a private tutor and then by journalism. In 1798 he and his brother Friedrich

founded a literary journal, *Das Athenaeum*, and over the next few years he built up a reputation as a leading exponent of Romantic ideas. These ideas were later systematically expounded in a famous series of lectures in Berlin and Vienna.

His marriage to Caroline Böhmer was dissolved, and in 1804 he formed an association with Madame de Staël, accompanying her on many journeys in Europe until her death in 1817. Thereafter he accepted a professorship at Bonn and devoted himself to the study of oriental languages.

Although Schlegel wrote poems and a classical play, his real importance is as a translator and publicist. His monumental translation of Shakespeare in verse (seventeen plays, 1797–1810) laid the foundation for Shakespeare's enormous popularity in Germany.

*1816:*
395  Lebensmelodien
409  Die verfehlte Stunde
410  Sprache der Liebe
*1818:*
628  Sonett I
629  Sonett II
711  Lob der Tränen
*1821:*
712  Die gefangenen Sänger
*1825:*
855  Wiedersehn
856  Abendlied für die Entfernte
9 songs

**SCHLEGEL, Karl Wilhelm Friedrich von**
(1772–1829). German poet and critic, brother of August Wilhelm von Schlegel. He was intended for commerce, but after a brief and unsuccessful experiment in a bank he secured his parents' permission to study at the university. He contributed to various periodicals and was co-founder of *Das Athenaeum* with his brother August. In 1804 he married Dorothea Veit, the daughter of Moses Mendelssohn and aunt of the composer. In 1808, the pair moved to Vienna, where Friedrich entered the government service, and they both converted to Roman Catholicism. In Vienna Schlegel was the centre of a circle of writers and philosophers which included Franz von Bruchmann and other members of the Schubert circle. It is not clear that Schubert ever met Schlegel, but there is no doubt that he was influenced by him. That influence was at its strongest in the years 1819–22, and it is to that period that most of the Schlegel songs belong.

The Romantic view of nature as the mediator between God and man which Schlegel embraced and expounded made a strong appeal to Schubert, and it is reflected not only in his songs but in the 'Great' C major Symphony. *Im Walde*, written in December 1820, is a rhapsodic paean of praise to nature as the immanent Spirit.

*1818:*
631  Blanka (or *Das Mädchen* I)
632  Vom Mitleiden Mariä

*1819:*
646  Die Gebüsche
649  Der Wanderer
652  Das Mädchen [II[
*1819–23:*
633  Der Schmetterling
634  Die Berge
*1820:*
684  Die Sterne
691  Die Vögel
692  Der Knabe
693  Der Fluss
694  Der Schiffer
708  Im Walde
745  (?) Die Rose
*(?) 1820–3:*
690  Abendröte
*1825:*
854  Fülle der Liebe
    16 songs

**SCHMIDT**, Georg Philipp (1766–1849), called 'Schmidt von Lübeck'. He studied law and medicine, practised as a doctor and joined the government service in Denmark. The poem which Schubert made famous was first published in 1808, but Schubert probably found it in an anthology called *Dichtungen für Kunstredner* ('Poems for Speaking Aloud') published in Vienna in 1815. In this anthology it was erroneously attributed to the Romantic poet Zacharias Werner, a mistake which Schubert repeated on the manuscript of his first draft.
  *October 1816:*
489, 493 Der Wanderer
    1 song

**SCHOBER**, Franz von (1796–1882). Occasional poet, dilettante, and friend of Schubert. Born in Sweden of a German father and an Austrian mother, Schober was educated in Austria and studied law in Vienna. His private means and *savoir faire* gave him a certain authority in the Schubert circle. When Schubert left home in 1816 to live in the inner city Schober provided him with a refuge; and he was glad to accept the hospitality of the Schober family again in later years, 1822–3, 1826 and 1827–8. Schober was a versatile dilettante of sophisticated tastes but no great talent, and Schubert's more serious-minded friends blamed him for the composer's misfortunes, and especially for his serious illness. He certainly knew as much as anybody about Schubert's private affairs, but he never found the time or the will to write down his recollections, though he did pass on a few sensational anecdotes verbally (*Memoirs* pp.264–6).
  Schober tried his hand at acting, writing, publishing, and living as a gentleman, but never settled. In later years he lived in Hungary, where he met Liszt and became his secretary for a few years, and in Dresden, where he died.

Schober's poetry is mostly insipid stuff, but it provided Schubert with the text of one of his greatest songs, and several fine ones. He also wrote the libretto for *Alfonso and Estrella*, Schubert's only full-length all-sung opera. His poems were published in 1865.
  *(?) 1815:*
143  Genügsamkeit
  *(?) 1816:*
361  Am Bach im Frühling
  *1817:*
547  An die Musik
546  Trost im Liede
551  Pax vobiscum
  *1822:*
758  Todesmusik
761  Schatzgräbers Begehr
  *1823:*
786  Viola
789  Pilgerweise
792  Vergissmeinnicht
  *1827:*
909  Jägers Liebeslied
910  Schiffers Scheidelied
    12 songs

**SCHOPENHAUER**, Johanna (1766–1838). German writer, novelist, and member of the Goethe circle in Weimar. The text of *Hippolits Lied* (890) occurs in her novel *Gabriele* (1821), but the author of the lyric is not Johanna but Friedrich von Gerstenberg (q.v.). She was the mother of the philosopher Arthur Schopenhauer.

**SCHREIBER**, Alois (1763–1841). Schoolmaster, drama critic, and professor of literature at Heidelberg. Schreiber came from Baden and was a prolific author. His poems were published in 1817, and all Schubert's settings of them date from the following year. They are noteworthy for their freshness of feeling, and for the fluency and independence of the piano writing.
  *1818:*
614  An den Mond in einer Herbstnacht
622  Der Blumenbrief
623  Das Marienbild
627  Das Abendrot
    4 songs

**SCHUBART**, Christian Friedrich Daniel (1739–91). German poet. His wild ways in youth and his uncompromising views led to his being withdrawn from Erlangen University and dismissed from his post as court organist at Ludwigsburg in 1773. He founded a journal, *Die deutsche Chronik*, at Augsburg but was arrested and imprisoned without trial for satirical attacks on the Duke of Württemberg and his mistress. After ten years in prison he was released and appointed to a musical post at court. Schubart was a fearless exponent of liberal ideas, and he paid a heavy price for being ahead of his time. His poems, mostly on pious, patriotic or political themes, were published in 1785.

The Schubert settings belong to 1816 and 1817 and include perhaps the best-known of all Schubert songs. In their different ways, all four are important and significant.

*1816:*
454 Grablied auf einen Soldaten
342 An mein Klavier
*1817:*
550 Die Forelle
518 An den Tod
   4 songs

**SCHUBERT, Franz** (1797–1828). The habit of writing verses to mark an occasion, to pay a compliment or to console a friend was very common in Schubert's day, and there is no doubt that he himself often wrote verses and sometimes set them to music. The survival of many personal albums filled with such tributes documents the practice. *Abschied von einem Freunde* was written in Schober's album, at a time when he had to leave Vienna for family reasons (see *Docs.* no.108). It may well be that some other texts which cannot be assigned to known authors may be by Schubert.

*August 1817:*
578 Abschied von einem Freunde
   1 song

**SCHÜCKING, Clemens August** (1759–90). Nothing seems to be known of him, except that he came from Münster.

*March 1811:*
5 Hagars Klage
   1 song

**SCHULZE, Ernst Konrad Friedrich** (1789–1817). German poet. He studied at Göttingen, where he fell in love with and became engaged to the daughter of a professor. She died in the following year. His hopes blighted, Schulze served in the War of Liberation. When he returned to Göttingen his health was already undermined and he died of tuberculosis in 1817.

His poetry, like his life, centres on the loss of his betrothed and is characterised by a deep sense of loss and alienation. His best-known work is a Romantic epic *Die bezauberte Rose* ('The Enchanted Rose'), which Schubert at one time planned to use as the basis for an opera. But the songs all come from a sequence called *Poetisches Tagebuch* ('Verse Journal') which was published in 1822 as part of Schulze's collected poems. These poignantly personal poems depict the tragic fate of a man who cannot come to terms with bitter reality. The Schulze songs were written in 1825 and 1826; their pessimism, no less than their driving rhythms, foreshadows *Winterreise*.

*1825:*
834 Im Walde

853 Auf der Brücke
860 An mein Herz
861 Der liebliche Stern
862 Um Mitternacht
   *1825/1826:*
876 Tiefes Leid
   *1826:*
882 Im Frühling
883 Lebensmut
884 Über Wildemann
874 O Quell, was strömst du rasch und wild
   10 songs

**SCHÜTZ, Christian Wilhelm von** (1776–1847). German Romantic dramatist. He was born in Berlin and was associated with Tieck, Arnim and other writers of the Berlin Romantic school, and later with Adam Müller and Heinrich von Kleist. He became a Roman Catholic in 1833.

The text of Schubert's two Schütz songs comes from the play *Lacrimas* (1803).

*September 1825:*
857 no. 1 Florio (=D2 no. 2)
857 no. 2 Delphine (=D2 no. 1)
   2 songs

**SCOTT, Sir Walter** (1771–1832). Scottish poet and novelist. The public's appetite for Scott's historical romances was insatiable in Schubert's time. His novels were adapted as plays and operas all over Europe, and Schubert was one of many composers who found inspiration in the verse romances. He read Scott during his holiday in the summer of 1823 (*Docs.* no.374) and two years later made a conscious plan to write a series of Scott songs and publish them with both English and German words. In this he was not altogether successful, because he was not accustomed to setting English words and the translations he used were sometimes so different metrically from the original text that the same tune would not fit both. In any event, the plan to publish these songs also in London was never put into effect.

The style of the Scott songs is akin to the epic style Schubert had used in his settings of Klopstock and makes full use of martial rhythms and horn calls. But he abandons the episodic form used earlier and is content to unify the songs with ostinato rhythms and melodic figures.

Translating Scott was a growth industry, and it is not always clear which translation Schubert used for his German text. For the *Lady of the Lake* songs he relied on the translation by Adam Storck (1819). See also SPIKER, Samuel Heinrich, MÜLLER, Karl Ludwig Methusalem.

*1825:*
830 Lied der Anne Lyle
831 Gesang der Norna
837 Ellens Gesang I

838 Ellens Gesang II
839 Ellens Gesang III
843 Lied des gefangenen Jägers
846 Normans Gesang
*(?) 1826:*
907 Romanze des Richard Löwenherz
8 songs

**SEIDL, Johann Gabriel** (1804–75).
Government official, poet and journalist, of
Vienna. Seidl was a popular author in
Schubert's day. He wrote the modern version of
the Austrian national anthem, and his poetry,
with its conventional sentiment and arch
humour, had a broad appeal. Schubert used the
edition of his poems published in 1826. His
collected works were published in six volumes
after his death.
*1826:*
870 Der Wanderer an den Mond
871 Das Zügenglöcklein
867 Wiegenlied
878 Am Fenster
879 Sehnsucht
880 Im Freien
*(?) 1828:*
Vier Refrain Lieder:
866 no.1 Die Unterscheidung
866 no.2 Bei dir allein
866 no.3 Die Männer sind méchant
866 no.4 Irdisches Glück
*October 1828:*
957 no.14 (2 965A) Die Taubenpost
11 songs

**SENN, Johann Chrysostomus** (1792–1857).
Patriot und poet, of the Austrian Tyrol, was the
son of a judge and supported the cause of
Tyrolese independence in 1809. He met
Schubert at the Imperial College. He was a
young man of strong liberal views and
courageous temperament. In 1814 he lost his
scholarship place at the college because he took
the lead in opposition to the authorities in a
row over the imprisonment of a fellow student
(*Memoirs* p.88). Later Senn came under
suspicion from the secret police. In March 1820
the police raided his rooms and arrested him
together with Schubert, Bruchmann and
Streinsberg. He was kept in prison for fourteen
months without trial and finally deported to
the Tyrol (*Docs.* no.162). In later years Senn
served as an officer in the Italian campaign of
1831, but his career had been ruined, and he
died poor and unbefriended.
The two Senn poems which Schubert set in
1822–3 were probably brought back in
manuscript to Vienna by Bruchmann, who
visited Senn at Innsbruck in September 1822.
*(?) Autumn 1822:*
743 Selige Welt
744 Schwanengesang
2 songs

**SHAKESPEARE, William** (1564–1616).
Schubert took the German texts of his three
Shakespeare songs from the Vienna
*Shakespeare*-Ausgabe of 1825, in which A. W.
von Schlegel's translations were supplemented
by new ones from Eduard von Bauernfeld und
Ferdinand Mayerhofer. The songs were written
at Währing in July 1826.
*July 1826:*
888 Trinklied
889 Ständchen
891 An Sylvia
3 songs

**SILBERT, Johann Petrus** (1772–1844).
German academic and occasional poet. He was
at Kolmar and studied at Mainz; he became
professor of French language and literature at
the Polytechnic Institute in Vienna. His poems
were published in 1819.
*February 1819:*
650 Abendbilder
651 Himmelsfunken
2 songs

**SPAUN, Josef von** (1788–1865). Austrian
government official. He was the eldest son of a
Linz lawyer and arrived at the Imperial College
two years before Schubert. He was the first to
recognise Schubert's genius, and he became a
close friend and a strong supporter of the composer throughout his youth and adolescence.
Through Spaun Schubert met Witteczek,
Mayrhofer, Schober and Vogl, all of whom were
to play a crucial role in his development. It was
Spaun who took the leading part in the plan to
have Schubert's song published in a series of
volumes arranged by authors. In 1816 Schubert
and Spaun lived together in Professor
Watteroth's house for a few weeks.
Spaun left Vienna in September 1821 to take
up a post in Linz, and he did not return until
the spring of 1826. He was thus out of touch
with Schubert during the most critical years of
his life, though the two exchanged news and
kept in touch through friends. Spaun had a
distinguished career as a state servant before
retiring in 1861. His various biographical
writings about Schubert are of first-rate
importance, and are all included in the
*Memoirs.*
*March 1817:*
545 Der Jüngling und der Tod
1 song

**SPIKER, Samuel Heinrich.** As translator of
Scott's **The Pirate** into German (Berlin, 1822)
he was responsible for the German text of the
*Gesang der Norna*, which Schubert set early in
1825 (831).

**STADLER, Albert** (1794–1888). Lawyer
und local government officer. Stadler was a
native of Steyr. He and Schubert were fellow

students at the Imperial College, 1812–13, and he remained in Vienna as a law student until 1817. During these early years he was in close contact with Schubert and made a collection of his songs in manuscript.

The two friends renewed their association in 1819, when Schubert and Vogl stayed in Steyr, and probably in 1823 and 1825. Stadler wrote occasional verses and also a few songs. In later years he became a local government officer in Salzburg, before retiring in 1876. His recollections of the composer are published in the *Memoirs*.

*July 1815:*
222  Lieb Minna
*March 1820:*
695  Namenstaglied
2 songs

**STOLBERG, Friedrich Leopold, Graf zu Stolberg-** (1750–1819). German poet. Born in Holstein as Danish subjects, Friedrich Stolberg and his brother Christian were educated at Halle and Göttingen, where they developed strongly liberal views and a liking for the new poetry of Klopstock and the Göttinger Hainbund. In 1775 they made a tour of Switzerland with Goethe and Bodmer. Stolberg held various diplomatic and administrative posts. After the death of his first wife in 1789 he turned increasingly to religion and abandoned the anti-authoritarian views of his youth. In 1800 he resigned all his official positions and he and his wife became Roman Catholics.

*1815:*
266  Morgenlied
276  Abendlied
372  An die Natur
*1816:*
144  Romanze
411  Daphne am Bach
412  Stimme der Liebe
416  Lied in der Abwesenheit
*1823*
774  Auf dem Wasser zu singen
788  Die Mutter Erde
9 songs

**STOLL, Josef Ludwig** (1778–1815). Journalist, of Vienna. He was the editor of the periodical *Prometheus*. The songs may have been occasioned by Stoll's death.

*October 1815:*
301  Lambertine
302  Labetrank der Liebe
303  An die Geliebte
3 songs

**STORCK, D. Adam.** A professor in Bremen who translated Scott's verse epic *The Lady of the Lake* into German (Essen, 1819). He was therefore the author of the German text of the five songs from that work which Schubert set in 1825: *Ellens Gesänge* (837, 838 and 839), the *Lied des gefangenen Jägers* (843), and *Normans Gesang* (846).

**SZÉCHÉNYI, Ludwig Count von** (1781–1855). Amateur poet and musician, born in Hungary. Széchényi became high steward to the Archduchess Sophie. He was a prominent member of the Philharmonic Society.

The songs were published at the end of 1821. They are sometimes attributed to 1817, but there is no substantial evidence to support so early a date. Széchényi was sufficiently well known and well to do to be a useful patron; it is more likely therefore that they belong to 1820 or early 1821.

*(?) 1821:*
514  Die abgeblühte Linde
515  Der Flug der Zeit
2 songs

**TIECK, Johann Ludwig** (1773–1853). German Romantic poet, novelist and critic. In the light of Tieck's importance to the Romantic movement it seems surprising that Schubert only once attempted to set a poem of his, and then never got beyond an unfinished sketch. Schwind, it is true, was enthusiastic about Tieck (as about much else), and the reading parties tried out a series of Tieck stories in 1828. But Tieck's influence was much stronger in the north than in Vienna. In 1825 Schober tried to interest Tieck in a production of *Alfonso und Estrella* at Dresden, but nothing came of it (*Docs.* no.575.)

*January 1819:*
645  Abend
1 song

**TIEDGE, Christoph August** (1752–1841). German philosophical poet. After an education at Halle and Magdeburg, he earned his living as a private tutor and private secretary until the turn of the century. In 1804 he accompanied the poetess Countess Elisa von der Recke on a tour of Italy, and from 1819 until her death he lived with her in Dresden. He was a prolific author, and his philosophical poem *Urania* was highly regarded in his day. The text of *An die Sonne* appeared in Becker's 'Pocketbook and Almanach of Sociable Pleasures' for 1795.

*August 1815:*
272  An die Sonne
1 song

**UHLAND, Johann Ludwig** (1787–1862). German Romantic poet, medievalist and philologist, of Tübingen. He read law, but developed an interest in ballads and folksong, and in medieval literature and mythology. He was appointed to a post in the government service in 1812, but finding government policy inconsistent with his liberal principles he resigned and set up his own practice at Stuttgart. His poems were published in 1815. In later years Uhland took an active part in political life, but he resigned in 1839 to devote himself to philological studies.

Uhland was an important influence on

younger Romantic poets. His *Wanderlieder* (1813) greatly impressed Wilhelm Müller, who followed his example with his own *Wanderlieder*.

Schubert's only Uhland setting is a favourite.

*September 1820:*
686  Frühlingsglaube
    1 song

**UZ, Johann Peter** (1720–96). German Anacreontic poet. He was a native of Ansbach and held various administrative posts there and in Nuremberg. His poetry reflects the rational complacent Christianity of the eighteenth century and celebrates the pleasures of life and love with amiable charm.

*June 1816:*
358  Die Nacht
363  An Chloen
446  Die Liebesgötter
448  Gott im Frühlinge
449  Der gute Hirt
    5 songs

**VITTORELLI, Jacopo Andrea** (1749–1835). Venetian author. Little is known about him. The two poems Schubert set were thought to be by Metastasio, but in recent years Vittorelli's authorship of them has been established by the Norwegian scholar Odd Udbye.

Vier Canzonen:
*January 1820:*
688 no.1  Non t'accostare all'urna
688 no.2  Guarda, che bianca luna
    2 songs

**WERNER, Friedrich Ludwig Zacharias** (1768–1823). German Romantic poet and dramatist, the son of a Königsberg professor. He graduated in law and held civil service posts until 1807, when he resigned and devoted himself to writing and travelling. He made his name with his historical dramas in the first decade of the century. His three marriages were dissolved. In 1810 he was received into the Catholic Church; three years later he was ordained. He became an honorary canon of St Stephen's, the cathedral church of Vienna.

*January 1817:*
521  Jagdlied
*(?) 1817:*
2 513A  Nur wer die Liebe kennt
*1820:*
685  Morgenlied
    3 songs

**WILLEMER, Marianne von** (1784–1860). German actress of uncertain origin who was a-dopted into the family of the Frankfurt banker J. J. Willemer as a girl of sixteen. In 1814, a few weeks before her marriage to Willemer, she met Goethe. A strong attraction grew up between them, and Goethe visited the couple several times in 1814 and 1815. She was the inspiration of the *Buch Suleika* in Goethe's *West-östlicher Divan*, and he actually incorporated some of her poems unacknowledged into that work. She is the real author of the two Suleika poems which Schubert set (717 and 720).

**WINKLER, Karl Gottfried** (1775–1856). German Romantic poet, journalist and publicist, of Dresden. He is better known by his pseudonym, Theodor Hell. Winkler was a prominent member of the Dresden circle of Romantic writers and artists. He earned his living first as an archivist and public official, then as secretary (later deputy director) of the Dresden Court Theatre. He was also active as a publisher and editor of journals, including the Dresden *Abendzeitung*.

Closely associated with Weber and Kind, he translated Camoens, Byron and Scribe, and made the German version of Weber's *Oberon*. He was also responsible for the libretto of *Die drei Pintos*.

*July 1816:*
456  Das Heimweh
    1 song

**ZETTLER, Alois** (1778–1828). Zettler, born in Moravia, went to Vienna in 1799 and became a teacher and then an official of the censorship department. His occasional poems appeared in various publications. They were collected and published in 1836.

*April 1815:*
D183  Trinklied
    1 song

# Addendum P.366

## ROMANZE Romance *(Der Vollmond strahlt)*
**Helmina von Chézy**
December 1823
F Minor D797 no.3b Peters I p.230

This famous aria from Schubert's incidental music for *Rosamunde* was a great success when it was sung by Emilie Neumann at the Theater an der Wien in December 1823, and it was published with piano accompaniment in March 1824. It has been a favourite recital number with contraltos ever since. As one of Schubert's most beautiful and evocative tunes it deserves at least an honorary mention in this book.

# *Appendices*

## I HOW MANY SCHUBERT SONGS?

How many songs did Schubert write? To this often-posed question there is no single authoritative and accepted answer. It is like asking: How many tall men are there in London? The answer depends on how you define your terms.

To begin at the beginning, this book is concerned with the songs for solo voice with piano accompaniment. But there is a long list of special cases and borderline cases, many of them ratified by past practice and hallowed by tradition. Here are some of them, with examples denoted by Deutsch numbers in brackets:

(a) Unfinished songs and sketches. There are too many of these to list, and they include some fine songs. Many have been edited and completed and published; some have been recorded.

(b) Song melodies with no title or text (1A, 311, 555, 916A).

(c) Lost songs which may — or may not — have once existed (204A, 863, 864, 990B, 990F).

(d) Duets with piano accompaniment, including solo songs which are sometimes sung as duets (282, 322, 542, 286, 352, 312, 877 no. 1, 126).

(e) Terzets with piano accompaniment (37, 277, 666, 441, 442, 930).

(f) Duets for unaccompanied voices or horns (199, 202, 203, 204, 205).

(g) Unaccompanied three-part songs and canons (147, and many contrapuntal exercises written as exercises for Salieri).

(h) Songs with accompaniment for piano and other instruments, or for instruments other than the piano (80, 81, 83, 482, 535, 943, 965).

(i) Songs for solo voice and chorus (148, 443, 387, 189, 822, 170, 492, 903, 183).

(j) Partsongs and choruses which were included in Series XX of the *Gesamtausgabe* (329A, 330, 377, 569, 643A).

Also included here may be some choruses masquerading as solo songs (234, 394).

(k) Arias and concerted numbers from the operas which have found their way into the songbooks arranged for piano accompaniment (239 nos. 3 and 6, 326 no. 12, 435 nos. 7 and 11, 647 no. 3, 732 nos. 12–16, 787 no. 2, 797 no. 3b).

Any attempt to make a tally of Schubert songs therefore involves finding one's way through a forest of special cases, and a consistent line is hard to draw. But there is a more serious source of confusion in the difficulty of distinguishing clearly between variants and new versions. In theory the distinction is plain enough. Nobody doubts that *Die Forelle* is one song, though at least five autographs survive, no two of which are exactly alike. Schubert was in the habit of writing out copies of favourite songs for his friends, usually from memory, and he did not hesitate to vary the details or the key when it suited his purpose or theirs. At the other end of the scale, there are two quite different versions of Goethe's *An den Mond* (259, 296); one is a quite ordinary and conventional setting in the eighteenth-century manner, and the other is a master-piece. But there is a grey area where the difference between variants and new versions is not so easy to define. The first two settings of *Der Jüngling am Bache* (30, 192) and *Nur wer die Sehnsucht kennt* (310 nos. 1 and 2) may fairly be regarded as variants, but the case of *Meeres Stille* (215A, 216) is more arguable, and what about *Der Taucher* (77, 111), which Deutsch listed as two songs, but which D2 regards as one? Are the six settings of *Geistes-Gruss* properly regarded as one song or six? Or perhaps two, since the last is substantially different from the first five? *Abends unter der Linde* (235, 237) is a genuine borderline case: the second setting, written two days after the first, is a clear reworking of the original idea, though the time-signature is different.

It is not to be wondered at, therefore, that the question, How many songs did Schubert write? receives as many different answers as there are experts. Series XX of the old *Gesamtausgabe*, completed in the 1890s, contains 603 songs. It included a number of songs which might more properly have been put elsewhere. Many songs have come to light since then. Reinhard van Hoorickx has listed 57 songs not included in the *Gesamtausgabe*, making a grand total of 660, but this takes in some lost songs, tunes without texts, and other dubious items. Maurice Brown (*Essays* p. 269) reached the even higher total of 708, but only by regarding all

published variants as separate songs.

In this book an attempt has been made to deal with the problem on a more conservative and rational basis. For the sake of completeness, many borderline cases are included or referred to in Part I — lost songs, operatic arias, choruses — which do not strictly speaking belong to the category of solo songs. In Part II, however, more strict criteria apply. The songs are listed and totalled under authors. Sketches and unfinished songs are included, but not lost songs, songs without text, operatic arias, partsongs or choruses and other doubtful starters. Versions are counted separately, but not variants. The grand total comes to 631, and the same criteria have been applied in the compilation of Appendix IV.

## II SCHUBERT'S TONALITIES

Schubert's instinctive awareness of the emotional colour of individual keys is an essential part of his genius for finding the best musical form for a particular text. No student of the songs can be unaware of the emotional potential in his hands of B minor or A minor, for instance; or, on the other hand, of the epic quality of C major or E flat. Any attempt to codify these emotional connotations, however, has to contend with the infinite variety of the songs and Schubert's indefatigable zest for experiment. He is famous for his freedom of modulation, justly so, but he is as likely, even in his mature years, to write a song like *Erstarrung*, which maintains the tonality of C minor for several pages, as one like *Todesmusik*, with six key changes in five pages. Many of his greatest and best known songs, like *An die Musik* or *Die Forelle*, are firmly rooted in a single key. Many more are based on a progressive

tonality of one kind or another; and again, the subtlety of his major/minor alternations seems to demand that a song like *Tränen-regen* should be regarded as in A major/A minor, rather than A major.

The keys quoted in the following lists adhere to those given in Part I, and normally agree with those quoted in the Thematic Catalogue. However, Schubert thought nothing of transposing his songs to suit individual singers, or the convenience of publishers. Moreover, the autograph, where it exists, and the first edition often differ in the key used. Not too much weight, therefore, should be attached to individual examples. The Deutsch number is quoted before each song.

Many episodic songs, with no obvious tonal unity, are omitted. Elsewhere the key given is the key in which the song begins, even in those cases where the tonality is progressive.

### I

C major is the key of clear morning (*Morgengruss*), of harmony with nature (*Meeresstille, Ständchen* 889), and sublimity (*Die Allmacht, Der entsühnte Orest*); it can also express the intoxication of first love, as in *Die erste Liebe* and *Will-kommen und Abschied*. Because C major represents normality and sanity, its anti-

thesis is the sinister or the intangible, and the contrast between the two is exploited with wonderful effect in *Dass sie hier gewesen*, which oscillates between an atonal chromaticism and C major, and *Am Meer*, where a similar tonal contrast symbolises th security of *Meeresstille* threatened by the bitterness of betrayal.

Logically enough, C minor stands for the sinister aspect of nature (*Der greise Kopf, Die Krähe*), or of people (*Der Jäger, Die Stadt*), or of the supernatural (*Der Geistertanz*), or infidelity (*Die Liebe hat gelogen*). *Gruppe aus dem Tartarus* is a special case, though the underlying tonality seems to be C minor rather than C major, in spite of the key signature.

## C MAJOR

957 (12) Am Meer
542 Antigone und Oedip
732 (13) Cavatine
623 Das Marienbild
775 Dass sie hier gewesen
588 Der Alpenjäger
699 Der entsühnte Orest
579 Der Knabe in der Wiege
514 Die abgeblühte Linde
852 Die Allmacht
563 Die Einsiedelei
182 Die erste Liebe
446 Die Liebesgötter
289 Die Sommernacht
413 Entzückung
455 Freude der Kinderjahre
808 Gondelfahrer
795 (3) Halt
902 (3) Il modo di prender ...
415 Klage (Die Sonne steigt)
298 Liane
508 Lebenslied

902 (1) L'Incanto degli occhi
215 (A) Meeres Stille (1)
216 Meeres Stille (2)
795 (8) Morgengruss
381 Morgenlied
752 Nachtviolen
392 Pflügerlied
165 Sängers Morgenlied (2)
170 Schwertlied
516 Sehnsucht (Mayrhofer)
35 (1) Serbato, O Dei custodi
630 Sonett III
889 Ständchen (Shakespeare)
274 Tischlerlied
234 Tischlied
888 Tischlied
287 Vaterlandslied
688 (1) Non t'accostare
261 Wer kauft Liebesgötter
767 Willkommen und Abschied
896 (B) Wolke und Quelle

## C MINOR

754 Aus 'Heliopolis' II
282 Cronnan
281 Das Mädchen von Inistore
15 Der Geistertanz (1)
116 Der Geistertanz (3)
911 (15) Die Krähe
795 (14) Der Jäger
638 Der Jüngling am Bache (3)
191 Des Mädchens Klage (2)
389 Des Mädchens Klage (3)
911 (14) Der greise Kopf
751 Die Liebe hat gelogen
957 (11) Die Stadt

445 Edone
911 (4) Erstarrung
454 Grablied für einen Soldaten
583 Gruppe aus dem Tartarus
957 (2) Kriegers Ahnung
830 Lied der Anne Lyle
846 Normans Gesang
467 Pflicht und Liebe
911 (10) Rast
121 Schäfers Klagelied
78 Son fra l'onde
595 Thekla (2)
260 Wonne der Wehmut

# II

D major is for Schubert important as a symphonic key. The songs in this key are comparatively few and, unusually, fewer than those in D minor, as well as including fewer masterpieces. *Im Dorfe* is a wonderfully assured and complex song both structurally and psychologically, and *Mein* represents a lyrical peak and a turning point in the earlier cycle. For the rest,

the great D major songs – *An die Musik, Der Blumenbrief, Marie, Fischerweise* – seem to be born not made, unblemished masterpieces of pure song.

The list of D minor songs, however, is full of powerful dramatic masterpieces, and there is hardly a negligible song among them. The basic idea seems to be man's courage and resolution in a struggle against fate (*An Schwager Krones, Lied des gefangenen Jägers*), the elements (*Der Strom, Über Wildemann*), conscience (*Der Kampf*) and death (*Der Tod und das Mädchen, Freiwilliges Versinken, Fahrt zum Hades*). The list also includes *Gretchen am Spinnrade*, and three of the finest songs of Romantic *Sehnsucht*, including Collin's *Wehmut*, perhaps the greatest of them all.

## D MAJOR

| | |
|---|---|
| 766 Am Flusse (2) | 351 Fischerlied |
| 905 An die Laute | 881 Fischerweise |
| 547 An die Musik | 911 (17) Im Dorfe |
| 411 Daphne am Bach | 909 Jägers Liebeslied |
| 174 Das war ich (2) | 239 (6) Liebe schwärmt ... |
| 926 Das Weinen | 273 Lilla an die Morgenröthe |
| 622 Der Blumenbrief | 711 Lob der Tränen |
| 932 Der Kreuzzug | 658 Marie |
| 794 Der Pilgrim | 795 (11) Mein |
| 149 Der Sänger | 687 Nachthymne |
| 694 Der Schiffer (Schlegel) | 76 Pensa che questo istante |
| 906 Der Vater mit dem Kind | 412 Stimme der Liebe (Stolberg) |
| 649 Der Wanderer (Schlegel) | |

## D MINOR

| | |
|---|---|
| 160 Am Flusse (1) | 911 (1) Gute Nacht |
| 369 An Schwager Kronos | 118 Gretchen am Spinnrade |
| 108 Der Abend | 728 Johanna Sebus |
| 490 Der Hirt | 843 Lied des gefangenen Jägers |
| 594 Der Kampf | 359 Nur wer die Sehnsucht kennt (2) |
| 367 Der König in Thule | 957 (4) Ständchen (Rellstab) |
| 256 Der Schatzgräber | 476 Rückweg |
| 565 Der Strom | 761 Schatzgräbers Begehr |
| 911 (18) Der stürmische Morgen | 52 Sehnsucht (1) (Schiller) |
| 531 Der Tod und das Mädchen | 879 Sehnsucht (Seidl) |
| 6 Des Mädchens Klage (1) | 884 Über Wildemann |
| 194 Die Mainacht | 772 Wehmut (Collin) |
| 466 Die Perle | 525 Wie Ulfru fischt |
| 526 Fahrt zum Hades | 492 Zum Punsche |
| 700 Freiwilliges Versunken | |

## III

The emotional associations of E major are with innocence and joy. *Seligkeit* and *An die Freude* are characteristic, but the uncomplicated happiness they represent is not to be confused with felicity, or with the contemplative joy of harmony with Nature and with God. The songs of innocence almost always confine themselves to E major, but there is also a philosophical dimension to this key, and in *Elysium, Im Walde, Grenzen der Menschheit* and *Rastlose Liebe* it is used as the basis for sustained and wide-ranging tonal adventures.

E minor symbolises sadness, depression (*Wasserflut, Tiefes Leid*) and nostalgia, but a psychological state rather than the philosophical concept of *Wehmut*. *Trockne Blumen*, which moves from minor to major, seems to cover the whole range of emotion from dejection to redemption.

## E MAJOR

241 Alles um Liebe
189 An die Freude
115 An Laura
943 Auf dem Strom
431 Blumenlied
627 Das Abendrot
442 Das grosse Halleluja
449 Der gute Hirt
911 (5) Der Lindenbaum
517 Der Schäfer und der Reiter
579 B Die Erde
229 Der Erscheinung
262 Die Fröhlichkeit
430 Die frühe Liebe
795 (20) Des Baches Wiegenlied
230 Die Täuschung
584 Elysium
434 Erntelied

607 Evangelium Johannis
857 Florio's Song ('Lacrimas')
233 Geist der Liebe
142 (6) Geistesgruss
716 Grenzen der Menschheit
240 Huldigung
708 Im Walde
483 Lied (Ferner von der grossen Stadt)
107 Lied aus der Ferne
549 Mahomets Gesang (1)
429 Minnelied
278 Ossians Lied nach der Falle Nathos
138 Rastlose Liebe
114 Romanze
443 Schlachtgesang
433 Seligkeit
410 Sprache der Liebe
501 Zufriedenheit (2)

## E MINOR

406 Abschied von der Harfe
911 (7) Auf dem Flusse
731 Der Blumen Schmerz
702 Der Jüngling auf dem Hügel
482 Der Sänger am Felsen
795 (18) Trockne Blumen
877 (2) Heiss mich nicht reden (2)

549 Herbst
902 (2) Il traditor deluso
957 (5) Aufenthalt
910 Schiffers Scheidelied
180 Sehnsucht der Liebe
876 Tiefes Leid
101 Totenopfer
911 (6) Wasserflut

## IV

F major is a pastoral key, often associated with evening, autumn, the stars, hope and consolation; also with sleep (*Schlaflied*), and the sleep of death (*Das Wirtshaus*).

The minor mode is used to express not so much a contrasted mood, as the same one more highly charged with feelings of regret, bitterness, or nostalgia; *Erster Verlust*, *Gefrorne Tränen*, and *Die junge Nonne*, for example.

## F MAJOR

382 Abendlied
495 Abendlied der Fürstin
856 Abendlied für die Entfernte
235 Abends unter der Linde (1)
237 Abends unter der Linde (2)
829 Abschied von der Erde
878 Am Fenster
283 An den Frühling
372 An die Natur
113 An Emma
99 Andenken
81 Auf den Sieg der Deutschen
297 Augenlied
155 Das Bild
309 Das gestörte Glück
456 Das Heimweh (Theodor Hell)

252 Das Mädchen aus der Fremde (2)
911 (21) Das Wirtshaus
524 Der Alpenjäger
560 Der Goldschmiedsgesell
30 Der Jüngling am Bache (1)
633 Der Schmetterling
805 Der Sieg
444 Die Gestirne
404 Die Herbstnacht
307 Die Sternenwelten
586 Erlafsee
562 Fischerlied (2)
896 Fröhliches Scheiden
520 Frohsinn
239 (3) Hin und wieder fliegen die Pfeile
295 Hoffnung (1) (Goethe)

521 Jagdlied
215 Jägers Abendlied (1)
436 Klage an den Mond
302 Labetrank der Liebe
266 Morgenlied
561 Nach einem Gewitter
551 Pax Vobiscum
17 (1) Quell' innocente figlio

527 Schlaflied
559 Schweizerlied
286 Selma und Selmar
187 Stimme der Liebe (1) (Matthisson)
533 Täglich zu singen
546 Trost im Liede
120 Trost in Tränen
304 Wiegenlied (Körner)

### F MINOR

193 An den Mond (Hölty)
458 Aus 'Diego Manazares'
15 (A) Der Geistertanz (2)
405 Der Herbstabend
192 Der Jüngling am Bache (2)
828 Die junge Nonne
409 Die verfehlte Stunde
778 (A) Die Wahlfahrt
226 Erster Verlust

911 (3) Gefrorne Tränen
831 Gesang der Norna
218 Grablied
317 Idens Schwanenlied
222 Lieb Minna
787 (2) Romanze
318 Schwangesang (Kosegarten)
842 Totengräbers Heimweh
228 Von Ida

## V

G major is an essentially lyrical key, associated with love (*Liebesbotschaft, Die Taubenpost, Liebesrausch*) and with serenity (*Im Frühling, Der Einsame*): the familiar right hand accompaniment figures of Romantic song, the running semiquavers and repeated chords in triplets, for instance, appear frequently in G major songs. But with Schubert, the shadow of mortality is always part of the light of joy; it is not surprising, therefore, that G major is also the tonality of *An die Nachtigall* (Claudius), *Die gefangenen Sänger*, and *Auflösung*.

G minor often expresses the fortitude of those whose lot is a battle against fate or the supernatural, *Erlkönig, Atlas, Amphiaraos, An Mignon*. Minor/major alternations play a special part in fine songs like *Beim Winde, Das Heimweh* (Pyrker), *Der Wandrer an den Mond*, and in the song cycles.

### G MAJOR

475 Abschied
153 Als ich sie erröten sah
344 Am ersten Maimorgen
363 An Chloen
765 An die Entfernte
303 An die Geliebte
497 An die Nachtigall (Claudius)
807 Auflösung
795 (4) Danksagung an den Bach
793 Das Geheimnis (2)
174 Das war ich (1)
291 Dem Unendlichen
800 Der Einsame
990 Der Graf von Habsburg
861 Der liebliche Stern
764 Der Musensohn
255 Der Rattenfänger
104 Die Befreier Europas
634 Die Berge
646 Die Gebüsche
712 Die gefangenen Sänger

522 Die Liebe
745 Die Rose
957 Die Taubenpost
866 (1) Die Unterscheidung
391 Die vier Weltalter
398 Frühlingslied
414 Geist der Liebe (Matthisson)
688 (2) Guarda, che bianca luna
257 Heidenröslein
502 Herbstlied
651 Himmelsfunken
882 Im Frühling
528 La Pastorella al Prato
395 Lebensmelodien
957 (1) Liebesbotschaft
352 Licht und Liebe
164 Liebesrausch (1)
179 Liebesrausch (2)
284 Lied (Es ist so angenehm)
503 Mailied
874 O Quell, was strömst du ...

163 Sängers Morgenlied (1)
123 Sehnsucht (Goethe)
507 Skolie
418 Stimme der Liebe (2)
73 Thekla (1)
758 Todesmusik

44 Totengräberlied
183 Trinklied
682 Über allen Zauber
855 Wiedersehn
795 (2) Wohin

## G MINOR

645 Abend
124 Am See (Mayrhofer)
122 Ammenlied
166 Amphiaraos
161 An Mignon
669 Beim Winde
957 (8) Der Atlas
795 (19) Der Müller und der Bach g/G
931 Der Wallensteiner
870 Der Wandrer an den Mond
911 (20) Der Wegweiser
785 Der zürnende Barde
534 Die Nacht
795 (15) Eifersucht und Stolz
923 Eine altschottische Ballade

33 (1) Entre l'uomo
328 Erlkönig
419 Julius An Theone
23 Klagelied
509 Leiden der Trennung
535 Lied
373 Lied (Mutter geht ...)
42 Misero pargoletto
911 (22) Mut
114 Romanze
911 (8) Rückblick
198 Seufzer
629 Sonett II
275 Totenkranz für ein Kind
632 Vom Mitleiden Mariae

# VI

The long list of songs in A major includes many of Schubert's most characteristic masterpieces, remarkable for their perfection of form and for complete equality of voice and keyboard: *An Sylvia, Der Jüngling an der Quelle, Ungeduld, Frühlingstraum, Die Nebensonnen, Dithyrambe*, and many others. It can be said that A major was the key which unlocked the essential Schubert, in that the sonata of 1819 in that key (D 664) was the first to marry concision with lyricism, and the 'Trout' Quintet in A màjor of the same year was the first to declare the seminal importance of the song in his instrumental work. Significantly, *An mein Klavier* is in the same key. The keyboard writing in songs like *Abendröte, An den Mond in einer Herbstnacht*, and *Das Lied im Grünen* often achieves a more pianistic quality than the sonatas.

A minor – the key of *Der Leiermann, Der Zwerg, Atys* and *Schöne Welt, wo bist du* – is firmly associated with disenchantment, alienation, and derangement. In this tonality Schubert wrote all the Harper's songs and many of Mignon's. It is also used to express the despair of unrequited love (*Du liebst mich nicht*), the remoteness of the stars (*Abendstern*), and ineluctable fate (*An mein Herz*).

Major/minor modulations have a special poignance in this tonality, e.g. *Tränenregen, Morgenlied.* Schubert often uses A major for his settings of playful, witty verses, e.g. *Liebhaber in allen Gestalten, Der Knabe, Die Vögel.*

## A MAJOR

276 Abendlied
690 Abendröte
904 Alinde
195 Amalia
587 An den Frühling (2)
468 An den Mond II (Hölty)
311 An den Mond
614 An den Mond in einer Herbstnacht
447 An den Schlaf

197 An die Apfelbäume
394 An die Harmonie
530 An eine Quelle
342 An mein Klavier
891 An Sylvia
151 Auf einen Kirchhof
917 Das Lied im Grünen
652 Das Mädchen
117 Das Mädchen aus der Fremde (1)

857 Delphine
515 Der Flug der Zeit
300 Der Jüngling an der Quelle
692 Der Knabe
141 Der Mondabend
213 Der Traum
742 Der Wachtelschlag
271 Der Weiberfreund
320 Der Zufriedene
795 (9) Des Müllers Blumen
393 Die Einsiedelei (1)
390 Die Entzückung an Laura
400 Die Knabenzeit
911 (23) Die Nebensonnen
50 Die Schatten

691 Die Vögel
801 Dithyrambe
911 (11) Frühlingstraum
552 Hänflings Liebeswerbung
662 Hymne IV
738 Im Haine
321 Kennst du das Land?
388 Laura am Klavier
698 Liebeslauschen
558 Liebhaber in allen Gestalten
822 Lied eines Kriegers
695 Namenstagslied
911 (19) Täuschung
362 Zufriedenheit

## A MINOR

650 Abendbilder
806 Abendstern
795 (5) Am Feierabend
654 An die Freunde
478 (3) An die Türen
860 An mein Herz
585 Atys
399 Auf den Tod einer Nachtigall (2)
631 Blanka
231 Das Sehnen
911 (24) Der Leiermann
771 Der Zwerg
933 Des Fischers Liebesglück
290 Die frühen Gräber
677 Die Götter Griechenlands

866 (3) Die Männer sind mechant
788 Die Mutter Erde
911 (2) Die Wetterfahne
770 Drang in die Ferne
756 Du liebst mich nicht
890 Hippolyts Lied
403 Ins stille Land
685 Morgenlied
481 Nur wer die Sehnsucht ... (3)
877 (4) Nur wer die Sehnsucht ... (4)
59 Verklärung
478 (2) Wer nie sein Brot ...
325 Wer sich der Einsamkeit ... (1)
478 (1) Wer sich der Einsamkeit ... (2)
401 Winterlied

# VII

E flat is indicative of awe and devotion. It may be awe in the presence of the sea (most of Schubert's 'on the water' songs are in E flat), or the stars, or the grave (*Ihr Grab, Litanei, Bei dem Grabe meines Vaters*), or of night (*In der Mitternacht*); it may also express pure devotion, as in *Du bist die Ruh* and the famous four-part setting of the 23rd Psalm. *An die Leier* and *Nachtstück* begin in C minor and move on to a solemn apostrophe in E flat. Other songs, *An die untergehende Sonne* and *Auf der Donau*, for instance, begin in E flat and move on to a rhapsodic climax. E flat also has epic connotations, especially in a mythical or historical context. Examples are *Ellens Gesang* II, *Ritter Toggenburg* and *Dido Abbandonata*.

## E FLAT MAJOR

957 (7) Abschied
746 Am See (Bruchmann)
116 An den Mond (1) (Goethe)
737 An die Leyer
272 An die Sonne (Tiedge)
457 An die untergehende Sonne
543 Auf dem See (Goethe)
553 Auf der Donau
496 Bei dem Grabe meines Vaters

263 Cora an die Sonne
350 Der Entfernten
254 Der Gott und die Bajadere
264 Der Morgenkuss
536 Der Schiffer (Mayrhofer)
510 Dido Abbandonata
911 (13) Die Post
939 Die Sterne (Leitner)
684 Die Sterne (F. Schlegel)

776 Du bist die Ruh
838 Ellens Gesang II
100 Geisternähe
955 Glaube, Hoffnung, und Liebe
322 Hermann und Thusnelda
463 Hochzeitslied
736 Ihr Grab
880 Im Freien

464 In der Mitternacht
301 Lambertine
911 (16) Letzte Hoffnung
206 Liebeständelei
343 Litanei auf das Fest aller Seelen
314 Nachtgesang
397 Ritter Toggenburg

## E FLAT MINOR

504 Am Grabe Anselmos
653 Bertas Lied in der Nacht

626 Blondel zu Marien
694 A Klage um Ali Bey

# VIII

It may be significant that the two songs Schubert wrote as concert pieces for Anna Milder, *Suleika* II and *Der Hirt auf dem Felsen*, are both in B flat. For while it is difficult to discover any consistent emotional tone in the songs in this key, they do exhibit a sort of rhythmic virtuosity. In content they range from the intensely poetic 'Ave Maria' and 'Über allen Gipfeln ist Ruh' to lighthearted spring songs and drinking songs. Schubert's mastery of movement, however, is everywhere apparent, and the rhythmical range is impressive, from songs which proceed from a single unchecked impetus (*Die Blumensprache, Frühlingssehnsucht, Im Walde, Das Wandern*) to those which suggest hesitation, or contemplation, or diffidence, like *Pause, Der blinde Knabe, Das Echo* and *Um Mitternacht*.

## B FLAT MAJOR

499 Abendlied (Claudius)
265 Abendständchen
258 Bundeslied
688 (3) Da quel sembiante
868/990 (C) Das Echo
219 Das Finden
795 (1) Das Wandern
833 Der blinde Knabe
225 Der Fischer (Goethe)
402 Der Flüchtling
965 Der Hirt auf dem Felsen
207 Der Liebende
938 Der Winterabend
832 Des Sängers Habe
519 Die Blumensprache
159 Die Erwartung
210 Die Liebe (Goethe)
673 Die Liebende schreibt
308 Die Macht der Liebe
313 Die Sterne (Kosegarten)
838 Ellens Gesang III
98 Erinnerung (Matthisson)
957 (3) Frühlingssehnsucht
171 Gebet während der Schlacht

491 Geheimnis (Mayrhofer)
922 Heimliches Lieben
637 Hoffnung (Schiller) (2)
227 Idens Nachtgesang
990 (A) Kaiser Maximilian
883 Lebensmut (Schulze)
937 Lebensmut (Rellstab)
109 Lied der Liebe
596 Lied eines Kindes
248 Lob der Tokayers
305 Mein Gruss an den Mai
795 (13) Mit dem grünen Lautenbande
188 Naturgenuss
795 (12) Pause
674 Prometheus
253 Punschlied
741 Sei mir gegrüsst
896 (A) Sie in jedem Liede
306 Skolie
628 Sonett I
717 Suleika II
862 Um Mitternacht
768 Wandrers Nachtlied II
639 Wiederschein

B FLAT MINOR

663  Der 13 Psalm
564  Gretchens Bitte
660  Hymne II
661  Hymne III

957 (9)  Ihr Bild
834  Im Walde (Schulze)
319  Luisens Antwort
688 (4)  Mio ben ricordati

## IX

Significantly, there are no songs in A flat major in either of the two major song cycles, and only one (*Das Fischermädchen*) among the Heine and Rellstab sets. The key is associated with secret happiness and private joy, and with a secure and reciprocated love. Typical are Kosegarten's Rosa songs, of which the best is perhaps *Das Rosenband*, Goethe's *Ganymede* and *Geheimes*, and Rückert's *Lachen und Weinen*. By extension, A flat also expresses

faith in the power of Nature to revive and renew, as in *Frühlingsglaube*, *Im Abendrot*, and *Lied an die Dioskuren*; and the masterly second setting of Goethe's *An den Mond* almost matches the subtlety and complexity of that great poem.

Two fine songs, notated in A flat, are really poised halfway between major and minor, *Auf dem Wasser zu singen* and *Schwanengesang* (Senn).

### A FLAT MAJOR

95  Adelaide
462  An Chloen
296  An den Mond (2) (Goethe)
315  An Rosa I
316  An Rosa II
288  An Sie
853  Auf der Brücke
866 (2)  Bei dir allein
957 (10)  Das Fischermädchen
250  Das Geheimnis (1)
532  Das Lied vom Reifen
280  Das Rosenband
871  Das Zugenglöcklein
707  Der zürnenden Diana
214  Die Laube
358  Die Nacht (Uz)
208  Die Nonne
186  Die Sterbende
450  Fragment aus dem Aeschylus

686  Frühlingsglaube
919  Frühlingslied
854  Fülle der Liebe
285  Furcht der Geliebten
544  Ganymede
719  Geheimes
799  Im Abendrot
777  Lachen und Weinen
360  Lied eines Schiffers an die Dioskuren
119  Nachtgesang (Goethe)
513 (A)  Nur wer die Liebe kennt
743  Selige Welt
469  So lasst mich scheinen (1)
465  Trauer der Liebe
715  Versunken
786  Viola
498  Wiegenlied (Anon)
867  Wiegenlied (Seidl)

### A FLAT MAJOR/MINOR

774  Auf dem Wasser zu singen

744  Schwanengesang (Senn)

## X

B minor and B major stand at the ambivalent centre of Schubert's emotional world. Together they represent what may be called the passion (in every sense of that word) inherent in the human condition: physical and mental suffering (*Der Leidende*, *Philoktet*), loneliness (*Einsamkeit*), alienation and derangement (*Der Doppelgänger*, *Die liebe Farbe*) – these

are all aspects of the minor mode, more common in Schubert than the major. On the reverse side of the medal, B major stands for erotic feeling in *Suleika* I, angry resentment against the nature of things in *Die böse Farbe*, Romantic obsession with night and with dreams, and death and transfiguration (*An den Tod*, *So lasst mich scheinen*). Many songs associated with the idea of death move towards a climax in B major, as in *Grablied für die Mutter*, *Vor meiner Wiege*, and *An die untergehende*

*Sonne*, signifying a kind of apotheosis of 'das mildre Land'.

### B MAJOR

| | |
|---|---|
| 477 Alte Liebe | 795 (6) Der Neugierige |
| 539 Am Strome | 102 Die Betende |
| 518 An den Tod | 795 (17) Die böse Farbe |
| 221 Der Abend | 827 Nacht und Träume |
| 693 Der Fluss | 877 (3) So lasst mich scheinen (3) |

### B MINOR

| | |
|---|---|
| 578 Abschied von einem Freunde | 911 (9) Irrlicht |
| 957 (3) Der Doppelgänger | 371 Klage (Trauer umfliesst mein Leben) |
| 432 Der Leidende | 416 Lied in der Abwesenheit |
| 713 Der Unglückliche | 877 (1) Nur wer die Sehnsucht kennt |
| 795 (16) Die liebe Farbe | 540 Philoktet |
| 247 Die Spinnerin | 907 Romanze des Richard Löwenherz |
| 911 (12) Einsamkeit | 636 Sehnsucht (Schiller) (2) |
| 616 Grablied für die Mutter | 727 So lasst mich scheinen (2) |
| 778 Greisengesang | 720 Suleika I |
| 726 Heiss mich nicht reden (1) | 729 Vor meiner Wiege |
| 957 (6) In der Ferne | |

## XI

F sharp is a Romantic key, conveying in Hölty's *An die Nachtigall* and in the first version of *Auf den Tod einer Nachtigall* a rapturous sense of the existential moment. Schubert's only song in F sharp major, *Die Mondnacht*, is an astonishingly predictive,

quasi-late Romantic song expressing a feeling of harmony with the beloved. The visionary *Schwestergruss* moves from minor to major and back again, and so does *Totengräberweise*.

### F SHARP MAJOR

238 Die Mondnacht

### F SHARP MINOR

| | |
|---|---|
| 196 An die Nachtigall (Hölty) | 762 Schwestergruss |
| 201 Auf den Tod einer Nachtigall (1) | 869 Totengräberweise |
| 789 Pilgerweise | |

## XII

C sharp minor is an important key, for it is the home of the 'Wanderer' theme; but it is not a lyrical key, and is normally used as a contrast to the relative major, E. *Genugsamkeit*, it is true, may be said to

be 'in' C sharp minor, though it ends in E. *Der Wanderer* moves after a wonderful introduction to E major, and *Der Jüngling und der Tod* moves on to D and finally to F.

### C SHARP MINOR

| | |
|---|---|
| 545 Der Jüngling und der Tod | 143 Genugsamkeit |
| 489 Der Wanderer | 721 Mahomets Gesang (2) |

## XIII

Two great songs in G flat major express a profound sense of peace and harmony with nature (*Wandrers Nachtlied* I) and with the beloved (*Nähe des Geliebten*), while Körner's *Der Morgenstern* strikes much the same note of contemplative joy.

### G FLAT

172  Der Morgenstern
251  Hoffnung (1) (Schiller)
573  Iphigenia
474  Lied des Orpheus

162  Nähe des Geliebten
500  Phidile
224  Wandrers Nachtlied I

## XIV

The emotional tone of D flat seems to be contemplative and introspective, but no very consistent thread can be detected in the few songs Schubert wrote in this key. There is an epic quality in *Memnon*, and also in Ellen's first song. *Die Forelle* we are so used to hearing in the bright key of D – in the Piano Quintet – that it is difficult to associate it with D flat.

### D FLAT

361  Am Bach im Frühling
550  Die Forelle
670  Die Sternennächte

837  Ellens Gesang I
368  Jägers Abendlied
541  Memnon

# III THEMATIC AND STYLISTIC LINKS BETWEEN THE SONGS AND THE INSTRUMENTAL WORKS

To say that Schubert's genius was essentially lyrical is not to belittle his achievement as an instrumental composer, but to define it. The great instrumental works of his middle and late years, from the 'Trout' Quintet on to the String Quintet of 1828, are dependent upon his earlier success as a songwriter, not merely in the obvious sense that most of them openly exploit the popularity of individual songs like *Der Wanderer, Die Forelle, Der Tod und das Mädchen,* and others; but also because they adapt the expressive freedom and 'inwardness' of Romantic song to the formal patterns of instrumental music in such a way that, as Schwind put it, these instrumental works 'stay in the mind, as songs do, fully sensuous and expressive' (Docs. no.443).

It is not surprising therefore that the thematic and stylistic links between songs and instrumental works are many and varied, and difficult to categorise. Only a full-scale study of the development of Schubert's musical idiom would do justice to the complexity of the subject. To take a single instance, the opening bars of his very first complete song, *Hagars Klage,* are based on a tonal sequence familiar from baroque music (the so-called 'Lamento topos'), which reappears not only in other songs, but in several instrumental works of his boyhood, including D8, D9, D24D, D46, D48. This seminal motif, which provides the thematic source for much of his fourth symphony (the 'Tragic'), also serves as the prototype for many of his songs of Sehnsucht and death. It consists essentially of a tonal descent from tonic minor to dominant major, based upon a firm chromatically descending bass line, a figure which Schubert raised to the level of great art in songs like *Wehmut* (Collin), *Nachtstück, Der Jüngling und der Tod, Die Liebe hat gelogen,* in the famous 'Wanderer' theme, and in many of the great songs and instrumental works of his last years.

The fact that these motivic cross-references may be for the most part entire[

sub-conscious only gives them added significance for the student of Schubert's musical language. On the other hand, many apparently deliberate self-borrowings and self-quotations are of incidental interest only. It really does not matter very much that Schubert used the tune of *Hänflings Liebeswerbung* as the third of his three *Deutsche* (D972), or that in the setting of Schiller's *Elysium* he 'quotes' the concluding bars from the first movement of his Piano Sonata in E major of August 1816. It is true that these self-borrowings may sometimes suggest an unconscious association of ideas. It seems significant, for instance, that the tune of *Täuschung* in *Winterreise* is borrowed from a scene in Schubert's opera *Alfonso und Estrella*, for both the song and the dramatic scene tell a tale of bewitchment. But in general a characteristic turn of phrase, a tonal sequence or an ostinato rhythm may tell us more about the emotional provenance of the great instrumental works than the conscious cross-references. In the Octet the implied allusions to 'Schöne Welt, wo bist du?' in the last movement are more significant than the fact that the variation movement is based on a tune from *Die Freunde von Salamanka*. It is the association with Schiller's words which counts in the former example; in the contemporary A minor String Quartet, the same phrase sets the emotional tone for the whole work.

These extra-musical clues to the emotional climate of Schubert's work can be found in most of the works of his maturity. Even in his last quartet, the Quartet in G major of 1826, they are not altogether absent, as is sometimes supposed. There are unmistakable echoes of *Winterreise* in the elegiac Andante, while the affinity with the Schulze songs is evident in the driving rhythms and in the tonal ambivalence of the outer movements. As for the 'Unfinished' Symphony, often regarded as an isolated peak unrelated to contemporary works, its psychological background is vividly illuminated by *Suleika I*, which reproduces several of its salient features, including the tonality and the ostinato rhythm, and *Der Zwerg*, in which the pianist's right-hand semiquaver movement is even closer to the symphony's first movement. The fact that Goethe's text, and Collin's, both deal with sexual obsession at least throws an interesting

light on the emotional world from which this great work emerged.

These latent affinities between the songs and the instrumental works are of special interest when they link works which are strictly contemporary. Some of the rhythmic and melodic features of the D major Piano Sonata, written at Gastein in August 1825, for instance, are reproduced in *Fülle der Liebe* (August 1825) and *Wiedersehn* (September 1825). More significantly perhaps, the sinuous unison theme which meanders through the first movement of the A minor Piano Sonata of May 1825, and appears to dominate its conclusion, is clearly related to a passage in the setting of Craigher's *Totengräbers Heimweh*. Since the song was written in the April of 1825, the self-quotation in the sonata can hardly be anything but a conscious recollection.

There are close thematic and stylistic links also between the songs and the piano works of Schubert's last years, though these are no more, generally speaking, than a recurrence of rhythmic patterns and turns of phrase. The four Impromptus opus 90 and the Moments Musicaux opus 94, in particular, are particularly rich in such allusions. Opus 90 no.1 in C minor is a kind of keyboard paraphrase of *Der Wegweiser*. No.3 closely resembles the middle (B major) section of *Vor meiner Wiege*. The sombre tone and repeated chords of the Trio of no.4 recall the middle section of *Kriegers Ahnung*. Opus 94 no.5 is a keyboard study based on the familiar gait of Leitner's *Die Sterne* – crotchet followed by two quavers. Again, the fact that all these songs seem to be concerned in one way or another with the prospect of death throws an interesting light on Schubert's state of mind during these final years.

Finally, no student of the last three piano sonatas can fail to recognise their lyrical allusiveness. The Andantino of the A major Sonata is a near relation of *Pilgerweise* (cf. the F sharp minor section of Opus 94 no.2). The Rondo Finale of the same work pays its tribute to *Im Frühling*. The resemblance between the long opening theme of the B flat Sonata and the tune of Mignon's song, *So lasst mich scheinen* (second setting, D727) has been noted by Einstein. But this seems less significant than the Schubertian fingerprints; the ominous bass trills, for instance, which look back to *Auf der Donau* and *Orpheus* and *Gebet während der Schlacht*, and the heart-easing cadence which makes so large a contribution to the poetry of this first movement (see, for instance, I 74–101, 301–29), and which is anticipated in the melodrama *Abschied von der Erde* (D 829, February 1826).

Given the complexity of the relationship between Schubert's songs and his instru-mental works, and the subjective element involved in the perception of stylistic resemblances, no schematic treatment of thematic cross-references can hope to be comprehensive. The following list includes some of the more obvious instances, and may serve at least as a basis for discussion, amendment and extension. No attempt is made to assess the significance of individual examples.

*Abschied von der Erde* Bars 9, 14, 29. Cf. similar cadences in opening Molto moderato of B flat Piano Sonata (960).

*An den Mond in einer Herbstnacht* Last four bars. Cf. main theme of Andante of A minor Piano Sonata (784) of 1823.

*Abendstern* One of several songs (cf. *Du liebst mich nicht, Suleika I, Der Zwerg*) based on a distinctive *Bewegung* – in 3/4 time – which Schubert used orchestrally in the 'Unfinished' Symphony.

*Auf der Donau* The doom-laden bass trills, and the chromatically descending bass line in the final bars, foreshadow the B flat Piano Sonata (960) and the Trio of the String Quintet.

*Aus Heliopolis I* The key, the pace, and the gait foreshadow the first movement of the A minor Piano Sonata (845) of 1825, and the Andante con moto of the 'Great' C major.

*Aus Heliopolis II* The relentless drive, and in particular the C major climax, anticipate the finale of the 'Great' C major.

*Bertas Lied in der Nacht* For the sinuous unison line at the beginning (indicative of loneliness and anxiety?), compare the A minor Piano Sonata (845) and the Trio of the String Quintet.

*Das Heimweh* (Pyrker) The G major section, marked *Geschwind*, echoes the Trio of the 'Great' C major Symphony.

*Der Doppelgänger* The motivic cell closely resembles the opening of the Agnus Dei of the E flat Mass of 1828.

*Der Leidende* (432) The tune of the first version is used in a section (Minore II) of the B flat Entre-Act (no.5) of the 'Rosamunde' music.

*Der Tod und das Mädchen* The second half was adapted and extended for use as the theme of the variation movement of the D minor String Quartet of 1824.

*Der Unglückliche* The atmospheric accompaniment echoes the Andante of the A major Piano Sonata at bar 12, and vaguely foreshadows the D major Sonata of August 1825.

*Der Wanderer* (Schmidt) The 'Wanderer theme' itself (bars 23–30) is derived from earlier variations on the 'Lamento' topos, and appears in various forms in many other songs and works expressive of Romantic *Sehnsucht*. It provides the thematic cell on which the 'Wanderer' Fantasie (760) is constructed.

*Der Wegweiser* The gait and melodic shape are identical with those of the first Impromptu opus 90 no.1.

*Der Zwerg* Apart from the change of tempo, the pianist's right-hand semi-quaver movement is identical with that of the (contemporary) 'Unfinished' Symphony at bar 9 of the opening Allegro moderato.

*Des Sängers Habe* The triplet movement in the accompaniment in bar 4 is strongly suggestive of the opening movement of the B flat Piano Trio (898).

*Die Betende* Thirteen years after this song was composed Schubert borrowed the tune for the sketch of Suleika's aria – no.10 (c) in *Der Graf von Gleichen* (918).

*Die Forelle* The tune was used as the theme of the variation movement of the Piano Quintet in A major (the 'Trout') of 1819.

*Die Götter Griechenlands* The setting of a verse from this Schiller poem – 'Schöne Welt, wo bist du ...' – was to become the text for Schubert's A minor String Quartet of 1824. It is quoted in the opening movement and in the Menuetto and sets the tone of wistful disenchantment for the work. There are also allusions to the theme in the last movement of the Octet in F.

*Die Freunde von Salamanka* The duet ('Gelagert unterm hellen Dach') from Act II of this Singspiel is used as the theme for the variation movement of the Octet.

*Die Mutter Erde* Bars 18–22 recall the Andante of the Piano Sonata in A of 1819.

*Die Sterne* (Leitner) The brisk dactylic rhythm dominates also the contemporary F minor Moment Musical, no.5 of Opus 94.

*Du liebst mich nicht* The plodding rhythm (cf. *Suleika I* and *Der Zwerg*, both also written shortly before the 'Unfinished' Symphony) suggests that this characteristic movement, with its opportunities for displaced accents, had erotic associations for Schubert. *Abendstern* and *Fülle der Liebe* have a similar gait.

*Einsamkeit* (Müller) There is a vague affinity between this song and the Andante un poco mosso of the¦ G major String Quartet, written shortly before. It can be traced in the slow four-in-a-bar pace (cf. the beginning of the middle section of the quartet movement), in the disruptive character of the middle section of both, and in the prevailing tone of stoical suffering and isolation.

*Elysium* Bars 31–3 are identical with the closing bars of the first movement of the E major Piano Sonata (D459) of August 1816.

*Fierabras* Schubert adapted the tune of the opening chorus of Act III in the second (E flat major) of his *Drei Klavierstücke* of 1828.

*Fülle der Liebe* There are unmistakable affinities between this song and the Andante con moto of the contemporary Piano Sonata in D major. Both were written in August 1825.

*Geist der Liebe* (Matthisson) The tune is used a few weeks later in the Romanze (no.7) of Schubert's incomplete opera *Die Bürgschaft*.

*Gute Nacht* The characteristic pacing rhythm (*In gehender Bewegung*) of this song is strongly felt in the Andante con moto of the second Piano Trio in E flat.

*Hagars Klage* The opening bars present a seminal motif which recurs in many contemporary instrumental works, and was later to become the thematic cell on which the fourth symphony (the 'Tragic') was largely based.

*Hänflings Liebeswerbung* The tune was used again in the third of *Drei Deutsche* (972).

*Hektors Abschied* The key, the tempo, and the opening phrase of this early song strangely foreshadow the main theme of the duet Fantasie in F minor of 1828.

*Ihr Bild* The spare unison descent from tonic minor to dominant major, and bars 6 and 7 in particular, anticipate the Schubert of the B flat Piano Sonata and the String Quintet.

*Im Frühling* Foreshadows the theme of the Rondo Finale of the Piano Sonata in A major (959).

*Klaglied* (Rochlitz) At bars 9–12 there is a curious but fortuitous anticipation of a sequence from the Andante of the B flat major Piano Trio.

*Pilgerweise* Cf. the Andantino of the Piano Sonata in A major (959).

*Schwanengesang* (Senn) Inhabits the same tonal country as the Impromptus Opus 142, Opus 90 no.4, and no.2 of the Moments Musicaux – A flat major and minor, C flat major/minor and D flat major/minor.

*Schwestergruss* The repeated quaver octaves in the tonality of F sharp minor/major, and the modulation to C sharp major towards the end, recall similar procedures in the first two movements of the B flat Piano Sonata (960).

*Sei mir gegrüsst* The tune is adapted to serve as the theme for a set of variations in the Andantino section of the Fantasie in C major for violin and piano, Opus 159.

*So lasst mich scheinen* (2) (727) Einstein points to the resemblance between the melodic shape of the singer's first phrase and the main theme of the opening Molto moderato of the last piano sonata, in B flat.

*Suleika I* The rhythmic affinity with the first movement of the 'Unfinished' Symphony has often been noticed. There is, however, a much closer link with the fragmentary Fantasie in C (D 605) for piano (probably dating from the summer of 1822).

*Täuschung* The tune is borrowed from the opening scene of Act II of *Alfonso und Estrella*, the section in B major.

*Todesmusik* The lay-out of the piano accompaniment in the B flat major section, with its repeated triplet chords, is strongly reminiscent of the opening move movement of the B flat Piano Trio Opus 99.

*Totengräbers Heimweh* The words 'Abandoned by all, cousin only to death, I wait on the brink with a cross in my hand, staring into the deep grave' are sung to a long-drawn unison phrase which plays an important part in the A minor Piano Sonata (845), written a few weeks later.

*Trockne Blumen* The tune is used as the theme for a set of variations for flute and piano (802) written in January 1824.

*Vor meiner Wiege* The middle (B major) section has the Chopinesque quality of the Impromptu in G flat, Opus 90 no.3.

*Wonne der Wehmut* The song shows a certain affinity with the Andante of the unfinished Sonata in C (the 'Reliquie') of 1825.

# IV THE SOLO SONGS: THE CREATIVE PATTERN

The following table shows the approximate number of songs composed month by month during Schubert's creative lifetime. The operative word is 'approximate': no authority or finality attaches to the individual figures, because many songs cannot be certainly dated within months, and quite a few cannot be assigned with confidence to any one year. In such cases I have simply made an informed guess. The composition of the song cycles, and possibly of other important works, stretched over several months; the date of the fair copy is not the date of composition, and it is quite impossible to assign dates to the individual songs. None the less, the vast majority of Schubert songs can be dated with reasonable confidence; and provided the figures are used with proper caution, interesting conclusions can be drawn from them.

The obvious one is that Schubert's creative energies fell into a regular seasonal pattern. Song-writing tended to be concentrated in the spring and autumn months, with peaks in March and October, while the summer months were more often devoted to large-scale orchestral and

| | Jan. | Feb. | March | April | May | June | July | Aug. | Sept. | Oct. | Nov. | Dec. | **Totals** |
|---|---|---|---|---|---|---|---|---|---|---|---|---|---|
| 1810 | | | | | | | | | | 1 | | | **1** |
| 1811 | | 1 | | | | | | | 2 | | 1 | | **4** |
| 1812 | | 1 | | | | | | | 4 | 2 | | | **7** |
| 1813 | 1 | | | 2 | 1 | | | 1 | 5 | 2 | | | **12** |
| 1814 | | | | 4 | 1 | | 3 | | 4 | 5 | 3 | 4 | **24** |
| 1815 | 2 | 10 | 6 | 7 | 17 | 10 | 17 | 28 | 14 | 24 | 3 | 4 | **142** |
| 1816 | 5 | 6 | 16 | 13 | 12 | 11 | 5 | 9 | 15 | 4 | 12 | 4 | **112** |
| 1817 | 11 | 6 | 14 | 7 | 9 | 1 | 1 | 2 | 7 | 4 | 3 | | **65** |
| 1818 | | | 1 | 2 | | 2 | | 2 | 1 | | 4 | 4 | **17** |
| 1819 | 2 | 7 | 1 | 1 | 4 | 1 | | | | 9 | 1 | | **26** |
| 1820 | 7 | 1 | 7 | 1 | | | | | | 1 | 1 | 2 | **20** |
| 1821 | 5 | 1 | 4 | 3 | | | | | 2 | | | | **15** |
| 1822 | 3 | | 1 | 4 | | | 2 | | | 4 | 9 | 10 | **33** |
| 1823 | 1 | | 4 | 1 | 3 | | | | | 10 | 10 | | **29** |
| 1824 | | | 4 | | | 1 | | | | | | 1 | **6** |
| 1825 | 4 | 2 | 2 | 7 | | | | 3 | 4 | | | 3 | **25** |
| 1826 | 4 | 1 | 15 | | | | 4 | | | | | | **24** |
| 1827 | 3 | 14 | | 1 | 3 | 1 | | | 2 | 12 | 10 | | **46** |
| 1828 | | 6 | 5 | 9 | | | | 1 | | 2 | | | **23** |
| **Totals** | **48** | **54** | **82** | **62** | **50** | **27** | **32** | **46** | **60** | **80** | **56** | **34** | **631** |

chamber works, or operas in his middle years. 1815 and, to a lesser extent, 1816 are exceptions to this pattern: in these astonishingly prolific years Schubert seemed to find song-writing as necessary as breathing. But the annual cycle of creativity is plain enough in other years, and its statistical basis would be even more pronounced if the years 1815 and 1816 were excluded.

The career pattern is also interesting. The thinnest years from the point of view of song production are the Zseliz years 1818 and 1824, and the 'opera years' 1820 and 1821. The reasons are obvious enough. The revival of song-writing activity in the autumn and winter of 1822 may have something to do with Schubert's illness and his consequent withdrawal from the social limelight. Schubert's decision to concentrate on traditional forms in 1824 and so 'pave the way for grand symphony' is reflected in the meagre song output of that year, and his preoccupation with the song cycle is reflected in the later figures. Without the songs of Müller, Heine and Rellstab, the years 1823, 1827 and 1828 would look very different.

# V SCHUBERT'S POETIC PROGRESS: THE CYCLICAL METHOD OF COMPOSITION

Such was Schubert's appetite for a good song-text, and so quick was his response to poetry, that once he had discovered a poet whose work kindled the creative spark he liked to go on setting one poem after another until the urge was, for the time being at least, satisfied. Then, more often than not, he would move on to find his inspiration elsewhere. It is thus possible, with a certain amount of selection and simplification, to represent his development as a succession of poetic phases, each one dominated by the work of one particular poet.

Of course, it is not quite as simple as that. In his early days, at any rate, he often used a variety of texts from different authors, though they may all have been culled from one anthology. On 25 August 1815, for instance, he appears to have set texts by Baumberg, Ratschky, Tiedge, an unknown author and Matthisson. But this is exceptional. Even in this most prolific years he preferred to work with one poet at a time. The pattern is further complicated by the fact that he returned again and again to the men of real stature – to Goethe, Schiller, Mayrhofer – although in such cases also he would return with a new onset of enthusiasm which would result in a group of four or five new songs. The lesser lights, Matthisson, Kosegarten and Jacobi for instance, he simply grew out of.

This cyclical method of composition is a recognition of the fact that Schubert's literary sensibility led him not simply to a poem but usually to a poet. He needed to find the right tone and style not just for a set of verses, but for each individual author. Indeed, he had a style for each poet, so that it is perfectly possible to discuss the stylistic characteristics of the Scott songs, the Heine songs, the Müller songs and so on, and to distinguish one from the other.

What follows is an attempt to isolate these successive creative phases and present them in a chronological sequence. Only those poets who played a significant part in Schubert's development are included; but although they are comparatively few – not many more than a quarter of the 115 poets represented in Schochow's comprehensive book on the song-texts – they account for more than half of the songs. The selection is not simply a matter of numbers, however; Matthäus von Collin, for instance, with three songs, is really more important than Kosegarten with twenty, because he inspired three of the greatest and most Romantic songs in the critical Schubert year of 1822. Even Platen, with only two songs, deserves to be included, though Fouqué, with five, is not. Deutsch numbers are given, but the implied dates are by no means always certain.

|  | *Author* | *Deutsch nos.* |
|---|---|---|
| *1811–13:* | Schiller | 6, 7, 30, 52, 73, 77 |
| *1814:* | | |
| April–Oct. | Matthisson | 95, 97–102, 107–9, 114–16 |
| *1814/15:* | | |
| Oct.–Feb. | Goethe | 118–21, 123, 126, 149, 160–2 |
| *1815:* | | |
| Feb.–May | Körner | 163–6, 170–2, 174, 179, 180, 206 |
| May–June | Hölty | 193, 194, 196–8, 201, 207, 208, 213, 214 |
| May–Oct. | Schiller | 189, 191, 192, 195, 246, 250–3, 283, 284, 312 |
| May–Aug. | Goethe | 138, 142, 210, 215, 215A, 216, 224–6, 234, 254–61, 247 |
| June–Oct. | Kosegarten | 219, 221, 227–31, 233, 235, 237, 238, 240, 241, 313–19 |
| August | Baumberg | 248, 263–5, 270 |
| Sept.–Oct. | Klopstock | 280, 285–91, 322 |
| *1815/16:* | | |
| June–Feb. | Ossian | 150, 217, 278, 281, 282, 293, 327, 375, 376 |
| *1816:* | | |
| Jan.–April | Stolberg | 144, 372, 411, 412, 416 |
| Feb. | Goethe | 367–9 |
| March | Salis-Seewis | 350, 351, 392–4, 403–6 |
| March–May | Schiller | 159, 388–91, 396, 397, 402 |
| March–April | A. W. von Schlegel | 395, 409, 410 |
| April | Matthisson | 413–15, 418 |
| May–Nov. | Hölty | 398–401, 429–31, 433, 434, 436, 468, 503 |
| June | Uz | 358, 363, 446, 448, 449 |
| June | Klopstock | 442–5 |
| Aug.–Sept. | Jacobi | 343, 462–6, 474 |
| Sept.–Oct. | Mayrhofer | 473, 475–7, 490–2 |
| Sept. | Goethe | 359, 469, 478, 479, 480 nos.1 and 2, 481 |
| *1816/17:* | | |
| Nov.–Feb. | Claudius | 496, 496A, 497, 499, 500, 501, 504, 530–3 |
| *1817:* | | |
| Jan.–May | Mayrhofer | 297, 516, 524–7, 539–42, 548, 553, 554, 516, 561, 699 |
| March–May | Goethe | 543, 544, 549, 558–60, 564 |
| July | Mayrhofer | 573 |
| Sept. | Mayrhofer | 536, 585, 586 |
| Aug.–Nov. | Schiller | 577, 583, 584, 587, 588, 594, 595 |
| *1818:* | | |
| April–Aug. | Schreiber | 614, 622, 623 |
| Nov.–Dec. | A. W. von Schlegel | 628, 629, 711 |
| *1819:* | | |
| March | Mayrhofer | 654 |
| May | Novalis | 658, 659–62 |
| Oct. | Goethe | 295, 296, 673, 674 |
| *1820:* | | |
| Jan. | Novalis | 687 |
| March | F. von Schlegel | 633, 634, 691–4, 745 |
| Dec. | Mayrhofer | 707 |
| Dec. | F. von Schlegel | 708 |
| *1821:* | | |
| Feb.–April | Goethe | 715, 716, 719–21, 726–8 |
| *1822:* | | |
| March–April | Mayrhofer | 360, 752–4 |
| April–July | Platen | 751, 756 |
| July–Nov. | Rückert | 741, 775–778A |
| Dec. | Goethe | 764–8 |
| Oct.–Dec. | M. von Collin | 771, 772, 827 |
| *1822/23:* | | |
| Nov.–Feb. | Bruchmann | 737, 738, 746, 762, 785 |
| *1823:* | | |
| May–Nov. | Müller | 795 (20 songs) |

| | Author | Deutsch nos. |
|---|---|---|
| *1824:* | | |
| March | Mayrhofer | 805–8 |
| *1825:* | | |
| Feb.–April | Scott | 830, 831, 837–9, 843, 846 |
| Jan. | Lappe | 799, 800 |
| March | Schulze | 834, 853 |
| *1825/26:* | | |
| Aug. | Pyrker | 851, 852 |
| Dec.–March | Schulze | 860–2, 874, 876, 882–4 |
| *1826:* | | |
| Jan. | Goethe | 877 (4 songs) |
| March | Seidl | 867, 870, 871, 878–80 |
| July | Shakespeare | 888, 889, 891 |
| *1827:* | | |
| Feb.–Oct. | Müller | 911 (24 songs) |
| *1827/28:* | | |
| Oct.–Jan. | Leitner | 896, 896A, 896B, 926, 927, 931–3, 938, 939 |
| *1828:* | | |
| (?) Feb.–March | Heine | 957 nos.8–13 |
| (?) March–April | Rellstab | 957 nos.1–7 |

# VI PUBLICATION OF THE SONGS

Schubert's solo songs were the most popular part of his output, and more than a quarter of them were published during his lifetime. The tables in the following pages give details of the early publications under four headings:

(1) Songs published as supplements to periodicals during his lifetime
(2) Songs published with opus numbers during his lifetime
(3) Songs published from the beginning of 1829 to 1843
(4) Songs published by Diabelli in the *Nachlass* (1830–50)

## (1) SOLO SONGS PUBLISHED AS SUPPLEMENTS TO PERIODICALS IN SCHUBERT'S LIFETIME

| Date | Song | Author | Publication |
|---|---|---|---|
| 6 Feb. 1818 | Erlafsee | Mayrhofer | *MTfFiG* [1] |
| 28 Sept. 1820 | Widerschein | Schlechta | *TzgV* [2] |
| 9 Dec. 1820 | Die Forelle | Schubart | *ZfK* |
| 30 June 1821 | An Emma | Schiller | *ZfK* |
| 8 Dec. 1821 | Der Blumen Schmerz | Majláth | *ZfK* |
| 7 May 1822 | Die Rose | F. von Schlegel | *ZfK* |
| 30 July 1822 | Der Wachtelschlag | Sauter | *ZfK* |
| 25 March 1823 | Drang in die Ferne | Leitner | *ZfK* |
| 30 Dec. 1823 | Auf dem Wasser zu singen | Stolberg | *ZfK* |
| 26 June 1824 | An den Tod | Schubart | *AMZ* (Vienna) |
| 11 Dec. 1824 | Die Erscheinung | Kosegarten | *Album musicale* [3] |
| 12 March 1825 | Der Einsame | Lappe | *ZfK* |
| 23 June 1827 | Trost im Liede | Schober | *ZfK* |
| 23 June 1827 | Wandrers Nachtlied II | Goethe | *ZfK* |
| 25 Sept. 1827 | Der blinde Knabe | Cibber, Craigher | *ZfK* |
| 16 Sept. 1828 | Im Frühling | Schulze | *ZfK* |

16 songs

[1] *Mahlerisches Taschenbuch für Freunde interessanter Gegenden* ('Pictorial Pocket-book for Friends of the Countryside'; published in Vienna)
[2] *Taschenbuch zum geselligen Vergnügen* ('Pocket-book of Sociable Pleasure'; published in Leipzig)
[3] Published by Sauer and Leidesdorf

## (2) **SOLO SONGS PUBLISHED WITH OPUS NUMBERS DURING SCHUBERT'S LIFETIME**

Titles in parentheses indicate that the song had been published previously. C and C = Cappi and Czerny; C and D = Cappi and Diabelli; LIV = Lithographic Institute, Vienna; S and L = Sauer and Leidesdorf

| Op. no. | Title | Author | Publisher | Date |
|---|---|---|---|---|
| 1 | Erlkönig | Goethe | C and D | 2 April 1821 |
| 2 | Gretchen am Spinnrade | Goethe | C and D | 30 April 1821 |
| 3 | Schäfers Klagelied<br>Meeresstille (2)<br>Heidenröslein<br>Jägers Abendlied (2) | Goethe | C and D | 29 May 1821 |
| 4 | Der Wanderer<br>Morgenlied<br>Wandrers Nachtlied I | Schmidt von Lübeck<br>Werner<br>Goethe | C and D | 29 May 1821 |
| 5 | Rastlose Liebe<br>Nähe des Geliebten<br>Der Fischer<br>Erster Verlust<br>Der König in Thule | Goethe | C and D | 9 July 1821 |
| 6 | Memnon<br>Antigone und Oedip<br>Am Grabe Anselmos | Mayrhofer<br><br>Claudius | C and D | 23 Aug. 1821 |
| 7 | Die abgeblühte Linde<br>Der Flug der Zeit<br>Der Tod und das Mädchen | Széchényi<br><br>Claudius | C and D | 27 Nov. 1821 |
| 8 | Der Jüngling auf dem Hügel<br>Sehnsucht<br>(Erlafsee)<br>Am Strome | Hüttenbrenner<br><br>Mayrhofer | C and D | 9 May 1822 |
| 12 | 3 Gesänge des Harfners | Goethe | C and D | 13 Dec. 1822 |
| 13 | Der Schäfer und der Reiter<br>Lob der Tränen<br>Der Alpenjäger | Fouqué<br>A. W. von Schlegel<br>Mayrhofer | C and D | 13 Dec. 1822 |
| 14 | Suleika I<br>Geheimes | Goethe | C and D | 13 Dec. 1822 |
| 19 | An Schwager Kronos<br>An Mignon<br>Ganymed | Goethe | Diabelli | 6 June 1825 |
| 20 | Sei mir gegrüsst<br>Frühlingsglaube<br>Hänflings Liebeswerbung | Rückert<br>Uhland<br>Kind | S and L | 10 April 1823 |
| 21 | Auf der Donau<br>Der Schiffer<br>Wie Ulfru fischt | Mayrhofer | S and L | 19 June 1823 |
| 22 | Der Zwerg<br>Wehmut | M. von Collin | S and L | 27 May 1823 |
| 23 | Die Liebe hat gelogen<br>Selige Welt<br>Schwanengesang<br>Schatzgräbers Begehr | Platen<br>Senn<br>Senn<br>Schober | S and L | 4 Aug. 1823 |
| 24 | Gruppe aus dem Tartarus (2)<br>Schlummerlied ( = Schlaflied) | Schiller<br>Mayrhofer | S and L | 27 Oct. 1823 |
| 25 | Die schöne Müllerin<br>(20 songs) | Müller | S and L | Feb.–Aug. 1824 |

| Op. no. | Title | Author | Publisher | Date |
|---|---|---|---|---|
| 31 | Suleika II | Goethe | Pennauer | 12 Aug. 1825 |
| 32 | (Die Forelle) | Schubart | Diabelli | 13 Jan. 1825 |
| 36 | Der zürnenden Diana<br>Nachtstück } | Mayrhofer | Cappi | 11 Feb. 1825 |
| 37 | Der Pilgrim<br>Der Alpenjäger } | Schiller | Cappi | 28 Feb. 1825 |
| 38 | Der Liedler | Kenner | Cappi | 9 May 1825 |
| 39 | Sehnsucht (2) | Schiller | Pennauer | 8 Feb. 1826 |
| 41 | (Der Einsame) | Lappe | Diabelli | 5 Jan. 1827 |
| 43 | Die junge Nonne<br>Nacht und Träume | Craigher<br>M. von Collin | Pennauer | 25 July 1825 |
| 44 | An die untergehende Sonne | Kosegarten | Diabelli | 5 Jan. 1827 |
| 52 | 5 songs from Scott's Lady of<br>the Lake | Scott | Artaria | 5 April 1826 |
| 56 | Willkommen und Abschied<br>An die Leyer<br>Im Haine | Goethe<br>Bruchmann<br>Bruchmann | Pennauer | 14 July 1826 |
| 57 | Der Schmetterling<br>Die Berge<br>An den Mond I } | F. von Schlegel<br><br>Hölty | Weigl | 6 April 1826 |
| 58 (56) | Hektors Abschied<br>(Emma) ( = An Emma)<br>Des Mädchens Klage (2) } | Schiller | Weigl | 6 April 1826 |
| 59 | Du liebst mich nicht<br>Dass sie hier gewesen<br>Du bist die Ruh<br>Lachen und Weinen } | Platen<br><br>Rückert | S and L | 21 Sept. 1826 |
| 60 | Greisengesang<br>Dithyrambe | Rückert<br>Schiller | C and C | 10 June 1826 |
| 62 | 4 songs from *Wilhelm Meister* | Goethe | Diabelli | 2 March 1827 |
| 65 | Lied eines Schiffers an die<br>Dioskuren<br>Der Wanderer<br>Heliopolis I ( = Aus<br>'Heliopolis' I) | Mayrhofer<br><br>A.W. von Schlegel<br>Mayrhofer | C and C | 24 Nov. 1826 |
| 68 | (Der Wachtelschlag) | Sauter | Diabelli | 16 May 1827 |
| 71 | (Drang in der Ferne) | Leitner | Diabelli | 2 March 1827 |
| 72 | (Auf dem Wasser zu singen) | Stolberg | Diabelli | 2 March 1827 |
| 73 | (Die Rose) | F. von Schlegel | Diabelli | 16 May 1827 |
| 79 | Das Heimweh<br>Die Allmacht } | Pyrker | Haslinger | 16 May 1827 |
| 80 | Der Wanderer an den Mond<br>Das Zügenglöcklein<br>Im Freien } | Seidl | Haslinger | 25 May 1827 |
| 81 | Alinde<br>An die Laute } | Rochlitz | Haslinger | 25 May 1827 |
| 83 | 3 Italian songs for bass voice | Metastasio | Haslinger | 12 Sept. 1827 |
| 85 | Lied der Anne Lyle<br>Gesang der Norna } | Scott | Diabelli | 14 March 1828 |
| 86 | Romanze des Richard Löwenherz | Scott | Diabelli | 14 March 1828 |
| 87 (84) | Der Unglückliche<br>Die Hoffnung ( = Hoffnung (2))<br>Der Jüngling am Bache (3) } | Pichler<br>Schiller | Pennauer | 6 Aug. 1827 |

| Op. no. | Title | Author | Publisher | Date |
|---|---|---|---|---|
| 88 | Abendlied für die Entfernte<br>Thekla: eine Geisterstimme (2)<br>Um Mitternacht<br>An die Musik | A. W. von Schlegel<br>Schiller<br>Schulze<br>Schober | Weigl | 12 Dec. 1827 |
| 89 | Winterreise<br>　Part I  12 songs<br>　Part II 12 songs | Müller | Haslinger | 14 Jan. 1828<br>30 Dec. 1828 |
| 92<br>(87) | Der Musensohn<br>Auf dem See<br>Geistes-Gruss | } Goethe | Leidesdorf | 11 July 1828 |
| 93<br>(90) | Im Walde<br>Auf der Brücke | } Schulze | Kienreich<br>(Graz) | 30 May 1828 |
| 95 | Vier Refrain Lieder | Seidl | Weigl | 13 Aug. 1828 |
| 96 | Die Sterne<br>Jägers Liebeslied<br>(Wandrers Nachtlied II)<br>Fischerweise | Leitner<br>Schober<br>Goethe<br>Schlechta | LIV | Summer 1828 |
| 97 | Glaube, Hoffnung und Liebe | Kuffner | Diabelli | 6 Oct. 1828 |
| 101 | (Im Frühling)<br>(Der blinde Knabe)<br>(Trost im Liede)<br>(Wandrers Nachtlied II) | Schulze<br>Cibber, Craigher<br>Schober<br>Goethe | Probst (Leipzig) | 12 Dec. 1828 |
| 105 | Widerspruch<br>Wiegenlied<br>Am Fenster<br>Sehnsucht | } Seidl | Czerny | 21 Nov. 1828 |
| 106 | Heimliches Leben<br>Das Weinen<br>Vor meiner Wiege<br>An Sylvia | Klenke<br>Leitner<br>Leitner<br>Shakespeare | LIV | Spring 1828 |

*Notes:*

(a) Schubert died on 19 November 1828. This section has been extended to include songs published in November and December of that year, which were almost certainly proof-read by the composer before his death.

(b) In the last years of his life Schubert used several different publishers, with the result that opus numbers sometimes got confused and had to be changed after publication. In such cases the original opus number is put in brackets after the corrected one.

(c) The titles in brackets do not count as new publications, because they are already included in Section 1.

(d) The total of songs first published with opus numbers in the composer's lifetime is thus 169, making a grand total of 185 solo songs with those published as supplements to periodicals, or 29% of his output.

The distribution of these publications over the years show that the upward trend in the popularity of his songs was maintained right up to the end of Schubert's life.

| | |
|---|---|
| 1818 | 1 |
| 1820 | 2 |
| 1821 | 22 |
| 1822 | 13 |
| 1823 | 16 |
| 1824 | 22 |
| 1825 | 12 |
| 1826 | 23 |
| 1827 | 25 |
| 1828 | 49 |
| **Total** | **185** |

## (3) SONGS PUBLISHED POSTHUMOUSLY OTHER THAN IN THE 'NACHLASS', 1829–1843

| Op. no. | Title | Author | Publisher | Date |
|---|---|---|---|---|
| 108 (93) | Über Wildemann<br>Todesmusik<br>(Erinnerung = Die Erscheinung) | Schulze<br>Schober<br>Kosegarten | Leidesdorf | 28 Jan. 1829 |
| 110 | Der Kampf | Schiller | Czerny | 31 Jan. 1829 |
| 111 | An die Freude<br>Lebensmelodien<br>Die vier Weltalter | Schiller<br>A. W. von Schlegel<br>Schiller | Czerny | 31 Jan. 1829 |
| 116 | Die Erwartung | Schiller | Leidesdorf | 13 April 1829 |
| — | Schwanengesang (14 songs) | Heine, Rellstab, Seidl | Haslinger | May 1829 |
| 115 | Das Lied im Grünen<br>Wonne der Wehmut<br>Sprache der Liebe | Reil<br>Goethe<br>A. W. von Schlegel | Leidesdorf | 16 June 1829 |
| 117 | Der Sänger | Goethe | Czerny | 19 June 1829 |
| 118 | Geist der Liebe<br>Der Abend<br>Tischlied<br>Lob des Tokayers<br>An die Sonne<br>Die Spinnerin | Kosegarten<br>Kosegarten<br>Goethe<br>Baumberg<br>Baumberg<br>Goethe | Czerny | 19 June 1829 |
| — | Beim Winde | Mayrhofer | *ZfK*, Suppl. | 23 June 1829 |
| 98 | An die Nachtigall<br>Wiegenlied<br>Iphigenia | Claudius<br>Author unknown<br>Mayrhofer | Diabelli | 10 Juli 1829 |
| 109 | Am Bach im Frühling<br>Genügsamkeit<br>An eine Quelle | Schober<br>Schober<br>Claudius | Diabelli | 10 July 1829 |
| 119 | Auf dem Strom | Rellstab | Leidesdorf | 27 Oct. 1829 |
| 124 | Delphine<br>Florio } | Schütz | Pennauer | 30 Oct. 1829 |
| 126 | Ballade | Kenner | Czerny | 5 Jan. 1830 |
| — | Der Wallensteiner<br>Lanzknecht beim<br>Trunk } | Leitner | Suppl. to a<br>Vienna almanac | Jan. 1830 |
| 129 | Der Hirt auf dem Felsen | Müller, Chézy | Haslinger | 1 June 1830 |
| 130 | Das Echo | Castelli | Weigl | 12 July 1830 |
| — | Fülle der Liebe | F. von Schlegel | *ZfK*, suppl. | 25 Sept. 1830 |
| 131 | Der Mondabend<br>Klaglied | Kumpf<br>Rochlitz | Czerny | 9 Nov. 1830 |
| 123 | Viola | Schober | Pennauer | 26 Nov. 1830 |
| — | Der Kreuzzug | Leitner | *AmA*,[1] suppl. | 5 Jan. 1832 |
| — | Die Liebende schreibt | Goethe | *ZfK*, suppl. | 26 June 1832 |
| — | Wiedersehen | A. W. von Schlegel | *LaÖ*,[2] suppl. | 1843 |

[1] *Allgemeiner musikalischer Anzeiger* (published in Vienna)
[2] *Lebensbilder aus Österreich*, ed. A. Schumacher

Number of songs newly published in this section: 52.

## (4) SONGS PUBLISHED BY DIABELLI IN THE 'NACHLASS', 1830–1850

At the time of his death, the bulk of Schubert's unpublished song manuscripts were in the hands of his brother Ferdinand, who sold them to Diabelli early in 1830. Later in the same year Diabelli announced his intention to publish them in a series of fortnightly parts (*Lieferungen*). The series began in July with the publication in five parts of the Ossian songs. In each of the first few years six books of songs were published, but later on the striking rate went down to two or three books a year.

Diabelli made a praiseworthy attempt to assemble the vast store of manuscripts at his disposal into some sensible order before publication. Songs were grouped sometimes by author (Matthisson, Goethe, Mayrhofer, Schulze, Klopstock, for instance) and sometimes by subject matter (*Geistliche Lieder*). But inevitably the choice had occasionally to be arbitrary.

The series was advertised as 'Franz Schubert's Posthumous Musical Poems [*Nachgelassene musikalische Dichtungen*] for Song and Pianoforte', but it soon became known as the *Nachlass*, and Diabelli used this title in the later parts.

Diabelli, himself a composer, took a positive view of an editor's responsibilities, and his frequent changes of key, insertion of piano introductions, and occasional interference with the text or the music or both have drawn a good deal of fire from critics. There is a full discussion of these points in Maurice Brown's 'The Posthumous Publication of the Songs', *Essays*, pp. 267–90.

In the following list the titles in parentheses indicate, as before, that the song had been published previously. Precise dates of publication are, in most cases, impossible to establish; unless marked with an asterisk, the dates given here are those of Diabelli's announcements of forthcoming publications. Brown (loc. cit.) has attempted a more precise dating for the individual volumes.

| Date | Book | Title | Author |
|------|------|-------|--------|
| 10 July | 1 | Die Nacht | |
| | 2 | Cronnan | |
| | | Kolmas Klage | |
| | 3 | Lodas Gespenst | James Macpherson |
| | 4 | Shilrik und Vinvela | (Ossian) |
| | | Ossians Lied nach dem Falle Nathos | |
| | | Das Mädchen von Inistore | |
| | 5 | Der Tod Oscars | |
| | 6 | Elysium | Schiller |
| 26 Oct. 1830 | 7 | Des Sängers Habe | Schlechta |
| | | Hippolits Lied | Gerstenberg |
| | | Abendröte | F. von Schlegel |
| | | Ständchen | Shakespeare |
| | 8 | Die Bürgschaft | Schiller |
| | 9 | Der zürnende Barde | Bruchmann |
| | | Am See | Bruchmann |
| | | Abendbilder | Silbert |
| | 10 | Geistliche Lieder ('Spiritual Songs') | |
| | | Dem Unendlichen | Klopstock |
| | | Die Gestirne | Klopstock |
| | | Das Marienbild | Schreiber |
| | | Vom Mitleiden Mariä | F. von Schlegel |
| | | Litanei (auf das Fest aller Seelen) | Jacobi |
| | | Pax vobiscum | Schober |
| | | Gebet während der Schlacht | Körner |
| | | Himmelsfunken | Silbert |
| | 11 | Orest auf Tauris | |
| | | Der entsühnte Orest | |
| | | Philoktet | Mayrhofer |
| | | Freiwilliges Versinken | |
| 16 June 1831 | 12 | Der Taucher | Schiller |
| 4 Jan. 1832 | 13 | An mein Herz | Schulze |
| | | Der liebliche Stern | |

| Date | Book | Title | Author |
|------|------|-------|--------|
| | 14 | Grenzen der Menschheit | Goethe |
| | | Fragment aus dem Aeschylus | Mayrhofer |
| | 15 | (Widerschein) | |
| | | Liebeslauschen | Schlechta |
| | | Totengräber-Weise | |
| 12 March 1832 | 16 | Waldesnacht ( = Im Walde) | F. von Schlegel |
| 5 May 1832 | 17 | Lebensmut | Schulze |
| | | Der Vater mit dem Kind | Bauernfeld |
| | | (An den Tod) | Schubart |
| | | Verklärung | Pope trans. Herder |
| 12 July 1832 | 18 | Pilgerweise | Schober |
| | | An den Mond in einer Herbstnacht | Schreiber |
| | | Fahrt zum Hades | Mayrhofer |
| 29 Oct. 1832 | 19 | Lied des Orpheus | Jacobi |
| | | Ritter Toggenburg | Schiller |
| 22 Dec. 1832 | 20 | Im Abendrot | Lappe |
| | | Szene aus Faust | Goethe |
| | | Kennst du das Land? | Goethe |
| 14 Feb. 1833 | 21 | Der Blumenbrief | Schreiber |
| | | Vergissmeinnicht | Schober |
| 4 June 1833 | 22 | Der Sieg | |
| | | Atys | |
| | | (Beim Winde) | Mayrhofer |
| | | Abendstern | |
| 27 July 1833 | 23 | Schwestergruss | Bruchmann |
| | | Liedesend | Mayrhofer |
| 25 Sept. 1833 | 24 | Schiffers Scheidelied | Schober |
| | | Totengräbers Heimweh | Craigher |
| 9 Oct. 1835 | 25 | (Fülle der Liebe) | F. von Schlegel |
| | | (Im Frühling) | Schulze |
| | | Trost in Tränen | Goethe |
| | 26 | Der Winterabend | Leitner |
| | 27 | (Der Wallensteiner Lanzknecht beim Trunk) | Leitner |
| 25 April 1837 | 28 | Hermann und Thusnelda | |
| | | Selma und Selmar | |
| | | Das Rosenband | Klopstock |
| | | Edone | |
| | | Die frühen Gräber | |
| *June 1838 | 29 | Stimme der Liebe | Stolberg |
| | | Die Mutter Erde | Stolberg |
| | | Gretchens Bitte | Goethe |
| | | Abschied von einem Freunde | Schubert |
| *1838 | 30 | Tiefes Leid | Schulze |
| | | Clärchens Lied ( = Die Liebe) | Goethe |
| | | Grablied für die Mutter | Author unknown |
| 13 June 1840 | 31 | Die Betende | |
| | | Der Geistertanz (3) | Matthisson |
| | | An Laura | |
| | 32 | Einsamkeit | Mayrhofer |
| 23 June 1842 | 33 | Der Schiffer | F. von Schlegel |
| | | Die gefangenen Sänger | A. W. von Schlegel |
| | 34 | Auflösung | Mayrhofer |
| | | Blondel zu Marien | Author unknown |
| | 35 | Die erste Liebe | Fellinger |
| | | Lied eines Kriegers | Author unknown |
| | 36 | Der Jüngling an der Quelle | Salis-Seewis |
| | | Lambertine | Stoll |
| | | Ihr Grab | Engelhardt |
| | 37 | Aus 'Heliopolis' II | Mayrhofer |
| | | Sehnsucht | Goethe |
| *c. New Year 1845 | 38 | Die Einsiedelei (1) | Salis-Seewis |
| | | Lebenslied | Matthisson |
| | | Versunken | Goethe |

| Date | Book | Title | Author |
|------|------|-------|--------|
| | 39 | Als ich sie erröten sah | Ehrlich |
| | | Das war ich (1) | Körner |
| | | Ins stille Land | Salis-Seewis |
| * c. 1842 | 40 | Das Mädchen II | F. von Schlegel |
| | | Bertas Lied in der Nacht | Grillparzer |
| | | An die Freunde | Mayrhofer |
| * c. 1847 | 41 | Licht und Liebe | M. von Collin |
| | | Das grosse Halleluja | Klopstock |
| * c. mid-1848 | 42 | Die Götter Griechenlands | Schiller |
| | | Das Finden | Kosegarten |
| | | Cora an die Sonne | Baumberg |
| | | Grablied | Kenner |
| | | Adelaide | Matthisson |
| * New Year 1849 | (43) | (Vocal quartet: Im gegenwärtigen Vergangenes) | Goethe |
| * c. mid-1849 | 44 | Trost | Mayrhofer |
| | | Die Nacht | Uz |
| | | Zum Punsche | Mayrhofer |
| 8 Jan. 1850 | 45 | Frohsinn | Castelli |
| | | Der Morgenkuss | Baumberg |
| | 46 | Epistel: musikalischer Schwank | M. von Collin |
| * New Year 1850 | 47 | Prometheus | |
| | | Wer kauft Liebesgötter | |
| | | Der Rattenfänger | Goethe |
| | | Nachtgesang | |
| | | An den Mond (1) | |
| * New Year 1850 | 48 | Die Sterne | F. von Schlegel |
| | | Erntelied | Hölty |
| | | Klage an den Mond | Hölty |
| | | Trinklied | Shakespeare |
| | | So lasst mich scheinen (3) | Goethe |
| | | Der Goldschmiedsgesell | Goethe |
| | | Tischlerlied | Author unknown |
| * c. 1850 | 49 | Auf der Riesenkoppe | Körner |
| | | Auf einen Kirchhof | Schlechta |
| * Late 1850 | 50 | An die Apfelbäume | Hölty |
| | | Der Leidende | Author unknown |
| | | Augenlied | Mayrhofer |

The total of songs published for the first time in the *Nachlass* is 125. With those published previously, this means that 362 songs were published by the middle of the century, well over half of Schubert's total output. But some 270 songs still remained unpublished. As already mentioned, the ten volumes of series XX (solo songs with piano) of the *Gesamtausgabe* included 603 songs, some of them variants. Series IV (Lieder) of the *Neue Ausgabe*, now in course of publication by Bärenreiter, is planned to include all the known songs and variants.

# VII SCHUBERT'S TEMPO INDICATIONS AND EXPRESSION MARKS

Up to September 1814 Schubert used the normal Italian forms in all his compositions, whether vocal or instrumental. However, as he came more directly under the influence of German poets like Schiller and Matthisson, and German composers like Beethoven, he changed to German when writing songs, though he continued to use the conventional Italian forms for instrumental compositions to the end of his life. His tempo indications and expression marks for the songs are often detailed and idiomatic, so that it is not always easy to provide a precise English equivalent. The following notes and glossary will, it is hoped, prove useful to students and song-lovers who have little or no knowledge of German.

## TEMPO INDICATIONS

The basic tempo indications are:

*langsam* — slow
*langsamer* — slower
*geschwind* — fast
*geschwinder* — faster
*schnell* — quick
*schneller* — quicker
*mässig* (also *gemässigt*) — at a moderate
pace (moderato)

Two others should be mentioned, though they have implications which go beyond metronomic speed:

*lebhaft* — lively
*bewegt* — animated, moving

All these are frequently qualified by the following:

*sehr* — very
*ziemlich* — fairly, suitably
*etwas* — quite, a little
*mässig* — moderately
*nicht zu* — not too

So, for example:

*sehr langsam* — very slow
*mässig geschwind* — moderately fast
*nicht zu schnell* — not too fast

*etwas bewegt* — a little (more) animated
*ziemlich geschwind* — fairly fast

These tempo markings are also used in combination with the verbs *werden* ('to become'), *wachsen* ('to grow') and *steigen* ('to rise'). So:

*geschwinder werdend* — getting faster

The German word for tempo is *Zeitmass*. So, for instance:

*im Zeitmasse* — in tempo
*im ersten Zeitmasse* — tempo primo

Of particular importance in any consideration of Schubert's expressive markings is the word Bewegung, which means movement or pulse, combined with the individual rhythmical characteristics of the song. Perhaps 'gait' is the nearest English equivalent. The word frequently appears in such phrases as:

*in sanfter Bewegung*—moving forward gently
*mit steigender Bewegung*—with mounting urgency
*mässig in gehende Bewegung* — at a moderate walking pace

## PEDAL MARKINGS

Schubert often uses the normal Italian terms for the use of the pedals, even in his songs, *Ped.*, *con Pedale*, *Pedale*, or even *mit Pedale* for the sustaining pedal, and *con sordini* ('with mutes') for the una corda or 'soft' pedal. But he also uses the German terms *mit gehobener Dämpfung* and *mit erhobener Dämpfung* ('with the dampers lifted') for the sustaining pedal, and *mit Verschiebung* ('with displacement') for the una corda.

## GLOSSARY

*Affekt* — emotion, passion (*mit steigendem Affekt*, with mounting passion)
*allmählich* — gradually
*Andacht* — devotion
*andächtig* — devout, rapt (*mit Andacht*)
*angenehm* — agreeable, pleasant
*Angst* — fear, anxiety
*ängstlich* — anxiously
*Anmut* — grace, sweetness
*Ausdruck* — expression

*bedauernd* — pitying, sorrowing
*behaglich* — agreeable, comfortable, cosy
*beinahe* — almost (*beinahe die vorige Bewegung*, almost the same tempo as before)
*bewegt/Bewegung* — (see above)
*bis* — up to, until (e.g. *bis Ende* 'to the end'). Not to be confused with the French word *bis*, meaning 'twice' or 'again'.

*declamiert* — declaimed
*doch* — yet, but (*Frisch, doch nicht zu schnell*, 'Lively, but not too quick')
*düster* — dusky, sombre

*eilig* — hurried
*Empfindung* — feeling, sensitivity (*mit Empfindung* 'with feeling', espressivo)
*entschlossen* — firm, determined
*ernst* — serious
*erzählend* — narrating, as though telling a story
*etwas* — quite, rather

*feierlich* — with ceremony, solemn, festive
*Feuer* — fire (*mit Feuer*, with ardour)
*freudig* — joyful
*freundlich* — amiably
*frisch* — brisk, fresh, lively

*froh und frei* — merry and free
*fromm* — pious, devout

*Gefühl*—feeling (*mit Gefühl*, with feeling)
*gehend* ⁻ walking, at a steady pace
(andante)
*geschwind* — fast
*Grauen* — horror, dread (*Mit Grauen*,
fearful)

*heilig* — sacred, holy (*mit heiliger
Rührung*, with sacred emotion)
*heiter* — serene, clear, bright
*herzlich* — sincere, heartfelt

*innig* — warm, tender
*Innigkeit* — fervour, 'inwardness' (A word
very often used of and by Romantic
composers, but for which there is no
precise equivalent)

*Jubel* — jubilation

*klagend* — plaintive, complaining
*Kraft* — strength (*mit aller Kraft*, at full
strength)
*kräftig* — strong
*kraftvoll* — vigorously

*langsam* — slow
*Laune* — humour, temper (*in guter Laune*,
in good humour)
*lebhaft* — lively
*Leidenschaft* — passion (*mit Leidenschaft*,
passionately)
*leise* — soft, gentle
*lieblich* — lovely, charming
*lustig* — merry, jolly, cheerful

*Majestät* — majesty
*majestätisch* — majestic
*mässig* — moderate, at a moderate pace
*munter* — sprightly, frisky, cheerful
*mutig* — spirited, plucky

*nachgehend* — following

*romanzenartig* — in the manner of a
romantic tale

*ruhig* — still, quiet, tranquil

*sanft* — soft, gentle
*schauerlich* — ghastly, gruesome, horrible
*scherzhaft* — in fun, facetious
*schleichend* — moving softly, creeping
*schmerzlich* — painful(ly)
*schnell* — quick
*schreitend* — striding
*schwärmerisch* — zealous, enthusiastic,
ecstatic
*Sehnsucht* — longing for that which lies
beyond reach, including happiness,
perfection, and the Infinite (*Langsam
mit schwärmerischen Sehnsucht*, slow
and with ecstatic longing)
*sehr* — very
*stark* — strong
*Stimme* — voice (*mit leiser Stimme*, in a
low voice)
*stürmisch* — stormy

*Takt* — beat, bar (*in Takte*, in strict time)
*taktlos* — not in strict time: *ad lib*
*tandelnd* — playful
*trauernd* — sorrowing, mourning
*traurig* — melancholy, mournful

*unruhig* — restless, uneasy, troubled
*unschuldig* — innocently

*vertrauensvoll* — trustfully, confidently
*vom Zeichen* — from the sign
*von Ferne* — from afar

*wachsend* — growing
*Wehmut* — sadness, melancholy
*wehmütig* — sadly
*wie oben* — as before
*wild* — fierce, wild
*Würde* — dignity (*mit stillen Würde*, with
quiet dignity)

*zart* — tender
*Zeitmass* — tempo (*Zeitmass des
Marsches*, in march time)
*ziemlich* — fairly
*zögernd* — lingering
*zurückhaltend* — holding back